PRAISE FOR THE MAJIPOOR CYCLE

Majipoor Chronicles

"If you like tales with an *Arabian Nights* piquancy, this book belongs in your hands."
    —*The Washington Post Book World*

"Majipoor is probably the finest creation of Silverberg's powerful imagination and certainly one of the most fully realized worlds of modern science fiction."
    —*Booklist*

Lord Valentine's Castle

"A surefire page-turner . . . a brilliant concept of the imagination."
    —*Chicago Sun-Times*

"An imaginative fusion of action, sorcery, and science fiction."
    —*The New York Times Book Review*

"[A] heady blend of rigorous SF world building and the poetic sensibility of fantasy fiction."
    —Sci Fi Weekly

"A grand, picaresque tale . . . by one of the great storytellers of the century. *Lord Valentine's Castle* has everything."
    —Roger Zelazny

"Silverberg has created a big planet, chockablock with life and potential."
    —*The Washington Post*

"This absorbing book is . . . successful in creating a wildly imaginative universe. It is also better written than most in this genre and deserves to be one of the year's hits, sci-fi or otherwise."
    —*People*

"In this richly imagined setting, Valentine not only learns about his world but about himself and his proper place in it. . . . Robert Silverberg's writing and imagination soar with nary a false step. It is truly an extraordinary tale, well told."
    —SFFaudio

The Majipoor Cycle

Lord Valentine's Castle
Majipoor Chronicles
Valentine Pontifex

ROBERT SILVERBERG

MAJIPOOR CHRONICLES

BOOK TWO OF THE MAJIPOOR CYCLE

A ROC BOOK

ROC
Published by New American Library, a division of
Penguin Group (USA) Inc., 375 Hudson Street,
New York, New York 10014, USA
Penguin Group (Canada), 90 Eglinton Avenue East, Suite 700, Toronto,
Ontario M4P 2Y3, Canada (a division of Pearson Penguin Canada Inc.)
Penguin Books Ltd., 80 Strand, London WC2R 0RL, England
Penguin Ireland, 25 St. Stephen's Green, Dublin 2,
Ireland (a division of Penguin Books Ltd.)
Penguin Group (Australia), 250 Camberwell Road, Camberwell, Victoria 3124,
Australia (a division of Pearson Australia Group Pty. Ltd.)
Penguin Books India Pvt. Ltd., 11 Community Centre, Panchsheel Park,
New Delhi - 110 017, India
Penguin Group (NZ), 67 Apollo Drive, Rosedale, Auckland 0632,
New Zealand (a division of Pearson New Zealand Ltd.)
Penguin Books (South Africa) (Pty.) Ltd., 24 Sturdee Avenue,
Rosebank, Johannesburg 2196, South Africa

Penguin Books Ltd., Registered Offices:
80 Strand, London WC2R 0RL, England

Published by Roc, an imprint of New American Library, a division of Penguin Group (USA)
Inc. Previously published in an Arbor House trade paperback edition. Published by arrangement with the author.

First Roc Trade Paperback Printing, September 2012
10 9 8 7 6 5 4 3 2 1

 REGISTERED TRADEMARK—MARCA REGISTRADA

ROC TRADE PAPERBACK ISBN: 978-0-451-46483-5

THE LIBRARY OF CONGRESS HAS CATALOGED THIS TITLE AS FOLLOWS:

Silverberg, Robert
Majipoor chronicles: a novel/by Robert Silverberg
1. Majipoor (Imaginary place)—Fiction.   I. Title
PS3569.I472 M3 1982
813'.54
ISBN: 0-87795-358-9

Set in Bell MT
Designed by Spring Hoteling

Printed in the United States of America

FOR KIRBY

Who may not have been driven all the way to despair by
this one, but who certainly got as far as the outlying suburbs.

Majipoor

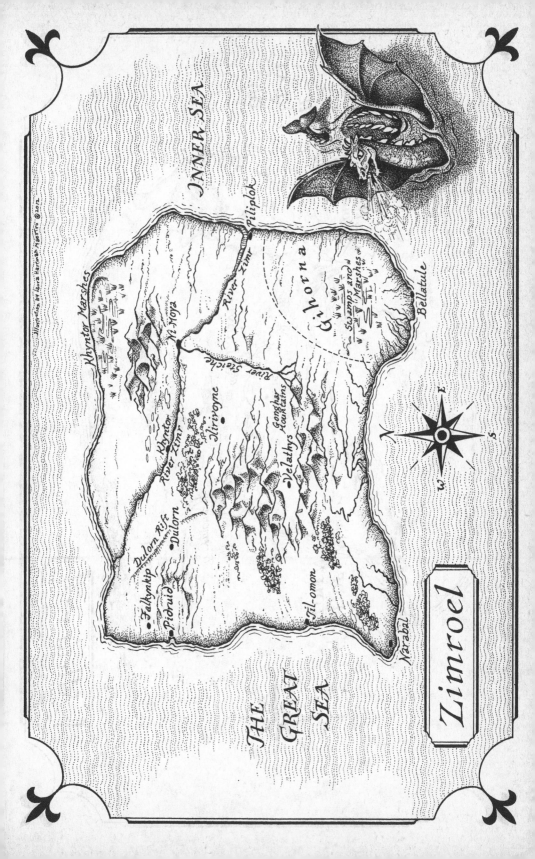

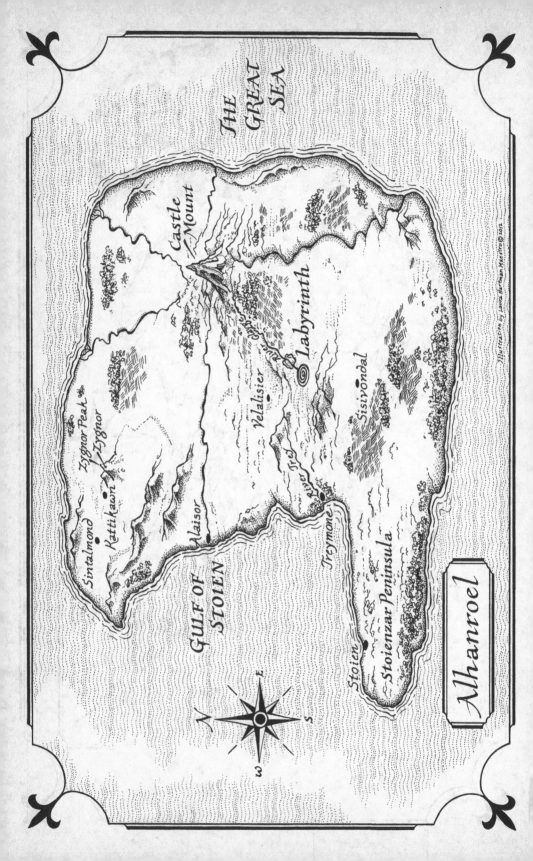

Glayge Valley
and Castle Mount

Castle

Makroprosopos

Pendiwane

River Glayge

Velalisier

Lake Roghoiz

Labyrinth

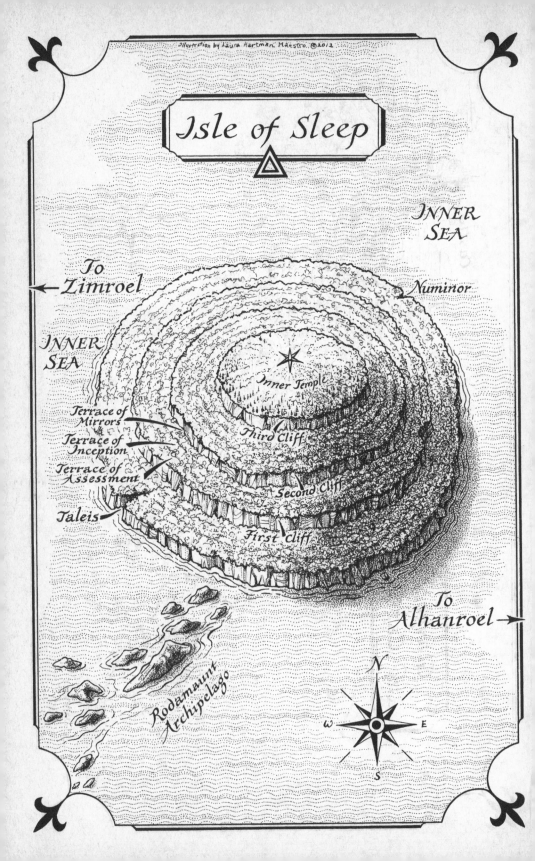

MAJIPOOR
CHRONICLES

PROLOGUE

In the fourth year of the restoration of the Coronal Lord Valentine a great mischief has come over the soul of the boy Hissune, a clerk in the House of Records of the Labyrinth of Majipoor. For the past six months it has been Hissune's task to prepare an inventory of the archives of the tax-collectors—an interminable list of documents that no one is ever going to need to consult—and it looks as though the job will keep him occupied for the next year or two or three. To no purpose, so far as Hissune can understand, since who could possibly care about the reports of provincial tax-collectors who lived in the reign of Lord Dekkeret or Lord Calintane or even the ancient Lord Stiamot? These documents had been allowed to fall into disarray, no doubt for good reason, and now some malevolent destiny has chosen Hissune to put them to rights, and so far as he can see, it is useless work, except that he will have a fine geography lesson, a vivid experience of the hugeness of Majipoor. So many provinces! So many cities! The three giant continents are divided and subdivided and further divided into thousands of municipal units, each with its millions of people, and as he toils, Hissune's mind overflows with names, the Fifty Cities of Castle Mount, the great urban districts of Zimroel, the mysterious desert settlements of Suvrael, a torrent of metropolises, a lunatic tribute to the fourteen thousand years of Majipoor's unceasing fertility: Pidruid, Narabal, Ni-moya, Alaisor, Stoien, Piliplok, Pendiwane, Amblemorn, Minimool, Tolaghai, Kangheez, Natu Gorvinu—so much, so much, so much! A million names of places! But when one is fourteen years old one can tolerate only a certain amount of geography, and then one begins to grow restless.

Restlessness invades Hissune now. The mischievousness that is never far from the surface in him wells up and overflows.

Close by the dusty little office in the House of Records where Hissune sifts and classifies his mounds of tax reports is a far more interesting place, the Register of Souls, which is closed to all but authorized personnel, and there are said to be not many authorized personnel. Hissune knows a good deal about that place. He knows a good deal about every part of the Labyrinth, even the forbidden places, especially the forbidden places—for has he not, since the age of eight, earned his living in the streets of the great underground capital by guiding bewildered tourists through the maze, using his wits to pick up a crown here and a crown there? "House of Records," he would tell the tourists. "There's a room in there where millions of people of Majipoor have left memory-readings. You pick up a capsule and put it in a special slot, and suddenly it's as if you were the person who made the reading, and you find yourself living in Lord Confalume's time, or Lord Siminave's, or out there fighting the Metamorph Wars with Lord Stiamot—but of course hardly anyone is allowed to consult the memory-reading room." Of course. But how hard would it be, Hissune wonders, to insinuate himself into that room on the pretext of needing data for his research into the tax archives? And then to live in a million other minds at a million other times, in all the greatest and most glorious eras of Majipoor's history—yes!

Yes, it would certainly make this job more tolerable if he could divert himself with an occasional peek into the Register of Souls.

From that realization it is but a short journey to the actual attempting of it. He equips himself with the appropriate passes—he knows where all the document-stampers are kept in the House of Records—and makes his way through the brightly lit curving corridors late one afternoon, dry-throated, apprehensive, tingling with excitement.

It has been a long time since he has known any excitement. Living by his wits in the streets was exciting, but he no longer does that; they have civilized him, they have housebroken him, they have given him a job. A *job*! *They*! And who are *they*? The Coronal himself, that's who! Hissune has not overcome his amazement over that. During the time when Lord Valentine was wandering in exile, displaced from his body and his throne by the usurper Barjazid, the Coronal had come to the Labyrinth, and Hissune had guided him, recognizing him somehow for what he truly was; and that had been the beginning of Hissune's downfall. For the next thing Hissune knew, Lord Valentine was on his way from the Labyrinth to Castle Mount to regain his crown, and then the usurper was overthrown, and then at the time of the second coronation Hissune found himself summoned, the Divine only knew why, to attend the ceremonies at Lord Valentine's Castle. What a time that was! Never before had he so much as been out of the Labyrinth to see the light of day, and now he was journeying in an official floater, up the valley of the Glayge past cities he had known only in dreams, and there was Castle Mount's thirty-mile-high bulk rising like another planet in the sky, and at last he was at the Castle, a grimy ten-year-old boy standing next to the Coronal and trading jokes with him—yes, that had been splendid, but Hissune was caught by surprise by what followed. The Coronal believed that Hissune had promise. The Coronal wished him to be trained for a government post. The Coronal admired the boy's energy and wit and enterprise. Fine. Hissune would become a protégé of the Coronal. Fine. Fine. Back to the Labyrinth, then—and into the House of Records! Not so fine. Hissune has always detested the bureaucrats, those mask-faced idiots who pushed papers about in the bowels of the Labyrinth, and now, by special favor of Lord Valentine, he has become such a person himself. Well, he supposes he has to do something by way of earning a living besides take tourists around—but he never imagined it would be this! *Report of the Collector of Revenue for the Eleventh District of the Province of Chorg, Prefecture of Bibiroon, 11th Pont. Kinniken Cor. Lord Ossier*—oh, no, no, not a lifetime of that! A month, six months, a year of doing his nice little job in the nice little House of Records, Hissune hopes, and then Lord Valentine might send for him and install him in the Castle as an aide-de-camp, and then at last life would have some value! But the Coronal seems to have forgotten him, as one might expect. He has an entire world of twenty or thirty billion people to govern, and what does one little boy of the Labyrinth matter? Hissune suspects that his life has already passed its most glorious peak, in his brief time on Castle Mount, and now by some miserable irony he has been metamorphosed into a clerk of the Pontificate, doomed to shuffle documents forever—

But there is the Register of Souls to explore.

Even though he may never leave the Labyrinth again, he might—if no one caught him—roam the minds of millions of folk long dead, explorers, pioneers, warriors, even Coronals and Pontifexes. That's some consolation, is it not?

He enters a small antechamber and presents his pass to the dull-eyed Hjort on duty.

Hissune is ready with a flow of explanations: special assignment from the Coronal, important historical research, need to correlate demographic details, necessary corroboration of data profile—oh, he's good at such talk, and it lies coiled waiting at the back of his tongue. But the Hjort says only, "You know how to use the equipment?"

"It's been a while. Perhaps you should show me again."

The ugly warty-faced fellow, many-chinned and flabby, gets slowly to his feet and leads Hissune to a sealed enclosure, which he opens by some deft maneuver of a thumblock. The Hjort indicates a screen and a row of buttons. "Your control console. Send for the capsules you want. They plug in here. Sign for everything. Remember to turn out the lights when you're done."

That's all there is to it. Some security system! Some guardian!

Hissune finds himself alone with the memory-readings of everyone who has ever lived on Majipoor.

Almost everyone, at any rate. Doubtless billions of people have lived and died without bothering to make capsules of their lives. But one is allowed every ten years, beginning at the age of twenty, to contribute to these vaults, and Hissune knows that although the capsules are minute, the merest flecks of data, there are miles and miles of them in the storage levels of the Labyrinth. He puts his hands to the controls. His fingers tremble.

Where to begin?

He wants to know everything. He wants to trek across the forests of Zimroel with the first explorers, he wants to drive back the Metamorphs, to sail the Great Sea, to slaughter sea-dragons off the Rodamaunt Archipelago, to—to—to—he shakes with a frenzy of yearning. Where to begin? He studies the keys before him. He can specify a date, a place, a specific person's identity—but with fourteen thousand years to choose from—no, more like eight or nine thousand, for the records, he knows, go back only to Lord Stiamot's time or a little before—how can he decide on a starting point? For ten minutes he is paralyzed with indecision.

Then he punches at random. Something early, he thinks. The continent of Zimroel; the time of the Coronal Lord Barhold, who had lived even before Stiamot; and the person—why, anyone! Anyone!

A small gleaming capsule appears in the slot.

Quivering in amazement and delight, Hissune plugs it into the playback outlet and dons the helmet. There are crackling sounds in his ears. Vague blurred streaks of blue and green and scarlet cross his eyes behind his closed lids. Is it working? Yes! Yes! He feels the presence of another mind! Someone dead nine thousand years, and that person's mind—*her* mind, she was a woman, a young woman—flows into Hissune's, until he cannot be sure whether he is Hissune of the Labyrinth or this other, this Thesme of Narabal—

With a little sobbing sound of joy he releases himself entirely from the self he has lived with for the fourteen years of his life and lets the soul of the other take possession of him.

ONE

Thesme and the Ghayrog

1

For six months now Thesme had lived alone in a hut that she had built
with her own hands, in the dense tropical jungle half a dozen miles or so
east of Narabal, in a place where the sea breezes did not reach and the
heavy humid air clung to everything like a furry shroud. She had never
lived by herself before, and at first she wondered how good she was going
to be at it; but she had never built a hut before, either, and she had done
well enough at that, cutting down slender sijaneel saplings, trimming
away the golden bark, pushing their slippery sharpened ends into the soft,
moist ground, lashing them together with vines, finally tying on five
enormous blue vramma leaves to make a roof. It was no masterpiece of
architecture, but it kept out the rain, and she had no need to worry about
cold. Within a month her sijaneel timbers, trimmed though they were,
had all taken root and were sprouting leathery new leaves along their
upper ends, just below the roof; and the vines that held them were still
alive, too, sending down fleshy red tendrils that searched for and found
the rich fertile soil. So now the house was a living thing, daily becoming
more snug and secure as the vines tightened and the sijaneels put on
girth, and Thesme loved it. In Narabal nothing stayed dead for long; the
air was too warm, the sunlight too bright, the rainfall too copious, and
everything quickly transformed itself into something else with the riot-
ous, buoyant ease of the tropics.

Solitude was turning out to be easy, too. She had needed very much
to get away from Narabal, where her life had somehow gone awry: too
much confusion, too much inner noise, friends who became strangers,

lovers who turned into foes. She was twenty-five years old and needed to stop, to take a long look at everything, to change the rhythm of her days before it shook her to pieces. The jungle was the ideal place for that. She rose early, bathed in a pond that she shared with a sluggish old gromwark and a school of tiny crystalline chichibors, plucked her breakfast from a thokka vine, hiked, read, sang, wrote poems, checked her traps for captured animals, climbed trees and sunbathed in a hammock of vines high overhead, dozed, swam, talked to herself, and went to sleep when the sun went down. In the beginning she thought there would not be enough to do, that she would soon grow bored, but that did not seem to be the case; her days were full and there were always a few projects to save for tomorrow.

At first she expected that she would go into Narabal once a week or so to buy staple goods, to pick up new books and cubes, to attend an occasional concert or a play, even to visit her family or those of her friends that she still felt like seeing. For a while she actually did go to town fairly often. But it was a sweaty, sticky trek that took half a day, nearly, and as she grew accustomed to her reclusive life, she found Narabal ever more jangling, ever more unsettling, with few rewards to compensate for the drawbacks. People there stared at her. She knew they thought she was eccentric, even crazy, always a wild girl and now a peculiar one, living out there by herself and swinging through the treetops. So her visits became more widely spaced. She went only when it was unavoidable. On the day she found the injured Ghayrog she had not been to Narabal for at least five weeks.

She had been roving that morning through a swampy region a few miles northeast of her hut, gathering the sweet yellow fungi known as calimbots. Her sack was almost full and she was thinking of turning back when she spied something strange a few hundred yards away: a creature of some sort with gleaming, metallic-looking gray skin and thick tubular limbs, sprawled awkwardly on the ground below a great sijaneel tree. It reminded her of a predatory reptile her father and brother once had killed in Narabal Channel, a sleek, elongated, slow-moving thing with curved claws and a vast toothy mouth. But as she drew closer she saw that this life-form was vaguely human in construction, with a massive rounded head, long arms, powerful legs. She thought it might be dead, but it stirred faintly when she approached and said, "I am damaged. I have been stupid and now I am paying for it."

"Can you move your arms and legs?" Thesme asked.

"The arms, yes. One leg is broken, and possibly my back. Will you help me?"

She crouched and studied it closely. It did look reptilian, yes, with shining scales and a smooth, hard body. Its eyes were green and chilly and did not blink at all; its hair was a weird mass of thick black coils that moved of their own accord in a slow writhing; its tongue was a serpent-tongue, bright scarlet, forked, flickering constantly back and forth between the narrow fleshless lips.

"What are you?" she asked.

"A Ghayrog. Do you know of my kind?"

"Of course," she said, though she knew very little, really. All sorts of non-human species had been settling on Majipoor in the past hundred years, a whole menagerie of aliens invited here by the Coronal Lord Melikand because there were not enough humans to fill the planet's immensities. Thesme had heard that there were four-armed ones and two-headed ones and tiny ones with tentacles and these scaly, snake-tongued, snake-haired ones, but none of the alien beings had yet come as far as Narabal, a town on the edge of nowhere, as distant from civilization as one could get. So this was a Ghayrog, then? A strange creature, she thought, almost human in the shape of its body and yet not at all human in any of its details, a monstrosity, really, a nightmare-being, though not especially frightening. She pitied the poor Ghayrog, in fact—a wanderer, doubly lost, far from its home world and far from anything that mattered on Majipoor. And badly hurt, too. What was she going to do with it? Wish it well and abandon it to its fate? Hardly. Go all the way into Narabal and organize a rescue mission? That would take at least two days, assuming anyone cared to help. Bring it back to her hut and nurse it to good health? That seemed the most likely thing to do, but what would happen to her solitude, then, her privacy, and how did one take care of a Ghayrog, anyway, and did she really want the responsibility? And the risk, for that matter: this was an alien being and she had no idea what to expect from it.

It said, "I am Vismaan."

Was that its name, its title, or merely a description of its condition? She did not ask. She said, "I am called Thesme. I live in the jungle an hour's walk from here. How can I help you?"

"Let me brace myself on you while I try to get up. Do you think you are strong enough?"

"Probably."

"You are female, am I right?"

She was wearing only sandals. She smiled and touched her hand lightly to her breasts and loins and said, "Female, yes."

"So I thought. I am male and perhaps too heavy for you."

Male? Between his legs he was as smooth and sexless as a machine. She supposed that Ghayrogs carried their sex somewhere else. And if they were reptiles, her breasts would indicate nothing to him about her sex. Strange, all the same, that he should need to ask.

She knelt beside him, wondering how he was going to rise and walk with a broken back. He put his arm over her shoulders. The touch of his skin against hers startled her: it felt cool, dry, rigid, smooth, as though he wore armor. Yet it was not an unpleasant texture, only odd. A strong odor came from him, swampy and bitter with an undertaste of honey. That she had not noticed it before was hard to understand, for it was pervasive and insistent; she decided she must have been distracted by the unexpectedness of coming upon him. There was no ignoring the odor now that she was aware of it, and at first she found it intensely disagreeable, though within moments it ceased to bother her.

He said, "Try to hold steady. I will push myself up."

Thesme crouched, digging her knees and hands into the soil, and to her amazement he succeeded in drawing himself upward with a peculiar coiling motion, pressing down on her, driving his entire weight for a moment between her shoulder blades in a way that made her gasp. Then he was standing, tottering, clinging to a dangling vine. She made ready to catch him if he fell, but he stayed upright.

"This leg is cracked," he told her. "The back is damaged but not, I think, broken."

"Is the pain very bad?"

"Pain? No, we feel little pain. The problem is functional. The leg will not support me. Can you find me a strong stick?"

She scouted about for something he might use as a crutch and spied, after a moment, the stiff aerial root of a vine dangling out of the forest canopy. The glossy black root was thick but brittle, and she bent it backward and forward until she succeeded in snapping off some two yards of it. Vismaan grasped it firmly, draped his other arm around Thesme, and cautiously put his weight on his uninjured leg. With difficulty he took a step, another, another, dragging the broken leg along. It seemed to Thesme that his body odor had changed: sharper, now, more vinegar, less honey. The strain of walking, no doubt. The pain was probably less trivial than he wanted her to think. But he was managing to keep moving, at any rate.

"How did you hurt yourself?" she asked.

"I climbed this tree to survey the territory just ahead. It did not bear my weight."

He nodded toward the slim, shining trunk of the tall sijaneel. The lowest branch, which was at least forty feet above her, was broken and hung down by nothing more than shreds of bark. It amazed her that he had survived a fall from such a height; after a moment she found herself wondering how he had been able to get so high on the slick, smooth trunk in the first place.

He said, "My plan is to settle in this area and raise crops. Do you have a farm?"

"In the jungle? No, I just live here."

"With a mate?"

"Alone. I grew up in Narabal, but I needed to get away by myself for a while." They reached the sack of calimbots she had dropped when she first noticed him lying on the ground, and she slung it over her shoulder. "You can stay with me until your leg has healed. But it's going to take all afternoon to get back to my hut this way. Are you sure you're able to walk?"

"I am walking now," he pointed out.

"Tell me when you want to rest."

"In time. Not yet."

Indeed it was nearly half an hour of slow and surely painful hobbling before he asked to halt, and even then he remained standing, leaning against a tree, explaining that he thought it unwise to go through the whole difficult process of lifting himself from the ground a second time. He seemed altogether calm and in relatively little discomfort, although it was impossible to read expression into his unchanging face and unblinking eyes: the constant flickering of his forked tongue was the only indicator of apparent emotion she could see, and she had no idea how to interpret those ceaseless darting movements. After a few minutes they resumed the walk. The slow pace was a burden to her, as was his weight against her shoulder, and she felt her own muscles cramping and protesting as they edged through the jungle. They said little. He seemed preoccupied with the need to exert control over his crippled body, and she concentrated on the route, searching for shortcuts, thinking ahead to avoid streams and dense undergrowth and other obstacles he would not be able to cope with. When they were halfway back to her hut a warm rain began to fall, and after that they were enveloped in hot clammy fog the rest of the way. She was nearly exhausted by the time her little cabin came into view.

"Not quite a palace," she said, "but it's all I need. I built it myself. You can lie down here." She helped him to her zanja-down bed. He sank onto it with a soft hissing sound that was surely relief. "Would you like something to eat?" she asked.

"Not now."

"Or to drink? No? I imagine you just want to get some rest. I'll go outside so you can sleep undisturbed."

"This is not my season of sleep," Vismaan said.

"I don't understand."

"We sleep only one part of the year. Usually in winter."

"And you stay awake all the rest of the time?"

"Yes," he said. "I am finished with this year's sleep. I understand it is different with humans."

"Extremely different," she told him. "I'll leave you to rest by yourself, anyway. You must be terribly tired."

"I would not drive you from your home."

"It's all right," Thesme said, and stepped outside. The rain was beginning again, the familiar, almost comforting rain that fell every few hours all day long. She sprawled out on a bank of dark, yielding rubbermoss and let the warm droplets of rain wash the fatigue from her aching back and shoulders.

A houseguest, she thought. And an alien one, no less. Well, why not? The Ghayrog seemed undemanding: cool, aloof, tranquil even in calamity. He was obviously more seriously hurt than he was willing to admit, and even this relatively short journey through the forest had been a struggle for him. There was no way he could walk all the way into Narabal in this condition. Thesme supposed that she could go into town and arrange for someone to come out in a floater to get him, but the idea displeased her. No one knew where she was living and she did not care to lead anyone here, for one thing. And she realized in some confusion that she did not want to give the Ghayrog up, that she wanted to keep him here and nurse him until he had regained his strength. She doubted that anyone else in Narabal would have given shelter to an alien, and that made her feel pleasantly perverse, set apart in still another way from the citizens of her native town. In the past year or two she had heard plenty of muttering about the offworlders who were coming to settle on Majipoor. People feared and disliked the reptilian Ghayrogs and the giant, hulking, hairy Skandars and the little tricky ones with the many tentacles—Vroons, were they?—and the rest of that bizarre crew, and even though aliens were still unknown in remote Narabal the hostility toward them was already there. Wild and eccentric Thesme, she thought, was just the kind who *would* take in a Ghayrog and pat his fevered brow and give him medicine and soup, or whatever you gave a Ghayrog with a broken leg. She had no real idea of how to care for him, but she did not intend to let that stop her. It occurred to her that she had never taken care of anyone in her life, for somehow there had been neither opportunity nor occasion; she was the youngest in her family and no one had ever allowed her any sort of responsibility, and she had not married or borne children or even kept pets, and during the stormy period of her innumerable turbulent love affairs she had never seen fit to visit any of her lovers while he was ill. Quite likely, she told herself, that was why she was suddenly so determined to keep this Ghayrog at her hut. One of the reasons she had quitted Narabal for the jungle was to live her life in a new way, to break with the uglier traits of the former Thesme.

She decided that in the morning she would go into town, find out if she could what kind of care the Ghayrog needed, and buy such medicines or provisions as seemed appropriate.

2

After a long while she returned to the hut. Vismaan lay as she had left him, flat on his back with arms stiff against his sides, and he did not seem to be moving at all, except for the perpetual serpentine writhing of his hair. Asleep? After all his talk of needing none? She went to him and peered down at the strange massive figure on her bed. His eyes were open, and she saw them tracking her.

"How do you feel?" she asked.

"Not well. Walking through the forest was more difficult than I realized."

She put her hand to his forehead. His hard, scaly skin felt cool. But the absurdity of her gesture made her smile. What was a Ghayrog's normal body temperature? Were they susceptible to fever at all, and if so, how could she tell? They were reptiles, weren't they? Did reptiles run high temperatures when they were sick? Suddenly it all seemed preposterous, this notion of nursing a creature of another world.

He said, "Why do you touch my head?"

"It's what we do when a human is sick. To see if you have a fever. I have no medical instruments here. Do you know what I mean by running a fever?"

"Abnormal body temperature. Yes. Mine is high now."

"Are you in pain?"

"Very little. But my systems are disarranged. Can you bring me some water?"

"Of course. And are you hungry? What sort of things do you normally eat?"

"Meat. Cooked. And fruits and vegetables. And a great deal of water."

She fetched a drink for him. He sat up with difficulty—he seemed much weaker than when he had been hobbling through the jungle; most likely he was suffering a delayed reaction to his injuries—and drained the bowl in three greedy gulps. She watched the furious movements of his forked tongue, fascinated. "More," he said, and she poured a second bowl. Her water-jug was nearly empty, and she went outside to fill it at the spring. She plucked a few thokkas from the vine, too, and brought them to him. He held one of the juicy blue-white berries at arm's length, as though that was the only way he could focus his vision properly on it, and rolled it experimentally between two of his fingers. His hands were almost human, Thesme observed, though there were two extra fingers and he had no fingernails, only lateral scaly ridges running along the first two joints.

"What is this fruit called?" he asked.

"Thokka. They grow on a vine all over Narabal. If you like them, I'll bring you as many as you want."

He tasted it cautiously. Then his tongue flickered more rapidly, and he devoured the rest of the berry and held out his hand for another. Now Thesme remembered the reputation of thokkas as aphrodisiacs, but she looked away to hide her grin, and chose not to say anything to him about that. He described himself as male, so the Ghayrogs evidently had sexes, but did they have sex? She had a sudden fanciful image of male Ghayrogs squirting milt from some concealed orifice into tubs into which female Ghayrogs climbed to fertilize themselves. Efficient but not very romantic, she thought, wondering if that was actually how they did it—fertilization at a distant remove, like fishes, like snakes.

She prepared a meal for him of thokkas and fried calimbots and the little many-legged, delicate-flavored hiktigans that she netted in the stream. All her wine was gone, but she had lately made a kind of fermented juice from a fat red fruit whose name she did not know, and she gave him some of that. His appetite seemed healthy. Afterward she asked him if she could examine his leg, and he told her she could.

The break was more than midway up, in the widest part of his thigh. Thick though his scaly skin was, it showed some signs of swelling there. Very lightly she put her fingertips to the place and probed. He made a barely audible hiss but otherwise gave no sign that she might be increasing his discomfort. It seemed to her that something was moving inside his thigh. The broken ends of the bone, was it? Did Ghayrogs *have* bones? She knew so little, she thought dismally—about Ghayrogs, about the healing arts, about anything.

"If you were human," she said, "we would use our machines to see the fracture, and we would bring the broken place together and bind it until it knitted. Is it anything like that with your people?"

"The bone will knit of its own," he replied. "I will draw the break together through muscular contraction and hold it until it heals. But I must remain lying down for a few days, so that the leg's own weight does not pull the break apart when I stand. Do you mind if I stay here that long?"

"Stay as long as you like. As long as you need to stay."

"You are very kind."

"I'm going into town tomorrow to pick up supplies. Is there anything you particularly want?"

"Do you have entertainment cubes? Music, books?"

"I have just a few here. I can get more tomorrow."

"Please. The nights will be very long for me as I lie here without sleeping. My people are great consumers of amusement, you know."

"I'll bring whatever I can find," she promised.

She gave him three cubes—a play, a symphony, a color composition—and went about her after-dinner cleaning. Night had fallen, early as always, this close to the equator. She heard a light rainfall beginning again outside. Ordinarily she would read for a while, until it grew too dark, and then lie down to sleep. But tonight everything was different. A mysterious reptilian creature occupied her bed; she would have to put together a new sleeping-place for herself on the floor; and all this conversation, the first she had had in so many weeks, had left her mind buzzing with unaccustomed alertness. Vismaan seemed content with his cubes. She went outside and collected bubblebush leaves, a double armful of them and then another, and strewed them on the floor near the door of her hut. Then, going to the Ghayrog, she asked if she could do anything for him; he answered by a tiny shake of his head, without taking his attention from the cube. She wished him a good night and lay down on her improvised bed. It was comfortable enough, more so than she had expected. But sleep was impossible. She turned this way and that, feeling cramped and stiff, and the presence of the other a few yards away seemed to announce itself by a tangible pulsation in her soul. And there was the Ghayrog's odor, too, pungent and inescapable. Somehow she had ceased noticing it while they ate, but now, with all her nerve-endings tuned to maximum sensitivity as she lay in the dark, she perceived it almost as she would a trumpet-blast unendingly repeated. From time to time she sat up and stared through the darkness at Vismaan, who lay motionless and silent. Then at some point slumber overtook her, for when the sounds of the new morning came to her, the many familiar piping and screeching melodies, and the early light made its way through the door-opening, she awakened into the kind of disorientation that comes often when one has been sleeping soundly in a place that is not one's usual bed. It took her a few moments to collect herself, to remember where she was and why.

He was watching her. "You spent a restless night. My being here disturbs you."

"I'll get used to it. How do you feel?"

"Stiff. Sore. But I am already beginning to mend, I think. I sense the work going on within."

She brought him water and a bowl of fruit. Then she went out into the mild misty dawn and slipped quickly into the pond to bathe. When she returned to the hut the odor hit her with new impact. The contrast between the fresh air of morning and the acrid Ghayrog-flavored atmosphere indoors was severe; yet soon it passed from her awareness once again.

As she dressed she said, "I won't be back from Narabal until nightfall. Will you be all right here by yourself?"

"If you leave food and water within my reach. And something to read."

"There isn't much. I'll bring more back for you. It'll be a quiet day for you, I'm afraid."

"Perhaps there will be a visitor."

"A visitor?" Thesme cried, dismayed. "Who? What sort of visitor? No one comes here! Or do you mean some Ghayrog who was traveling with you and who'll be out looking for you?"

"Oh, no, no. No one was with me. I thought, possibly friends of yours—"

"I have no friends," said Thesme solemnly.

It sounded foolish to her the instant she said it—self-pitying, melodramatic. But the Ghayrog offered no comment, leaving her without a way of retracting it, and to hide her embarrassment she busied herself elaborately in the job of strapping on her pack.

He was silent until she was ready to leave. Then he said, "Is Narabal very beautiful?"

"You haven't seen it?"

"I came down the inland route from Til-omon. In Til-omon they told me how beautiful Narabal is."

"Narabal is nothing," Thesme said. "Shacks. Muddy streets. Vines growing over everything, pulling the buildings apart before they're a year old. They told you that in Til-omon? They were joking with you. The Til-omon people despise Narabal. The towns are rivals, you know—the two main tropical ports. If anyone in Til-omon told you how wonderful Narabal is, he was lying, he was playing games with you."

"But why do that?"

Thesme shrugged. "How would I know? Maybe to get you out of Til-omon faster. Anyway, don't look forward to Narabal. In a thousand years it'll be something, I suppose, but right now it's just a dirty frontier town."

"All the same, I hope to visit it. When my leg is stronger, will you show me Narabal?"

"Of course," she said. "Why not? But you'll be disappointed, I promise you. And now I have to leave. I want to get the walk to town behind me before the hottest part of the day."

3

As she made her way briskly toward Narabal she envisioned herself turning up in town one of these days with a Ghayrog by her side. How they'd love that, in Narabal! Would she and Vismaan be pelted with rocks and clots of mud? Would people point and snicker, and snub her when she tried to greet them? Probably. There's that crazy Thesme, they would say to each other, bringing aliens to town, running around with snaky Ghayrogs, probably doing all sorts of unnatural things with them out in the jungle. Yes. Yes. Thesme smiled. It might be fun to promenade about Narabal with Vismaan. She would try it as soon as he was capable of making the long trek through the jungle.

The path was no more than a crudely slashed track, blaze-marks on the trees and an occasional cairn, and it was overgrown in many places. But she had grown skilled at jungle travel and she rarely lost her way for long; by late morning she reached the outlying plantations, and soon Narabal itself was in view, straggling up one hillside and down another in a wobbly arc along the seashore.

Thesme had no idea why anyone had wanted to put a city here—halfway around the world from anywhere, the extreme southwest point of Zimroel. It was some idea of Lord Melikand's, the same Coronal who had invited all the aliens to settle on Majipoor, to encourage development on the western continent. In Lord Melikand's time Zimroel had only two cities, both of them terribly isolated, virtual geographic accidents founded in the earliest days of human settlement on Majipoor, before it became apparent that the other continent was going to be the center of Majipoori life. There was Pidruid up in the northwest, with its wondrous climate and its spectacular natural harbor, and there was Piliplok all the way across on the eastern coast, where the hunters of the migratory sea-dragons had their base. But now also there was a little outpost called

Ni-moya on one of the big inland rivers, and Til-omon had sprung up on the western coast at the edge of the tropical belt, and evidently some settlement was being founded in the central mountains, and supposedly the Ghayrogs were building a town a thousand miles or so east of Pidruid, and there was Narabal down here in the steaming rainy south, at the tip of the continent with sea all around. If one stood by the shore of Narabal Channel and looked toward the water one felt the terrible weight of the knowledge that at one's back lay thousands of miles of wilderness, and then thousands of miles of ocean, separating one from the continent of Alhanroel where the real cities were. When she was young Thesme had found it frightening to think that she lived in a place so far from the centers of civilized life that it might as well be on some other planet; and other times Alhanroel and its thriving cities seemed merely mythical to her, and Narabal the true center of the universe. She had never been anywhere else, and had no hope of it. Distances were too great. The only town within reasonable reach was Til-omon, but even that was far away, and those who had been there said it was much like Narabal, anyway, only with less rain and the sun standing constantly in the sky like a great boring, inquisitive green eye.

In Narabal she felt inquisitive eyes on her wherever she turned: everyone staring, as though she had come to town naked. They all knew who she was—wild Thesme who had run off to the jungle—and they smiled at her and waved and asked her how everything was going, and behind those trivial pleasantries were the eyes, intent and penetrating and hostile, drilling into her, plumbing her for the hidden truths of her life. *Why do you despise us? Why have you withdrawn from us? Why are you sharing your house with a disgusting snake-man?* And she smiled and waved back, and said, "Nice to see you again," and "Everything's just fine," and replied silently to the probing eyes, *I don't hate anybody. I just needed to get away from myself. I'm helping the Ghayrog because it's time I helped someone and he happened to come along.* But they would never understand.

No one was at home at her mother's house. She went to her old room and stuffed her pack with books and cubes, and ransacked the medicine cabinet for drugs that she thought might do Vismaan some good, one to reduce inflammation, one to promote healing, a specific for high fever, and some others—probably all useless to an alien, but worth trying, she supposed. She wandered through the house, which was becoming strange to her even though she had lived in it nearly all her life. Wooden floors instead of strewn leaves—real transparent windows—doors on hinges—a cleanser, an actual mechanical cleanser with knobs and handles!—all those *civilized* things, the million and one humble little things that humanity had invented so many thousands of years ago on another world, and from which she had blithely walked away to live in her humid little hut with live branches sprouting from its walls—

"Thesme?"

She looked up, taken by surprise. Her sister Mirifaine had come in: her twin, in a manner of speaking—same face, same long, thin arms and legs, same straight brown hair, but ten years older, ten years more reconciled to the patterns of her life, a married woman, a mother, a hard worker. Thesme had always found it distressing to look at Mirifaine. It was like looking in a mirror and seeing herself old.

Thesme said, "I needed a few things."

"I was hoping you'd decided to move back home."

"What for?"

Mirifaine began to reply—most likely some standard homily, about resuming normal life, fitting into society and being useful, et cetera, et cetera—but Thesme saw her shift direction while all that was still unspoken, and Mirifaine said finally, "We miss you, love."

"I'm doing what I need to do. It's been good to see you, Mirifaine."

"Won't you at least stay the night? Mother will be back soon—she'd be delighted if you were here for dinner—"

"It's a long walk. I can't spend more time here."

"You look good, you know. Tanned, healthy. I suppose being a hermit agrees with you, Thesme."

"Yes. Very much."

"You don't mind living alone?"

"I adore it," Thesme said. She began to adjust her pack. "How are you, anyway?"

A shrug. "The same. I may go to Til-omon for a while."

"Lucky you."

"I think so. I wouldn't mind getting out of the mildew zone for a little holiday. Holthus has been working up there all month, on some big scheme to build new towns in the mountains—housing for all these aliens that are starting to move in. He wants me to bring the children up, and I think I will."

"Aliens?" Thesme said.

"You don't know about them?"

"Tell me."

"The offworlders that have been living up north are starting to filter this way, now. There's one kind that looks like lizards with human arms and legs that's interested in starting farms in the jungles."

"Ghayrogs."

"Oh, you've heard of them, then? And another kind, all puffy and warty, frog-faced ones with dark gray skins—they do practically all the government jobs now in Pidruid, Holthus says, the customs-inspectors and market clerks and things like that—well, they're being hired down here, too, and Holthus and some syndicate of Til-omon people are planning housing for them inland—"

"So that they won't smell up the coastal cities?"

"What? Oh, I suppose that's part of it—nobody knows how they'll fit in here, after all—but really I think it's just that we don't have accommodations for a lot of immigrants in Narabal, and I gather it's the same in Til-omon, and so—"

"Yes, I see," said Thesme. "Well, give everyone my love. I have to begin heading back. I hope you enjoy your holiday in Til-omon."

"Thesme, please—"

"Please what?"

Mirifaine said sadly, "You're so brusque, so distant, so chilly! It's been months since I've seen you, and you barely tolerate my questions, you look at me with such anger—anger for what, Thesme? Have I ever hurt you? Was I ever anything other than loving? Were any of us? You're such a mystery, Thesme."

Thesme knew it was futile to try once more to explain herself. No one understood her, no one ever would, least of all those who said they loved her. Trying to keep her voice gentle, she said, "Call it an overdue adolescent rebellion, Miri. You were all very kind to me. But nothing was working right and I had to run away." She touched her fingertips lightly to her sister's arm. "Maybe I'll be back one of these days."

"I hope so."

"Just don't expect it to happen soon. Say hello to everybody for me," said Thesme, and went out.

She hurried through town, uneasy and tense, afraid of running into her mother or any of her old friends and especially any of her former lovers; and as she carried out her errands she looked about furtively, like a thief, more than once ducking into an alleyway to avoid someone she needed to avoid. The encounter with Mirifaine had been disturbing enough. She had not realized, until Mirifaine had said it, that she had been showing anger; but Miri was right, yes, Thesme could still feel the dull throbbing residue of fury within her. These people, these dreary little people with their little ambitions and their little fears and their little prejudices, going through the little rounds of their meaningless days—they infuriated her. Spilling out over Majipoor like a plague, nibbling at the unmapped forests, staring at the enormous uncrossable ocean, founding ugly muddy towns in the midst of astounding beauty, and never once questioning the purpose of anything—that was the worst of it, their bland unquestioning natures. Did they never once look up at the stars and ask what it all meant, this outward surge of humanity from Old Earth, this replication of the mother world on a thousand conquered planets? Did they care? This could *be* Old Earth for all it mattered, except that that was a tired, drab, plundered, forgotten husk of a world and this, even after centuries and centuries of human occupation, was still beautiful; but long ago Old Earth had no doubt been as beautiful as Majipoor was now; and in five thousand more years Majipoor would be the same way, with hideous cities stretching for hundreds of miles wherever you looked, and traffic everywhere, and filth in the rivers, and the animals wiped out and the poor cheated Shapeshifters penned up in reservations somewhere, all the old mistakes carried out once again on a virgin world. Thesme boiled with an indignation so fierce it amazed her. She had never known that her quarrel with the world was so cosmic. She had thought it was merely a matter of failed love affairs and raw nerves and muddled personal goals, not this irate dissatisfaction with the entire human universe that had so suddenly overwhelmed her. But the rage held its power in her. She wanted to seize Narabal and push it into the ocean. But she could not do that, she could not change a thing, she could not halt for a moment the spread of what they called civilization here; all she could do was flee, back to her jungle, back to the interlacing vines and the steamy, foggy air and the shy creatures of the marshes, back to her hut, back to her lame Ghayrog, who was himself part of the tide that was overwhelming the planet but for whom she would care, whom she would even cherish, because the others of her kind disliked or even hated him, and so she could use him as one of her ways of distinguishing herself from *them*, and because also he needed her just now and no one had ever needed her before.

Her head was aching and the muscles of her face had gone rigid, and she realized she was walking with her shoulders hunched, as if to relax them would be to surrender to the way of life that she had repudiated. As swiftly as she could, she escaped once again from Narabal; but it was not until she had been on the jungle trail for two hours, and the last outskirts of the town were well behind her, that she began to feel the tensions ebbing. She paused at a little lake she knew and stripped and soaked herself in its cool depths to rid herself of the last taint of town, and then, with her going-to-town clothes slung casually over her shoulder, she marched naked through the jungle to her hut.

4

Vismaan lay in bed and did not seem to have moved at all while she was gone. "Are you feeling better?" she asked. "Were you able to manage by yourself?"

"It was a very quiet day. There is somewhat more of a swelling in my leg."

"Let me see."

She probed it cautiously. It *did* seem puffier, and he pulled away slightly as she touched him, which probably meant that there was real trouble in there, if the Ghayrog sense of pain was as weak as he claimed. She debated the merit of getting him into Narabal for treatment. But he seemed unworried, and she doubted that the Narabal doctors knew much about Ghayrog physiology anyway. Besides, she wanted him here. She unpacked the medicines she had brought from town and gave him the ones for fever and inflammation, and then prepared fruits and vegetables for his dinner. Before it grew too dark she checked the traps at the edge of the clearing and found a few small animals in them, a young sigimoin and a couple of mintuns. She wrung their necks with a practiced hand— it had been terribly hard at first, but meat was important to her and no one else was likely to do her killing for her, out here—and dressed them for roasting. Once she had the fire started she went back inside. Vismaan was playing one of the new cubes she had brought him, but he put it aside when she entered.

"You said nothing about your visit to Narabal," he remarked.

"I wasn't there long. Got what I needed, had a little chat with one of my sisters, came away edgy and depressed, felt better as soon as I was in the jungle."

"You have great hatred for that place."

"It's worth hating. Those dismal boring people, those ugly squat little buildings—" She shook her head. "Oh: my sister told me that they're going to found some new towns inland for offworlders, because so many are moving south. Ghayrogs, mainly, but also some other kind with warts and gray skins—"

"Hjorts," said Vismaan.

"Whatever. They like to work as customs-inspectors, she told me. They're going to be settled inland because no one wants them in Tilomon or Narabal, is my guess."

"I have never felt unwanted among humans," the Ghayrog said.

"Really? Maybe you haven't noticed. I think there's a great deal of prejudice on Majipoor."

"It has not been evident to me. Of course, I have never been in Narabal, and perhaps it is stronger there than elsewhere. Certainly in the north there is no difficulty. You have never been in the north?"

"No."

"We find ourselves welcome among humans in Pidruid."

"Is that true? I hear that the Ghayrogs are building a city for themselves somewhere east of Pidruid, quite a way east, on the Great Rift. If everything's so wonderful for you in Pidruid, why settle somewhere else?"

Vismaan said calmly, "It is we who are not altogether comfortable living with humans. The rhythms of our lives are so different from yours—our habits of sleep, for instance. We find it difficult living in a city that goes dormant eight hours every night, when we ourselves remain awake. And there are other differences. So we are building Dulorn. I hope you see it someday. It is quite marvelously beautiful, constructed entirely from a white stone that shines with an inner light. We are very proud of it."

"Why don't you live there, then?"

"Is your meat not burning?" he asked.

She reddened and ran outside, barely in time to snatch dinner from the spits. A little sullenly she sliced it and served it, along with some thokkas and a flask of wine she had bought that afternoon in Narabal. Vismaan sat up, with some awkwardness, to eat.

He said after a while, "I lived in Dulorn for several years. But that is very dry country, and I come from a place on my planet that is warm and wet, like Narabal. So I journeyed down here to find fertile lands. My distant ancestors were farmers, and I thought to return to their ways. When I heard that in the tropics of Majipoor one could raise six harvests a year, and that there was land everywhere for the claiming, I set out to explore the territory."

"Alone?"

"Alone, yes. I have no mate, though I intend to obtain one as soon as I am settled."

"And you'll raise crops and market them in Narabal?"

"So I intend. On my home world there is scarcely any wild land anywhere, and hardly enough remaining for agriculture. We import most of our food—do you know that? And so Majipoor has a powerful appeal for us, this gigantic planet with its sparse population and its great wilderness awaiting development. I am very happy to be here. And I think that you are not right, about our being unwelcome among your fellow citizens. You Majipoori are kind and gentle folk, civil, law-abiding, orderly."

"Even so: if anyone knew I was living with a Ghayrog, they'd be shocked."

"Shocked? Why?"

"Because you're an alien. Because you're a reptile."

Vismaan made an odd snorting sound. Laughter? "We are not reptiles! We are warm-blooded, we nurse our young—"

"Reptilian, then. *Like* reptiles."

"Externally, perhaps. But we are nearly as mammalian as you, I insist."

"Nearly?"

"Only that we are egg-layers. But there are some mammals of that sort, too. You much mistake us if you think—"

"It doesn't really matter. Humans perceive you as reptiles, and we aren't comfortable with reptiles, and there's always going to be awkwardness between humans and Ghayrogs because of that. It's a tradition that goes back into prehistoric times on Old Earth. Besides—" She caught herself just as she was about to make a reference to the Ghayrog odor. "Besides," she said clumsily, "you look scary."

"More so than a huge shaggy Skandar? More so than a Su-Suheris with two heads?" Vismaan turned toward her and fixed his unsettling lidless eyes on her. "I think you are telling me that *you* are uncomfortable with Ghayrogs yourself, Thesme."

"No."

"The prejudices of which you speak have never been visible to me. This is the first time I have heard of them. Am I troubling to you, Thesme? Shall I go?"

"No. No. You're completely misunderstanding me. I want you to stay here. I want to help you. I feel no fear of you at all, no dislike, nothing negative whatever. I was only trying to tell you—trying to explain about the people in Narabal, how they feel, or how I think they feel, and—" She took a long gulp of her wine. "I don't know how we got into all of this. I'm sorry. I'd like to talk about something else."

"Of course."

But she suspected that she had wounded him, or at least aroused some discomfort in him. In his cool alien way he seemed to have considerable insight, and maybe he was right, maybe it was her own prejudice that was showing, her own uneasiness. She had bungled all of her relationships with humans; quite conceivably she was incapable of getting along with anyone, she thought, human or alien, and had shown Vismaan in a thousand unconscious ways that her hospitality was merely a willed act, artificial and half reluctant, intended to cover an underlying dislike for his presence here. Was that so? She understood less and less of her own motivations, it appeared, as she grew older. But wherever the truth might lie, she did not want him to feel like an intruder here. In the days ahead, she resolved, she would find ways of showing him that her taking him in and caring for him were genuinely founded.

She slept more soundly that night than the one before, although she was still not accustomed to sleeping on the floor in a pile of bubblebush leaves or having someone with her in the hut, and every few hours she awakened. Each time she did, she looked across at the Ghayrog, and saw him each time busy with the entertainment cubes. He took no notice of her. She tried to imagine what it was like to do all of one's sleeping in a single three-month stretch, and to spend the rest of one's time constantly awake; it was, she thought, the most alien thing about him. And to lie there hour after hour, unable to stand, unable to sleep, unable to hide from the discomfort of the injury, making use of whatever diversion was available to consume the time—few torments could be worse. And yet his mood never changed: serene, unruffled, placid, impassive. Were all Ghayrogs like that? Did they never get drunk, lose their tempers, brawl in the streets, bewail their destinies, quarrel with their mates? If Vismaan was a fair sample, they had no human frailties. But, then, she reminded herself, they were not human.

5

In the morning she gave the Ghayrog a bath, sponging him until his scales glistened, and changed his bedding. After she had fed him she went off for the day, in her usual fashion; but she felt guilty wandering the jungle by herself while he remained marooned in the hut, and wondered if she should have stayed with him, telling him stories or drawing him into a conversation to ease his boredom. But she was aware that if she were constantly at his side they would quickly run out of things to talk about, and very likely get on each other's nerves; and he had dozens of entertainment cubes to help him ward off boredom, anyway. Perhaps he preferred to be alone most of the time. In any case she needed solitude herself, more than ever now that she was sharing her hut with him, and she made a long reconnaissance that morning, gathering an assortment of berries and roots for dinner. At midday it rained, and she squatted under a vramma tree whose broad leaves sheltered her nicely. She let her eyes go out of focus and emptied her mind of everything, guilts, doubts, fears, memories, the Ghayrog, her family, her former lovers, her unhappiness, her loneliness. The peace that settled over her lasted well into the afternoon.

She grew used to having Vismaan living with her. He continued to be easy and undemanding, amusing himself with his cubes, showing great patience with his immobility. He rarely asked her questions or initiated any sort of talk, but he was friendly enough when she spoke with him, and told her about his home world—shabby and horribly overpopulated, from the sound of things—and about his life there, his dream of settling on Majipoor, his excitement when he first saw the beauty of his adopted planet. Thesme tried to visualize him showing excitement. His snaky hair jumping around, perhaps, instead of just coiling slowly. Or maybe he registered emotion by changes of body odor.

On the fourth day he left the bed for the first time. With her help he hauled himself upward, balancing on his crutch and his good leg and tentatively touching the other one to the ground. She sensed a sudden sharpness of his aroma—a kind of olfactory wince—and decided that her theory must be right, that Ghayrogs did show emotion that way.

"How does it feel?" she asked. "Tender?"

"It will not bear my weight. But the healing is proceeding well. Another few days and I think I will be able to stand. Come, help me walk a little. My body is rusting from so little activity."

He leaned on her and they went outside, to the pond and back at a slow, wary hobble. He seemed refreshed by the little journey. To her surprise she realized that she was saddened by this first show of progress, because it meant that soon—a week, two weeks?—he would be strong enough to leave, and she did not want him to leave. *She did not want him to leave.* That was so odd a perception that it astonished her. She longed for her old reclusive life, the privilege of sleeping in her own bed and going about her forest pleasures without worrying about whether her guest was being sufficiently well amused and all of that; in some ways she was finding it more and more irritating to have the Ghayrog around. And yet, and yet, and yet, she felt downcast and disturbed at the thought that he would shortly leave her. How strange, she thought, how peculiar, how very Thesme-like.

Now she took him walking several times a day. He still could not use the broken leg, but he grew more agile without it, and he said that the swelling was abating and the bone appeared to be knitting properly. He began to talk of the farm he would establish, the crops, the ways of clearing the jungle.

One afternoon at the end of the first week Thesme, as she returned from a calimbot-gathering expedition in the meadow where she had first found the Ghayrog, stopped to check her traps. Most were empty or contained the usual small animals; but there was a strange violent thrashing in the underbrush beyond the pond, and when she approached the trap she had placed there she discovered she had caught a bilantoon. It was the biggest creature she had ever snared. Bilantoons were found all over western Zimroel—elegant fast-moving little beasts with sharp hooves, fragile legs, a tiny upturned tufted tail—but the Narabal form was a giant, twice the size of the dainty northern one. It stood as high as a man's waist, and was much prized for its tender and fragrant meat. Thesme's first impulse was to let the pretty thing go: it seemed much too beautiful to kill, and much too big, also. She had taught herself to slaughter little things that she could seize in one hand, but this was another matter entirely, a major animal, intelligent-looking and noble, with a life that it surely valued, hopes and needs and yearnings, a mate probably waiting somewhere nearby. Thesme told herself that she was being foolish. Droles and mintuns and sigimoins also very likely were eager to go on living, certainly as eager as this bilantoon was, and she killed them without hesitation. It was a mistake to romanticize animals, she knew—especially when in her more civilized days she had been willing to eat their flesh quite gladly, if slain by other hands. The bilantoon's bereaved mate had not mattered to her then.

As she drew nearer she saw that the bilantoon in its panic had broken one of its delicate legs, and for an instant she thought of splinting it and keeping the creature as a pet. But that was even more absurd. She could not adopt every cripple the jungle brought her. The bilantoon would never calm down long enough for her to examine its leg; and if by some miracle she did manage to repair it, the animal would probably run away the first chance that it got. Taking a deep breath, she came around behind the struggling creature, caught it by its soft muzzle, and snapped its long graceful neck.

The job of butchering it was bloodier and more difficult than Thesme expected. She hacked away grimly for what seemed like hours, until Vismaan called from within the hut to find out what she was doing.

"Getting dinner ready," she answered. "A surprise. A great treat: roast bilantoon!"

She chuckled quietly. She sounded so wifely, she thought, as she crouched here with blood all over her naked body, sawing away at haunches and ribs, while a reptilian alien creature lay in her bed waiting for his dinner.

But eventually the ugly work was done and she had the meat smoldering over a smoky fire, as one was supposed to do, and she cleansed herself in the pond and set about collecting thokkas and boiling some ghumba-root and opening the remaining flasks of her new Narabal wine. Dinner was ready as darkness came, and Thesme felt immense pride in what she had achieved.

She expected Vismaan to gobble it without comment, in his usual phlegmatic way, but no: for the first time she thought she detected a look of animation on his face—a new sparkle in the eyes, maybe, a different pattern of tongue-flicker. She decided she might be getting better at reading his expressions. He gnawed the roast bilantoon enthusiastically, praised its flavor and texture, and asked again and again for more. For each serving she gave him she took one for herself, forcing the meat down until she was glutted and going onward anyway well past satiation, telling herself that whatever was not consumed now would spoil before morning. "The meat goes so well with the thokkas," she said, popping another of the blue-white berries into her mouth.

"Yes. More, please."

He calmly devoured whatever she set before him. Finally she could eat no more, nor could she even watch him. She put what remained within his reach, took a last gulp of the wine, shuddered a little, laughed as a few drops trickled down her chin and over her breasts. She sprawled out on the bubblebush leaves. Her head was spinning. She lay facedown, clutching the floor, listening to the sounds of biting and chewing going on and on and on not far away. Then even the Ghayrog was done feasting, and all was still. Thesme waited for sleep, but sleep would not come. She grew dizzier, until she feared being flung in some terrible centrifugal arc through the side of the hut. Her skin was blazing, her nipples felt hard and sore. I have had much too much to drink, she thought, and I have eaten too many thokkas. Seeds and all, the most potent way, a dozen berries at least, their fiery juice now coursing wildly through her brain.

She did not want to sleep alone, huddled this way on the floor.

With exaggerated care Thesme rose to her knees, steadied herself, and crawled slowly toward the bed. She peered at the Ghayrog, but her eyes were blurred and she could make out only a rough outline of him.

"Are you asleep?" she whispered.

"You know that I would not be sleeping."

"Of course. Of course. Stupid of me."

"Is something wrong, Thesme?"

"Wrong? No, not really. Nothing wrong. Except—it's just that—" She hesitated. "I'm drunk—do you know? Do you understand what being drunk means?"

"Yes."

"I don't like being on the floor. Can I lie beside you?"

"If you wish."

"I have to be very careful. I don't want to bump into your bad leg. Show me which one it is."

"It's almost healed, Thesme. Don't worry. Here: lie down." She felt his hand closing around her wrist and drawing her upward. She let herself float, and drifted easily to his side. She could feel the strange, hard, shell-like skin of him against her from breast to hip, so cool, so scaly, so smooth. Timidly she rubbed her hand across his body. Like a fine piece of luggage, she thought, digging her fingertips in a little, probing the powerful muscles beneath the rigid surface. His odor changed, becoming spicy, piercing.

"I like the way you smell," she murmured.

She buried her forehead against his chest and held tight to him. She had not been in bed with anyone for months and months, almost a year, and it was good to feel him so close. Even a Ghayrog, she thought. Even a Ghayrog. Just to have the contact, the closeness. It feels so good.

He touched her.

She had not expected that. The entire nature of their relationship was that she cared for him and he passively accepted her services. But suddenly his hand—cool, ridged, scaly, smooth—was passing over her body. Brushing lightly across her breasts, trailing down her belly, pausing at her thighs. What was this? Was Vismaan making *love* to her? She thought of his sexless body, like a machine. He went on stroking her. This is very weird, she thought. Even for Thesme, she told herself, this is an extremely weird thing. He is not human. And I—

And I am very lonely—

And I am very drunk—

"Yes, please," she said softly. "Please."

She hoped only that he would continue stroking her. But then he slipped one arm about her shoulders and lifted her easily, gently, rolling her over on top of him and lowering her, and she felt the unmistakable jutting rigidity of maleness against her thigh. What? Did he carry a concealed penis somewhere beneath his scales, that he let slide out when it was needed for use? And was he going to—

Yes.

He seemed to know what to do. Alien he might be, uncertain at their first meeting even whether she was male or female, and nevertheless he plainly understood the theory of human lovemaking. For an instant, as she felt him entering her, she was engulfed by terror and shock and revulsion, wondering if he would hurt her, if he would be painful to receive, and thinking also that this was grotesque and monstrous, this coupling of human and Ghayrog, something that quite likely had never happened before in the history of the universe. She wanted to pull herself free and run out into the night. But she was too dizzy, too drunk, too confused to move; and then she realized that he was not hurting her at all, that he was sliding in and out like some calm clockwork device, and that waves of pleasure were spreading outward from her loins, making her tremble and sob and gasp and press herself against that smooth leathery carapace of his—

She let it happen, and cried out sharply at the best moment, and afterward lay curled up against his chest, shivering, whimpering a little, gradually growing calm. She was sober now. She knew what she had done, and it amazed her, but more than that it amused her. Take *that*, Narabal! The Ghayrog is my lover! And the pleasure had been so intense, so extreme. Had there been any pleasure in it for him? She did not dare ask. How did one tell if a Ghayrog had an orgasm? Did they have them at all? Would the concept mean anything to him? She wondered if he had made love to human women before. She did not dare ask that, either. He had been so capable—not exactly skilled, but definitely very certain about what needed to be done, and he had done it rather more competently than many men she had known, though whether it was because he had had experience with humans or simply because his clear, cool mind could readily calculate the anatomical necessities, she did not know, and she doubted that she would ever know.

He said nothing. She clung to him and drifted into the soundest sleep she had had in weeks.

6

In the morning she felt strange but not repentant. They did not talk about what had passed between them that night. He played his cubes; she went out at dawn for a swim to clear her throbbing head, and tidied some of the debris left from their bilantoon feast, and made breakfast for them, and afterward she took a long walk toward the north, to a little mossy cave, where she sat most of the morning, replaying in her mind the texture of his body against her and the touch of his hand on her thighs and the wild shudder of ecstasy that had run through her body. She could not say that she found him in any way attractive. Forked tongue, hair like live snakes, scales all over his body—no, no, what had happened last night had not had anything whatever to do with physical attraction, she decided. Then why had it happened? The wine and the thokkas, she told herself, and her loneliness, and her readiness to rebel against the conventional values of the citizens of Narabal. Giving herself to a Ghayrog was the finest way she knew of showing her defiance for all that those people believed. But of course such an act of defiance was meaningless unless they found out about it. She resolved to take Vismaan to Narabal with her as soon as he was able to make the trip.

After that they shared her bed every night. It seemed absurd to do otherwise. But they did not make love the second night, or the third, or the fourth; they lay side by side without touching, without speaking. Thesme would have been willing to yield herself if he had reached out for her, but he did not. Nor did she choose to approach him. The silence between them became an embarrassment to her, but she was afraid to break it for fear of hearing things that she did not want to hear—that he had disliked their lovemaking, or that he regarded such acts as obscene and unnatural and had done it that once only because she seemed so insistent, or that he was aware that she felt no true desire for him but was merely using him to make a point in her ongoing warfare against convention. At the end of the week, troubled by the accumulated tensions of so many unspoken uncertainties, Thesme risked rolling against him when she got into the bed, taking trouble to make it seem accidental, and he embraced her easily and willingly, gathering her into his arms without hesitation.

After that they made love on some nights and did not on others, and it was always a random and unpremeditated thing, casual, almost trivial, something they occasionally did before she went to sleep, with no more mystery or magic about it than that. It brought her great pleasure every time. The alienness of his body soon became invisible to her.

He was walking unaided now and each day he spent more time taking exercise. First with her, then by himself, he explored the jungle trails, moving cautiously at the beginning but soon striding along with only a slight limp. Swimming seemed to further the healing process, and for hours at a time he paddled around Thesme's little pond, annoying the gromwark that lived in a muddy burrow at its edge; the slow-moving old creature crept from its hiding-place and sprawled out at the pond's rim like some bedraggled bristly sack that had been discarded there. It eyed the Ghayrog glumly and would not return to the water until he was done with his swim. Thesme consoled it with tender green shoots that she plucked upstream, far beyond the reach of the gromwark's little sucker-feet.

"When will you take me to Narabal?" Vismaan asked her one rainy evening.

"Why not tomorrow?" she replied.

That night she felt unusual excitement, and pressed herself insistently against him.

They set out at dawn in light rain showers that soon gave way to brilliant sunshine. Thesme adopted a careful pace, but soon it was apparent that the Ghayrog was fully healed, and before long she was walking swiftly. Vismaan had no difficulty keeping up. She found herself chattering—telling him the names of every plant or animal they encountered, giving him bits of Narabal's history, talking about her brothers and sisters and people she knew in town. She was desperately eager to be seen by them with him—*look, this is my alien lover, this is the Ghayrog I've been sleeping with*—and when they came to the outskirts she began looking around intently, hoping to find someone familiar; but scarcely anyone seemed to be visible on the outer farms, and she did not recognize those who were. "Do you see how they're staring at us?" she whispered to Vismaan, as they passed into a more thickly inhabited district. "They're afraid of you. They think you're the vanguard of some sort of alien invasion. And they're wondering what I'm doing with you, why I'm being so civil to you."

"I see none of that," said Vismaan. "They appear curious about me, yes. But I detect no fear, no hostility. Is it because I am unfamiliar with human facial expressions? I thought I had learned to interpret them quite well."

"Wait and see," Thesme told him. But she had to admit to herself that she might be exaggerating things a little, or even more than a little. They were nearly in the heart of Narabal, now, and some people had glanced at the Ghayrog in surprise and curiosity, yes, but they had quickly softened their stares, while others had merely nodded and smiled as though it were the most ordinary thing in the world to have some kind of offworld creature walking through the streets. Of actual hostility she could find none. That angered her. These mild, sweet people, these bland, amiable people, were not at all reacting as she had expected. Even when she finally met familiar people—Khanidor, her oldest brother's best friend, and Hennimont Sibroy who ran the little inn near the waterfront, and the woman from the flower-shop—they were nothing other than cordial as Thesme said, "This is Vismaan, who has been living with me lately." Khanidor smiled as though he had always known Thesme to be the sort of person who would set up housekeeping with an alien, and spoke of the new towns for Ghayrogs and Hjorts that Mirifaine's husband was planning to build. The innkeeper reached out jovially to shake Vismaan's hand and invited him down for some wine on the house, and the flower-shop woman said over and over, "How interesting, how interesting! We hope you like our little town!" Thesme felt patronized by their cheerfulness. It was as if they were going out of their way not to let her shock them—as if they had already taken all the wildness from Thesme that they were going to take, and now would accept anything, anything at all from her, without caring, without surprise, without comment. Perhaps they misunderstood the nature of her relationship with the Ghayrog and thought he was merely boarding with her. Would they give her the reaction she wanted if she came right out and said they were lovers, that his body had been inside hers, that they had done that which was unthinkable between human and alien? Probably not. Probably even if she and the Ghayrog lay down and coupled in Pontifex Square it would cause no stir in this town, she thought, scowling.

And did Vismaan like their little town? It was, as always, difficult to detect emotional response in him. They walked up one street and down another, past the haphazardly planned plazas and the flat-faced scruffy shops and the little lopsided houses with their overgrown gardens, and he said very little. She sensed disappointment and disapproval in his silence, and for all her own dislike of Narabal, she began to feel defensive about the place. It was, after all, a young settlement, an isolated outpost in an obscure corner of a second-class continent, just a few generations old. "What do you think?" she asked finally. "You aren't very impressed by Narabal, are you?"

"You warned me not to expect much."

"But it's even more dismal than I led you to expect, isn't it?"

"I do find it small and crude," he said. "After one has seen Pidruid, or even—"

"Pidruid's thousands of years old."

"—Dulorn," he went on. "Dulorn is extraordinarily beautiful even now, when it is just being built. But of course the white stone they use there is—"

"Yes," she said. "Narabal ought to be built out of stone, too, because this climate is so damp that wooden buildings fall apart, but there hasn't been time yet. Once the population's big enough, we can quarry in the mountains and put together something marvelous here. Fifty years from now, a hundred, when we have a proper labor force. Maybe if we got some of those giant four-armed aliens to work here—"

"Skandars," said Vismaan.

"Skandars, yes. Why doesn't the Coronal send us ten thousand Skandars?"

"Their bodies are covered with thick hair. They will find this climate difficult. But doubtless Skandars will settle here, and Vroons, and Su-Suheris, and many, many wet-country Ghayrogs like me. It is a very bold thing your government is doing, encouraging offworld settlers in such numbers. Other planets are not so generous with their land."

"Other planets are not so large," Thesme said. "I think I've heard that even with all the huge oceans we have, Majipoor's land mass is still three or four times the size of any other settled planet. Or something like that. We're very lucky, being such a big world, and yet having such gentle gravity, so that humans and humanoids can live comfortably here. Of course, we pay a high price for that, not having anything much in the way of heavy elements, but still—oh. Hello." The tone of her voice changed abruptly, dropping off to a startled blurt. A slim young man, very tall, with pale wavy hair, had nearly collided with her as he emerged from the bank on the corner, and now he stood gaping at her, and she at him. He was Ruskelorn Yulvan, Thesme's lover for the four months just prior to her withdrawal into the jungle, and the person in Narabal she was least eager to see. But if there had to be a confrontation with him, she intended to make the most of it; and, seizing the initiative after her first moment of confusion, she said, "You look well, Ruskelorn."

"And you. Jungle life must agree with you."

"Very much. It's been the happiest seven months of my life. Ruskelorn, this is my friend Vismaan, who's been living with me the past few weeks. He had an accident while scouting for farmland near my place—broke his leg falling out of a tree—and I've been looking after him."

"Very capably, I imagine," Ruskelorn Yulvan said evenly. "He seems to be in excellent condition." To the Ghayrog he said, "Pleased to meet you," in a way that made it seem as though he might actually mean it.

Thesme said, "He comes from a part of his planet where the climate is a lot like Narabal's. He tells me that there'll be plenty of his country-people settling down here in the tropics in the next few years."

"So I've heard." Ruskelorn Yulvan grinned and said, "You'll find it amazingly fertile territory. Eat a berry at breakfast time and toss the seed away, you'll have a vine as tall as a house by nightfall. That's what everyone says, so it must be true."

The light and casual manner of his speaking infuriated her. Did he not realize that this scaly alien creature, this offworlder, this Ghayrog, was his replacement in her bed? Was he immune to jealousy, or did he simply not understand the real situation? With a ferocious silent intensity she attempted to convey the truth of things to Ruskelorn Yulvan in the most graphic possible way, thinking fierce images of herself in Vismaan's arms, showing Ruskelorn Yulvan the alien hands of Vismaan caressing her breasts and thighs and flicking his little scarlet two-pronged tongue lightly over her closed eyelids, her nipples, her loins. But it was useless. Ruskelorn was no more of a mind-reader than she. *He is my lover,* she thought, *he enters me, he makes me come again and again, I can't wait to get back to the jungle and tumble into bed with him,* and all the while Ruskelorn Yulvan stood there smiling, chatting politely with the Ghayrog, discussing the potential for raising niyk and glein and stajja in these parts, or perhaps lusavender-seed in the swampier districts, and only after a good deal of that did he turn his glance back toward Thesme and ask, as placidly as though he were asking the day of the week, whether she intended to live in the jungle indefinitely.

She glared. "So far I prefer it to life in town. Why?"

"I wondered if you missed the comforts of our splendid metropolis, that's all."

"Not yet, not for a moment. I've never been happier."

"Good. I'm so pleased for you, Thesme." Another serene smile. "How nice to have run into you. How good to have met you," he said to the Ghayrog, and then he was gone.

Thesme smoldered with rage. He had not cared, he had not cared in the slightest; she could be coupling with Ghayrogs or Skandars or the gromwark in the pond for all it mattered to him! She had wanted him to be wounded or at least shocked, and instead he had simply been polite. Polite! It must be that he, like all the others, failed to comprehend the real state of affairs between her and Vismaan—that it was simply inconceivable to them that a woman of human stock would offer her body to a reptilian offworlder, and so they did not consider—they did not even suspect—

"Have you seen enough of Narabal now?" she asked the Ghayrog.

"Enough to realize that there is little to see."

"How does your leg feel? Are you ready to begin the journey back?"

"Have you no errands to perform in town?"

"Nothing important," she said. "I'd like to go."

"Then let us go," he answered.

His leg did seem to be giving him some trouble—the muscles stiffening, probably; that was a taxing hike even for someone in prime condition, and he had traveled only much shorter distances since his recovery—but in his usual uncomplaining way he followed her toward the jungle road. This was the worst time of day to be making the trip, with the sun almost straight overhead and the air moist and heavy from the first gatherings of what would be this afternoon's rainfall. They walked slowly, pausing often, though never once did he say he was tired; it was Thesme herself who was tiring, and she pretended that she wanted to show him some geological formation here, some unusual plant there, in order to manufacture occasions to rest. She did not want to admit fatigue. She had suffered enough mortification today.

The venture into Narabal had been a disaster for her. Proud, defiant, rebellious, scornful of Narabal's conventional ways, she had hauled her Ghayrog lover to town to flaunt him before the tame city-dwellers, and they had not cared. Were they such puddings that they could not guess at the truth? Or had they seen instantly through her pretensions, and were determined to give her no satisfaction? Either way she felt outraged, humiliated, defeated—and very foolish. And what about the bigotry she imagined she had found earlier among the Narabal folk? Were they not threatened by the influx of these aliens? They had all been so charming to Vismaan, so friendly. Perhaps, Thesme thought gloomily, the prejudice was in her mind alone and she had misinterpreted the remarks of others, and in that case it had been stupid to give herself to the Ghayrog, it had accomplished nothing, flouted no Narabal decorum, served no purpose at all in the private war she had been fighting against those people. It had only been a strange and willful and grotesque event.

Neither she nor the Ghayrog spoke during the long, slow, uncomfortable return to the jungle. When they reached her hut he went inside and she bustled about ineffectually in the clearing, checking traps, pulling berries from vines, setting things down and forgetting what she had done with them.

After a while she entered the hut and said to Vismaan, "I think you may as well leave."

"Very well. It *is* time for me to be on my way."

"You can stay here tonight, of course. But in the morning—"

"Why not leave now?"

"It'll be dark soon. You've already walked so many miles today—"

"I have no wish to trouble you. I will go now, I think."

Even now she found it impossible to read his feelings. Was he surprised? Hurt? Angry? He showed her nothing. He offered no gestures of farewell, either, but simply turned and began walking at a steady pace toward the interior of the jungle. Thesme watched him, throat dry, heart pounding, until he disappeared beyond the low-hanging vines. It was all she could do to keep herself from running after him. But then he was gone, and soon the tropical night descended.

She rummaged together a sort of dinner for herself, but she ate very little, thinking, He is out there sitting in the darkness, waiting for the morning to come. They had not even said good-bye. She could have made some little joke, warning him to stay out of sijaneel trees, or he could have thanked her for all she had done on his behalf, but instead there had been nothing, just her dismissal of him and his calm uncomplaining departure. An alien, she thought, and his ways were alien. And yet, when they had been together in bed, and he had touched her and held her and drawn her body down on top of his—

It was a long bleak night for her. She lay huddled in the crudely sewn zanja-down bed that they had so lately shared, listening to the night rain hammering on the vast blue leaves that were her roof, and for the first time since she had entered the jungle, she felt the pain of loneliness. Until this moment she had not realized how much she had valued the bizarre parody of domesticity that she and the Ghayrog had enacted here; but now that was over, and she was alone again, somehow more alone than she had been before, and far more cut off from her old life in Narabal than before, also, and he was out there, unsleeping in the darkness, unsheltered from the rain. I am in love with an alien, she told herself in wonderment, I am in love with a scaly *thing* that speaks no words of endearment and asks hardly any questions and leaves without saying thank you or good-bye. She lay awake for hours, crying now and then. Her body felt tense and clenched from the long walk and the day's frustrations; she drew her knees to her breasts and stayed that way a long while, and then put her hands between her legs and stroked herself, and finally there came a moment of release, a gasp and a little soft moan, and sleep after that.

7

In the morning she bathed and checked her traps and assembled a breakfast and wandered over all the familiar trails near her hut. There was no sign of the Ghayrog. By midday her mood seemed to be lifting, and the afternoon was almost cheerful for her; only as nightfall approached, the time of solitary dinner, did she begin to feel the bleakness descending again. But she endured it. She played the cubes she had brought from home for him, and eventually dropped into sleep, and the next day was a better day, and the next, and the one after that.

Gradually Thesme's life returned to normal. She saw nothing of the Ghayrog and he started to slip from her mind. As the solitary weeks went by she rediscovered the joy of solitude, or so it seemed to her, but then at odd moments she speared herself on some sharp and painful memory of him—the sight of a bilantoon in a thicket or the sijaneel tree with the broken branch or the gromwark sitting sullenly at the edge of the pond—and she realized that she still missed him. She roved the jungle in wider and wider circles, not quite knowing why, until at last she admitted to herself that she was looking for him.

It took her three more months to find him. She began seeing indications of settlement off to the southeast—an apparent clearing, visible two or three hilltops away, with what looked like traces of new trails radiating from it—and in time she made her way in that direction and across a considerable river previously unknown to her, to a zone of felled trees, beyond which was a newly established farm. She skulked along its perimeter and caught sight of a Ghayrog—it was Vismaan, she was certain of that—tilling a field of rich black soil. Fear swept her spirit and left her weak and trembling. Could it be some other Ghayrog? No, no, no, she was sure it was he; she even imagined she detected a little limp. She ducked down out of sight, afraid to approach him. What could she say to him? How could she justify having come this far to seek him out, after having so coolly dismissed him from her life? She drew back into the underbrush and came close to turning away altogether. But then she found her courage and called his name.

He stopped short and looked around.

"Vismaan? Over here! It's Thesme!"

Her cheeks were blazing, her heart pounded terrifyingly. For one dismal instant she was convinced that this was a strange Ghayrog, and apologies for her intrusion were already springing to her lips. But as he came toward her she knew that she had not been mistaken.

"I saw the clearing and thought it might be your farm," she said, stepping out of the tangled brush. "How have you been, Vismaan?"

"Quite excellent. And yourself?"

She shrugged. "I get along. You've done wonders here, Vismaan. It's only been a few months, and look at all this!"

"Yes," he said. "We have worked hard."

"We?"

"I have a mate now. Come: let me introduce you to her, and show you what we have accomplished here."

His tranquil words withered her. Perhaps they were meant to do that—instead of showing any sort of resentment or pique over the way she had sent him out of her life, he was taking his revenge in a more diabolical fashion, through utter dispassionate restraint. But more likely, she thought, he felt no resentment and saw no need for revenge. His view of all that had passed between them was probably entirely unlike hers. Never forget that he is an alien, she told herself.

She followed him up a gentle slope and across a drainage ditch and around a small field that was obviously newly planted. At the top of the hill, half hidden by a lush kitchen-garden, was a cottage of sijaneel timbers not very different from her own, but larger and somewhat more angular in design. From up here the whole farm could be seen, occupying three faces of the little hill. Thesme was astounded at how much he had managed to do—it seemed impossible to have cleared all this, to have built a dwelling, to have made ready the soil for planting, even to have begun planting, in just these few months. She remembered that Ghayrogs did not sleep; but had they no need of rest?

"Turnome!" he called. "We have a visitor, Turnome!"

Thesme forced herself to be calm. She understood now that she had come looking for the Ghayrog because she no longer wanted to be alone, and that she had had some half-conscious fantasy of helping him establish his farm, of sharing his life as well as his bed, of building a true relationship with him; she had even, for one flickering instant, seen herself on a holiday in the north with him, visiting wonderful Dulorn, meeting his countrymen. All that was foolish, she knew, but it had had a certain crazy plausibility until the moment when he told her he had a mate. Now she struggled to compose herself, to be cordial and warm, to keep all absurd hints of rivalry from surfacing—

Out of the cottage came a Ghayrog nearly as tall as Vismaan, with the same gleaming pearly armor of scales, the same slowly writhing serpentine hair; there was only one outward difference between them, but it was a strange one indeed, for the Ghayrog woman's chest was festooned with dangling tubular breasts, a dozen or more of them, each tipped with a dark green nipple. Thesme shivered. Vismaan had said Ghayrogs were mammals, and the evidence was impossible to refute, but the reptilian look of the woman was if anything heightened by those eerie breasts, which made her seem not mammalian but weirdly hybrid and incomprehensible. Thesme looked from one to the other of these creatures in deep discomfort.

Vismaan said, "This is the woman I told you about, who found me when I hurt my leg, and nursed me back to health. Thesme: my mate Turnome."

"You are welcome here," said the Ghayrog woman solemnly.

Thesme stammered some further appreciation of the work they had done on the farm. She wanted only to escape, now, but there was no getting away; she had come to call on her jungle neighbors, and they insisted on observing the niceties. Vismaan invited her in. What was next? A cup of tea, a bowl of wine, some thokkas and grilled mintun? There was scarcely anything inside the cottage except a table and a few cushions and, in the far corner, a curious high-walled woven container of large size, standing on a three-legged stool. Thesme glanced toward it and quickly away, thinking without knowing why that it was wrong to display curiosity about it; but Vismaan took her by the elbow and said, "Let us show you. Come: look." She peered in.

It was an incubator. On a nest of moss were eleven or twelve leathery round eggs, bright green with large red speckles.

"Our firstborn will hatch in less than a month," Vismaan said.

Thesme was swept by a wave of dizziness. Somehow this revelation of the true alienness of these beings stunned her as nothing else had, not the chilly stare of Vismaan's unblinking eyes nor the writhing of his hair nor the touch of his skin against her naked body nor the sudden amazing sensation of him moving inside her. Eggs! A litter! And Turnome already puffing up with milk to nurture them! Thesme had a vision of a dozen tiny lizards clinging to the woman's many breasts, and horror transfixed her: she stood motionless, not even breathing, for an endless moment, and then she turned and bolted, running down the hillside, over the drainage ditch, right across, she realized too late, the newly planted field, and off into the steaming, humid jungle.

8

She did not know how long it was before Vismaan appeared at her door. Time had gone by in a blurred flow of eating and sleeping and weeping and trembling, and perhaps it was a day, perhaps two, perhaps a week, and then there he was, poking his head and shoulders into the hut and calling her name.

"What do you want?" she asked, not getting up.

"To talk. There were things I had to tell you. Why did you leave so suddenly?"

"Does it matter?"

He crouched beside her. His hand rested lightly on her shoulder.

"Thesme, I owe you apologies."

"For what?"

"When I left here, I failed to thank you for all you had done for me. My mate and I were discussing why you had run away, and she said you were angry with me, and I could not understand why. So she and I explored all the possible reasons, and when I described how you and I had come to part, Turnome asked me if I had told you that I was grateful for your help, and I said no, I had not, I was unaware that such things were done. So I have come to you. Forgive me for my rudeness, Thesme. For my ignorance."

"I forgive you," she said in a muffled voice. "Will you go away, now?"

"Look at me, Thesme."

"I'd rather not."

"Please. Will you?" He tugged at her shoulder.

Sullenly she turned to him.

"Your eyes are swollen," he said.

"Something I ate must have disagreed with me."

"You are still angry. Why? I have asked you to understand that I meant no discourtesy. Ghayrogs do not express gratitude in quite the same way humans do. But let me do it now. You saved my life, I believe. You were very kind. I will always remember what you did for me when I was injured. It was wrong of me not to have told you that before."

"And it was wrong of me to throw you out like that," she said in a low voice. "Don't ask me to explain why I did, though. It's very complicated. I'll forgive you for not thanking me if you'll forgive me for making you leave like that."

"No forgiveness was required. My leg had healed; it was time for me to go, as you pointed out; I went on my way and found the land I needed for my farm."

"It was that simple, then?"

"Yes. Of course."

She got to her feet and stood facing him. "Vismaan, why did you have sex with me?"

"Because you seemed to want it."

"That's all?"

"You were unhappy and did not seem to wish to sleep alone. I hoped it would comfort you. I was trying to do the friendly thing, the compassionate thing."

"Oh. I see."

"I believe it gave you pleasure," he said.

"Yes. Yes. It did give me pleasure. But you didn't desire me, then?"

His tongue flickered in what she thought might be the equivalent of a puzzled frown.

"No," he said. "You are human. How can I feel desire for a human? You are so different from me, Thesme. On Majipoor my kind are called aliens, but to me *you* are the alien—is that not so?"

"I suppose. Yes."

"But I was very fond of you. I wished your happiness. In that sense I had desire for you. Do you understand? And I will always be your friend. I hope you will come to visit us, and share in the bounty of our farm. Will you do that, Thesme?"

"I—yes, yes, I will."

"Good. I will go now. But first—"

Gravely, with immense dignity, he drew her to him and enfolded her in his powerful arms. Once again she felt the strange smooth rigidity of his alien skin; once again the little scarlet tongue fluttered across her eyelids in a forked kiss. He embraced her for a long moment.

When he released her he said, "I am extremely fond of you, Thesme. I can never forget you."

"Nor I you."

She stood in the doorway, watching until he disappeared from sight beyond the pond. A sense of ease and peace and warmth had come over her spirit. She doubted that she ever would visit Vismaan and Turnome and their litter of little lizards, but that was all right: Vismaan would understand. Everything was all right. Thesme began to gather her possessions and stuff them into her pack. It was still only midmorning, time enough to make the journey to Narabal.

She reached the city just after the afternoon showers. It was over a year since she had left it, and a good many months since her last visit; and she was surprised by the changes she saw now. There was a boomtown bustle to the place, new buildings going up everywhere, ships in the Channel, the streets full of traffic. And the town seemed to have been invaded by aliens—hundreds of Ghayrogs, and other kinds, too, the warty ones that she supposed were Hjorts, and enormous double-shouldered Skandars, a whole circus of strange beings going about their business and taken absolutely for granted by the human citizens. Thesme found her way with some difficulty to her mother's house. Two of her sisters were there, and her brother Dalkhan. They stared at her in amazement and what seemed like fear.

"I'm back," she said. "I know I look like a wild animal, but I just need my hair trimmed and a new tunic and I'll be human again."

She went to live with Ruskelorn Yulvan a few weeks later, and at the end of the year they were married. For a time she thought of confessing to him that she and her Ghayrog guest had been lovers, but she was afraid to do it, and eventually it seemed unimportant to bring it up at all. She did, finally, ten or twelve years later, when they had dined on roast bilantoon at one of the fine new restaurants in the Ghayrog quarter of town, and she had had much too much of the strong golden wine of the north, and the pressure of old associations was too powerful to resist. When she had finished telling him the story she said, "Did you suspect any of that?" And he said, "I knew it right away, when I saw you with him in the street. But why should it have mattered?"

TWO

The Time of the Burning

*F*or weeks after that astounding experience Hissune does not dare return to the Register of Souls. It was too powerful, too raw; he needs time to digest, to absorb. He had lived months of that woman's life in an hour in that cubicle, and the experience blazes in his soul. Strange new images tumble tempestuously through his consciousness now.

The jungle, first of all—Hissune has never known anything but the carefully controlled climate of the subterranean Labyrinth, except for the time he journeyed to the Mount, the climate of which is in a different way just as closely regulated. So he was amazed by the humidity, the denseness of the foliage, the rain showers, the bird-sounds and insect-sounds, the feel of wet soil beneath bare feet. But that is only a tiny slice of what he has taken in. To be a woman—how astonishing! And then to have an alien for a lover—Hissune has no words for that; it is simply an event that has become part of him, incomprehensible, bewildering. And when he has begun to work his way all through that there is much more for his meditations: the sense of Majipoor as a developing world, parts of it still young, unpaved streets in Narabal, wooden shacks, not at all the neat and thoroughly tamed planet he inhabits, but a turbulent and mysterious land with many dark regions. Hissune mulls these things hour upon hour, while mindlessly arranging his meaningless revenue archives, and gradually it occurs to him that he has been forever transformed by that illicit interlude in the Register of Souls. He can never be only Hissune again; he will always be, in some unfathomable way, not just Hissune but also the woman Thesme who lived and died nine *thousand years ago on another continent, in a hot steamy place that Hissune will never see.*

Then, of course, he hungers for a second jolt of the miraculous Register. A different official is on duty this time, a scowling little Vroon whose mask is askew, and Hissune has to wave his documents around very quickly to get inside. But his glib mind is a match for any of these sluggish civil servants, and soon enough he is in the cubicle, punching out coordinates with swift fingers. Let it be the time of Lord Stiamot, he decides. The final days of the conquest of the Metamorphs by the armies of the human settlers of Majipoor. Give me a soldier of Lord Stiamot's army, he tells the hidden mind of the recording vaults. And perhaps I'll have a glimpse of Lord Stiamot himself!

THE DRY FOOTHILLS WERE burning along a curving crest from Milimorn to Hamifieu, and even up here, in his eyrie fifty miles east on Zygnor Peak, Group Captain Eremoil could feel the hot blast of the wind and taste the charred flavor of the air. A dense crown of murky smoke rose over the entire range. In an hour or two the fliers would extend the fireline from Hamifieu down to that little town at the base of the valley, and tomorrow they'd torch the zone from there south to Sintalmond. And then this entire province would be ablaze, and woe betide any Shapeshifters who lingered in it.

"It won't be long now," Viggan said. "The war's almost over."

Eremoil looked up from his charts of the northwestern corner of the continent and stared at the subaltern. "Do you think so?" he asked vaguely.

"Thirty years. That's about enough."

"Not thirty. Five thousand years, six thousand, however long it's been since humans first came to this world. It's been war all the time, Viggan."

"For a lot of that time we didn't realize we were fighting a war, though."

"No," Eremoil said. "No, we didn't understand. But we understand now, don't we, Viggan?"

He turned his attention back to the charts, bending low, squinting, peering. The oily smoke in the air was bringing tears to his eyes and blurring his vision, and the charts were very finely drawn. Slowly he drew his pointer down the contour lines of the foothills below Hamifieu, checking off the villages on his report-sheets.

Every village along the arc of flame was marked on the charts, he hoped, and officers had visited each to bring notice of the burning. It would go hard for him and those beneath him if the mappers had left any place out, for Lord Stiamot had issued orders that no human lives were to be lost in this climactic drive: all settlers were to be warned and given time to evacuate. The Metamorphs were being given the same warning. One did not simply roast one's enemies alive, Lord Stiamot had said repeatedly. One aimed only to bring them under one's control, and just now fire seemed to be the best means of doing that. Bringing the fire itself under control afterward might be a harder job, Eremoil thought, but that was not the problem of the moment.

"Kattikawn—Bizfern—Domgrave—Byelk—so many little towns, Viggan. Why do people want to live up here, anyway?"

"They say the land is fertile, sir. And the climate is mild, for such a northerly district."

"Mild? I suppose, if you don't mind half a year without rain." Eremoil coughed. He imagined he could hear the crackling of the distant fire through the tawny knee-high grass. On this side of Alhanroel it rained all winter long and then rained not at all the whole summer: a challenge for farmers, one would think, but evidently they had surmounted it, considering how many agricultural settlements had sprouted along the slopes of these hills and downward into the valleys that ran to the sea. This was the height of the dry season now, and the region had been baking under summer sun for months—dry, dry, dry, the dark soil cracked and gullied, the winter-growing grasses dormant and parched, the thick-leaved shrubs folded and waiting. What a perfect time to put the place to the torch and force one's stubborn enemies down to the edge of the ocean, or into it! But no lives lost, no lives lost—Eremoil studied his lists. "Chikmoge—Fualle—Daniup—Michimang—" Again he looked up. To the subaltern he said, "Viggan, what will you do after the war?"

"My family owns lands in the Glayge Valley. I'll be a farmer again, I suppose. And you, sir?"

"My home is in Stee. I was a civil engineer—aqueducts, sewage conduits, other such fascinating things. I can be that again. When did you last see the Glayge?"

"Four years ago," said Viggan.

"And five for me, since Stee. You were at the Battle of Treymone, weren't you?"

"Wounded. Slightly."

"Ever killed a Metamorph?"

"Yes, sir."

Eremoil said, "Not I. Never once. Nine years a soldier, never a life taken. Of course, I've been an officer. I'm not a good killer, I suspect."

"None of us are," said Viggan. "But when they're coming at you, changing shape five times a minute, with a knife in one hand and an axe in the other—or when you know they've raided your brother's land and murdered your nephews—"

"Is that what happened, Viggan?"

"Not to me, sir. But to others, plenty of others. The atrocities—I don't need to tell you how—"

"No. No, you don't. What's this town's name, Viggan?"

The subaltern leaned over the charts. "Singaserin, sir. The lettering's a little smudged, but that's what it says. And it's on our list. See, here. We gave them notice day before yesterday."

"I think we've done them all, then."

"I think so, sir," said Viggan.

Eremoil shuffled the charts into a stack, put them away, and looked out again toward the west. There was a distinct line of demarcation between the zone of the burning and the untouched hills south of it, dark green and seemingly lush with foliage. But the leaves of those trees were shriveled and greasy from months without rain, and those hillsides would explode as though they had been bombed when the fire reached them. Now and again he saw little bursts of flame, no more than puffs of sudden brightness as though from the striking of a light. But it was a trick of distance, Eremoil knew; each of those tiny flares was the eruption of a vast new territory as the fire, carrying itself now by airborne embers where the fliers themselves were not spreading it, devoured the forests beyond Hamifieu.

Viggan said, "Messenger here, sir."

Eremoil turned. A tall young man in a sweaty uniform had clambered down from a mount and was staring uncertainly at him.

"Well?" he said.

"Captain Vanayle sent me, sir. Problem down in the valley. Settler won't evacuate."

"He'd better," Eremoil said, shrugging. "What town is it?"

"Between Kattikawn and Bizfern, sir. Substantial tract. The man's name is Kattikawn, too, Aibil Kattikawn. He told Captain Vanayle that he holds his land by direct grant of the Pontifex Dvorn, that his people have been here thousands of years, and that he isn't going to—"

Eremoil sighed and said, "I don't care if he holds his land by direct grant of the Divine. We're burning that district tomorrow and he'll fry if he stays there."

"He knows that, sir."

"What does he want us to do? Make the fire go around his farm, eh?" Eremoil waved his arm impatiently. "Evacuate him, regardless of what he is or isn't going to do."

"We've tried that," said the messenger. "He's armed and he offered resistance. He says he'll kill anyone who tries to remove him from his land."

"Kill?" Eremoil said, as though the word had no meaning. *"Kill?* Who talks of killing other human beings? The man is crazy. Send fifty troops and get him on his way to one of the safe zones."

"I said he offered resistance, sir. There was an exchange of fire. Captain Vanayle believes that he can't be removed without loss of life. Captain Vanayle asks that you go down in person to reason with the man, sir."

"That *I*—"

Viggan said quietly, "It may be the simplest way. These big landholders can be very difficult."

"Let Vanayle go to him," Eremoil said.

"Captain Vanayle has already attempted to parley with the man, sir," the messenger said. "He was unsuccessful. This Kattikawn demands an audience with Lord Stiamot. Obviously that's impossible, but perhaps if you were to go—"

Eremoil considered it. It was absurd for the commanding officer of the district to undertake such a task. It was Vanayle's direct responsibility to clear the territory before tomorrow's burning; it was Eremoil's to remain up here and direct the action. On the other hand, clearing the territory was ultimately Eremoil's responsibility also, and Vanayle had plainly failed to do it, and sending in a squad to make a forcible removal would probably end in Kattikawn's death and the deaths of a few soldiers, too, which was hardly a useful outcome. Why not go? Eremoil nodded slowly. Protocol be damned: he would not stand on ceremony. He had nothing significant left to do this afternoon and Viggan could look after any details that came up. And if he could save one life, one stupid, stubborn old man's life, by taking a little ride down the mountainside—

"Get my floater," he said to Viggan.

"Sir?"

"Get it. Now, before I change my mind. I'm going down to see him."

"But Vanayle has already—"

"Stop being troublesome, Viggan. I'll only be gone a short while. You're in command here until I get back, but I don't think you'll have to work very hard. Can you handle it?"

"Yes, sir," the subaltern said glumly.

It was a longer journey than Eremoil expected, nearly two hours down the switchbacked road to the base of Zygnor Peak, then across the uneven sloping plateau to the foothills that ringed the coastal plain. The air was hotter though less smoky down there; shimmering heat waves spawned mirages and made the landscape seem to melt and flow. The road was empty of traffic, but he was stopped again and again by panicky migrating beasts, strange animals of species that he could not identify, fleeing wildly from the fire zone ahead. Shadows were beginning to lengthen by the time Eremoil reached the foothill settlements. Here the fire was a tangible presence, like a second sun in the sky; Eremoil felt the heat of it against his cheek, and a fine grit settled on his skin and clothing.

The places he had been checking on his lists now became uncomfortably real to him: Byelk, Domgrave, Bizfern. One was just like the next, a central huddle of shops and public buildings, an outer residential rim, a ring of farms radiating outward beyond that, each town tucked in its little valley where some stream cut down out of the hills and lost itself on the plain. They were all empty now, or nearly so, just a few stragglers left, the others already on the highways leading to the coast. Eremoil supposed that he could walk into any of these houses and find books, carvings, souvenirs of holidays abroad, even pets, perhaps, abandoned in grief; and tomorrow all this would be ashes. But this territory was infested with Shapeshifters. The settlers here had lived for centuries under the menace of an implacable savage foe that flitted in and out of the forests in masquerade, disguised as one's friend, one's lover, one's son, on errands of murder, a secret quiet war between the dispossessed and those who had come after them, a war that had been inevitable since the early outposts on Majipoor had grown into cities and sprawling agricultural territories that consumed more and more of the domain of the natives. Some remedies involve drastic cautery: in this final convulsion of the struggle between humans and Shapeshifters there was no help for it, Byelk and Domgrave and Bizfern must be destroyed so that the agony could end. Yet that did not make it easy to face abandoning one's home, Eremoil thought, nor was it even particularly easy to destroy someone else's home, as he had been doing for days, unless one did it from a distance, from a comfortable distance where all this torching was only a strategic abstraction.

Beyond Bizfern the foothills swung westward a long way, the road following their contour. There were good streams here, almost little rivers, and the land was heavily forested where it had not been cleared for planting. Yet even here the months without rain had left the forests terribly combustible, drifts of dead fallen leaves everywhere, fallen branches, old cracked trunks.

"This is the place, sir," the messenger said.

Eremoil beheld a box canyon, narrow at its mouth and much broader within, with a stream running down its middle. Against the gathering shadows he made out an impressive manor, a great white building with a roof of green tiles, and beyond that what seemed to be an immense acreage of crops. Armed guards were waiting at the mouth of the canyon. This was no simple farmer's spread; this was the domain of one who regarded himself as a duke. Eremoil saw trouble in store.

He dismounted and strode toward the guards, who studied him coldly and held their energy-throwers at the ready. To one that seemed the most imposing he said, "Group Captain Eremoil to see Aibil Kattikawn."

"The Kattikawn is awaiting Lord Stiamot," was the flat, chilly reply.

"Lord Stiamot is occupied elsewhere. I represent him today. I am Group Captain Eremoil, commanding officer in this district."

"We are instructed to admit only Lord Stiamot."

"Tell your master," Eremoil said wearily, "that the Coronal sends his regrets and asks him to offer his grievances to Group Captain Eremoil instead."

The guard seemed indifferent to that. But after a moment he spun around and entered the canyon. Eremoil watched him walking unhurriedly along the bank of the stream until he disappeared in the dense shrubbery of the plaza before the manor-house. A long time passed; the wind changed, bringing a hot gust from the fire zone, a layer of dark air that stung the eyes and scorched the throat. Eremoil envisioned a coating of black gritty particles on his lungs. But from here, in this sheltered place, the fire itself was invisible.

Eventually the guard returned, just as unhurriedly.

"The Kattikawn will see you," he announced.

Eremoil beckoned to his driver and his guide, the messenger. But Kattikawn's guard shook his head.

"Only you, Captain."

The driver looked disturbed. Eremoil waved her back. "Wait for me here," he said. "I don't think I'll be long."

He followed the guard down the canyon path to the manor-house.

From Aibil Kattikawn he expected the same sort of hard-eyed welcome that the guards had offered; but Eremoil had underestimated the courtesy a provincial aristocrat would feel obliged to provide. Kattikawn greeted him with a warm smile and an intense, searching stare, gave him what seemed to be an unfeigned embrace, and led him into the great house, which was sparsely furnished but elegant in its stark and rugged way. Exposed beams of oiled black wood dominated the vaulted ceilings; hunting trophies loomed high on the walls; the furniture was massive and plainly ancient. The whole place had an archaic air. So too did Aibil Kattikawn. He was a big man, much taller than the lightly built Eremoil and broad through the shoulders, a breadth dramatically enhanced by the heavy steetmoy-fur cloak he wore. His forehead was high, his hair gray but thick, rising in heavy ridges; his eyes were dark, his lips thin. In every aspect he was of the most imposing presence.

When he had poured bowls of some glistening amber wine and they had had the first sips, Kattikawn said, "So you need to burn my lands?"

"We must burn this entire province, I'm afraid."

"A stupid stratagem, perhaps the most foolish thing in the whole history of human warfare. Do you know how valuable the produce of this district is? Do you know how many generations of hard work have gone into building these farms?"

"The entire zone from Milimorn to Sintalmond and beyond is a center of Metamorph guerrilla activity, the last one remaining in Alhanroel. The Coronal is determined to end this ugly war finally, and it can only be done by smoking the Shapeshifters out of their hiding-places in these hills."

"There are other methods."

"We have tried them and they have failed," Eremoil said.

"Have you? Have you tried moving from inch to inch through the forests searching for them? Have you moved every soldier on Majipoor in here to conduct the mopping-up operations? Of course not. It's too much trouble. It's much simpler to send out those fliers and set the whole place on fire."

"This war has consumed an entire generation of our lives."

"And the Coronal grows impatient toward the end," said Kattikawn. "At my expense."

"The Coronal is a master of strategy. The Coronal has defeated a dangerous and almost incomprehensible enemy and has made Majipoor safe for human occupation for the first time—all but this district."

"We have managed well enough with these Metamorphs skulking all around us, Captain. I haven't been massacred yet. I've been able to handle them. They haven't been remotely as much of a threat to my welfare as my own government seems to be. Your Coronal, Captain, is a fool."

Eremoil controlled himself. "Future generations will hail him as a hero among heroes."

"Very likely," said Kattikawn. "That's the kind that usually gets made into heroes. I tell you that it was not necessary to destroy an entire province in order to round up the few thousand aborigines that remain at large. I tell you that it is a rash and shortsighted move on the part of a tired general who is in a hurry to return to the ease of Castle Mount."

"Be that as it may, the decision has been taken, and everything from Milimorn to Hamifieu is already ablaze."

"So I have noticed."

"The fire is advancing toward Kattikawn village. Perhaps by dawn the outskirts of your own domain will be threatened. During the day we'll continue the incendiary attacks past this region and on south as far as Sintalmond."

"Indeed," said Kattikawn calmly.

"This area will become an inferno. We ask you to abandon it while you still have time."

"I choose to remain, Captain."

Eremoil let his breath out slowly. "We cannot be responsible for your safety if you do."

"No one has ever been responsible for my safety except myself."

"What I'm saying is that you'll die, and die horribly. We have no way of laying down the fire-line in such a way as to avoid your domain."

"I understand."

"You ask us to murder you, then."

"I ask nothing of the sort. You and I have no transaction at all. You fight your war; I maintain my home. If the fire that your war requires should intrude on the territory I call my own, so much the worse for me, but no murder is involved. We are bound on independent courses, Captain Eremoil."

"Your reasoning is strange. You will die as a direct result of our incendiary attack. Your life will be on our souls."

"I remain here of free will, after having been duly warned," said Kattikawn. "My life will be on my own soul alone."

"And your people's lives? They'll die, too."

"Those who choose to remain, yes. I've given them warning of what is about to happen. Three have set out for the coast. The rest will stay. Of their own will, and not to please me. This is our place. Another bowl of wine, Captain?"

Eremoil refused, then instantly changed his mind and proffered the empty bowl. Kattikawn, as he poured, said, "Is there no way I can speak with Lord Stiamot?"

"None."

"I understand the Coronal is in this area."

"Half a day's journey, yes. But he is inaccessible to such petitioners."

"By design, I imagine." Kattikawn smiled. "Do you think he's gone mad, Eremoil?"

"The Coronal? Not at all."

"This burning, though—such a desperate move, such an idiotic move. The reparations he'll have to pay afterward—millions of royals; it'll bankrupt the treasury; it'll cost more than fifty castles as grand as the one he's built on top of the Mount. And for what? Give us two or three more years and we'd have the Shapeshifters tamed."

"Or five or ten or twenty," said Eremoil. "This must be the end of the war, now, this season. This ghastly convulsion, this shame on everyone, this stain, this long nightmare—"

"Oh, you think the war's been a mistake, then?"

Eremoil quickly shook his head. "The fundamental mistake was made long ago, when our ancestors chose to settle on a world that was already inhabited by an intelligent species. By our time we had no choice but to crush the Metamorphs, or else retreat entirely from Majipoor, and how could we do that?"

"Yes," Kattikawn said, "how could we give up the homes that had been ours and our forebears' for so long, eh?"

Eremoil ignored the heavy irony. "We took this planet from an unwilling people. For thousands of years we attempted to live in peace with them, until we admitted that coexistence was impossible. Now we are imposing our will by force, which is not beautiful, but the alternatives are even worse."

"What will Lord Stiamot do with the Shapeshifters he has in his internment camps? Plow them under as fertilizer for the fields he's burned?"

"They'll be given a vast reservation in Zimroel," said Eremoil. "Half a continent to themselves—that's hardly cruelty. Alhanroel will be ours, and an ocean between us. Already the resettlement is under way. Only your area remains unpacified. Lord Stiamot has taken upon himself the terrible burden of responsibility for a harsh but necessary act, and the future will hail him for it."

"I hail him now," said Kattikawn. "O wise and just Coronal! Who in his infinite wisdom destroys this land so that his world need not have the bother of troublesome aborigines lurking about. It would have been better for me, Eremoil, if he had been less noble of spirit, this hero-king of yours. Or more noble, perhaps. He'd seem much more wondrous to me if he'd chosen some slower method of conquering these last holdouts. Thirty years of war—what's another two or three?"

"This is the way he has chosen. The fires are approaching this place as we speak."

"Let them come. I'll be here, defending my house against them."

"You haven't seen the fire zone," Eremoil said. "Your defense won't last ten seconds. The fire eats everything in its way."

"Quite likely. I'll take my chances."

"I beg you—"

"You beg? Are you a beggar, then? What if I were to beg? I beg you, Captain, spare my estate!"

"It can't be done. I beg you indeed: retreat, and spare your life and the lives of your people."

"What would you have me do, go crawling along that highway to the coast, and live in some squalid little cabin in Alaisor or Bailemoona? Wait on table at an inn, or sweep the streets, or curry mounts in a stable? This is my place. I would rather die here in ten seconds tomorrow than live a thousand years in cowardly exile." Kattikawn walked to the window. "It grows dark, Captain. Will you be my guest for dinner?"

"I am unable to stay, I regret to tell you."

"Does this dispute bore you? We can talk of other things. I would prefer that."

Eremoil reached for the other man's great paw of a hand. "I have obligations at my headquarters. It would have been an unforgettable pleasure to accept your hospitality. I wish it were possible. Will you forgive me for declining?"

"It pains me to see you leave unfed. Do you hurry off to Lord Stiamot?"

Eremoil was silent.

"I would ask you to gain me an audience with him," said Kattikawn.

"It can't be done, and it would do no good. Please: leave this place tonight. Let us dine together, and then abandon your domain."

"This is my place, and here I remain," Kattikawn said. "I wish you well, Captain, a long and harmonious life. And I thank you for this conversation." He closed his eyes a moment and inclined his head: a tiny bow, a delicate dismissal. Eremoil moved toward the door of the great hall. Kattikawn said, "The other officer thought he would pull me out of here by force. You had more sense, and I compliment you. Farewell, Captain Eremoil."

Eremoil searched for appropriate words, found none, and settled for a gesture of salute.

Kattikawn's guards led him back to the mouth of his canyon, where Eremoil's driver and the messenger waited, playing some game with dice by the side of the floater. They snapped to attention when they saw Eremoil, but he signaled them to relax. He looked off to the east, at the great mountains that rose on the far side of the valley. In these northerly latitudes, on this summer night, the sky was still light, even to the east, and the heavy bulk of Zygnor Peak lay across the horizon like a black wall against the pale gray of the sky. South of it was its twin, Mount

Haimon, where the Coronal had made his headquarters. Eremoil stood for a time studying the two mighty peaks, and the foothills below them, and the pillar of fire and smoke that ascended on the other side, and the moons just coming into the sky; then he shook his head and turned and looked back toward Aibil Kattikawn's manor, disappearing now in the shadows of the late dusk. In his rise through the army ranks Eremoil had come to know dukes and princes and many other high ones that a mere civil engineer does not often meet in private life, and he had spent more than a little time with the Coronal himself and the intimate circle of advisers around him, and yet he thought he had never encountered anyone quite like this Kattikawn, who was either the most noble or the most misguided man on the planet, and perhaps both.

"Let's go," he said to the driver. "Take the Haimon road."

"The Haimon, sir?"

"To the Coronal, yes. Can you get us there by midnight?"

The road to the southern peak was much like the Zygnor road, but steeper and not as well paved. In darkness its twists and turns would probably be dangerous at the speed Eremoil's driver, a woman of Stoien, was risking; but the red glow of the fire zone lit up the valley and the foothills and much reduced the risks. Eremoil said nothing during the long journey. There was nothing to say: how could the driver or the messenger-lad possibly understand the nature of Aibil Kattikawn? Eremoil himself, on first hearing that one of the local farmers refused to leave his land, had misunderstood that nature, imagining some crazy old fool, some stubborn fanatic blind to the realities of his peril. Kattikawn was stubborn, surely, and possibly he could be called a fanatic, but he was none of the other things, not even crazy, however crazy his philosophy might seem to those, like Eremoil, who lived by different codes.

He wondered what he was going to tell Lord Stiamot.

No use rehearsing: words would come, or they would not. He slipped after a time into a kind of waking sleep, his mind lucid but frozen, contemplating nothing, calculating nothing. The floater, moving lightly and swiftly up the dizzying road, climbed out of the valley and into the jagged country beyond. At midnight it was still in the lower reaches of

Mount Haimon, but no matter: the Coronal was known to keep late hours, often not to sleep at all. Eremoil did not doubt he would be available.

Somewhere on the upper slopes of Haimon he dropped without any awareness of it into real sleep, and he was surprised and confused when the messenger shook him gently awake, saying, "This is Lord Stiamot's camp, sir." Blinking, disoriented, Eremoil found himself still sitting erect, his legs cramped, his back stiff. The moons were far across the sky and the night now was black except for the amazing fiery gash that tore across it to the west. Awkwardly Eremoil scrambled from the floater. Even now, in the middle of the night, the Coronal's camp was a busy place, messengers running to and fro, lights burning in many of the buildings. An adjutant appeared, recognized Eremoil, gave him an exceedingly formal salute. "This visit comes as a surprise, Captain Eremoil!"

"To me also, I'd say. Is Lord Stiamot in the camp?"

"The Coronal is holding a staff meeting. Does he expect you, Captain?"

"No," said Eremoil. "But I need to speak with him."

The adjutant was undisturbed by that. Staff meetings in the middle of the night, regional commanders turning up unannounced for conferences—well, why not? This was war, and protocols were improvised from day to day. Eremoil followed the man through the camp to an octagonal tent that bore the starburst insignia of the Coronal. A ring of guards surrounded the place, as grim and dedicated-looking as those who had held the mouth of Kattikawn's canyon. There had been four attempts on Lord Stiamot's life in the past eighteen months—all Metamorphs, all thwarted. No Coronal in Majipoor's history had ever died violently, but none had ever waged war, either, before this one.

The adjutant spoke with the commander of the guard; suddenly Eremoil found himself at the center of a knot of armed men, with lights shining maddeningly into his eyes and fingers digging painfully into his arms. For an instant the onslaught astonished him. But then he regained his poise and said, "What is this? I am Group Captain Eremoil."

"Unless you're a Shapeshifter," one of the men said.

"And you think you'd find that out by squeezing me and blinding me with your glare?"

"There are ways," said another.

Eremoil laughed. "None that ever proved reliable. But go on: test me, and do it fast. I must speak with Lord Stiamot."

They did indeed have tests. Someone gave him a strip of green paper and told him to touch his tongue to it. He did, and the paper turned orange. Someone else asked for a snip of his hair, and set fire to it. Eremoil looked on in amazement. It was a month since he had last been to the Coronal's camp, and none of these practices had been employed then; there must have been another assassination attempt, he decided, or else some quack scientist had come among them with these techniques. So far as Eremoil knew, there was no true way to distinguish a Metamorph from an authentic human when the Metamorph had taken on human form, except through dissection, and he did not propose to submit to that.

"You pass," they said at last. "You can go in."

But they accompanied him. Eremoil's eyes, dazzled already, adjusted with difficulty to the dimness of the Coronal's tent, but after a moment he saw half a dozen figures at the far end, and Lord Stiamot among them. They seemed to be praying. He heard murmured invocations and responses, bits of the old scripture. Was this the sort of staff meetings the Coronal held now? Eremoil went forward and stood a few yards from the group. He knew only one of the Coronal's attendants, Damlang of Bibiroon, who was generally considered second or third in line for the throne; the others did not seem even to be soldiers, for they were older men, in civilian dress, with a soft citified look about them, poets, dream-speakers perhaps, certainly not warriors. But the war was almost over.

The Coronal looked in Eremoil's direction without seeming to notice him.

Eremoil was startled by Lord Stiamot's harried, ragged look. The Coronal had been growing visibly older all through the past three years of the war, but the process seemed to have accelerated now: he appeared shrunken, colorless, frail, his skin parched, his eyes dull. He might have been a hundred years old, and yet he was no older than Eremoil himself, a man in middle life. Eremoil could remember the day Stiamot had come to the throne, and how Stiamot had vowed that day to end the madness of this constant undeclared warfare with the Metamorphs, to collect the planet's ancient natives and remove them from the territories settled by mankind. Only thirty years, and the Coronal looked the better part of a century older; but he had spent his reign in the field, as no Coronal before him had done and probably none after him ever would do, campaigning in the Glayge Valley, in the hotlands of the south, in the dense forests of the northeast, in the rich plains along the Gulf of Stoien, year after year encircling the Shapeshifters with his twenty armies and penning them in camps. And now he was nearly finished with the job, just the guerrillas of the northwest remaining at liberty—a constant struggle, a long fierce life of war, with scarcely time to return to the tender springtime of Castle Mount for the pleasures of the throne. Eremoil had occasionally wondered, as the war went on and on, how Lord Stiamot would respond if the Pontifex should die, and he be called upward to the other kingship and be forced to take up residence in the Labyrinth: would he decline, and retain the Coronal's crown so that he might remain in the field? But the Pontifex was in fine health, so it was said, and here was Lord Stiamot now a tired little old man, looking to be at the edge of the grave himself. Eremoil understood abruptly what Aibil Kattikawn had failed to comprehend, why it was that Lord Stiamot was so eager to bring the final phase of the war to its conclusion regardless of cost.

The Coronal said, "Who do we have there? Is that Finiwain?"

"Eremoil, my lord. In command of the forces carrying out the burning."

"Eremoil. Yes. Eremoil. I recall. Come, sit with us. We are giving thanks to the Divine for the end of the war, Eremoil. These people have come to me from my mother the Lady of the Isle, who guards us in dreams, and we will spend the night in songs of praise and gratitude, for in the morning the circle of fire will be complete. Eh, Eremoil? Come, sit, sing with us. You know the songs to the Lady, don't you?"

Eremoil heard the Coronal's cracked and frayed voice with shock. That faded thread of dry sound was all that remained of his once majestic tone. This hero, this demigod, was withered and ruined by his long campaign; there was nothing left of him; he was a spectre, a shadow. Seeing him like this, Eremoil wondered if Lord Stiamot had ever been the mighty figure of memory, or if perhaps that was only mythmaking and propaganda, and the Coronal had all along been less than met the eye.

Lord Stiamot beckoned. Eremoil reluctantly moved closer.

He thought of what he had come here to say. *My lord, there is a man in the path of the fire who will not move and will not allow himself to be moved, and who cannot be moved without the loss of life, and, my lord, he is too fine a man to be destroyed in this way. So I ask you, my lord, to halt the burning, perhaps to devise some alternative strategy, so that we may seize the Metamorphs as they flee the fire zone but do not need to extend the destruction beyond the point it already reaches, because—*

No.

He saw the utter impossibility of asking the Coronal to delay the end of the war a single hour. Not for Kattikawn's sake, not for Eremoil's sake, not for the sake of the holy Lady his mother could the burning be halted now, for these were the last days of the war and the Coronal's need to proceed to the end was the overriding force that swept all else before it. Eremoil might try to halt the burning on his own authority, but he could not ask the Coronal for approval.

Lord Stiamot thrust his head toward Eremoil.

"What is it, Captain? What bothers you? Here. Sit by me. Sing with us, Captain. Raise your voice in thanksgiving."

They began a hymn, some tune Eremoil did not know. He hummed along, improvising a harmony. After that they sang another, and another, and that one Eremoil did know; he sang, but in a hollow and tuneless way. Dawn could not be far off now. Quietly he moved into the shadows and out of the tent. Yes, there was the sun, beginning to cast the first greenish light along the eastern face of Mount Haimon, though it would be an hour or more before its rays climbed the mountain wall and illuminated the doomed valleys to the southwest. Eremoil yearned for a week of sleep. He looked for the adjutant and said, "Will you send a message for me to my subaltern on Zygnor Peak?"

"Of course, sir."

"Tell him to take charge of the next phase of the burning and proceed as scheduled. I'm going to remain here during the day and will return to my headquarters this evening, after I've had some rest."

"Yes, sir."

Eremoil turned away and looked toward the west, still wrapped in night except where the terrible glow of the fire zone illuminated it. Probably Aibil Kattikawn had been busy all this night with pumps and hoses, wetting down his lands. It would do no good, of course; a fire of that magnitude takes all in its path, and burns until no fuel is left. So Kattikawn would die and the tiled roof of the manor-house would collapse, and there was no helping it. He could be saved only at the risk of the lives of innocent soldiers, and probably not even then; or he could be saved if Eremoil chose to disregard the orders of Lord Stiamot, but not for long. So he will die. After nine years in the field, Eremoil thought, I am at last the cause of taking a life, and he is one of our own citizens. So be it. So be it.

He remained at the lookout post, weary but unable to move on, another hour or so, until he saw the first explosions of flame in the foothills near Bizfern, or maybe Domgrave, and knew that the morning's incendiary bombing had begun. The war will soon be over, he told himself. The last of our enemies now flee toward the safety of the coast, where they will be interned and transported overseas, and the world will be quiet again. He felt the warmth of the summer sun on his back and the warmth of the spreading fires on his cheeks. The world will be quiet again, he thought, and went to find a place to sleep.

THREE

In the Fifth Year of the Voyage

That one was quite different from the first. Hissune is less amazed by it, less shattered; it is a sad and moving tale, but it does not rock his soul's depths the way the embrace of human and Ghayrog had done. Yet he has learned a great deal from it about the nature of responsibility, about the conflicts that arise between opposing forces neither of which can be said to be in the wrong, and about the meaning of true tranquillity of spirit. Then too he has discovered something about the process of mythmaking: for in all the history of Majipoor there has been no figure more godlike than Lord Stiamot, the shining warrior-king who broke the strength of the sinister aboriginal Shapeshifters, and eight thousand years of idolization have transformed him into an awesome being of great majesty and splendor. That Lord Stiamot of myth still exists in Hissune's mind, but it has been necessary to move him to one side in order to make room for the Stiamot he has seen through Eremoil's eyes—that weary, pallid, withered little man, old before his time, who burned his soul to a husk in a lifetime of battle. A hero? Certainly, except perhaps to the Metamorphs. But a demigod? No, a human being, very human, all frailty and fatigue. It is important never to forget that, Hissune tells himself, and in that moment he realizes that these stolen minutes in the Register of Souls are providing him with his true education, his doctoral degree in life.

It is a long while before he feels ready to return for another course. But in time the dust of the tax archives begins to seep to the depths of his being and he craves a diversion, an adventure. So, too, back to the Register. Another legend

*needs exploring; for once, long ago, a shipload of madmen set out to sail across
the Great Sea—folly if ever folly had been conceived, but glorious folly, and
Hissune chooses to take passage aboard that ship and discover what befell its
crew. A little research produces the captain's name: Sinnabor Lavon, a native
of Castle Mount. Hissune's fingers lightly touch the keys, giving date, place,
name, and he sits back, poised, expectant, ready to go to sea.*

IN THE FIFTH YEAR of the voyage, Sinnabor Lavon noticed the first strands
of dragon-grass coiling and writhing in the sea alongside the hull of the
ship.

He had no idea of what it was, of course, for no one on Majipoor had
ever seen dragon-grass before. This distant reach of the Great Sea had
never been explored. But he did know that this was the fifth year of the
voyage, for every morning Sinnabor Lavon had carefully noted the date
and the ship's position in his log, so that the explorers would not lose their
psychological bearings on this boundless and monotonous ocean. Thus
he was certain that this day lay in the twentieth year of the Pontificate of
Dizimaule, Lord Arioc being Coronal, and that this was the fifth year
since the *Spurifon* had set out from the port of Til-omon on her journey
around the world.

He mistook the dragon-grass for a mass of sea-serpents at first. It
seemed to move with an inner force, twisting, wriggling, contracting,
relaxing. Against the calm dark water it gleamed with a shimmering
richness of color, each strand iridescent, showing glints of emerald and
indigo and vermilion. There was a small patch of it off the port side and
a somewhat broader streak of it staining the sea to starboard.

Lavon peered over the rail to the lower deck and saw a trio of shaggy
four-armed figures below: Skandar crewmen, mending nets, or pretending to. They met his gaze with sour, sullen looks. Like many of the crew,
they had long ago grown weary of the voyage. "You, there!" Lavon yelled.
"Put out the scoop! Take some samples of those serpents!"

"Serpents, Captain? What serpents you mean?"

"There! There! Can't you see?"

The Skandars glanced at the water, and then, with a certain patronizing solemnity, up at Sinnabor Lavon. "You mean that grass in the water?"

Lavon took a closer look. Grass? Already the ship was beyond the first patches, but there was more ahead, larger masses of it, and he squinted, trying to pick individual strands out of the tangled drifts. The stuff moved, as serpents might move. But yet Lavon saw no heads, no eyes. Well, possibly grass, then. He gestured impatiently and the Skandars, in no hurry, began to extend the jointed boom-mounted scoop with which biological specimens were collected.

By the time Lavon reached the lower deck a dripping little mound of the grass was spread on the boards and half a dozen staffers had gathered about it: First Mate Vormecht, Chief Navigator Galimoin, Joachil Noor and a couple of her scientists, and Mikdal Hasz, the chronicler. There was a sharp ammoniac smell in the air. The three Skandars stood back, ostentatiously holding their noses and muttering, but the others, pointing, laughing, poking at the grass, appeared more excited and animated than they had seemed for weeks.

Lavon knelt beside them. No doubt of it, the stuff was seaweed of some sort, each flat fleshy strand about as long as a man, about as wide as a forearm, about as thick as a finger. It twitched and jerked convulsively, as though on strings, but its motions grew perceptibly slower from moment to moment as it dried, and the brilliant colors were fading quickly.

"Scoop up some more," Joachil Noor told the Skandars. "And this time, dump it in a tub of sea-water to keep it alive."

The Skandars did not move. "The stench—such a filthy stench—" one of the hairy beings grunted.

Joachil Noor walked toward them—the short wiry woman looked like a child beside the gigantic creatures—and waved her hand brusquely. The Skandars, shrugging, lumbered to their task.

Sinnabor Lavon said to her, "What do you make of it?"

"Algae. Some unknown species, but everything's unknown this far out at sea. The color changes are interesting. I don't know whether they're caused by pigment fluctuations or simply result from optical tricks, the play of light over the shifting epidermal layers."

"And the movements? Algae don't have muscles."

"Plenty of plants are capable of motion. Minor oscillations of electrical current, causing variances in columns of fluid within the plant's structure—you know the sensitivos of northwestern Zimroel? You shout at them and they cringe. Sea-water's an excellent conductor; these algae must pick up all sorts of electrical impulses. We'll study them carefully." Joachil Noor smiled. "I tell you, they come as a gift from the Divine. Another week of empty sea and I'd have jumped overboard."

Lavon nodded. He had been feeling it too: that hideous killing boredom, that frightful choking feeling of having condemned himself to an endless journey to nowhere. Even he, who had given seven years of his life to organizing this expedition, who was willing to spend all the rest of it carrying it to completion, even he, in this fifth year of the voyage, paralyzed by listlessness, numb with apathy—

"Tonight," he said, "give us a report, eh? Preliminary findings. Unique new species of seaweed."

Joachil Noor signaled and the Skandars hoisted the tub of seaweed to their broad backs and carried it off toward the laboratory. The three biologists followed.

"There'll be plenty of it for them to study," said Vormecht. The first mate pointed. "Look, there! The sea ahead is thick with it!"

"Too thick, perhaps?" Mikdal Hasz said.

Sinnabor Lavon turned to the chronicler, a dry-voiced little man with pale eyes and one shoulder higher than the other. "What do you mean?"

"I mean fouled rotors, Captain, if the seaweed gets much thicker. There are tales from Old Earth that I've read, of oceans where the weeds were impenetrable, where ships became hopelessly enmeshed, their crews living on crabs and fishes and eventually dying of thirst, and the vessels drifting on and on for hundreds of years with skeletons aboard—"

Chief Navigator Galimoin snorted. "Fantasy. Fable."

"And if it happens to us?" asked Mikdal Hasz.

Vormecht said, "How likely is that?"

Lavon realized they were all looking at him. He stared at the sea. Yes, the weeds did appear thicker; beyond the bow they gathered in bunched clumps, and their rhythmic writhings made the flat and listless surface of the water seem to throb and swell. But broad channels lay between each clump. Was it possible that these weeds could engulf so capable a ship as the *Spurifon*? There was silence on the deck. It was almost comic: the dread menace of the seaweed, the tense officers divided and contentious, the captain required to make the decision that might mean life or death—

The true menace, Lavon thought, is not seaweed but boredom. For months the journey had been so uneventful that the days had become voids that had to be filled with the most desperate entertainments. Each dawn the swollen bronze-green sun of the tropics rose out of Zimroel, by noon it blazed overhead out of a cloudless sky, in the afternoon it plunged toward the inconceivably distant horizon, and the next day it was the same. There had been no rain for weeks, no changes of any kind in the weather. The Great Sea filled all the universe. They saw no land, not even a scrap of island this far out, no birds, no creatures of the water. In such an existence an unknown species of seaweed became a delicious novelty. A ferocious restlessness was consuming the spirits of the voyagers, these dedicated and committed explorers who once had shared Lavon's vision of an epic quest and who now were grimly and miserably enduring the torment of knowing that they had thrown away their lives in a moment of romantic folly. No one had expected it to be like this, when they had set out to make the first crossing in history of the Great Sea that occupied nearly half of their giant planet. They had imagined daily adventure, new beasts of fantastic nature, unknown islands, heroic storms, a sky riven by lightning and daubed with clouds of fifty unfamiliar hues. But not this, this grinding sameness, this unvarying repetition of days. Lavon had already begun to calculate the risks of mutiny, for it might be seven or nine or eleven more years before they made landfall on the shores of far-off Alhanroel, and he doubted that there were many on board who had the heart to see it through to the end. There must be dozens who had begun to dream dreams of turning the ship around and heading back to Zimroel; there were times when he dreamed of it himself. Therefore let us seek risks, he thought, and if need be let us manufacture them out of fantasy. Therefore let us brave the peril, real or imagined, of the seaweed. The possibility of danger will awaken us from our deadly lethargy.

"We can cope with seaweed," Lavon said. "Let's move onward."

Within an hour he was beginning to have doubts. From his pacing-place on the bridge he stared warily at the ever-thickening seaweed. It was forming little islands now, fifty or a hundred yards across, and the channels between were narrower. All the surface of the sea was in motion, quivering, trembling. Under the searing rays of an almost vertical sun the seaweed grew richer in color, sliding in a manic way from tone to tone as if pumped higher by the inrush of solar energy. He saw creatures moving about in the tight-packed strands: enormous crablike things, many-legged, spherical, with knobby green shells, and sinuous serpentine animals something like squid, harvesting other life-forms too small for Lavon to see.

Vormecht said nervously, "Perhaps a change of course—"

"Perhaps," Lavon said. "I'll send a lookout up to tell us how far this mess extends."

Changing course, even by a few degrees, held no appeal for him. His course was set; his mind was fixed; he feared that any deviation would shatter his increasingly frail resolve. And yet he was no monomaniac, pressing ahead without regard to risk. It was only that he saw how easy it would be for the people of the *Spurifon* to lose what was left of their dedication to the immense enterprise on which they had embarked.

This was a golden age for Majipoor, a time of heroic figures and mighty deeds. Explorers were going everywhere, into the desert barrens of Suvrael and the forests and marshes of Zimroel and the virgin outlands of Alhanroel, and into the archipelagoes and island clusters that bordered the three continents. The population was expanding rapidly, towns were turning into cities and cities into improbably great metropolises, non-human settlers were pouring in from the neighboring worlds to seek their fortunes, everything was excitement, change, growth. And Sinnabor Lavon had chosen for himself the craziest feat of all, to cross the Great Sea by ship. No one had ever attempted that. From space one could see that the giant planet was half water, that the continents, huge though they were, were cramped together in a single hemisphere and all the other face of the world was a blankness of ocean. And though it was some thousands of years since the human colonization of Majipoor had begun, there had been work aplenty to do on land, and the Great Sea had been left to itself and to the armadas of sea-dragons that untiringly crossed it from west to east in migrations lasting decades.

But Lavon was in love with Majipoor and yearned to embrace it all. He had traversed it from Amblemorn at the foot of Castle Mount to Tilomon on the other shore of the Great Sea; and now, driven by the need to close the circle, he had poured all his resources and energies into outfitting this awesome vessel, as self-contained and self-sufficient as an island, aboard which he and a crew as crazy as himself intended to spend a decade or more exploring that unknown ocean. He knew, and probably they knew, too, that they had sent themselves off on what might be an impossible task. But if they succeeded, and brought their argosy safely into harbor on Alhanroel's eastern coast where no ocean-faring ship had ever landed, their names would live forever.

"Hoy!" cried the lookout suddenly. "Dragons ho! Hoy! Hoy!"

"Weeks of boredom," Vormecht muttered, "and then everything at once!"

Lavon saw the lookout, dark against the dazzling sky, pointing rigidly north-northwest. He shaded his eyes and followed the outstretched arm. Yes! Great humped shapes, gliding serenely toward them, flukes high, wings held close to their bodies or in a few cases magnificently outspread—

"Dragons!" Galimoin called. "Dragons—look!" shouted a dozen other voices at once.

The *Spurifon* had encountered two herds of sea-dragons earlier in the voyage: six months out, among the islands that they had named the Stiamot Archipelago, and then two years after that, in the part of the ocean that they had dubbed the Arioc Deep. Both times the herds had been large ones, hundreds of the huge creatures, with many pregnant cows, and they had stayed far away from the *Spurifon*. But these appeared to be only the outliers of their herd, no more than fifteen or twenty of them, a handful of giant males and the others adolescents hardly forty feet in length. The writhing seaweed now looked inconsequential as the dragons neared. Everyone seemed to be on deck at once, almost dancing with excitement.

Lavon gripped the rail tightly. He had wanted risk for the sake of diversion: well, here was risk. An angry adult sea-dragon could cripple a ship, even one so well defended as the *Spurifon*, with a few mighty blows. Only rarely did they attack vessels that had not attacked them first, but it had been known to happen. Did these creatures imagine that the *Spurifon* was a dragon-hunting ship? Each year a new herd of sea-dragons passed through the waters between Piliplok and the Isle of Sleep, where hunting them was permitted, and fleets of dragon-ships greatly thinned their numbers then; these big ones, at least, must be survivors of that gamut, and who knew what resentments they harbored? The *Spurifon*'s harpooners moved into readiness at a signal from Lavon.

But no attack came. The dragons seemed to regard the ship as a curiosity, nothing more. They had come here to feed. When they reached the first clumps of seaweed they opened their immense mouths and began to gulp the stuff down by the bale, sucking in along with it the squid-things and the crab-things and all the rest. For several hours they grazed noisily amid the seaweed; and then, as if by common agreement, they slipped below the surface and within minutes were gone.

A great ring of open sea now surrounded the *Spurifon*.

"They must have eaten tons of it," Lavon murmured. "Tons!"

"And now our way is clear," said Galimoin.

Vormecht shook his head. "No. See, Captain? The dragon-grass, farther out. Thicker and thicker and thicker!"

Lavon stared into the distance. Wherever he looked there was a thin dark line along the horizon.

"Land," Galimoin suggested. "Islands—atolls—"

"On every side of us?" Vormecht said scornfully. "No, Galimoin. We've sailed into the middle of a continent of this dragon-grass stuff. The opening that the dragons ate for us is just a delusion. We're trapped!"

"It's only seaweed," Galimoin said. "If we have to, we'll cut our way through it."

Lavon eyed the horizon uneasily. He was beginning to share Vormecht's discomfort. A few hours ago the dragon-grass had amounted to mere isolated strands, then scattered patches and clumps; but now, although the ship was for the moment in clear water, it did indeed look as if an unbroken ring of the seaweed had come to enclose them fore and aft. And yet could it possibly become thick enough to block their passage?

Twilight was descending. The warm heavy air grew pink, then quickly gray. Darkness rushed down upon the voyagers out of the eastern sky.

"We'll send out boats in the morning and see what there is to see," Lavon announced.

That evening after dinner Joachil Noor reported on the dragon-grass: a giant alga, she said, with an intricate biochemistry, well worth detailed investigation. She spoke at length about its complex system of color-nodes, its powerful contractile capacity. Everyone on board, even some who had been lost in fogs of hopeless depression for weeks, crowded around to peer at the specimens in the tub, to touch them, to speculate and comment. Sinnabor Lavon rejoiced to see such liveliness aboard the *Spurifon* once again after these weeks of doldrums.

He dreamed that night that he was dancing on the water, performing a vigorous solo in some high-spirited ballet. The dragon-grass was firm and resilient beneath his flashing feet.

An hour before dawn he was awakened by urgent knocking at his cabin door. A Skandar was there—Skeen, standing third watch. "Come quickly—the dragon-grass, Captain—"

The extent of the disaster was evident even by the faint pearly gleams of the new day. All night the *Spurifon* had been on the move and the dragon-grass had been on the move, and now the ship lay in the heart of a tight-woven fabric of seaweed that seemed to stretch to the ends of the universe. The landscape that presented itself as the first green streaks of morning tinted the sky was like something out of a dream: a single unbroken carpet of a trillion trillion knotted strands, its surface pulsing, twitching, throbbing, trembling, and its colors shifting everywhere through a restless spectrum of deep assertive tones. Here and there in this infinitely entangled webwork its inhabitants could be seen variously scuttling, creeping, slithering, crawling, clambering, and scampering. From the densely entwined masses of seaweed rose an odor so piercing it seemed to go straight past the nostrils to the back of the skull. No clear water was in sight. The *Spurifon* was becalmed, stalled, as motionless as if in the night she had sailed a thousand miles overland into the heart of the Suvrael desert.

Lavon looked toward Vormecht—the first mate, so querulous and edgy all yesterday, now bore a calm look of vindication—and toward Chief Navigator Galimoin, whose boisterous confidence had given way to a tense and volatile frame of mind, obvious from his fixed, rigid stare and the grim clamping of his lips.

"I've shut the engines down," Vormecht said. "We were sucking in dragon-grass by the barrel. The rotors were completely clogged almost at once."

"Can they be cleared?" Lavon asked.

"We're clearing them," said Vormecht. "But the moment we start up again, we'll be eating seaweed through every intake."

Scowling, Lavon looked to Galimoin and said, "Have you been able to measure the area of the seaweed mass?"

"We can't see beyond it, Captain."

"And have you sounded its depth?"

"It's like a lawn. We can't push our plumbs through it."

Lavon let his breath out slowly. "Get boats out right away. We need to survey what we're up against. Vormecht, send two divers down to find out how deep the seaweed goes, and whether there's some way we can screen our intakes against it. And ask Joachil Noor to come up here."

The little biologist appeared promptly, looking weary but perversely cheerful. Before Lavon could speak she said, "I've been up all night studying the algae. They're metal-fixers, with a heavy concentration of rhenium and vanadium in their—"

"Have you noticed that we're stopped?"

She seemed indifferent to that. "So I see."

"We find ourselves living out an ancient fable, in which ships are caught by impenetrable weeds and become derelicts. We may be here a long while."

"It will give us a chance to study this unique ecological province, Captain."

"The rest of our lives, perhaps."

"Do you think so?" asked Joachil Noor, startled at last.

"I have no idea. But I want you to shift the aim of your studies, for the time being. Find out what kills these weeds, aside from exposure to the air. We may have to wage biological warfare against them if we're ever going to get out of here. I want some chemical, some method, some scheme, that'll clear them away from our rotors."

"Trap a pair of sea-dragons," Joachil Noor said at once, "and chain one to each side of the bow, and let them eat us free."

Sinnabor Lavon did not smile. "Think about it more seriously," he said, "and report to me later."

He watched as two boats were lowered, each bearing a crew of four. Lavon hoped that the outboard motors would be able to keep clear of the dragon-grass, but there was no chance of that: almost immediately the blades were snarled, and it became necessary for the boatmen to unship the oars and beat a slow, grueling course through the weeds, while pausing occasionally to drive off with clubs the fearless giant crustaceans that wandered over the face of the choked sea. In fifteen minutes the boats were no more than a hundred yards from the ship. Meanwhile a pair of divers clad in breathing-masks had gone down, one Hjort, one human, hacking openings in the dragon-grass alongside the ship and vanishing into the clotted depths. When they failed to return after half an hour Lavon said to the first mate, "Vormecht, how long can men stay underwater wearing those masks?"

"About this long, Captain. Perhaps a little longer for a Hjort, but not much."

"So I thought."

"We can hardly send more divers after them, can we?"

"Hardly," said Lavon bleakly. "Do you imagine the submersible would be able to penetrate the weeds?"

"Probably not."

"I doubt it, too. But we'll have to try it. Call for volunteers."

The *Spurifon* carried a small underwater vessel that it employed in its scientific research. It had not been used in months, and by the time it could be readied for descent more than an hour had passed; the fate of the

two divers was certain; and Lavon felt the awareness of their deaths settling about his spirit like a skin of cold metal. He had never known anyone to die except from extreme old age, and the strangeness of accidental
mortality was a hard thing for him to comprehend, nearly as hard as the
knowledge that he was responsible for what had happened.

Three volunteers climbed into the submersible and it was winched
overside. It rested a moment on the surface of the water; then its opera-
tors thrust out the retractable claws with which it was equipped, and like
some fat glossy crab it began to dig its way under. It was a slow business,
for the dragon-grass clung close to it, reweaving its sundered web almost
as fast as the claws could rip it apart. But gradually the little vessel
slipped from sight.

Galimoin was shouting something over a bullhorn from another
deck. Lavon looked up and saw the two boats he had sent out, struggling
through the weeds perhaps half a mile away. By now it was mid-morning
and in the glare it was hard to tell which way they were headed, but it
seemed they were returning.

Alone and silent Lavon waited on the bridge. No one dared approach
him. He stared down at the floating carpet of dragon-grass, heaving
here and there with strange and terrible life-forms, and thought of
the two drowned men and the others in the submersible and the ones
in the boats, and of those still safe aboard the *Spurifon*, all enmeshed in
the same grotesque plight. How easy it would have been to avoid this,
he thought; and how easy to think such thoughts. And how futile.

He held his post, motionless, well past noon, in the silence and the
haze and the heat and the stench. Then he went to his cabin. Later in the
day Vormecht came to him with the news that the crew of the submersible had found the divers hanging near the stilled rotors, shrouded in
tight windings of dragon-grass, as though the weeds had deliberately set
upon and engulfed them. Lavon was skeptical of that; they must merely
have become tangled in it, he insisted, but without conviction. The submersible itself had had a hard time of it and had nearly burned out its
engines in the effort to sink fifty feet. The weeds, Vormecht said, formed
a virtually solid layer for a dozen feet below the surface. "What about the
boats?" Lavon asked, and the first mate told him that they had returned

safely, their crews exhausted by the work of rowing through the knotted weeds. In the entire morning they had managed to get no more than a mile from the ship, and they had seen no end to the dragon-grass, not even an opening in its unbroken weave. One of the boatmen had been attacked by a crab-creature on the way back, but had escaped with only minor cuts.

During the day there was no change in the situation. No change seemed possible. The dragon-grass had seized the *Spurifon* and there was no reason for it to release the ship, unless the voyagers compelled it to, which Lavon did not at present see how to accomplish.

He asked the chronicler Mikdal Hasz to go among the people of the *Spurifon* and ascertain their mood. "Mainly calm," Hasz reported. "Some are troubled. Most find our predicament strangely refreshing: a challenge, a deviation from the monotony of recent months."

"And you?"

"I have my fears, Captain. But I want to believe we will find a way out. And I respond to the beauty of this weird landscape with unexpected pleasure."

Beauty? Lavon had not thought to see beauty in it. Darkly he stared at the miles of dragon-grass, bronze-red under the bloody sunset sky. A red mist was rising from the water, and in that thick vapor the creatures of the algae were moving about in great numbers, so that the enormous raftlike weed-structures were constantly in tremor. Beauty? A sort of beauty indeed, Lavon conceded. He felt as if the *Spurifon* had become stranded in the midst of some huge painting, a vast scroll of soft fluid shapes, depicting a dreamlike, disorienting world without landmarks, on whose liquid surface there was unending change of pattern and color. So long as he could keep himself from regarding the dragon-grass as the enemy and destroyer of all he had worked to achieve, he could to some degree admire the shifting glints and forms all about him.

He lay awake much of the night searching without success for a tactic to use against this vegetable adversary.

Morning brought new colors in the weed, pale greens and streaky yellows under a discouraging sky burdened with thin clouds. Five or six colossal sea-dragons were visible a long way off, slowly eating a path for

themselves through the water. How convenient it would be, Lavon reflected, if the *Spurifon* could do as much!

He met with his officers. They too had noticed last night's mood of
general tranquillity, even fascination. But they detected tensions beginning to rise this morning. "They were already frustrated and homesick,"
said Vormecht, "and now they see a new delay here of days or even
weeks."

"Or months or years or forever," snapped Galimoin. "What makes
you think we'll ever get out?"

The navigator's voice was ragged with strain and cords stood out
along the sides of his thick neck. Lavon had long ago sensed an instability somewhere within Galimoin, but even so he was not prepared for the
swiftness with which Galimoin had been undone by the onset of the
dragon-grass.

Vormecht seemed amazed by it also. The first mate said in surprise,
"You told us yourself the day before yesterday, 'It's only seaweed. We'll
cut our way through it.' Remember?"

"I didn't know then what we were up against," Galimoin growled.

Lavon looked toward Joachil Noor. "What about the possibility that
this stuff is migratory, that the whole formation will sooner or later
break up and let us go?"

The biologist shook her head. "It could happen. But I see no reason
to count on it. More likely this is a quasi-permanent ecosystem. Currents
might carry it to other parts of the Great Sea, but in that case they'd
carry us right along with it."

"You see?" Galimoin said glumly. "Hopeless!"

"Not yet," said Lavon. "Vormecht, what can we do about using the
submersible to mount screens over the intakes?"

"Possibly. Possibly."

"Try it. Get the fabricators going on some sort of screens right away.
Joachil Noor, what are your thoughts on a chemical counterattack against
the seaweed?"

"We're running tests," she said. "I can't promise anything."

No one could promise anything. They could only think and work
and wait and hope.

Designing screens for the intakes took a couple of days; building them took five more. Meanwhile Joachil Noor experimented with methods of killing the grass around the ship, without apparent result.

In those days not only the *Spurifon* but time itself seemed to stand still. Daily, Lavon took his sightings and made his log entries; the ship was actually traveling a few miles a day, moving steadily south-southwest, but it was going nowhere in relation to the entire mass of algae: to provide a reference point they marked the dragon-grass around the ship with dyes, and there was no movement in the great yellow and scarlet stains as the days went by. And in this ocean they could drift forever with the currents and not come within reach of land.

Lavon felt himself fraying. He had difficulty maintaining his usual upright posture; his shoulders now were beginning to curve, his head felt like a deadweight. He felt older; he felt old. Guilt was eroding him. On him was the responsibility for having failed to pull away from the dragon-grass zone the moment the danger was apparent; only a few hours would have made the difference, he told himself, but he had let himself be diverted by the spectacle of the sea-dragons and by his idiotic theory that a bit of peril would add spice to what had become a lethally bland voyage. For that he assailed himself mercilessly, and it was not far from there to blaming himself for having led these unwitting people into this entire absurd and futile journey. A voyage lasting ten or fifteen years, from nowhere to nowhere? Why? Why?

Yet he worked at maintaining morale among the others. The ration of wine—limited, for the ship's cellars had to last out the voyage—was doubled. There were nightly entertainments. Lavon ordered every research group to bring its oceanographic studies up to date, thinking that this was no moment for idleness on anyone's part. Papers that should have been written months or even years before, but which had been put aside in the long slow progress of the cruise, now were to be completed at once. Work was the best medicine for boredom, frustration, and—a new and growing factor—fear.

When the first screens were ready, a volunteer crew went down in the submersible to attempt to weld them to the hull over the intakes. The job, a tricky one at best, was made more complicated by the need to do it entirely with the little vessel's extensor claws. After the loss of the two divers Lavon would not risk letting anyone enter the water except in the submersible. Under the direction of a skilled mechanic named Duroin Klays the work proceeded day after day, but it was a thankless business. The heavy masses of dragon-grass, nudging the hull with every swell of the sea, frequently ripped the fragile mountings loose, and the welders made little progress.

On the sixth day of the work Duroin Klays came to Lavon with a sheaf of glossy photographs. They showed patterns of orange splotches against a dull gray background.

"What is this?" Lavon asked.

"Hull corrosion, sir. I noticed it yesterday and took a series of underwater shots this morning."

"Hull corrosion?" Lavon forced a smile. "That's hardly possible. The hull's completely resistant. What you're showing me here must be barnacles or sponges of some sort, or—"

"No, sir. Perhaps it's not clear from the pictures," said Duroin Klays. "But you can tell very easily when you're down in the submersible. It's like little scars, eaten into the metal. I'm quite sure of it, sir."

Lavon dismissed the mechanic and sent for Joachil Noor. She studied the photographs a long while and said finally, "It's altogether likely."

"That the dragon-grass is eating into the hull?"

"We've suspected the possibility of it for a few days. One of our first findings was a sharp pH gradient between this part of the ocean and the open sea. We're sitting in an acid bath, Captain, and I'm sure it's the algae that are secreting the acids. And we know that they're metal-fixers whose tissues are loaded with heavy elements. Normally they pull their metals from sea-water, of course. But they must regard the *Spurifon* as a gigantic banquet table. I wouldn't be surprised to find that the reason the dragon-grass became so thick so suddenly in our vicinity is that the algae have been flocking from miles around to get in on the feast."

"If that's the case, then it's foolish to expect the algae jam to break up of its own accord."

"Indeed."

Lavon blinked. "And if we remain locked in it long enough, the dragon-grass will eat holes right through us?"

The biologist laughed and said, "That might take hundreds of years. Starvation's a more immediate problem."

"How so?"

"How long can we last eating nothing but what's currently in storage on board?"

"A few months, I suppose. You know we depend on what we can catch as we go along. Are you saying—"

"Yes, Captain. Everything in the ecosystem around us right now is probably poisonous to us. The algae absorb oceanic metals. The small crustaceans and fishes eat the algae. The bigger creatures eat the smaller ones. The concentration of metallic salts gets stronger and stronger as we go up the chain. And we—"

"Won't thrive on a diet of rhenium and vanadium."

"And molybdenum and rhodium. No, Captain. Have you seen the latest medical reports? An epidemic of nausea, fever, some circulatory problems—how have *you* been feeling, Captain? And it's only the beginning. None of us yet has a serious buildup. But in another week, two weeks, three—"

"May the Lady protect us!" Lavon gasped.

"The Lady's blessings don't reach this far west," said Joachil Noor. She smiled coolly. "I recommend that we discontinue all fishing at once and draw on our stores until we're out of this part of the sea. And that we finish the job of screening the rotors as fast as possible."

"Agreed," said Lavon.

When she had left him he stepped to the bridge and looked gloomily out over the congested, quivering water. The colors today were richer than ever, heavy umbers, sepias, russets, indigos. The dragon-grass was thriving. Lavon imagined the fleshy strands slapping up against the hull, searing the gleaming metal with acid secretions, burning it away molecule by molecule, converting the ship to ion soup and greedily drinking it. He shivered. He could no longer see beauty in the intricate textures of the seaweed. That dense and tightly interwoven mass of algae stretching toward the horizon now meant only stink and decay to him, danger and death, the bubbling gases of rot and the secret teeth of destruction. Hour by hour the flanks of the great ship grew thinner, and here she still sat, immobilized, helpless, in the midst of the foe that consumed her.

Lavon tried to keep these new perils from becoming general knowledge. That was impossible, of course: there could be no secrets for long in a closed universe like the *Spurifon*. His insistence on secrecy did at least serve to minimize open discussion of the problems, which could lead so swiftly to panic. Everyone knew, but everyone pretended that he alone realized how bad things were.

Nevertheless the pressure mounted. Tempers were short; conversations were strained; hands shook, words were slurred, things were dropped. Lavon remained apart from the others as much as his duties would allow. He prayed for deliverance and sought guidance in dreams, but Joachil Noor seemed to be right: the voyagers were beyond the reach of the loving Lady of the Isle whose counsel brought comfort to the suffering and wisdom to the troubled.

The only new glimmer of hope came from the biologists. Joachil Noor suggested that it might be possible to disrupt the electrical systems of the dragon-grass by conducting a current through the water. It sounded doubtful to Lavon, but he authorized her to put some of the ship's technicians to work on it.

And finally the last of the intake screens was in place. It was late in the third week of their captivity.

"Start the rotors," Lavon ordered.

The ship throbbed with renewed life as the rotors began to move. On the bridge the officers stood frozen: Lavon, Vormecht, Galimoin, silent, still, barely breathing. Tiny wavelets formed along the bow. The *Spurifon* was beginning to move! Slowly, stubbornly, the ship began to cut a path through the close-packed masses of writhing dragon-grass—

—and shuddered, and bucked, and fought, and the throb of the rotors ceased—

"The screens aren't holding!" Galimoin cried in anguish.

"Find out what's happening," Lavon told Vormecht. He turned to Galimoin, who was standing as though his feet had been nailed to the deck, trembling, sweating, muscles rippling weirdly about his lips and cheeks. Lavon said gently, "It's probably only a minor hitch. Come, let's have some wine, and in a moment we'll be moving again."

"No!" Galimoin bellowed. "I felt the screens rip loose. The dragon-grass is eating them."

More urgently Lavon said, "The screens will hold. By this time to-morrow we'll be far from here, and you'll have us on course again for Alhanroel—"

"We're lost!" Galimoin shouted, and broke away suddenly, arms flail-ing as he ran down the steps and out of sight. Lavon hesitated. Vormecht returned, looking grim: the screens had indeed broken free, the rotors were fouled, the ship had halted again. Lavon swayed. He felt infected by Galimoin's despair. His life's dream was ending in failure, an absurd ca-tastrophe, a mocking farce.

Joachil Noor appeared. "Captain, do you know that Galimoin's gone berserk? He's up on the observation deck, wailing and screaming and dancing and calling for a mutiny."

"I'll go to him," said Lavon.

"I felt the rotors start. But then—"

Lavon nodded. "Fouled again. The screens ripped loose." As he moved toward the catwalk he heard Joachil Noor say something about her electrical project, that she was ready to make the first full-scale test, and he replied that she should begin at once, and report to him as soon as there were any encouraging results. But her words went quickly out of his mind. The problem of Galimoin occupied him entirely.

The chief navigator had taken up a position on the high platform to starboard where once he had made his observations and calculations of latitudes and longitudes. Now he capered like a deranged beast, strutting back and forth, flinging out his arms, shouting incoherently, singing rau-cous snatches of balladry, denouncing Lavon as a fool who had deliber-ately led them into this trap. A dozen or so members of the crew were gathered below, listening, some jeering, some calling out their agreement, and others were arriving quickly: this was the sport of the moment, the day's divertissement. To Lavon's horror he saw Mikdal Hasz making his way out onto Galimoin's platform from the far side. Hasz was speaking in low tones, beckoning to the navigator, quietly urging him to come down; and several times Galimoin broke off his harangue to look toward Hasz and growl a threat at him. But Hasz kept advancing. Now he was just a yard or two from Galimoin, still speaking, smiling, holding out his open hands as if to show that he carried no weapons.

"Get away!" Galimoin roared. "Keep back!"

Lavon, edging toward the platform himself, signaled to Hasz to keep out of reach. Too late: in a single frenzied moment the infuriated Galimoin lunged at Hasz, scooped the little man up as if he were a doll, and hurled him over the railing into the sea. A cry of astonishment went up from the onlookers. Lavon rushed to the railing in time to see Hasz, limbs flailing, crash against the surface of the water. Instantly there was convulsive activity in the dragon-grass. Like maddened eels the fleshy strands swarmed and twisted and writhed; the sea seemed to boil for a moment; and then Hasz was lost to view.

A terrifying dizziness swept through Lavon. He felt as though his heart filled his entire chest, crushing his lungs, and his brain was spinning in his skull. He had never seen violence before. He had never heard of an instance in his lifetime of the deliberate slaying of one human by another. That it should have happened on his ship, by one of his officers upon another, in the midst of this crisis, was intolerable, a mortal wound. He moved forward like one who walks while dreaming and laid his hands on Galimoin's powerful, muscular shoulders and with a strength he had never had before he shoved the navigator over the rail, easily, unthinkingly. He heard a strangled wail, a splash; he looked down, amazed, appalled, and saw the sea boiling a second time as the dragon-grass closed over Galimoin's thrashing body.

Slowly, numbly, Lavon descended from the platform.

He felt dazed and flushed. Something seemed broken within him. A ring of blurred figures surrounded him. Gradually he discerned eyes, mouths, the patterns of familiar faces. He started to say something, but no words would come, only sounds. He toppled and was caught and eased to the deck. Someone's arm was around his shoulders; someone was giving him wine. "Look at his eyes," he heard a voice say. "He's gone into shock!" Lavon began to shiver. Somehow—he was unaware of being lifted—he found himself in his cabin, with Vormecht bending over him and others standing behind.

.The first mate said quietly, "The ship is moving, Captain."

"What? What? Hasz is dead. Galimoin killed Hasz and I killed Galimoin."

"It was the only possible thing to do. The man was insane."

"I *killed* him, Vormecht."

"We couldn't have kept a madman locked up on board for the next ten years. He was dangerous to us all. His life was forfeit. You had the power. You acted rightly."

"We do not kill," Lavon said. "Our barbarian ancestors took each other's lives, on Old Earth long ago, but we do not kill. *I* do not kill. We were beasts once, but that was in another era, on a different planet. I killed him, Vormecht."

"You are the captain. You had the right. He threatened the success of the voyage."

"Success? Success?"

"The ship is moving again, Captain."

Lavon stared, but could barely see. "What are you saying?"

"Come. Look."

Four massive arms enfolded him and Lavon smelled the musky tang of Skandar fur. The giant crewman lifted him and carried him to the deck, and put him carefully down. Lavon tottered, but Vormecht was at his side, and Joachil Noor. The first mate pointed toward the sea. A zone of open water bordered the *Spurifon* along the entire length of her hull.

Joachil Noor said, "We dropped cables into the water and gave the dragon-grass a good jolt of current. It shorted out their contractile systems. The ones closest to us died instantly and the rest began to pull back. There's a clear channel in front of us as far as we can see."

"The voyage is saved," said Vormecht. "We can go onward now, Captain!"

"No," Lavon said. He felt the haze and confusion lifting from his mind. "Who's navigator now? Have him turn the ship back toward Zimroel."

"But—"

"Turn her around! Back to Zimroel!"

They were gaping at him, bewildered, stunned. "Captain, you're not yourself yet. To give such an order, in the very moment when all is well again—you need to rest, and in a few hours you'll feel—"

"The voyage is ended, Vormecht. We're going back."

"No!"

"No? Is this a mutiny, then?" Their eyes were blank. Their faces were expressionless. Lavon said, "Do you really want to continue? Aboard a doomed ship with a murderer for a captain? You were all sick of the voyage before any of this happened. Don't you think I knew that? You were hungry for home. You didn't dare say it, is all. Well, now I feel as you do."

Vormecht said, "We've been at sea five years. We may be halfway across. It might take us no longer to reach the farther shore than to return."

"Or it might take us forever," said Lavon. "It does not matter. I have no heart for going forward."

"Tomorrow you may think differently, Captain."

"Tomorrow I will still have blood on my hands, Vormecht. I was not meant to bring this ship safely across the Great Sea. We bought our freedom at the cost of four lives; but the voyage was broken by it."

"Captain—"

"Turn the ship around," said Lavon.

WHEN THEY CAME TO him the next day, pleading to be allowed to continue the voyage, arguing that eternal fame and immortality awaited them on the shores of Alhanroel, Lavon calmly and quietly refused to discuss it with them. To continue now, he told them again, was impossible. So they looked at one another, those who had hated the voyage and yearned to be free of it and who in the euphoric moment of victory over the dragon-grass had changed their minds, and they changed their minds again, for without the driving force of Lavon's will there was no way of going on. They set their course to the east and said no more about the crossing of the Great Sea. A year afterward they were assailed by storms and severely thrown about, and in the following year there was a bad encounter with sea-dragons that severely damaged the ship's stern; but yet they continued, and of the hundred and sixty-three voyagers who had left Til-omon long before, more than a hundred were still alive, Captain Lavon among them, when the *Spurifon* came limping back into her home port in the eleventh year of the voyage.

FOUR

Calintane Explains

*H*issune is downcast for days after that. He knows, of course, that the voyage failed: no ship has ever crossed the Great Sea, and no ship ever will, for the idea is absurd and realization of it is probably impossible. But to fail in such a way, to go so far and then turn back, not out of cowardice or because of illness or famine but rather from sheer moral despair—Hissune finds that hard to comprehend. He would never turn back. Through the fifteen years of his life he has always gone steadily forward toward whatever he perceived as his goal, and those who faltered along their own routes have always seemed to him idle and weak. But, then, he is not Sinnabor Lavon; and, too, he has never taken a life. Such a deed of violence might shake anyone's soul. For Sinnabor Lavon he feels a certain contempt, and a great deal of pity, and then, the more he considers the man, seeing him from within, a kind of admiration replaces the contempt, for he realizes that Sinnabor Lavon was no weakling but in fact a person of enormous moral strength. That is a startling insight, and Hissune's depression lifts the moment he reaches it. My education, he thinks, continues.

All the same he has gone to Sinnabor Lavon's records in search of adventure and diversion, not such sober-minded philosophizing. He has not found quite what he sought. But a few years afterward, he knows, there was an event in this very Labyrinth that had diverted everyone most extremely, and that even after more than six thousand years still reverberates through history as one of the strangest events Majipoor has seen. When his duties permit, Hissune takes the time to do a bit of historical research; and then he returns to the Register of

Souls to enter the mind of a certain young official at the court of the Pontifex Arioc of bizarre repute.

ON THE MORNING AFTER the day when the crisis had reached its climax and the final lunacies had occurred, a strange hush settled over the Labyrinth of Majipoor, as if everyone were too stunned even to speak. The impact of yesterday's extraordinary events was just beginning to be felt, although even those who had witnessed what had taken place could not yet fully believe it. All the ministries were closed that morning, by order of the new Pontifex. The bureaucrats both major and minor had been put to extreme strain by the recent upheavals, and they were set at liberty to sleep it off, while the new Pontifex and the new Coronal—each amazed by the unanticipated attainment of kingship that had struck him with thunderclap force—withdrew to their private chambers to contemplate their astounding transformations. Which gave Calintane at last an opportunity to see his beloved Silimoor. Apprehensively—for he had treated her shabbily all month, and she was not an easily forgiving sort—he sent her a note that said, *I know I am guilty of shameful neglect, but perhaps now you begin to understand. Meet me for lunch at the café by the Court of Globes at midday and I will explain everything.*

She had a quick temper at the best of times. It was virtually her only fault, but it was a severe one, and Calintane feared her wrath. They had been lovers a year; they were nearly betrothed to be betrothed; all the senior officials at the Pontifical court agreed he was making a wise match. Silimoor was lovely and intelligent and knowledgeable in political matters, and of good family, with three Coronals in her ancestry, including no less than the fabled Lord Stiamot himself. Plainly she would be an ideal mate for a young man destined for high places. Though still some distance short of thirty, Calintane had already attained the outer rim of the inner circle about the Pontifex, and had been given responsibilities well beyond his years. Indeed, it was those very responsibilities that had kept him from seeing or even speaking at any length to Silimoor lately. For which he expected her to berate him, and for which he hoped without much conviction that she would eventually pardon him.

All this past sleepless night he had rehearsed in his weary mind a long speech of extenuation that began, "As you know, I've been preoccupied with urgent matters of state these last weeks, too delicate to discuss in detail with you, and so—" And as he made his way up the levels of the Labyrinth to the Court of Globes for his rendezvous with her, he continued to roll the phrases about. The ghostly silence of the Labyrinth this morning made him feel all the more edgy. The lowest levels, where the government offices were, seemed wholly deserted, and higher up just a few people could be seen, gathering in little knotted groups in the darkest corners, whispering and muttering as though there had been a coup d'etat, which in a sense was not far wrong. Everyone stared at him. Some pointed. Calintane wondered how they recognized him as an official of the Pontificate, until he remembered that he was still wearing his mask of office. He kept it on anyway, as a kind of shield against the glaring artificial light, so harsh on his aching eyes. Today the Labyrinth seemed stifling and oppressive. He longed to escape its somber subterranean depths, those levels upon levels of great spiraling chambers that coiled down and down. In a single night the place had become loathsome to him.

On the level of the Court of Globes he emerged from the lift and cut diagonally across that intricate vastness, decorated with its thousands of mysteriously suspended spheres, to the little cafe on the far side. The midday hour struck just as he entered it. Silimoor was already there—he knew she would be; she used punctuality to express displeasure—at a small table along the rear wall of polished onyx. She rose and offered him not her lips but her hand, also as he expected. Her smile was precise and cool. Exhausted as he was, he found her beauty almost excessive: the short golden hair arrayed like a crown, the flashing turquoise eyes, the full lips and high cheekbones, an elegance too painful to bear, just now. "I've missed you so," he said hoarsely.

"Of course. So long a separation—it must have been a dreadful burden—"

"As you know, I've been preoccupied with urgent matters of state these last weeks, too delicate to discuss in detail with you, and so—"

The words sounded impossibly idiotic in his own ears. It was a relief when she cut him off, saying smoothly, "There's time for all that, love. Shall we have some wine?"

"Please. Yes."

She signaled. A liveried waiter, a haughty-looking Hjort, came to take the order, and stalked away.

Silimoor said, "And won't you even remove your mask?"

"Ah. Sorry. It's been such a scrambled few days—"

He set aside the bright yellow strip that covered his nose and eyes and marked him as the Pontifex's man. Silimoor's expression changed as she saw him clearly for the first time; the look of serenely self-satisfied fury faded and something close to concern appeared on her face. "Your eyes are so bloodshot—your cheeks are so pale and drawn—"

"I've had no sleep. It's been a crazy time."

"Poor Calintane."

"Do you think I kept away from you because I *wanted* to? I've been caught up in this insanity, Silimoor."

"I know. I can see how much of a strain it's been."

He realized suddenly that she was not mocking him, that she was genuinely sympathetic, that in fact this was possibly going to be easier than he had been imagining.

He said, "The trouble with being ambitious is that you get engulfed in affairs far beyond your control, and you have no choice but to let yourself be swept along. You've heard what the Pontifex Arioc did yesterday?"

She stifled a laugh. "Yes, of course. I mean, I've heard the rumors. Everyone has. Are they true? Did it really happen?"

"Unfortunately, it did."

"How marvelous, how perfectly marvelous! But such a thing turns the world upside down, doesn't it? It affects you in some dreadful way?"

"It affects you, and me, and everyone in the world," said Calintane, with a gesture that reached beyond the Court of Globes, beyond the Labyrinth itself, encompassing the entire planet beyond these claustrophobic depths, from the awesome summit of Castle Mount to the far-off cities of the western continent. "Affects us all to a degree that I hardly understand yet myself. But let me tell you the story from the beginning—"

PERHAPS YOU WERE NOT aware that the Pontifex Arioc has been behaving strangely for months. I suppose there's something about the pressures of high office that eventually drives people crazy, or perhaps you have to be at least partly mad in the first place to aspire to high office. But you know that Arioc was Coronal for thirteen years under Dizimaule, and now he's been Pontifex a dozen years more, and that's a long time to hold that sort of power. Especially living here in the Labyrinth. The Pontifex must yearn for the outside world now and then, I'd imagine—to feel the breezes on Castle Mount or hunt gihornas in Zimroel or just to swim in a real river anywhere—and here he is miles and miles underground in this maze, presiding over his rituals and his bureaucrats until the end of his life.

One day about a year ago Arioc suddenly began talking about making a grand processional of Majipoor. I was in attendance at court that day, along with Duke Guadeloom. The Pontifex called for maps and started laying out a journey down the river to Alaisor, over to the Isle of Sleep for a pilgrimage and a visit to the Lady at Inner Temple, then across to Zimroel, with stops at Piliplok, Ni-moya, Pidruid, Narabal, you know, *everywhere*, a tour that would last at least five years. Guadeloom gave me a funny look and gently pointed out to Arioc that it's the Coronal who makes grand processionals, not the Pontifex, and that Lord Struin had only just come back from one a couple of years ago.

"Then I am forbidden to do so?" the Pontifex asked.

"Not precisely forbidden, your majesty, but custom dictates—"

"That I remain a prisoner in the Labyrinth?"

"Not at all a prisoner, your majesty, but—"

"But I am rarely if ever to venture into the upper world?"

And so on. I must say my sympathies were with Arioc; but remember that I am not, like you, a native of the Labyrinth, only one whose government duties have brought him here, and I do find life underground a little unnatural at times. At any rate Guadeloom did convince his majesty that a grand processional was out of the question. But I could see the restlessness in the Pontifex's eyes.

The next thing that happened was that his majesty started slipping out by night to wander around the Labyrinth by himself. No one knows how often he did it before we found out what was going on, but we began to hear odd rumors that a masked figure who looked much like the Pontifex had been seen in the small hours lurking about in the Court of Pyramids or the Hall of Winds. We regarded that as so much nonsense, until the night when some flunky of the bedchamber imagined he had heard the Pontifex ring for service and went in and found the room empty. I think you will remember that night, Silimoor, because I was spending it with you and one of Guadeloom's people hunted me down and made me leave, claiming that an urgent meeting of the high advisers had been convened and my services were needed. You were quite upset— furious, I'd say. Of course what the meeting was about was the disappearance of the Pontifex, though later we covered it up by claiming it was a discussion of the great wave that had devastated so much of Stoienzar.

We found Arioc about four hours past midnight. He was in the Arena—you know, that stupid empty thing that the Pontifex Dizimaule built in one of *his* crazier moments—sitting crosslegged at the far side, playing a zootibar and singing songs to an audience of five or six ragged little boys. We brought him home. A few weeks later he got out again and managed to get as far up as the Court of Columns. Guadeloom discussed it with him: Arioc insisted that it is important for a monarch to go among his people and hear their grievances, and he cited precedents as far back as the kings of Old Earth. Quietly Guadeloom began posting guards in the royal precincts, supposedly to keep assassins out—but who would assassinate a Pontifex? The guards were put there to keep Arioc in. But though the Pontifex is eccentric, he's far from stupid, and despite the guards he slipped out twice more in the next couple of months. It was becoming a critical problem. What if he vanished for a week? What if he got out of the Labyrinth entirely, and went for a stroll in the desert?

"Since we can't seem to prevent him from roaming," I said to Guadeloom, "why don't we give him a companion, someone who'll go on his adventures with him and at the same time see to it that no harm comes to him?"

"An excellent idea," the duke replied. "And I appoint you to the post. The Pontifex is fond of you, Calintane. And you are young enough and agile enough to be able to extricate him from any trouble into which he may stumble."

That was six weeks ago, Silimoor. You will surely recall that I suddenly ceased spending my nights with you at that time, pleading an increase of responsibilities at court, and thus our estrangement began. I could not tell you what duty it was that now occupied my nights, and I could only hope you did not suspect me of having shifted my affections to another. But I can now reveal that I was compelled to take up lodgings close by the bedchamber of the Pontifex and give him attendance every night; that I began to do most of my sleeping at random hours of the day; and that by one stratagem and another I became companion to Arioc on his nocturnal jaunts.

It was taxing work. I was in truth the Pontifex's keeper, and we both knew it, but I had to take care not to underscore the fact by unduly imposing my will on him. And yet I had to guard him from rough playmates and risky excursions. There are rogues, there are brawlers, there are hotheads; no one would knowingly harm the Pontifex but he might easily come by accident between two who meant to harm each other. In my rare moments of sleep I sought the guidance of the Lady of the Isle— may she rest in the bosom of the Divine—and she came to me in a blessed sending, and told me that I must make myself the Pontifex's friend if I meant not to be his jailer. How fortunate we are to have the counsel of so kind a mother in our dreams! And so I dared to initiate more than a few of Arioc's adventures myself. "Come, let us go out tonight," I said to him, which would have frozen Guadeloom's blood, had he known. It was my idea to take the Pontifex up into the public levels of the Labyrinth for a night of taverns and marketplaces—masked, of course, beyond chance of recognition. I led him into mysterious alleyways where gamblers lived, but gamblers known to me, who posed no threats. And it was I who on the boldest night of all actually guided him beyond the walls of the Labyrinth itself. I knew it was what he most desired, and even he feared to attempt it, so I proposed it to him as my secret gift, and he and I took the private royal passageway upward that emerges at the Mouth of Waters.

We stood together so close to the River Glayge that we could feel the cool air that blows down from Castle Mount, and we looked up at the blazing stars. "I have not been out here in six years," said the Pontifex. He was trembling and I think he was weeping behind his mask; and I, who had not seen the stars either for much too long, was nearly as deeply moved. He pointed to this one and that, saying it was the star of the world from which the Ghayrog folk came, and this the star of the Hjorts, and that one there, that trifling dot of light, was none other than the sun of Old Earth. Which I doubted, since I had been taught otherwise in school, but he was in such joy that I could not contradict him then. And he turned to me and gripped my arm and said in a low voice, "Calintane, I am the supreme ruler of this whole colossal world, and I am nothing at all, a slave, a prisoner. I would give everything to escape this Labyrinth and spend my last years in freedom under the stars."

"Then why not abdicate?" I suggested, astounded at my audacity.

He smiled. "It would be cowardice. I am the elect of the Divine, and how can I reject that burden? I am destined to be a Power of Majipoor to the end of my days. But there must be some honorable way to free myself from this subterranean misery."

And I saw that the Pontifex was neither mad nor wicked nor capricious, but only lonely for the night and the mountains and the moons and the trees and the streams of the world he had been forced to abandon so that the government might be laid upon him.

Next came word, two weeks ago, that the Lady of the Isle, Lord Struin's mother and the mother of us all, had fallen ill and was not likely to recover. This was an unusual crisis that created major constitutional problems, for of course the Lady is a Power of rank equal to Pontifex and Coronal, and replacing her should hardly be done casually. Lord Struin himself was reported to be on his way from Castle Mount to confer with the Pontifex—foregoing a journey to the Isle of Sleep, for he could not possibly reach it in time to bid his mother farewell. Meanwhile Duke Guadeloom, as high spokesman of the Pontificate and chief officer of the court, had begun to compile a list of candidates for the post, which would be compared with Lord Struin's list to see if any names were on both. The counsel of the Pontifex Arioc was necessary in all of this, and we thought that would be beneficial to him in his present unsettled state by involving him more deeply in imperial matters. In at least a technical sense the dying Lady was his wife, for under the formalities of our succession law he had adopted Lord Struin as his son when choosing him to be Coronal; of course the Lady had a lawful husband of her own somewhere on Castle Mount, but you understand the legalities of the custom, do you not? Guadeloom informed the Pontifex of the impending death of the Lady and a round of governmental conferences began. I did not take part in these, since I am not of that level of authority or responsibility.

I am afraid we assumed that the gravity of the situation might cause Arioc to become less erratic in his behavior, and at least unconsciously we must have relaxed our vigilance. On the very night that the news of the death of the Lady reached the Labyrinth, the Pontifex slipped away alone for the first time since I had been assigned to keep watch over him. Past the guards, past me, past his servants—out into the interminable intricate complexities of the Labyrinth, and no one could find him. We searched all night and half the next day. I was beside myself with terror, both for him and for my career. In the greatest of apprehension I sent officers out each of the seven mouths of the Labyrinth to search that bleak and torrid desert outside; I myself visited all the rakish haunts to which I had introduced him; Guadeloom's staff prowled in places unknown to me; and throughout all this we sought to keep the populace from knowing that the Pontifex was missing. I think we must have succeeded in that.

We found him in midafternoon of the day after his disappearance. He was in a house in the district known as Stiamot's Teeth in the first ring of the Labyrinth and he was disguised in women's clothes. We might never have found him at all but for some quarrel over an unpaid bill, which brought proctors to the scene, and when the Pontifex was unable to identify himself satisfactorily and a man's voice was heard coming from a supposed woman the proctors had the sense to summon me, and I hurried to take custody of him. He looked appallingly strange in his robes and his bangles, but he greeted me calmly by name, acting perfectly composed and rational, and said he hoped he had not caused me great inconvenience.

I expected Guadeloom to demote me. But the duke was in a forgiving mood, or else he was too bound up in the larger crisis to care about my lapse, for he said nothing whatever about the fact that I had let the Pontifex get out of his bedchamber. "Lord Struin arrived this morning," Guadeloom told me, looking harried and weary. "Naturally he wanted to meet with the Pontifex at once, but we told him that Arioc was asleep and it was unwise to disturb him—this while half my people were out searching for him. It pains me to lie to the Coronal, Calintane."

"The Pontifex is genuinely asleep in his chambers now," I said.

"Yes. Yes. And there he will stay, I think."

"I will make every effort to see to that."

"That's not what I mean," said Guadeloom. "The Pontifex Arioc is plainly out of his mind. Crawling through laundry chutes, creeping around the city at night, decking himself out in female finery—it goes beyond mere eccentricity, Calintane. Once we have this business of the new Lady out of the way, I'm going to propose that we confine him permanently to his quarters under strong guard—for his own protection, Calintane, his own protection—and hand the Pontifical duties over to a regency. There's precedent for that. I've been through the records. When Barhold was Pontifex he fell ill of swamp fever and it affected his mind, and—"

"Sir," I said, "I don't believe the Pontifex is insane."

Guadeloom frowned. "How else could you characterize one who does what he's been doing?"

"They are the acts of a man who has been king too long, and whose soul rebels against all that he must continue to bear. But I have come to know him well, and I venture to say that what he expresses by these escapades is a torment of the soul, but not any kind of madness."

It was an eloquent speech and, if I have to say it myself, courageous, for I am a junior counsellor and Guadeloom was at that moment the third most powerful figure in the realm, behind only Arioc and Lord Struin. But there comes a time when one must put diplomacy and ambition and guile aside, and simply speak the plain truth; and the idea of confining the unhappy Pontifex like a common lunatic, when he already suffered great pain from his confinement in the Labyrinth alone, was horrifying to me. Guadeloom was silent a long while and I suppose I should have been frightened, speculating whether I would be dismissed altogether from his service or simply sent down to the record-keeping halls to spend the remainder of my life shuffling papers, but I was calm, totally calm, as I awaited his reply.

Then came a knock at the door: a messenger, bearing a note sealed with the great starburst that was the Coronal's personal seal. Duke Guadeloom ripped it open and read the message and read it again, and read it a third time, and I have never seen such a look of incredulity and horror pass over a human face as crossed his then. His hands were shaking; his face was without color.

He looked at me and said in a strangled voice, "This is in the Coronal's own hand, informing me that the Pontifex has left his quarters and has gone to the Place of Masks, where he has issued a decree so stupefying that I cannot bring myself to frame the words with my own lips." He handed me the note. "Come," he said, "I think we should hasten to the Place of Masks."

He ran out, and I followed, trying desperately to glance at the note as I went. But Lord Struin's handwriting is jagged and difficult, and Guadeloom was moving with phenomenal speed, and the corridors were winding and the way poorly lit; so I could only get a snatch of the content here and there, something about a proclamation, a new Lady designated, an abdication. Whose abdication if not that of the Pontifex Arioc? Yet he had said to me out of the depths of his spirit that it would be cowardice to turn his back on the destiny that had chosen him to be a Power of the realm.

Breathless, I came to the Place of Masks, a zone of the Labyrinth that I find disturbing at the best of times, for the great slit-eyed faces that rise on those gleaming marble plinths seem to me figures out of nightmare. Guadeloom's footsteps clattered on the stone floor, and mine doubled the sound of his a good way behind, for though he was more than twice my age he was moving like a demon. Up ahead I heard shouts, laughter, applause. And then I saw a gathering of perhaps a hundred fifty citizens, among whom I recognized several of the chief ministers of the Pontificate. Guadeloom and I barged into the group and halted only when we saw figures in the green-and-gold uniform of the Coronal's service, and then the Coronal himself. Lord Struin looked furious and dazed at the same time, a man in shock.

"There is no stopping him," the Coronal said hoarsely. "He goes from hall to hall, repeating his proclamation. Listen: he begins again!"

And I saw the Pontifex Arioc at the head of the group, riding on the shoulders of a colossal Skandar servant. His majesty was dressed in flowing white robes of the female style, with a splendid brocaded border, and on his breast lay a glowing red jewel of wondrous immensity and radiance.

"Whereas a vacancy has developed among the Powers of Majipoor!" cried the Pontifex in a marvelously robust voice. "And whereas it is needful that a new Lady of the Isle of Sleep! Be appointed herewith and swiftly! So that she may minister to the souls of the people! By appearing in their dreams to give aid and comfort! And! Whereas! It is my earnest desire! To yield up the burden of the Pontificate that I have borne these twelve years!

"Therefore—

"I do herewith! Using the supreme powers at my command! Proclaim that I be acclaimed hereafter as a member of the female sex! And as Pontifex I do name as Lady of the Isle the woman Arioc, formerly male!"

"Madness," muttered Duke Guadeloom.

"This is the third time I have heard it, and still I cannot believe it," said the Coronal Lord Struin.

"—and do herewith simultaneously abdicate my Pontifical throne! And call upon the dwellers of the Labyrinth! To fetch for the Lady Arioc a chariot! To transport her to the port of Stoien! And thence to the Isle of Sleep so that she may bring her consolations to you all!"

And in that moment the gaze of Arioc turned toward me, and his eyes for an instant met mine. He was flushed with excitement and his forehead gleamed with sweat. He recognized me, and he smiled, and he *winked*, an undeniable wink, a wink of joy, a wink of triumph. Then he was carried away out of my sight.

"This must be stopped," Guadeloom said.

Lord Struin shook his head. "Listen to the cheering! They love it.

The crowd grows larger as he goes from level to level. They'll sweep him up to the top and out the Mouth of Blades and off to Stoien before this day is out."

"You are Coronal," said Guadeloom. "Is there nothing you can do?"

"Overrule the Pontifex, whose every command I have sworn to serve? Commit treason before hundreds of witnesses? No, no, no, Guadeloom, what's done is done, preposterous as it may be, and now we must live with it."

"All hail the Lady Arioc!" a booming voice bellowed.

"All hail! The Lady Arioc! All hail! All hail!"

I watched in utter disbelief as the procession moved on through the Place of Masks, heading for the Hall of Winds or the Court of Pyramids beyond. We did not follow, Guadeloom and the Coronal and I. Numb, silent, we stood motionless as the cheering, gesticulating figures disappeared. I was abashed to be among these great men of our realm at so humiliating a moment. It was absurd and fantastic, this abdication and appointment of a Lady, and they were shattered by it.

At length Guadeloom said thoughtfully, "If you accept the abdication as valid, Lord Struin, then you are Coronal no longer, but must make ready to take up residence here in the Labyrinth, for you are now our Pontifex."

Those words fell upon Lord Struin like mighty boulders. In the frenzy of the moment he had evidently not thought Arioc's deed through even to its first consequence.

His mouth opened but no words came forth. He opened and closed his hands as though making the starburst gesture in his own honor, but I knew it was only an expression of bewilderment. I felt shivers of awe, for it is no small thing to witness a transfer of succession, and Struin was wholly unprepared for it. To give up the joys of Castle Mount in the midst of life, to exchange its brilliant cities and splendid forests for the gloom of the Labyrinth, to put aside the starburst crown for the senior diadem—no, he was not ready at all, and as the truth of it came home to him, his face turned ashen and his eyelids twitched madly.

After a very long while he said, "So be it, then. I am the Pontifex. And who, I ask you, is to be Coronal in my place?"

I suppose it was a rhetorical question. Certainly I gave no answer, and neither did Duke Guadeloom.

Angrily, roughly, Struin said again, "Who is to be Coronal? I ask you!"

His gaze was on Guadeloom.

I tell you, I was near to destroyed by being witness of these events, that will never be forgotten if our civilization lasts another ten thousand years. But how much more of an impact all this must have had on them! Guadeloom fell back, spluttering. Since Arioc and Lord Struin both were relatively young men, little speculation on the succession to their thrones had taken place; and though Guadeloom was a man of power and majesty, I doubt that he had ever expected himself to reach the heights of Castle Mount, and certainly not in any such way as this. He gaped like a gaffed gromwark and could not speak, and in the end it was I who reacted first, going down on my knee, making the starburst to him, crying out in a choked voice, "Guadeloom! Lord Guadeloom! Hail, Lord Guadeloom! Long life to Lord Guadeloom!"

Never again will I see two men so astonished, so confused, so instantly altered, as were the former Lord Struin, now Pontifex, and the former Duke Guadeloom, now Coronal. Struin was stormy-faced with rage and pain, Lord Guadeloom half broken with amazement.

There was another huge silence.

Then Lord Guadeloom said in an oddly quavering voice, "If I am Coronal, custom demands that my mother be named the Lady of the Isle, is that not so?"

"How old is your mother?" Struin asked.

"Quite old. Ancient, one could say."

"Yes. And neither prepared for the tasks of the Ladyship nor strong enough to bear them."

"True," said Lord Guadeloom.

Struin said, "Besides, we have a new Lady this day, and it would not do to select another so soon. Let us see how well her Ladyship Arioc conducts herself in Inner Temple before we seek to put another in her place, eh?"

"Madness," said Lord Guadeloom.

"Madness indeed," said the Pontifex Struin. "Come, let us go to the Lady, and see her safely off to her Isle."

I went with them to the upper reaches of the Labyrinth, where we found ten thousand people hailing Arioc as he or she, barefoot and in splendid robes, made ready to board the chariot that would conduct her or him to the port of Stoien. It was impossible to get close to Arioc, so close was the press of bodies. "Madness," said Lord Guadeloom over and over. "Madness, madness!"

But I knew otherwise, for I had seen Arioc's wink, and I understood it completely. This was no madness at all. The Pontifex Arioc had found his way out of the Labyrinth, which was his heart's desire. Future generations, I am sure, will think of him as a synonym for folly and absurdity; but I know that he was altogether sane, a man to whom the crown had become an agony and whose honor forbade him simply to retire into private life.

And so it is, after yesterday's strange events, that we have a Pontifex and a Coronal and a Lady, and they are none of them the ones we had last month, and now you understand, beloved Silimoor, all that has befallen our world.

CALINTANE FINISHED SPEAKING AND took a long draft of his wine. Silimoor was staring at him with an expression that seemed to him a mixture of pity and contempt and sympathy.

"You are like small children," she said at last, "with your titles and your royal courts and your bonds of honor. Nevertheless I understand, I think, what you have experienced and how it has unsettled you."

"There is one thing more," said Calintane.

"Yes?"

"The Coronal Lord Guadeloom, before he took to his chambers to begin the task of comprehending these transformations, appointed me his chancellor. He will leave next week for Castle Mount. And I must be at his side, naturally."

"How splendid for you," said Silimoor coolly.

"I ask you therefore to join me there, to share my life at the Castle," he said as measuredly as he could.

Her dazzling turquoise eyes stared frostily into his.

"I am native to the Labyrinth," she answered. "I love dearly to dwell in its precincts."

"Is that my answer, then?"

"No," said Silimoor. "You will have your answer later. Much like your Pontifex and your Coronal, I require time to accustom myself to great changes."

"Then you *have* answered!"

"Later," she said, and thanked him for the wine and for the tale he had told, and left him at the table. Calintane eventually rose, and wandered like a spectre through the depths of the Labyrinth in an exhaustion beyond all exhaustion, and heard the people buzzing as the news spread— Arioc the Lady now, Struin the Pontifex, Guadeloom the Coronal—and it was to him like the droning of insects in his ears. He went to his chamber and tried to sleep, but no sleep came, and he fell into gloom over the state of his life, fearing that this sour period of separation from Silimoor had done fatal harm to their love, and that despite her oblique hint to the contrary she would reject his suit. But he was wrong. For, a day later, she sent word that she was ready to go with him, and when Calintane took up his new residence at Castle Mount she was at his side, as she still was many years later when he succeeded Lord Guadeloom as Coronal. His reign in that post was short but cheerful, and during his time he accomplished the construction of the great highway at the summit of the Mount that bears his name; and when in old age he returned to the Labyrinth as Pontifex himself it was without the slightest surprise, for he had lost all capacity for surprise that day long ago when the Pontifex Arioc had proclaimed himself to be the Lady of the Isle.

FIVE

The Desert of Stolen Dreams

*S*o the legend of Arioc has obscured the truth of him, Hissune sees now, as
legend has obscured truth in so many other ways. For in the distortions of
time Arioc has come to seem grotesque, whimsical, a clown of sudden instability;
and yet if the testimony of Lord Calintane means anything, it was not that way
at all. A suffering man sought freedom and chose an outlandish way to attain
it: no clown, no madman at all. Hissune, himself trapped in the Labyrinth and
longing to taste the fresh air without, finds the Pontifex Arioc an unexpectedly
congenial figure—his brother in spirit across the thousands of years.

For a long while thereafter Hissune does not go to the Register of Souls.
The impact of those illicit journeys into the past has been too powerful; his head
buzzes with stray strands out of the souls of Thesme and Calintane and Sinnabor Lavon and Group Captain Eremoil, so that when all of them set up a
clamor at once he has difficulty locating Hissune, and that is dismaying. Besides, he has other things to do. After a year and a half he has finished with
the tax documents, and by then he has established himself so thoroughly in the
House of Records that another assignment is waiting for him, a survey of the
distribution of aboriginal population groups in present-day Majipoor. He
knows that Lord Valentine has had some problems with Metamorphs—that in
fact it was a conspiracy of the Shapeshifter folk that tumbled him from his
throne in that weird event of a few years back—and he remembers from what
he had overheard among the great ones on Castle Mount during his visit there
that it is Lord Valentine's plan to integrate them more fully into the life of the

planet, if that can be done. So Hissune suspects that these statistics he has been asked to compile have some function in the grand strategy of the Coronal, and that gives him a private pleasure.

It gives him, too, occasion for ironic smiles. For he is shrewd enough to see what is happening to the street-boy Hissune. That agile and cunning urchin who caught the Coronal's eye seven years ago is now an adolescent bureaucrat, transformed, tamed, civil, sedate. So be it, he thinks: one does not remain fourteen years old forever, and a time comes to leave the streets and become a useful member of society. Even so he feels some regret for the loss of the boy he had been. Some of that boy's mischief still bubbles in him; only some, but enough. He finds himself thinking weighty thoughts about the nature of society on Majipoor, the organic interrelationship of the political forces, the concept that power implies responsibility, that all beings are held together in harmonious union by a sense of reciprocal obligation. The four great Powers of the realm—the Pontifex, the Coronal, the Lady of the Isle, the King of Dreams—how, Hissune wonders, have they been able to work so well together? Even in this profoundly conservative society, where over thousands of years so little has changed, the harmony of the Powers seems miraculous, a balance of forces that must be divinely inspired. Hissune has had no formal education; there is no one to whom he can turn for knowledge of such things; but nevertheless, there is the Register of Souls, with all the teeming life of Majipoor's past held in a wondrous suspension, ready to release its passionate vitality at a command. It is folly not to explore that pool of knowledge now that such questions trouble his mind. So once again Hissune forges the documents; once again he slides himself glibly past the slow-witted guardians of the archives; once again he punches the keys, seeking now not only amusement and the joy of the forbidden but also an understanding of the evolution of his planet's political institutions. What a serious young man you are becoming, he tells himself, as the dazzling lights of many colors throb in his mind and the dark, intense presence of another human being, long dead but forever timeless, invades his soul.

1

Suvrael lay like a glowing sword across the southern horizon—an iron band of dull red light, sending shimmering heat-pulsations into the air. Dekkeret, standing at the bow of the freighter on which he had made the long dreary sea journey, felt a quickening of the pulse. Suvrael at last! That dreadful place, that abomination of a continent, that useless and miserable land, now just a few days away, and who knew what horrors would befall him there? But he was prepared. Whatever happens, Dekkeret believed, happens for the best, in Suvrael as on Castle Mount. He was in his twentieth year, a big burly man with a short neck and enormously broad shoulders. This was the second summer of Lord Prestimion's glorious reign under the great Pontifex Confalume.

It was as an act of penance that Dekkeret had undertaken the voyage to the burning wastes of barren Suvrael. He had committed a shameful deed—certainly not intending it, at first barely realizing the shame of it—while hunting in the Khyntor Marches of the far northland, and some sort of expiation seemed necessary to him. That was in a way a romantic and flamboyant gesture, he knew, but he could forgive himself that. If he did not make romantic and flamboyant gestures at twenty, then when? Surely not ten or fifteen years from now, when he was bound to the wheel of his destinies and had settled snugly in for the inevitable bland, easy career in Lord Prestimion's entourage. This was the moment, if ever. So, then, to Suvrael to purge his soul, no matter the consequences.

His friend and mentor and hunting companion in Khyntor, Akbalik, had not been able to understand. But of course Akbalik was no romantic, and a long way beyond twenty, besides. One night in early spring, over a few flasks of hot golden wine in a rough mountain tavern, Dekkeret had announced his intention and Akbalik's response had been a blunt snorting laugh. "Suvrael?" he had cried. "You judge yourself too harshly. There's no sin so foul that it merits a jaunt in Suvrael."

And Dekkeret, stung, feeling patronized, had slowly shaken his head. "Wrongness lies on me like a stain. I'll burn it from my soul under the hotland sun."

"Make the pilgrimage to the Isle instead, if you think you need to do something. Let the blessed Lady heal your spirit."

"No. Suvrael."

"Why?"

"To suffer," said Dekkeret. "To take myself far from the delights of Castle Mount, to the least pleasant place on Majipoor, to a dismal desert of fiery winds and loathsome dangers. To mortify the flesh, Akbalik, and show my contrition. To lay upon myself the discipline of discomfort and even pain—*pain*, do you know what that is?—until I can forgive myself. All right?"

Akbalik, grinning, dug his fingers into the thick robe of heavy black Khyntor furs that Dekkeret wore. "All right. But if you must mortify, mortify thoroughly. I assume you'll not take this from your body all the while you're under the Suvraelu sun."

Dekkeret chuckled. "There are limits," he said, "to my need for discomfort." He reached for the wine. Akbalik was nearly twice Dekkeret's age, and doubtless found his earnestness funny. So did Dekkeret, to a degree; but that did not swerve him.

"May I try once more to dissuade you?"

"Pointless."

"Consider the waste," said Akbalik anyway. "You have a career to look after. Your name is frequently heard at the Castle now. Lord Prestimion has said high things of you. A promising young man, due to climb far, great strength of character, all that kind of noise. Prestimion's young; he'll rule a long while; those who are young in his early days will rise as he rises. And here you are, deep in the wilds of Khyntor playing when you should be at court, and already planning another and more reckless trip. Forget this Suvrael nonsense, Dekkeret, and return to the Mount with me. Do the Coronal's bidding, impress the great ones with your worth, and build for the future. These are wonderful times on Majipoor, and it will be splendid to be among the wielders of power as things unfold. Eh? Eh? Why throw yourself away in Suvrael? No one knows of this—ah—*sin* of yours, this one little lapse from grace—"

"*I* know."

"Then promise never to do it again, and absolve yourself."

"It's not so simple," Dekkeret said.

"To squander a year or two of your life, or perhaps lose your life entirely, on a meaningless, useless journey to—"

"Not meaningless. Not useless."

"Except on a purely personal level it is."

"Not so, Akbalik. I've been in touch with the people of the Pontificate and I've wangled an official appointment. I'm on a mission of inquiry. Doesn't that sound grand? Suvrael isn't exporting its quota of meat and livestock and the Pontifex wants to know why. You see? I continue to further my career even while going off on what seems to you a wholly private adventure."

"So you've already made arrangements."

"I leave on Fourday next." Dekkeret reached his hand toward his friend. "It'll be at least two years. We'll meet again on the Mount. What do you say, Akbalik, the games at High Morpin, two years from Winterday?"

Akbalik's calm gray eyes fastened intently on Dekkeret's. "I will be there," he said slowly. "I pray that you'll be, too."

That conversation lay only some months in the past; but to Dekkeret now, feeling the throbbing heat of the southern continent reaching toward him over the pale green water of the Inner Sea, it seemed incredibly long ago, and the voyage infinitely long. The first part of the journey had been pleasing enough—down out of the mountains to the grand metropolis of Ni-moya, and then by riverboat down the Zimr to the port of Piliplok on the eastern coast. There he had boarded a freighter, the cheapest transport he could find, bound for the Suvraelu city of Tolaghai, and then it had been south and south and south all summer long, in a ghastly little cabin just downwind from a hold stuffed with bales of dried baby sea-dragons, and as the ship crossed into the tropics the days presented a heat unlike anything he had ever known, and the nights were little better; and the crew, mostly a bunch of shaggy Skandars, laughed at his discomfort and told him that he had better enjoy the cool weather while he could, for real heat was waiting for him in Suvrael. Well, he had wanted to suffer, and his wish was being amply granted already, and worse to come. He did not complain. He felt no regret. But his comfortable life among the young knights of Castle Mount had not prepared him for sleepless nights with the reek of sea-dragon in his nostrils like stilettos, nor for the stifling heat that engulfed the ship a few weeks out of Piliplok, nor for the intense boredom of the unchanging seascape. The planet was so impossibly *huge*, that was the trouble. It took forever to get from anywhere to anywhere. Crossing from his native continent of Alhanroel to the western land of Zimroel had been a big enough project, by riverboat to Alaisor from the Mount, then by sea to Piliplok and up the river into the mountain marches, but he had had Akbalik with him to lighten the time, and there had been the excitement of his first major journey, the strangeness of new places, new foods, new accents. And he had had the hunting expedition to look forward to. But this? This imprisonment aboard a dirty creaking ship stuffed with parched meat of evil odor? This interminable round of empty days without friends, without duties, without conversation? If only some monstrous sea-dragon would heave into view, he thought, and enliven the journey with a bit of peril; but no, no, the dragons in their migrations were elsewhere, one great herd said to be in western waters out by Narabal just now and another midway between Piliplok and the Rodamaunt Archipelago, and Dekkeret saw none of the vast beasts, not even a few stragglers. What made the boredom worse was that it did not seem to have any value as catharsis. He was suffering, true, and suffering was what he imagined would heal him of his wound, but yet the awareness of the terrible thing he had done in the mountains did not seem to diminish at all. He was hot and bored and restless, and guilt still clawed at him, and still he tormented himself with the ironic knowledge that he was being praised by no less than the Coronal Lord Prestimion for great strength of character while he could find only weakness and cowardice and foolishness in himself. Perhaps it takes more than humidity and boredom and foul odors to cure one's soul, Dekkeret decided. At any rate he had had more than enough of the process of getting to Suvrael, and he was ready to begin the next phase of his pilgrimage into the unknown.

2

Every journey ends, even an endless one. The hot wind out of the south intensified day after day until the deck was too hot to walk and the bare-foot Skandars had to swab it down every few hours; and then suddenly the burning mass of sullen darkness on the horizon resolved itself into a shoreline and the jaws of a harbor. They had reached Tolaghai at last.

All of Suvrael was tropical; most of its interior was desert, oppressed perpetually by a colossal weight of dry dead air around the periphery of which searing cyclones whirled; but the fringes of the continent were more or less habitable, and there were five major cities along the coasts, of which Tolaghai was the largest and the one most closely linked by commerce to the rest of Majipoor. As the freighter entered the broad harbor, Dekkeret was struck by the strangeness of the place. In his brief time he had seen a great many of the giant world's cities—a dozen of the fifty on the flanks of Castle Mount, and towering windswept Alaisor, and the vast, astounding, white-walled Ni-moya, and magnificent Piliplok, and many others—and never had he beheld a city with the harsh, myste-rious, forbidding look of this one. Tolaghai clung like a crab to a low ridge along the sea. Its buildings were flat, squat things of sun-dried orange brick, with mere slits for windows, and there were only sparse plantings around them, dismaying angular palms, mainly, that were all bare trunk with tiny feathery crowns far overhead. Here at midday the streets were almost deserted. The hot wind blew sprays of sand over the cracked paving-stones. To Dekkeret the city seemed like some sort of prison outpost, brutal and ugly, or perhaps a city out of time, belonging to some prehistoric folk of a regimented and authoritarian race. Why had anyone chosen to build a place so hideous? Doubtless it was out of mere efficiency, ugliness like this being the best way to cope with the climate of the land, but still, still, Dekkeret thought, the challenges of heat and drought might surely have called forth some less repellent architecture.

In his innocence Dekkeret thought he could simply go ashore at once, but that was not how things worked here. The ship lay at anchor for more than an hour before the port officials, three glum-looking Hjorts, came aboard. Then followed a lengthy business with sanitary inspections and cargo manifests and haggling over docking fees; and finally the dozen or so passengers were cleared for landing. A porter of the Ghayrog race seized Dekkeret's luggage and asked the name of his hotel. He replied that he had not booked one, and the reptilian-looking creature, tongue flickering and black fleshy hair writhing like a mass of serpents, gave him an icy, mocking look and said, "What will you pay? Are you rich?"

"Not very. What can I get for three crowns a night?"

"Little. Bed of straw. Vermin on the walls."

"Take me there," said Dekkeret.

The Ghayrog looked as startled as a Ghayrog is capable of looking. "You will not be happy there, fine sir. You have the bearing of lordship about you."

"Perhaps so, but I have a poor man's purse. I'll take my chances with the vermin."

Actually the inn turned out to be not as bad as he feared: ancient, squalid, and depressing, yes, but so was everything else in sight, and the room he received seemed almost palatial after his lodgings on the ship. Nor was there the reek of sea-dragon flesh here, only the arid, piercing flavor of Suvraelu air, like the stuff within a flask that had been sealed a thousand years. He gave the Ghayrog a half-crown piece, for which he had no thanks, and unpacked his few belongings.

In late afternoon Dekkeret went out. The stifling heat had dropped not at all, but the thin, cutting wind seemed less fierce now, and there were more people in the streets. All the same the city felt grim. This was the right sort of place for doing a penance. He loathed the blank-faced brick buildings, he hated the withered look of the landscape, and he missed the soft sweet air of his native city of Normork on the lower slopes of Castle Mount. Why, he wondered, would anyone choose to live here, when there was opportunity aplenty on the gentler continents? What starkness of the soul drove some millions of his fellow citizens to scourge themselves in the daily severities of life on Suvrael?

The representatives of the Pontificate had their offices on the great blank plaza fronting the harbor. Dekkeret's instructions called upon him to present himself there, and despite the lateness of the hour he found the place open, for in the searing heat all citizens of Tolaghai observed a midday closing and transacted business well into evening. He was left to wait a while in an antechamber decorated with huge white ceramic portraits of the reigning monarchs, the Pontifex Confalume shown in full face with a look of benign but overwhelming grandeur, and young Lord Prestimion the Coronal in profile, eyes aglitter with intelligence and dynamic energy. Majipoor was fortunate in her rulers, Dekkeret thought. When he was a boy he had seen Confalume, then Coronal, holding court in the wondrous city of Bombifale high up the Mount, and he had wanted to cry out from sheer joy at the man's calmness and radiant strength. A few years later Lord Confalume succeeded to the Pontificate and went to dwell in the subterranean recesses of the Labyrinth, and Prestimion had been made Coronal—a very different man, equally impressive but all dash and vigor and impulsive power. It was while Lord Prestimion was making the grand processional through the cities of the Mount that he had spied the young Dekkeret in Normork and had chosen him, in his random unpredictable way, to join the knights in training in the High Cities. Which seemed an epoch ago, such great changes having occurred in Dekkeret's life since then. At eighteen he had allowed himself fantasies of ascending the Coronal's throne himself one day; but then had come his ill-starred holiday in the mountains of Zimroel, and now, scarcely past twenty, fidgeting in a dusty outer office in this drab city of cheerless Suvrael, he felt he had no future at all, only a barren stretch of meaningless years to use up.

A pudgy sour-faced Hjort appeared and announced, "The Archiregimand Golator Lasgia will see you now."

That was a resonant title; but its owner proved to be a slender dark-skinned woman not greatly older than Dekkeret, who gave him careful scrutiny out of large, glossy, solemn eyes. In a perfunctory way she offered him greeting with the hand-symbol of the Pontificate and took the document of his credentials from him. "The Initiate Dekkeret," she murmured. "Mission of inquiry, under commission of the Khyntor provincial superstrate. I don't understand, Initiate Dekkeret. Do you serve the Coronal or the Pontifex?"

Uncomfortably Dekkeret said, "I am of Lord Prestimion's staff, a very low echelon. But while I was in Khyntor Province a need arose at the office of the Pontificate for an investigation of certain things in Suvrael, and when the local officials discovered that I was bound for Suvrael anyway, they asked me in the interests of economy to take on the job even though I was not in the employ of the Pontifex. And—"

Tapping Dekkeret's papers thoughtfully against her desktop, Golator Lasgia said, "You were bound for Suvrael anyway? May I ask why?"

Dekkeret flushed. "A personal matter, if you please."

She let it pass. "And what affairs of Suvrael can be of such compelling interest to my Pontifical brothers of Khyntor, or is my curiosity on that subject also misplaced?"

Dekkeret's discomfort grew. "It has to do with an imbalance of trade," he answered, barely able to meet her cool, penetrating gaze. "Khyntor is a manufacturing center; it exchanges goods for the livestock of Suvrael; for the past two years the export of blaves and mounts out of Suvrael has declined steadily, and now strains are developing in the Khyntor economy. The manufacturers are encountering difficulty in carrying so much Suvraelu credit."

"None of this is news to me."

"I've been asked to inspect the rangelands here," said Dekkeret, "in order to determine whether an upturn in livestock production can soon be expected."

"Will you have some wine?" Golator Lasgia asked unexpectedly.

Dekkeret, adrift, considered the proprieties. While he faltered she produced two flasks of golden, deftly snapped their seals, and passed one to him. He took it with a grateful smile. The wine was cold, sweet, with a faint sparkle.

"Wine of Khyntor," she said. "Thus we contribute to the Suvraelu trade deficit. The answer, Initiate Dekkeret, is that in the final year of the Pontifex Prankipin a terrible drought struck Suvrael—you may ask, Initiate, how we can tell the difference here between a year of drought and a year of normal rainfall, but there is a difference, Initiate, there is a significant difference—and the grazing districts suffered. There was no way of feeding our cattle, so we butchered as many as the market could hold, and sold much of the remaining stock to ranchers in western Zimroel. Not long after Confalume succeeded to the Labyrinth, the rains returned and the grass began to grow in our savannas. But it takes several years to rebuild the herds. Therefore the trade imbalance will continue a time longer, and then will be cured." She smiled without warmth. "There. I have spared you the inconvenience of an uninteresting journey to the interior."

Dekkeret found himself perspiring heavily. "Nevertheless I must make it, Archiregimand Golator Lasgia."

"You'll learn nothing more than I've just told you."

"I mean no disrespect. But my commission specifically requires me to see with my own eyes—"

She closed hers a moment. "To reach the rangelands just now will involve you in great difficulties, extreme physical discomfort, perhaps considerable personal danger. If I were you, I'd remain in Tolaghai, sampling such pleasures as are available here, and dealing with whatever personal business brought you to Suvrael; and after a proper interval, write your report in consultation with my office and take yourself back to Khyntor."

Immediate suspicions blossomed in Dekkeret. The branch of the government she served was not always cooperative with the Coronal's people; she seemed quite transparently trying to conceal something that was going on in Suvrael; and, although his mission of inquiry was only the pretext for his voyage to this place and not his central task, all the same he had his career to consider, and if he allowed a Pontifical Archiregimand to bamboozle him too easily here it would go badly for him later. He wished he had not accepted the wine from her. But to cover his confusion he allowed himself a series of suave sips, and at length said, "My sense of honor would not permit me to follow such an easy course."

"How old are you, Initiate Dekkeret?"

"I was born in the twelfth year of Lord Confalume."

"Yes, your sense of honor would still prick you, then. Come, look at this map with me." She rose briskly. She was taller than he expected, nearly his own height, which gave her a fragile appearance. Her dark, tightly coiled hair emitted a surprising fragrance, even over the aroma of the strong wine. Golator Lasgia touched the wall and a map of Suvrael in brilliant ochre and auburn hues sprang into view. "This is Tolaghai," she said, tapping the northwest corner of the continent. "The grazing lands are here." She indicated a band that began six or seven hundred miles inland and ran in a rough circle surrounding the desert at the heart of Suvrael. "From Tolaghai," she went on, "there are three main routes to the cattle country. This is one. At present it is ravaged by sandstorms and no traffic can safely use it. This is the second route: we are experiencing certain difficulties with Shapeshifter bandits there, and it is also closed to travelers. The third way lies here, by Khulag Pass, but that road has fallen into disuse of late, and an arm of the great desert has begun to encroach on it. Do you see the problems?"

As gently as he could Dekkeret said, "But if it is the business of Suvrael to raise cattle for export, and all the routes between the grazing lands and the chief port are blocked, is it correct to say that a lack of pasture is the true cause of the recent shortfalls of cattle exports?"

She smiled. "There are other ports from which we ship our produce in this current situation."

"Well, then, if I go to one of those, I should find an open highway to the cattle country."

Again she tapped the map. "Since last winter the port of Natu Gorvinu has been the center of the cattle trade. This is it, in the east, under the coast of Alhanroel, about six thousand miles from here."

"Six thousand—"

"There is little reason for commerce between Tolaghai and Natu Gorvinu. Perhaps once a year a ship goes from one to the other. Overland the situation is worse, for the roads out of Tolaghai are not maintained east of Kangheez—" she indicated a city perhaps a thousand miles away—"and beyond that, who knows? This is not a heavily settled continent."

"Then there's no way to reach Natu Gorvinu?" Dekkeret said, stunned.

"One. By ship from Tolaghai to Stoien on Alhanroel, and from Stoien to Natu Gorvinu. It should take you only a little over a year. By the time you reach Suvrael again and penetrate the interior, of course, the crisis that you've come to investigate will probably be over. Another flask of the golden, Initiate Dekkeret?"

Numbly he accepted the wine. The distances stupefied him. Another horrendous voyage across the Inner Sea, all the way back to his native continent of Alhanroel, only to turn around and cross the water a third time, sailing now to the far side of Suvrael, and then to find, probably, that the ways to the interior had meanwhile been closed out there, and— no. No. There was such a thing as carrying a penance too far. Better to abandon the mission altogether than subject himself to such absurdities.

While he hesitated Golator Lasgia said, "The hour is late and your problems need longer consideration. Have you plans for dinner, Initiate Dekkeret?"

Suddenly, astoundingly, her somber eyes gleamed with mischief of a familiar kind.

3

In the company of the Archiregimand Golator Lasgia, Dekkeret discovered that life in Tolaghai was not necessarily as bleak as first superficial inspection had indicated. By floater she returned him to his hotel—he could see her distaste at the look of the place—and instructed him to rest and cleanse himself and be ready in an hour. A coppery twilight had descended, and by the time the hour had elapsed, the sky was utterly black, with only a few alien constellations cutting jagged tracks across it, and the crescent hint of one or two moons down near the horizon. She called for him punctually. In place of her stark official tunic she wore now something of clinging mesh, almost absurdly seductive. Dekkeret was puzzled by all this. He had had his share of success with women, yes, but so far as he knew he had given her no sign of interest, nothing but the most formal of respect; and yet she clearly was assuming a night of intimacy. Why? Certainly not his irresistible sophistication and physical appeal, nor any political advantage he could confer on her, nor any other rational motive. Except one, that this was a foul backwater outpost where life was stale and uncomfortable, and he was a youthful stranger who might provide a woman herself still young with a night's amusement. He felt used by that, but otherwise he could see no great harm in it. And after months at sea he was willing to run a little risk in the name of pleasure.

They dined at a private club on the outskirts of town, in a garden elegantly decorated with the famous creature-plants of Stoienzar and other flowering wonders that had Dekkeret calculating how much of Tolaghai's modest water supply was diverted toward keeping this one spot flourishing. At other tables, widely separated, were Suvraelinu in handsome costume, and Golator Lasgia nodded to this one and that, but no one approached her, nor did they stare unduly at Dekkeret. From within the building blew a cool, refreshing breeze, the first he had felt in weeks, as though some miraculous machine of the ancients, some cousin to the ones that generated the delicious atmosphere of Castle Mount, were at work in there. Dinner was a magnificent affair of lightly fermented fruits and tender, juicy slabs of a pale green–fleshed fish, accompanied by a fine dry wine of Amblemorn, no less, the very fringes of Castle Mount. She drank freely, as did he; they grew bright-eyed and animated; the chilly formality of the interview in her office dropped away. He learned that she was nine years his senior, that she was a native of moist, lush Narabal on the western continent, that she had entered the service of the Pontifex when still a girl, and had been stationed in Suvrael for the past ten years, rising upon Confalume's accession to the Pontificate to her present high administrative post in Tolaghai.

"Do you *like* it here?" he asked.

She shrugged. "One gets accustomed to it."

"I doubt that I would. To me Suvrael is merely a place of torment, a kind of purgatory."

Golator Lasgia nodded. "Exactly."

There was a flash from her eyes to his. He did not dare ask for amplification; but something told him that they had much in common.

He filled their glasses once again and permitted himself the perils of a calm, knowing smile.

She said, "Is it purgatory you seek here?"

"Yes."

She indicated the lavish gardens, the empty wine-flasks, the costly dishes, the half-eaten delicacies. "You have made a poor start, then."

"Milady, dinner with you was no part of my plan."

"Nor mine. But the Divine provides, and we accept. Yes? Yes?" She leaned close. "What will you do now? The voyage to Natu Gorvinu?"

"It seems too heavy an enterprise."

"Then do as I say. Stay in Tolaghai until you grow weary of it; then return and file your report. No one will be the wiser in Khyntor."

"No. I must go inland."

Her expression grew mocking. "Such dedication! But how will you do it? The roads from here are closed."

"You mentioned the one by Khulag Pass, that had fallen into disuse. Mere disuse doesn't seem as serious as deadly sandstorms, or Shape-shifter bandits. Perhaps I can hire a caravan leader to take me that way."

"Into the desert?"

"If needs be."

"The desert is haunted," said Golator Lasgia casually. "You should forget that idea. Call the waiter over: we need more wine."

"I think I've had enough, milady."

"Come, then. We'll go elsewhere."

Stepping from the breeze-cooled garden to the dry, hot night air of the street was a shock; but quickly they were in her floater, and not long after they were in a second garden, this one in the courtyard of her official residence, surrounding a pool. There were no weather-machines here to ease the heat, but the Archiregimand had another way, dropping her gown and going to the pool. Her lean, supple body gleamed a moment in the starlight; then she dived, sliding nearly without a splash beneath the surface. She beckoned to him and quickly he joined her.

Afterward they embraced on a bed of close-cropped thick-bladed grass. It was almost as much like wrestling as lovemaking, for she clasped him with her long muscular legs, tried to pinion his arms, rolled over and over with him, laughing, and he was amazed at the strength of her, the playful ferocity of her movements. But when they were through testing one another they moved with more harmony, and it was a night of little sleep and much exertion.

Dawn was an amazement: without warning, the sun was in the sky like a trumpet-blast, roasting the surrounding hills with shafts of hot light.

They lay limp, exhausted. Dekkeret turned to her—by cruel morning light she looked less girlish than she had under the stars—and said abruptly, "Tell me about this haunted desert. What spirits will I meet there?"

"How persistent you are!"

"Tell me."

"There are ghosts there that can enter your dreams and steal them. They rob your soul of joy and leave fears in its place. By day they sing in the distance, confusing you, leading you from the path with their clatter and their music."

"Am I supposed to believe this?"

"In recent years many who have entered that desert have perished there."

"Of dream-stealing ghosts."

"So it is said."

"It will make a good tale to tell when I return to Castle Mount, then."

"*If* you return," she said.

"You say that not everyone who has gone into that desert has died of it. Obviously not, for someone has come out to tell the tale. Then I will hire a guide, and take my chances among the ghosts."

"No one will accompany you."

"Then I'll go alone."

"And certainly die." She stroked his powerful arms and made a little purring sound. "Are you so interested in dying, so soon? Dying has no value. It confers no benefits. Whatever peace you seek, the peace of the grave is not it. Forget the desert journey. Stay here with me."

"We'll go together."

She laughed. "I think not."

It was, Dekkeret realized, madness. He had doubts of her tales of ghosts and dream-stealers, unless what went on in that desert was some trickery of the rebellious Shapeshifter aborigines, and even then he doubted it. Perhaps all her tales of danger were only ruses to keep him longer in Tolaghai. Flattering if true, but of no help in his quest. And she was right about death being a useless form of purgation. If his adventures in Suvrael were to have meaning, he must succeed in surviving them.

Golator Lasgia drew him to his feet. They bathed briefly in the pool; then she led him within, to the most handsomely appointed dwelling he had seen this side of Castle Mount, and gave him a breakfast of fruits and dried fish.

Suddenly, in midmorning, she said, "*Must* you go into the interior?"

"An inner need drives me in that direction."

"Very well. We have in Tolaghai a certain scoundrel who often ventures inland by way of Khulag Pass, or so he claims, and seems to survive it. For a purse full of royals he'll no doubt guide you there. His name is Barjazid; and if you insist, I'll summon him and ask him to assist you."

4

"Scoundrel" seemed the proper word for Barjazid. He was a lean and disreputable-looking little man, shabbily dressed in an old brown robe and worn leather sandals, with an ancient necklace of mismatched sea-dragon bones at his throat. His lips were thin, his eyes had a feverish glaze, his skin was burned almost black by the desert sun. He stared at Dekkeret as though weighing the contents of his purse.

"If I take you," said Barjazid in a voice altogether lacking in resonance but yet not weak, "you will first sign a quitclaim absolving me of any responsibility to your heirs, in the event of your death."

"I have no heirs," Dekkeret replied.

"Kinfolk, then. I won't be hauled into the Pontifical courts by your father or your elder sister because you've perished in the desert."

"Have you perished in the desert yet?"

Barjazid looked baffled. "An absurd question."

"You go into that desert," Dekkeret persisted, "and you return alive. Yes? Well then, if you know your trade, you'll come out alive again this time, and so will I. I'll do what you do and go where you go. If you live, I live. If I perish, you'll have perished, too, and my family will have no lien."

"I can withstand the power of the stealers of dreams," said Barjazid. "This I know from ample tests. How do you know you'll prevail over them as readily?"

Dekkeret helped himself to a new serving of Barjazid's tea, a rich infusion brewed from some potent shrub of the sandhills. The two men squatted on mounds of haigus-hide blankets in the musty backroom of a shop belonging to Barjazid's brother's son: it was evidently a large clan. Dekkeret sipped the sharp, bitter tea reflectively and said, after a moment, "Who are these dream-stealers?"

"I cannot say."

"Shapeshifters, perhaps?"

Barjazid shrugged. "They have not bothered to tell me their pedigree. Shapeshifters, Ghayrogs, Vroons, ordinary humans—how would I know? In dreams all voices are alike. Certainly there are tribes of Shapeshifters loose in the desert, and some of them are angry folk given to mischief, and perhaps they have the skill of touching minds along with the skill of altering their bodies. Or perhaps not."

"If the Shapeshifters have closed two of the three routes out of Tolaghai, the Coronal's forces have work to do here."

"This is no affair of mine."

"The Shapeshifters are a subjugated race. They must not be allowed to disrupt the daily flow of life on Majipoor."

"It was you who suggested that the dream-stealers were Shapeshifters," Barjazid pointed out acidly. "I myself have no such theory. And who the dream-stealers are is not important. What is important is that they make the lands beyond Khulag Pass dangerous for travelers."

"Why do you go there, then?"

"I am not likely ever to answer a question that begins with *why*," said Barjazid. "I go there because I have reason to go there. Unlike others, I seem to return alive."

"Does everyone else who crosses the pass die?"

"I doubt it. I have no idea. Beyond question many have perished since the dream-stealers first were heard from. At the best of times that desert has been perilous." Barjazid stirred his tea. He began to appear restless. "If you accompany me, I'll protect you as best I can. But I make no guarantees for your safety. Which is why I demand that you give me legal absolution from responsibility."

Dekkeret said, "If I sign such a paper it would be signing a death warrant. What would keep you from murdering me ten miles beyond the pass, robbing my corpse, and blaming it all on the dream-stealers?"

"By the Lady, I am no murderer! I am not even a thief."

"But to give you a paper saying that if I die on the journey you are not to be blamed—might that not tempt even an honest man beyond all limits?"

Barjazid's eyes blazed with fury. He gestured as though to bring the interview to an end. "What goes beyond limits is your audacity," he said, rising and tossing his cup aside. "Find another guide, if you fear me so much."

Dekkeret, remaining seated, said quietly, "I regret the suggestion. I ask you only to see my position: a stranger and a young man in a remote and difficult land, forced to seek the aid of those he does not know to take him into places where improbable things happen. I must be cautious."

"Be even more cautious, then. Take the next ship for Stoien and return to the easy life of Castle Mount."

"I ask you again to guide me. For a good price, and nothing more about signing a quitclaim to my life. How much is your fee?"

"Thirty royals," Barjazid said.

Dekkeret grunted as though he had been struck below the ribs. It had cost him less than that to sail from Piliplok to Tolaghai. Thirty royals was a year's wage for someone like Barjazid; to pay it would require Dekkeret to draw on an expensive letter of credit. His impulse was to respond with knightly scorn, and offer ten; but he realized that he had forfeited his bargaining strength by objecting to the quitclaim. If he haggled now over the price as well, Barjazid would simply terminate the negotiations.

He said at length, "So be it. But no quitclaim."

Barjazid gave him a sour look. "Very well. No quitclaim, as you insist."

"How is the money to be paid?"

"Half now, half on the morning of departure."

"Ten now," said Dekkeret, "and ten on the morning of departure, and ten on the day of my return to Tolaghai."

"That makes a third of my fee conditional on your surviving the trip. Remember that I make no guarantee of that."

"Perhaps my survival becomes more likely if I hold back a third of the fee until the end."

"One expects a certain haughtiness from one of the Coronal's knights, and one learns to ignore it as a mere mannerism, up to a point. But I think you have passed the point." Once again Barjazid made a gesture of dismissal. "There is too little trust between us. It would be a poor idea for us to travel together."

"I meant no disrespect," said Dekkeret.

"But you ask me to leave myself to the mercies of your kinfolk if you perish, and you seem to regard me as an ordinary cutthroat or at best a brigand, and you feel it necessary to arrange my fee so that I will have less motivation to murder you." Barjazid spat. "The other face of haughtiness is courtesy, young knight. A Skandar dragon-hunter would have shown me more courtesy. I did not seek your employ, bear in mind. I will not humiliate myself to aid you. If you please—"

"Wait."

"I have other business this morning."

"Fifteen royals now," said Dekkeret, "and fifteen when we set forth, as you say. Yes?"

"Even though you think I'll murder you in the desert?"

"I became too suspicious because I didn't want to appear too innocent," said Dekkeret. "It was tactless for me to have said the things I said. I ask you to hire yourself to me on the terms agreed."

Barjazid was silent.

From his purse Dekkeret drew three five-royal coins. Two were pieces of the old coinage, showing the Pontifex Prankipin with Lord

Confalume. The third was a brilliant newly minted one, bearing Confalume as Pontifex and the image of Lord Prestimion on the reverse. He extended them toward Barjazid, who selected the new coin and examined it with great curiosity.

"I have not seen one of these before," he said. "Shall we call in my brother's son for an opinion of its authenticity?"

It was too much. "Do you take me for a passer of false money?" Dekkeret roared, leaping to his feet and looming ferociously over the small man. Rage throbbed in him; he came close to striking Barjazid.

But he perceived that the other was altogether fearless and unmoving in the face of his wrath. Barjazid actually smiled, and took the other two coins from Dekkeret's trembling hand.

"So you too have little liking for groundless accusations, eh, young knight?" Barjazid laughed. "Let us have a treaty, then. You'll not expect me to assassinate you beyond Khulag Pass, and I'll not send your coins out to the money changer's for an appraisal, eh? Well? Is it agreed?"

Dekkeret nodded wearily.

"Nevertheless this is a risky journey," said Barjazid, "and I would not have you too confident of a safe return. Much depends on your own strength when the time of testing comes."

"So be it. When do we leave?"

"Fiveday, at the sunset hour. We depart the city from Pinitor Gate. Is that place known to you?"

"I'll find it," Dekkeret said. "Till Fiveday, at sunset." He offered the little man his hand.

5

Fiveday was three days hence. Dekkeret did not regret the delay, for that gave him three more nights with the Archiregimand Golator Lasgia; or so he thought, but in fact it happened otherwise. She was not at her office by the waterfront on the evening of Dekkeret's meeting with Barjazid, nor would her aides transmit a message to her. He wandered the torrid city disconsolately until long after dark, finding no companionship at all, and ultimately ate a drab and gritty meal at his hotel, still hoping that Golator Lasgia would miraculously appear and whisk him away. She did not, and he slept fitfully and uneasily, his mind obsessed by the memories of her smooth flanks, her small firm breasts, her hungry, aggressive mouth. Toward dawn came a dream, vague and unreadable, in which she and Barjazid and some Hjorts and Vroons performed a complex dance in a roofless sandswept stone ruin, and afterward he fell into a sound sleep, not awakening until midday on Seaday. The entire city appeared to be in hiding then, but when the cooler hours came he went round to the Archiregimand's office once again, once again not seeing her, and then spent the evening in the same purposeless fashion as the night before. As he gave himself up to sleep he prayed fervently to the Lady of the Isle to send Golator Lasgia to him. But it was not the function of the Lady to do such things, and all that did reach him in the night was a bland and cheering dream, perhaps a gift of the blessed Lady but probably not, in which he dwelled in a thatched hut on the shores of the Great Sea by Tilomon and nibbled on sweet purplish fruits that squirted juice to stain his cheeks. When he awakened he found a Hjort of the Archiregimand's staff waiting outside his room, to summon him to the presence of Golator Lasgia.

That evening they dined together late, and went to her villa again, for a night of lovemaking that made their other one seem like a month of chastity. Dekkeret did not ask her at any time why she had refused him these two nights past, but as they breakfasted on spiced gihorna-skin and golden wine, both he and she vigorous and fresh after having had no sleep whatever, she said, "I wish I had had more time with you this week, but at least we were able to share your final night. Now you'll go to the Desert of Stolen Dreams with my taste on your lips. Have I made you forget all other women?"

"You know the answer."

"Good. Good. You may never embrace a woman again; but the last was the best, and few are so lucky as that."

"Were you so certain I'll die in the desert, then?"

"Few travelers return," she said. "The chances of my seeing you again are slight."

Dekkeret shivered faintly—not out of fear, but in recognition of Golator Lasgia's inner motive. Some morbidity in her evidently had led her to snub him those two nights, so that the third would be all the more intense, for she must believe that he would be a dead man shortly after and she wanted the special pleasure of being his last woman. That chilled him. If he were going to die before long, Dekkeret would just as soon have had the other two nights with her as well; but apparently the subtleties of her mind went beyond such crass notions. He bade her a courtly farewell, not knowing if they would meet again or even if he wished it, for all her beauty and voluptuary skills. Too much that was mysterious and dangerously capricious lay coiled within her.

Not long before sunset he presented himself at Pinitor Gate on the city's southeastern flank. It would not have surprised him if Barjazid had reneged on their agreement, but no, a floater was waiting just outside the pitted sandstone arch of the old gate, and the little man stood leaning against the vehicle's side. With him were three companions: a Vroon, a Skandar, and a slender, hard-eyed young man who was obviously Barjazid's son.

At a nod from Barjazid the giant four-armed Skandar took hold of Dekkeret's two sturdy bags and stowed them with a casual flip in the floater's keep. "Her name," said Barjazid, "is Khaymak Gran. She is unable to speak, but far from stupid. She has served me many years, since I found her tongueless and more than half dead in the desert. The Vroon is Serifain Reinaulion, who often speaks too much, but knows the desert tracks better than anyone of this city." Dekkeret exchanged brusque salutes with the small tentacular being. "And my son, Dinitak, will also accompany us," Barjazid said. "Are you well rested, Initiate?"

"Well enough," Dekkeret answered. He had slept most of the day, after his unsleeping night.

"We travel mainly by darkness, and camp in heat of day. My understanding is that I am to take you through Khulag Pass, across the wasteland known as the Desert of Stolen Dreams, and to the edge of the grazing lands around Ghyzyn Kor, where you have certain inquiries to make among the herdsmen. And then back to Tolaghai. Is this so?"

"Exactly," Dekkeret said.

Barjazid made no move to enter the floater. Dekkeret frowned; and then he understood. From his purse he produced three more five-royal pieces, two of them old ones of the Prankipin coinage, the third a shining coin of Lord Prestimion. These he handed to Barjazid, who plucked forth the Prestimion coin and tossed it to his son. The boy eyed the bright coin suspiciously. "The new Coronal," said Barjazid. "Make yourself familiar with his face. We'll be seeing it often."

"He will have a glorious reign," said Dekkeret. "He will surpass even Lord Confalume in grandeur. Already a wave of new prosperity sweeps the northern continents, and they were prosperous enough before. Lord Prestimion is a man of vigor and decisiveness, and his plans are ambitious."

Barjazid said, with a shrug, "Events on the northern continents carry very little weight here, and somehow prosperity on Alhanroel or Zimroel has a way of mattering hardly at all to Suvrael. But we rejoice that the Divine has blessed us with another splendid Coronal. May he remember, occasionally, that there is a southern land also, and citizens of his realm dwelling in it. Come, now: time to be traveling."

6

The Pinitor Gate marked an absolute boundary between city and desert. To one side there was a district of low, sprawling villas, walled and faceless; to the other was only barren waste beyond the city's perimeter. Nothing broke the emptiness of the desert but the highway, a broad cobbled track that wound slowly upward toward the crest of the ridge that encircled Tolaghai.

The heat was intolerable. By night the desert was perceptibly cooler than by day, but scorching all the same. Though the great blazing eye of the sun was gone, the orange sands, radiating the stored heat of the day toward the sky, shimmered and sizzled with the intensity of a banked furnace. A strong wind was blowing—with the coming of the darkness, Dekkeret had noticed, the flow of the wind reversed, blowing now from the heart of the continent toward the sea—but it made no difference:

shore-wind or sea-wind, both were oppressive streams of dry, baking air that offered no mercies.

In the clear, arid atmosphere, the light of the stars and moons was unusually bright, and there was an earthly glow as well, a strange ghostly greenish radiance that rose in irregular patches from the slopes flanking the highway. Dekkeret asked about it. "From certain plants," said the Vroon. "They shine with an inner light in the darkness. To touch such a plant is always painful and often fatal."

"How am I to know them by daylight?"

"They look like pieces of old string, weathered and worn, sprouting in bunches from clefts in the rock. Not all the plants of such a form are dangerous, but you would do well to avoid any of them."

"And any other," Barjazid put in. "In this desert the plants are well defended, sometimes in surprising ways. Each year our garden teaches us some ugly new secret."

Dekkeret nodded. He did not plan to stroll about out there, but if he did, he would make it his rule to touch nothing.

The floater was old and slow, the grade of the highway steep. Through the broiling night the car labored unhurriedly onward. There was little conversation within. The Skandar drove, with the Vroon beside her, and occasionally Serifain Reinaulion made some comment on the condition of the road; in the rear compartment the two Barjazids sat silently, leaving Dekkeret alone to stare with growing dismay at the infernal landscape. Under the merciless hammers of the sun the ground had a beaten, broken look. Such moisture as winter had brought this land had long ago been sucked forth, leaving gaunt, angular fissures. The surface of the ground was pockmarked where the unceasing winds had strafed it with sand particles, and the plants, low and sparsely growing things, were of many varieties but all appeared twisted, tortured, gnarled, and knobby. To the heat Dekkeret gradually found himself growing accustomed: it was simply there, like one's skin, and after a time one came to accept it. But the deathly ugliness of all that he beheld, the dry, rough, spiky, uncaring bleakness of everything, numbed his soul. A landscape that was hateful was a new concept to him, almost an inconceivable one. Wherever he had gone on Majipoor he had known only beauty. He thought of his home city of Normork spread along the crags of the Mount, with its winding boulevards and its wondrous stone wall and its gentle midnight rains. He thought of the giant city of Stee higher on the Mount, where once he had walked at dawn in a garden of trees no taller than his ankle, with leaves of a green hue that dazzled his eyes. He thought of High Morpin, that glimmering miracle of a city devoted wholly to pleasure, that lay almost in the shadow of the Coronal's awesome castle atop the Mount. And the rugged forested wilds of Khyntor, and the brilliant white towers of Ni-moya, and the sweet meadows of the Glayge Valley—how beautiful a world this is, Dekkeret thought, and what marvels it holds, and how terrible this place I find myself in now!

He told himself that he must alter his values and strive to discover the beauties of this desert, or else it would paralyze his spirit. Let there be beauty in utter dryness, he thought, and beauty in menacing angularity, and beauty in pockmarks, and beauty in ragged plants that shine with a pale green glow by night. Let spiky be beautiful, let bleak be beautiful, let harsh be beautiful. For what is beauty, Dekkeret asked himself, if not a learned response to things beheld? Why is a meadow intrinsically more beautiful than a pebbled desert? Beauty, they say, is in the eye of the beholder; therefore re-educate your eye, Dekkeret, lest the ugliness of this land kill you.

He tried to make himself love the desert. He pulled such words as "bleak" and "dismal" and "repellent" from his mind as though pulling fangs from a wild beast, and instructed himself to see this landscape as tender and comforting. He made himself admire the contorted strata of the exposed rock faces and the great gouges of the dry washes. He found aspects of delight in the bedraggled, beaten shrubs. He discovered things to esteem in the small, toothy, nocturnal creatures that occasionally scuttered across the road. And as the night wore on, the desert did become less hateful to him, and then neutral, and at last he believed he actually could see some beauty in it; and by the hour before dawn he had ceased to think about it at all.

Morning came suddenly: a shaft of orange flame breaking against the mountain wall to the west, a limb of bright red fire rising over the opposite rim of the range, and then the sun, its yellow face tinged more with bronzy-green than in the northern latitudes, bursting into the sky like an untethered balloon. In this moment of apocalyptic sunrise Dekkeret was startled to find himself thinking in sharp pain of the Archiregimand Golator Lasgia, wondering whether she was watching the dawn, and with whom; he savored the pain a little, and then, banishing the thought, said to Barjazid, "It was a night without phantoms. Is this desert not supposed to be haunted?"

"Beyond the pass is where the real trouble begins," the little man replied.

They rode onward through the early hours of the day. Dinitak served a rough breakfast, dry bread and sour wine. Looking back, Dekkeret saw a mighty view, the land sloping off below him like a great tawny apron, all folds and cracks and wrinkles, and the city of Tolaghai barely visible as a huddled clutter at the bottom end, with the vastness of the sea to the north rolling on to the horizon. The sky was without clouds, and the blue of it was so enhanced by the terra-cotta hue of the land that it seemed almost to be a second sea above him. Already the heat was rising. By midmorning it was all but unendurable, and still the Skandar driver moved impassively up the breast of the mountain. Dekkeret dozed occasionally, but in the cramped vehicle sleep was impossible. Were they going to drive all night and then all day, too? He asked no questions. But just as weariness and discomfort were reaching intolerable levels in him, Khaymak Gran abruptly swung the floater to the left, down a short spur of the road, and brought it to a halt.

"Our first day's camp," Barjazid announced.

Where the spur ended, a high flange of rock reared out of the desert floor, forming an overarching shelter. In front of it, protected by shadows at this time of day, was a wide sandy area that had obviously been used many times as a campsite. At the base of the rock formation Dekkeret saw a dark spot where water mysteriously seeped from the ground, not exactly a gushing spring but useful and welcome enough to parched travelers in this terrible desert. The place was ideal. And plainly the entire first day's journey had been timed to bring them here before the worst of the heat descended.

The Skandar and young Barjazid pulled straw mats from some compartment of the floater and scattered them on the sand; the midday meal was offered, chunks of dried meat, a bit of tart fruit, and warm Skandar mead; then, without a word, the two Barjazids and the Vroon and the Skandar sprawled out on their mats and dropped instantly into sleep. Dekkeret stood alone, probing between his teeth for a bit of meat caught there. Now that he could sleep, he was not at all sleepy. He wandered the edge of the campsite, staring into the sun-blasted wastes just outside the area in shadow. Not a creature could be seen, and even the plants, poor shabby things, seemed to be trying to pull themselves into the ground. The mountains rose steeply above him to the south; the pass could not be far off. And then? And then?

He tried to sleep. Unwanted images plagued him. Golator Lasgia hovered above his mat, so close that he felt he could seize her and draw her down to him, but she bobbed away and was lost in the heat-haze. For the thousandth time he saw himself in that forest in the Khyntor Marches, pursuing his prey, aiming, suddenly trembling. He shook that off and found himself scrambling along the great wall at Normork, with cool delectable air in his lungs. But these were not dreams, only idle fantasies and fugitive memories; sleep would not come for a long time, and when it did, it was deep and dreamless and brief.

Strange sounds awakened him: humming, singing, musical instruments in the distance, the faint but distinct noises of a caravan of many travelers. He thought he heard the tinkle of bells, the booming of drums. For a time he lay still, listening, trying to understand. Then he sat up, blinked, looked around. Twilight had come. He had slept away the hottest part of the day, and the shadows now encroached from the other side. His four companions were up and packing the mats. Dekkeret cocked an ear, seeking the source of the sounds. But they seemed to come from everywhere, or from nowhere. He remembered Golator Lasgia's tale of the ghosts of the desert that sing by day, confusing travelers, leading them from the true path with their clatter and their music.

To Barjazid he said, "What are those sounds?"

"Sounds?".

"You don't hear them? Voices, bells, footfalls, the humming of many travelers?"

Barjazid looked amused. "You mean the desert-songs."

"Ghost-songs?"

"They could be that. Or merely the sounds of wayfarers coming down the mountain, rattling chains, striking gongs. Which is more probable?"

"Neither is probable," said Dekkeret gloomily. "There are no ghosts in the world I inhabit. But there are no wayfarers on this road except ourselves."

"Are you sure, Initiate?"

"That there are no wayfarers, or no ghosts?"

"Either."

Dinitak Barjazid, who had been standing to one side taking in this interchange, approached Dekkeret and said, "Are you frightened?"

"The unknown is always disturbing. But at this point I feel more curiosity than fear."

"I will gratify your curiosity, then. As the heat of the day diminishes, the rocky cliffs and the sands give up their warmth, and in cooling they contract and release sounds. Those are the drums and bells you hear. There are no ghosts in this place," the boy said.

The elder Barjazid made a brusque gesture. Serenely the boy moved away.

"You didn't want him to tell me that, did you?" Dekkeret asked. "You prefer me to think that there are ghosts all about me."

Smiling, Barjazid said, "It makes no difference to me. Believe whichever explanation you find more cheering. You will meet a sufficiency of ghosts, I assure you, on the far side of the pass."

7

All Starday evening they climbed the winding road up the face of the mountain, and near midnight came to Khulag Pass. Here the air was cooler, for they were thousands of feet above sea level and warring winds brought some relief from the swelter. The pass was a broad notch in the mountain wall, surprisingly deep; it was early Sunday morning before they completed its traversal and began their descent into the greater desert of the interior.

Dekkeret was stunned by what lay before him. By bright moonlight he beheld a scene of unparalleled bleakness that made the lands on the cityward side of the pass look like gardens. That other desert was a rocky one, but this was sandy, an ocean of dunes broken here and there by open patches of hard pebble-strewn ground. There was scarcely any vegetation, none at all in the duned places and the merest of sorry scraggles elsewhere. And the heat! Upward out of the dark bowl ahead there came currents of stupefying hot blasts, air that seemed stripped of all nourishment, air that had been baked to death. It astounded him that somewhere in that furnace there could be grazing lands. He tried to remember the map in the Archiregimand's office: the cattle country was a belt that flanked the continent's innermost zone of desert, but here below Khulag Pass an arm of the central wastes had somehow encroached—that was it. On the far side of this band of formidable sterility lay a green zone of grass and browsing beasts, or so he prayed.

Through the early morning hours they headed down the inner face of the mountains and onto the great central plateau. By first light Dekkeret noticed an odd feature far downslope, an oval patch of inky darkness sharply outlined against the buff breast of the desert, and as they drew nearer he saw that it was an oasis of sorts, the dark patch resolving itself into a grove of slender long-limbed trees with tiny violet-flushed leaves. This place was the second day's campsite. Tracks in the sand showed where other parties had camped; there was scattered debris under the trees; in a clearing at the heart of the grove were half a dozen crude shelters made of heaped-up rocks topped with old dried boughs. Just beyond, a brackish stream wound between the trees and terminated in a small stagnant pool, green with algae. And a little way beyond that was a second pool, apparently fed by a stream that ran wholly underground, the waters of which were pure. Between the two pools Dekkeret saw a curious construction, seven round-topped stone columns as high as his waist, arranged in a double arc. He inspected them.

"Shapeshifter work," Barjazid told him.

"A Metamorph altar?"

"So we think. We know the Shapeshifters often visit this oasis. We find little Piurivar souvenirs here—prayer sticks, bits of feathers, small, clever wickerwork cups."

Dekkeret stared about uneasily at the trees as if he expected them to transform themselves momentarily into a party of savage aborigines. He had had little contact with the native race of Majipoor, those defeated and displaced indigenes of the forests, and what he knew of them was mainly rumor and fantasy, born of fear, ignorance, and guilt. They once had had great cities, that much was certain—Alhanroel was strewn with the ruins of them, and in school Dekkeret had seen views of the most famous of all, vast stone Velalisier not far from the Labyrinth of the Pontifex; but those cities had died thousands of years ago, and with the coming of the human and other races to Majipoor the native Piurivars had been forced back into the darker places of the planet, mainly a great wooded reservation in Zimroel somewhere southeast of Khyntor. To his knowledge Dekkeret had seen actual Metamorphs only two or three times, frail greenish folk with strange blank-featured faces, but of course they slid from one form to another in mimicry of a marvelously easy kind, and for all he knew this little Vroon here was a secret Shapeshifter, or Barjazid himself.

He said, "How can Shapeshifters or anyone else survive in this desert?"

"They're resourceful people. They adapt."

"Are there many of them here?"

"Who can know? I've encountered a few scattered bands, fifty, seventy-five all told. Probably there are others. Or perhaps I keep meeting the same ones over and over again in different guises, eh?"

"A strange people," Dekkeret said, rubbing his hand idly over the smooth stone dome atop the nearest of the altar-columns. With astonishing speed Barjazid grasped Dekkeret's wrist and pulled it back.

"Don't touch those!"

"Why not?" said Dekkeret, amazed.

"Those stones are holy."

"To you?"

"To those who erected them," said Barjazid dourly. "We respect them. We honor the magic that may be in them. And in this land one never casually invites the vengeance of one's neighbors."

Dekkeret stared in astonishment at the little man, at the columns, at the two pools, the graceful sharp-leaved trees that surrounded them. Even in the heat he shivered. He looked out, beyond the borders of the little oasis, to the swaybacked dunes all around, to the dusty ribbon of road that disappeared southward into the land of mysteries. The sun was climbing quickly now and its warmth was like a terrible flail pounding the sky, the land, the few vulnerable travelers wandering in this awful place. He glanced back, to the mountains he had just passed through, a huge and ominous wall cutting him off from what passed for civilization on this torrid continent. He felt frighteningly alone here, weak, lost.

Dinitak Barjazid appeared, tottering under a great load of flasks that he dropped almost at Dekkeret's feet. Dekkeret helped the boy fill them from the pure pool, a task that took an unexpectedly long while. He sampled the water himself: cool, clear, with a strange metallic taste, not displeasing, that Dinitak said came from dissolved minerals. It took a dozen trips to carry all the flasks to the floater. There would be no more sources of fresh water, Dinitak explained, for several days.

They lunched on the usual rough provisions and afterward, as the heat rose toward its overwhelming midday peak, they settled on the straw mats to sleep. This was the third day that Dekkeret had slept by day and by now his body was growing attuned to the change; he closed his eyes, commended his soul to the beloved Lady of the Isle, Lord Prestimion's holy mother, and tumbled almost instantly into heavy slumber.

This time dreams came.

He had not dreamed properly for more days than he cared to remember. To Dekkeret as to all other folk of Majipoor, dreams were a central part of existence, nightly providing comfort, reassurance, instruction, clarification, guidance and reprimands, and much else. From childhood one was trained to make one's mind receptive to the messengers of sleep, to observe and record one's dreams, to carry them with one through the night and into the waking hours beyond. And always there was the benevolent, omnipresent figure of the Lady of the Isle of Sleep hovering over one, helping one explore the workings of one's spirit and through her sendings offering direct communication to each of the billions of souls that dwelled on vast Majipoor.

Dekkeret now saw himself walking on a mountain ridge that he perceived to be the crest of the range they had lately crossed. He was by himself and the sun was impossibly great, filling half the sky; yet the heat was not troublesome. So steep was the slope that he could look straight down over the edge, down and down and down for what seemed hundreds of miles, and he beheld a roaring smoking cauldron beneath him, a surging volcanic crater in which red magma bubbled and churned. That immense vortex of subterranean power did not frighten him; indeed it exerted a strange pull, a blatant appeal, so that he yearned to plunge himself into it, to dive to its depths and swim in its molten heart. He began to descend, running and skipping, often leaving the ground and floating, drifting, flying down the immense hillside, and as he drew nearer he thought he saw faces in the throbbing lava, Lord Prestimion, and the Pontifex, and Barjazid's face, and Golator Lasgia's—and were those Metamorphs, those strange, sly, half-visible images near the periphery? The core of the volcano was a stew of potent figures. Dekkeret ran toward them in love, thinking, Take me into you, here I am, here I come; and when he perceived, behind all the others, a great white disk that he understood to be the loving countenance of the Lady of the Isle, a deep and powerful bliss invaded his soul, for he knew this now to be a sending, and it was many months since last the kind Lady had touched his sleeping mind.

Sleeping but aware, watching the Dekkeret within the dream, he awaited the consummation, the joining of dream-Dekkeret to dream-Lady, the immolation in the volcano that would bring some revelation of truth, some instant of knowledge leading to joy. But then a strangeness crossed the dream like some spreading veil. The colors faded; the faces dimmed; he continued to run down the side of the mountain wall, but now he stumbled often, he tripped and sprawled, he abraded his hands and knees against hot desert rocks, and he was losing the path entirely, moving sideways instead of downward, unable to progress. He had been on the verge of a moment of delight, and somehow it was out of reach now and he felt only distress, uneasiness, shock. The ecstasy that seemed to be the promise of the dream was draining from it. The brilliant colors yielded to an all-encompassing gray, and all motion ceased: he stood frozen on the mountain face, staring rigidly down at a dead crater, and the sight of it made him tremble and pull his knees to his chest, and he lay there sobbing until he woke.

He blinked and sat up. His head pounded and his eyes felt raw, and there was a dismal tension in his chest and shoulders. This was not what dreams, even the most terrifying of dreams, were supposed to provide: such a gritty residue of malaise, confusion, fear. It was early afternoon and the blinding sun hung high above the treetops. Nearby him lay Khaymak Gran and the Vroon, Serifain Reinaulion; a bit farther away was Dinitak Barjazid. They seemed sound asleep. The elder Barjazid was nowhere in view. Dekkeret rolled over and pressed his cheeks into the warm sand beside his mat and attempted to let the tension ease from him. Something had gone wrong in his sleep, he knew; some dark force had meddled in his dream, had stolen the virtue from it and given him pain in exchange. So this was what they meant by the haunting of the desert? This was dream-stealing? He drew himself together in a knotted ball. He felt soiled, used, invaded. He wondered if it would be like this every sleep-period now, as they penetrated deeper into this awful desert; he wondered whether it might get even worse.

After a time Dekkeret returned to sleep. More dreams came, stray blurred scraps without rhythm or design. He ignored them. When he woke, the day was ending and the desert-sounds, the ghost-sounds, were nibbling at his ears, tinklings and murmurings and far-off laughter. He felt more weary than if he had not slept at all.

8

The others showed no sign of having been disturbed as they slept. They greeted Dekkeret upon rising in their usual manners—the huge taciturn Skandar woman not at all, the little Vroon with amiable buzzing chirps and much coiling and interlacing of tentacles, the two Barjazids with curt nods—and if they were aware that one member of their party had been

visited with torments in his dreams, they said nothing of it. After breakfast the elder Barjazid held a brief conference with Serifain Reinaulion
concerning the roads they were to travel that night, and then they were
off into the moonlit darkness once again.

I will pretend that nothing out of the ordinary happened, Dekkeret
resolved. I will not let them know that I am vulnerable to these phantoms.

But it was a short-lived resolution. As the floater was passing
through a region of dry lakebeds out of which odd gray-green stony
humps projected by the thousands, Barjazid turned to him suddenly and
said, breaking a long silence, "Did you dream well?"

Dekkeret knew he could not conceal his fatigue. "I have had better
rest," he muttered.

Barjazid's glossy eyes were fixed inexorably on his. "My son says you
moaned in your sleep, that you rolled over many times and clutched your
knees. Did you feel the touch of the dream-stealers, Initiate?"

"I felt the presence of a troubling power in my dreams. Whether this
was the touch of the dream-stealers I have no way of knowing."

"Will you describe the sensations?"

"Are you a dream-speaker then, Barjazid?" Dekkeret snapped in
sudden anger. "Why should I let you probe and poke in my mind? My
dreams are my own!"

"Peace, peace, good knight. I meant no intrusion."

"Let me be, then."

"Your safety is my responsibility. If the demons of this wasteland
have begun to reach your spirit, it is in your own interest to inform me."

"Demons, are they?"

"Demons, ghosts, phantoms, disaffected Shapeshifters, whatever
they are," Barjazid said impatiently. "The beings that prey on sleeping
travelers. Did they come to you or did they not?"

"My dreams were not pleasing."

"I ask you to tell me in what way."

Dekkeret let his breath out slowly. "I felt I was having a sending
from the Lady, a dream of peace and joy. And gradually it changed its
nature; do you see? It darkened and became chaotic, and all the joy was
taken from it, and I ended the dream worse than when I entered it."

Nodding earnestly, Barjazid said, "Yes, yes, those are the symptoms. A touch on the mind, an invasion of the dream, a disturbing overlay, a taking of energy."

"A kind of vampirism?" Dekkeret suggested. "Creatures that lie in wait in this wasteland and tap the life-force from unwary travelers?"

Barjazid smiled. "You insist on speculations. I make no hypotheses of any kind, Initiate."

"Have you felt their touch in your own sleep?"

The small man stared at Dekkeret strangely. "No. No, never."

"Never? Are you immune?"

"Seemingly so."

"And your boy?"

"It has befallen him several times. It happens to him only rarely out here, one time out of fifty, perhaps. But the immunity is not hereditary, it appears."

"And the Skandar? And the Vroon?"

"They too have been touched," said Barjazid. "On infrequent occasions. They find it bothersome but not intolerable."

"Yet others have died from the dream-stealers' touch."

"More hypothesis," said Barjazid. "Most travelers passing this way in recent years have reported experiencing strange dreams. Some of them have lost their way and have failed to return. How can we know whether there is a connection between the disturbing dreams and the losing of the way?"

"You are a very cautious man," Dekkeret said. "You leap to no conclusions."

"And I have survived to a fair old age, while many who were more rash have returned to the Source."

"Is mere survival the highest achievement you think one can attain?"

Barjazid laughed. "Spoken like a true knight of the Castle! No, Initiate, I think there's more to living than mere avoidance of death. But survival helps, eh, Initiate? Survival's a good basic requirement for those who go on to do high deeds. The dead don't achieve a thing."

Dekkeret did not care to pursue that theme. The code of values of a knight-initiate and of such a one as Barjazid were hardly comparable;

and, besides, there was something wily and mercurial about Barjazid's style of argument that made Dekkeret feel slow and stolid and hulking, and he disliked exposing himself to that feeling. He was silent a moment. Then he said, "Do the dreams get worse as one gets deeper into the desert?"

"So I am given to understand," said Barjazid.

Yet as the night waned and the time for making camp arrived, Dekkeret found himself ready and even eager to contend once more with the phantoms of sleep. They had camped this day far out on the bowl of the desert, in a low-lying area where much of the sand had been swept aside by scouring winds, and the underlying rock shield showed through. The dry air had a weird crackle to it, a kind of wind-borne buzz, as if the force of the sun were stripping the particles of matter bare in this place. It was only an hour before midday by the time they were ready for sleep. Dekkeret settled calmly on his mat of straw and, without fear, offered his soul on the verge of slumber to whatever might come. In his order of knighthood he had been trained in the customary notions of courage, naturally, and was expected to meet challenges without fear, but he had been little tested thus far. On placid Majipoor one must work hard to find such challenges, going into the untamed parts of the world, for in the settled regions life is orderly and courteous; therefore Dekkeret had gone abroad, but he had not done well by his first major trial, in the forests of the Khyntor Marches. Here he had another chance. These foul dreams held forth to him, in a way, the promise of redemption.

He gave himself up to sleep.

And quickly dreamed. He was back in Tolaghai, but a Tolaghai curiously transformed, a city of smooth-faced alabaster villas and dense green gardens, though the heat was still of tropical intensity. He wandered up one boulevard and down the next, admiring the elegance of the architecture and the splendor of the shrubbery. His clothing was the traditional green and gold of the Coronal's entourage, and as he encountered the citizens of Tolaghai making their twilight promenades he bowed gracefully to them, and exchanged with them the starburst finger-symbol that acknowledged the Coronal's authority. To him now came the slender figure of the lovely Archiregimand Golator Lasgia. She smiled, she took him by the hand, she led him to a place of cascading fountains where cool spray drifted through the air, and there they put their clothing aside and bathed, and rose naked from the sweet-scented pool, and strolled, feet barely touching the ground, into a garden of plants with arching stems and great glistening, many-lobed leaves. Without words she encouraged him onward, along shadowy avenues bordered by rows of close-planted trees. Golator Lasgia moved just ahead of him, an elusive and tantalizing figure, floating only inches out of his reach and then gradually widening the distance to feet and yards. At first it seemed hardly a difficult task to overtake her, but he made no headway at it, and had to move faster and faster to keep within sight of her. Her rich olive-hued skin gleamed by early moonlight, and she glanced back often, smiling brilliantly, tossing her head to urge him to keep up. But he could not. She was nearly an entire length of the garden ahead of him now. With growing desperation he impelled himself toward her, but she was dwindling, disappearing, so far ahead of him now that he could barely see the play of muscles beneath her glowing bare skin, and as he rushed from one pathway of the garden to the next he became aware of an increase in the temperature, a sudden and steady change in the air, for somehow the sun was rising here in the night and its full force was striking his shoulders. The trees were wilting and drooping. Leaves were falling. He struggled to remain upright. Golator Lasgia was only a dot on the horizon now, still beckoning to him, still smiling, still tossing her head, but she grew smaller and smaller, and the sun was still climbing, growing stronger, searing, incinerating, withering everything within its reach. Now the garden was a place of gaunt bare branches and rough, cracked, arid soil. A dreadful thirst had come over him, but there was no water here, and when he saw figures lurking behind the blistered and blackened trees—Metamorphs, they were, subtle tricky creatures that would not hold their shapes still, but flickered and flowed in a maddening way—he called out to them for something to drink, and was given only light tinkling laughter to ease his dryness. He staggered on. The fierce pulsing light in the heavens was beginning to roast him; he felt his skin hardening, crackling, crisping, splitting. Another moment of this and he would be charred. What had become of Golator Lasgia? Where were the smiling, bowing, starburst-making townspeople? He saw no garden now. He was in the desert, lurching and stumbling through a torrid baking wasteland where even shadows burned. Now real terror rose in him, for even as he dreamed he felt the pain of the heat, and the part of his soul that was observing all this grew alarmed, thinking that the power of the dream might well be so great as to reach up to injure his physical self. There were tales of such things, people who had perished in their sleep of dreams that had overwhelming force. Although it went against his training to terminate a dream prematurely, although he knew he must ordinarily see even the worst of horrors through to its ultimate revelation, Dekkeret considered awakening himself for safety's sake, and nearly did; but then he saw that as a species of cowardice and vowed to remain in the dream even if it cost him his life. He was down on his knees now, groveling in the fiery sands, staring with strange clarity at mysterious, tiny, golden-bodied insects that were marching in single file across the rims of the dunes toward him: ants, they were, with ugly swollen jaws, and each in turn clambered up his body and took a tiny nip, the merest bite, and clung and held on, so that within moments thousands of the minute creatures were covering his skin. He brushed at them but could not dislodge them. Their pincers held and their heads came loose from their bodies: the sand about him was black now with headless ants, but they spread over his skin like a cloak, and he brushed and brushed with greater vigor while still more ants mounted him and dug their jaws in. He grew weary of brushing at them. It was actually cooler in this cloak of ants, he thought. They shielded him from the worst force of the sun, although they too stung and burned him, but not as painfully as did the sun's rays. Would the dream never end? He attempted to take control of it himself, to turn the stream of onrushing ants into a rivulet of cool pure water, but that did not work, and he let himself slip back into the nightmare and went crawling wearily onward over the sands.

And gradually Dekkeret became aware that he was no longer dreaming.

There was no boundary between sleep and wakefulness that he could detect, except that eventually he realized that his eyes were open and that his two centers of consciousness, the dreamer who observed and the dream-Dekkeret who suffered, had merged into one. But he was still in the desert, under the terrible midday sun. He was naked. His skin felt raw and blistered. And there were ants crawling on him, up his legs as far as his knees, minute pale ants that indeed were nipping their tiny pincers into his flesh. Bewildered, he wondered if he had tumbled into some layer of dream beneath dream, but no, so far as he could tell this was the waking world, this was the authentic desert and he was out in the midst of it. He stood up, brushing the ants away—and as in the dream they gripped him even at the cost of their heads—and looked about for the campsite.

He could not see it. In his sleep he had wandered out onto the bare scorching anvil of the open desert and he was lost. Let this be a dream still, he thought fiercely, and let me awaken from it in the shade of Barjazid's floater. But there was no awakening. Dekkeret understood now how lives were lost in the Desert of Stolen Dreams.

"Barjazid?" he called. *"Barjazid!"*

9

Echoes came back to him from the distant hills. He called again, two, three times, and listened to the reverberations of his own voice, but heard no reply. How long could he survive out here? An hour? Two? He had no water, no shelter, not even a scrap of clothing. His head was bare to the sun's great blazing eye. It was the hottest part of the day. The landscape looked the same in all directions, flat, a shallow bowl swept by hot winds. He searched for his own footprints, but the trail gave out within yards, for the ground was hard and rocky here and he had left no imprint. The camp might lie anywhere about, hidden from him by the slightest of rises in the terrain. He called out again for help and again heard only echoes. Perhaps if he could find a dune he would bury himself to his neck, and wait out the heat that way, and by darkness he might locate the camp by its campfire; but he saw no dunes. If there were a high place here that would give him a sweeping view, he would mount it and search the horizon for the camp. But he saw no hillocks. What would Lord Stiamot do in such a situation, he wondered, or Lord Thimin, or one of the other great warriors of the past? What is Dekkeret going to do? This was a foolish way to die, he thought, a useless, nasty, ugly death. He turned and turned and turned again, scanning every way. No clues; no point in walking at all, not knowing where he was going. He shrugged and crouched in a place where there were no ants. There was no dazzlingly clever ploy that he could use to save himself. There was no inner resource that would bring him, against all the odds, to safety. He had lost himself in his sleep, and he would die just as Golator Lasgia had said he would, and that was all there was to it. Only one thing remained to him, and that was strength of character: he would die quietly and calmly, without tears or anger, without raging against the forces of fate. Perhaps it would take an hour. Perhaps less. The important thing was to die honorably, for when death is inevitable there's no sense making a botch of it.

He waited for it to come.

What came instead—ten minutes later, half an hour, an hour, he had no way of knowing—was Serifain Reinaulion. The Vroon appeared like a mirage out of the east, trudging slowly toward Dekkeret struggling under the weight of two flasks of water, and when he was within a hundred yards or so he waved two of his tentacles and called, "Are you alive?"

"More or less. Are you real?"

"Real enough. And we've been searching for you half the afternoon." In a flurry of rubbery limbs the small creature pushed one of the flasks upward into Dekkeret's hands. "Here. Sip it. Don't gulp. *Don't gulp.* You're so dehydrated you'll drown if you're too greedy."

Dekkeret fought the impulse to drain the flask in one long pull. The Vroon was right: sip, sip, be moderate, or harm will come. He let the water trickle into his mouth, swished it around, soaked his swollen tongue in it, finally let it down his throat. *Ah.* Another cautious sip. Another, then a fair swallow. He grew a little dizzy. Serifain Reinaulion beckoned for the flask. Dekkeret shook him off, drank again, rubbed a little of the water against his cheeks and lips.

"How far are we from the camp?" he asked finally.

"Ten minutes. Are you strong enough to walk, or shall I go back for the others?"

"I can walk."

"Let's get started, then."

Dekkeret nodded. "One more little sip—"

"Carry the flask. Drink whenever you like. If you get weak, tell me and we'll rest. Remember, I can't carry you."

The Vroon headed off slowly toward a low sandy ridge perhaps five hundred yards to the east. Feeling wobbly and light-headed, Dekkeret followed, and was surprised to see the ground trending upward; the ridge was not all that low, he realized, but some trick of the glare had made him think otherwise. In fact it rose to two or three times his own height, high enough to conceal two lesser ridges on the far side. The floater was parked in the shadow of the farther one.

Barjazid was the only person at the camp. He glanced up at Dekkeret with what looked like contempt or annoyance in his eyes and said, "Went for a stroll, did you? At noontime?"

"Sleepwalking. The dream-stealers had me. It was like being under a spell." Dekkeret was shivering as the sunburn began to disrupt his body's heat-shedding systems. He dropped down alongside the floater and huddled under a light robe. "When I woke I couldn't see camp. I was sure that I would die."

"Half an hour more and you would have. You must be two-thirds fried as it is. Lucky for you my boy woke up and saw that you had disappeared."

Dekkeret pulled the robe tighter around him. "Is that how they die out here? By sleepwalking at midday?"

"One of the ways, yes."

"I owe you my life."

"You've owed me your life since we crossed Khulag Pass. Going on your own you'd have been dead fifty times already. But thank the Vroon, if you have to thank anyone. He did the real work of finding you."

Dekkeret nodded. "Where's your son? And Khaymak Gran? Out looking for me also?"

"On their way back," said Barjazid. And indeed the Skandar and the boy appeared only moments later. Without a glance at him the Skandar flung herself down on her sleeping-mat; Dinitak Barjazid grinned slyly at Dekkeret and said, "Had a pleasant walk?"

"Not very. I regret the inconvenience I caused you."

"As do we."

"Perhaps I should sleep tied down from now on."

"Or with a heavy weight sitting on your chest," Dinitak suggested. He yawned. "Try to stay put until sundown, at least. Will you?"

"So I intend," said Dekkeret.

But it was impossible for him to fall asleep. His skin itched in a thousand places from the bites of the insects, and the sunburn, despite a cooling ointment that Serifain Reinaulion gave him, made him miserable. There was a dry, dusty feeling in his throat that no amount of water seemed to cure, and his eyes throbbed painfully. As though probing an irritating sore he ran through his memories of his desert ordeal again and again—the dream, the heat, the ants, the thirst, the awareness of imminent death. Rigorously he searched for moments of cowardice and found none. Dismay, yes, and anger, and discomfort, but he had no recollection of panic or fear. Good. Good. The worst part of the experience, he decided, had not been the heat and thirst and peril but the dream, the dark and disturbing dream, the dream that had once again begun in joy and midway had undergone a somber metamorphosis. To be denied the solace of healthy dreams is a kind of death-in-life, he thought, far worse than perishing in a desert, for dying occupies only a single moment but dreaming affects all of one's time to come. And what knowledge was it that these bleak Suvraelu dreams were imparting? Dekkeret knew that when dreams came from the Lady they must be studied intently, if necessary with the aid of one who practices the art of dream-speaking, for they contain information vital to the proper conduct of one's life; but these dreams were hardly of the Lady, seeming rather to emanate from some other dark Power, some sinister and oppressive force more adept at taking than giving. Shapeshifters? It could be. What if some tribe of them had, through deceit, obtained one of the devices by which the Lady of the Isle is able to reach the minds of her flock, and lurked here in the hot heartland of Suvrael preying on unwary travelers, stealing from their souls, draining their vitality, imposing an unknown and unfathomable revenge one by one upon those who had stolen their world?

As the afternoon shadows lengthened he found himself at last slipping back into sleep. He fought it, fearing the touch of the invisible intruders on his soul once again. Desperately he held his eyes open, staring across the darkening wasteland and listening to the eerie hum and buzz of the desert-sounds; but it was impossible to fend off exhaustion longer. He drifted into a light, uneasy slumber, broken from time to time by dreams that he sensed came neither from the Lady nor from any other external force, but merely floated randomly through the strata of his weary mind, bits of patternless incident and stray incomprehensible images. And then someone was shaking him awake—the Vroon, he realized. Dekkeret's mind was foggy and slow. He felt numbed. His lips were cracked, his back was sore. Night had fallen, and his companions were already at work closing down their camp. Serifain Reinaulion offered Dekkeret a cup of some sweet, thick, blue-green juice, and he drank it in a single draft.

"Come," the Vroon said. "Time to be going onward."

10

Now the desert changed again and the landscape grew violent and rough. Evidently there had been great earthquakes here, and more than one, for the land lay fractured and upheaved, with mighty blocks of the desert floor piled at unlikely angles against others, and huge sprawls of talus at the feet of the low shattered cliffs. Through this chaotic zone of turbulence and disruption there was only a single passable route—the wide, gently curving bed of a long-extinct river whose sandy floor swerved in long easy bends between the cracked and sundered rock-heaps. The large moon was full and there was almost a daylight brilliance to the grotesque scene. After some hours of passing through a terrain so much the same from one mile to the next that it seemed almost as though the floater were not moving at all, Dekkeret turned to Barjazid and said, "And how long will it be before we reach Ghyzyn Kor?"

"This valley marks the boundary between desert and grazing lands."
Barjazid pointed toward the southwest, where the riverbed vanished between two towering craggy peaks that rose like daggers from the desert
floor. "Beyond that place—Munnerak Notch—the climate is altogether
different. On the far side of the mountain wall sea-fogs enter by night
from the west, and the land is green and fit for grazing. We will camp
halfway to the Notch tomorrow, and pass through it the day after. By
Seaday at the latest you'll be at your lodgings in Ghyzyn Kor."

"And you?" Dekkeret asked.

"My son and I have business elsewhere in the area. We'll return to
Ghyzyn Kor for you after—three days? Five?"

"Five should be sufficient."

"Yes. And then the return journey."

"By the same route?"

"There is no other," said Barjazid. "They explained to you in Tolaghai, did they not, that access to the rangelands was cut off, except by
way of this desert? But why should you fear this route? The dreams
aren't so awful, are they? And so long as you do no more roaming in your
sleep, you'll not be in any danger here."

It sounded simple enough. Indeed, he felt sure he could survive the
trip; but yesterday's dream had been sufficient torment, and he looked
without cheer upon what might yet come. When they made camp the
next morning Dekkeret found himself again uneasy about entrusting
himself to sleep at all. For the first hour of the rest-period he kept himself
awake, listening to the metallic clangor of the bare tumbled rocks as they
stretched and quivered in the midday heat, until at last sleep came up
over his mind like a dense black cloud and took him unawares.

And in time a dream possessed him, and it was, he knew at its outset,
going to be the most terrible of all.

Pain came first—an ache, a twinge, a pang, then without warning a
racking explosion of dazzling light against the walls of his skull, making
him grunt and clutch his head. The agonizing spasm passed swiftly,
though, and he felt the soft sleep presence of Golator Lasgia about him,
soothing him, cradling him against her breasts. She rocked him and
murmured to him and eased him until he opened his eyes and sat up and

looked around, and saw that he was out of the desert, free of Suvrael itself. He and Golator Lasgia were in some cool forest glade where giant
trees with perfectly straight yellow-barked trunks rose to incomprehensible heights, and a swiftly flowing stream, studded with rocky outcrop-
pings, tumbled and roared wildly past almost at their feet. Beyond the
stream the land dropped sharply away, revealing a distant valley, and, on
the far side of it, a great gray, saw-toothed, snowcapped mountain that
Dekkeret recognized instantly as one of the nine vast peaks of the Khyntor Marches.

"No," he said. "This is not where I want to be."

Golator Lasgia laughed, and the pretty tinkling sound of it was
somehow sinister in his ears, like the delicate sounds the desert made at
twilight. "But this is a dream, good friend! You must take what comes, in
dreams!"

"I will direct my dream. I have no wish to return to the Khyntor
Marches. Look: the scene changes. We are on the Zimr, approaching the
river's great bend. See? See? The city of Ni-moya sparkling there before us?"

Indeed he saw the huge city, white against the green backdrop of
forested hills. But Golator Lasgia shook her head.

"There is no city here, my love. There is only the northern forest.
Feel the wind? Listen to the song of the stream. Here—kneel, scoop up
the fallen needles on the ground. Ni-moya is far away, and we are here
to hunt."

"I beg you, let us be in Ni-moya."

"Another time," said Golator Lasgia.

He could not prevail. The magical towers of Ni-moya wavered and
grew transparent and were gone, and there remained only the yellow-
boled trees, the chilly breezes, the sounds of the forest. Dekkeret trembled. He was the prisoner of this dream and there was no escape.

And now five hunters in rough black haigus-hide robes appeared and
made perfunctory gestures of deference and held forth weapons to him,
the blunt, dull tube of an energy-thrower and a short, sparkling poniard
and a blade of a longer kind with a hooked tip. He shook his head, and
one of the hunters came close and grinned mockingly at him, a gap-

toothed grin out of a wide mouth stinking from dried fish. Dekkeret recognized her face, and looked away in shame, for she was the hunter who had died on that other day in the Khyntor Marches a thousand thousand years ago. If only she were not here now, he thought, the dream might be bearable. But this was diabolical torture, to force him to live through all this once again.

Golator Lasgia said, "Take the weapons from her. The steetmoy are running and we must be after them."

"I have no wish to—"

"What folly, to think that dreams respect wishes! The dream *is* your wish. Take the weapons."

Dekkeret understood. With chilled fingers he accepted the blades and the energy-thrower and stowed them in the proper places on his belt. The hunters smiled and grunted things at him in the thick, harsh dialect of the north. Then they began to run along the bank of the stream, moving in easy loping bounds, touching the ground no more than one stride out of five; and willy-nilly Dekkeret ran with them, clumsily at first, then with much the same floating grace. Golator Lasgia, by his side, kept pace easily, her dark hair fluttering about her face, her eyes bright with excitement. They turned left, into the heart of the forest, and fanned out in a crescent formation that widened and curved inward to confront the prey.

The prey! Dekkeret could see three white-furred steetmoy gleaming like lanterns deep in the forest. The beasts prowled uneasily, growling, aware of intruders but still unwilling to abandon their territory—big creatures, possibly the most dangerous wild animals on Majipoor, quick and powerful and cunning, the terrors of the northlands. Dekkeret drew his poniard. Killing steetmoy with energy-throwers was no sport, and might damage too much of their valuable fur besides: one was supposed to get to close range and kill them with one's blade, preferably the poniard, if necessary the hooked machete.

The hunters looked to him. Pick one, they were saying, choose your quarry. Dekkeret nodded. The middle one, he indicated. They were smiling coldly. What did they know that they were not telling him? It had been like this that other time, too, the barely concealed scorn of the mountainfolk for the pampered lordlings who were seeking deadly amusements in their forests; and that outing had ended badly. Dekkeret hefted his poniard. The dream-steetmoy that moved nervously beyond those trees were implausibly enormous, great heavy-haunched immensities that clearly could not be slain by one man alone, wielding only hand-weapons, but here there was no turning back, for he knew himself to be bound upon whatever destiny the dream offered him. Now with hunting-horns and hand-clapping the hired hunters commenced to stampede the prey; the steetmoy, angered and baffled by the sudden blaring, strident sounds, rose high, whirled, raked trees with their claws, swung around, and more in disgust than fear began to run.

The chase was on.

Dekkeret knew that the hunters were separating the animals, driving the two rejected ones away to allow him a clear chance at the one he had chosen. But he looked neither to the right nor the left. Accompanied by Golator Lasgia and one of the hunters, he rushed forward, giving pursuit as the steetmoy in the center went rumbling and crashing through the forest. This was the worst part, for although humans were faster, steetmoy were better able to break through barriers of under-brush, and he might well lose his quarry altogether in the confusions of the run. The forest here was fairly open; but the steetmoy was heading for cover, and soon Dekkeret found himself struggling past saplings and vines and low brush, barely able to keep the retreating white phantom in view. With singleminded intensity he ran and hacked with the machete and clambered through thickets. It was all so terribly familiar, so much of an old story, especially when he realized that the steetmoy was doubling back, was looping through the trampled part of the forest as if planning a counterattack—

The moment would soon be at hand, the dreaming Dekkeret knew, when the maddened animal would blunder upon the gap-toothed hunter, would seize the mountain woman and hurl her against a tree, and Dekkeret, unwilling or unable to halt, would go plunging onward, continuing the chase, leaving the woman where she lay, so that when the squat thick-snouted scavenging beast emerged from its hole and began to rip her belly apart there would be no one to defend her, and only later, when things were more quiet and there was time to go back for the injured hunter, would he begin to regret the callous, uncaring focus of concentration that had allowed him to ignore his fallen companion for the sake of keeping sight of his prey. And afterward the shame, the guilt, the unending self-accusations—yes, he would go through all that again as he lay here asleep in the stifling heat of the Suvraelu desert, would he not?

No.

No, it was not that simple at all, for the language of dreams is complex, and in the thick mists that suddenly enfolded the forest, Dekkeret saw the steetmoy swing around and lash the gap-toothed woman and knock her flat, but the woman rose and spat out a few bloody teeth and laughed, and the chase continued, or rather it twisted back on itself to the same point, the steetmoy bursting forth unexpectedly from the darkest part of the woods and striking at Dekkeret himself, knocking his poniard and his machete from his hands, rearing high overhead for the deathblow, but not delivering it, for the image changed and it was Golator Lasgia who lay beneath the plunging claws while Dekkeret wandered aimlessly nearby, unable to move in any useful direction, and then it was the huntswoman who was the victim once more, and Dekkeret again, and suddenly and improbably old pinch-faced Barjazid, and then Golator Lasgia. As Dekkeret watched, a voice at his elbow said, "What does it matter? We each owe the Divine a death. Perhaps it was more important for you then to follow your prey." Dekkeret stared. The voice was the voice of the gap-toothed hunter. The sound of it left him dazed and shaking. The dream was becoming bewildering. He struggled to penetrate its mysteries.

Now he saw Barjazid standing at his side in the dark, cool forest glade. The steetmoy once more was savaging the mountain woman.

"Is this the way it truly was?" Barjazid asked.

"I suppose so. I didn't see it."

"What did you do?"

"Kept on going. I didn't want to lose the animal."

"You killed it?"

"Yes."

"And then?"

"Came back. And found her. Like that—"

Dekkeret pointed. The snuffling scavenger was astride the woman. Golator Lasgia stood nearby, arms folded, smiling.

"And then?"

"The others came. They buried their companion. We skinned the steetmoy and rode back to camp."

"And then? And then? And then?"

"Who are you? Why are you asking me this?"

Dekkeret had a flashing view of himself beneath the scavenger's fanged snout.

Barjazid said, "You were ashamed?"

"Of course. I put the pleasures of my sport ahead of a human life."

"You had no way of knowing she was injured."

"I sensed it. I saw it, but I didn't *let* myself see it. Do you understand? I knew she was hurt. I kept on going."

"Who cared?"

"I cared."

"Did her tribesmen seem to care?"

"I cared."

"And so? And so? And so?"

"It mattered to me. Other things matter to them."

"You felt guilty?"

"Of course."

"You *are* guilty. Of youth, of foolishness, of naïveté."

"And are you my judge?"

"Of course I am," said Barjazid. "See my face?" He tugged at his seamed, weatherbeaten jowls, pulled and twisted until his leathery desert-tanned skin began to split, and the face ripped away like a mask, revealing another face beneath, a hideous, ironic, distorted face twisted with convulsive, mocking laughter, and the other face was Dekkeret's own.

11

In that moment Dekkeret experienced a sensation as of a bright needle of piercing light driving downward through the roof of his skull. It was the most intense pain he had ever known, a sudden intolerable spike of racking anguish that burned through his brain with monstrous force. It lit a flare in his consciousness by whose baleful light he saw himself grimly illuminated, fool, romantic, boy, sole inventor of a drama about which no one else cared, inventing a tragedy that had an audience of one, seeking purgation for a sin without context, which was no sin at all except perhaps the sin of self-indulgence. In the midst of his agony Dekkeret heard a great gong tolling far away and the dry rasping sound of Barjazid's demonic laughter; then with a sudden wrenching twist he pulled free of sleep and rolled over, quivering, shaken, still afflicted by the lancing thrust of the pain, although it was beginning to fade as the last bonds of sleep dropped from him.

He struggled to rise and found himself enveloped in thick musky fur, as if the steetmoy had seized him and was crushing him against its breast. Powerful arms gripped him—*four* arms, he realized, and as Dekkeret completed the journey up out of dreams he understood that he was in the embrace of the giant Skandar woman, Khaymak Gran. Probably he had been crying out in his sleep, thrashing and flailing about, and as he scrambled to his feet she had decided he was off on another sleepwalking excursion and was determined to prevent him from going. She was hugging him with rib-cracking force.

"It's all right," he muttered, tight against her heavy gray pelt. "I'm awake! I'm not going anywhere!"

Still she clung to him.

"You're—hurting—me—"

He fought for breath. In her great awkward solicitousness she was apt to kill him with motherly kindness. Dekkeret pushed, even kicked, twisted, hammered at her with his head. Somehow as he wriggled in her grasp he threw her off balance, and they toppled together, she beneath him; at the last moment her arms opened, allowing Dekkeret to spin away. He landed on both knees and crouched where he fell, aching in a dozen places and befuddled by all that had happened in the last few moments. But not so befuddled that when he stood up he failed to see Barjazid, on the far side of the floater, hastily removing some sort of mechanism from his forehead, some slender crownlike circlet, and attempting to conceal it in a compartment of the floater.

"What was that?" Dekkeret demanded.

Barjazid looked uncharacteristically flustered. "Nothing. A toy, only."

"Let me see."

Barjazid seemed to signal. Out of the corner of his eye Dekkeret saw Khaymak Gran getting to her feet and beginning to reach for him again, but before the ponderous Skandar could manage it Dekkeret had skipped out of the way and darted around the floater to Barjazid's side. The little man was still busy with his intricate bit of machinery. Dekkeret, looming over him as the Skandar had loomed over Dekkeret, swiftly caught Barjazid's hand and yanked it up behind his back. Then he plucked the mechanism from its storage case and examined it.

Everyone was awake now. The Vroon stared goggle-eyed at what was going on; and young Dinitak, producing a knife that was not much unlike the one in Dekkeret's dream, glared up at him and said, "Let go of my father."

Dekkeret swung Barjazid around to serve as a shield.

"Tell your son to put that blade away," he said.

Barjazid was silent.

Dekkeret said, "He drops the blade or I smash this thing in my hand. Which?"

Barjazid gave the order in a low growling tone. Dinitak pitched the knife into the sand almost at Dekkeret's feet, and Dekkeret, taking one step forward, pulled it to him and kicked it behind him. He dangled the mechanism in Barjazid's face: a thing of gold and crystal and ivory, elaborately fashioned, with mysterious wires and connections.

"What is this?" Dekkeret said.

"I told you. A toy. Please—give it to me, before you break it."

"What is the function of this toy?"

"It amuses me while I sleep," said Barjazid hoarsely.

"In what way?"

"It enhances my dreams and makes them more interesting."

Dekkeret took a closer look at it. "If I put it on, will it enhance my dreams?"

"It will only harm you, Initiate."

"Tell me what it does for you."

"That is very hard to describe," Barjazid said.

"Work at it. Strive to find the words. How did you become a figure in my dream, Barjazid? You had no business being in that particular dream."

The little man shrugged. He said uncomfortably, "Was I in your dream? How would I know what was happening in your dream? Anyone can be in anybody's dream."

"I think this machine may have helped put you there. And may have helped you know what I was dreaming."

Barjazid responded only with glum silence.

Dekkeret said, "Describe the workings of this machine, or I'll grind it to scrap in my hand."

"Please—"

Dekkeret's thick, strong fingers closed on one of the most fragile-looking parts of the device. Barjazid sucked in his breath; his body went taut in Dekkeret's grip.

"Well?" Dekkeret said.

"Your guess is right. It—it lets me enter sleeping minds."

"Truly? Where did you get such a thing?"

"My own invention. A notion that I have been perfecting over a number of years."

"Like the machines of the Lady of the Isle?"

"Different. More powerful. She can only speak to minds; I can read dreams, control the shape of them, take command of a person's sleeping mind to a great degree."

"And this device is entirely of your own making. Not stolen from the Isle."

"Mine alone," Barjazid murmured.

A torrent of rage surged through Dekkeret. For an instant he wanted to crush Barjazid's machine in one quick squeeze and then to grind Barjazid himself to pulp. Remembering all of Barjazid's half-truths and evasions and outright lies, thinking of the way Barjazid had meddled in his dreams, how he had wantonly distorted and transformed the healing rest Dekkeret so sorely needed, how he had interposed layers of fears and torments and uncertainties into that Lady-sent gift, his own true blissful rest, Dekkeret felt an almost murderous fury at having been invaded and manipulated in this fashion. His heart pounded, his throat went dry, his vision blurred. His hand tightened on Barjazid's bent arm until the small man whimpered and mewed. Harder—harder—break it off—

No.

Dekkeret reached some inner peak of anger and held himself there a moment, and then let himself descend the farther slope toward tranquillity. Gradually, he regained his steadiness, caught his breath, eased the drumming in his chest. He held tight to Barjazid until he felt altogether calm. Then he released the little man and shoved him forward against the floater. Barjazid staggered and clung to the vehicle's curving side. All color seemed to have drained from his face. Tenderly he rubbed his bruised arm, and glanced up at Dekkeret with an expression that seemed to be compounded equally of terror and pain and resentment.

With care Dekkeret studied the curious instrument, gently rubbing the tips of his fingers over its elegant and complicated parts. Then he moved as if to put it on his own forehead.

Barjazid gasped. "Don't!"

"What will happen? Will I damage it?"

"You will. And yourself as well."

Dekkeret nodded. He doubted that Barjazid was bluffing, but he did not care to find out.

After a moment he said, "There are no Shapeshifter dream-stealers hiding in this desert, is that right?"

"That is so," Barjazid whispered.

"Only you, secretly experimenting on the minds of other travelers. Yes?"

"Yes."

"And causing them to die."

"No," Barjazid said. "I intended no deaths. If they died, it was because they became alarmed, became confused, because they panicked and ran off into dangerous places—because they began to wander in their sleep, as you did—"

"But they died because you had meddled in their minds."

"Who can be sure of that? Some died, some did not. I had no desire to have anyone perish. Remember, when *you* wandered away, we searched diligently for you."

"I had hired you to guide and protect me," said Dekkeret. "The others were innocent strangers whom you preyed on from afar—is that not so?"

Barjazid was silent.

"You knew that people were dying as a direct result of your experiments, and you went on experimenting."

Barjazid shrugged.

"How long were you doing this?"

"Several years."

"And for what reason?"

Barjazid looked toward the side. "I told you once, I would never answer a question of that sort."

"And if I break your machine?"

"You will break it anyway."

"Not so," Dekkeret replied. "Here. Take it."

"*What?*"

Dekkeret extended his hand, with the dream-machine resting on his palm. "Go on. Take it. Put it away. I don't want the thing."

"You're not going to kill me?" Barjazid said in wonder.

"Am I your judge? If I catch you using that device on me again, I'll kill you sure enough. But otherwise, no. Killing is not my sport. I have one sin on my soul as it is. And I need you to get me back to Tolaghai, or have you forgotten that?"

"Of course. Of course." Barjazid looked astounded at Dekkeret's mercy.

Dekkeret said, "Why would I want to kill you?"

"For entering your mind—for interfering with your dreams—"

"Ah."

"For putting your life at risk on the desert."

"That, too."

"And yet you aren't eager for vengeance?"

Dekkeret shook his head. "You took great liberties with my soul, and that angered me, but the anger is past and done with. I won't punish you. We've had a transaction, you and I, and I've had my money's worth from you, and this thing of yours has been of value to me." He leaned close and said in a low, earnest voice, "I came to Suvrael full of doubt and confusion and guilt, looking to purge myself through physical suffering. That was foolishness. Physical suffering makes the body uncomfortable and strengthens the will, but it does little for the wounded spirit. You gave me something else, you and your mind-meddling toy. You tormented me in dreams and held up a mirror to my soul, and I saw myself clearly. How much of that last dream were you really able to read, Barjazid?"

"You were in a forest—in the north—"

"Yes."

"Hunting. One of your companions was injured by an animal, yes? Is that it?"

"Go on."

"And you ignored her. You continued the chase. And afterward, when you went back to see about her, it was too late, and you blamed yourself for her death. I sensed the great guilt in you. I felt the power of it radiating from you."

"Yes," Dekkeret said. "Guilt that I'll bear forever. But there's nothing that can be done for her now, is there?" An astonishing calmness had spread through him. He was not altogether sure what had happened, except that in his dream he had confronted the events of the Khyntor forest at last, and had faced the truth of what he had done there and what he had not done, had understood, in a way that he could not define in words, that it was folly to flagellate himself for all his lifetime over a single act of carelessness and unfeeling stupidity, that the moment had come to put aside all self-accusation and get on with the business of his life. The process of forgiving himself was under way. He had come to Suvrael to be purged and somehow he had accomplished that. And he owed Barjazid thanks for that favor. To Barjazid he said, "I might have saved her, or maybe not; but my mind was elsewhere, and in my foolishness I passed her by to make my kill. But wallowing in guilt is no useful means of atonement, eh, Barjazid? The dead are dead. My services must be offered to the living. Come: turn this floater and let's begin heading back toward Tolaghai."

"And what about your visit to the rangelands? What about Ghyzyn Kor?"

"A silly mission. It no longer matters, these questions of meat shortages and trade imbalances. Those problems are already solved. Take me to Tolaghai."

"And then?"

"You will come with me to Castle Mount. To demonstrate your toy before the Coronal."

"No!" Barjazid cried in horror. He looked genuinely frightened for the first time since Dekkeret had known him. "I beg you—"

"Father?" said Dinitak.

Under the midday sun the boy seemed ablaze with light. There was a wild and fiery look of pride on his face.

"Father, go with him to Castle Mount. Let him show his masters what we have here."

Barjazid moistened his lips. "I fear—"

"Fear nothing. Our time is now beginning."

Dekkeret looked from one to the other, from the suddenly timid and shrunken old man to the transfigured and glowing boy. He sensed that historic things were happening, that mighty forces were shifting out of balance and into a new configuration, and this he barely comprehended, except to know that his destinies and those of these desertfolk were tied in some way together; and the dream-reading machine that Barjazid had created was the thread that bound their lives.

Barjazid said huskily, "What will happen to me on Castle Mount, then?"

"I have no idea," said Dekkeret. "Perhaps they'll take your head and mount it atop Lord Siminave's Tower. Or perhaps you'll find yourself set up on high as a Power of Majipoor. Anything might happen. How would

I know?" He realized that he did not care, that he was indifferent to Barjazid's fate, that he felt no anger at all toward this seedy little tinkerer with minds, but only a kind of perverse abstract gratitude for Barjazid's having helped rid him of his own demons. "These matters are in the Coronal's hands. But one thing is certain, that you will go with me to the Mount, and this machine of yours with us. Come, now, turn the floater, take me to Tolaghai."

"It is still daytime," Barjazid muttered. "The heart of the day rages at its highest."

"We'll manage. Come: get us moving, and fast! We have a ship to catch in Tolaghai, and there's a woman in that city I want to see again, before we set sail!"

12

These events happened in the young manhood of him who was to become the Coronal Lord Dekkeret in the Pontificate of Prestimion. And it was the boy Dinitak Barjazid who would be the first to rule in Suvrael over the minds of all the sleepers of Majipoor, with the title of King of Dreams.

SIX

The Soul-Painter and
the Shapeshifter

It has become an addiction. Hissune's mind is opening now in all directions, and the Register of Souls is the key to an infinite world of new understanding. When one dwells in the Labyrinth one develops a peculiar sense of the world as vague and unreal, mere names rather than concrete places: only the dark and hermetic Labyrinth has substance, and all else is vapor. But Hissune has journeyed by proxy to every continent now, he has tasted strange foods and seen weird landscapes, he has experienced extremes of heat and cold, and in all that he has come to acquire a comprehension of the complexity of the world that, he suspects, very few others have had. Now he goes back again and again. No longer does he have to bother with forged credentials; he is so regular a user of the archives that a nod is sufficient to get him within, and then he has all the million yesterdays of Majipoor at his disposal. Often he stays with a capsule for only a moment or two, until he has determined that it contains nothing that will move him farther along the road to knowledge. Sometimes of a morning he will call up and dismiss eight, ten, a dozen records in rapid succession. True enough, he knows, that every being's soul contains a universe; but not all universes are equally interesting, and that which he might learn from the innermost depths of one who spent his life sweeping the streets of Piliplok or murmuring prayers in the entourage of the Lady of the Isle does not seem immediately useful to him, when he considers other possibilities. So he summons capsules and rejects them and summons again, dipping here and there into Majipoor's past, and keeps at it until he finds himself in contact with a mind that promises real revelation.

Even Coronals and Pontifexes can be bores, he has discovered. But there are always wondrous unexpected finds—a man who fell in love with a Metamorph, for example—

IT WAS A SURFEIT of perfection that drove the soul-painter Therion Nismile from the crystalline cities of Castle Mount to the dark forests of the western continent. All his life he had lived amid the wonders of the Mount, traveling through the Fifty Cities according to the demands of his career, exchanging one sort of splendor for another every few years. Dundilmir was his native city—his first canvases were scenes of the Fiery Valley, tempestuous and passionate with the ragged energies of youth—and then he dwelled some years in marvelous Canzilaine of the talking statues, and afterward in Stee the awesome, whose outskirts were three days' journey across, and in golden Halanx at the very fringes of the Castle, and for five years at the Castle itself, where he painted at the court of the Coronal Lord Thraym. His paintings were prized for their calm elegance and their perfection of form, which mirrored the flawlessness of the Fifty Cities to the ultimate degree. But the beauty of such places numbs the soul, after a time, and paralyzes the artistic instincts. When Nismile reached his fortieth year he found himself beginning to identify perfection with stagnation; he loathed his own most famous works; his spirit began to cry out for upheaval, unpredictability, transformation.

The moment of crisis overtook him in the gardens of Tolingar Barrier, that miraculous park on the plain between Dundilmir and Stipool. The Coronal had asked him for a suite of paintings of the gardens, to decorate a pergola under construction on the Castle's rim. Obligingly Nismile made the long journey down the slopes of the enormous mountain, toured the forty miles of park, chose the sites where he meant to work, set up his first canvas at Kazkas Promontory, where the contours of the garden swept outward in great, green, symmetrical, pulsating scrolls. He had loved this place when he was a boy. On all of Majipoor there was no site more serene, more orderly, for the Tolingar gardens were composed of plants bred to maintain themselves in transcendental tidiness. No gardener's shears touched these shrubs and trees; they grew of their own accord in graceful balance, regulated their own spacing and rate of replacement, suppressed all weeds in their environs, and controlled their proportions so that the original design remained forever unbreached. When they shed their leaves or found it needful to drop an entire dead bough, enzymes within dissolved the cast-off matter quickly into useful compost. Lord Havilbove, more than a hundred years ago, had been the founder of this garden; his successors Lord Kanaba and Lord Sirruth had continued and extended the program of genetic modification that governed it; and under the present Coronal Lord Thraym its plan was wholly fulfilled, so that now it would remain eternally perfect, eternally balanced. It was that perfection which Nismile had come to capture.

He faced his blank canvas, drew breath deep down into his lungs, and readied himself for entering the trance state. In a moment his soul, leaping from his dreaming mind, would in a single instant imprint the unique intensity of his vision of this scene on the psychosensitive fabric. He glanced one last time at the gentle hills, the artful shrubbery, the delicately angled leaves—and a wave of rebellious fury crashed against him, and he quivered and shook and nearly fell. This immobile landscape, this static, sterile beauty, this impeccable and matchless garden, had no need of him; it was itself as unchanging as a painting, and as lifeless, frozen in its own faultless rhythms to the end of time. How ghastly! How hateful! Nismile swayed and pressed his hands to his pounding skull. He heard the soft surprised grunts of his companions, and when he opened his eyes he saw them all staring in horror and embarrassment at the blackened and bubbling canvas. "Cover it!" he cried, and turned away. Everyone was in motion at once; and in the center of the group Nismile stood statue-still. When he could speak again he said quietly, "Tell Lord Thraym I will be unable to fulfill his commission."

And so that day in Dundilmir he purchased what he needed and began his long journey to the lowlands, and out into the broad, hot floodplain of the Iyann River, and by riverboat interminably along the sluggish Iyann to the western port of Alaisor; and at Alaisor he boarded, after a wait of weeks, a ship bound for Numinor on the Isle of Sleep, where he tarried a month. Then he found passage on a pilgrim-ship sailing to Piliplok on the wild continent of Zimroel. Zimroel, he was sure, would not oppress him with elegance and perfection. It had only eight or nine cities, which in fact were probably little more than frontier towns. The entire interior of the continent was wilderness, into which Lord Stiamot had driven the aboriginal Metamorphs after their final defeat four thousand years ago. A man wearied of civilization might be able to restore his soul in such surroundings.

Nismile expected Piliplok to be a mudhole, but to his surprise it turned out to be an ancient and enormous city, laid out according to a maddeningly rigid mathematical plan. It was ugly but not in any refreshing way, and he moved on by riverboat up the Zimr. He journeyed past great Ni-moya, which was famous even to inhabitants of the other continent, and did not stop there; but at a town called Verf he impulsively left the boat and set forth in a hired wagon into the forests to the south. When he had traveled so deep into the wilderness that he could see no trace of civilization, he halted and built a cabin beside a swift dark stream. It was three years since he had left Castle Mount. Through all his journey he had been alone and had spoken to others only when necessary, and he had not painted at all.

Here Nismile felt himself beginning to heal. Everything in this place was unfamiliar and wonderful. On Castle Mount, where the climate was artificially controlled, an endless sweet springtime reigned, the unreal air was clear and pure, and rainfall came at predictable intervals. But now he was in a moist and humid rain-forest, where the soil was spongy and yielding, clouds and tongues of fog drifted by often, showers were frequent, and the vegetation was a chaotic, tangled anarchy, as far removed as he could imagine from the symmetries of Tolingar Barrier. He wore little clothing, learned by trial and error what roots and berries and shoots were safe to eat, and devised a wickerwork weir to help him catch the slender crimson fish that flashed like skyrockets through the stream. He walked for hours through the dense jungle, savoring not only its strange beauty but also the tense pleasure of wondering if he could find his way back to his cabin. Often he sang, in a loud erratic voice; he had never sung on Castle Mount. Occasionally he started to prepare a canvas, but always he put it away unused. He composed nonsensical poems, vo-luptuous strings of syllables, and chanted them to an audience of slender towering trees and incomprehensibly intertwined vines. Sometimes he wondered how it was going at the court of Lord Thraym, whether the Coronal had hired a new artist yet to paint the decorations for the per-gola, and if the halatingas were blooming now along the road to High Morpin. But such thoughts came rarely to him.

He lost track of time. Four or five or perhaps six weeks—how could he tell?—went by before he saw his first Metamorph.

The encounter took place in a marshy meadow two miles upstream from his cabin. Nismile had gone there to gather the succulent scarlet bulbs of mud-lilies, which he had learned to mash and roast into a sort of bread. They grew deep, and he dug them by working his arm into the muck to the shoulder and groping about with his cheek pressed to the ground. He came up muddy-faced and slippery, clutching a dripping handful, and was startled to find a figure calmly watching him from a distance of a dozen yards.

He had never seen a Metamorph. The native beings of Majipoor were perpetually exiled from the capital continent, Alhanroel, where Nismile had spent all his years. But he had an idea of how they looked, and he felt sure this must be one: an enormously tall, fragile, sallow-skinned being, sharp-faced, with inward-sloping eyes and barely perceptible nose and stringy, rubbery hair of a pale greenish hue. It wore only a leather loin-harness and a short, sharp dirk of some polished black wood was strapped to its hip. In eerie dignity the Metamorph stood balanced with one frail long leg twisted around the shin of the other. It seemed both sinister and gentle, menacing and comic. Nismile chose not to be alarmed.

"Hello," he said. "Do you mind if I gather bulbs here?"

The Metamorph was silent.

"I have the cabin down the stream. I'm Therion Nismile. I used to be a soul-painter, when I lived on Castle Mount."

The Metamorph regarded him solemnly. A flicker of unreadable ex-pression crossed its face. Then it turned and slipped gracefully into the jungle, vanishing almost at once.

Nismile shrugged. He dug down for more mud-lily bulbs.

A week or two later he met another Metamorph, or perhaps the same one, this time while he was stripping bark from a vine to make rope for a bilantoon-trap. Once more the aborigine was wordless, materializing quietly like an apparition in front of Nismile and contemplating him from the same unsettling one-legged stance. A second time Nismile tried to draw the creature into conversation, but at his first words it drifted off, ghostlike. "Wait!" Nismile called. "I'd like to talk with you. I—" But he was alone.

A few days afterward he was collecting firewood when he became aware yet again that he was being studied. At once he said to the Meta-morph, "I've caught a bilantoon and I'm about to roast it. There's more meat than I need. Will you share my dinner?" The Metamorph smiled— he took that enigmatic flicker for a smile, though it could have been anything—and as if by way of replying underwent a sudden astonishing shift, turning itself into a mirror image of Nismile, stocky and muscular, with dark penetrating eyes and shoulder-length black hair. Nismile blinked wildly and trembled; then, recovering, he smiled, deciding to take the mimicry as some form of communication, and said, "Marvelous! I can't begin to see how you people do it!" He beckoned. "Come. It'll take an hour and a half to cook the bilantoon, and we can talk until then. You understand our language, don't you? Don't you?" It was bizarre beyond measure, this speaking to a duplicate of himself. "Say something, eh? Tell me: is there a Metamorph village somewhere nearby? *Piurivar*," he cor-rected, remembering the Metamorphs' name for themselves. "Eh? A lot of Piurivars hereabouts, in the jungle?" Nismile gestured again. "Walk with me to my cabin and we'll get the fire going. You don't have any wine, do you? That's the only thing I miss, I think, some good strong wine, the heavy stuff they make in Muldemar. Won't taste that ever again, I guess, but there's wine in Zimroel, isn't there? Eh? Will you say something?" But the Metamorph responded only with a grimace, per-haps intended as a grin, that twisted the Nismile-face into something harsh and strange; then it resumed its own form between one instant and the next and with calm floating strides went walking away.

Nismile hoped for a time that it would return with a flask of wine, but he did not see it again. Curious creatures, he thought. Were they angry that he was camped in their territory? Were they keeping him under surveillance out of fear that he was the vanguard of a wave of human settlers? Oddly, he felt himself in no danger. Metamorphs were generally considered to be malevolent; certainly they were disquieting beings, alien and unfathomable. Plenty of tales were told of Metamorph raids on outlying human settlements, and no doubt the Shapeshifter folk harbored bitter hatred for those who had come to their world and dispossessed them and driven them into these jungles; but yet Nismile knew himself to be a man of goodwill, who had never done harm to others and wanted only to be left to live his life, and he fancied that some subtle sense would lead the Metamorphs to realize that he was not their enemy. He wished he could become their friend. He was growing hungry for conversation after all this time of solitude, and it might be challenging and rewarding to exchange ideas with these strange folk; he might even paint one. He had been thinking again lately of returning to his art, of experiencing once more that moment of creative ecstasy as his soul leaped the gap to the psychosensitive canvas and inscribed on it those images that he alone could fashion. Surely he was different now from the increasingly unhappy man he had been on Castle Mount, and that difference must show itself in his work. During the next few days he rehearsed speeches designed to win the confidence of the Metamorphs, to overcome that strange shyness of theirs, that delicacy of bearing which blocked any sort of contact. In time, he thought, they would grow used to him, they would begin to speak, to accept his invitation to eat with him, and then perhaps they would pose—

But in the days that followed he saw no more Metamorphs. He roamed the forest, peering hopefully into thickets and down mistswept lanes of trees, and found no one. He decided that he had been too forward with them and had frightened them away—so much for the malevolence of the monstrous Metamorphs!—and after a while he ceased to expect further contact with them. That was disturbing. He had not missed companionship when none seemed likely, but the knowledge that there were intelligent beings somewhere in the area kindled an awareness of loneliness in him that was not easy to bear.

One damp and warm day several weeks after his last Metamorph encounter Nismile was swimming in the cool, deep pond formed by a natural dam of boulders half a mile below his cabin when he saw a pale slim figure moving quickly through a dense bower of blue-leaved bushes by the shore. He scrambled out of the water, barking his knees on the rocks. "Wait!" he shouted. "Please—don't be afraid—don't go—" The figure disappeared, but Nismile, thrashing frantically through the underbrush, caught sight of it again in a few minutes, leaning casually now against an enormous tree with vivid red bark.

Nismile stopped short, amazed, for the other was no Metamorph but a human woman.

She was slender and young and naked, with thick auburn hair, narrow shoulders, small high breasts, bright playful eyes. She seemed altogether unafraid of him, a forest-sprite who had obviously enjoyed leading him on this little chase. As he stood gaping at her, she looked him over unhurriedly, and with an outburst of clear tinkling laughter said, "You're all scratched and torn! Can't you run in the forest any better than that?"

"I didn't want you to get away."

"Oh, I wasn't going to go far. You know, I was watching you for a long time before you noticed me. You're the man from the cabin, right?"

"Yes. And you—where do you live?"

"Here and there," she said airily.

He stared at her in wonder. Her beauty delighted him, her shamelessness astounded him. She might almost be a hallucination, he thought. Where had she come from? What was a human being, naked and alone, doing in this primordial jungle?

Human?

Of course not, Nismile realized, with the sudden sharp grief of a child who has been given some coveted treasure in a dream, only to awaken aglow and perceive the sad reality. Remembering how effortlessly the Metamorph had mimicked him, Nismile comprehended the dismal probability: this was some prank, some masquerade. He studied her intently, seeking a sign of Metamorph identity, a flickering of the projection, a trace of knife-sharp cheekbones and sloping eyes behind the cheerfully impudent face. She was convincingly human in every degree.

But yet—how implausible to meet one of his own kind here, how much more likely that she was a Shapeshifter, a deceiver—

He did not want to believe that. He resolved to meet the possibility of deception with a conscious act of faith, in the hope that that would make her be what she seemed to be.

"What's your name?" he asked.

"Sarise. And yours?"

"Nismile. Where *do* you live?"

"In the forest."

"Then there's a human settlement not far from here?"

She shrugged. "I live by myself." She came toward him—he felt his muscles growing taut as she moved closer, and something churning in his stomach, and his skin seemed to be blazing—and touched her fingers lightly to the cuts the vines had made on his arms and chest. "Don't those scratches bother you?"

"They're beginning to. I should wash them."

"Yes. Let's go back to the pool. I know a better way than the one you took. Follow me!"

She parted the fronds of a thick clump of ferns and revealed a narrow, well-worn trail. Gracefully she sprinted off, and he ran behind her, delighted by the ease of her movements, the play of muscles in her back and buttocks. He plunged into the pool a moment after her and they splashed about. The chilly water soothed the stinging of the cuts. When they climbed out, he yearned to draw her to him and enclose her in his arms, but he did not dare. They sprawled on the mossy bank. There was mischief in her eyes.

He said, "My cabin isn't far."

"I know."

"Would you like to go there?"

"Some other time, Nismile."

"All right. Some other time."

"Where do you come from?" she asked.

"I was born on Castle Mount. Do you know where that is? I was a soul-painter at the Coronal's court. Do you know what soul-painting is?

It's done with the mind and a sensitive canvas, and—I could show you. I could paint you, Sarise. I take a close look at something, I seize its essence with my deepest consciousness, and then I go into a kind of trance, almost a waking dream, and I transform what I've seen into something of my own and hurl it on the canvas. I capture the truth of it in one quick blaze of transference—" He paused. "I could show you best by making a painting of you."

She scarcely seemed to have heard him.

"Would you like to touch me, Nismile?"

"Yes. Very much."

The thick turquoise moss was like a carpet. She rolled toward him and his hand hovered above her body, and then he hesitated, for he was certain still that she was a Metamorph playing some perverse Shapeshifter game with him, and a heritage of thousands of years of dread and loathing surfaced in him, and he was terrified of touching her and discovering that her skin had the clammy, repugnant texture that he imagined Metamorph skin to have, or that she would shift and turn into a creature of alien form the moment she was in his arms. Her eyes were closed, her lips were parted, her tongue flickered between them like a serpent's: she was waiting. In terror he forced his hand down to her breast. But her flesh was warm and yielding and it felt very much the way the flesh of a young human woman should feel, as well as he could recall after these years of solitude. With a soft little cry she pressed herself into his embrace. For a dismaying instant the grotesque image of a Metamorph rose in his mind, angular and long-limbed and noseless, but he shoved the thought away fiercely and gave himself up entirely to her lithe and vigorous body.

For a long time afterward they lay still, side by side, hands clasped, saying nothing. Even when a light rain shower came they did not move, but simply allowed the quick, sharp sprinkle to wash the sweat from their skins. He opened his eyes eventually and found her watching him with keen curiosity.

"I want to paint you," he said.

"No."

"Not now. Tomorrow. You'll come to my cabin, and—"

"No."

"I haven't tried to paint in years. It's important to me to begin again. And I want very much to paint you."

"I want very much not to be painted," she said.

"Please."

"No," she said gently. She rolled away and stood up. "Paint the jungle. Paint the pool. Don't paint me, all right, Nismile? All right?"

He made an unhappy gesture of acceptance.

She said, "I have to leave now."

"Will you tell me where you live?"

"I already have. Here and there. In the forest. Why do you ask these questions?"

"I want to be able to find you again. If you disappear, how will I know where to look?"

"I know where to find you," she said. "That's enough."

"Will you come to me tomorrow? To my cabin?"

"I think I will."

He took her hand and drew her toward him. But now she was hesitant, remote. The mysteries of her throbbed in his mind. She had told him nothing, really, but her name. He found it too difficult to believe that she, like he, was a solitary of the jungle, wandering as the whim came; but he doubted that he could have failed to detect, in all these weeks, the existence of a human village nearby. The most likely explanation still was that she was a Shapeshifter, embarked for who knew what reason on an adventure with a human. Much as he resisted that idea, he was too rational to reject it completely. But she *looked* human, she *felt* human, she *acted* human. How good were these Metamorphs at their transformations? He was tempted to ask her outright whether his suspicions were correct, but that was foolishness; she had answered nothing else, and surely she would not answer that. He kept his questions to himself. She pulled her hand gently free of his grasp and smiled and made the shape of a kiss with her lips, and stepped toward the fern-bordered trail and was gone.

Nismile waited at his cabin all the next day. She did not come. It scarcely surprised him. Their meeting had been a dream, a fantasy, an interlude beyond time and space. He did not expect ever to see her again. Toward evening he drew a canvas from the pack he had brought with him and set it up, thinking he might paint the view from his cabin as twilight purpled the forest air; he studied the landscape a long while, testing the verticals of the slender trees against the heavy horizontal of a thick, sprawling yellow-berried bush, and eventually shook his head and put his canvas away. Nothing about this landscape needed to be captured by art. In the morning, he thought, he would hike upstream past the meadow to a place where fleshy red succulents sprouted like rubbery spikes from a deep cleft in a great rock: a more promising scene, perhaps.

But in the morning he found excuses for delaying his departure, and by noon it seemed too late to go. He worked in his little garden plot instead—he had begun transplanting some of the shrubs whose fruits or greens he ate—and that occupied him for hours. In late afternoon a milky fog settled over the forest. He went in; and a few minutes later there was a knock at the door.

"I had given up hope," he told her.

Sarise's forehead and brows were beaded with moisture. The fog, he thought, or maybe she had been dancing along the path. "I promised I'd come," she said softly.

"Yesterday."

"This is yesterday," she said, laughing, and drew a flask from her robe. "You like wine? I found some of this. I had to go a long distance to get it. Yesterday."

It was a young gray wine, the kind that tickles the tongue with its sparkle. The flask had no label, but he supposed it to be some Zimroel wine, unknown on Castle Mount. They drank it all, he more than she— she filled his cup again and again—and when it was gone they lurched outside to make love on the cool, damp ground beside the stream, and fell into a doze afterward, she waking him in some small hour of the night and leading him to his bed. They spent the rest of the night pressed close to one another, and in the morning she showed no desire to leave. They went to the pool to begin the day with a swim; they embraced again on the turquoise moss; then she guided him to the gigantic red-barked tree where he had first seen her, and pointed out to him a colossal yellow fruit, three or four yards across, that had fallen from one of its enormous branches. Nismile looked at it doubtfully. It had split open, and its interior was a scarlet custardy stuff, studded with huge, gleaming black seeds. "Dwikka," she said. "It will make us drunk." She stripped off her robe and used it to wrap great chunks of the dwikka-fruit, which they carried back to his cabin and spent all morning eating. They sang and laughed most of the afternoon. For dinner they grilled some fish from Nismile's weir, and later, as they lay arm in arm watching the night descend, she asked him a thousand questions about his past life, his painting, his boyhood, his travels, about Castle Mount, the Fifty Cities, the Six Rivers, the royal court of Lord Thraym, the royal Castle of uncountable rooms. The questions came from her in a torrent, the newest one rushing forth almost before he had dealt with the last. Her curiosity was inexhaustible. It served, also, to stifle his; for although there was much he yearned to know about her—everything—he had no chance to ask it, and just as well, for he doubted she would give him answers.

"What will we do tomorrow?" she asked, finally.

So they became lovers. For the first few days they did little but eat and swim and embrace and devour the intoxicating fruit of the dwikka-tree. He ceased to fear, as he had at the beginning, that she would disappear as suddenly as she had come to him. Her flood of questions subsided, after a time, but even so he chose not to take his turn, preferring to leave her mysteries unpierced.

He could not shake his obsession with the idea that she was a Metamorph. The thought chilled him—that her beauty was a lie, that behind it she was alien and grotesque—especially when he ran his hands over the cool, sweet smoothness of her thighs or breasts. He had constantly to fight away his suspicions. But they would not leave him. There were no human outposts in this part of Zimroel and it was too implausible that this girl—for that was all she was, a girl—had elected, as he had, to take up a hermit's life here. Far more likely, Nismile thought, that she was native to this place, one of the unknown number of Shapeshifters who slipped like phantoms through these humid groves. When she slept he sometimes watched her by faint starlight to see if she began to lose human form. Always she remained as she was; and even so, he suspected her.

And yet, and yet, it was not in the nature of Metamorphs to seek human company or to show warmth toward them. To most people of Majipoor the Metamorphs were ghosts of a former era, revenants, unreal, legendary. Why would one seek him out in his seclusion, offer itself to him in so convincing a counterfeit of love, strive with such zeal to brighten his days and enliven his nights? In a moment of paranoia he imagined Sarise reverting in the darkness to her true shape and rising above him as he slept to plunge a gleaming dirk into his throat: revenge for the crimes of his ancestors. But what folly such fantasies were! If the Metamorphs here wanted to murder him, they had no need of such elaborate charades.

It was almost as absurd to believe that she was a Metamorph as to believe that she was not.

To put these matters from his mind he resolved to take up his art again. On an unusually clear and sunny day he set out with Sarise for the rock of the red succulents, carrying a raw canvas. She watched, fascinated, as he prepared everything.

"You do the painting entirely with your mind?" she asked.

"Entirely. I fix the scene in my soul, I transform and rearrange and heighten, and then—you'll see."

"It's all right if I watch? I won't spoil it?"

"Of course not."

"But if someone else's mind gets into the painting—"

"It can't happen. The canvases are tuned to me." He squinted, made frames with his fingers, moved a few feet this way and that. His throat was dry and his hands were quivering. So many years since last he had done this: would he still have the gift? And the technique? He aligned the canvas and touched it in a preliminary way with his mind. The scene was a good one, vivid, bizarre, the color contrasts powerful ones, the compositional aspects challenging, that massive rock, those weird meaty red plants, the tiny yellow floral bracts at their tips, the forest-dappled sunlight—yes, yes, it would work, it would amply serve as the vehicle through which he could convey the texture of this dense tangled jungle, this place of shapeshifting—

He closed his eyes. He entered trance. He hurled the picture to the canvas.

Sarise uttered a small surprised cry.

Nismile felt sweat break out all over; he staggered and fought for breath; after a moment he regained control and looked toward the canvas.

"How beautiful!" Sarise murmured.

But he was shaken by what he saw. Those dizzying diagonals—the blurred and streaked colors—the heavy greasy sky, hanging in sullen loops from the horizon—it looked nothing like the scene he had tried to capture, and, far more troublesome, nothing like the work of Therion Nismile. It was a dark and anguished painting, corrupted by unintended discords.

"You don't like it?" she asked.

"It isn't what I had in mind."

"Even so—how wonderful, to make the picture come out on the canvas like that—and such a lovely thing—"

"You think it's lovely?"

"Yes, of course! Don't you?"

He stared at her. This? Lovely? Was she flattering him, or merely ignorant of prevailing tastes, or did she genuinely admire what he had done? This strange tormented painting, this somber and alien work—

Alien.

"You don't like it," she said, not a question this time.

"I haven't painted in almost four years. Maybe I need to go about it slowly, to get the way of it right again—"

"I spoiled your painting," Sarise said.

"You? Don't be silly."

"My mind got mixed into it. My way of seeing things."

"I told you that the canvases are tuned to me alone. I could be in the midst of a thousand people and nothing of them would affect the painting."

"But perhaps I distracted you, I swerved your mind somehow."

"Nonsense."

"I'll go for a walk. Paint another one while I'm gone."

"No, Sarise. This one is splendid. The more I look at it, the more pleased I am. Come—let's go home; let's swim and eat some dwikka and make love. Yes?"

He took the canvas from its mount and rolled it. But what she had said affected him more than he would admit. Some kind of strangeness *had* entered the painting, no doubt of it. What if she had managed somehow to taint it, her hidden Metamorph soul radiating its essence into his spirit, coloring the impulses of his mind with an alien hue—

They walked downstream in silence. When they reached the meadow of the mud-lilies where Nismile had seen his first Metamorph, he heard himself blurt, "Sarise, I have to ask you something."

"Yes?"

He could not halt himself. "You aren't human, are you? You're really a Metamorph, right?"

She stared at him wide-eyed, color rising in her cheeks.

"Are you serious?"

He nodded.

"Me a Metamorph?" She laughed, not very convincingly. "What a wild idea!"

"Answer me, Sarise. Look into my eyes and answer me."

"It's too foolish, Therion."

"Please. Answer me."

"You want me to prove I'm human? How could I?"

"I want you to tell me that you're human. Or that you're something else."

"I'm human," she said.

"Can I believe that?"

"I don't know. Can you? I've given you your answer." Her eyes flashed with mirth. "Don't I feel human? Don't I act human? Do I seem like an imitation?"

"Perhaps I'm unable to tell the difference."

"Why do you think I'm a Metamorph?"

"Because only Metamorphs live in this jungle," he said. "It seems—

logical. Even though—despite—" He faltered. "Look, I've had my answer. It was a stupid question and I'd like to drop the subject. All right?"

"How strange you are! You must be angry with me. You do think I
spoiled your painting."

"That's not so."

"You're a very poor liar, Therion."

"All right. *Something* spoiled my painting. I don't know what. It
wasn't the painting I intended."

"Paint another one, then."

"I will. Let me paint you, Sarise."

"I told you I didn't want to be painted."

"I need to. I need to see what's in my own soul, and the only way I
can know—"

"Paint the dwikka-tree, Therion. Paint the cabin."

"Why not paint you?"

"The idea makes me uncomfortable."

"You aren't giving me a real answer. What is there about being
painted that—"

"Please, Therion."

"Are you afraid I'll see you on the canvas in a way that you won't
like? Is that it? That I'll get a different answer to my questions when I
paint you?"

"Please."

"Let me paint you."

"No."

"Give me a reason, then."

"I can't," she said.

"Then you can't refuse." He drew a canvas from his pack. "Here, in
the meadow, now. Go on, Sarise. Stand beside the stream. It'll take only
a moment—"

"No, Therion."

"If you love me, Sarise, you'll let me paint you."

It was a clumsy bit of blackmail, and it shamed him to have attempted it; and angered her, for he saw a harsh glitter in her eyes that

he had never seen before. They confronted each other for a long, tense moment.

Then she said in a cold, flat voice, "Not here, Therion. At the cabin. I'll let you paint me there, if you insist."

Neither of them spoke the rest of the way home.

He was tempted to forget the whole thing. It seemed to him that he had imposed his will by force, that he had committed a sort of rape, and he almost wished he could retreat from the position he had won. But there would never now be any going back to the old easy harmony between them; and he had to have the answers he needed. Uneasily he set about preparing a canvas.

"Where shall I stand?" she asked.

"Anywhere. By the stream. By the cabin."

In a slouching slack-limbed way she moved toward the cabin. He nodded and dispiritedly began the final steps before entering trance. Sarise glowered at him. Tears were welling in her eyes.

"I love you," he cried abruptly, and went down into trance, and the last thing he saw before he closed his eyes was Sarise altering her pose, coming out of her moody slouch, squaring her shoulders, eyes suddenly bright, smile flashing.

When he opened his eyes the painting was done and Sarise was staring timidly at him from the cabin door.

"How is it?" she asked.

"Come. See for yourself."

She walked to his side. They examined the picture together, and after a moment Nismile slipped his arm around her shoulder. She shivered and moved closer to him.

The painting showed a woman with human eyes and Metamorph mouth and nose, against a jagged and chaotic background of clashing reds and oranges and pinks.

She said quietly, "Now do you know what you wanted to know?"

"Was it you in the meadow? And the other two times?"

"Yes."

"Why?"

"You interested me, Therion. I wanted to know all about you. I had never seen anything like you."

"I still don't believe it," he whispered.

She pointed toward the painting. "Believe it, Therion."

"No. No."

"You have your answer now."

"I *know* you're human. The painting lies."

"No, Therion."

"Prove it for me. Change for me. Change now." He released her and stepped a short way back. "Do it. Change for me."

She looked at him sadly. Then, without perceptible transition, she turned herself into a replica of him, as she had done once before: the final proof, the unanswerable answer. A muscle quivered wildly in his cheek. He watched her unblinkingly and she changed again, this time into something terrifying and monstrous, a nightmarish gray pockmarked balloon of a thing with flabby skin and eyes like saucers and a hooked black beak; and from that she went to the Metamorph form, taller than he, hollow-chested and featureless, and then she was Sarise once more, cascades of auburn hair, delicate hands, and firm, strong thighs.

"No," he said. "Not that one. No more counterfeits."

She became the Metamorph again.

He nodded. "Yes. That's better. Stay that way. It's more beautiful."

"Beautiful, Therion?"

"I find you beautiful. Like this. As you really are. Deception is always ugly."

He reached for her hand. It had six fingers, very long and narrow, without fingernails or visible joints. Her skin was silky and faintly glossy, and it felt not at all as he had expected. He ran his hands lightly over her slim, practically fleshless body. She was altogether motionless.

"I should go now," she said at last.

"Stay with me. Live here with me."

"Even now?"

"Even now. In your true form."

"You still want me?"

"Very much," he said. "Will you stay?"

She said, "When I first came to you, it was to watch you, to study you, to play with you, perhaps even to mock and hurt you. You are the enemy, Therion. Your kind must always be the enemy. But as we began to live together I saw there was no reason to hate you. Not *you*, you as a special individual—do you understand?"

It was the voice of Sarise coming from those alien lips. How strange, he thought, how much like a dream.

She said, "I began to want to be with you. To make the game go on forever—do you follow? But the game had to end. And yet I still want to be with you."

"Then stay, Sarise."

"Only if you truly want me."

"I've told you that."

"I don't horrify you?"

"No."

"Paint me again, Therion. Show me with a painting. Show me love on the canvas, Therion, and then I'll stay."

HE PAINTED HER DAY after day, until he had used every canvas, and hung them all about the interior of the cabin, Sarise and the dwikka-tree, Sarise in the meadow, Sarise against the milky fog of evening, Sarise at twilight, green against purple. There was no way he could prepare more canvases, although he tried. It did not really matter. They began to go on long voyages of exploration together, down one stream and another, into distant parts of the forest, and she showed him new trees and flowers, and the creatures of the jungle, the toothy lizards and the burrowing golden worms and the sinister ponderous amorfibots sleeping away their days in muddy lakes. They said little to one another; the time for answering questions was over and words were no longer needed.

Day slipped into day, week into week, and in this land of no seasons it was difficult to measure the passing of time. Perhaps a month went by, perhaps six. They encountered nobody else. The jungle was full of Metamorphs, she told him, but they were keeping their distance, and she hoped they would leave them alone forever.

One afternoon of steady drizzle he went out to check his traps, and when he returned an hour later he knew at once something was wrong. As he approached the cabin four Metamorphs emerged. He felt sure that one was Sarise, but he could not tell which one. "Wait!" he cried, as they moved past him. He ran after them. "What do you want with her? Let her go! Sarise? Sarise? Who are they? What do they want?"

For just an instant one of the Metamorphs flickered and he saw the girl with the auburn hair, but only for an instant; then there were four Metamorphs again, gliding like ghosts toward the depths of the jungle. The rain grew more intense, and a heavy fog-bank drifted in, cutting off all visibility. Nismile paused at the edge of the clearing, straining desperately for sounds over the patter of the rain and the loud throb of the stream. He imagined he heard weeping; he thought he heard a cry of pain, but it might have been any other sort of forest-sound. There was no hope of following the Metamorphs into that impenetrable zone of thick white mist.

He never saw Sarise again, nor any other Metamorph. For a while he hoped he would come upon Shapeshifters in the forest and be slain by them with their little polished dirks, for the loneliness was intolerable now. But that did not happen, and when it became obvious that he was living in a sort of quarantine, cut off not only from Sarise—if she was still alive—but from the entire society of the Metamorph folk, he found himself unable any longer to dwell in the clearing beside the stream. He rolled up his paintings of Sarise and carefully dismantled his cabin and began the long and perilous journey back to civilization. It was a week before his fiftieth birthday when he reached the borders of Castle Mount. In his absence, he discovered, Lord Thraym had become Pontifex and the new Coronal was Lord Vildivar, a man of little sympathy with the arts. Nismile rented a studio on the riverbank at Stee and began to paint again. He worked only from memory: dark and disturbing scenes of jungle life, often showing Metamorphs lurking in the middle distance. It was not the sort of work likely to be popular on the cheerful and airy world of Majipoor, and Nismile found few buyers at first. But in time his paintings caught the fancy of the Duke of Qurain, who had begun to weary of sunny serenity and perfect proportion. Under the duke's patronage Nismile's work grew fashionable, and in the later years of his life there was a ready market for everything he produced.

He was widely imitated, though never successfully, and he was the subject of many critical essays and biographical studies. "Your paintings are so turbulent and strange," one scholar said to him. "Have you devised some method of working from dreams?"

"I work only from memory," said Nismile.

"From painful memory, I would be so bold as to venture."

"Not at all," answered Nismile. "All my work is intended to help me recapture a time of joy, a time of love, the happiest and most precious moment of my life." He stared past the questioner into distant mists, thick and soft as wool, that swirled through clumps of tall slender trees bound by a tangled network of vines.

SEVEN

Crime and Punishment

That one takes him back to the beginning of his explorations of these ar-chives. Thesme and the Ghayrog all over again, another forest romance, the love of human and non-human. Yet the similarities are all on the surface, for these were very different people in very different circumstances. Hissune comes away from the tale with what he thinks is a reasonably good understand-ing of the soul-painter Therion Nismile—some of whose works, he learns, are still on display in the galleries of Lord Valentine's Castle—but the Metamorph is a mystery to him still, as great a mystery perhaps as she had been to Nismile. He checks the index for recordings of Metamorph souls, but is unsurprised to find that there are none. Do the Shapeshifters refuse to record, or is the appa-ratus incapable of picking up the emanations of their minds, or are they merely banned from the archives? Hissune does not know and he is unable to find out. In time, he tells himself, all things will be answered. Meanwhile there is much more to discover. The operations of the King of Dreams, for instance—he needs to learn much more about those. For a thousand years the descendants of the Barjazids have had the task of lashing the sleeping minds of criminals; Hissune wonders how it is done. He prowls the archives, and before long fortune deliv-ers up to him the soul of an outlaw, disguised drearily as a tradesman of the city of Stee—

THE MURDER WAS AMAZINGLY easy to commit. Little Gleim was standing by the open window of the little upstairs room of the tavern in Vugel where he and Haligome had agreed to meet. Haligome was near the couch. The discussion was not going well. Haligome asked Gleim once more to reconsider.

Gleim shrugged and said, "You're wasting your time and mine. I don't see where you have any case at all."

At that moment it seemed to Haligome that Gleim and Gleim alone stood between him and the tranquillity of life that he felt he deserved, that Gleim was his enemy, his nemesis, his persecutor. Calmly Haligome walked toward him, so calmly that Gleim evidently was not in the least alarmed, and with a sudden smooth motion he pushed Gleim over the windowsill.

Gleim looked amazed. He hung as if suspended in midair for a surprisingly long moment; then he dropped toward the swiftly flowing river just outside the tavern, hit the water with scarcely a splash, and was carried away rapidly toward the distant foothills of Castle Mount. In an instant he was lost to view.

Haligome looked at his hands as though they had just sprouted on his wrists. He could not believe they had done what they had done. Again he saw himself walking toward Gleim; again he saw Gleim standing bewildered on air; again he saw Gleim vanish into the dark river. Probably Gleim was already dead. If not, then within another minute or two. They would find him sooner or later, Haligome knew, washed up on some rocky shore down by Canzilaine or Perimor, and somehow they would identify him as a merchant of Gimkandale, missing the past week or ten days. But would there be any reason for them to suspect he had been murdered? Murder was an uncommon crime. He could have fallen. He could have jumped. Even if they managed to prove—the Divine only knew how—that Gleim had gone unwillingly to his death, how could they demonstrate that he had been pushed from the window of a tavern in Vugel by Sigmar Haligome of the city of Stee? They could not, Haligome told himself. But that did not change the essential truth of the situation, which was that Gleim had been murdered and Haligome was his murderer.

His murderer? That new label astonished Haligome. He had not come here to kill Gleim, only to negotiate with him. But the negotiations had been sour from the start. Gleim, a small, fastidious man, refused entirely to admit liability over a matter of defective equipment, and said that it must have been Haligome's inspectors who were at fault. He refused to pay a thing, or even to show much sympathy for Haligome's awkward financial plight. At that final bland refusal Gleim appeared to swell until he filled all the horizon, and all of him was loathsome, and Haligome wished only to be rid of him, whatever the cost. If he had stopped to think about his act and its consequences he would not, of course, have pushed Gleim out the window, for Haligome was not in any way a murderous man. But he had not stopped to think, and now Gleim was dead and Haligome's life had undergone a grotesque redefinition: he had transformed himself in a moment from Haligome the jobber of precision instruments to Haligome the murderer. How sudden! How strange! How terrifying!

And now?

Trembling, sweating, dry-throated, Haligome closed the window and dropped down on the couch. He had no idea of what he was supposed to do next. Report himself to the imperial proctors? Confess, surrender, and enter prison, or wherever it was that criminals were sent? He had no preparation for any of this. He had read old stories of crimes and punishments, ancient myths and fables, but so far as he knew murder was an extinct crime and the mechanisms for its detection and expiation had long ago rusted away. He felt prehistoric; he felt primeval. There was that famous story of a sea-captain of the remote past who had pushed a crazed crewman overboard during an ill-fated expedition across the Great Sea, after that crewman had killed someone else. Such tales had always seemed wild and implausible to Haligome. But now, effortlessly, unthinkingly, he had made himself a legendary figure, a monster, a taker of human life. He knew that nothing would ever again be the same for him.

One thing to do was to get away from the tavern. If someone had seen Gleim fall—not likely, for the tavern stood flush against the riverbank; Gleim had gone out a back window and had been swallowed up at once by the rushing flow—there was no point in standing around here waiting for investigators to arrive. Quickly he packed his one small suitcase, checked to see that nothing of Gleim's was in the room, and went downstairs. There was a Hjort at the desk. Haligome produced a few crowns and said, "I'd like to settle my account."

He resisted the impulse to chatter. This was not the moment to make clever remarks that might imprint him on the Hjort's memory. Pay your bill and clear out fast, he thought. Was the Hjort aware that the visitor from Stee had entertained a guest in his room? Well, the Hjort would quickly enough forget that, and the visitor from Stee as well, if Haligome gave him no reason to remember. The clerk totaled the figures; Haligome handed over some coins; to the Hjort's mechanical "Please come again" Haligome made an equally mechanical reply, and then he was out on the street, walking briskly away from the river. A strong sweet breeze was blowing downslope. The sunlight was bright and warm. It was years since Haligome had last been in Vugel, and at another time he might well have taken a few hours to tour its famous jeweled plaza, its celebrated soul-painting murals, and the other local wonders, but this was not the moment for tourism. He hurried to the transit terminal and bought a one-way ticket back to Stee.

Fear, uncertainty, guilt, and shame rode with him on the journey around the flank of Castle Mount from city to city.

The familiar sprawling outskirts of gigantic Stee brought him some repose. To be home meant to be safe. With each new day of his entry into Stee he felt more comfort. There was the mighty river for which the city was named, tumbling in astonishing velocity down the Mount. There were the smooth, shining facades of the Riverwall Buildings, forty stories high and miles in length. There was Kinniken Bridge; there was Thimin Tower; there was the Field of Great Bones. Home! The enormous vitality and power of Stee, throbbing all about him as he made his way from the central terminal to his suburban district, comforted him greatly. Surely here in what had become the greatest city of Majipoor—vastly expanded, thanks to the beneficence of its native son who was now the Coronal Lord Kinniken—Haligome was safe from the dark consequences, whatever they might be, of the lunatic deed he had committed in Vugel.

He embraced his wife, his two young daughters, his sturdy son. They could readily see his fatigue and tension, it appeared, for they treated him with a kind of exaggerated delicacy, as though he had become newly fragile on his journey. They brought him wine, a pipe, slippers; they bustled round, radiating love and goodwill; they asked him nothing about how his trip had gone, but regaled him instead with local gossip. Not until dinner did he say at last, "I think Gleim and I worked everything out. There's reason to be hopeful."

He nearly believed it himself.

Was there any way the murder could be laid to him, if he simply kept quiet about it? He doubted that there could have been witnesses. It would not be hard for the authorities to discover that he and Gleim had agreed to meet in Vugel—neutral ground—to discuss their business disagreements, but what did that prove? "Yes, I saw him in some tavern near the river," Haligome could say. "We had lunch and drank a lot of wine and came to an understanding, and then I went away. He looked pretty wobbly when I left, I must say." And poor Gleim, flushed and staggering with a bellyful of the strong wine of Muldemar, must have leaned too far out the window afterward, perhaps for a view of some elegant lord and lady sailing past on the river—no, no, no, let *them* do all the speculating, Haligome told himself. "We met for lunch and reached a settlement, and then I went away," and nothing more than that. And who could prove it had been otherwise?

He returned to his office the next day and went about his business as though nothing unusual had happened in Vugel. He could not allow himself the luxury of brooding over his crime. Things were precarious: he was close to bankrupt, his credit overextended, his plausibility with his prime accounts sadly diminished. All that was Gleim's doing. Once you ship shoddy goods, though, you go on suffering for it for a long time, no matter how blameless you may be. Having had no satisfaction from Gleim—and not likely to get any, now—Haligome's only recourse was to strive with intense dedication to rebuild the confidence of those whom he supplied with precision instruments, while at the same time struggling to hold off his creditors until matters returned to equilibrium.

Keeping Gleim out of his mind was difficult. Over the next few days his name kept coming up, and Haligome had to work hard to conceal his reactions. Everyone in the trade seemed to understand that Gleim had taken Haligome for a fool, and everyone was trying to seem sympathetic.

That in itself was encouraging. But to have every conversation somehow wander around to Gleim—Gleim's iniquities, Gleim's vindictiveness, Gleim's tightfistedness—threw Haligome constantly off balance. The name was like a trigger. *"Gleim!"* and he would go rigid. *"Gleim!"* and muscles would throb in his cheeks. *"Gleim!"* and he would thrust his hands out of sight behind him, as if they bore the imprint of the dead man's aura. He imagined himself saying to some client, in a moment of sheer weariness, "I killed him, you know. I pushed him out a window when I was in Vugel." How easily the words would flow from his lips, if only he relaxed his control!

He thought of making a pilgrimage to the Isle to cleanse his soul. Later, perhaps: not now, for now he had to devote every waking moment to his business affairs, or his firm would collapse and his family would fall into poverty. He thought also of confessing and coming quickly to some understanding with the authorities that would allow him to atone for the crime without disrupting his commercial activities. A fine, maybe—though how could he afford a fine now? And would they let him off so lightly? In the end he did nothing at all except to try to shove the murder out of his consciousness, and for a week or ten days that actually seemed to work. And then the dreams began.

The first one came on Starday night in the second week of summer, and Haligome knew instantly that it was a sending of a dark and painful kind. He was in his third sleep, the deepest of the night just before the mind's ascent into dawn, and he found himself crossing a field of gleaming and slippery yellow teeth that churned and writhed beneath his feet. The air was foul, swamp air of a discouraging grayish hue, and ropy strands of some raw meaty substance dangled from the sky, brushing against his cheeks and arms and leaving sticky tracks that burned and throbbed. There was a ringing in his ears: the harsh, tense silence of a malign sending, that makes it seem as though the world has been drawn far too tight on its drawstrings, and beyond that a distant jeering laughter. An intolerably bright light seared the sky. He was traversing a mouthplant, he realized—one of those hideous carnivorous floral monsters of far-off Zimroel, that he once had seen exhibited in a show of curios at the Kinniken Pavilion. But those were only three or four yards in diameter, and this was the size of a goodly suburb, and he was trapped in its diabolical core, running as fast as he could to keep from slipping down into those mercilessly grinding teeth.

So this is how it will be, he thought, floating above his dream and bleakly surveying it. This is the first sending, and the King of Dreams will torment me hereafter.

There was no hiding from it. The teeth had eyes, and the eyes were the eyes of Gleim, and Haligome was scrambling and sliding and sweating, and now he pitched forward and tumbled against a bank of the remorseless teeth and they nipped his hand, and when he was able to get to his feet again he saw that the bloody hand was no longer his own familiar one, but had been transformed into the small, pale hand of Gleim, fitting badly on his wrist. Again Haligome fell, and again the teeth nipped at him, and again came an unwelcome metamorphosis, and again, and again, and he ran onward, sobbing and moaning, half Gleim, half Haligome, until he broke from his sleep and discovered himself sitting up, trembling, sweat soaked, clutching his astounded wife's thigh as though it were a lifeline.

"Don't," she murmured. "You're hurting me. What is it? What is it?"

"Dream—very bad—"

"A sending?" she asked. "Yes, it must have been. I can smell the odor of it in your sweat. Oh, Sigmar, what was it?"

He shuddered. "Something I ate. The sea-dragon meat—it was too dry, too old—"

He left the bed unsteadily and poured a little wine, which calmed him. His wife stroked him and bathed his feverish forehead and held him until he relaxed a little, but he feared going back to sleep, and lay awake until dawn, staring into the gray darkness. The King of Dreams! So this was to be his punishment. Bleakly he considered things. He had always believed that the King of Dreams was only a fable to keep children in line. Yes, yes, they said that he lived in Suvrael, that the title was the hereditary holding of the Barjazid family, that the King and his minions scanned the night air for the guilts of sleepers, and found the souls of the unworthy and tormented them, but was it so? Haligome had never known anyone to have a sending from the King of Dreams. He thought he might once have had one from the Lady, but he was not sure of that, and in any case that was different. The Lady offered only the most general kind of visions. The King of Dreams was said to inflict real pain; but could the King of Dreams really monitor the entire teeming planet, with its billions of citizens, not all of them virtuous?

Possibly it was only indigestion, Haligome told himself.

When the next night and the next passed calmly, he allowed himself to believe that the dream had been no more than a random anomaly. The King might only be a fable after all. But on Twoday came another unmistakable sending.

The same silent ringing sound. The same fierce, glaring light illuminating the landscape of sleep. Images of Gleim; laughter; echoes; swellings and contractions of the fabric of the cosmos; a wrenching giddiness blasting his spirit with terrible vertigo. Haligome whimpered. He buried his face against the pillow and fought for breath. He dared not awaken, for if he surfaced he would inevitably reveal his distress to his wife, and she would suggest that he take his dreams to a speaker, and he could not do that. Any speaker worth her fee would know at once that she was joining her soul with the soul of a criminal, and what would happen to him then? So he suffered his nightmare until the force of it was spent, and only then he awakened, to lie limp and quivering until the coming of the day.

That was Twoday's nightmare. Fourday's was worse: Haligome soared and dropped and was impaled on the ultimate summit of Castle Mount, spear-sharp and cold as ice, and lay there for hours while gihorna-birds with the face of Gleim ripped at his belly and bombarded his dripping wounds with blazing droppings. Fiveday he slept reasonably well, though he was tense, on guard for dreams; Starday too brought no sendings; Sunday found him swimming through oceans of clotted blood while his teeth loosened and his fingers turned to strips of ragged dough; Moonday and Twoday brought milder horrors, but horrors all the same; on Seaday morning his wife said, "These dreams of yours will not relent. Sigmar, what have you done?"

"Done? I've done nothing!"

"I feel the sendings surging through you night after night."

He shrugged. "Some mistake has been made by the Powers that govern us. It must happen occasionally: dreams meant for some child-molester of Pendiwane are delivered to a jobber of precision instruments in Stee. Sooner or later they'll see the error and leave me alone."

"And if they don't?" She gave him a penetrating glance. "And if the dreams are meant for you?"

He wondered if she knew the truth. She was aware that he had gone to Vugel to confer with Gleim; possibly, though it was hard to imagine how, she had learned that Gleim had never returned to his home in Gimkandale; her husband now was receiving sendings of the King of Dreams; she could draw her own conclusions all too readily. Could it be? And if so, what would she do? Denounce her own husband? Though she loved him, she might well do that, for if she let herself harbor a murderer, she might bring the vengeance of the King upon her own sleep as well.

He said, "If the dreams continue, I will ask the officials of the Pontifex to intercede on my behalf."

Of course he could not do that. He tried instead to grapple with the dreams and repress them, so that he would arouse no suspicion in the woman who slept by his side. In his pre-sleep meditations he instructed himself to be calm, to accept what images might come, to regard them only as fantasies of a disordered soul, and not as realities with which he needed to cope. And yet when he found himself floating over a red sea of fire, dipping now and then ankle-deep, he could not keep from screaming; and when needles grew outward from his flesh and burst through his skin so that he looked like a manculain, that untouchable spiny beast of the torrid southlands, he whimpered and begged for mercy in his sleep; and when he strolled through the immaculate gardens of Lord Havilbove by Tolingar Barrier and the flawless shrubs became mocking, toothy, hairy things of sinister ugliness, he wept and broke into torrents of sweat that made the mattress reek. His wife asked no more questions, but she eyed him uneasily and seemed constantly on the verge of demanding how long he intended to tolerate these intrusions on his spirit.

He could scarcely operate his business. Creditors hovered; manufacturers balked at extending further credit; customer complaints swirled about him like dead and withered autumn leaves. Secretly he burrowed in the libraries for information about the King of Dreams and his powers, as though this were some strange new disease that he had contracted and about which he needed to learn everything. But the information was scanty and obvious: the King was an agency of the government, a Power equal in authority to the Pontifex and the Coronal and the Lady of the Isle, and for hundreds of years it had been his role to impose punishment on the guilty.

There has been no trial, Haligome protested silently—

But he knew none was needed, and plainly the King knew that, too. And as the dread dreams continued, grinding down Haligome's soul and fraying his nerves to threads, he saw that there was no hope of withstanding these sendings. His life in Stee was ended. One moment of rashness and he had made himself an outcast, doomed to wander across the vast face of the planet, searching for someplace to hide.

"I need a rest," he told his wife. "I will travel abroad a month or two, and regain my inner peace." He called his son to his side—the boy was almost a man; he could handle the responsibilities now—and turned the business over to him, giving him in an hour a list of maxims that had taken him half a lifetime to learn. Then, with such little cash as he could squeeze from his greatly diminished assets, he set forth out of his splendid native city, aboard the third-class floater bound for—at random—Normork, in the ring of Slope Cities near the foot of Castle Mount. An hour into his journey he resolved never to call himself Sigmar Haligome again, and renamed himself Miklan Forb. Would that be sufficient to divert the force of the King of Dreams?

Perhaps so. The floater drifted across the face of Castle Mount, lazily descending from Stee to Normork by way of Lower Sunbreak, Bibiroon Sweep, and Tolingar Barrier, and at each night's hostelry he went to bed clutching his pillow with terror, but the only dreams that came were the ordinary ones of a tired and fretful man, without that pecular ghastly intensity that typified sendings of the King. It was pleasant to observe that the gardens of Tolingar Barrier were symmetrical and perfectly tidy, nothing at all like the hideous wastelands of his dream. Haligome began to relax a bit. He compared the gardens with the dream-images, and was surprised to see that the King had provided him with a rich and detailed and accurate view of those gardens just before transforming them into horror, complete to the most minute degree; but he had never before seen them, which meant that the sending had transmitted into his mind an entire cluster of data new to him, whereas ordinary dreams merely called upon that which already was recorded there.

That answered a question that had troubled him. He had not known whether the King was simply liberating the detritus of his unconscious, stirring the murky depths from afar, or was actually beaming imagery into it. Evidently the latter was the case. But that begged another query: were the nightmares specifically designed for Sigmar Haligome, crafted by specialists to stir his particular terrors? Surely there could not be personnel enough in Suvrael to handle that job. But if there were, it meant that they were monitoring him closely, and it was folly to think he could hide from them. He preferred to believe that the King and his minions had a roster of standard nightmares—send him the teeth, send him the gray greasy blobs, now send him the sea of fire—that were brought forth in succession for each malefactor, an impersonal and mechanical operation. Possibly even now they were aiming some grisly phantasms at his empty pillow in Stee.

He came up past Dundilmir and Stipool to Normork, that somber and hermetic walled city perched atop the formidable fangs of Normork Crest. It had not consciously occurred to him before that Normork, with its huge circumvallation of cyclopean blocks of black stone, had the appropriate qualities for a hiding-place: protected, secure, impregnable. But of course not even the walls of Normork could keep out the vengeful shafts of the King of Dreams, he realized.

The Dekkeret Gate, an eye in the wall fifty feet high, stood open as always, the one breach in the fortification, polished black wood bound with a Coronal's ransom of iron bands. Haligome would have preferred that it be closed and triple-locked as well, but of course the great gate was open, for Lord Dekkeret, constructing it in the thirtieth year of his auspicious reign, had decreed that it be closed only at a time when the world was in peril, and these days under the happy guidance of Lord Kinniken and the Pontifex Thimin everything flourished on Majipoor, save only the troubled soul of the former Sigmar Haligome, who called himself Miklan Forb. As Forb he found cheap lodgings on the slopeside quarter of the city, where Castle Mount reared up behind like a second wall of immeasurable height. As Forb he took a job with the maintenance crew that patrolled the city wall day after day, digging the tenacious wireweed out from between the unmortared masonry. As Forb he sank down into sleep each night fearful of what would come, but what came, week after week, was only the blurred and meaningless dreamery of ordinary slumber. For nine months he lived submerged in Normork, wondering if he had escaped the hand of Suvrael; and then one night after a pleasant meal and a flask of fine crimson wine of Bannikanniklole he tumbled into bed feeling entirely happy for the first time since long before his baleful meeting with Gleim, and dropped unwarily to sleep, and a sending of the King came to him and seized his soul by the throat and flailed him with monstrous images of melting flesh and rivers of slime. When the dream was done with him he awoke weeping, for he knew that there was no hiding for long from the avenging Power that pursued him.

Yet life as Miklan Forb had been good for nine months of peace. With his small savings he bought a ticket downslope to Amblemorn, where he became Degrail Gilalin, and earned ten crowns a week as a bird-limer on the estate of a local prince. He had five months of freedom from torment, until the night when sleep brought him the crackle of silence and the fury of limitless light and the vision of an arch of disembodied eyes strung like a bridge across the universe, all those eyes watching only him. He journeyed along the River Glayge to Makroprosopos, where he lived a month unscathed as Ogvorn Brill before the coming of a dream of crystals of fiery metal multiplying like hair in his throat. Overland through the arid inlands he went as part of a caravan to the market city of Sisivondal, which was a journey of eleven weeks. The King of Dreams found him in the seventh of those and sent him out screaming at night to roll about in a thicket of whipstaff plants, and that was no dream, for he was bleeding and swollen when he finally broke free from the plants, and had to be carried to the next village for medicines. Those with whom he traveled knew that he was one who had sendings of the King, and they left him behind; but eventually he found his way to Sisivondal, a drab and monochromatic place so different from the splendid cities of Castle Mount that he wept each morning at the sight of it. But all the same he stayed there six months without incident. Then the dreams came back and drove him westward, a month here and six weeks there, through nine cities and as many identities, until at last to Alaisor on the coast, where he had a year of tranquillity under the name of Badril Maganorn, gutting fish in a dockside market. Despite his forebodings he allowed himself to begin believing that the King was at last done with him, and he speculated on the possibility of returning to his old life in Stee, from which he had now been absent almost four years. Was four years of punishment not enough for an unpremeditated, almost accidental crime?

Evidently not. Early in his second year at Alaisor he felt the familiar ominous buzz of a sending throbbing behind the wall of his skull, and there came upon him a dream that made all the previous ones seem like children's holiday theatricals. It began in the bleak wastelands of Suvrael, where he stood on a jagged peak looking across a dry and blasted valley at a forest of sigupa trees that gave off an emanation fatal to all life that came within ten miles, even unwary birds and insects that flew above the thick, drooping branches. His wife and children could be seen in the valley, marching steadily toward the deadly trees; he ran toward them, in sand that clung like molasses, and the trees stirred and beckoned, and his loved ones were swallowed up in their dark radiance and fell and vanished entirely. But he continued onward until he was within the grim perimeter. He prayed for death, but he alone was immune to the trees. He came among them, each isolated and remote from the others, and nothing growing about them, no shrubs nor vines nor ground-covers, merely a long array of ugly leafless trees standing like palisades in the midst of nowhere. That was all there was to the dream, but it carried a burden of frightfulness far beyond all the grotesqueries of image that he had endured before, and it went on and on, Haligome wandering forlorn and solitary among those barren trees as though in an airless void, and when he awakened his face was withered and his eyes were quivering as if he had aged a dozen years between night and dawn.

He was defeated utterly. Running was useless; hiding was futile. He belonged to the King of Dreams forever.

No longer did he have the strength to keep creating new lives and identities for himself in these temporary refuges. When daybreak cleared the terror of the forest dream from his spirit he staggered to the temple of the Lady on Alaisor Heights, and asked to be allowed to make the pilgrimage to the Isle of Sleep. He gave his name as Sigmar Haligome. What had he left to conceal?

He was accepted, as everyone is, and in time he boarded a pilgrim-ship bound for Numinor on the northeastern flank of the Isle. Occasional sendings harassed him during the sea-crossing, some of them merely irritating, a few of terrible impact, but when he woke and trembled and wept there were other pilgrims to comfort him, and somehow now that he had surrendered his life to the Lady, the dreams, even the worst of them, mattered little. The chief pain of the sendings, he knew, is the disruption they bring to one's daily life: the haunting, the strangeness. But now he had no life of his own to be disrupted, so what did it matter that he opened his eyes to a morning of trembling? He was no longer a jobber of precision instruments or a digger of wireweed sprouts or a limer of birds; he was nothing, he was no one, he had no self to defend against the incursions of his foe. In the midst of a flurry of sendings a strange kind of peace came over him.

In Numinor he was received into the Terrace of Assessment, the outer rim of the Isle, where for all he knew he would spend the rest of his life. The Lady called her pilgrims inward step by step, according to the pace of their invisible inner progress, and one whose soul was stained by murder might remain forever in some menial role on the edge of the holy domain. That was all right. He wanted only to escape the sendings of the King, and he hoped that sooner or later he would come under the protection of the Lady and be forgotten by Suvrael.

In soft pilgrim-robes he toiled as a gardener in the outermost terrace for six years. His hair was white, his back was stooped; he learned to tell weed-seedlings from blossom-seedlings; he suffered from sendings every month or two at first, and then less frequently, and though they never left him entirely he found them increasingly unimportant, like the twinges of some ancient wound. Occasionally he thought of his family, who doubtless thought him dead. He thought also of Gleim, eternally frozen in astonishment, hanging in midair before he fell to his death. Had there ever been such a person, and had Haligome truly killed him? It seemed unreal now; it was so terribly long ago. Haligome felt no guilt for a crime whose very existence he was coming to doubt. But he remembered a business quarrel, and an arrogant refusal by the other merchant to see his frightening dilemma, and a moment of blind rage in which he had struck out at his enemy. Yes, yes, it had all happened; and, thought Haligome, Gleim and I both lost our lives in that moment of fury.

Haligome performed his tasks faithfully, did his meditation, visited dream-speakers—it was required here, but they never offered comments or interpretations—and took holy instruction. In the spring of his seventh year he was summoned inward to the next stage on the pilgrimage, the Terrace of Inception, and there he remained month after month, while other pilgrims moved through and past to the Terrace of Mirrors beyond. He said little to anyone, made no friends, and accepted in resignation the sendings that still came to him at widely spaced intervals.

In his third year at the Terrace of Inception he noticed a man of middle years staring at him in the dining-hall, a short and frail man with an oddly familiar look. For two weeks this newcomer kept Haligome under close surveillance, until at last Haligome's curiosity was too strong to control; he made inquiries and was told that the man's name was Goviran Gleim.

Of course. Haligome went to him during an hour of free time and said, "Will you answer a question?"

"If I can."

"Are you a native of the city of Gimkandale on Castle Mount?"

"I am," said Goviran Gleim. "And you, are you a man of Stee?"

"Yes," said Haligome.

They were silent for some time. Then at last Haligome said, "So you have been pursuing me all these years?"

"Why no. Not at all."

"It is only coincidence that we are both here?"

Goviran Gleim said, "I think there is no such thing as coincidence, in fact. But it was not by my conscious design that I came to the place where you were."

"You know who I am, and what I have done?"

"Yes."

"And what do you want of me?" asked Haligome.

"Want? Want?" Gleim's eyes, small and dark and gleaming like those of his long-dead father, looked close into Haligome's. "What do I want? Tell me what happened in the city of Vugel."

"Come. Walk with me," said Haligome.

They passed through a close-clipped blue-green hedge and into the garden of alabandinas that Haligome tended, thinning the buds to make for larger blooms. In these fragrant surroundings Haligome described, speaking flatly and quietly, the events that he had never described to anyone and that had become nearly unreal to him: the quarrel, the meeting, the window, the river. No emotion was apparent on the face of Goviran Gleim during the recitation, although Haligome searched the other man's features intently, trying to read his purpose.

When he was done describing the murder, Haligome waited for a response. There was none.

Ultimately Gleim said, "And what happened to you afterward? Why did you disappear?"

"The King of Dreams whipped my soul with evil sendings, and put me in such torment that I took up hiding in Normork; and when he found me there I went on, fleeing from place to place, and eventually in my flight I came to the Isle as a pilgrim."

"And the King still follows you?"

"From time to time I have sendings," said Haligome. He shook his head. "But they are useless. I have suffered, I have done penance, and it has been meaningless, for I feel no guilt for my crime. It was a moment of madness, and I have wished a thousand thousand times that it had never occurred, but I can find in myself no responsibility for your father's death: he goaded me to frenzy, and I pushed, and he fell, but it was not an act that bears any connection to the way I conducted the other aspects of my life, and it was therefore not mine."

"You feel that, do you?"

"Indeed. And these years of tormented dreams—what good did they do? If I had refrained from killing out of fear of the King, the whole system of punishment would be justified; but I gave no thought to anything, least of all the King of Dreams, and I therefore see the code under which I have been punished as a futile one. So too with my pilgrimage: I came here not so much to atone as to hide from the King and his sendings, and I suppose I have essentially achieved that. But neither my atonement nor my sufferings will bring your father back to life, so all this charade has been without purpose. Come: kill me and get it over with."

"Kill you?" said Gleim.

"Isn't that what you intend?"

"I was a boy when my father vanished. I am no longer young now, and you are older still, and all this is ancient history. I wanted only to know the truth of his death, and I know it now. Why kill you? If it would bring my father back to life, perhaps I would, but, as you yourself point out, nothing can do that. I feel no anger toward you and I have no wish to experience torment at the hands of the King. For me, at least, the system is a worthy deterrent."

"You have no wish to kill me," said Haligome, amazed.

"None."

"No. No. I see. Why should you kill me? That would free me from a life that has become one long punishment."

Gleim again looked astounded. "Is that how you see it?"

"You condemn me to life, yes."

"But your punishment ended long ago! The grace of the Lady is on you now. Through my father's death you have found your way to her!"

Haligome could not tell whether the other man was mocking him or truly meant his words.

"You see grace in me?" he asked.

"I do."

Haligome shook his head. "The Isle and all it stands for are nothing to me. I came here only to escape the onslaughts of the King. I have at last found a place to hide, and no more than that."

Gleim's gaze was steady. "You deceive yourself," he said, and walked away, leaving Haligome stunned and dazed.

Could it be? Was he purged of his crime, and had not understood that? He resolved that if that night a sending of the King came to him—

and he was due, for it had been nearly a year since the last one—he would walk to the outer edge of the Terrace of Assessment and throw himself into the sea. But what came that night was a sending of the Lady, a warm and gentle dream summoning him inward to the Terrace of Mirrors. He still did not understand fully, and doubted that he ever would. But his dream-speaker told him in the morning to go on at once to that shining terrace that lay beyond, for the next stage of his pilgrimage had commenced.

EIGHT

Among the Dream-Speakers

Often now Hissune finds that one adventure demands immediate explanation by another; and when he has done with the somber but instructive tale of the murderer Sigmar Haligome he understands a great deal of the workings of the agencies of the King of Dreams, but of the dream-speakers themselves, those intermediaries between the sleeping and waking worlds, he knows very little at all. He has never consulted one; he regards his own dreams more as theatrical events than as messages of guidance. This is counter to the central spiritual tradition of the world, he knows, but much that he does and thinks runs counter to those traditions. He is what he is, a child of the streets of the Labyrinth, a close observer of his world but not a wholehearted subscriber to all of its ways.

There is in Zimroel, or was, a famous dream-speaker named Tisana, whom Hissune had met while attending the second enthronement of Lord Valentine. She was a fat old woman of the city of Falkynkip, and evidently she had played some part in Lord Valentine's rediscovery of his lost identity; Hissune knows nothing about that, but he recalls with some discomfort the old woman's penetrating eyes, her powerful and vigorous personality. For some reason she had taken a fancy to the boy Hissune: he remembers standing beside her, dwarfed by her, hoping that she would not get the notion of embracing him, for she would surely crush him in her vast bosom. She said then, "And here's another little lost princeling!" What did that mean? A dream-speaker might tell him, Hissune occasionally thinks, but he does not go to dream-speakers. He wonders if Tisana has left a recording in the Register of Souls. He checks the archives. Yes, yes, there is one. He summons it and discovers quickly that it was made early in her life, some fifty years ago, when she was only learning her craft, and there are no others of hers on file. Nearly he sends it back. But something of Tisana's flavor lingers in his mind after only a moment of her recording. He might yet learn from her, he decides, and dons the helmet once more, and lets the vehement soul of the young Tisana enter his consciousness.

ON THE MORNING OF the day before Tisana's Testing it suddenly began to rain, and everyone came running out of the chapter-house to see it, the novices and the pledgeds and the consummates and the tutors, and even the old Speaker-Superior Inuelda herself. Rain was a rare event here in the desert of Velalisier Plain. Tisana emerged with all the others, and stood watching the large clear drops descending on a slanting course from the single black-edged cloud that hovered high above the chapter-house's great spire, as though tethered to it. The drops hit the parched sandy ground with an audible impact: dark spreading stains, oddly far apart, were forming on the pale reddish soil. Novices and pledgeds and consummates and tutors flung aside their cloaks and frolicked in the downpour. "The first in well over a year," someone said.

"An omen," murmured Freylis, the pledged who was Tisana's closest friend in the chapter-house. "You will have an easy Testing."

"Do you really believe such things?"

"It costs no more to see good omens than bad," Freylis said.

"A useful motto for a dream-speaker to adopt," said Tisana, and they both laughed.

Freylis tugged at Tisana's hand. "Come dance with me out there!" she urged.

Tisana shook her head. She remained in the shelter of the overhang, and all Freylis' tugging was to no avail. Tisana was a tall woman, sturdy, big-boned, and powerful; Freylis, fragile and slight, was like a bird beside her. Dancing in the rain hardly suited Tisana's mood just now. Tomorrow would bring the climax to seven years of training; she still had no idea whatever of what was going to be required of her at the ritual, but she was perversely certain that she would be found unworthy and sent back to her distant provincial town in disgrace; her fears and dark forebodings were a ballast of lead in her spirit, and dancing at such a time seemed an impossible frivolity.

"Look there," Freylis cried. "The Superior!"

Yes, even the venerable Inuelda was out in the rain, dancing with stately abandon, the gaunt, leathery, white-haired old woman moving in wobbly but ceremonious circles, skinny arms outspread, face upturned ecstatically. Tisana smiled at the sight. The Superior spied Tisana lurking on the portico and grinned and beckoned to her, the way one would beckon to a sulky child who will not join the game. But the Superior had taken her own Testing so long ago she must have forgotten how awesome it loomed; no doubt she was unable to understand Tisana's somber preoccupation with tomorrow's ordeal. With an apologetic little gesture Tisana turned and went within. From behind her came the abrupt drumming of a heavy downpour, and then sharp silence. The strange little storm was over.

Tisana entered her cell, stooping to pass under the low arch of blue stone blocks, and leaned for a moment against the rough wall, letting the tension drain from her. The cell was tiny, barely big enough for a mattress, a washbasin, a cabinet, a workbench, and a little bookcase, and Tisana, solid and fleshy, with the robust, healthy body of the farm-girl she once had been, nearly filled the little room. But she had grown accustomed to its crampedness and found it oddly comforting. Comforting, too, were the routines of the chapter-house, the daily round of study and manual labor and instruction and—since she had attained the rank of a consummate—the tutoring of novices. At the time the rainfall began Tisana had been brewing the dream-wine, a chore that had occupied an hour of every morning for her for the past two years, and now, grateful for the difficulties of the task, she returned to it. On this uneasy day it was a welcome distraction.

All the dream-wine used on Majipoor was produced right here, by the pledgeds and consummates of the chapter-house of Velalisier. Making it called for fingers quicker and more delicate than Tisana's, but she had become adept all the same. Laid out before her were the little vials of herbs, the minuscule gray muorna-leaves and the succulent vejloo-roots and the dried berries of the sithereel and the rest of the nine-and-twenty ingredients that produced the trance out of which came the understanding of dreams. Tisana busied herself with the grinding and the mixing of them—it had to be done in a precise order, or the chemical reactions would go awry—and then the kindling of the flame, the char-ring, the reduction to powder, the dissolving into the brandy and the stirring of the brandy into the wine. After a while the intensity of her concentration helped her grow relaxed and even cheerful again.

As she worked she became aware of soft breathing behind her.

"Freylis?"

"Is it all right to come in?"

"Of course. I'm almost finished. Are they still dancing?"

"No, no, everything's back to normal. The sun is shining again."

Tisana swirled the dark heavy wine in the flask. "In Falkynkip, where I grew up, the weather is also hot and dry. Nevertheless, we don't drop everything and go cavorting the moment the rain comes."

"In Falkynkip," Freylis said, "people take everything for granted. A Skandar with eleven arms wouldn't excite them. If the Pontifex came to town and did handstands in the plaza it wouldn't draw a crowd."

"Oh? You've been there?"

"Once, when I was a girl. My father was thinking of going into ranching. But he didn't have the temperament for it, and after a year or so we went back to Til-omon. He never stopped talking about the Falkynkip people, though, how slow and stolid and deliberate they are."

"And am I like that, too?" Tisana asked, a little mischievously.

"You're—well—extremely stable."

"Then why am I so worried about tomorrow?"

The smaller woman knelt before Tisana and took both her hands in hers. "You have nothing to worry about," she said gently.

"The unknown is always frightening."

"It's only a test, Tisana!"

"The last test. What if I bungle it? What if I reveal some terrible flaw of character that shows me absolutely unfit to be a speaker?"

"What if you do?" Freylis asked.

"Why, then I've wasted seven years. Then I creep back to Falkynkip like a fool, without a trade, without skills, and I spend the rest of my life pushing slops on somebody's farm."

Freylis said, "If the Testing shows that you're not fit to be a speaker, you have to be philosophical about it. We can't let incompetents loose in people's minds, you know. Besides, you're *not* unfit to be a speaker, and the Testing isn't going to be any problem for you, and I don't understand why you're so worked up about it."

"Because I have no clue to what it will be like."

"Why, they'll probably do a speaking with you. They'll give you the wine and they'll look in your mind and they'll see that you're strong and wise and good, and they'll bring you out of it and the Superior will give you a hug and tell you you've passed, and that'll be all."

"Are you sure? Do you know?"

"It's a reasonable guess, isn't it?"

Tisana shrugged. "I've heard other guesses. That they do something to you that brings you face to face with the worst thing you've ever done. Or the thing that most frightens you in all the world. Or the thing that you most fear other people will find out about you. Haven't you heard those stories?"

"Yes."

"If this were the day before *your* Testing, wouldn't you be a little edgy, then?"

"They're only stories, Tisana. Nobody knows what the Testing is really like, except those who've passed it."

"And those who've failed."

"Do you know that anyone has failed?"

"Why—I assume—"

Freylis smiled. "I suspect they weed out the failures long before they get to be consummates. Long before they get to be pledgeds, even." She arose and began to toy with the vials of herbs on Tisana's workbench. "Once you're a speaker, will you go back to Falkynkip?"

"I think so."

"You like it there that much?"

"It's my home."

"It's such a big world, Tisana. You could go to Ni-moya, or Piliplok, or stay over here in Alhanroel, live on Castle Mount, even—"

"Falkynkip will suit me," said Tisana. "I like the dusty roads. I like the dry brown hills. I haven't seen them in seven years. And they need speakers in Falkynkip. They don't in the great cities. Everybody wants to be a speaker in Ni-moya or Stee, right? I'd rather have Falkynkip."

Slyly Freylis asked, "Do you have a lover waiting there?"

Tisana snorted. "Not likely! After seven years?"

"I had one in Til-omon. We were going to marry and build a boat and sail all the way around Zimroel, take three or four years doing it, and then maybe go up the river to Ni-moya and settle there and open a shop in the Gossamer Galleria."

That startled Tisana. In all the time she had known Freylis, they had never spoken of these things.

"What happened?"

Quietly Freylis said, "I had a sending that told me I should become a dream-speaker. I asked him how he felt about that. I wasn't even sure I would do it, you know, but I wanted to hear what he thought, and the moment I told him, I saw the answer, because he looked stunned and amazed and a little angry, as if my becoming a dream-speaker would interfere with his plans. Which of course it would. He said I should give him a day or two to mull it over. That was the last I saw of him. A friend of his told me that that very night he had a sending telling him to go to Pidruid, and he went in the morning, and later on he married an old sweetheart he ran into up there, and I suppose they're still talking about building a boat and sailing it around Zimroel. And I obeyed my sending and did my pilgrimage and came here, and here I am, and next month I'll be a consummate and if all goes well next year I'll be a full-fledged speaker. And I'll go to Ni-moya and set up my speaking in the Grand Bazaar."

"Poor Freylis!"

"You don't have to feel sorry for me, Tisana. I'm better off for what happened. It only hurt for a little while. He was worthless, and I'd have found it out sooner or later, and either way I'd have ended up apart from him, except this way I'll be a dream-speaker and render service to the Divine, and the other way I'd have been nobody useful at all. Do you see?"

"I see."

"And I didn't really need to be anybody's wife."

"Nor I," said Tisana. She sniffed her batch of new wine and approved it and began to clean off her workbench, fussily capping the vials and arranging them in a precise order. Freylis was so kind, she thought, so gentle, so tender, so understanding. The womanly virtues. Tisana could find none of those traits in herself. If anything, her soul was more like what she imagined a man's to be, thick, rough, heavy, strong, capable of withstanding all sorts of stress but not very pliant and certainly insensitive to nuance and matters of delicacy. Men were not really like that, Tisana knew, any more than women were invariably models of subtlety and perception, but yet there was a certain crude truth to the notion, and Tisana had always believed herself to be too big, too robust, too foursquare, to be truly feminine. Whereas Freylis, small and delicate and volatile, quicksilver soul and hummingbird mind, seemed to her to be almost of a different species. And Freylis, Tisana thought, would be a superb dream-speaker, intuitively penetrating the minds of those who came to her for interpretations and telling them, in the way most useful to them, what they most needed to know. The Lady of the Isle and the King of Dreams, when in their various ways they visited the minds of sleepers, often spoke cryptically and mystifyingly; it was the speaker's task to serve as interlocutor between those awesome Powers and the billions of people of the world, deciphering and interpreting and guiding. There was terrifying responsibility in that. A speaker could shape or reshape a person's life. Freylis would do well at it: she knew exactly where to be stern and where to be flippant and where consolation and warmth were needed. How had she learned those things? Through engagement with life, no doubt of it, through experience with sorrow and disappointment and failure and defeat. Even without knowing many details of Freylis' past, Tisana could see in the slender woman's cool gray eyes the look of costly knowledge, and it was that knowledge, more than any tricks and techniques she would learn in the chapter-house, that would equip her for her chosen profession. Tisana had grave doubts of her own vocation for dream-speaking, for she had managed to miss all the passionate turmoil that shaped the Freylises of the world. Her life had been too placid, too easy, too—what had Freylis said?—*stable*. A Falkynkip sort of life, up with the sun, out to the chores, eat and work and play and go to sleep well fed and well tired out. No tempests, no upheavals, no high ambitions that led to great downfalls. No real pain, and so how could she truly understand the sufferings of those who suffered? Tisana thought of Freylis and her treacherous lover, betraying her on an instant's notice because her half-formed plans did not align neatly with his; and then she thought of her own little barnyard romances, so light, so casual, mere companionship, two people mindlessly coming together for a while and just as mindlessly parting, no anguish, no torment. Even when she made love, which was supposed to be the ultimate communion, it was a simple, trivial business, a grappling of healthy, strapping bodies, an easy joining, a little thrashing and pumping, gasps and moans, a quick shudder of pleasure, then release and parting. Nothing more. Somehow Tisana had slid through life unscarred, untouched, undeflected. How, then, could she be of value to others? Their confusions and conflicts would be meaningless to her. And, she saw, maybe that was what she feared about the Testing: that they would finally look into her soul and see how unfit she was to be a speaker because she was so uncomplicated and innocent, that they would uncover her deception at last. How ironic that she was worried now because she had lived a worry-free life! Her hands began to tremble. She held them up and stared at them: peasant hands—big, stupid, coarse, thick-fingered hands, quivering as though on drawstrings. Freylis, seeing the gesture, pulled Tisana's hands down and gripped them with her own, barely able to span them with her frail and tiny fingers. "Relax," she whispered fiercely. "There's nothing to fret about!"

Tisana nodded. "What time is it?"

"Time for you to be with your novices and me to be making my observances."

"Yes. Yes. All right, let's be about it."

"I'll see you later. At dinner. And I'll keep dream-vigil with you tonight, all right?"

"Yes," Tisana said. "I'd like that very much."

They left the cell. Tisana hastened outside, across the courtyard to the assembly-room where a dozen novices waited for her. There was no trace now of the rain: the harsh desert sun had boiled away every drop. At midday even the lizards were hiding. As she approached the far side of the cloister, a senior tutor emerged, Vandune, a Piliplokki woman nearly as old as the Superior. Tisana smiled at her and went on; but the tutor halted and called back to her, "Is tomorrow your day?"

"I'm afraid so."

"Have they told you who'll be giving you your Testing?"

"They've told me nothing," said Tisana. "They've left me guessing about the whole thing."

"As it should be," Vandune said. "Uncertainty is good for the soul."

"Easy enough for you to say," Tisana muttered, as Vandune trudged away. She wondered if she herself would ever be so cheerily heartless to candidates for the Testing, assuming she passed and went on to be a tutor. Probably. Probably. One's perspective changes when one is on the other side of the wall, she thought, remembering that when she was a child she had vowed always to understand the special problems of children when she became an adult, and never to treat the young with the sort of blithe cruelty that all children receive at the hands of their unthinking elders; she had not forgotten the vow, but, fifteen or twenty years later, she had forgotten just what it was that was so special about the condition of childhood, and she doubted that she showed any great sensitivity to them despite everything. So, too, most likely, with this.

She entered the assembly-room. Teaching at the chapter-house was done mainly by the tutors, who were fully qualified dream-speakers voluntarily taking a few years from their practices to give instruction; but the consummates, the final-year students who were speakers in all but the last degree, were required also to work with the novices by way of gaining experience in dealing with people. Tisana taught the brewing of dream-wine, theory of sendings, and social harmonics. The novices looked up at her with awe and respect as she took her place at the desk. What could they know of her fears and doubts? To them she was a high initiate of their rite, barely a notch or two below the Superior Inuelda.

She had mastered all the skills they were struggling so hard to comprehend. And if they were aware of the Testing at all, it was merely as a vague dark cloud on the distant horizon, no more relevant to their immediate concerns than old age and death.

"Yesterday," Tisana began, taking a deep breath and trying to make herself seem cool and self-possessed, an oracle, a fount of wisdom, "we spoke of the role of the King of Dreams in regulating the behavior of society on Majipoor. You, Meliara, raised the issue of the frequent malevolence of the imagery in sendings of the King, and questioned the underlying morality of a social system based on chastisement through dreams. I'd like us to address that issue today in more detail. Let us consider a hypothetical person—say, a sea-dragon hunter from Piliplok—who in a moment of extreme inner stress commits an act of unpremeditated but severe violence against a fellow member of her crew, and—"

The words came rolling from her in skeins. The novices scribbled notes, frowned, shook their heads, scribbled notes even more frantically. Tisana remembered from her own novitiate that desperate feeling of being confronted with an infinity of things to learn, not merely techniques of the speaking itself but all kinds of subsidiary nuances and concepts. She hadn't anticipated any of that, and probably neither had the novices before her. But of course Tisana had given little thought to the difficulties that becoming a dream-speaker might pose for her. Anticipatory worrying, until this business of the Testing had arisen, had never been her style. One day seven years ago a sending had come upon her from the Lady, telling her to leave her farm and bend herself toward dream-speaking, and without questioning it she had obeyed, borrowing money and going off on the long pilgrimage to the Isle of Sleep for the preparatory instruction, and then, receiving permission there to enroll at the Velalisier chapter-house, journeying onward across the interminable sea to this remote and forlorn desert where she had lived the past four years. Never doubting, never hesitating.

But there was so much to learn! The myriad details of the speaker's relationship with her clients, the professional etiquette, the responsibilities, the pitfalls. The method of mixing the wine and merging minds. The ways of couching interpretations in usefully ambiguous words. And

the dreams themselves! The types, the significances, the cloaked mean-
ings! The seven self-deceptive dreams and the nine instructive dreams,
the dreams of summoning, the dreams of dismissal, the three dreams of
transcendence of self, the dreams of postponement of delight, the dreams
of diminished awareness, the eleven dreams of torment, the five dreams
of bliss, the dreams of interrupted voyage, the dreams of striving, the
dreams of good illusions, the dreams of harmful illusions, the dreams of
mistaken ambition, the thirteen dreams of grace—Tisana had learned
them all, had made the whole list part of her nervous system the way the
multiplication table and the alphabet were, had rigorously experienced
each of the many types through month upon month of programmed
sleep, and so in truth she was an adept, she was an initiate, she had attained all that these wide-eyed unformed youngsters here were striving
to know, and yet all the same, tomorrow the Testing might undo her
completely, which none of them could possibly comprehend.

Or could they? The lesson came to its end and Tisana stood at her
desk for a moment, numbly shuffling papers, as the novices filed out. One
of them, a short, plump, fair-haired girl from one of the Guardian Cities
of Castle Mount, paused before her a moment—dwarfed by her, as most
people were—and looked up and touched her fingertips lightly to Tisana's forearm, a moth-wing caress, and whispered shyly, "It'll be easy for
you tomorrow. I'm certain of it." And smiled and turned away, cheeks
blazing, and was gone.

So they knew, then—some of them. That benediction remained with
Tisana like a candle's glow through all the rest of the day. A long dreary
day it was, too, full of chores that could not be shirked, though she would
have preferred to go off by herself and walk in the desert instead of doing
them. But there were rituals to perform and observances to make and
some heavy digging at the site of the new chapel of the Lady, and in the
afternoon another class of novices to face, and then a little solitude before
dinner, and finally dinner itself, at sundown. By then it seemed to Tisana
that this morning's little rainstorm had happened weeks ago, or perhaps
in a dream.

Dinner was a tense business. She had almost no appetite, something
unheard-of for her. All around her in the dining-hall surged the warmth

and vitality of the chapter-house, laughter, gossip, raucous singing, and Tisana sat isolated in the midst of it as if surrounded by an invisible sphere of crystal. The older women were elaborately ignoring the fact that this was the eve of her Testing, while the younger ones, trying to do the same, could not help stealing little quick glances at her, the way one covertly looks at someone who suddenly has been called upon to bear some special burden. Tisana was not sure which was worse, the bland pretense of the consummates and tutors or the edgy curiosity of the pledgeds and novices. She toyed with her food. Freylis scolded her as one would scold a child, telling her she would need strength for tomorrow. At that Tisana managed a thin laugh, patting her firm fleshy middle and saying, "I've stored up enough already to last me through a dozen Testings."

"All the same," Freylis replied. "Eat."

"I can't. I'm too nervous."

From the dais came the sound of a spoon tinkling against a glass. Tisana looked up. The Superior was rising to make an announcement.

In dismay Tisana muttered, "The Lady keep me! Is she going to say something in front of everybody about my Testing?"

"It's about the new Coronal," said Freylis. "The news arrived this afternoon."

"What new Coronal?"

"To take the place of Lord Tyeveras, now that he's Pontifex. Where have you been? For the past five weeks—"

"—and indeed this morning's rain was a sign of sweet tidings and a new springtime," the Superior was saying.

Tisana forced herself to follow the old woman's words.

"A message has come to me today that will cheer you all. We have a Coronal again! The Pontifex Tyeveras has selected Malibor of Bombifale, who this night on Castle Mount will take his place upon the Confalume Throne!"

There was cheering and table-pounding and making of starburst signs. Tisana, like one who walks in sleep, did as the others were doing. A new Coronal? Yes, yes, she had forgotten, the old Pontifex had died some months back and the wheel of state had turned once more; Lord

Tyeveras was Pontifex now and there was a new man this very day atop
Castle Mount. "Malibor! Lord Malibor! Long live the Coronal!" she
shouted, along with the rest, and yet it was unreal and unimportant to
her. A new Coronal? One more name on the long, long list. Good for
Lord Malibor, whoever he may be, and may the Divine treat him kindly:
his troubles are only now beginning. But Tisana hardly cared. One was
supposed to celebrate at the outset of a reign. She remembered getting
tipsy on fireshower wine when she was a little girl and the famous Kinniken had died, bringing Lord Ossier into the Labyrinth of the Pontifex
and elevating Tyeveras to Castle Mount. And now Lord Tyeveras was
Pontifex and somebody else was Coronal, and some day, no doubt, Tisana
would hear that this Malibor had moved on to the Labyrinth and there
was another eager young Coronal on the throne. Though these events
were supposed to be terribly important, Tisana could not at the moment
care at all what the king's name happened to be, whether Malibor or
Tyeveras or Ossier or Kinniken. Castle Mount was far away, thousands
of miles, for all she knew did not even exist. What loomed as high in her
life as Castle Mount was the Testing. Her obsession with her Testing
overshadowed everything, turning all other events into wraiths. She
knew that was absurd. It was something like the bizarre intensifying of
feeling that comes over one when one is ill, when the entire universe
seems to center on the pain behind one's left eye or the hollowness in
one's gut, and nothing else has any significance. Lord Malibor? She
would celebrate his rising some other time.

"Come," Freylis said. "Let's go to your room."

Tisana nodded. The dining-hall was no place for her tonight. Conscious that all eyes were on her, she made her way unsteadily down the
aisle and out into the darkness. A dry, warm wind was blowing, a rasping
wind, grating against her nerves. When they reached Tisana's cell, Freylis lit the candles and gently pushed Tisana down on the bed. From the
cabinet she took two wine-bowls, and from under her robe she drew a
small flask.

"What are you doing?" Tisana asked.

"Wine. To relax you."

"Dream-wine?"

"Why not?"

Frowning, Tisana said, "We aren't supposed to—"

"We aren't going to do a speaking. This is just to relax you, to bring us closer together so that I can share my strength with you. Yes? Here." She poured the thick, dark wine into the bowls and put one into Tisana's hand. "Drink. Drink it, Tisana." Numbly Tisana obeyed. Freylis drank her own, quickly, and began to remove her clothes. Tisana looked at her in surprise. She had never had a woman for a lover. Was that what Freylis wanted her to do now? Why? This is a mistake, Tisana thought. On the eve of my Testing, to be drinking dream-wine, to be sharing my bed with Freylis—

"Get undressed," Freylis whispered.

"What are you going to do?"

"Keep dream-vigil with you, silly. As we agreed. Nothing more. Finish your wine and get your robe off!"

Freylis was naked now. Her body was almost like a child's, straight-limbed, lean, with pale clear skin and small girlish breasts. Tisana dropped her own clothes to the floor. The heaviness of her flesh embarrassed her, the powerful arms, the thick columns of her thighs and legs. One was always naked when one did speakings, and one quickly came not to care about baring one's body, but somehow this was different, intimate, personal. Freylis poured a little more wine for each of them. Tisana drank without protest. Then Freylis seized Tisana's wrists and knelt before her and stared straight into her eyes and said, in a tone both affectionate and scornful, "You big fool, you've got to stop worrying about tomorrow! The Testing is *nothing*. Nothing." She blew out the candles and lay down alongside Tisana. "Sleep softly. Dream well." Freylis curled herself up in Tisana's bosom and clasped herself close against her, but she lay still, and in moments she was asleep.

So they were not to become lovers. Tisana felt relief. Another time, perhaps—why not?—but this was no moment for such adventures. Tisana closed her eyes and held Freylis as one might hold a sleeping child. The wine made a throbbing in her, and a warmth. Dream-wine opened one mind to another, and Tisana was keenly sensitive now to Freylis's spirit beside her, but this was no speaking and they had not done the focusing exercises that created the full union; from Freylis came only broad undefined emanations of peace and love and energy. She was strong, far stronger than her slight body led one to think, and as the dream-wine took deeper hold of Tisana's mind she drew increasing comfort from the nearness of the other woman. Slowly drowsiness overtook her. Still she fretted—about the Testing, about what the others would think about their going off together so early in the evening, about the technical violation of regulations that they had committed by sharing the wine this way—and eddying currents of guilt and shame and fear swirled through her spirit for a time. But gradually she grew calm. She slept. With a speaker's trained eye she kept watch on her dreams, but they were without form or sequence, the images mysteriously imprecise, a blank horizon illuminated by a vague and distant glow, and now perhaps the face of the Lady, or of the Superior Inuelda, or of Freylis, but mainly just a band of warm consoling light. And then it was dawn and some bird was shrieking on the desert, announcing the new day.

Tisana blinked and sat up. She was alone. Freylis had put away the candles and washed the wine-bowls, and had left a note on the table—no, not a note, a drawing, the lightning-bolt symbol of the King of Dreams within the triangle-within-triangle symbol of the Lady of the Isle, and around that a heart, and around that a radiant sun: a message of love and good cheer.

"Tisana?"

She went to the door. The old tutor Vandune was there.

"Is it time?" Tisana asked.

"Time and then some. The sun's been up for twenty minutes. Are you ready?"

"Yes," Tisana said. She felt oddly calm—ironic, after this week of fears. But now that the moment was at hand there no longer was anything to fear. Whatever would be, would be, and if she were to be found lacking in her Testing, so be it; it would be for the best.

She followed Vandune across the courtyard and past the vegetable plot and out of the chapter-house grounds. A few people were already up and about, but did not speak to them. By the sea-green light of early day they marched in silence over the crusted desert sands, Tisana checking her pace to keep just to the rear of the older woman. They walked east-ward and southward, without a word passing between them, for what felt like hours and hours, miles and miles. Out of the emptiness of the desert there began to appear now the outlying ruins of the ancient Metamorph city of Velalisier, that vast and haunted place of forbidding scope and majesty, thousands of years old and long since accursed and abandoned by its builders. Tisana thought she understood. For the Testing, they would turn her loose in the ruins and let her wander among the ghosts all day. But could that be it? So childish, so simpleminded? Ghosts held no terrors for her. And they should be doing this by night, besides, if they meant to frighten her. Velalisier by day was just a thing of humps and snags of stone, fallen temples, shattered columns, sand-buried pyramids.

They came at last to a kind of amphitheater, well preserved, ring upon ring of stone seats radiating outward in a broad arc. In the center stood a stone table and a few stone benches, and on the table sat a flask and a wine-bowl. So this was the place of the Testing! And now, Tisana guessed, she and old Vandune would share the wine and lie down to-gether on the flat sandy ground, and do a speaking, and when they rose Vandune would know whether or not to enroll Tisana of Falkynkip in the roster of dream-speakers.

But that was not how it would be, either. Vandune indicated the flask and said, "It holds dream-wine. I will leave you here. Pour as much of the wine as you like, drink, look into your soul. Administer the Testing to yourself."

"I?"

Vandune smiled. "Who else can test you? Go. Drink. In time I will return."

The old tutor bowed and walked away. Tisana's mind brimmed with questions, but she held them back, for she sensed that the Testing had already begun and that the first part of it was that no questions could be asked. In puzzlement she watched as Vandune passed through a niche in the amphitheater wall and disappeared into an alcove. There was no sound after that, not even a footfall. In the crushing silence of the empty city the sand seemed to be roaring, but silently. Tisana frowned, smiled, laughed—a booming laugh that stirred far-off echoes. The joke was on her! Devise your own Testing—that was the thing! Let them dread the day, then march them into the ruins and tell them to run the show themselves! So much for dread anticipation of fearsome ordeals, so much for the phantoms of the soul's own making.

But how—

Tisana shrugged. Poured the wine, drank. Very sweet, perhaps wine of another year. The flask was a big one. All right: I'm a big woman. She gave herself a second draft. Her stomach was empty; she felt the wine almost instantly churning her brains. Yet she drank a third.

The sun was climbing fast. The edge of its forelimb had reached the top of the amphitheater wall.

"Tisana!" she cried. And to her shout she replied, "Yes, Tisana?"

Laughed. Drank again.

She had never before had dream-wine in solitude. It was always taken in the presence of another—either while doing a speaking, or else with a tutor. Drinking it now alone was like asking questions of one's reflection. She felt the kind of confusion that comes from standing between two mirrors and seeing one's image shuttled back and forth to infinity.

"Tisana," she said, "this is your Testing. Are you fit to be a dream-speaker?"

And she answered, "I have studied four years, and before that I spent three more making the pilgrimage to the Isle. I know the seven self-deceptive dreams and the nine instructive dreams, the dreams of summoning, the dreams of—"

"All right. Skip all that. Are you fit to be a dream-speaker?"

"I know how to mix the wine and how to drink it."

"Answer the question. Are you fit to be a dream-speaker?"

"I am very stable. I am tranquil of soul."

"You are evading the question."

"I am strong and capable. I have little malice in me. I wish to serve the Divine."

"What about serving your fellow beings?"

"I serve the Divine by serving them."

"Very elegantly put. Who gave you that line, Tisana?"

"It just came to me. May I have some more wine?"

"All you like."

"Thank you," Tisana said. She drank. She felt dizzy but yet not drunk, and the mysterious mind-linking powers of the dream-wine were absent, she being alone and awake. She said, "What is the next question?"

"You still haven't answered the first one."

"Ask the next one."

"There is only one question, Tisana. Are you fit to be a dream-speaker? Can you soothe the souls of those who come to you?"

"I will try."

"Is that your answer?"

"Yes," Tisana said. "That is my answer. Turn me loose and let me try. I am a woman of goodwill. I have the skills and I have the desire to help others. And the Lady has commanded me to be a dream-speaker."

"Will you lie down with all who need you? With humans and Ghayrogs and Skandars and Liimen and Vroons and all others of all the races of the world?"

"All," she said.

"Will you take their confusions from them?"

"If I can, I will."

"Are you fit to be a dream-speaker?"

"Let me try, and then we will know," said Tisana.

Tisana said, "That seems fair. I have no further questions."

She poured the last of the wine and drank it. Then she sat quietly as the sun climbed and the heat of the day grew. She was altogether calm, without impatience, without discomfort. She would sit this way all day and all night, if she had to. What seemed like an hour went by, or a little more, and then suddenly Vandune was before her, appearing without warning.

The old woman said softly, "Is your Testing finished?"

"Yes."

"How did it go?"

"I have passed it," said Tisana.

Vandune smiled. "Yes. I was sure that you would. Come, now. We must speak with the Superior, and make arrangements for your future, Speaker Tisana."

They returned to the chapter-house as silently as they had come, walking quickly in the mounting heat. It was nearly noon when they emerged from the zone of ruins. The novices and pledgeds who had been working in the fields were coming in for lunch. They looked uncertainly at Tisana, and Tisana smiled at them, a bright reassuring smile.

At the entrance to the main cloister Freylis appeared, crossing Tisana's path as though by chance, and gave her a quick worried look.

"Well?" Freylis asked tensely.

Tisana smiled. She wanted to say, It was nothing, it was a joke, a formality, a mere ritual, the real Testing took place long before this. But Freylis would have to discover those things for herself. A great gulf now separated them, for Tisana was a speaker now and Freylis still merely a pledged. So Tisana simply said, "All is well."

"Good. Oh, good, Tisana, good! I'm so happy for you!"

"I thank you for your help," said Tisana gravely.

A shadow suddenly crossed the courtyard. Tisana looked up. A small black cloud, like yesterday's, had wandered into the sky, some strayed fragment, no doubt, of a storm out by the far-off coast. It hung as if hooked to the chapter-house's spire, and, as though some latch had been pulled back, it began abruptly to release great heavy raindrops. "Look," Tisana said. "It's raining again! Come, Freylis! Come, let's dance!"

NINE

A Thief in Ni-moya

*T*oward the close of the seventh year of the restoration of Lord Valentine, word reaches the Labyrinth that the Coronal soon will be arriving on a visit—news that sends Hissune's pulse rate climbing and his heart to pounding. Will he see the Coronal? Will Lord Valentine remember him? The Coronal once took the trouble to summon him all the way to Castle Mount for his recrowning; surely the Coronal still thinks of him, surely Lord Valentine has some recollection of the boy who—

Probably not, Hissune decides. His excitement subsides; his cool rational self regains control. If he catches sight of Lord Valentine at all during his visit, that will be extraordinary, and if Lord Valentine knows who he is, that will be miraculous. Most likely the Coronal will dip in and out of the Labyrinth without seeing anyone but the high ministers of the Pontifex. They say he is off on a grand processional toward Alaisor, and thence to the Isle to visit his mother, and a stop at the Labyrinth is obligatory on such an itinerary. But Hissune knows that Coronals tend not to enjoy visits to the Labyrinth, which remind them uncomfortably of the lodgings that await them when it is their time to be elevated to the senior kingship. And he knows, too, that the Pontifex Tyeveras is a ghost-creature, more dead than alive, lost in impenetrable dreams within the cocoon of his life-support systems, incapable of rational human speech, a symbol rather than a man, who ought to have been buried years ago but who is kept in maintenance so that Lord Valentine's time as Coronal can be prolonged. That is fine for Lord Valentine and doubtless for Majipoor, Hissune thinks; not so

good for old Tyeveras. But such matters are not his concern. He returns to the
Register of Souls, still speculating idly about the coming visit of the Coronal,
and idly he taps for a new capsule, and what comes forth is the recording of a
citizen of Ni-moya, which begins so unpromisingly that Hissune would have
rejected it, but that he desires a glimpse of that great city of the other continent.
For Ni-moya's sake he allows himself to live the life of a little shopkeeper—and
soon he has no regrets.

1

Inyanna's mother had been a shopkeeper in Velathys all her life, and so
had Inyanna's mother's mother, and it was beginning to look as though
that would be Inyanna's destiny, too. Neither her mother nor her mother's
mother had seemed particularly resentful of such a life, but Inyanna, now
that she was nineteen and sole proprietor, felt the shop as a crushing
burden on her back, a hump, an intolerable pressure. She thought often
of selling out and seeking her real fate in some other city far away, Piliplok or Pidruid or even the mighty metropolis of Ni-moya, far to the
north, that was said to be wondrous beyond the imagination of anyone
who had not beheld it.

But times were dull and business was slow and Inyanna saw no pur-
chasers for the shop on the horizon. Besides, the place had been the center of her family's life for generations, and simply to abandon it was
not an easy thing to do, no matter how hateful it had become. So every
morning she rose at dawn and stepped out on the little cobbled terrace
to plunge herself into the stone vat of rainwater that she kept there
for bathing, and then she dressed and breakfasted on dried fish and
wine and went downstairs to open the shop. It was a place of general
merchandise—bolts of cloth and clay pots from the south coast and barrels of spices and preserved fruits and jugs of wine and the keen cutlery
of Narabal and slabs of costly sea-dragon meat and the glittering fili-
greed lanterns that they made in Til-omon, and many other such things.
There were scores of shops just like hers in Velathys; none of them did

particularly well. Since her mother's death, Inyanna had kept the books and managed the inventory and swept the floor and polished the counters and filled out the governmental forms and permits, and she was weary of all that. But what other prospects did life hold? She was an unimportant girl living in an unimportant, rainswept, mountain-girt city, and she had no real expectation that any of that would change over the next sixty or seventy years.

Few of her customers were humans. Over the decades, this district of Velathys had come to be occupied mainly by Hjorts and Liimen—and a good many Metamorphs, too, for the Metamorph province of Piurifayne lay just beyond the mountain range north of the city and a considerable number of the shapeshifting folk had filtered down into Velathys. She took them all for granted, even the Metamorphs, who made most humans uneasy. The only thing Inyanna regretted about her clientele was that she did not get to see many of her own kind, and so, although she was slender and attractive, tall, sleek, almost boyish-looking, with curling red hair and striking green eyes, she rarely found lovers and had never met anyone she might care to live with. Sharing the shop would ease much of the labor. On the other hand, it would cost her much of her freedom, too, including the freedom to dream of a time when she did not keep a shop in Velathys.

One day after the noon rains two strangers entered the shop, the first customers in hours. One was short and thick-bodied, a little round stub of a man, and the other, pale and gaunt and elongated, with a bony face all knobs and angles, looked like some predatory creature of the mountains. They wore heavy white tunics with bright orange sashes, a style of dress that was said to be common in the grand cities of the north, and they looked about the store with the quick scornful glances of those accustomed to a far finer level of merchandise.

The short one said, "Are you Inyanna Forlana?"

"I am."

He consulted a document. "Daughter of Forlana Hayorn, who was the daughter of Hayorn Inyanna?"

"You have the right person. May I ask—"

"At last!" cried the tall one. "What a long dreary trail this has been! If you knew how long we've searched for you! Up the river to Khyntor, and then around to Dulorn, and across these damnable mountains—does it ever stop raining down here?—and then from house to house, from shop to shop, all across Velathys, asking this one, asking that one—"

"And I am who you seek?"

"If you can prove your ancestry, yes."

Inyanna shrugged. "I have records. But what business do you have with me?"

"We should introduce ourselves," said the short one. "I am Vezan Ormus and my colleague is called Steyg, and we are officials of the staff of his majesty the Pontifex Tyeveras, Bureau of Probate, Ni-moya." From a richly tooled leather purse Vezan Ormus withdrew a sheaf of documents; he shuffled them purposefully and said, "Your mother's mother's elder sister was a certain Saleen Inyanna, who in the twenty-third year of the Pontificate of Kinniken, Lord Ossier being then Coronal, settled in the city of Ni-moya and married one Helmyot Gavoon, third cousin to the duke."

Inyanna stared blankly. "I know nothing of these people."

"We are not surprised," said Steyg. "It was some generations ago. And doubtless there was little contact between the two branches of the family, considering the great gulf in distance and in wealth."

"My grandmother never mentioned rich relatives in Ni-moya," said Inyanna.

Vezan Ormus coughed and searched in the papers. "Be that as it may. Three children were born to Helmyot Gavoon and Saleen Inyanna, of whom the eldest, a daughter, inherited the family estates. She died young in a hunting mishap and the lands passed to her only son, Gavoon Dilamayne, who remained childless and died in the tenth year of the Pontificate of Tyeveras, that is to say, nine years ago. Since then the property has remained vacant while the search for legitimate heirs has been conducted. Three years ago it was determined—"

"That I am heir?"

"Indeed," said Steyg blandly, with a broad, bony smile.

Inyanna, who had seen the trend of the conversation for quite some time, was nevertheless astounded. Her legs quivered, her lips and mouth went dry, and in her confusion she jerked her arm suddenly, knocking down and shattering an expensive vase of Alhanroel ware. Embarrassed by all that, she got herself under control and said, "What is it I'm supposed to have inherited, then?"

"The grand house known as Nissimorn Prospect, on the northern shore of the Zimr at Ni-moya, and estates at three places in the Steiche Valley, all leased and producing income," said Steyg.

"We congratulate you," said Vezan Ormus.

"And I congratulate you," replied Inyanna, "on the cleverness of your wit. Thank you for these moments of amusement; and now, unless you want to buy something, I beg you let me get on with my bookkeeping, for the taxes are due and—"

"You are skeptical," said Vezan Ormus. "Quite properly. We come with a fantastic story and you are unable to absorb the impact of our words. But look: we are men of Ni-moya. Would we have dragged ourselves thousands of miles down to Velathys for the sake of playing jokes on shopkeepers? See—here—" He fanned out his sheaf of papers and pushed them toward Inyanna. Hands trembling, she examined them. A view of the mansion—dazzling—and an array of documents of title, and a genealogy, and a paper bearing the Pontifical seal with her name inscribed on it—

She looked up, stunned, dazed.

In a faint furry voice she said, "What must I do now?"

"The procedures are purely routine," Steyg replied. "You must file affidavits that you are in fact Inyanna Forlana, you must sign papers agreeing that you will make good the accrued taxes on the properties out of accumulated revenues once you have taken possession, you will have to pay the filing fees for transfer of title, and so on. We can handle all of that for you."

"Filing fees?"

"A matter of a few royals."

Her eyes widened. "Which I can pay out of the estate's accumulated revenues?"

"Unfortunately, no," said Vezan Ormus. "The money must be paid *before* you have taken title, and, of course, you have no access to the revenues of the estate until you have taken title, so—"

"An annoying formality," Steyg said. "But a trifling one, if you take the long view."

2

All told the fees came to twenty royals. That was an enormous sum for Inyanna, nearly her whole savings; but a study of the documents told her that the revenues of the agricultural lands alone were nine hundred royals a year, and then there were the other assets of the estate, the mansion and its contents, the rents and royalties on certain riverfront properties—

Vezan Ormus and Steyg were extremely helpful in the filling out of the forms. She put the CLOSED FOR BUSINESS sign out, not that it mattered much in this slow season, and all afternoon they sat beside her at her little desk upstairs, passing things to her for her to sign, and stamping them with impressive-looking Pontifical seals. Afterward she celebrated by taking them down to the tavern at the foot of the hill for a few rounds of wine. Steyg insisted on buying the first, pushing her hand away and plunking down half a crown for a flask of choice palm-wine from Pidruid. Inyanna gasped at the extravagance—she ordinarily drank humbler stuff—but then she remembered that she had come into wealth, and when the flask was gone she ordered another herself. The tavern was crowded, mainly with Hjorts and a few Ghayrogs, and the bureaucrats from the northland looked uncomfortable amid all these non-humans, sometimes holding their fingers thoughtfully over their noses as if to filter out the scent of alien flesh. Inyanna, to put them at their ease, told them again and again how grateful she was that they had taken the trouble to seek her out in the obscurity of Velathys.

"But it is our job!" Vezan Ormus protested. "On this world we each must give service to the Divine by playing our parts in the intricacies of daily life. Land was sitting idle; a great house was unoccupied; a deserving heir lived drably in ignorance. Justice demands that such inequities be righted. To us falls the privilege of doing so."

"All the same," said Inyanna, flushed with wine and leaning almost coquettishly close now to one man, now to the other, "You have undergone great inconvenience for my sake, and I will always be in your debt. May I buy you another flask?"

It was well past dark when they finally left the tavern. Several moons were out, and the mountains that ringed the city, outlying fangs of the great Gonghar range, looked like jagged pillars of black ice in the chilly glimmer. Inyanna saw her visitors to their hostelry, at the edge of Dekkeret Plaza, and in her winy wooziness came close to inviting herself in for the night. But seemingly they had no yearning for that, were perhaps made even a little wary at the possibility, and she found herself smoothly and expertly turned away at the door. Wobbling a little, she made the long steep climb to her house and stepped out on the terrace to take the night air. Her head was throbbing. Too much wine, too much talk, too much startling news! She looked about her at her city, row upon row of small stucco-walled tile-roofed buildings descending the sloping bowl of Velathys Basin, a few ragged strands of parkland, some plazas and mansions, the duke's ramshackle castle slung along the eastern ridge, the highway like a girdle encircling the town, then the lofty and oppressive mountains beginning just beyond, the marble quarries like raw wounds on their flanks—she could see it all from her hilltop nest. Farewell! Neither an ugly city nor a lovely one, she thought: just a place, quiet, damp, dull, chilly, ordinary, known for its fine marble and its skilled stonemasons and not much else, a provincial town on a provincial continent. She had been resigned to living out her days here. But now, now that miracles had invaded her life, it seemed intolerable to have to spend as much as another hour here, when shining Ni-moya was waiting. Ni-moya, Ni-moya, Ni-moya!

She slept only fitfully. In the morning she met with Vezan Ormus and Steyg in the notary's office behind the bank and turned over to them her little sack of well-worn royal pieces, most of them old, some very old, with the faces of Kinniken and Thimin and Ossier on them, and even one coin of the reign of great Confalume, a coin hundreds of years old. In return they gave her a single sheet of paper: a receipt, acknowledging payment of twenty royals that they were to expend on her behalf for filing fees. The other documents, they explained, must go back with them to be countersigned and validated. But they would ship everything to her once the transfer was complete, and then she could come to Ni-moya to take possession of her property.

"You will be my guests," she told them grandly, "for a month of hunting and feasting, when I am in my estates."

"Oh, no," said Vezan Ormus softly. "It would hardly be appropriate for such as we to mingle socially with the mistress of Nissimorn Prospect. But we understand the sentiment, and we thank you for the gesture."

Inyanna asked them to lunch. But they had to move on, Steyg replied. They had other heirs to contact, probate work to carry out in Narabal and Til-omon and Pidruid; many months would pass before they saw their homes and wives in Ni-moya again. And did that mean, she asked, suddenly dismayed, that no action would be taken on the filing of her claim until they had finished their tour? "Not at all," said Steyg. "We will ship your documents to Ni-moya by direct courier tonight. The processing of the claim will begin as soon as possible. You should hear from our office in—oh, shall we say seven to nine weeks?"

She accompanied them to their hotel, and waited outside while they packed, and saw them into their floater, and stood waving in the street as they drove off toward the highway that led to the southwest coast. Then she reopened the shop. In the afternoon there were two customers, one buying eight weights' worth of nails and the other asking for false satin, three yards at sixty weights the yard, so the entire day's sales were less than two crowns, but no matter. Soon she would be rich.

A month went by and no news came from Ni-moya. A second month, and still there was silence.

The patience that had kept Inyanna in Velathys for nineteen years was the patience of hopelessness, of resignation. But now that great changes were before her, she had no patience left. She fidgeted, she paced, she made notations on the calendar. The summer, with its virtually daily rains, came to an end, and the dry, crisp autumn began, when the leaves turned fiery in the foothills. No word. The heavy torrents of winter began, with masses of moist air drifting south out of the Zimr Valley across the Metamorph lands and colliding with the harsh mountain winds. There was snow in the highest rims of the Gonghars, and streams of mud ran through the streets of Velathys. No word out of Nimoya, and Inyanna thought of her twenty royals, and terror began to mingle with annoyance in her soul. She celebrated her twentieth birthday alone, bitterly drinking soured wine and imagining what it would be like to command the revenues of Nissimorn Prospect. Why was it taking so long? No doubt Vezan Ormus and Steyg had properly forwarded the documents to the offices of the Pontifex; but just as surely her papers were sitting on some dusty desk, awaiting action, while weeds grew in the gardens of her estate.

On Winterday Eve Inyanna resolved to go to Ni-moya and take charge of the case in person.

The journey would be expensive and she had parted with her savings. To raise the money she mortgaged the shop to a family of Hjorts. They gave her ten royals; they were to pay themselves interest by selling off her inventory at their own profit; if the entire debt should be repaid before she returned, they would continue to manage the place on her behalf, paying her a royalty. The contract greatly favored the Hjorts, but Inyanna did not care: she knew, but told no one, that she would never again see the shop, nor these Hjorts, nor Velathys itself, and the only thing that mattered was having the money to go to Ni-moya.

It was no small trip. The most direct route between Velathys and Ni-moya lay across the Shapeshifter province of Piurifayne, and to enter that was dangerous and rash. Instead she had to make an enormous detour, westward through Stiamot Pass, then up the long, broad valley that was the Dulorn Rift, with the stupendous mile-high wall of Velathys Scarp rising on the right for hundreds of miles; and once she reached the city of Dulorn itself she would still have half the vast continent of Zimroel to cross, by land and by riverboat, before coming to Ni-moya. But

Inyanna saw all that as a glorious gaudy adventure, however long it might take. She had never been anywhere, except once when she was ten, and her mother, enjoying unusual prosperity one winter, had sent her to spend a month in the hotlands south of the Gonghars. Other cities, although she had seen pictures of them, were as remote and implausible to her as other worlds. Her mother once had been to Til-omon on the coast, which she said was a place of brilliant sunlight like golden wine, and soft never-ending summer weather. Her mother's mother had been as far as Narabal, where the tropical air was damp and heavy and hung about you like a mantle. But the rest—Pidruid, Piliplok, Dulorn, Ni-moya, and all the others—were only names to her, and the idea of the ocean was almost beyond her imagining, and it was utterly impossible for her really to believe that there was another continent entirely beyond the ocean, with ten great cities for every city of Zimroel, and thousands of millions of people, and a baffling lair beneath the desert called the Labyrinth, where the Pontifex lived, and a mountain thirty miles high, at the summit of which dwelled the Coronal and all his princely court. Thinking about such things gave her a pain in the throat and a ringing in the ears. Awesome and incomprehensible Majipoor was too gigantic a sweetmeat to swallow at a single gulp; but nibbling away at it, a mile at a time, was wholly wondrous to someone who had only once been beyond the boundaries of Velathys.

So Inyanna noted in fascination the change in the air as the big transport floater drifted through the pass and down into the flatlands west of the mountains. It was still winter down there—the days were short, the sunlight pale and greenish—but the breeze was mild and thick, lacking a wintry edge, and there was a sweet, pungent fragrance on it. She saw in surprise that the soil here was dense and crumbly and spongy, much unlike the shallow, rocky, sparkling stuff around her home, and that in places it was an amazing bright red hue for miles and miles. The plants were different—fat-leaved, glistening—and the birds had unfamiliar plumage, and the towns that lined the highway were airy and open, farming villages nothing at all like dark, ponderous, gray Velathys, with audacious little wooden houses fancifully ornamented with scrollwork and painted in bright splashes of yellow and blue and scarlet. It was

terribly unfamiliar, too, not to have the mountains on all sides, for Velathys nestled in the bosom of the Gonghars, but now she was in the wide
depressed plateau that lay between the mountains and the far-off coastal
strip, and when she looked to the west she could see so far that it was
almost frightening, an unbounded vista dropping off into infinity. On her
other side she had Velathys Scarp, the outer wall of the mountain chain,
but even that was a strangeness, a single, solid, grim, vertical barrier
only occasionally divided into individual peaks that ran endlessly north.
But eventually the Scarp gave out, and the land changed profoundly once
again as she continued northward into the upper end of the Dulorn Rift.
Here the colossal sunken valley was rich in gypsum, and the low rolling
hills were white as if with frost. The stone had an eerie texture, spider-
web stuff with a mysterious chilly sheen. In school she had learned that
all of the city of Dulorn was built of this mineral, and they had shown
pictures of it, spires and arches and crystalline facades blazing like cold
fire in the light of day. That had seemed mere fable to her, like the tales
of Old Earth from which her people were said to have sprung. But one
day in late winter Inyanna found herself staring at the outskirts of the
actual city of Dulorn and she saw that the fable had been no work of
fancy. Dulorn was far more beautiful and strange than she had been able
to imagine. It seemed to shine with an inner light of its own, while the
sunlight, refracted and shattered and deflected by the myriad angles and
facets of the lofty baroque buildings, fell in gleaming showers to the
streets.

So this was a city! Beside it, Inyanna thought, Velathys was a bog.
She would have stayed here a month, a year, forever, going up one street
and down the next, staring at the towers and bridges, peering into the
mysterious shops so radiant with costly merchandise, so much unlike her
own pitiful little place. These hordes of snaky-faced people—this was a
Ghayrog city, millions of the quasi-reptilian aliens and just a scattering
of the other races—moving with such purposefulness, pursuing profes-
sions unknown to simple mountainfolk—the luminous posters advertis-
ing Dulorn's famous Perpetual Circus—the elegant restaurants and
hotels and parks—all of it left Inyanna numb with awe. Surely there was
nothing on Majipoor to compare with this place! Yet they said Ni-moya

was far greater, and Stee on Castle Mount superior to them both, and then also the famous Piliplok, and the port of Alaisor, and—so much, so much!

But half a day was all she had in Dulorn, while the floater was discharging its passengers and being readied for the next leg of its route. That was like no time at all. A day later, as she journeyed eastward through the forests between Dulorn and Mazadone, she found herself not sure whether she had truly seen Dulorn or only dreamed that she had been there.

New wonders presented themselves daily—places where the air was purple, trees the size of hills, thickets of ferns that sang. Then came long stretches of dull indistinguishable cities, Cynthion, Mazadone, Thagobar, and many more. Aboard the floater passengers came and went, drivers were changed every nine hundred miles or so, and only Inyanna went on and on and on, country girl off seeing the world, getting glassy-eyed now and foggy-brained from the endlessly unrolling vista. There were geysers to be seen shortly, and hot lakes, and other thermal wonders: Khyntor, this was, the big city of the midlands, where she was to board the riverboat for Ni-moya. Here the River Zimr came down out of the northwest, a river as big as a sea, so that it strained the eyes to look from bank to bank. In Velathys, Inyanna had known only mountain streams, quick and narrow. They gave her no preparation for the huge curving monster of dark water that was the Zimr.

On the breast of that monster Inyanna now sailed for weeks, past Verf and Stroyn and Lagomandino and fifty other cities whose names were mere noises to her. The riverboat became the whole of her world. In the valley of the Zimr seasons were gentle and it was easy to lose track of the passing of time. It seemed to be springtime, though she knew it must be summer, and late summer at that, for she had been embarked on this journey more than half a year. Perhaps it would never end; perhaps it was her fate merely to drift from place to place, experiencing nothing, coming to ground nowhere. That was all right. She had begun to forget herself. Somewhere there was a shop that had been hers, somewhere there was a great estate that would be hers, somewhere there was a young woman named Inyanna Forlana who came from Velathys, but all that had dissolved into mere motion as she floated onward across unending Majipoor.

Then one day for the hundredth time some new city began to come in view along the Zimr's shores, and there was sudden stirring aboard the boat, a rushing to the rails to stare into the misty distance. Inyanna heard them muttering, "Ni-moya! Ni-moya!" and knew that her voyage had reached its end, that her wandering was over, that she was coming into her true home and birthright.

3

She was wise enough to know that to try to fathom Ni-moya on the first day made no more sense than trying to count the stars. It was a metropolis twenty times the size of Velathys, sprawling for hundreds of miles along both banks of the immense Zimr, and she sensed that one could spend a lifetime here and still need a map to find one's way around. Very well. She refused to let herself be awed or overwhelmed by the grotesque excessiveness of everything she saw about her here. She would conquer this city step by single step. In that calm decision was the beginning of her transformation into a true Ni-moyan.

Nevertheless there was still the first step to be taken. The riverboat had docked at what seemed to be the southern bank of the Zimr. Clutching her one small satchel, Inyanna stared out over a vast body of water—the Zimr here was swollen by its meeting with several major tributaries—and saw cities on every shore. Which one was Ni-moya? Where would the Pontifical offices be? How would she find her lands and mansion? Glowing signs directed her to ferries, but their destinations were places called Gimbeluc and Istmoy and Strelain and Strand Vista: suburbs, she guessed. There was no sign for a ferry to Ni-moya because *all* these places were Ni-moya.

"Are you lost?" a thin, sharp voice said.

Inyanna turned and saw a girl who had been on the riverboat, two or three years younger than herself, with a smudged face and stringy hair bizarrely dyed lavender. Too proud or perhaps too shy to accept help from her—she was not sure which—Inyanna shook her head brusquely and glanced away, feeling her cheeks go hot and red.

The girl said, "There's a public directory back of the ticket windows," and vanished into the ferry-bound hordes.

Inyanna joined the line outside the directory, came at last to the communion booth, and poked her head into the yielding contact hood. "Directory," a voice said.

Inyanna replied smoothly, "Office of the Pontifex. Bureau of Probate."

"There is no listing for such a bureau."

Inyanna frowned. "Office of the Pontifex, then."

"853 Rodamaunt Promenade, Strelain."

Vaguely troubled, she bought a ferry ticket to Strelain: one crown twenty weights. That left her with exactly two royals, perhaps enough for a few weeks' expenses in this costly place. After that? I am the inheritor of Nissimorn Prospect, she told herself airily, and boarded the ferry. But she wondered why the Bureau of Probate's address was unlisted.

It was midafternoon. The ferry, with a blast of its horn, glided serenely out from its slip. Inyanna clung to the rail, peering in wonder at the city on the far shore, every building a radiant white tower, flat-roofed, rising in level upon level toward the ridge of gentle green hills to the north. A map was mounted on a post near the stairway to the lower decks. Strelain, she saw, was the central district of the city, just opposite the ferry depot, which was named Nissimorn. The men from the Pontifex had told her that her estate was on the northern shore; therefore, since it was called Nissimorn Prospect and must face Nissimorn, it should be in Strelain itself, perhaps somewhere in that forested stretch of the shore to the northeast. Gimbeluc was a western suburb, separated from Strelain by a many-bridged subsidiary river; Istmoy was to the east; up from the south came the River Steiche, nearly as great as the Zimr itself, and the towns along its bank were named—

"Your first time?" It was the lavender-haired girl again. Inyanna smiled nervously. "Yes. I'm from Velathys. Country girl, I guess."

"You seem afraid of me."

"Am I? Do I?"

"I won't bite you. I won't even swindle you. My name's Liloyve. I'm a thief in the Grand Bazaar."

"Did you say *thief?*"

"It's a recognized profession in Ni-moya. They don't license us yet, but they don't interfere much with us, either, and we have our own official registry, like a regular guild. I've been down in Lagomandino, selling stolen goods for my uncle. Are you too good for me, or just very timid?"

"Neither," said Inyanna. "But I've come a long way alone, and I'm out of the habit of talking to people, I think." She forced another smile. "You're really a thief?"

"Yes. But not a pickpocket. You look so worried! What's your name, anyway?"

"Inyanna Forlana."

"I like the sound of that. I've never met an Inyanna before. You've traveled all the way from Velathys to Ni-moya? What for?"

"To claim my inheritance," Inyanna answered. "The property of my grandmother's sister's grandson. An estate known as Nissimorn Prospect, on the north shore of—"

Liloyve giggled. She tried to smother it, and her cheeks belled out, and she coughed and clapped a hand over her mouth in what was almost a convulsion of mirth. But it passed swiftly and her expression changed to a softer one of pity. Gently she said, "Then you must be of the family of the duke, and I should beg your pardon for approaching you so rudely here."

"The family of the duke? No, of course not. Why do you—"

"Nissimorn Prospect is the estate of Calain, who is the duke's younger brother."

Inyanna shook her head. "No. My grandmother's sister's—"

"Poor thing, no need to pick your pocket. Someone's done it already!"

Inyanna clutched at her satchel.

"No," Liloyve said. "I mean, you've been taken, if you think you've inherited Nissimorn Prospect."

"There were papers with the Pontifical seal. Two men of Ni-moya brought them in person to Velathys. I may be a country girl, but I'm not so great a fool as to make this journey without proof. I had my suspicions, yes, but I saw the documents. I've filed for title! Twenty royals, it cost, but the papers were in order!"

Liloyve said, "Where will you stay, when we reach Strelain?"

"I've given that no thought. An inn, I suppose."

"Save your crowns. You'll need them. We'll put you up with us in the Bazaar. And in the morning you can take things up with the imperial proctors. Maybe they can help you recover some of what you've lost, eh?"

4

That she had been the victim of swindlers had been in Inyanna's mind from the start, like a low nagging buzz droning beneath lovely music, but she had chosen not to hear that buzz, and even now, with the buzz grown to a monstrous roar, she compelled herself to remain confident. This scruffy little bazaar-girl, this self-admitted professional thief, doubtless had the keenly honed mistrustfulness of one who lived by her wits in a hostile universe, and saw fraud and malevolence on all sides, possibly even where none existed. Inyanna was aware that she might have led herself through gullibility into a terrible error, but it was pointless to lament so soon. Perhaps she *was* somehow of the duke's family after all, or perhaps Liloyve was confused about the ownership of Nissimorn Prospect; or, if in fact she had come to Ni-moya on a fool's chase, consuming her last few crowns in the fruitless journey, at least now she was in Ni-moya rather than Velathys, and that in itself was cause for cheer.

As the ferry pulled into the Strelain slip, Inyanna had her first view of central Ni-moya at close range. Towers of dazzling white came down almost to the water's edge, rising so steeply and suddenly that they seemed unstable, and it was hard to understand why they did not topple into the river. Night was beginning to fall. Lights glittered everywhere. Inyanna maintained the calmness of a sleepwalker in the face of the city's splendors. I have come home, she told herself over and over. I am home, this city is my home, I feel quite at home here. All the same she took care to stay close beside Liloyve as they made their way through swarming mobs of commuters, up the passageway to the street.

At the gate of the terminal stood three huge metallic birds with jeweled eyes—a gihorna with vast wings outspread, a great, silly, long-legged hazenmarl, and some third one that Inyanna did not know, with an enormous pouched beak curved like a sickle. The mechanical figures moved slowly, craning their heads, fluffing their wings. "Emblems of the city," Liloyve said. "You'll see them everywhere, the big silly boobies! A fortune in precious jewels in their eyes, too."

"And no one steals them?"

"I wish I had the nerve. I'd climb right up there and snatch them. But it's a thousand years' bad luck, so they say. The Metamorphs will rise again and cast us out, and the towers will fall, and a lot of other nonsense."

"But if you don't believe the legends, why don't you steal the gems?"

Liloyve laughed her snorting little laugh. "Who'd buy them? Any dealer would know what they were, and with a curse on them there'd be no takers, and a world of trouble for the thief, and the King of Dreams whining in your head until you wanted to scream. I'd rather have a pocketful of colored glass than the eyes of the birds of Ni-moya. Here, get in!" She opened the door of a small street-floater parked outside the terminal and shoved Inyanna to a seat. Settling in beside her, Liloyve briskly tapped out a code on the floater's pay-plate and the little vehicle took off. "We can thank your noble kinsman for this ride," she said.

"What? Who?"

"Calain, the duke's brother. I used his pay-code. It was stolen last month and a lot of us are riding free, courtesy of Calain. Of course, when the bills come in his chancellor will get the number changed, but until then—you see?"

"I am very naïve," said Inyanna. "I still believe that the Lady and the King see our sins while we sleep, and send dreams to discourage such things."

"So you are meant to believe," Liloyve replied. "Kill someone and you'll hear from the King of Dreams, no question of it. But there are how many people on Majipoor? Eighteen billion? Thirty? Fifty? And the King has time to foul the dreams of everyone who steals a ride in a street-floater? Do you think so?"

"Well—"

"Or even those who falsely sell title to other people's palaces?"

Inyanna's cheeks flamed and she turned away.

"Where are we going now?" she asked in a muffled voice.

"We're already there. The Grand Bazaar. Out!"

Inyanna followed Liloyve into a broad plaza bordered on three sides by lofty towers and on the fourth by a low, squat-looking building fronted by a multitude of shallow-rising stone steps. Hundreds of people in elegant white Ni-moyan tunics, perhaps thousands, were rushing in and out of the building's wide mouth, over the arch of which the three emblematic birds were carved in high relief, with jewels again in their eyes.

Liloyve said, "This is Pidruid Gate, one of thirteen entrances. The Bazaar itself covers fifteen square miles, you know—a little like the Labyrinth, though it isn't as far underground, just at street level mainly, snaking all over the city, through the other buildings, under some of the streets, between buildings—a city within a city, you might say. My people have lived in it for hundreds of years. Hereditary thieves, we are. Without us the shopkeepers would be in bad trouble."

"I was a shopkeeper in Velathys. We have no thieves there, and I think we never felt the need for any," said Inyanna dryly as they allowed themselves to be swept along up the shallow steps and into the gate of the Grand Bazaar.

"It's different here," said Liloyve.

The Bazaar spread in every direction—a maze of narrow arcades and passages and tunnels and galleries, brightly lit, divided and subdivided into an infinity of tiny stalls. Overhead, a single continuous skein of yellow sparklecloth stretched into the distance, casting a brilliant glow from its own internal luminescence. That one sight astounded Inyanna more than anything else she had seen so far in Ni-moya, for she had sometimes carried sparklecloth in her shop, at three royals the roll, and such a roll was good for decorating no more than a small room; her soul quailed at the thought of fifteen square miles of sparklecloth, and her mind, canny as it was in such matters, could not at all calculate the cost. Ni-moya! Such excess could be met only with the defense of laughter.

They proceeded inward. One little streetlet seemed just like the next, every one bustling with shops for porcelains and fabrics and tableware and clothes, for fruits and meats and vegetables and delicacies, each with a wine-shop and a spice-shop and a gallery of precious stones, and a vendor selling grilled sausages and one selling fried fish, and the like. Yet Liloyve seemed to know precisely which fork and channel to take, which of the innumerable identical alleys led toward her destination, for she moved purposefully and swiftly, pausing only occasionally to acquire their dinner by deftly snatching a stick of fish from one counter or a globelet of wine from another. Several times the vendor saw her make the theft, and only smiled.

Mystified, Inyanna said, "They don't mind?"

"They know me. But I tell you, we thieves are highly regarded here. We are a necessity."

"I wish I understood that."

"We maintain order in the Bazaar—do you see? No one steals here but us, and we take only what we need, and we patrol the place against amateurs. How would it be, in these mobs, if one customer out of ten filled his purse with merchandise? But we move among them, filling our own purses, and also halting *them*. We are a known quantity. Do you see? Our own takings are a kind of tax on the merchants, a salary of sorts that they pay us, to regulate the others who throng the passages. *Here, now!*" Those last words were directed not to Inyanna but to a boy of about twelve, dark-haired and eel-slim, who had been rummaging through hunting knives in an open bin. With a swift swoop Liloyve caught the boy's hand and in the same motion seized hold of the writhing tentacles of a Vroon no taller than the boy, standing a few feet away in the shadows. Inyanna heard Liloyve speaking in low, fierce tones, but could not make out a single word; the encounter was over in moments, and the Vroon and the boy slunk miserably away.

"What happened then?" Inyanna asked.

"They were stealing knives, the boy passing them to the Vroon. I told them to get out of the Bazaar right away, or my brothers would cut the Vroon's wrigglers off and feed them to the boy roasted in stinnim-oil."

"Would such a thing be done?"

"Of course not. It would be worth a life of sour dreams to anyone who did it. But they got the point. Only authorized thieves steal in this place. You see? We are the proctors here, in a way of speaking. We are indispensable. And here—this is where I live. You are my guest."

5

Liloyve lived underground, in a room of whitewashed stone that was one of a chain of seven or eight such rooms beneath a section of the Grand Bazaar devoted to merchants of cheeses and oils. A trapdoor and a suspended ladder of rope led to the subterranean chambers; and the moment Inyanna began the downward climb, all the noise and frenzy of the Bazaar became impossible to perceive, and the only reminder of what lay above was the faint but unarguable odor of red Stoienzar cheese that penetrated even the stone walls.

"Our den," Liloyve said. She sang a quick lilting melody and people came trailing in from the far rooms—shabby, shifty people, mostly small and thin, with a look about them much the same as Liloyve's, as of having been manufactured from second-rate materials. "My brothers Sidoun and Hanoun," she said. "My sister Medill Faryun. My cousins Avayne, Amayne, and Athayne. And this is my uncle Agourmole, who heads our clan. Uncle, this is Inyanna Forlana, from Velathys, who was sold Nissimorn Prospect for twenty royals by two traveling rogues. I met her on the riverboat. She'll live with us and become a thief."

Inyanna gasped. "I—"

Agourmole, courtly and elaborately formal, made a gesture of the Lady, by way of blessing. "You are one of us. Can you wear a man's clothing?"

Bewildered, Inyanna said, "Yes, I imagine so, but I don't under—"

"I have a younger brother who is registered with our guild. He lives in Avendroyne among the Shapeshifters, and has not been seen in

Ni-moya for years. You will take his name and place. It is simpler that way than gaining a new registration. Give me your hand." She let him take it. His palms were moist and soft. He looked up into her eyes and said in a low, intense tone, "Your true life is just commencing. All that has gone before has been only a dream. Now you are a thief in Ni-moya and your name is Kulibhai." Winking, he added, "Twenty royals is an excellent price for Nissimorn Prospect."

"Those were only the filing fees," said Inyanna. "They told me I had inherited it, through my mother's mother's sister."

"If it is true, you must hold a grand feast for us there, once you are in possession, to repay our hospitality. Agreed?" Agourmole laughed. "Avayne! Wine for your uncle Kulibhai! Sidoun, Hanoun, find clothes for him! Music, someone! Who's for a dance? Show some life! Medill, prepare the guest bed!" The little man pranced about irrepressibly, barking orders. Inyanna, swept along by his vehement energies, accepted a cup of wine, allowed herself to be measured for a tunic by one of Liloyve's brothers, struggled to commit to memory the flood of names that had swept across her mind. Others now were coming into the room, more humans, three pudgy-cheeked gray-faced Hjorts, and, to Inyanna's amazement, a pair of slender, silent Metamorphs. Accustomed though she was to dealing with Shapeshifters in her shopkeeping days, she had not expected to find Liloyve and her family actually sharing their quarters with these mysterious aborigines. But perhaps thieves, like Metamorphs, deemed themselves a race apart on Majipoor, and the two were drawn readily to one another.

An impromptu party buzzed about her for hours. The thieves seemed to be vying for her favor, each in turn cozying up to her, offering some little trinket, some intimate tale, some bit of confidential gossip. To the child of a long line of shopkeepers, thieves were natural enemies; and yet these people, seedy outcasts though they might be, seemed warm and friendly and open, and they were her only allies against a vast and indifferent city. Inyanna had no wish to take up their profession, but she knew that fortune might have done worse by her than to throw her in with Liloyve's folk.

She slept fitfully, dreaming vaporous fragmentary dreams and several times waking in total confusion, with no idea where she was. Eventually exhaustion seized her and she dropped into deep slumber. Usually it was dawn that woke her, but dawn was a stranger in this cave of a place, and when she awakened it might have been any time of day or night.

Liloyve smiled at her. "You must have been terribly tired."

"Did I sleep too long?"

"You slept until you were finished sleeping. That must have been the right amount, eh?"

Inyanna looked around. She saw traces of the party—flasks, empty globelets, stray items of clothing—but the others were gone. Off on their morning rounds, Liloyve explained. She showed Inyanna where to wash and dress, and then they went up into the maelstrom of the Bazaar. By day it was as busy as it had been the night before, but somehow it looked less magical in ordinary light, its texture less dense, its atmosphere less charged with electricity: it was no more than a vast crowded emporium, where last night it had seemed to Inyanna an enigmatic self-contained universe. They paused only to steal their breakfasts at three or four counters, Liloyve brazenly helping herself and passing the take to an abashed and hesitant Inyanna, and then—making their way through the impossible intricacy of the maze, which Inyanna was sure she would never master—they emerged abruptly into the clear fresh air of the surface world.

"We have come out at Piliplok Gate," said Liloyve. "From here it's only a short walk to the Pontificate."

A short walk but a stunning one, for around every corner lay new wonders. Up one splendid boulevard Inyanna caught sight of a brilliant stream of radiance, like a second sun sprouting from the pavement. This, said Liloyve, was the beginning of the Crystal Boulevard, that blazed by day and by night with the glint of revolving reflectors. Across another street and she had a view of what could only be the palace of the Duke of Ni-moya, far to the east down the great slope of the city, at the place where the Zimr made its sudden bend. It was a slender shaft of glassy stone atop a broad many-columned base, huge even at this enormous distance, and surrounded by a park that was like a carpet of green. One more turn and Inyanna beheld something that resembled the loosely woven chrysalis of some fabulous insect, but a mile in length, hanging suspended above an immensely wide avenue. "The Gossamer Galleria," said Liloyve, "where the rich ones buy their playthings. Perhaps some day you'll scatter your royals in its shops. But not today. Here we are: Rodamaunt Promenade. We'll see soon enough about your inheritance."

The street was a grand curving one lined on one side by flat-faced towers all the same height, and on the other by an alternation of great buildings and short ones. These, apparently, were government offices. Inyanna was daunted by the complexity of it all, and might have wandered outside in confusion for hours, not daring to enter; but Liloyve penetrated the mysteries of the place with a series of quick inquiries and led Inyanna within, through the corridors and windings of a maze hardly less intricate than the Grand Bazaar itself, until at length they found themselves sitting on a wooden bench in a large and brightly lit waiting room, watching names flick on and off on a bulletin board overhead. In half an hour Inyanna's appeared on the board.

"Is this the Bureau of Probate?" she asked, as they went in.

"Apparently there's no such thing," said Liloyve. "These are the proctors. If anyone can help you, they can."

A dour-faced Hjort, bloated and goggle-eyed like most of his kind, asked for her problem, and Inyanna, hesitant at first, then voluble, poured out the story: the strangers from Ni-moya, the astounding tale of the grand inheritance, the documents, the Pontifical seal, the twenty royals in filing fees. The Hjort, as the story unfolded, slumped behind his desk, kneaded his jowls, disconcertingly swiveled his great globular eyes one at a time. When she was done he took her receipt from her, ran his thick fingers thoughtfully over the ridges of the imperial seal it bore, and said gloomily, "You are the nineteenth claimant to Nissimorn Prospect who has presented herself in Ni-moya this year. There will be more, I am afraid. There will be many more."

"Nineteenth?"

"To my knowledge. Others may not have bothered to report the fraud to the proctors."

"The fraud," Inyanna repeated. "Is that it? The documents they showed me, the genealogy, the papers with my name on it—they traveled all the way from Ni-moya to Velathys simply to swindle me of twenty royals?"

"Oh, not simply to swindle *you*," said the Hjort. "Probably there are three or four heirs to Nissimorn Prospect in Velathys, and five in Narabal, and seven in Til-omon, and a dozen in Pidruid—it's not hard to get genealogies, you know. And forge the documents, and fill in the blanks. Twenty royals from this one, thirty perhaps from that, a nice livelihood if you keep moving, you see?"

"But how is this possible? Such things are against the law!"

"Yes," the Hjort agreed wearily. "And the King of Dreams—"

"Will punish them severely—you may be sure of it. Nor will we fail to apply civil penalties once we apprehend them. You will give us great assistance by describing them to us."

"And my twenty royals?"

The Hjort shrugged.

Inyanna said, "There's no hope that I can recover a thing?"

"None."

"But I've lost everything, then!"

"On behalf of his majesty I offer my most sincere regrets," said the Hjort, and that was that.

Outside, Inyanna said sharply to Liloyve, "Take me to Nissimorn Prospect!"

"But surely you don't believe—"

"That it is really mine? No, of course not. But I want to see it! I want to know what sort of place it was that was sold to me for my twenty royals!"

"Why torment yourself?"

"Please," Inyanna said.

"Come, then," said Liloyve.

She hailed a floater and gave it its instructions. Wide-eyed, Inyanna stared in wonder as the little vehicle bore them through the noble avenues of Ni-moya. In the warmth of the midday sun everything seemed bathed with light, and the city glowed, not with the frosty light of crystalline

Dulorn but with a pulsing, throbbing, sensuous splendor that reverberated from every whitewashed wall and street. Liloyve described the most significant of the places they were passing. "This is the Museum of Worlds," she said, indicating a great structure crowned by a tiara of angular glass domes. "Treasures of a thousand planets, even some things of Old Earth. And this is the Chamber of Sorcery, also a museum of sorts, given over to magic and dreaming. I have never been in it. And there—see the three birds of the city out front?—is the City Palace, where the mayor lives." They turned downhill, toward the river. "The floating restaurants are in this part of the harbor," she said, with a grand wave of her hand. "Nine of them, like little islands. They say you can have dishes from every province of Majipoor there. Someday we'll eat at them, all nine, eh?"

Inyanna smiled sadly. "It would be nice to think so."

"Don't worry. We have all our lives before us, and a thief's life is a comfortable one. I mean to roam every street of Ni-moya in my time, and you can come with me. There's a Park of Fabulous Beasts out in Gimbeluc, off in the hills, you know, with creatures that are extinct in the wilds everywhere, sigimoins and ghalvars and dimilions and everything, and there's the Opera House, where the municipal orchestra plays—you know about our orchestra? A thousand instruments, nothing like it in the universe—and then there's—oh. Here we are!"

They dismounted from the floater. Inyanna saw that they were nearly at the river's edge. Before her lay the Zimr, the great river so wide at this point that she could barely see across it, and only dimly could she make out the green line of Nissimorn on the horizon. Just to her left was a palisade of metal spikes twice the height of a man, set eight or ten feet apart and linked by a gauzy, almost invisible webbing that gave off a deep and sinister humming sound. Within that fence was a garden of striking beauty, low elegant shrubs abloom with gold and turquoise and scarlet blossoms, and a lawn so closely cropped it might well have been sprayed against the ground. Farther beyond, the land began to rise, and the house itself sat upon a rocky prominence overlooking the harbor: a mansion of wonderful size, white-walled in the Ni-moya manner, which made much use of the techniques of suspension and lightness typical of

Ni-moyan architecture, with porticoes that seemed to float and balconies cantilevered out for wondrous distances. Short of the Ducal Palace itself—visible not far down the shore, rising magnificently on its pedestal—Nissimorn Prospect seemed to Inyanna to be the most beautiful single building she had seen in all of Ni-moya thus far. And it was this that she thought she had inherited! She began to laugh. She sprinted along the palisade, pausing now and again to contemplate the great house from various angles, and laughter poured from her as though someone had told her the deepest truth of the universe, the truth that holds the secrets of all other truths and so must necessarily evoke a torrent of laughter. Liloyve followed her, calling out for her to wait, but Inyanna ran as one possessed. Finally she came to the front gate, where two mammoth Skandars in immaculate white livery stood guard, all their arms folded in an emphatic, possessive way. Inyanna continued to laugh; the Skandars scowled; Liloyve, coming up behind, plucked at Inyanna's sleeve and urged her to leave before there was trouble.

"Wait," she said, gasping. She went up to the Skandars. "Are you servants of Calain of Ni-moya?"

They looked at her without seeing her, and said nothing.

"Tell your master," she went on, undisturbed, "that Inyanna of Velathys was here, to see the house, and sends her regrets that she could not come to dine. Thank you."

"Come!" Liloyve whispered urgently.

Anger was beginning to replace indifference on the hairy faces of the huge guards. Inyanna saluted them graciously, and broke into laughter again, and gestured to Liloyve; and together they ran back to the floater, Liloyve too finally joining in the uncontrollable mirth.

6

It was a long time before Inyanna saw the sunlight of Ni-moya again, for now she took up her new life as a thief in the depths of the Grand Bazaar. At first she had no intent of adopting the profession of Liloyve and her family. But practical considerations soon overruled her niceties of morality. She had no way of returning to Velathys, nor, after these first few glimpses of Ni-moya, had she any real wish to do so. Nothing waited for her there except a life of peddling glue and nails and false satin and lanterns from Til-omon. To stay in Ni-moya, though, required a livelihood. She knew no trade except shopkeeping, and without capital she could hardly open a shop here. Quite soon all her money would be exhausted; she would not live off the charity of her new friends; she had no other prospects; they were offering her a niche in their society; and somehow it seemed acceptable to take up a life of thieving, alien though that was to her former nature, now that she had been robbed of all her savings by the fast-talking swindlers. So she let herself be garbed in a man's tunic— she was tall enough, and a little awkward of bearing, enough to carry the deception off plausibly—and under the name of Kulibhai, brother to the master thief Agourmole, entered the guild of thieves.

Liloyve was her mentor. For three days Inyanna followed her through the Bazaar, watching closely as the lavender-haired girl skimmed merchandise here and there. Some of it was done as crudely as donning a cloak in a shop and vanishing suddenly into the crowds; some involved quick sleight-of-hand in the bins and counters; and some required elaborate deceptions, bamboozling some delivery boy with a promise of kisses or better, while an accomplice made off with his barrow of goods. At the same time there was the obligation to prevent freelance theft. Twice in the three days, Inyanna saw Liloyve do that—the hand on the wrist, the cold, angry glare, the sharp whispered words, resulting both times in the look of fear, the apologies, the hasty withdrawal. Inyanna wondered if she would ever have the courage to do that. It seemed harder than thieving itself; and she was not at all sure she could bring herself to steal, either.

On the fourth day Liloyve said, "Bring me a flask of dragon-milk and two of the golden wine of Piliplok."

Inyanna said, appalled, "But they must sell for a royal apiece!"

"Indeed."

"Let me begin by stealing sausages."

"It's no harder to steal rare wines," said Liloyve. "And considerably more profitable."

"I am not ready."

"You only think you aren't. You've seen how it's done. You can do it yourself. Your fears are needless. You have the soul of a thief, Inyanna."

Furiously Inyanna said, "How can you say such a—"

"Softly, softly. I meant it as a compliment!"

Inyanna nodded. "Even so. I think you are wrong."

"I think you underestimate yourself," said Liloyve. "There are aspects of your character more apparent to others than to yourself. I saw them displayed the day we visited Nissimorn Prospect. Go, now: steal me a flask of Piliplok golden, and one of dragon-milk, and no more chatter. If you are ever to be a thief of our guild, today is your beginning."

There was no avoiding it. But there was no reason to risk doing it alone. Inyanna asked Liloyve's cousin Athayne to accompany her, and together they went swaggering down to a wine-shop in Ossier Lane— two young bucks of Ni-moya off to buy themselves some jollity. A strange calmness came over Inyanna. She allowed herself to think of no irrelevancies, such as morality, property rights, or the fear of punishment; there was only the task at hand to consider, a routine job of thievery. Once her profession had been shopkeeping, and now it was shoplooting, and it was useless to complicate the situation with philosophical hesitations.

A Ghayrog was behind the wine-shop counter: icy eyes that never blinked, glossy, scaly skin, writhing, fleshy hair. Inyanna, making her voice as deep as she could, inquired after the price of dragon-milk in globelet, flask, and duple. Meanwhile Athayne busied himself among the cheap red midcountry wines. The Ghayrog quoted prices. Inyanna expressed shock. The Ghayrog shrugged. Inyanna held a flask aloft, studied the pale blue fluid, scowled, and said, "It is murkier than the usual quality."

"It varies from year to year. And from dragon to dragon."

"One would think these things would be made standard."

"The effect is standard," said the Ghayrog, with the chilly reptilian Ghayrog equivalent of a leer and a smirk. "A few sips of that, my fellow, and you'll be good for the whole night!"

"Let me think about it a moment," said Inyanna. "A royal's no little sum, no matter how wonderful the effects."

It was the signal to Athayne, who turned and said, "This Mazadone stuff—is it really three crowns the duple? I'm certain that last week it sold for two."

"If you can find it at two, buy it at two," the Ghayrog answered.

Athayne scowled, moved as if to put the bottle back on the shelf, lurched and stumbled, and knocked half a row of globelets over. The Ghayrog hissed in anger. Athayne, bellowing his regrets, clumsily tried to set things to rights, knocking still more bottles down. The Ghayrog scurried to the display, yelling. He and Athayne bumbled into one another in their attempts to restore order, and in that moment Inyanna popped the flask of dragon-milk into her tunic, tucked one of Piliplok golden beside it, and, saying loudly, "I'll check the prices elsewhere, I think," walked out of the shop. That was all there was to it. She forced herself not to break into a run, although her cheeks were blazing and she was certain that the passersby all knew her for a thief, and that the other shopkeepers in the row would come storming out to seize her, and that the Ghayrog himself would be after her in a moment. But without difficulty she made her way to the corner, turned to her left, saw the street of facepaints and perfumes, went the length of it, and entered the place of oils and cheeses where Liloyve was waiting.

"Take these," Inyanna said. "They burn holes in my breast."

"Well done," Liloyve told her. "We'll drink the golden tonight, in your honor!"

"And the dragon-milk?"

"Keep it," said Liloyve. "Share it with Calain, the night you are invited to dine at Nissimorn Prospect."

That night Inyanna lay awake for hours, afraid to sleep, for sleep brought dreams and in dreams came punishments. The wine was gone, but the dragon-milk flask lay beneath her pillow, and she felt the urge to slip off in the night and return it to the Ghayrog. Centuries of shopkeeper ancestors weighed against her soul. A thief, she thought, a thief, a thief, I have become a thief in Ni-moya. By what right did I take those things?

By what right, she answered herself, did those two steal my twenty royals? But what had that to do with the Ghayrog? If *they* steal from me, and I use that as license to steal from *him*, and he goes to another's goods, where does it end, how does society survive? The Lady forgive me, she thought. The King of Dreams will whip my spirit. But at last she slept; she could not keep from sleeping forever; and the dreams that came to her were dreams of wonder and majesty, as she glided disembodied through the grand avenues of the city, past the Crystal Boulevard, the Museum of Worlds, the Gossamer Galleria, to Nissimorn Prospect, where the duke's brother took her hand. The dream bewildered her, for she could not in any way see it as a dream of punishment. Where was morality? Where was proper conduct? This went counter to all she believed. Yet it was as though destiny had intended her to be a thief. Everything that had happened to her in the past year had aimed her toward that. So perhaps it was the will of the Divine that she become what she had become. Inyanna smiled at that. What cynicism! But so be it. She would not fight destiny.

7

She stole often and she stole well. That first tentative, terrifying venture into thievery was followed by many more over the days that followed. She roved freely through the Grand Bazaar, sometimes with accomplices, sometimes alone, helping herself to this and that and this and that. It was so easy that it came to seem almost not like crime. The Bazaar was always crowded: Ni-moya's population, they said, was close to thirty million, and it seemed that all of them were in the Bazaar all the time. There was a constant crushing flow of people. The merchants were harried and careless, bedeviled always by questions, disputes, bargainers, inspectors. There was little challenge in moving through the river of beings, taking as she pleased.

Most of the booty was sold. A professional thief might keep the occasional item for her own use, and meals were always taken on the job, but nearly everything was stolen with an eye toward immediate resale. That was mainly the responsibility of the Hjorts who lived with Agourmole's family. There were three of them, Beyork, Hankh, and Mozinhunt, and they were part of a wide-ranging network of disposers of stolen goods, a chain of Hjorts that passed merchandise briskly out of the Bazaar and into wholesale channels that often eventually resold it to the merchants from whom it had been taken. Inyanna learned quickly what things were in demand by these people and what were not to be bothered with.

Because Inyanna was new to Ni-moya she had a particularly easy time of it. Not all the merchants of the Grand Bazaar were complacent about the guild of thieves, and some knew Liloyve and Athayne and Sidoun and the others of the family by sight, ordering them out of their shops the moment they appeared. But the young man who called himself Kulibhai was unknown in the Bazaar, and so long as Inyanna picked over a different section of the all but infinite place every day, it would be many years before her victims became familiar with her.

The dangers in her work came not so much from the shopkeepers, though, as from thieves of other families. They did not know her, either, and their eyes were quicker than the merchants'—so that three times in her first ten days Inyanna was apprehended by some other thief. It was terrifying at first to feel a hand closing on her wrist; but she remained cool, and, confronting the other without panic, she said simply, "You are infringing. I am Kulibhai, brother to Agourmole." Word spread swiftly. After the third such event, she was not troubled again.

To make such arrests herself was troublesome. At first she had no way of telling the legitimate thieves from the improper ones, and she hesitated to seize the wrist of some who, for all she knew, had been pilfering in the Bazaar since Lord Kinniken's time. It became surprisingly easy for her to detect thievery in progress, but if she had no other thief of Agourmole's clan with her to consult, she took no action. Gradually she came to recognize many of the licensed thieves of other families, but yet nearly every day she saw some unfamiliar figure rummaging through a merchant's goods, and finally, after some weeks in the Bazaar, she felt moved to act. If she found herself apprehending a true thief, she could always beg pardon; but the essence of the system was that she not only stole but also policed, and she knew she was failing in that duty. Her first arrest was that of a grimy girl taking vegetables; there was hardly time to say a word, for the girl dropped her take and fled in terror. The next one turned out to be a veteran thief distantly related to Agourmole, who amiably explained Inyanna's mistake; and the third, unauthorized but also unfrightened, responded to Inyanna's words with spitting curses and muttered threats, to which Inyanna replied calmly and untruthfully that seven other thieves of the guild were observing them and would take immediate action in the event of trouble. After that she felt no qualms, and acted freely and confidently whenever she believed it was appropriate.

Nor did the thieving itself trouble her conscience, after the beginning. She had been reared to expect the vengeance of the King of Dreams if she wandered into sin—nightmares, torments, a fever of the soul whenever she closed her eyes—but either the King did not regard this sort of pilferage and purloinment as sin, or else he and his minions were so busy with even greater criminals that they had no time to get around to her. Whatever the reason, the King sent her no sendings. Occasionally she dreamed of him, fierce old ogre beaming bad news out of the burning wastelands of Suvrael, but that was nothing unusual; the King entered everybody's dreams from time to time, and it meant very little. Sometimes, too, Inyanna dreamed of the blessed Lady of the Isle, the gentle mother of the Coronal Lord Malibor, and it seemed to her that that sweet woman was shaking her head sadly, as though to say she was woefully disappointed in her child Inyanna. But it was within the powers of the Lady to speak more strongly to those who had strayed from her path, and that she did not seem to be doing. In the absence of moral correction Inyanna quickly came to have a casual view of her profession. It was not crime; it was merely redistribution of goods. No one seemed to be greatly injured by it, after all.

In time she took as her lover Sidoun, the older brother of Liloyve. He was shorter than Inyanna, and so bony that it was a sharp business to embrace him; but he was a gentle and thoughtful man, who played prettily on the pocket-harp and sang old ballads in a clear light tenor, and the more often she went out thieving with him the more agreeable she found his company. Some rearrangements of the sleeping-quarters in Agourmole's den were made, and they were able to spend their nights together. Liloyve and the other thieves seemed to find this development charming.

In Sidoun's company she roved farther and farther through the great city. So efficient were they as a team that often they had their day's quota of larceny done in an hour or two, and that left them free for the rest of the day, for it would not do to exceed one's quota: the social contract of the Grand Bazaar allowed the thieves to take only so much, and no more, with impunity. So it was that Inyanna began to make excursions to the delightful outer reaches of Ni-moya. One of her favorite places was the Park of Fabulous Beasts in the hilly suburb of Gimbeluc, where she could roam among animals of other eras, that had been crowded out of their domains by the spread of civilization on Majipoor. Here she saw such rarities as the wobbly-legged dimilions, fragile long-necked leaf-chompers twice as high as a Skandar, and the dainty, tiptoeing sigimoins with a thickly furred tail at either end, and the awkward big-beaked zampidoon birds that once had darkened the sky over Ni-moya with their great flocks, and now existed only in the park and as one of the city's official emblems. Through some magic that must have been devised in ancient times, voices came from the ground whenever one of these creatures sauntered by, telling onlookers its name and original habitat. Then too the park had lovely secluded glades, where Inyanna and Sidoun could walk hand in hand, saying little, for Sidoun was not a man of many words.

Some days they went on boat-rides out into the Zimr and over to the Nissimorn side, and occasionally down the gullet of the nearby River Steiche, which, if followed long enough, would bring them to the forbidden Shapeshifter territory. But that was many weeks' journey upriver, and they traveled only as far as the little Liiman fishing villages a short way south of Nissimorn, where they bought fresh-caught fish and held picnic on the beach and swam and lay in the sun. Or on moonless evenings they went to the Crystal Boulevard, where the revolving reflectors cast dazzling patterns of ever-changing light, and peered in awe at the exhibit cases maintained by the great companies of Majipoor, a streetside museum of costly goods, so magnificent and so opulently displayed that not even the boldest of thieves would dare to attempt an entry. And often they dined at one of the floating restaurants, frequently taking Liloyve with them, for she loved those places above all else in the city. Each island was a miniature of some far territory of the planet, its characteristic plants and animals thriving there, and its special foods and wines a feature: one of windy Piliplok, where those who had the price dined on seadragon meat, and one of humid Narabal with its rich berries and succulent ferns, and one of great Stee on Castle Mount, and a restaurant of Stoien and one of Pidruid and one of Til-omon—but none of Velathys, Inyanna learned without surprise, nor was the Shapeshifter capital of Ilirivoyne favored with an island, nor harsh sun-blasted Tolaghai on Suvrael, for Tolaghai and Ilirivoyne were places that most folk of Majipoor did not care to think about, and Velathys was simply beneath notice.

Of all the places that Inyanna visited with Sidoun on these leisurely afternoons and evenings, though, her favorite was the Gossamer Galleria. That mile-long arcade, hanging high above street level, contained the finest shops of Ni-moya, which is to say the finest in all the continent of Zimroel, the finest outside the rich cities of Castle Mount. When they went there, Inyanna and Sidoun put on their most elegant clothes, that they had stolen from the best stalls in the Grand Bazaar—nothing at all to compare with what the aristocrats wore, but superior by far to their daily garb. Inyanna enjoyed getting out of the male costumes that she wore in her role as Kulibhai the thief, and dressing in slinky and clinging robes of purples and greens, and letting her long red hair tumble free. With her fingertips lightly touching Sidoun's, she made the grand promenade of the Galleria, indulging in pleasant fantasies as they inspected the eye-jewels and feather-masks and polished amulets and metal trinkets that were available, for a double handful of shining royal-pieces, to the truly wealthy. None of these things would ever be hers, she knew, for a thief who thieved well enough to afford such luxuries would be a danger to the stability of the Grand Bazaar; but it was joyous enough merely to see the treasures of the Gossamer Galleria, and to pretend.

It was on one of these outings to the Gossamer Galleria that In-yanna strayed into the orbit of Calain, brother to the duke.

8

She had no notion that that was what she was doing, of course. All she thought she was doing was conducting a little innocent flirtation, as part of the adventure into fantasy that a visit to the Galleria ought to be. It was a mild night in late summer and she was wearing one of her lightest gowns, a sheer fabric less substantial even than the webbing of which the Galleria was woven; and she and Sidoun were in the shop of dragon-bone carvings, examining the extraordinary thumbnail-sized masterpieces of a Skandar boat-captain who produced intricacies of interwoven slivers of ivory of the highest implausibility, when four men in the robes of nobility came in. Sidoun at once faded into a dark corner, for he knew that his clothing and his bearing and the cut of his hair marked him as no equal to these; but Inyanna, conscious that the lines of her body and the cool gaze of her green eyes could compensate for all sorts of deficiencies of manner, boldly held her place at the counter. One of the men glanced at the carving in her hand and said, "If you buy that, you'll be doing well for yourself."

"I have not made up my mind," Inyanna replied.

"May I see it?"

She dropped it lightly into his palm, and at the same time let her eyes make contact brazenly with his. He smiled, but gave his attention mainly to the ivory piece, a map-globe of Majipoor fashioned from many sliding panels of bone. After a moment he said to the proprietor, "The price?"

"It is a gift," answered the other, a slender and austere Ghayrog.

"Indeed. And also from me to you," said the nobleman, spilling the bauble back into the hand of the amazed Inyanna. Now his smile was more intimate. "You are of this city?" he asked quietly.

"I live in Strelain," she said.

"Do you dine often at the Narabal Island?"

"When the mood takes me."

"Good. Will you be there at sunset tomorrow? There will be someone there eager to make your acquaintance."

Hiding her bewilderment, Inyanna bowed. The nobleman bowed and turned away; he purchased three of the little carvings, dropping a purse of coins on the counter; then they departed. Inyanna stared in astonishment at the precious thing in her hand. Sidoun, emerging from the shadows, whispered, "It's worth a dozen royals! Sell it back to the keeper!"

"No," she said. To the proprietor she said, "Who was that man?"

"You are unfamiliar with him?"

"I would not have asked you his name if I knew it."

"Yes. Yes." The Ghayrog made little hissing sounds. "He is Durand Livolk, the duke's chamberlain."

"And the other three?"

"Two are in the duke's service, and the third is a companion to the duke's brother Calain."

"Ah," said Inyanna. She held forth the ivory globe. "Can you mount this on a chain?"

"It will take only a moment."

"And the price for a chain worthy of the object?"

The Ghayrog gave her a long calculating look. "The chain is only accessory to the carving; and since the carving was a gift, so too with the chain." He fitted delicate golden links to the ivory ball, and packed the trinket in a box of shining stickskin.

"At least twenty royals, with the chain!" Sidoun muttered, amazed, when they were outside. "Take it across to that shop and sell it, Inyanna!"

"It was a gift," she said coolly. "I will wear it tomorrow night, when I dine at the Narabal Island."

She could not go to dinner in the gown she had worn that evening, though; and finding another just as sheer and costly in the shops of the Grand Bazaar required two hours of diligent work the next day. But in the end she came upon one that was the next thing to nakedness, yet cloaked everything in mystery; and that was what she wore to the Narabal Island, with the ivory carving dangling between her breasts.

At the restaurant there was no need to give her name. As she stepped off the ferry she was met by a somber and dignified Vroon in ducal livery, who conducted her through the lush groves of vines and ferns to a shadowy bower, secluded and fragrant, in a part of the island cut off by dense plantings from the main restaurant area. Here three people awaited her at a gleaming table of polished nightflower wood beneath a vine whose thick hairy stems were weighed down by enormous globular blue flowers. One was Durand Livolk, who had given her the ivory carving. One was a woman, slender and dark-haired, as sleek and glossy as the tabletop itself. And the third was a man of about twice Inyanna's age, delicately built, with thin close-pursed lips and soft features. All three were dressed with such magnificence that Inyanna cringed at her own fancied shabbiness. Durand Livolk rose smoothly, went to Inyanna's side, and murmured, "You look even more lovely this evening. Come: meet some friends. This is my companion, the Lady Tisiorne. And this—"

The frail-looking man got to his feet. "I am Calain of Ni-moya," he said simply, in a gentle and feathery voice.

Inyanna felt confused, but only for a moment. She had thought the duke's chamberlain had wanted her himself; now she understood that Durand Livolk had merely been procuring her for the duke's brother. That knowledge sparked an instant's indignation in her, but it died quickly away. Why take offense? How many young women of Ni-moya had the chance to dine on the Narabal Island with the brother of the duke? If to another it might seem that she was being used, so be it; she meant to do a little using herself, in this interchange.

A place was ready for her beside Calain. She took it and the Vroon instantly brought a tray of liqueurs, all unfamiliar ones, of colors that blended and swirled and phosphoresced. She chose one at random: it had the flavor of mountain mists, and caused an immediate tingling in her cheeks and ears. From overhead came the patter of light rainfall, landing on the broad glossy leaves of the trees and vines, but not on the diners. The rich tropical plantings of this island, Inyanna knew, were maintained by frequent artificial rainfall that duplicated the climate of Narabal.

Calain said, "Do you have favorite dishes here?"

"I would prefer that you order for me."

"If you wish. Your accent is not of Ni-moya."

"Velathys," she replied. "I came here only last year."

"A wise move," said Durand Livolk. "What prompted it?"

Inyanna laughed. "I think I will tell that story another time, if I may."

"Your accent is charming," said Calain. "We rarely meet Velathyntu folk here. Is it a beautiful city?"

"Hardly, my lord."

"Nestling in the Gonghars, though—surely it must be beautiful to see those great mountains all around you."

"That may be. One comes to take such things for granted when one spends all one's life among them. Perhaps even Ni-moya would begin to seem ordinary to one who had grown up here."

"Where do you live?" asked the woman Tisiorne.

"In Strelain," said Inyanna. And then, mischievously, for she had had another of the liqueurs and was feeling it, she added, "In the Grand Bazaar."

"*In* the Grand Bazaar?" said Durand Livolk.

"Yes. Beneath the street of the cheesemongers."

Tisiorne said, "And for what reason do you make your home there?"

"Oh," Inyanna answered lightly, "to be close to the place of my employment."

"In the street of the cheesemongers?" said Tisiorne, horror creeping into her tone.

"You misunderstand. I am employed in the Bazaar, but not by the merchants. I am a thief."

The word fell from her lips like a lightning-bolt crashing on the mountaintops. Inyanna saw the sudden startled look pass from Calain to Durand Livolk, and the color rising in Durand Livolk's face. But these people were aristocrats, and they had aristocratic poise. Calain was the first to recover from his amazement. Smiling coolly, he said, "A profession that calls for grace and deftness and quick-wittedness, I have always believed." He touched his glass to Inyanna's. "I salute you, thief who says she's a thief. There's an honesty in that which many others lack."

The Vroon returned, bearing a vast porcelain bowl filled with pale blue berries, waxen-looking, with white highlights. They were thokkas, Inyanna knew—the favorite fruit of Narabal, said to make the blood run hot and the passions to rise. She scooped a few from the bowl; Tisiorne carefully chose a single one; Durand Livolk took a handful, and Calain more than that. Inyanna noticed that the duke's brother ate the berries seeds and all, said to be the most effective way. Tisiorne discarded the seeds of hers, which brought a wry grin from Durand Livolk. Inyanna did not follow Tisiorne's fashion.

Then there were wines, and morsels of spiced fish, and oysters floating in their own fluids, and a plate of intricate little fungi of soft pastel hues, and eventually a haunch of aromatic meat—the leg of the giant bilantoon of the forests just east of Narabal, said Calain. Inyanna ate sparingly, a nip of this, a bit of that. It seemed the proper thing to do, and also the most sensible. Some Skandar jugglers came by after a while, and did wondrous things with torches and knives and hatchets, drawing hearty applause from the four diners. Calain tossed the rough four-armed fellows a gleaming coin—a five-royal piece, Inyanna saw, astounded. Later it rained again, though not on them, and still later, after another round of liqueurs, Durand Livolk and Tisiorne gracefully excused themselves and left Calain and Inyanna sitting alone in the misty darkness.

Calain said, "Are you truly a thief?"

"Truly. But it was not my original plan. I owned a shop of general wares in Velathys."

"And then?"

"I lost it through a swindle," she said. "And came penniless to Nimoya, and needed a profession, and fell in with thieves, who seemed thoughtful and sympathetic people."

"And now you have fallen in with much greater thieves," said Calain. "Does that trouble you?"

"Do you regard yourself, then, as a thief?"

"I hold high rank through luck of birth alone. I do not work, except to assist my brother when he needs me. I live in splendor beyond most people's imaginings. None of this is deserved. Have you seen my home?"

"I know it quite well. From the outside, of course, only."

"Would you care to see the interior of it tonight?"

Inyanna thought briefly of Sidoun, waiting in the whitewashed stone room below the street of the cheesemongers.

"Very much," she said. "And when I've seen it, I'll tell you a little story about myself and Nissimorn Prospect and how it happened that I first came to Ni-moya."

"It will be most amusing, I'm sure. Shall we go?"

"Yes," Inyanna said. "But would it cause difficulties if I stopped first at the Grand Bazaar?"

"We have all night," said Calain. "There is no hurry."

The liveried Vroon appeared, and lit the way for them through the jungled gardens to the island's dock, where a private ferry waited. It conveyed them to the mainland; a floater had been summoned meanwhile, and shortly Inyanna arrived at the plaza of Pidruid Gate. "I'll be only a moment," Inyanna whispered, and, wraithlike in her fragile and clinging gown, she drifted swiftly through the crowds that even at this hour still thronged the Bazaar. Down into the underground den she went. The thieves were gathered around a table, playing some game with glass counters and ebony dice. They cheered and applauded as she made her splendid entrance, but she responded only with a quick tense smile, and drew Sidoun aside. In a low voice she said, "I am going out again, and I will not be back this night. Will you forgive me?"

"It's not every woman who catches the fancy of the duke's chamberlain."

"Not the duke's chamberlain," she said. "The duke's brother." She brushed her lips lightly against Sidoun's. He was glassy-eyed with surprise at her words. "Tomorrow let's go to the Park of Fabulous Beasts, yes, Sidoun?" She kissed him again and moved on, to her bedroom, and drew the flask of dragon-milk out from under her pillow, where it had been hidden for months. In the central room she paused at the gaming-table, leaned close beside Liloyve, and opened her hand, showing her the flask. Liloyve's eyes widened. Inyanna winked and said, "Do you remember what I was saving this for? You said, to share it with Calain when I went to Nissimorn Prospect. And so—"

Liloyve gasped. Inyanna winked and kissed her and went out.

Much later that night, as she drew forth the flask and offered it to the duke's brother, she wondered in sudden panic whether it might be a vast breach of etiquette to be offering him an aphrodisiac this way, perhaps implying that its use might be advisable. But Calain showed no offense. He was, or else pretended to be, touched by her gift; he made a great show of pouring the blue milk into porcelain bowls so dainty they were nearly transparent; with the highest of ceremony he put one bowl in her hand, lifted the other himself, and signaled a salute. The dragon-milk was strange and bitter, difficult for Inyanna to swallow; but she got it down, and almost at once felt its warmth throbbing in her thighs. Calain smiled. They were in the Hall of Windows of Nissimorn Prospect, where a single band of gold-bound glass gave a three-hundred-sixty-degree view of the harbor of Ni-moya and the distant southern shore of the river. Calain touched a switch. The great window became opaque. A circular bed rose silently from the floor. He took her by the hand and drew her toward it.

9

To be the concubine of the duke's brother seemed a high enough ambition for a thief out of the Grand Bazaar. Inyanna had no illusions about her relationship with Calain. Durand Livolk had chosen her for her looks alone, perhaps something about her eyes, her hair, the way she held herself. Calain, though he had expected her to be a woman somewhat closer to his own class, had evidently found something charming about being thrown together with someone from the bottom rung of society, and so she had had her evening at the Narabal Island and her night at Nissimorn Prospect; it had been a fine interlude of fantasy, and in the morning she would return to the Grand Bazaar with a memory to last her the rest of her life, and that would be that.

Only that was not that.

There was no sleep for them all that night—was it the effect of the dragon-milk, she wondered, or was he like that always?—and at dawn they strolled naked through the majestic house, so that he could show her its treasures, and as they breakfasted on a veranda overlooking the garden he suggested an outing that day to his private park in Istmoy. So it was not to be an adventure of a single night, then. She wondered if she should send word to Sidoun at the Bazaar, telling him she would not return that day, but then she realized that Sidoun would not need to be told. He would interpret her silence correctly. She meant to cause him no pain, but on the other hand she owed him nothing but common courtesy. She was embarked now on one of the great events of her life, and when she returned to the Grand Bazaar it would not be for Sidoun's sake, but merely because the adventure was over.

As it happened, she spent the next six days with Calain. By day they sported on the river in his majestic yacht, or strolled hand in hand through the private game-park of the duke, a place stocked with surplus beasts from the Park of Fabulous Beasts, or simply lay on the veranda of Nissimorn Prospect, watching the sun's track across the continent from Piliplok to Pidruid. And by night it was all feasting and revelry, dinner now at one of the floating islands, now at some great house of Ni-moya, one night at the Ducal Palace itself. The duke was very little like Calain: a much bigger man, and a good deal older, with a wearied and untender manner. Yet he managed to be charming to Inyanna, treating her with grace and gravity and never once making her feel like a street-girl his brother had scooped out of the Bazaar. Inyanna sailed through these events with the kind of cool acceptance one displays in dreams. To show awe, she knew, would be coarse. To pretend to an equal level of rank and sophistication would be even worse. But she arrived at a demeanor that was restrained without being humble, agreeable without being forward, and it seemed to be effective. In a few days it began to seem quite natural to her that she should be sitting at table with dignitaries who were lately returned from Castle Mount with bits of gossip about Lord Malibor the Coronal and his entourage, or who could tell stories of having hunted in the northern marches with the Pontifex Tyeveras when he was Coronal under Ossier, or who had newly come back from meetings at Inner Temple with the Lady of the Isle. She grew so self-assured in the company of these great ones that if anyone had turned to her and said, "And you, milady, how have you passed the recent months?" she would have replied easily, "As a thief in the Grand Bazaar," as she had done that first night on the Narabal Island. But the question did not arise: at this level of society, she realized, one never idly indulged one's curiosity with others, but left them to unveil their histories to whatever degree they preferred.

And therefore when on the seventh day Calain told her to prepare to return to the Bazaar, she neither asked him if he had enjoyed her company nor whether he had grown tired of her. He had chosen her to be his companion for a time; that time was now ended, and so be it. It had been a week she would never forget.

Going back to the den of the thieves was a jolt, though. A sumptuously outfitted floater took her from Nissimorn Prospect to the Grand Bazaar's Piliplok Gate, and a servant of Calain's placed in her arms the little bundle of treasures Calain had given her during their week together. Then the floater was gone and Inyanna was descending into the sweaty chaos of the Bazaar, and it was like awakening from a rare and magical dream. As she passed through the crowded lanes no one called out to her, for those who knew her in the Bazaar knew her in her male guise of Kulibhai, and she was dressed now in women's clothes. She moved through the swirling mobs in silence, bathed still in the aura of the aristocracy and moment by moment giving way to an inrushing feeling of depression and loss as it became clear to her that the dream was over, that she had re-entered reality. Tonight Calain would dine with the visiting Duke of Mazadone, and tomorrow he and his guests would sail up the Steiche on a fishing expedition, and the day after that—well, she had no idea, but she knew that she, on that day, would be filching laces and flasks of perfume and bolts of fabric. For an instant, tears surged into her eyes. She forced them back, telling herself that this was foolishness, that she ought not lament her return from Nissimorn Prospect but rather rejoice that she had been granted a week there.

No one was in the thieves' rooms except the Hjort Beyork and one of the Metamorphs. They merely nodded as Inyanna came in. She went to her chamber and donned the Kulibhai costume. But she could not bring herself so soon to return to her thieving. She stowed her packet of jewels and trinkets, Calain's gifts, carefully under her bed. By selling them she could earn enough to exempt her from her profession for a year or two; but she did not plan to part even with the smallest of them. Tomorrow, she resolved, she would go back into the Bazaar. For now, though, she lay facedown on the bed she again shared with Sidoun, and when tears came again she let them come, and after a while she rose, feeling more calm, and washed and waited for the others to appear.

Sidoun welcomed her with a nobleman's poise. No questions about her adventures, no hint of resentment, no sly innuendos: he smiled and took her hand and told her he was pleased she had come back, and offered her a sip of a wine of Alhanroel he had just stolen, and told her a couple of stories of things that had happened in the Bazaar while she was away. She wondered if he would feel inhibited in their lovemaking by the knowledge that the last man to touch her body had been a duke's brother, but no, he reached for her fondly and unhesitatingly when they were in bed, and his gaunt, bony body pressed warmly and jubilantly against her. The next day, after their rounds in the Bazaar, they went together to the Park of Fabulous Beasts, and saw for the first time the gossimaule of Glayge, that was so slender it was nearly invisible from the side, and they followed it a little way until it vanished, and laughed as though they had never been separated.

The other thieves regarded Inyanna with some awe for a few days, for they knew where she had been and what she must have been doing, and that laid upon her the strangeness that came from moving in exalted circles. But only Liloyve dared to speak directly to her of it, and she only once, saying, "What did he see in you?"

"How would I know? It was all like a dream."

"I think it was justice."

"What do you mean?"

"That you were wrongfully promised Nissimorn Prospect, and this was by way of making atonement to you. The Divine balances the good and the evil—do you see?" Liloyve laughed. "You've had your twenty royals' worth out of those swindlers, haven't you?"

Indeed she had, Inyanna agreed. But the debt was not yet fully paid, she soon discovered. On Starday next, working her way through the booths of the moneychangers and skimming off the odd coin here and there, she was startled suddenly by a hand on her wrist, and wondered what fool of a thief, failing to recognize her, was trying to make arrest. But it was Liloyve. Her face was flushed and her eyes were wide. "Come home right away!" she cried.

"What is it?"

"Two Vroons waiting for you. You are summoned by Calain, and they say you are to pack all your belongings, for you will not be returning to the Grand Bazaar."

10

So it happened that Inyanna Forlana of Velathys, formerly a thief, took up residence in Nissimorn Prospect as companion to Calain of Ni-moya. Calain offered no explanation, nor did she seek one. He wanted her by his side, and that was explanation enough. For the first few weeks she still expected to be told each morning to make ready to go back to the Bazaar, but that did not occur, and after a while she ceased to consider the possibility. Wherever Calain went, she went: to the Zimr Marshes to hunt the gihorna, to glittering Dulorn for a week at the Perpetual Circus, to Khyntor for the Festival of Geysers, even into mysterious, rainy Piurifayne to explore the shadowy homeland of the Shapeshifters. She who had spent all her first twenty years in shabby Velathys came to take it quite for granted that she should be traveling about like a Coronal making the grand processional, with the brother of a royal duke at her side; but yet she never quite lost her perspective, never failed to see the irony and incongruity of the strange transformations her life had undergone.

Nor was it surprising to her even when she found herself seated at table next to the Coronal himself. Lord Malibor had come to Ni-moya on a visit of state, for it behooved him to travel in the western continent every eight or ten years, by way of showing the people of Zimroel that they weighed equally in their monarch's thoughts with those of his home continent of Alhanroel. The duke provided the obligatory banquet, and Inyanna was placed at the high table, with the Coronal to her right and Calain at her left, and the duke and his lady at Lord Malibor's far side. Inyanna had been taught the names of the great Coronals in school, of course, Stiamot and Confalume and Prestimion and Dekkeret and all the rest, and her mother often had told her that it was on the very day of her birth when news came to Velathys that the old Pontifex Ossier was dead, that Lord Tyeveras had succeeded him and had chosen a man of the city of Bombifale, one Malibor, to be the new Coronal; and eventually the new coinage had trickled into her province, showing this Lord Malibor, a broad-faced man with wide-set eyes and heavy brows. But that such people as Coronals and Pontifexes actually existed had been a matter of some doubt to her through all those years, and yet here she was with her elbow an inch from Lord Malibor's, and the only thing she marveled at was how very much this burly and massive man in imperial green and gold resembled the man whose face was on the coins. She had expected the portraits to be less precise.

It seemed sensible to her that the conversations of Coronals would revolve wholly around matters of state. But in fact Lord Malibor seemed to talk mainly of the hunt. He had gone to this remote place to slay that rare beast, and to that inaccessible and uncongenial place to take the head of this difficult creature, and so on and so on; and he was constructing a new wing of the Castle to house all his trophies. "In a year or two," said the Coronal, "I trust you and Calain will visit me at the Castle. The trophy-room will be complete by then. It will please you, I know, to see such an array of creatures, all of them prepared by the finest taxidermists of Castle Mount." Inyanna did indeed look forward to visiting Lord Malibor's Castle, for the Coronal's enormous residence was a legendary place that entered into everyone's dreams, and she could imagine nothing more wonderful than to ascend to the summit of lofty Castle Mount and wander that great building, thousands of years old, exploring its thousands of rooms. But she was only repelled by Lord Malibor's obsession with slaughter. When he talked of killing amorfibots and ghalvars and sigimoins and steetmoy, and of the extreme effort he expended in those kill-ings, Inyanna was reminded of Ni-moya's Park of Fabulous Beasts, where by order of some milder Coronal of long ago those same animals were protected and cherished; and that put her in mind of quiet, gaunt Sidoun, who had gone with her so often to that park, and had played so sweetly on his pocket-harp. She did not want to think of Sidoun, to whom she owed nothing but for whom she felt a guilty affection, and she did not want to hear of the killing of rare creatures so that their heads might adorn Lord Malibor's trophy-room. Yet she managed to listen politely to the Coronal's tales of carnage and even to make an amiable comment or two.

Toward dawn, when they were finally back at Nissimorn Prospect and preparing for bed, Calain said to her, "The Coronal is planning to hunt next for sea-dragons. He seeks one known as Lord Kinniken's dragon, that was measured once at more than three hundred feet in length."

Inyanna, who was tired and not cheerful, shrugged. Sea-dragons, at least, were far from rare, and it would be no cause for grief if the Coronal harpooned a few. "Is there room in his trophy-house for a dragon that size?"

"For its head and wings, I imagine. Not that he stands much chance of getting it. The Kinniken's been seen only four times since Lord Kinniken's day, and not for seventy years. But if he doesn't find that one, he'll get another. Or drown in the attempt."

"Is there much chance of that?"

Calain nodded. "Dragon-hunting's dangerous business. He'd be wiser not to try. But he's killed just about everything that moves on land, and no Coronal's ever been out in a dragon-ship, and so he'll not be discouraged from it. We leave for Piliplok at the end of the week."

"*We?*"

"Lord Malibor has asked me to join him on the hunt." With a rueful smile he said, "In truth he wanted the duke, but my brother begged off, claiming duties of state. So he asked me. One does not easily refuse such things."

"Do I accompany you?" Inyanna asked.

"We have not planned it that way."

"Oh," she said quietly. After a moment she asked, "How long will you be gone?"

"The hunt lasts three months, usually. During the season of the southerly winds. And then the time to reach Piliplok, and outfit the vessel, and to return—it would be six or seven months all told. I'll be home by spring."

"Ah. I see."

Calain came to her side and drew her against him. "It will be the longest separation we will ever endure. I promise you that."

She wanted to say, Is there no way you can refuse to go? Or, Is there some way I can be allowed to go with you? But she knew how useless that was, and what a violation of the etiquette by which Calain lived. So Inyanna made no further protest. She took Calain into her arms, and they embraced until sunrise.

On the eve of his departure for the port of Piliplok, where the dragon-ships made harbor, Calain summoned her to his study on the highest level of Nissimorn Prospect and offered her a thick document to sign.

"What is this?" she asked, without picking it up.

"Articles of marriage between us."

"This is a cruel joke, milord."

"No joke, Inyanna. No joke at all."

"But—"

"I would have discussed the matter with you this winter, but then the damnable dragon-voyage arose, and left me no time. So I have rushed things a little. You are no mere concubine to me: this paper formalizes our love."

"Is our love something that needs formality?"

Calain's eyes narrowed. "I am going off on a risky and foolhardy adventure, from which I expect to return, but while I am at sea my fate will not be in my own hands. As my companion you have no legal rights of inheritance. As my wife—"

Inyanna was stunned. "If the risk is so great, abandon the voyage, milord!"

"You know that's impossible. I must bear the risk. And so I would provide for you. Sign it, Inyanna."

She stared a long time at the document, a draft of many pages. Her eyes would not focus properly and she neither could nor would make out the words that some scribe had indited in the most elegant of calligraphy. Wife to Calain? It seemed almost monstrous to her, a shattering of all proprieties, a stepping beyond every boundary. And yet—and yet—

He waited. She could not refuse.

In the morning he departed in the Coronal's entourage for Piliplok, and all that day Inyanna roamed the corridors and chambers of Nissimorn Prospect in confusion and disarray. That night the duke thoughtfully invited her for dinner; the next, Durand Livolk and his lady escorted her to dine at the Pidruid Island, where a shipment of fireshower-palm wine had arrived. Other invitations followed, so that her life was a busy one, and the months passed. It was midwinter now. And then came word that a great sea-dragon had fallen upon the ship of Lord Malibor and sent it to the bottom of the Inner Sea. Lord Malibor was dead, and all those who had sailed with him, and a certain Voriax had been named Coronal. And under the terms of Calain's will, his widow Inyanna Forlana had come into full ownership of the great estate known as Nissimorn Prospect.

11

When the period of mourning was over and she had an opportunity to make arrangements for such matters, Inyanna called for one of her stewards and ordered rich gifts of money to be delivered to the Grand Bazaar, for the thief Agourmole and all members of his family. It was Inyanna's way of saying that she had not forgotten them. "Tell me their exact words when you hand the purses to them," she ordered the steward, hoping they would send back some warm remembrances of the old times together, but the man reported that none of them had said anything of interest, that they had simply expressed surprise and gratitude toward the Lady Inyanna, except for the man named Sidoun, who had refused his gift and could not be urged to accept it. Inyanna smiled sadly and had Sidoun's twenty royals distributed to children in the streets, and after that she had no further contact with the thieves of the Grand Bazaar, nor did she ever go near the place.

Some years later, while visiting the shops of the Gossamer Galleria, the Lady Inyanna observed two suspicious-looking men in the shop of the dragon-bone carvings. From their movements and the way they exchanged glances, it seemed quite clear to her that they were thieves, maneuvering to create a diversion that would allow them to plunder the shop. Then she looked at them more closely and realized that she had encountered them before, for one was a short thick-framed man, and the other tall and knobby-faced and pale. She gestured to her escorts, who moved quietly into position about the two.

Inyanna said, "One of you is Steyg, and one is called Vezan Ormus, but I have forgotten which of you is which. On the other hand, I remember the other details of our meeting quite well."

The thieves looked at one another in alarm. The taller one said, "Milady, you are mistaken. My name is Elakon Mirj, and my friend is called Thanooz."

"These days, perhaps. But when you visited Velathys long ago you went by other names. I see that you've graduated from swindling to thievery, eh? Tell me this: how many heirs to Nissimorn Prospect did you discover, before the game grew dull?"

Now there was panic in their eyes. They seemed to be calculating the chances of making a break past Inyanna's men toward the door; but that would have been rash. The guards of the Gossamer Galleria had been notified and were gathered just outside.

The shorter thief, trembling, said, "We are honest merchants, milady, and nothing else."

"You are incorrigible scoundrels," said Inyanna, "and nothing else. Deny it again and I'll have you shipped to Suvrael for penal servitude!"

"Milady—"

"Speak the truth," Inyanna said.

Through chattering teeth the taller one replied, "We admit the charge. But it was long ago. If we have injured you, we will make full restitution."

"Injured me? Injured me?" Inyanna laughed. "Rather, you did me the greatest service anyone could have done. I feel only gratitude toward you; for know that I was Inyanna Forlana the shopkeeper of Velathys, whom you cheated out of twenty royals, and now I am the Lady Inyanna of Ni-moya, mistress of Nissimorn Prospect. And so the Divine protects the weak and brings good out of evil." She beckoned to the guards. "Convey these two to the imperial proctors, and say that I will give testimony against them later, but that I ask mercy for them, perhaps a sentence of three months of road-mending, or something similar. And afterward I think I'll take the two of you into my service. You are worthless rogues, but clever ones, and it's better to keep you close at hand, where you can be watched, than to let you go loose to prey on the unwary." She waved her hand. They were led away.

Inyanna turned to the keeper of the shop. "I regret the interruption," she said. "Now, these carvings of the emblems of the city, that you think are worth a dozen royals apiece—what would you say to thirty royals for the lot, and maybe the little carving of the bilantoon thrown in to round things off—"

TEN

Voriax and Valentine

O *f all the vicarious lives Hissune has experienced in the Register of Souls,*
that of Inyanna Forlana seems perhaps the closest to his heart. In part it
is because she is a woman of modern times and so the world in which she
dwelled seems less alien to him than those of the soul-painter or the sea-captain
or Thesme of Narabal. But the main reason Hissune feels kinship with the one-
time shopkeeper of Velathys is that she began with practically nothing, and lost
even that, and nevertheless came to achieve power and grandeur and, Hissune
suspects, a measure of contentment. He understands that the Divine helps those
who helped themselves, and Inyanna seems much like him in that respect. Of
course, luck was with her—she caught the attention of the right people at the
right moment, and they saw her nicely along her journey; but does one not also
shape one's own luck? Hissune, who had been in the right place when Lord
Valentine in his wanderings came to the Labyrinth years ago, believes that. He
wonders what surprises and delights fortune has in store for him, and how he
can better shape his own destinies to achieve something higher than the clerkship
in the Labyrinth that has been his lot so long. He is eighteen, now, and that
seems very old for commencing his rise to greatness. But he reminds himself that
Inyanna, at his age, was peddling clay pots and bolts of cloth on the wrong side
of Velathys, and she came to inherit Nissimorn Prospect. No telling what waits
for him. Why, at any moment Lord Valentine might send for him—Lord Val-
entine, who arrived at the Labyrinth the week before, and is lodged now in those
luxurious chambers reserved for the Coronal when he is in residence at the

capital of the Pontificate—Lord Valentine might summon him and say, "Hissune, you've served long enough in this grubby place. From now on you live beside me on Castle Mount!"

At any moment, yes. But Hissune has heard nothing from the Coronal and expects to hear nothing. It is a pretty fantasy, but he will not torment himself with false hopes. He goes about his dreary work and mulls all that he has learned in the Register of Souls, and a day or two after sharing the life of the thief of Ni-moya he returns to the Register and with the greatest boldness he has ever displayed he inquires of the archival index whether there is on file a recording of the soul of Lord Valentine. It is impudence, he knows, and dangerous tempting of fate; Hissune will not be surprised if lights flash and bells ring and armed guards come to seize the prying young upstart who without the slightest shred of authority is attempting to penetrate the mind and spirit of the Coronal himself. What does surprise him is the actual event: the vast machine simply informs him that a single record of Lord Valentine is available, made long ago, in his earliest manhood. Hissune, shameless, does not hesitate. Quickly he punches the activator keys.

THEY WERE TWO BLACK-HAIRED, black-bearded men, tall and strong, with dark flashing eyes and wide shoulders and an easy look of authority about them, and anyone could see at a single glance that they must be brothers. But there were differences. One was a man and one was still to some degree a boy, and that was evident not only from the sparseness of the younger one's beard and the smoothness of his face, but from a certain warmth and playfulness and gaiety in his eyes. The older one was more stern, more austere of expression, more imperious, as though he bore terrible responsibilities that had left their mark on him. In a way that was true; for he was Voriax of Halanx, elder son of the High Counsellor Damiandane, and it had been commonly said of him on Castle Mount since his childhood that he was sure to be Coronal one day.

Of course there were those who said the same thing about his younger brother Valentine—that he was a fine boy of great promise, that he had the making of a king about him. But Valentine had no illusions about such compliments. Voriax was the older by eight years, and, beyond any doubt, if either of them went to dwell in the Castle it would be Voriax. Not that Voriax had any guarantees of the succession, despite what everyone said. Their father Damiandane had been one of Lord Tyeveras' closest advisers, and he too had universally been expected to be the next Coronal. But when Lord Tyeveras became Pontifex, he had reached all the way down the Mount to the city of Bombifale to choose Malibor as his successor. No one had anticipated that, for Malibor was only a provincial governor, a coarse man more interested in hunting and games than in the burdens of administration. Valentine had not yet been born then, but Voriax had told him that their father had never uttered a word of disappointment or dismay at being passed over for the throne, which perhaps was the best indication that he had been qualified to be chosen.

Valentine wondered whether Voriax would behave so nobly if the starburst crown were denied him after all, and went instead to some other high prince of the Mount—Elidath of Morvole, say, or Tunigorn, or Stasilaine, or to Valentine himself. How odd that would be! Sometimes Valentine covertly said the names to hear their sound: Lord Stasilaine, Lord Elidath, Lord Tunigorn. Lord Valentine, even! But such fantasies were idle folly. Valentine had no wish to displace his brother, nor was it likely to happen. Barring some unimaginable prank of the Divine or some bizarre whim of Lord Malibor, it was Voriax who would reign when it became Lord Malibor's time to be Pontifex, and the knowledge of that destiny had imprinted itself on Voriax's spirit and showed in his conduct and bearing.

The complexities of the court were far from Valentine's mind now. He and his brother were on holiday in the lower ranges of Castle Mount— a trip long postponed, for Valentine had suffered a terrible fracture of the leg the year before last while riding with his friend Elidath in the pygmy forest below Amblemorn, and only lately had he been sufficiently recovered for another such strenuous journey. Down the vast mountain he and Voriax had gone, making a grand and wonderful tour, possibly the last long holiday Valentine was apt to have before he entered the world of adult obligations. He was seventeen, now, and because he belonged to that select group of princelings from whom Coronals were chosen, there was much he must learn of the techniques of government, so that he would be ready for whatever might be asked of him.

And so he had gone with Voriax—who was escaping his own duties, and glad of it, for the sake of helping his brother celebrate his return to health—from the family estate in Halanx to the nearby pleasure-city of High Morpin, to ride the juggernauts and career through the power-tunnels. Valentine insisted on doing the mirror-slides, too, by way of testing the strength in his shattered leg, and just the merest look of uncertainty crossed Voriax's face, as if he doubted that Valentine could handle such sports but was too tactful to say it. When they stepped out on the slides Voriax hovered close by Valentine's elbow, irritatingly protective, and when Valentine moved away a few steps Voriax moved with him, until Valentine turned and said, "Do you think I will fall, brother?"

"There is little chance of that."

"Then why stand so close? Is it you that fears falling?" Valentine laughed. "Be reassured, then. I'll reach you soon enough to catch you."

"You are ever thoughtful, brother," said Voriax. And then the slides began to turn and the mirrors glowed brightly, and there was no time for more banter. Indeed Valentine felt a moment's uneasiness, for the mirror-slide was not for invalids and his injury had left him with a slight but infuriating limp that disturbed his coordination; but quickly he caught the rhythm of it and he stayed upright easily, sustaining his balance even in the wildest gyrations, and when he went whirling past Voriax he saw the anxiety gone from his brother's face. Yet the essence of the episode gave Valentine much to think about, as he and Voriax traveled on down the Mount to Tentag for the tree-dancing festival, and then to Ertsud Grand and Minimool, and onward past Gimkandale to Furible to witness the mating flight of the stone birds. While they had been waiting for the mirror-slides to start moving Voriax had been a concerned and loving guardian, and yet at the same time a bit condescending, a bit smothering: his fraternal care for Valentine's safety seemed to Valentine yet another way for Voriax to be maintaining authority over him, and Valentine, at the threshold of full manhood, did not at all like that. But he understood that brotherhood was part love and part warfare, and he kept his annoyance to himself.

From Furible they passed through Bimbak East and Bimbak West, pausing in each city to stand before one of the twin mile-high towers that made even the haughtiest swaggerer feel like an ant, and beyond Bimbak East they took the path that led to Amblemorn, where a dozen wild streams came together to become the potent River Glayge. On the downslope side of Amblemorn was a place some miles across where the soil was hard-packed and chalky-white, and trees that elsewhere grew to pierce the sky were dwarfed eerie things here, no taller than a man and no thicker than a girl's wrist. It was in this pygmy forest that Valentine had come to grief, goading his mount too hard in a place where treacherous roots snaked over the ground. The mount had lost its footing, Valentine had been thrown, his leg had been horribly bent between two slender but unyielding trees whose trunks had the toughness of a thousand years, and months of anguish and frustration had followed while the bones slowly knit and an irreplaceable year of being young slipped away from him. Why had they come back here now? Voriax prowled the weird forest as if searching for hidden treasure. At last he turned to Valentine and said, "This place seems enchanted."

"The explanation is simple. The roots of the trees are unable to penetrate very deeply into this useless gray soil; they take the best grip they can, for this is Castle Mount where everything grows, but they are starved for nourishment, and so—"

"Yes, I understand," said Voriax coolly. "I didn't say the place *is* enchanted, only that it *seems* that way. A legion of Vroon wizards couldn't have created anything so ugly. Yet I'm glad to be seeing it at last. Shall we ride through it?"

"How subtle you are, Voriax."

"Subtle? I fail to see—"

"Suggesting that I take another try at crossing the place that nearly cost me my leg."

Voriax's ruddy face turned even more florid. "I hardly think you'd fall again."

"Surely not. But you think I may think so, and you've long believed that the way to conquer fear is to take the offensive against whatever it is you dread, and so you maneuver me into a second race here, to burn away any lingering timidity this forest may have instilled in me. It is the opposite of what you were doing when we went on the mirror-slides, but it amounts to the same thing, does it not?"

"I understand none of this," said Voriax. "Do you have some sort of fever today?"

"Not at all. Shall we race?"

"I think not."

Valentine, baffled, pounded one fist against another. "But you just suggested it!"

"I suggested a ride," Voriax answered. "But you seem full of mysterious angers and defiance, and you accuse me of maneuvering and manipulating you where no such things were intended. If we cross the forest while you're in such a mood, you'll certainly fall again, and probably smash your other leg. Come: we'll go on into Amblemorn."

"Voriax—"

"Come."

"I want to ride through the forest." Valentine's eyes were steady on his brother's. "Will you ride with me, or do you prefer to wait here?"

"With you, I suppose."

"Now tell me to be careful and watch out for hidden roots."

A muscle flickered in annoyance in Voriax's cheek, and he let out a long sigh of exasperation. "You are no child. I would not say such a thing to you. Besides, if I thought you needed such advice, I'd deny you as my brother and cast you forth."

He stirred his mount and rode off furiously down the narrow avenues between the pygmy trees.

Valentine followed after a moment, riding hard, striving to close the gap between them. The path was difficult and here and there he saw obstacles as menacing as the one that had brought him down when he rode here with Elidath; but his mount was sure-footed and there was no need to pull back on the reins. Though the memory of his fall was bright in him, Valentine felt no fear, only a sort of heightened alertness: if he fell again, he knew he would fall less disastrously. He wondered if he might not be overreacting to Voriax. Perhaps he was too touchy, too sensitive, too quick to defend himself against the imagined overprotectiveness of his older brother. Voriax was in training to be lord of the world, after all; he could not help but seem to assume responsibility for everyone and everything, especially his younger brother. Valentine resolved to be less zealous in his defense of his autonomy.

They passed through the forest and into Amblemorn, oldest of the cities of Castle Mount, an ancient place of tangled streets and vine-encrusted walls. It was here, twelve thousand years ago, that the conquest of the Mount had begun—the first bold and foolish ventures into the bleak, airless wastes of the thirty-mile-high excrescence that jutted from Majipoor's flank. For one who had lived all his life amid its Fifty Cities and their eternal fragrant springtime, it was hard now to imagine a time when the Mount was bare and uninhabitable; but Valentine knew the story of the pioneers edging up the titanic slopes, carrying the machines that brought warmth and air to the great mountain, transforming it over centuries into a fairyland realm of beauty, crowned at last by the small rugged keep at the summit that Lord Stiamot had established eight thousand years ago, and that had grown by incredible metamorphosis into the vast, incomprehensible Castle where Lord Malibor dwelled today. He and Voriax paused in awe before the monument in Amblemorn marking the old timber-line:

ABOVE HERE ALL WAS BARREN ONCE

A garden of wondrous halatinga trees with crimson-and-gold flowers surrounded the shaft of polished black Velathyntu marble that bore the inscription.

A day and a night and a day and a night in Amblemorn, and then Voriax and Valentine descended through the valley of the Glayge to a place called Ghiseldorn, off the main roads. At the edge of a dark and dense forest a settlement had sprung up here a few thousand people who had retreated from the great cities; they lived in tents of black felt, made from the fleece of the wild blaves that grazed in the meadows beside the river, and had little to do with their neighbors. Some said that they were witches and wizards; some that they were a stray tribe of Metamorphs that had escaped the ancient expulsion of their kind from Alhanroel, and perpetually wore human form; the truth, Valentine suspected, was that these folk were simply not at home in the world of commerce and striving that was Majipoor, and had come here to live their own way in their own community.

By late afternoon he and Voriax reached a hill from which they could see the forest of Ghiseldorn and the village of black tents just beyond it. The forest seemed unwelcoming—pingla-trees, short and thick-trunked, with their plump branches emerging at sharp angles and interlacing to form a tight canopy, admitting no light. Nor did the village appear to beckon. The ten-sided tents, widely spaced, looked like giant insects of a peculiar geometry, pausing for the moment before continuing an inexorable migration across a landscape to which they were utterly indifferent. Valentine had felt a powerful curiosity about Ghiseldorn and its folk, but now that he was here he was less eager to penetrate its mysteries.

He glanced over at Voriax and saw the same doubts on his brother's face.

"What shall we do?" Valentine asked.

"Camp on this side of the forest, I think. In the morning we can approach the village and see what our reception is like."

"Would they attack us?"

"Attack? I doubt it very much. I think they're even more peaceful than the rest of us. But why intrude if we're not wanted? Why not respect their seclusion?" Voriax pointed to a half-moon of grassy ground at the edge of a stream. "What do you say to making our camp there?"

They halted, set the mounts to pasture, unrolled their packs, gathered succulent sprouts for dinner. While they foraged for firewood Valentine said suddenly, "If Lord Malibor were chasing some rare beast through the forest here, would he give any thought to the privacy of the Ghiseldorn folk?"

"Nothing prevents Lord Malibor from pursuing his prey."

"Exactly. The thought would never occur to him. I think you will be a far finer Coronal than Lord Malibor, Voriax."

"Don't talk foolishness."

"It isn't foolishness. It's a sensible opinion. Everyone agrees that Lord Malibor is crude and thoughtless. And when it's your turn—"

"Stop this, Valentine."

"You *will* be Coronal," Valentine said. "Why pretend otherwise? It's certain to happen, and soon. Tyeveras is very old; Lord Malibor will move on to the Labyrinth in two or three years; and when he does, he'll surely name you Coronal. He's not so stupid as to fly in the face of all his advisers. And then—"

Voriax caught Valentine by the wrist and leaned close. There was anguish and annoyance in his eyes. "This kind of chatter brings only bad luck. I ask you to stop."

"May I say one more thing?"

"I want no more speculation about who is to be Coronal."

Valentine nodded. "This is not speculation, but a question from brother to brother, that has been on my mind for some time. I don't say you will become Coronal, but I would like to know if you *wish* to become Coronal. Have they consulted you at all? Are you eager for the burden? Just answer me that, Voriax."

After a long silence Voriax said, "It is a burden no one dares refuse."

"But do you want it?"

"If destiny brings it to me, should I say no?"

"You aren't answering me. Look at us now: young, healthy, happy, free. Aside from our responsibilities at court, which are hardly over-whelming, we can do as we please, go anywhere in the world we like, a voyage to Zimroel, a pilgrimage to the Isle, a holiday in the Khyntor Marches, anything, anywhere. To give all that up for the sake of wearing the starburst crown, and signing a million decrees, and making grand processionals with all those speeches, and someday to have to live at the bottom of the Labyrinth—why, Voriax? Why would anyone want to do that? Do *you* want to do that?"

"You are still a child," said Voriax.

Valentine pulled back as though slapped. Condescension again! But then he realized that this had been merited, that he was asking naïve, puerile questions. He forced his anger to subside and said, "I thought I had moved somewhat into manhood."

"Somewhat. But you still have much to learn."

"Doubtless." He paused. "All right, you accept the inevitability of the kingship, if the kingship should come to you. But do you *want* it, Voriax, do you truly crave it, or is it only your breeding and your sense of duty that lead you to prepare yourself for the throne?"

Voriax said slowly, "I am not preparing myself for the throne, but only for a role in the government of Majipoor, as you also are doing, and yes, it is a matter of breeding and a sense of duty, for I am a son of the High Counsellor Damiandane, as I believe you also to be. If the throne is offered to me, I will accept it proudly and discharge its burdens as capably as I can. I spend no time craving the kingship and even less time speculating on whether it will come to me. And I find this conversation tiresome in the extreme and I would be grateful if you permitted me to gather firewood in silence."

He glared at Valentine and turned away.

Questions blossomed in Valentine like alabandinas in summer, but he suppressed them all, for he saw Voriax's lips quivering and knew that he had already gone beyond a boundary. Voriax was ripping angrily at the fallen branches, pulling twigs free with a vehemence not at all necessary, for the wood was dry and brittle. Valentine did not attempt again to breach his brother's defenses, though he had learned only a little of what he wanted to know. He suspected, from Voriax's defensiveness, that Voriax did indeed hunger for the kingship and devoted all his waking hours to training himself for it; and he had an inkling, but only an inkling, of why he should want it. For its own sake, for the power and the glory? Well, why not? And for fulfillment of a destiny that called certain people to high obligations? Yes, that, too. And doubtless to atone for the slight that had been shown their father when *he* had been passed over for the crown. But still, but still, to give up one's freedom merely to rule the world—it was a mystery to Valentine, and in the end he decided that Voriax was right, that these were things he could not fully comprehend at the age of seventeen.

He carried his load of firewood back to the campsite and began kindling a blaze. Voriax joined him soon, but he said nothing, and a chill of estrangement lingered between the brothers that gave Valentine great distress. He wished he could apologize to Voriax for having probed so deeply, but that was impossible, for he had never been graceful at such things with Voriax, nor Voriax with him. He still felt that brother could talk to brother concerning the most intimate matters without giving offense. But on the other hand this frostiness was hard to bear, and if prolonged would poison their holiday together. Valentine searched for a way of regaining amity and after a moment chose one that had worked well enough when they were younger.

He went to Voriax, who was carving the meat for their meal in a gloomy, sullen way, and said, "While we wait for the water to boil, will you wrestle with me?"

Voriax glanced up, startled. "What?"

"I feel the need for exercise."

"Climb those pingla-trees, then, and dance on their branches."

"Come. Take a few falls with me, Voriax."

"It would not be right."

"Why? If I overthrew you, would that offend your dignity even further?"

"Careful, Valentine!"

"I spoke too sharply. Forgive me." Valentine went into a wrestler's crouch and held out his hands. "Please? Some quick holds, a bit of sweat before dinner—"

"Your leg is only newly healed."

"But healed it is. You can use your full strength on me, as I will on you, and never fear."

"And if the leg snaps again, and we a day's journey from any city worth the name?"

"Come, Voriax," Valentine said impatiently. "You fret too much! Come, show me you still can wrestle!" He laughed and slapped his palms together and beckoned, and slapped his hands again, and thrust his grinning face almost against the nose of Voriax, and pulled his brother to his feet, and then Voriax yielded and began to grapple with him.

Something was wrong. They had wrestled often enough, ever since Valentine had been big enough to fight his brother as an equal, and Valentine knew all of Voriax's moves, his little tricks of balance and timing. But the man he wrestled with now seemed a complete stranger. Was this some Metamorph sneaked upon him in the guise of Voriax? No, no, no; it was the leg, Valentine realized, Voriax was holding back his strength, was being deliberately gentle and awkward, was once again patronizing him. In surprising rage Valentine lunged and, although in this early moment of the bout etiquette called on them only to be testing and probing one another, he seized Voriax with the intent to throw him, and forced him to one knee. Voriax stared in amazement. As Valentine caught his breath and gathered his strength to drive his brother's shoulders against the ground, Voriax rallied and pressed upward, unleashing for the first time all his formidable strength: he nearly went down anyway before Valentine's onslaught, but at the last moment he rolled free and sprang to his feet.

They circled one another warily.

Voriax said, "I see I underestimated you. Your leg must be entirely healed."

"So it is, as I've told you many times. I merely limp a little, which makes no difference. Come here, Voriax: come within reach again."

He beckoned. They sprang for one another and locked chest against chest, neither able to budge the other, and stayed that way for what seemed to Valentine an hour or more, though probably it was only minutes. Then he drove Voriax back a few inches, and then Voriax dug in and resisted, and forced Valentine back the same distance. They grunted and sweated and strained, and grinned at one another in the midst of the struggle. Valentine took the keenest pleasure in that grin of Voriax, for it meant that they were brothers again, that the chill between them was thawed, that he was forgiven for his impertinence. In that moment he yearned to embrace Voriax instead of wrestling with him; and in that same moment of relaxed tension, Voriax shoved at him, twisted, pivoted, drew him to the ground, pinned his midsection with his knee, and clamped his hands against Valentine's shoulders. Valentine held himself firm, but there was no withstanding Voriax for long at this stage: steadily Voriax pushed Valentine downward until his shoulder blades pressed against the cool, moist ground.

"Your match," Valentine said, gasping, and Voriax rolled free, lying beside him as laughter overtook them both. "I'll whip you the next one!"

How good it felt, even in defeat, to have regained his brother's love!

Abruptly Valentine heard the sound of applause coming from not very far away. He sat up and stared about in the twilight, and saw the figure of a woman, sharp-featured and with extraordinarily long, straight black hair, standing by the edge of the forest. Her eyes were bright and wicked, her lips were full, her clothes were of a strange style—mere strips of tanned leather crudely tacked together. She seemed quite old to Valentine, perhaps as much as thirty.

"I watched you," she said, coming toward them with no trace of fear. "At first I thought it was a real quarrel, but then I saw it was for sport."

"At first it was a real quarrel," said Voriax. "But also it was sport, always. I am Voriax of Halanx, and this is Valentine, my brother."

She looked from one to the other. "Yes, of course, brothers. Anyone could see that. I am called Tanunda, and I am of Ghiseldorn. Shall I tell you your fortunes?"

"Are you a witch, then?" Valentine asked.

There was merriment in her eyes. "Yes, yes, certainly, a witch. What else?"

"Come, then, foretell for us!" cried Valentine.

"Wait," said Voriax. "I have no liking for sorceries."

"You are too sober by half," Valentine said. "What harm can it do? We visit Ghiseldorn, the city of wizards; should we not then have our destinies read? What are you afraid of? It's a game, Voriax, only a game!" He walked toward the witch and said, "Will you stay with us for dinner?"

"Valentine—"

Valentine glanced boldly at his brother and laughed. "I'll protect you against evil, Voriax! Have no fear!" And in a lower voice he said, "We've traveled alone long enough, brother. I'm hungry for company."

"So I see," murmured Voriax.

But the witch was attractive and Valentine was insistent and shortly Voriax appeared to grow less uneasy about her presence; he carved a third portion of meat for her, and she went into the forest and came back with fruits of the pingla and showed them how to roast them to make their juice run into the meat and give a pleasingly dark and smoky flavor to it. Valentine felt his head swimming somewhat after a time, and he doubted that the few sips of wine he had had could be responsible, so quite probably it was the juice of the pinglas; the thought crossed his mind that there might be some treachery here, but he rejected it, for the dizziness that was overtaking him was an amiable and even exciting one and he saw no peril in it. He looked across at Voriax, wondering if his brother's more suspicious nature would arise to darken their feast, but Voriax, if he was feeling the effects of the juice at all, appeared only to be made more congenial by it: he laughed loudly at everything, he swayed and clapped his thighs, he leaned close to the witch-woman and shouted raucous things into her face. Valentine helped himself to more meat. Night was falling, now, a sudden blackness settling over the camp, stars abruptly blazing out of a sky lit only by one small sliver of moon. Valentine imagined he could hear distant singing and discordant chanting, though it seemed to him that Ghiseldorn must be too far away for such sounds to carry through the dense woods: a fantasy, he decided, stirred by these intoxicating fruits.

The fire burned low. The air grew cool. They huddled close together, Valentine and Voriax and Tanunda, and body pressed against body in what was at first an innocent way and then not so innocent. As they entwined, Valentine caught his brother's eye, and Voriax winked, as if he were saying, *We are men together tonight, and we will take our pleasure together, brother.* Now and then with Elidath or Stasilaine, Valentine had shared a woman, three tumbling merrily in a bed built for two, but never with Voriax; Voriax, who was so conscious of his dignity, his superiority, his high position, so there was special delight for Valentine in this game now. The Ghiseldorn witch had shed her leather garments and showed a lean and supple body by firelight. Valentine had feared that her flesh would be repellent, she being so much older than he, older even than Voriax by some years, but he saw now that that was the foolishness of inexperience for she seemed altogether beautiful to him. He reached for her and encountered Voriax's hand against her flank; he slapped at it playfully, as he would at a buzzing insect, and both brothers laughed, and above their deep laughter came the silvery chuckling of Tanunda, and all three rolled about in the dewy grass.

Valentine had never known so wild a night. Whatever drug was in the pingla-juice worked on him to free him of all inhibition and to spur his energies, and with Voriax it must have been the same. To Valentine the night became a sequence of fragmentary images, of sequences of events unlinked to others. Now he lay sprawled with Tanunda's head in his lap, stroking her gleaming brow while Voriax embraced her, and he listened to their mingled gasps with a strange pleasure; and then it was he who held the witch tight, and Voriax was somewhere close at hand but he could not tell where; and then Tanunda lay sandwiched between the two men for some giddy grappling; and somehow they went from there to the stream, and bathed and splashed and laughed, and ran naked and shivering to the dying fire, and made love again, Valentine and Tanunda, Voriax and Tanunda, Valentine and Tanunda and Voriax, flesh calling to flesh until the first grayish strands of morning broke the darkness.

All three were awake as the sun burst into the sky. Great swathes of the night were gone from Valentine's memory, and he wondered if he had slept unknowing from time to time, but now his mind was weirdly clear, his eyes were wide, as though this were the middle of the day. Voriax was the same, and the grinning naked witch who sprawled between them.

"Now," she said, "the telling of fortunes!"

Voriax made an uneasy sound, a rasping of the throat, but Valentine said quickly, "Yes! Yes! Prophesy for us!"

"Gather the pingla-seeds," she said.

They were scattered all about, glossy black nuts with splashes of red on them. Valentine scooped up a dozen of them, and even Voriax collected a few; these they gave to Tanunda, who had found a handful also, and she began to roll them in her fists and scatter them like dice on the ground. Five times she cast them, and scooped them up and cast again; then she cupped her hands and allowed a line of seeds to fall in a circle, and threw the remaining ones within that circle, and peered close a long while, squatting with face to the ground to study the patterns. At length she looked up. The wanton deviltry was gone from her face; she looked strangely altered, very solemn and some years older.

"You are high-born men," she said. "But that could be seen from the way you carry yourselves. The seeds tell me much more. I see great perils ahead for both of you."

Voriax looked away, scowling, and spat.

"You are skeptical, yes," she said. "But you each face dangers. You—"

she indicated Voriax—"must be wary of forests, and you—" a glance at Valentine—"of water, of oceans." She frowned. "And of much else, I think, for your destiny is a mysterious one and I am unable to read it clearly. Your line is broken—not by death, but by something stranger, some change, a great transformation—" She shook her head. "It is puzzling to me. I can be of no other help."

Voriax said, "Beware of forests, beware of oceans—beware of nonsense!"

"You will be king," said Tanunda.

Voriax caught his breath sharply. The anger fled his face and he gaped at her.

Valentine smiled and clapped his brother's back and said, "You see? You see?"

"And you also will be king," the witch said.

"What?" Valentine was bewildered. "What foolishness is this? Your seeds deceive you!"

"If they do, it is for the first time," said Tanunda. She gathered the fallen seeds and flung them quickly into the stream, and wrapped her strips of leather about her body. "A king and a king, and I have enjoyed my night's sport with you both, your majesties-to-be. Shall you go on to Ghiseldorn today?"

"I think not," said Voriax, without looking at her.

"Then we will not meet again. Farewell!"

She moved swiftly toward the forest. Valentine stretched out a hand toward her, but said nothing, only squeezed the air helplessly with his trembling fingers, and then she was gone. He turned toward Voriax, who was scuffing angrily at the embers of the fire. All the joy of the night's revelry had fled.

"You were right," Valentine said. "We should not have let her dabble in prophecy at our expense. Forests! Oceans! And this madness of our both being kings!"

"What does she mean?" asked Voriax. "That we will share the throne as we shared her body this night past?"

"It will not be," said Valentine.

"Never has there been joint rule in Majipoor. It makes no sense! It is unthinkable! If I am to be king, Valentine, how are you also to be king?"

"You are not listening to me. I tell you, pay no attention to it, brother. She was a wild woman who gave us a night of drunken pleasure. There's no truth in prophecy."

"She said I was to be king."

"And so you probably shall be. But it was only a lucky guess."

"And if not? And if she is a genuine seer?"

"Why, then, you will be king!"

"And you? If she spoke truly about me, then you too must be Coronal, and how——"

"No," Valentine said. "Prophets often speak in riddles and ambiguities. She means something other than the literal. You are to be Coronal, Voriax, it is the common knowledge—and there is some other meaning to the thing she predicted for me, or else there is no meaning at all."

"This frightens me, Valentine."

"If you are to be Coronal there is nothing to fear. Why do you grimace like that?"

"To share the throne with one's brother——" He worried at the idea as at a sore tooth, refusing to move away from it.

"It will not be," said Valentine. He scooped up a fallen garment, found it to belong to Voriax, and tossed it to him. "You heard me speak yesterday. It goes beyond my understanding why anyone would covet the throne. Certainly I am no threat to you in that regard." He seized his brother's wrist. "Voriax, Voriax, you look so dire! Can the words of a forest-witch affect you so? I swear this to you: when you are Coronal, I will be your servant, and never your rival. By our mother who is to be the Lady of the Isle do I swear it. And I tell you that what passed here this night is not to be taken seriously."

"Perhaps not," Voriax said.

"Certainly not," said Valentine. "Shall we leave this place now, brother?"

"I think so."

"She used her body well, do you not agree?"

Voriax laughed. "That she did. It saddens me a little to think I'll never embrace her again. But no, I would not care to hear more of her lunatic soothsaying, however wondrous the movements of her hips may be. I've had my fill of her, and of this place, I think. Shall we pass Ghiseldorn by?"

"I think so," Valentine said. "What cities lie along the Glayge near here?"

"Jerrik is next, where many Vroons are settled, and Mitripond, and a place called Gayles. I think we should take lodging in Jerrik, and amuse ourselves with some gambling for a few days."

"To Jerrik, then."

"Yes, to Jerrik. And say no more concerning the kingship to me, Valentine."

"Not a word, I promise." He laughed and threw his arms around Voriax. "Brother! I thought several times on this journey that I had lost you altogether, but I see that all is well, that I have found you again!"

"We were never lost to one another," said Voriax, "not for an instant. Come, now: pack your things, and onward to Jerrik!"

THEY NEVER SPOKE AGAIN of their night with the witch and of the things she had foretold. Five years later, when Lord Malibor perished while hunting sea-dragons, Voriax was chosen as Coronal, to no one's surprise, and Valentine was the first to kneel in homage before his brother. By then Valentine had virtually forgotten the troublesome prophecy of Tanunda, though not the taste of her kisses and the feel of her flesh. Both of them kings? How, after all, could that be, since only one man could be Coronal at a time? Valentine rejoiced for his brother Lord Voriax and was content to be what he was. And by the time he understood the full meaning of the prophecy, which was not that he would rule jointly with Voriax but that he would succeed him on the throne, though never before on Majipoor had brother followed brother in such a way, it was impossible for him to embrace Voriax and reassure him of his love, for Voriax was lost to him forever, struck down by a hunter's stray bolt in the forest, and Valentine was brotherless and alone as in awe and amazement he mounted the steps of the Confalume Throne.

ELEVEN

Those final moments, that epilogue that some scribe had appended to the young Valentine's soul-record, leave Hissune dazed. He sits motionless a long while; then he rises as if in a dream and begins to leave the cubicle. Images out of that frenzied night in the forest revolve in his stunned mind: the rival brothers, the bright-eyed witch, the bare grappling bodies, the prophecy of kingship. Yes, two kings! And Hissune has spied on them in the most vulnerable moment of their lives! He feels abashed, a rare emotion for him. Perhaps the time has come for a holiday from the Register of Souls, he thinks: the power of these experiences sometimes is overwhelming, and he may well require some months of recuperation. His hands shake as he steps through the doorway.

One of the usual functionaries of the Register admitted him an hour earlier, a plump and wall-eyed man named Penagorn, and he is still at his desk; but another person stands beside him, a tall, straight-backed individual in the green-and-gold uniform of the Coronal's staff, who studies Hissune severely and says, "May I see your identification, please?"

So this is the moment he has dreaded. They have found him out—unauthorized use of the archives—and he is to be arrested. Hissune offers his card. Probably they have known of his illegal intrusions here for a long time, but have simply been waiting for him to commit the ultimate atrocity, the playing of the Coronal's own recording. Very likely that one bears an alarm, Hissune thinks, that silently summons the minions of the Coronal, and now—

"You are the one we seek," says the man in green and gold. "Please come with me."

Silently Hissune follows—out of the House of Records and across the great plaza to the entrance to the lowest levels of the Labyrinth, and past a checkpoint to a waiting floater-car, and then downward, downward, into mysterious realms Hissune has never entered. He sits motionless, numb. All the world presses down on this place; layer upon layer of the Labyrinth spirals over his head. Where are they now? Is this place the Court of Thrones, where the high ministers hold sway? Hissune does not dare ask, and his escort says not a word. Through gate after gate, passage upon passage; then the floater-car halts; six more in the uniforms of Lord Valentine's staff emerge; they conduct him into a brightly lit room and stand flanking him.

A door opens, sliding into a recess, and a golden-haired man, wide-shouldered and tall, clad in a simple white robe, enters the room. Hissune gasps.

"Your lordship—"

"Please. Please. We can do without all that bowing, Hissune. You *are* Hissune, aren't you?"

"I am, my lord. Somewhat older."

"Eight years ago, was that it? Yes, eight. You were this high. And now a man. Well, I suppose I'm foolish to be surprised, but I suspected a boy even now. You're eighteen?"

"Yes, my lord."

"How old were you when you started poking about in the Register of Souls?"

"You know of that, then, my lord?" Hissune whispers, turning crimson, staring at his feet.

"Fourteen, were you? I think that's what they told me. I've had you watched, you know. It was three or four years ago that they sent word to me that you had bluffed your way into the Register. Fourteen, pretending to be a scholar. I imagine you saw a great many things that boys of fourteen don't ordinarily see."

Hissune's cheeks blaze. Through his mind rolls the thought, *An hour ago, my lord, I saw you and your brother coupling with a long-haired witch of*

Ghiseldorn. He would let himself be swallowed in the depths of the world before he says such a thing aloud. But he is certain that Lord Valentine knows it anyway, and that awareness is crushing to Hissune. He cannot look up. This golden-haired man is not the Valentine of the soul-record, for that had been the dark-haired Valentine, later magicked out of his body in the way that everyone now has heard, and these days the Coronal wears other flesh; but the person within is the same, and Hissune has spied on him, and there is no hiding the truth of that.

Hissune is silent.

Lord Valentine says, "Possibly I should take that back. You always were precocious. The Register probably didn't show you many things that you hadn't seen on your own."

"It showed me Ni-moya, my lord," Hissune says in a croaking, barely audible voice. "It showed me Suvrael, and the cities of Castle Mount, and the jungles outside Narabal—"

"Places, yes. Geography. It's useful to know all that. But the geography of the soul—you learned that your own way, eh? Look up at me. I'm not angry with you."

"No?"

"It was by my orders that you had free access to the Register. Not so you could gawk at Ni-moya, and not so you could spy on people making love, particularly. But so you could get a comprehension of what Majipoor really is, so you could experience a millionth millionth part of the totality of this world of ours. It was your education, Hissune. Am I right?"

"That was how I saw it, my lord. Yes. There was so much I wanted to know."

"Did you learn it all?"

"Not nearly. Not a millionth millionth part."

"Too bad. Because you'll no longer have access to the Register."

"My lord? Am I to be punished?"

Lord Valentine smiles oddly. "Punished? No, that's not the right word. But you'll be leaving the Labyrinth, and chances are you'll not be back here for a very long time, not even when I'm Pontifex, and may that day not come soon. I've named you to my staff, Hissune. Your training period's over. I want to put you to work. You're old enough now, I think. You have family here still?"

"My mother, two sisters—"

"Provided for. Whatever they need. Say good-bye to them and pack your things. Can you leave with me in three days?"

"Three—days—"

"For Alaisor. The grand processional is demanded of me again. And then the Isle. We skip Zimroel this time. Back to the Mount in seven or eight months, I hope. You'll have a suite at the Castle. Some formal instruction—that won't be unpleasant for you, will it? Fancier clothes to wear. You saw all this coming, didn't you? You know I marked you for great things, when you were only a ragged little boy fleecing tourists?" The Coronal laughs. "It's late. I'll send for you again in the morning. There's much for us to discuss."

He extends his fingertips toward Hissune, a courtly little gesture. Hissune bows, and when he dares to look up, Lord Valentine is gone. So. So. It has come to pass after all, his dream, his fantasy. Hissune does not allow any expression to enter his face. Rigid, somber, he turns to the green-and-gold escort, and follows them to the corridors, and they convey him up into the public levels of the Labyrinth. There they leave him. But he cannot go to his room now. His mind is racing, feverish, wild with amazement. From its depths come surging all those long-vanished folk he has come to know so well, Nismile and Sinnabor Lavon, Thesme, Dekkeret, Calintane, poor anguished Haligome, Eremoil, Inyanna Forlana, Vismaan, Sarise. Part of him now, embedded forever in his soul. He feels as though he has devoured the entire planet. What will become of him now? Aide to the Coronal? A glittering new life on Castle Mount? Holidays in High Morpin and Stee, and the great ones of the realm as his companions? Why, he might be Coronal himself some day! Lord Hissune! He laughs at his own monstrous presumption. And yet, and yet, and yet, why not? Had Calintane expected to be Coronal? Had Dekkeret? Had Valentine? But one must not think of such things, Hissune tells himself. One must work, and learn, and live one's life a moment at a time, and one's destiny will shape itself.

He realizes that he has somehow become lost—he, who at the age of ten was the most skillful guide the Labyrinth had. He has wandered in his daze from level to level, and half the night is gone, and he has no idea now where he is. And then he sees that he is in the uppermost level of the Labyrinth, on the desert side, near the Mouth of Blades. In fifteen minutes he can be outside the Labyrinth entirely. To go out there is not something he normally yearns to do; but this night is special, and he does not resist as his feet take him toward the gateway of the underground city. He comes to the Mouth of Blades and stares a long while at the rusted swords of some antique era that were set across its front to mark the boundary; then he steps past them and out into the hot, dry wasteland beyond. Like Dekkeret roaming that other, and far more terrible desert, he strides into the emptiness, until he is a good distance from the teeming hive that is the Labyrinth, and stands alone under the cool, brilliant stars. So many of them! And one is Old Earth, from which all the billions and billions of humankind had sprung so long ago. Hissune stands as if entranced. Through him pours an overwhelming sense of all the long history of the cosmos, rushing upon him like an irresistible river. The Register of Souls contains the records of enough lives to keep him busy for half of eternity, he thinks, and yet what is in it is just the merest fraction of everything that has existed on all those worlds of all those stars. He wants to seize and engulf it all and make it part of him as he had made those other lives part of him, and of course that cannot be done, and even the thought of it dizzies him. But he must give up such notions now, and forswear the temptations of the Register. He holds himself still until his mind has ceased its whirling. I will be quite calm now, he tells himself. I will regain control over my feelings. He allows himself one final look toward the stars, and searches among them, in vain, for the sun of Old Earth. Then he shrugs and swings about and slowly walks back toward the Mouth of Blades. Lord Valentine will send for him again in the morning. It is important to get some sleep before then. A new life is about to begin for him. I will live on Castle Mount, he thinks, and I will be an aide to the Coronal, and who knows what will happen to me after that? But whatever happens will be the right thing, as it was for Dekkeret, for Thesme, for Sinnabor Lavon, even for Haligome, for all of those whose souls are part of my soul now.

Hissune stands just outside the Mouth of Blades for a moment, only a moment, and the moment stretches, and the stars begin to fade, and the first light of dawn comes, and then a mighty sunrise takes possession of the sky, and all the land is flooded with light. He does not move. The warmth of the sun of Majipoor touches his face, as so rarely has it done in his life until now. The sun . . . the sun . . . the glorious, blazing, fiery sun . . . the mother of the worlds . . . He reaches out his arms to it. He embraces it. He smiles and drinks in its blessing. Then he turns and goes down into the Labyrinth for the last time.

Photo by Allen Batson

Robert Silverberg has won five Nebula Awards, four Hugo Awards, and the prestigious Prix Apollo. He is the author of more than one hundred science fiction and fantasy novels—including the bestselling Majipoor Cycle and the classics *Dying Inside* and *A Time of Changes*—and more than sixty nonfiction works. Mr. Silverberg's Majipoor Cycle, set on perhaps the grandest and greatest world ever imagined, is considered one of the jewels in the crown of speculative fiction.

The Future of China-Russia Relations

★

Edited by James Bellacqua

THE UNIVERSITY PRESS OF KENTUCKY

Scholarly publisher for the Commonwealth,
serving Bellarmine University, Berea College, Centre
College of Kentucky, Eastern Kentucky University,
The Filson Historical Society, Georgetown College,
Kentucky Historical Society, Kentucky State University,
Morehead State University, Murray State University,
Northern Kentucky University, Transylvania University,
University of Kentucky, University of Louisville,
and Western Kentucky University.
All rights reserved.

Editorial and Sales Offices: The University Press of Kentucky
663 South Limestone Street, Lexington, Kentucky 40508-4008
www.kentuckypress.com

      14 13 12 11 10   5 4 3 2 1

Library of Congress Cataloging-in-Publication Data

The future of China-Russia relations / edited by James Bellacqua.
     p.   cm.
  Includes bibliographical references and index.
  ISBN 978-0-8131-2563-3 (hardcover : alk. paper)
  1. China—Relations—Russia (Federation) 2. Russia
(Federation)—Relations—China. I. Bellacqua, James (James A.)
  JZ1730.A57R8 2010
  303.48'251047—dc22
                              2009044735

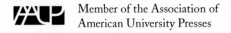

Contents

Part Four. China, Russia, and Regional Issues: Central Asia, Japan, and the Two Koreas

Part Five. China, Russia, and Regional Issues: Taiwan

Illustrations and Tables

Figures

Maps

Abbreviations

ABM	Anti-Ballistic Missile Treaty
AEW	airborne early warning
ALB	air-land battle
APEC	Asia-Pacific Economic Cooperation
ASEAN	Association of Southeast Asian Nations
ASW	antisubmarine warfare
AWACS	Airborne Warning and Control System
b/d	barrels per day
bcm	billion cubic meters
BMD	ballistic missile defense
BMP	Boyevaya Mashina Pekhoty (a Russian infantry fighting vehicle)
BRIC	Brazil, Russia, India, and China
BTC	Baku-Tblisi-Ceyhan pipelines
Btu	British thermal unit
C^3I	command, control, communications, and intelligence
CASS	Chinese Academy of Social Sciences
CAST	Centre for Analysis of Strategies and Technologies (Russia)
CICA	Conference on Interaction and Confidence-Building Measures in Asia
c.i.f.	cost, insurance, and freight
CIS	Commonwealth of Independent States
CITIC	China International Trust and Investment Company
CMC	Central Military Commission (China)
CNOOC	China National Offshore Oil Corporation
CNPC	China National Petroleum Corporation

COMECON	Council for Mutual Economic Assistance
COSTIND	Commission of Science, Technology, and Industry for National Defense (China)
CST	Collective Security Treaty
CSTO	Collective Security Treaty Organization
CVID	Comprehensive Verifiable and Irreversible Disarmament
DPP	Democratic Progressive Party (Taiwan)
ESPO	East Siberia–Pacific Ocean pipeline
ETIM	East Turkestan Islamic Movement
FDI	foreign direct investment
f.o.b.	free on board
GLONASS	Global Navigation Satellite System
GUUAM	Georgia, Ukraine, Uzbekistan, Azerbaijan, and Moldova
HEU	highly enriched uranium
IAEA	International Atomic Energy Agency
ICBM	intercontinental ballistic missile
IEA	International Energy Agency
IFV	infantry fighting vehicles
IMF	International Monetary Fund
IMU	Islamic Movement of Uzbekistan
ISAF	International Security in Afghanistan Forces
KEDO	Korean Peninsula Energy Development Organization
LDPR	Liberal Democratic Party of Russia
LNG	liquefied natural gas
LTR	light water reactors
MBT	main battle tanks
MFA	Ministry of Foreign Affairs
MGIMO	Moscow State Institute of International Relations
MND	Ministry of National Defense (China)
MOD	Ministry of Defense (Russia)
MOU	memorandum of understanding
MTC	military-technological cooperation
MTC	Moscow-Taipei Economic and Cultural Coordination Commission
NATO	North Atlantic Treaty Organization
NDRC	National Development and Reform Commission (China)
NGO	nongovernmental organization

NMD	national missile defense
NOC	national oil company
NPT	Non-Proliferation Treaty
OECD	Organization for Economic Cooperation and Development
OPEC	Organization of Petroleum Exporting Countries
PAP	People's Armed Police (China)
PLA	People's Liberation Army (China)
PLAAF	People's Liberation Army Air Force (China)
PLAN	People's Liberation Army Navy (China)
PRC	People's Republic of China
RATS	Regional Anti-Terrorist Structure
ROC	Republic of China (Taiwan)
SAM	surface-to-air missile
SCO	Shanghai Cooperation Organization
SEPA	State Environmental Protection Agency (China)
SIPRI	Stockholm International Peace Research Institute
SORT	Strategic Offensive Reduction Treaty
TCOG	Trilateral Coordination and Oversight Group
TMC	Taipei-Moscow Economic and Cultural Coordination Commission
TRA	Taiwan Relations Act (Russia; United States)
VTsIOM	Russian Public Opinion Research Center
WHO	World Health Organization
WTO	World Trade Organization

Introduction

Contemporary Sino-Russian Relations
Thirteen Years of a "Strategic Partnership"

James Bellacqua

In April 1996, Russian president Boris Yeltsin and his Chinese counterpart, Jiang Zemin, signed documentation formally establishing a "strategic partnership" between the Russian Federation and the People's Republic of China (PRC). The formation of this partnership was the product of what Gilbert Rozman describes in this book as the "sustained upward trend" in bilateral relations and was symbolically significant in illustrating just how far these two nations had come in their ties with one another. A relationship based on economic dependence and military alliance that began in 1950 ultimately broke down over ideological disputes between Mao Zedong and Nikita Khrushchev, culminating in a messy divorce of the two Communist giants in 1960. Ties remained frosty for the next three decades before finally being normalized in 1989. In the intervening years, the Sino-Soviet relationship could best be characterized as one of minimal interactions and mutual hostility.

Today these ideological disputes of the past are a distant memory. Thirteen years after it was established, the Sino-Russian strategic partnership not only is alive but appears to be taking on some practical manifestations. During the first decade of the partnership, Russia became a major source of arms for the PRC, although sales have slowed in recent years. Bilateral trade volume, albeit small, is increasing and Russia has become a growing source of energy for China. The two cooperate on the development of China's space program and civil aviation sector, and they have conducted joint military exercises under the auspices of the Shanghai Cooperation Organization (SCO). China and Russia have similar views on a number of international and regional security issues and have worked together on occasions where their respective interests are aligned. In late 2008, the two nations finally resolved the last stretch of their long-standing border dispute, which had led to armed conflict in the past.[1] The two states also created mechanisms for holding annual meetings between the countries' presidents and prime ministers.

Apart from a brief stop in Kazakhstan, the first overseas trip by new Russian president Dmitri Medvedev was a visit to the PRC.

At first glance, such interactions may not be surprising, given how much China and Russia seem to have in common. Prior to the onset of the 2008–2009 global financial crisis, both countries were experiencing robust economic growth fueled by their exports—Russia of oil and gas, and China of just about everything else. At the same time, both nations characterize themselves as "developing countries," with China still struggling to lift hundreds of millions of people out of poverty and Russia trying to diversify its economy away from a heavy dependence on raw material exports. The governments of both nations are stable, authoritarian, and administratively centralized, yet both are challenged to keep their distant regions under control. China and Russia are both proud, sensitive countries, eminently conscious of their global position, status, and degree of influence. They are equally conscious of their impact on global affairs and often vote the same at the UN Security Council, where both are permanent members with a veto.

A closer look, however, reveals a number of key differences. China is clearly a rising power, while Russia appears to be gradually declining in terms of its interaction with the rest of the world. The PRC has become a major player in global trade, is more integrated into the global economic system, and has better ties with the rest of the world. Beijing comes to the developing world, for instance, armed with preferential loans and infrastructure projects in the hopes of locking up energy resources and other raw materials to aid its economic development. In contrast, Russia's efforts to reach out to the rest of the world are hindered by the fact that it has little to sell besides oil, gas, chemicals, and metals. Politically, China remains a one-party state, while Russia chooses its leaders through popular, yet often stage-managed, elections. Russia has made efforts to keep its business elites out of the political process, while the Chinese Communist Party has attempted to bring them in.

In terms of demographics, China is the world's most populous nation and is still growing, while Russia's population is shrinking at an alarming rate of 700,000 a year.[2] Richard Lotspeich points out that Russia's population is only slightly more than 10 percent of China's, and the gap is widening.

The two are also culturally distant. Geographically, although Russia is the largest country by territory in continental Asia, its population centers are situated in the west—i.e., European Russia. The country is thus culturally oriented toward Europe and has minimal links to East Asia. China, by comparison, is oriented to the Asia-Pacific. Despite top-down efforts at promoting cultural exchanges, such as the "Year of China in Russia" and vice versa, few would characterize Chinese and Russian cultures as complementary, and ordinary citizens have little in common with one another.

What Does It All Mean?

These closer ties between China and Russia have caused unease, both in the Asia-Pacific region and in Washington. Questions persist over whether the Sino-Russian strategic partnership poses a threat to the West. Some have speculated that the strategic partnership may be a precursor to an outright military alliance between the two powers. Will the SCO, for example, evolve into a security alliance to challenge NATO, or will it emerge as a vehicle for Chinese and Russian military control? Conversely, others have postulated that the strategic partnership is long on rhetoric and short on substance. Do China and Russia simply have too many divergent interests and differences to make the strategic partnership work?

This volume was written with an eye toward answering these and other questions about the current state and future prospects of the relationship between China and Russia. It is the output of a February 2007 conference we convened at CNA in Alexandria, Virginia, on the topic. In this book, we examine how each side views the other across a wide range of issues and address the implications of this important relationship for the United States. These issues are not confined to the security dimensions of bilateral relations but also include the political relationship, economic interactions, and defense ties. We also explore the energy courtship between the two nations, along with each country's interests and policies on the key regional security issues: Central Asia, the Korean Peninsula, and Taiwan. On each of these topics, we examine both the Russian and the Chinese perspectives, identifying the common interests that bring the two countries closer as well as the divergent interests that pull them apart.

This book is organized into five sections and contains chapters by an impressive collection of authors, each of whom is a recognized expert in his or her respective field of study. In the first section, Gilbert Rozman looks at the overall state of play between China and Russia, and offers his thoughts on where he believes the relationship is headed. This is followed by chapters from Andrew Kuchins and Elizabeth Wishnick, who examine Russian and Chinese perspectives on the partnership. The second section features chapters from Richard Lotspeich and Erica Downs on economic and energy ties, respectively. In the third section, Kevin Ryan and Jing-dong Yuan assess

Russian and Chinese perspectives on the bilateral military relationship. The fourth section looks at Chinese and Russian interests vis-à-vis two key regional issues, with chapters from Charles Ziegler on Central Asia and Leszek Buszynski on the Korean Peninsula. This volume concludes with a discussion about Taiwan, in which Jeanne Wilson examines Russia's views on Taiwan and Shelley Rigger describes China's expectations of Russia with regard to support on the Taiwan issue.

Overarching Themes

In a marked contrast to Sino-Soviet ties during the Cold War, ideological factors are now largely absent from the China-Russia relationship. Only with the possible exception of shared suspicions over perceived U.S. domination of the international order does a shared ideological affinity still play a role in bilateral ties. Today it is primarily pragmatic considerations on issues of common ground that ultimately drive the Sino-Russian relationship forward. This common ground can be found in both countries' views on regional security issues, their growing economic interactions, their shared benefits from sales of military armaments, and their similar approaches to energy diversification.

Nonetheless, it is also important to keep in mind the equally numerous areas in which China's and Russia's interests conflict. For each area of common ground listed above, there are also divergent interests at play that often prevent cooperation from reaching its true potential. In Rozman's words, these "overlapping but not identical" interests play a significant role in hindering efforts by the two countries to fully develop a stable and predictable relationship.

International Affairs

Beijing and Moscow share broadly similar views of the world, and neither is particularly comfortable with perceived U.S. leadership of the international order. Both are suspicious of Washington's intentions, and they have worked together on occasion in an effort to balance U.S. interests. Both are also highly sensitive to issues of sovereignty, possibly because they have their own independence-minded regions to worry about. Shared outlooks such as these have given rise to practical cooperation between the two nations. Not only are they both veto-wielding permanent members of the UN Security Council with similar voting patterns, but they have also worked in concert at other multilateral forums and have adopted similar stances on a range of international issues. These include the role of the UN, opposition to missile defense and the weaponization of space, and the problematic situations in Sudan, Iran, and the Democratic People's Republic of Korea (DPRK).

Nonetheless, there are clearly limits to this cooperation, particularly when the two countries' interests are not aligned. During the recent conflict between Russia and Georgia, for example, China and Russia clearly did not see eye to eye. Beijing refused to endorse Moscow's conduct at the August 2008 SCO summit in Dushanbe. As Charles Ziegler observes, this stood in contrast to the views of the four Central Asian states in the SCO, which, one month later at a session of the Collective Security Treaty Organization (CSTO) in Moscow, sided with Russia in the dispute, although all four nations stopped short of endorsing independence for the two breakaway regions of South Ossetia and Abkhazia.

It should be pointed out that China's neutrality on the issue was not altogether surprising; Beijing often tries to stay out of disputes in which it feels it has no interests. Moreover, Russia's conduct vis-á-vis Georgia violated one of Beijing's core foreign policy priorities—noninterference in the sovereign affairs of another state. China has its own secession-minded regions (Taiwan, Tibet, and Xinjiang) and has always been unlikely to support any action that might set a precedent in that regard. For its part, although Russia may very well lend rhetorical support for China in the event of a similar conflict erupting over Taiwan, it is doubtful that Russian involvement would manifest in more practical or substantive actions (beyond weapons sales, of course). As Jeanne Wilson argues in this book, Russia is unwilling to be dragged into a conflict where it has virtually no national interests and where there is a very real risk of a military confrontation with the United States.

Central Asia

The two nations have similar priorities with regard to the five former Soviet republics of Central Asia. China and Russia each share long borders with the region and have an interest in its stability. Countering terrorism is a critical concern for both Beijing and Moscow, both of which support U.S.-led efforts to depose the Taliban in Afghanistan. At the same time, both countries also hope to balance U.S. influence in the region and neither was particularly sad to see the United States evicted from air bases in Kyrgyzstan and Uzbekistan. In terms of energy resources, China and Russia have been keen to develop the region's sizeable oil and gas fields in Kazakhstan and Turkmenistan.

However, these similar strategic objectives have resulted in competition as much as in cooperation. The two countries disagree, for example, on their preferred multilateral institution for engaging the region. Although Russia is a member of the SCO, it views the body as a Chinese invention and has sought to work around it. Moscow's preferred medium for engaging the region is the CSTO, a regional security bloc that is composed of seven former Soviet republics and excludes China. Additionally, China and Russia directly compete for access to and development of the region's energy resources. Russia is highly dependent on natural gas from Central Asia to meet its export commitments. Moscow, therefore, hopes to retain a monopoly on the region's pipelines and keep them heading west. For its part, China wants access to the oil and gas resources of Central Asia, and is already building pipelines heading east out of the region in cooperation with Kazakhstan and Turkmenistan.

Arms Sales

Until recently, Russian sales of armaments to the Chinese People's Liberation Army (PLA) were a major component of the partnership. An embargo on U.S. and EU weapons sales to China, imposed in the wake of the bloody suppression of the 1989 Tiananmen Square protests, forced Beijing to turn to Moscow to help modernize the PLA. Moscow has also benefited, as the exports to China have helped keep Russia's sizeable military-industrial complex afloat in the difficult post–Cold War economic climate. Kevin Ryan writes that in 2005 China accounted for 40 percent of all Russian military exports.

Although the sale of military armaments might appear to be a natural area of cooperation, further sales have been hampered by Russia's concerns that it is actively aiding the military development of a country that may one day constitute a challenge to its national security. Jing-dong Yuan observes that arms sales have slowed substantially, with no significant orders being placed since 2006. This may stem from Chinese aspirations of producing the equipment themselves once they obtain the designs or the possibility that the PLA is already saturated with Russian hardware imports (see Yuan's chapter for a list of sales through 2008). Nonetheless, China likely wishes to buy more products from Russia to aid the PLA's modernization, such as advanced military technology. However, Russia's concerns that its own technology could someday be used against it, coupled with the prospect of Beijing's gaining access to Russian proprietary information or learning to reengineer its technology for domestic production, may be contributing to Moscow's unwillingness to make such sales. It is interesting to note that while Russia has refused to supply the PLA with certain types of military equipment, such as the Tu-22M Backfire supersonic tactical strike bomber, it has been willing to sell them to India. One conference participant suggested that this largely reflects the fact that the Russian General Staff, which has to approve all weapons sales, views Beijing as a potential threat while holding no such suspicions about New Delhi.

Energy Strategies

The countries also share what Erica Downs describes as "complementary energy strategies." Russia has the oil and gas that China so desperately wants to fuel and sustain its economic growth and development. Moreover, both countries seek greater diversity in their present energy interactions with other nations: Russia hopes to diversify its consumer base away from Western Europe, and China aims to reduce its dependence on Middle Eastern suppliers and its overreliance on the Strait of Malacca, through which nearly 80 percent of its oil imports must transit.[3]

Despite the presence of complementary energy diversification priorities, however, bilateral energy ties have traditionally been one of the weaker areas of cooperation throughout the partnership's duration. Russia's energy infrastructure is oriented to the West, and Moscow has been hesitant to commit to the development of pipelines to bring East Siberian oil to China. Although the two sides signed a deal in February 2009 to finish constructing a pipeline to the Chinese border, discussions on the subject have been ongoing since 2001 and several previous agreements have unraveled in the process. Russian hesitation stems, in part, from unease over the fact that any pipeline constructed to East Asia might not be commercially viable. If that proved to be the case, then Russia might be forced into an overreliance on China as an energy-export destination, and thus be subjected to pressure from Beijing on the price and volume of any oil or gas it supplied. An alternative Japanese proposal to extend the pipeline to the Pacific Ocean has also delayed progress, as, until recently, Moscow seemed unable to decide between the two. As a result, what appear to be promising opportunities for cooperation in the energy sector have gone largely unfulfilled.

Economic Interaction

At the time of writing, bilateral trade was also fast becoming problematic despite top-down efforts at its promotion. As arms exports from Russia have waned, the balance of trade has swung in China's favor. In 2007, Beijing amassed a $9 billion trade surplus with its northern neighbor, a development that has not sat well with Moscow. Russian leaders have expressed dismay that China buys little more than raw materials, and have called on Beijing to increase imports of Russian machine tools and electronic products.

Russia's perceptions of China as a "threat" have also contributed to the two countries' failure to develop deeper economic integration, especially along the border. Because most of Russia's population and major centers of economic production are in the western part of the country, the economically depressed Far Eastern part of the Russian Federation is said to feel demographically and economically vulnerable as China's clout and population continue to grow. Although it may appear to outside observers that a solution to the problems of Russia's aging, thinly populated, and dying Far East would be an influx of young, inexpensive labor from an overpopulated China, where arable land is scarce and unemployment is rising, this has not been the case. Moscow has been reluctant to liberalize regulations on visas and immigration, while some local politicians have fanned xenophobic views on the subject. For China's part, setbacks on these and other issues have led some in the PRC to characterize Russia as both "unreliable" and "unpredictable."

Concluding Impressions

So, what are we to make of the Sino-Russian strategic partnership? Are we witnessing the formation of a new security alliance destined to challenge American leadership in the early twenty-first century? Or do the two countries' numerous differences and conflicting interests prevent their joint partnership from taking on any substance? This book suggests that the reality is neither of these things. To understand contemporary Sino-Russian relations, it is best to dispense with the strategic partnership formulation altogether, as it gives rise to the temptation to magnify the partnership's strengths or overstate the inherent differences between the two countries. Therefore, rather than view contemporary Sino-Russian relations through the prism of their strategic partnership, the scholarship in this volume makes the case that we should simply view China-Russia relations for what they are: a pragmatic relationship that is based on shared common interests, but is not without its fault lines.

Nonetheless, as the Sino-Russian strategic partnership evolves, it is important to keep in mind that this is not a relationship between equals. In a break from the past, Russia is increasingly becoming the "junior partner" in the relationship. Since the end of the Cold War, Russia has shifted its focus toward regional issues, whereas China's global footprint is rapidly expanding, largely as a result of its increasing economic influence. During our 2007 conference, participants generally agreed that both sides were cognizant of the shifting balance of power in the relationship.

As to the question of whether China and Russia have formed a military alliance, there is no evidence to suggest that this is the case or that they are planning to do so. It is equally doubtful as to whether such an arrangement would be in either country's national interest. Russia arguably has no desire to be dragged into a military confrontation over Taiwan, while China's recent conduct regarding the Russian invasion of Georgia shows that there are clear limits to the bilateral strategic partnership when it conflicts with Beijing's core sovereignty concerns. The SCO has conducted some combined military exercises in recent years, but it is difficult to see this body evolving into a security counterweight to NATO, particularly if the SCO expands to take on new members.

Finally, it is worth keeping in mind that for both China and Russia, relations with the United States may be more important than their ties with one another. Despite the anti-American rhetoric that emanates out of Beijing and Moscow from time to time, China and Russia both have a strong interest in maintaining stable ties with Washington. All three share an interest in cooperating on issues of common concern, such as countering terrorism, resolving global conflicts, and curbing the spread of weapons of mass destruction.

Economically, in an era of globalization, both China and Russia have felt the impact of the global economic slowdown triggered by America's subprime mortgage crisis. China and the United States, for example, have now become so intertwined economically that each is looking to the other for relief—China needs the United States to start spending again, and the United States needs China to finance it. Although Sino-Russian trade may be growing, it remains only one-eighth of the PRC's trade with the United States.[4] Russia, for its part, remains highly dependent on foreign investment and assistance to help stabilize, develop, and diversify its economy. Although China and Russia may cringe at U.S. economic, technological, and military prominence in the international order, such resentment is not indicative of a desire to confront Washington directly, either together or alone.

Notes

1. "Press Release: Minister of Foreign Affairs Sergey Lavrov's Upcoming Visit to China," Russian Federation Ministry of Foreign Affairs, 22 July 2008; "China, Russia Complete Border Survey, Determination," Xinhua, 21 July 2008; "Island's Return Marks End of Border Dispute," *China Daily*, 15 October 2008, http://www.chinadaily.com.cn/language_tips/cdaudio/2008-10/15/content_7108496.htm.

2. *Demographic Policy in Russia: From Reflection to Action*, report prepared by the United Nations in the Russian Federation, 30 April 2008, http://www.undp.ru/index.phtml?iso=RU&lid=1&cmd=news&id=493.

3. Peh Shing Huei, "Rebirth of the Chinese Armada—An Aircraft Carrier Will Signal China's Rise as a World Military Power," *The Straits Times*, 24 December 2008.

4. *Direction of Trade Statistics Database* (Washington, D.C.: International Monetary Fund, 2008), on-line service, accessed 7 August 2008.

Part One

★

The Making of a Strategic Partnership

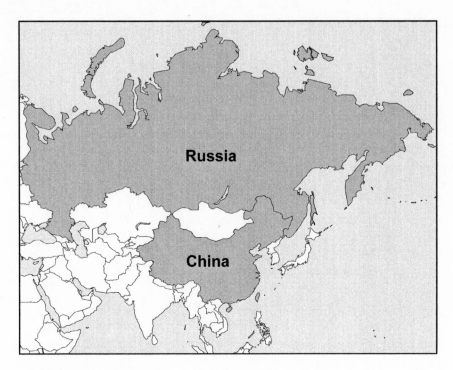

Map 1.1. China and Russia.

1

The Sino-Russian Strategic Partnership

How Close? Where To?

Gilbert Rozman

The Sino-Soviet dispute reached its full intensity in 1966–1976, and we have observed a sustained upward trend in relations between Beijing and Moscow in the three decades since. Snapshots of ties in 1976–1978, 1986–1988, 1996–1998, and 2006–2008 show continuous improvement even if momentum was at times interrupted by a succession of barriers. As we enter the fourth decade of advancing relations, the focus turns to three lingering questions: First, to what extent does unevenness in bilateral ties complicate the strategic partnership? Second, in what ways do domestic changes and national identities still restrain relations? And third, how does the ongoing great power realignment in Asia impinge on evolving relations? Many have underestimated this relationship, but extrapolating also may not suffice at a time when new strains reflect the dual rise of these two great powers, one as the reputed next superpower and the other as an energy behemoth for a thirsty world.

In 1976–1978, Mao Zedong's death and Deng Xiaoping's ascendance opened the way to reconciliation between leaders in Moscow and Beijing, but this opportunity was only slowly grasped. Normalization talks began in 1982 but were unable to achieve any momentum. At first division in China, then incompetent Soviet leadership was most responsible amid skewed debates on both sides, where ideologues trumped experts.[1] Mikhail Gorbachev's "new thinking" in 1986–1988 laid the foundation for normalization, but it was treated with suspicion even before the backlash from Beijing's 1989 domestic crackdown. Liberal moves in Moscow undermined any realist or ideological consensus, complicating relations until gradually, at the end of 1992, they began to be repaired. Failure to seize the opportunities in this reform era was the fault of both sides, notably Beijing's narrow view of socialist political reform and great power reconciliation, and limited appreciation in Moscow of where China was heading.[2] In 1996–1998, Boris Yeltsin shifted direction and, with Jiang Zemin, forged a strategic partnership; this advanced, but haltingly, while he remained president. This stuttering reconciliation even continued in the first years of Vladimir Putin's presidency. More than Chinese reticence, Russian hesitancy about favoring one partner slowed progress in drawing the two closer.[3] Only from 2003 do we observe a notable quickening of the pace of improvement, broadening as well the scope of bilateral relations to reach a new peak in 2006–2008, when Putin put emphasis on them. This emphasis continued under his successor, Dmitry Medvedev, whose first trip abroad was to Beijing. Viewing this upturn against the background of sustained improvement in relations over three decades, we are better able to assess the basis for further progress in these relations.

Each of these decades saw barriers limit rapid improvement in bilateral ties, but also some success in removing existing serious impediments. *Ideological barriers* fell in the post-Mao decade, as Beijing dropped the label "revisionism" and Moscow overcame backsliding seen in the label "Maoism without Mao." Indeed, the Chinese sought common ground in pursuit of "reform socialism," but the dismantling of the socialist model in the two societies was not in sync for any sort of ideology to resurface as adhesive glue for this dyad.[4] Moscow's decade of radical transformation served to lower *realist barriers,* first removing China's "three fundamental obstacles" (all military occupations and buildups around its borders), then the border dispute, leaving only a need to clean up loose ends through final demarcation, and, last, short-term concern about mutual security threats. By the mid-1990s, shared strategic interests had become the driving force for closer ties. Finally, in the decade of strategic partnership, barriers were falling to a wide-ranging relationship. The two parties learned to overcome differences over the uncertain status of the Russian Far East, migration, bilateral economic ties, energy, multilateralism in Central Asia, the Korean Peninsula, East Asian regionalism, and linkages to three other great powers—the United States, Japan, and India. While none of these ten sometimes divisive issues was resolved to the point that it could not complicate relations anew, the results in 2003–2008 brought an all-around partnership, in which arms sales have played a major role and where there is considerable potential for reshaping the geopolitical landscape of Asia.[5]

To assess the strength of this relationship as it enters its fourth decade of moving beyond the Sino-Soviet split, we need answers to the three questions identified above. First, among the issues that have troubled relations, are some still likely to disturb a trajectory of continued improvement in ties? This requires examining unevenness in the all-around partnership. Second, from the point of view of domestic change and national identities in the two states, are there any factors likely to have an impact on bilateral ties? Over the past sixty years since Josef Stalin and Mao first faced each other in the aftermath of World War II, it is these forces that have mattered most. Third, as we look ahead to the emergence of a new Asian system of great power relations, how will the Sino-Russian partnership be impacted in the context of multiple strategic triangles, not only the classic triangle involving the United States? Amid shifts in strategy as separate regions of Asia become closely intertwined and crises of nuclear weapons proliferation arouse urgent appeals for multilateral cooperation, we must pay close attention to the two large continental powers whose reach extends to virtually all areas of Asia. This requires broadening our vision to appreciate how Sino-Russian relations fit into unprecedented regional reordering. After all, great power identities and relations are the principal driving forces in this partnership.

Unevenness in the Sino-Russian Strategic Partnership

Since the 1980s, political leaders driven by realist power calculations have spurred normalization forward, intermittently boosted by economic interests alert to opportunities for trade, while overcoming public apathy or even distrust. Thus, political ties grew warm from the mid-1990s, economic ties were cool but became warmer, and cultural ties largely stayed cold despite repeated attempts to heat them from above. Wariness in the Russian Far East over alleged territorial demands, illicit immigration, loss of control of economic assets, and excessive dependency forged an atmosphere of suspicion and even revival of the pre-1917 alarm known as the "yellow peril."[6] When this type of thinking started to be fanned in 1993 by demagogues in the region (notably Governor Yevgeny Nazdratenko of Primorsky Krai), some contrasted it with more sober reasoning in Moscow—but the same concerns were echoed in discussions there about how to preserve sovereignty and full control over the Russian Far East and even Siberia in the face of unfavorable demographic, economic, and balance of power trends. The Chinese have been well aware of the sensitivity of this debate about "quiet expansionism" and have sought with some success to nullify its impact on bilateral relations.[7] At the same time, they have closely followed changes in Russian strategy to the outside world, welcoming Putin's impact.[8]

Putin has done many things to reduce tensions over the Russian Far East, even if his record is not unambiguous and critical decisions remain. He removed Nazdratenko and made it clear that similar interference by governors in international relations would not be tolerated. The final border demarcation that transferred to China part of an island next to Khabarovsk in the fall of 2004 was an act of statesmanship made easier by the pragmatic, forward-looking negotiating posture of the Chinese authorities. Economic ties have advanced, compared to the 1994–1999 stagnation following the chaotic "border fever" after the collapse of the Soviet Union. Rumors of rampant migration are less often repeated in alarmist tones, despite continuing concern about the inclinations of businesses and officials to rely on Chinese labor or even turn the other way as the Chinese gain a foothold in local communities, backed by legal and illegal payments. In regional capitals there is a new realism about working together, and making deals beneficial to both sides. Cross-border issues have a lower profile. In mid-2006 Ambassador Liu Guchang rightly celebrated the fifth anniversary of the Treaty of Good-Neighborliness and Friendly Cooperation for the significant progress achieved in bilateral relations.[9]

Even so, remaining problems keep cross-border ties more problematic than cross-national relations. One is the criminalization of the border crossings, indicated by serious underreporting of imports from China (often assessed by gross volume, then regarded as not having been taxed at all when they reach the intended market elsewhere in Russia) and of exports from Russia, such as lumber, marine products, and precious metals. After earlier attempts to establish new controls over border trade, Putin in 2006 purged the existing bureaucracy and launched a clean-up, to uncertain results. A second problem is divergence between China and Russia on cross-border zones, whether it be the long unrealized bridge between Blagoveshchensk and Heihe that could normalize ties between these paired cities or the industrial zone championed by Governor Sergei Darkin between Primorsky Krai and Heilongjiang Province before Russia insisted on controls to prevent competition between Chinese-produced goods and what Russians produce.[10] The Chinese keep seeking better access to markets, while the Russians fear freer trade or a loss of monopolies controlled by special interests. Agreements on joint projects are not necessarily fulfilled, even today after many gains in economic ties have been realized.

Third, the most visible problem before 2009 was uncertainty about the terminus of the oil pipeline from western Siberia (which began construction in 2006) and about the construction of a gas pipeline to Northwest China that will require agreed gas prices.[11] Attention focuses on the intervention by Japan from late 2002 to change the terminus from Daqing to the coast and Putin's agreement in principle, in contradiction of assurances already given to China's leaders. The matter is viewed as a test for Khabarovsky and Primorsky krais, which are strenuously lobbying for the Pacific route. Plentiful energy is their way out of what has widely been called the "crisis of the Russian Far East," where the much ballyhooed potential of opening to the Asia-Pacific region has been little realized. Their leaders see Northeast China's gain—plus shorter transportation routes for Siberian energy than those that swing over the hump of Heilongjiang and through the major cities of the Russian Far East—as their region's loss, relegating it to eventual oblivion without the wherewithal to withstand the growing imbalance with their vibrant neighbors inside China. Complaints abound about the structure of bilateral trade and lack of investment from China in manufacturing.[12] Thus, in his final months as president Putin stressed to South Korea's new president, Lee Myung-bak (who had just declared "energy diplomacy" a priority), the promise of working together on the development of resources in Asiatic Russia, and he hosted Japanese prime minister Yasuo Fukuda in a joint call for developing oil fields whose output would flow along the pipeline under construction to the Pacific coast. When Medvedev went to Beijing at the start of his presidency, the gas pipeline issue was on the agenda but remained unresolved. Only when Russia was battered by the financial crisis in 2009 did it yield to China on the oil pipeline route, in return for a larger loan.

The potential for trouble in bilateral relations over energy arose when Junichiro Koizumi made a late offer to Putin to pay a large share of the cost of an oil pipeline to the Pacific coast in place of one that the Chinese thought had already been promised to go to Daqing. Putin was leaning strongly toward the Japanese offer, recognizing that it provided more price flexibility with a diverse market and that it served the interests of the major cities in the Russian Far East. Yet, as construction was beginning on the first stage of the pipeline to Skovorodino by the border with China, there was still much speculation that the final leg would proceed to Daqing, for which China was ready to pay the cost. In the meantime, Putin had reasserted state control over oil firms and foreign-invested projects, treating energy as a strategic resource to be wielded on behalf of national power. Japan had waited until December 2006 to hint at a possible compromise offer to settle its territorial dispute with Russia over the southern Kuril Islands after backing away in 2001 from moves in that direction, and it was not satisfied with gaps in information about how much oil was available and how any deal would be structured. At fault was Russia's cavalier treatment of international investors, never preparing a detailed plan for the pipeline to convince the Japanese government and then alienating energy companies with threats of steep penalties, such as for supposed environmental violations, which they used to renegotiate contracts. Yet, as oil prices kept soaring, Russia's assets were ever more coveted and China's bargaining position became less convincing. Moreover, contradictory statements on the pipeline plans suggest that Russia's strategy may be changing and no longer aligned with that of its Chinese consumer.[13] Yet, after oil prices plummeted China had the upper hand, even if Russia still insisted that it would build a pipeline to the Pacific in a second stage, assuming oil supplies sufficed.[14]

The gap between political and economic ties, while narrowed by the six-fold rise in trade since the late 1990s, also should not be dismissed as a limiting factor in relations. Again it is the Russian side that poses more barriers to normal exchange based on market forces and that is more dissatisfied with how things are proceeding. Given China's enormous appetite for natural resources and Russia's poor competitiveness in industrial production (with some exceptions where low domestic energy prices give it an edge), many Russians are troubled by a division of labor seen as very favorable to China. Over the past decade Russian negotiators have at times pressed the Chinese to make nonmarket trade-offs, agreeing to buy such high-value exports as civilian aircraft and nuclear power stations in return for some Russian purchases or arms exports. Resistance to moves by Chinese firms to invest in Russia's energy sector presaged strong-arm tactics to make earlier domestic and foreign investors accept the return to a decisive Russian state control. Bilateral economic ties do not yet satisfy Russians on the diversity of their exports and Chinese on the growth of market forces. Vested interests linking the two economies, often with the Russian state sector in the forefront, such as in arms sales, have expanded, but they pale compared to Chinese business connections to other states, where commercial interests suffice. Discord over pricing of gas and oil in long-term agreements left various negotiations on hold.[15] A similar struggle ensued over arms sales, leading to a decline in Russian exports after years of bickering over such matters as shoddy parts and stolen technology.

Cultural ties continue to undermine efforts to boost the soft power of each state in the other. Xenophobia in Russia is not subsiding, even if it identifies many targets besides Chinese. Fascination across China with other parts of the world keeps growing, offering many more appealing destinations for students and tourists than Russia. Vice tourism to cities such as Vladivostok in Russia and consumer tourism to market centers such as Suifenhe in China meet existing demand, but do little to overcome the cultural gap. While Putin's daughter may study Chinese, in neither country is study of the other's language and culture rising rapidly enough to suggest that orientations toward the West will change. Yet, the "Year of Russia" in China was marked in March 2006 with Putin's fourth official visit to the country, in November with a large ceremony involving Prime Minister Mikhail Fradkov, and throughout the year with a panoply of exchanges to highlight mutual cultural appreciation.[16] Yet, such efforts (as had been seen in the "year of friendship between the young people of the two countries") do not suffice to build a firm foundation for mutual trust.[17] Given greater anxieties, the "Year of China" in Russia in 2007 posed a sterner test, and it left little imprint, as rising Russian self-confidence with economic advances and political stability did not provide adequate reason to increase reliance on or trust in China.

While Sino-Russian relations remain unbalanced, they are less so. Economic and cultural troubles that plagued relations in the 1990s are much reduced. China's deliberate strategy of strengthening ties since 1992 and Putin's emboldened challenge against the United States and the West since 2003 have laid markers for the future. Yet, the driving forces that brought the two sides closer together may be losing steam: fear of U.S. unipolarity and containment has diminished in China; Russia's marginalization is no longer a source of alarm; and both countries are assertively advancing their great power claims in ways that may bring them more directly into competition. Elements of unevenness in their relations—a lack of reassurance through shared values, awareness that bilateral economic ties are secondary to the ties each is forging with other states, and rising assertiveness on matters of regional security where interests do not coincide—suggest that the next decade will be marked by greater challenges. The political drive, along with the strategic imperative, for close relations is likely to persist to some degree, but precisely in these areas strains may put a brake on the upward trend between Moscow and Beijing visible over the past three decades. Problems in overcoming unevenness in relations could well spill over into more open disagreements where strategic interests diverge in neighboring areas of Asia.

Domestic Change and National Identities

Realist identities are ascendant in both China and Russia. Each is intent on more moves to maximize its power: China after thirty years of building up its comprehensive national power to what some argue is now second only to that of the United States, and Russia after an extended plunge from the Soviet Union's superpower pedestal recovering part of what it lost along with its self-respect and determination to flex its power. A major cause of the Sino-Soviet split was Mao's failure to pursue a realist course amid the utopianism of the Great Leap Forward and his embrace of an extreme version of communist ideology. Delays in achieving and capitalizing on normalization are seen as reflecting Leonid Brezhnev's ideological rigidity (in the hands of Mikhail Suslov and China-overseer O. B. Rakhmanin) and then Gorbachev and Yeltsin's "idealistic" pursuit of the West. They also were influenced by

China's deep suspicion of Gorbachev's way of thinking, compounded by the dual impact of the collapse of the communist bloc and the purge of political reformers in China after June 1989.[18] In China since that time and in Putin's entourage after he consolidated power, there is no sign of a leader who would forsake realism.

Great power identities have gained ground at the expense of communist claims that held sway through the 1970s and various Western-leaning alternatives (humanism, convergent modernization, globalization, etc.) that built a considerable following in the 1980s.[19] They have merged with legacies of traditional nationalism (anachronistically linked to Confucianism in China, and more aptly with tsarist thought in Russia). The search for the "Russian idea" launched by Yeltsin produced an amalgam of heroes, from Peter I to Stalin, whose buildup of national power looms in the minds of Russians as their greatest legacy. Similarly, the Chinese spiritual vacuum much discussed in the 1980s and thought by many to be exacerbated by the coercion of 1989 gave rise to the patriotic education movement of Jiang Zemin in the 1990s and then Hu Jintao's intensification of realist thinking. Putin and Hu were each consumed with increasing his nation's influence and capacity for power projection, leading both to focus on the lone superpower and various openings created by George W. Bush for countering the global reach of the United States. That effort to counter the U.S. reach does not, however, exclude cooperation with the United States, especially by Hu, who has recognized in the crises diverting America's attention opportunities to win assent to China's "peaceful rise."

September 11 might have served as the defining moment for transforming international relations by building a coalition of great powers to face terrorism. Instead, Bush's axis of evil speech and subsequent strategy toward the three demonized states of Iraq, North Korea, and Iran provided the background for China and Russia to redefine their realist strategies in opposition to the United States. To be sure, they threw their support behind Bush in the war with the Taliban in Afghanistan, and they made clear their opposition to nuclear weapons in the other three states. Yet, they rejected unilateral U.S. ultimatums, insisting on working for a compromise solution in each case. With the United States ignoring their views on Iraq and with the Iran situation only gradually heading toward a confrontation, the North Korean nuclear crisis as well as steps to shape a new balance of power in East Asia revealed their realist inclinations most clearly.[20] The Six-Party Talks and the Shanghai Cooperation Organization (SCO) were striking examples of Sino-Russian realist cooperation, but they may be losing that potential as the two countries' interests increasingly come into conflict.

Chinese and Russian interests on the Korean Peninsula are far from overlapping. Russians fear Chinese domination of the peninsula, at the price of their marginalization as well as of railroad construction bypassing the Russian Far East. Some suggest that only Russians are the true supporters of a united and independent Korea.[21] In January 2003, Putin sent his emissary to Pyongyang to put Moscow at the center of any negotiations, and as talks began in August it was Kim Jong-il who insisted on Russia's inclusion, making these the Six-Party Talks, but then the North became upset by Russian behavior at the first-round talks that they saw as being supportive of U.S. goals. Only in 2004, from the second round, do we see a more passive Russia apt to defer to China, as both states faulted U.S. negotiating as ideological and serving only to drive the North toward more extreme behavior. They strongly supported the 19 September 2005 Joint Statement of general principles and then blocked attempts in July and October 2006 for tough, intrusive sanctions against the North while pushing for renewed incentives that led to new Six-Party Talks on 18 December. Avoiding regime collapse offers the best hope of limiting U.S. power and laying a foundation for multilateral security cooperation. Above all, China and Russia do not define the standoff between the United States and North Korea in moral terms, but as a realist challenge over the regional power balance and eventual Korean reunification. The deal reached on 13 February 2007 at the Six-Party Talks tested North Korean and U.S. flexibility through difficult negotiations, but also left Beijing and especially Moscow more on the sidelines as they scrambled to realize their own interests on the Korean Peninsula. For instance, at the port of Rajin, near the three-way intersection of borders, Russia is planning a railway line to Vladivostok as China prepares a highway to Hunchun. Rather than the North Korean terminus emerging as a regional transport nexus, the North appeared to be reviving its "balancing" strategy after finding that not only were China and South Korea eager to compete with little coordination between them but also that China and Russia were prone to revive their own competition there. In 2009, however, it defiantly tested missiles and a nuclear weapon, causing the other states to agree on United Nations Security Council sanctions. China and Russia cooperated to narrow their scope and make use of force against the North less likely.

The SCO had started as the Shanghai Organization with limited goals and much uncertainty that China and Russia could cooperate closely in dealing with the potentially contested territory of Central Asia. It was assumed that Russia regarded China as the most likely transgressor into its sphere of influence, worrying about being squeezed out by China's economic dynamism. Accepting U.S. bases in the region to prosecute the war in Afghanistan, Putin seemed to support a more open Central Asia. Yet, in 2005 China and Russia jointly backed Uzbekistan's call for the United States to remove its military base and urged Kyrgyzstan to act as well. The SCO expanded its mission, granting observer status to various nearby states while leaving China along with Russia in the forefront. It was accelerating military cooperation, as in the November 2006 Beijing forum of military officials. In this case, too, realism targeted U.S. power rather than each other's. Looking back on the old strategic triangle which Washington had successfully manipulated as the pivot during crucial years, Beijing and Moscow were intent on developing their dyad and facing Washington from a position of greater strength. Yet, the SCO faced serious unmet challenges in both economic and military integration.[22] China's economic aspirations for the organization contrasted with Russia's interest in reasserting its influence as if the Soviet Union could be revived. Above all, pursuit of Central Asian energy resources found Russia intent on fortifying its traditional spheres of influence with pipelines leading to the north, and China focused on securing new supplies with pipelines leading to the east. The SCO became a backdrop to this intensified struggle. For Russia, its very identity as a great power demanded reassertion of dominance over the states and resources of Central Asia, where a large Russian diaspora remained. For China, its rise is predicated on extending its influence along all of its borders, starting with economic ties.

Central Asia is not only a battleground for energy, but also an arena of clashing aspirations for influence. Some observers, blinded by the apparent momentum in the SCO, have overlooked the intensity of the competition in Central Asia. While the agenda of the SCO expands and its scope broadens, including the addition of observer states and military exercises, the reality is that Russia has stepped up efforts to block the spread of China's influence in Central Asia as well as in the Russian Far East. It is more receptive to the economic activities of Japan and South Korea, fearing that Chinese entrepreneurs could be the first wave of an economic takeover or mass migration. Due to market forces still subject to substantial controls and narrow interpretations of national identity in Russia, the Chinese find it much easier to find common rules or understanding with countries to their east and south than with the remnants of the former Soviet Union. Beijing's deference to Moscow has so far limited open clashes over Central Asia. As Moscow aims to assert more control and Beijing has even more economic clout, more tension is likely.

A renewed clash of national identities would not take the form of the ideological struggle of the past. The age of sudden identity shifts at the insistence of charismatic top officials appears to be over. Memories of the legacy of Stalin and Mao, despite some nostalgia, and the travails of dismantling the traditional communist model in the 1980s and early 1990s make such shifts implausible. Globalization suggests to some optimists in the West the decline of nationalism or even the embrace of a common set of universal values, stimulating talk of the end of Cold War thinking in which great power balancing occurs. Yet, after China's leadership became obsessed with boosting comprehensive national power, similar nationalistic reasoning took hold among Russia's leadership. No sign of serious challenge due to a power struggle or generational change is in sight. Difficult internal problems exist in both societies, but they stand little chance of becoming a reason for scapegoating the other or of impacting bilateral relations. National identities as great powers with certain entitlements could, however, lead the two states toward mutual recriminations. China is obsessed with sovereignty, as it looks back to history to justify its borders and conceptualize its place in the regional order. Of late, it has raised concerns in both Koreas with claims about the ancient Koguryo state and elsewhere, including India, as Tibetan demonstrations aroused not only harsh repression but also exaggerated historical claims about sovereignty. Given Russian suspicions of China's view of history, whether applied to the Russian Far East or even to neighboring areas such as Mongolia, the potential exists for misunderstanding. At the same time, Russian nationalism tinged with Soviet expansionist reasoning has kept growing and could turn against China, as it has against other countries. If preoccupation with the United States and the West diminishes, other targets of nationalism may rise to the forefront, and Sino-Russian trust remains too uncertain to prevent mutual targeting.

Great Power Realignment in Asia

The notion of Asia had seemed little more than a geographer's convenience, as linkages among its various parts by land and sea remained rare until Western ships came calling in the sixteenth century and especially Western military superiority forced open all corners of the continent in the nineteenth. China and Russia had started regular contacts in the eighteenth century and became closely intertwined only after the middle of the nineteenth. In the first wave of military competition centered on Northeast Asia in the 1890s and 1900s, China served as transit route and battleground for Russian ambitions, but those were blocked by Japan. In the second wave of competition, from the export of Soviet communism in the 1920s to the Korean War in the 1950s, leaders in Moscow sought to transform China into a force to spread their worldview and power. For a time, Japan again gained the upper hand, taking an even more aggressive approach, then the United States blocked the spread of world communism and eventually divided the two communist leaders with moves toward peaceful coexistence, but it was China's own rejection of this arrangement that cut short Moscow's expansionist drive. The current third wave of intensive competition for reordering Asia differs in at least four important respects: (1) China is the driving force; (2) many great powers (existing or emerging) and middle powers are active; (3) war and military buildups play a role, but other factors matter too; and (4) virtually all of Asia plus a few other actors are involved, seen in the range of organizations—the East Asian Summit, the SCO and its observer states, and the Six-Party Talks among them—established since the start of this century. Sino-Russian ties are part of this Asian reorganization that is far from running its course.

In Northeast Asia, Sino-Russian relations were scarcely tested by other countries over the past decade because of three factors. First, Japan alienated both states, obsessed as it was with historical issues and demonstrating little flexibility in its strategic thinking toward Asia. Despite an energy initiative in 2003 to induce Russia to build an oil pipeline to the coast rather than to Northeast China, Japan's preoccupation with its territorial claims and its concentration on the alliance with the United States left ties with Russia in limbo. Second, before the 2007 Joint Agreement the United States and North Korea faced each other as implacable antagonists. This meant that in the Six-Party Talks when Washington applied pressure on Pyongyang, Moscow backed Beijing's effort to persuade Washington to take a softer line. Differences over how to deal with regional security and reunification were obscured by shared interest in bolstering North Korea and reaching a compromise in which the United States normalized relations with it. Third, little movement occurred in establishing a regional framework in which Seoul, as the region's middle power, would strive to achieve reconciliation among the great powers and Washington would realize the advantages of supplementing its bilateral alliances with a regional security framework. In 2008–2009, however, all of these factors were in flux, and that uncertainty impacted Sino-Russian relations.

North Korea's October 2006 nuclear test showed the limits of U.S. intransigence, and the Bush administration's abrupt change in policy left in doubt the rationale for Sino-Russian coordination. Differences in strategies toward both North and South Korea became more apparent. The gap was revealed between Russia's interest in a north-south corridor, as it invested in railroad reconstruction from Vladivostok to the port complex of Rajin-Sonbong and sought South Korean support as part of a plan for a rail line all the way down the peninsula, and China's east-west orientation. China sought corridors both across the south to Pyongyang through the border city of Sinuiju and across the north with a highway construction plan to the Rajin-Sonbong complex. Ready to boost Vladivostok as its gateway to the Pacific and host to the APEC summit in 2012, Russia seemed newly eager for foreign investment and closer regional ties, responding to Japan's overtures aimed at Medvedev's expressed openness to international economic integration and to South Korean president Lee Myung-bak's new "energy diplomacy." Above all, Japan has the potential, perhaps together with the United States and South Korea, to refocus Russian attention on a multilateral regional approach, reducing the one-sided reliance on China.

To date, Japan's behavior has contributed to closer Sino-Russian ties despite moments in 1989–1992 and 1997–2003 when it seemed that it stood a good chance of driving a wedge between them. A compromise proposal for resolving the southern Kuril Islands territorial dispute (splitting the total area of the four islands in half, with Japan getting three islands and half of the largest, Etorofu) by Foreign Minister Taro Aso seems to have been an uncoordinated appeal to both sides for more sober thinking, but it did not signal a new strategic approach.[23] Japan has sided strongly with the United States, and the current pattern is likely to continue, with this alliance representing one pole in Asia while the Sino-Russian strategic partnership serves as the opposite pole for two states obsessed with achieving security through a strategic balance in the region.[24] Yet, as seen in the back-to-back visits of Yasuo Fukuda to Russia and Hu Jintao to Japan in the spring of 2008, Japan can improve ties with both states and exert leverage that can both assist U.S. moves toward multilateralism—Deputy Secretary of State John Negroponte was in Beijing discussing a Northeast Asian peace and security mechanism on the heels of Hu's visit to Japan—and complicate Sino-Russian ties.

South Korea is a middle power and has groped for room to maneuver between the United States and China and between Japan and China. Russia could be a natural partner, as was seen in recurrent high Korean hopes for improved ties at the time of Yeltsin's visit to Seoul in 1992 after thumbing his nose at Japan, in Kim Dae-jung's visit to Moscow in 1999 as part of preparing the ground for the Sunshine Policy, and in Roh Moo-hyun's visit to Putin's dacha in 2004 as Roh struggled with the dead-end diplomacy of the Six-Party Talks. In 2008, Lee Myung-bak showed interest in conjunction with his high priority for "energy diplomacy." Russian analysts often stress the high degree of overlap between the interests of the two states in Northeast Asia, and Putin's 2001 visit to Kim Dae-jung accentuated shared interest in transportation, energy, and security—all with strategic implications for the shape of regional integration.[25] Yet, given the South's alliance with the United States and rapid economic integration with China, Russia has hesitated to make it a target for realizing strategic objectives. Roh also recognized that romanticized views of Russia's role raise suspicions elsewhere about existing commitments. This impasse may have started to change after the February 2007 compromise on the nuclear crisis. Lee's upgrading of ties with both the United States and Japan left doubts about the strength of ties with China. Even if China maintains a big edge over Russia in ties with South Korea, the changing search for regional balance may lead to maneuvering that will affect relations between China and Russia, especially with North Korea's uncertain role in the background.[26]

Another significant actor is India, being courted on all sides. For the foreseeable future it is unlikely to abandon its autonomy or cast its lot with one pole. The potential exists, however, should the United States and Japan temper their strategy and China and Pakistan retain their close ties, for India to draw closer to the U.S.-Japan pole. This puts some strain on Russia, long accustomed to treating India as its closest great power partner and eager, since Yevgeny Primakov's time as Yeltsin's foreign minister, to forge a troika with China and India. If Japan appeals to Russia from one side and India from another, each reinforcing internal fears that exclusive ties to China would leave Russia as a junior partner, realist balancing might be further enhanced. After all, soon preoccupation with U.S. unilateralism and establishment of a multipolar world may give way to recognition that Asia is already realizing multipolarity and Russia's leverage rises by keeping many directions open. Traditional ties with India have a special hold on Russian strategists, as seen in Putin's early 2007 visit to New Delhi, even as China's rapid rise leaves India with other suitors eager to build close partnerships.[27] After Washington and Tokyo, New Delhi arguably has the most potential to influence the strength of the Sino-Russian partnership.

Iran is a middle power with growing capacity to shape events in the Middle East and affect great power relations. China has generally followed Russia's lead in dealing with proposals for sanctions over Iran's nuclear development program. Yet, the arguably more hostile view of Moscow toward the United States and the existing world order may lead Russia to stand in the way of efforts to contain Iranian assertiveness in ways that China would be hesitant to support. If the United States expands its strategic dialogue with China and if Japan has success in easing tensions with China, then a compromise offer to Iran may leave room for China's support. To be sure, Chinese ties with Iran and oil dependency on it make any move to pressure China or overcome Sino-Russian coordination difficult.[28] Russia might shift to a more critical stance. Uncertainty over Iran's export of revolution in the Middle East and apparent interest in gaining control over the region's energy resources—as well as Tehran's nuclear weapons aspirations—casts a shadow that could cloud Sino-Russian relations.

If we set aside the tendency to treat the Association of Southeast Asian Nations (ASEAN) as a unitary actor on strategic issues, then the search for middle powers in Southeast Asia and beyond leads first to Indonesia and, in the eyes of some, next to Australia. As Russia seeks entry into the East Asian Summit, these are two voices along with those of China, Japan, and India that matter. Even if prospects for this new organization from 2005 are uncertain, the fact that the East Asian Summit's annual meeting in December follows those of ASEAN and ASEAN + 3 means that this is a venue that opens the door for the Northeast Asian states to strategizing about Southeast Asia and to exploration of the tantalizing topic of forging an East Asian community. Putin's current strategy of reliance on China in Asia does not necessarily win Russia backing for entrance into the East Asian Summit, while it arouses doubt in Australia and Indonesia about how constructive its role would be in an organization already in danger of overexpansion and excessive polarization between China and Japan. As host at the inaugural East Asian Summit, Malaysia invited Russia to be present and Putin made a pitch for inclusion, but the sixteen members did not reach consensus on that.

China and Russia face each other across a divide that stretches from South Asia through the states of Central Asia and Mongolia, and on to Northeast Asia, where limited opening of the long, eastern section of their border puts them in direct contact on an unprecedented scale. Cooperation in these locations tests the degree to which shared interests are really pursued. On the whole, China seeks resources to fuel its voracious appetite for everything that makes it the "factory to the world," preferring to do the processing, for example, of Russian timber in its own sawmills and furniture factories. In contrast, Russia aims to make industrial production the mainstay of the resurgence of its Far East, intensifying control over its own oil and gas exports, but also maneuvering to ensure that Central Asian oil and gas, much of which crosses its borders, is not brought under Chinese control. Russians often accuse China of seeking to turn the Asiatic expanses of their country into a "colonial" resource base supplying only raw materials to Chinese companies, which receive the lion's share of the jobs and profits from their transformation. As the prices on oil, gas, minerals, lumber, and other primary products have risen dramatically, the value of Russian exports has multiplied. Many Russians remain dissatisfied, however, still insisting on changing the composition of trade. Even as bilateral trade in 2007 reached $48 billion, a six-fold increase in just a decade, the struggle over economic relations remains unresolved. China fared better at the start of the global economic crisis, but Russia's position soon improved as oil prices rebounded. In the background, these economic ties are treated as ways to build influence that will determine the geopolitics of Asia as it becomes integrated.

Great power realignment around China's rise leaves unclear the degree to which Sino-Russian ties will become a nucleus within Asia, as U.S.-Japan ties are, or whether Russia will be split away from China to some degree through its ties with another great or middle power. Russia's lack of an overall regional strategy, including a long-term strategy for the Russian Far East, leaves its intentions uncertain.[29] Others too have not developed their own strategies sufficiently to make clear what they might seek from Russia and how they would proceed. Given these circumstances, Russia may be prone to stick close to China in the coming years. U.S. leadership focused on multilateralism, reduced nationalism in favor of realism in Japan, and new signs of assertiveness in China would all be conducive to Russia's taking steps to balance China's rise. Yet, they would likely occur gradually without any design to undermine the hard-won strategic partnership.

Conclusion

A decade ago the unbalanced nature of bilateral ties and uncertainty over national identities and domestic politics left doubt about prospects for the upward trend in Sino-Russian relations continuing unabated, but the state of great power relations pointed the way to another decade of improving ties. Now some earlier reasons for doubt are gone, but the state of global and regional power relations is changing in ways that put pressure on their strategic partnership. A fourth decade of care to prevent any serious setbacks is likely; yet, a turning point may emerge if some of the unrealized possibilities since the end of the Cold War finally occur against the backdrop of an uneven partnership, national identities skewed toward building unilateral power, and accelerated reordering of the balance of power in Asia. Just as abnormal prolongation of the Sino-Soviet split ended, so too may the abnormal advance of the Sino-Russian strategic partnership without forthright acknowledgment that they are also competitors in pursuit of clashing national interests.

The chances are greater that Russia will reconsider its expanding partnership with China than vice versa. After all, China is becoming the dominant force in the relationship and its priority of recovering Taiwan gives it a prime objective other than multipolarity. For Russia there have been a series of temptations over the past two decades that suggest it could still be convinced to seek balance in Asia that would attenuate its reliance on China. The United States and the European Union succeeded for a time in turning it toward the West. Japan gave it hope on more than one occasion that a breakthrough to full normalization through a deal over territory and a peace treaty could be achieved. Russian interest at times has focused on the Korean Peninsula with talk of South Korea becoming a special partner. In Central and South Asia it is still far from clear that Russian concerns about China's inroads might not lead to serious policy readjustments. India continues to have a special hold on Russia. All of these forces have failed in recent years to deter Russia's leaders from turning ever more toward China, and we should avoid the temptation of imagining that they will soon have a different impact. Instead, we should consider the possibility of gradual strategic rethinking once the United States and Japan agree on a new approach cognizant of Russia's aims.

There exists no cause for alarm about a Sino-Russian alliance or a renewed split marked by hostility. Efforts to check direct challenges to the existing world and regional order by each country can continue without serious concern that they will be driven into each other's arms. At the same time, encouragement for a multilateral security framework in Northeast Asia can offer reassurance to both that will make it easier to explore other interests and allow Sino-Russian ties to shed some of their protective gloss and become more normal. Success in the Six-Party Talks, leading to a more active working group focused on a multilateral security framework in which Russia has the lead role, a forward-looking Japanese posture that could result in a territorial compromise and a jump start to relations with Russia, and joint support for a long-term energy arrangement that could take advantage of the oil pipeline to the Pacific could all be steps in refocusing the Sino-Russian strategic partnership. Since 2007 there have been signs of a new strategic calculus originating from Washington and a new focus on strategic thinking toward Asia in Tokyo, which have produced new understandings with Beijing. An opportunity now exists for the Obama administration as well as new leaders in Japan and in South Korea to engage Moscow in talks about its regional strategy. While not in danger of a sharp downturn, Sino-Russian relations, strained across the Asian continental divide, are likely to reflect the outcome of these still uncertain efforts.

Notes

1. Gilbert Rozman, "Moscow's China-Watchers in the Post-Mao Era: The Response to a Changing China," *China Quarterly* 94 (June 1983): 215–41; Gilbert Roz-

man, *A Mirror for Socialism: Soviet Criticisms of China* (Princeton, N.J.: Princeton Univ. Press, 1985); Wu Lengxi, *The Ten-Year War of Words, 1956–66: Sino-Soviet Relations* [Shinian lunzhan, 1956–1966: Zhongsu guanxi] (Beijing: Central Literary Publishing House [Zhongyang wenxian chubanshe], 1999); Alexander Lukin, *The Bear Watches the Dragon: Russia's Perceptions of China and the Evolution of Russian-Chinese Relations since the Eighteenth Century* (Armonk, N.Y.: Sharpe, 2003); Sergey Radchenko, "The China Puzzle: Soviet Policy towards the People's Republic of China in the 1960s" (Doctoral diss., London School of Economics and Political Science, 2005).

2. Gilbert Rozman, "China's Soviet-Watchers in the 1980s: A New Era in Scholarship," *World Politics* 37, no. 4 (July 1985): 435–74; Gilbert Rozman, *The Chinese Debate about Soviet Socialism, 1978–1985* (Princeton, N.J.: Princeton Univ. Press, 1987); Gilbert Rozman, "Chinese Studies in Russia and Their Impact, 1985–1992," *Asian Research Trends*, no. 4 (1994): 143–60; Elizabeth Wishnick, *Mending Fences: The Evolution of Moscow's China Policy from Brezhnev to Yeltsin* (Seattle: Univ. of Washington Press, 2001).

3. Gilbert Rozman, "The Sino-Russian Strategic Partnership: Will It Endure?" *Demokratizatsiya* 6, no. 2 (spring 1998): 396–415; Gilbert Rozman, "Sino-Russian Relations in the 1990s: A Balance Sheet," *Post-Soviet Affairs* 14, no. 2 (spring 1998): 93–113; Gilbert Rozman, "Sino-Russian Mutual Assessments," in *Rapprochement or Rivalry? Russia-China Relations in a Changing Asia*, ed. Sherman Garnett, 147–74 (Armonk, N.Y.: Sharpe, 2000); Gilbert Rozman, "A New Sino-Russian-American Triangle?" *Orbis* 44, no. 4 (fall 2000): 541–55; Jeanne L. Wilson, *Strategic Partners: Russian-Chinese Relations in the Post-Soviet Era* (Armonk, N.Y.: Sharpe, 2004).

4. Gilbert Rozman, "The Comparative Study of Socialism in China: The Social Sciences at a Crossroads," *Social Research* 54, no. 4 (winter 1987): 631–61; Gilbert Rozman, "Stages in the Reform and Dismantling of Communism in China and the Soviet Union," in *Dismantling Communism: Common Causes and Regional Variations*, ed. Gilbert Rozman, 15–58 (Baltimore: Johns Hopkins Univ. Press, 1992); Yan Sun, *The Chinese Reassessment of Socialism, 1976–1992* (Princeton, N.J.: Princeton Univ. Press, 1995).

5. Robert H. Donaldson and John A. Donaldson, "The Arms Trade in Russian-Chinese Relations: Identity, Domestic Politics, and Geopolitical Positioning," *International Studies Quarterly* 47, no. 4 (December 2003): 709–32.

6. *Zheltaia opasnost'* (Vladivostok: Voron, 1996); Gilbert Rozman, "The Crisis of the Russian Far East: Who Is to Blame?" *Problems of Post-Communism* 44, no. 5 (September/October 1997): 3–12; Gilbert Rozman, "Troubled Choices for the Russian Far East: Decentralization, Open Regionalism, and Internationalism," *Journal of East Asian Affairs* 11, no. 2 (summer/fall 1997): 537–69; V. G. Gel'bras, *Rossiia v usloviiakh global'noi Kitaiskoi migratsii* (Moscow: Muravei, 2004).

7. Gilbert Rozman, "Turning Fortresses into Free Trade Zones," in *Rapprochement or Rivalry? Russia-China Relations in a Changing Asia*, ed. Sherman Garnett, 177–202 (Armonk, N.Y.: Sharpe, 2000); Gilbert Rozman, "Northeast China: Wait-

ing for Regionalism," *Problems of Post-Communism* 45, no. 4 (July–August 1998): 3–13.

8. Li Jingjie and Zheng Yu, eds., *Russia and the Contemporary World* [Eluosi yu dangdai shijie] (Beijing: World Knowledge Publishing House [Shijie zhishi chubanshe], 1996); Feng Shaolei and Xiang Lanxin, eds., *Putin's Foreign Policy* [Pujing waijiao] (Shanghai: Shanghai People's Publishing House [Shanghai renmin chubanshe], 2004); and Fan Jianzhong et al., *Contemporary Russia: Political Development and Progress and Foreign Strategic Choices* [Dangdai Eluosi: Zhengzhi fazhan jinchen yu duiwai zhanlue xuanze] (Beijing: World Publishing House [Shishi chubanshe], 2004).

9. Liu Guchang, "Five Years of the Treaty of Good-Neighborliness, Friendship, and Cooperation," *Far Eastern Affairs* 34, no. 3 (2006): 1–8.

10. Gilbert Rozman, "Strategic Thinking about the Russian Far East: A Resurgent Russia Eyes Its Future in Northeast Asia," *Problems of Post-Communism* 55, no. 1 (January/February 2008): 36–48.

11. Shoichi Itoh, "The Pacific Pipeline at a Crossroads: Dream Project or Pipe Dream?" *ERINA Report* 73 (January 2007): 31–62.

12. Viktor Ishaev, "Sotrudnichestvo Rossiiskogo Dal'nego Vostoka i Zabaikal'ia s Kitaem," *Rossiia Kitai XXI vek* (January 2007): 6–9.

13. Yu Bin, "China-Russian Relations: What Follows China's 'Russia Year'?" *Comparative Connections* (January 2007), www.csis.org/pacfor/ccejournal.html.

14. Torrey Clark, "Russia Moves Siberia Oil Link Route, Raising Costs $846 Million," *Bloomberg,* 29 April 2008.

15. Yu Bin, "China-Russia Relations: From Election Politics to Economic Posturing," *Comparative Connections* (April 2008), www.csis.org/pacfor/ccejournal. html.

16. Yu Bin, "China-Russian Relations: What Follows China's 'Russia Year'?" *Comparative Connections* (January 2007), www.csis.org/pacfor/ccejournal.html.

17. Yu Bin, "China and Russia: Normalizing Their Strategic Partnership," in *Power Shift: China and Asia's New Dynamics,* ed. David Shambaugh, 241 (Berkeley: Univ. of California Press, 2005).

18. Gilbert Rozman, "China's Concurrent Debate about the Gorbachev Era," in *China Learns from the Soviet Union, 1949 to the Present,* ed. Thomas Bernstein and Li Hua-yu (Lanham, Md.: Lexington Books, 2009).

19. Gilbert Rozman, "China's Quest for Great Power Identity," *Orbis* 43, no. 3 (summer 1999): 383–402; Christopher R. Hughes, *Chinese Nationalism in the Global Era* (London: Routledge, 2006); Andrei P. Tsyganov, *Russia's Foreign Policy: Change and Continuity in National Identity* (Lanham, Md.: Rowman and Littlefield, 2006); and Gilbert Rozman, Kazuhiko Togo, and Joseph P. Ferguson, eds., *Russian Strategic Thought toward Asia* (New York: Palgrave, 2006).

20. Gilbert Rozman, "The Geopolitics of the North Korean Nuclear Crisis," in *Strategic Asia 2003–04: Fragility and Crisis,* ed. Richard J. Ellings and Aaron L. Friedberg, 245–61 (Seattle: National Bureau of Asian Research, 2003); Gilbert Roz-

man, *Northeast Asia's Stunted Regionalism: Bilateral Distrust in the Shadow of Globalization* (Cambridge: Cambridge Univ. Press, 2004).

21. Gilbert Rozman, *Strategic Thinking about the Korean Nuclear Crisis: Four Parties Caught between North Korea and the United States* (New York: Palgrave, 2007).

22. Kimberly Marten, "Central Asia: Military Modernization and the Great Game," in *Strategic Asia 2005–06: Military Modernization in an Era of Uncertainty,* ed. Ashley J. Tellis and Michael Wills, 209–35 (Seattle: National Bureau of Asian Research, 2005); Dina R. Spechler and Martin C. Spechler, "Trade, Energy, and Security in the Central Asian Arena," in *Strategic Asia 2006–07: Trade, Interdependence, and Security,* ed. Ashley J. Tellis and Michael Wills, 205–38 (Seattle: National Bureau of Asian Research, 2006); Elizabeth Van Wie Davis and Rouben Azizian, eds., *Islam, Oil and Geopolitics: Central Asia after September 11* (Lanham, Md.: Rowman and Littlefield, 2007).

23. *Sankei shimbun,* 15 December 2006, 2.

24. Chinese Institute of Contemporary International Relations, *An Evaluation of International Strategy and the Security Situation in 2003/04* [Guoji zhanlue yu anquan xingshi pinggu 2003/04] (Beijing: Current Events Press [Shishi chubanshe], 2004); M. Iu Panchenko, *Rossiisko-Kitaiskie otnosheniia i obespechenie bezopasnosti v ATR* (Moscow: Nauchnaia kniga, 2005).

25. Nodari Simoniia, ed., *Polveka bez voiny i bez mira: Koreiskii poluostrov glazami Rossiiskikh uchenykh* (Moscow: IMEMO, 2003).

26. Jae Ho Chung, *Between Ally and Partner: Korea-China Relations and the United States* (New York: Columbia Univ. Press, 2007); Gilbert Rozman, "South Korea and the Sino-Japanese Rivalry: A Middle Power's Options within the East Asian Core Triangle," *Pacific Review* 20, no. 2 (June 2007): 197–220.

27. Robert G. Sutter, *China's Rise in Asia: Promises and Perils* (Lanham, Md.: Rowman and Littlefield, 2005).

28. John W. Garver, *China and Iran: Ancient Partners in a Post-Imperial World* (Seattle: Univ. of Washington Press, 2006).

29. Gilbert Rozman, "Russia in Northeast Asia: In Search of a Strategy," in *Twenty-First Century Russian Foreign Policy and the Shadow of the Past,* ed. Robert Legvold, 343–92 (New York: Columbia Univ. Press, 2007).

2

Russian Perspectives on China

Strategic Ambivalence

Andrew Kuchins

The Russian perspective on China is shaped by a complex amalgamation of geopolitical, economic, historical, and cultural factors that add up to a profound ambivalence toward their rapidly growing neighbor. Despite this ambivalence, Russian policy toward China for the past two decades under Boris Yeltsin, Vladimir Putin, and now Dmitri Medvedev has been driven mainly by pragmatic considerations, resulting in a gradual rapprochement and thickening of the relationship. As the Russian economy staged a remarkable recovery over the last decade, and Putin brought to politics the aura of an authoritarian stabilization, Russia's sensitivities of demographic and economic vulnerability to the rising superpower to its southeast have diminished somewhat. The "strategic partnership" established in 1996 by Boris Yeltsin and Jiang Zemin, which appeared long on rhetoric and thin on substance when Putin assumed power in 2000, has taken on considerable weight as economic and political cooperation have grown. Moscow has no desire to establish an alliance with Beijing, but growing irritation in U.S.-Russia and Europe-Russia relations has redounded to the benefit of China-Russia relations. One still hears Russian concerns about ending up as China's "junior partner" or nothing more than a natural resource appendage [pridatka], but increasingly less so as Russian confidence has increased thanks to a virtual macroeconomic revolution in recent years. Much like the Chinese political elite, Russian leaders and experts recognize that the unbalanced alliance of the 1950s and then the total breakdown in relations in the 1960s and 1970s were tremendous mistakes for Russian/Soviet national interests.[1]

The Russian perspectives on China are very indicative of Russia's identity and view of its place in the world as a uniquely *Eurasian* power.[2] As the massive geographical space in between Europe and Asia, Russia's identity historically has been dual from the Asiatic legacy of the Mongol period beginning in the thirteenth century with intermittent attempts of *westernizing* reforms from Peter the Great to Catherine the Great to Alexander II to Mikhail Gorbachev to Yeltsin. Historically, Asia has occupied a special place in the Russian imagination and in their version of *Manifest Destiny*, as a vast region key for Russia's development and global role. Dostoevsky famously wrote about this in 1881 after the Russian forces defeated the Turkmen in their quest to conquer Central Asia:

> What for? What Future? What is the need of the future seizure of Asia? What's our business there? This is necessary because Russia is not only in Europe, but also in Asia; because the Russian is not only a European, but also an Asiatic. Not only that: in our coming destiny, perhaps it is precisely Asia that represents our way out. . . .
>
> In Europe we were hangers-on and slaves, whereas to Asia we shall go as masters. In Europe we were Asiatics, whereas in Asia we, too, are Europeans. Our civilizing mission in Asia will bribe our spirit and drive us thither. It is only necessary that the movement should start. Build two railroads: begin with the one to Siberia, and then to Central Asia, and at once you will see the consequences.[3]

Of course, for much of its history, especially during the nineteenth and twentieth centuries when interaction between China and Russia grew significantly as part of a first wave of globalization, Russia viewed itself as the superior. During the brief period of the Sino-Soviet alliance during the 1950s, the Soviets (and often their Chinese comrades as well) described themselves as the "elder brother." Now, it finds itself as the weaker of the two partners for the first time since the Russians began to settle Siberia in the seventeenth century.

Today, China represents the dominant counterpoint to Russia's orientation politically, economically, and culturally toward the West with the United States and Europe. When the first post-Soviet government headed by Yeltsin and Yegor Gaidar took power at the end of 1991, their very strong, pro-Western foreign policy orientation immediately provoked a national debate between *Westernizers* and *Eurasianists* that echoed the mid-nineteenth-century debate about Russian identity between *Westernizers* and *Slavophiles*.[4] The Eurasianist position, notably articulated by future Foreign Minister Yevgeny Primakov and then Chairman of the Supreme Soviet's Committee on International Relations Vladimir Lukin, held that Russia must not overly rely on the prospects of an illusory alliance with the West, but must balance its ties with the West by simultaneously strengthening its presence in Asia and especially with China.[5] Shortly after becoming president in 2000, during his first tour of Asia, which included a visit to China, Vladimir Putin elegantly summarized the importance of balance in Russian foreign policy when he said, "Asia is very important for Russia . . . Russia is both a European and an Asiatic state. *It is like a bird and can only fly well if it uses both wings.*"[6]

Russian perspectives on China and international relations more broadly tend toward traditional *realpolitik* considerations of the dynamics between rising and falling great powers.[7] In this *realist* framework, Russian considerations about China are often derivative of what is going on in U.S.-Russian relations and Moscow's ties with the West. In the 1990s, when Russia was unhappy with U.S. support for NATO expansion, the war in Kosovo, and the development of a national missile defense (NMD), the Yeltsin administration gravitated more closely to Beijing. In recent years, the United States' support for democracy promotion and increased influence in the post-Soviet states has also driven the Putin administration to seek closer ties with China. Repeatedly Yeltsin and Putin have invoked improving ties with China as an alternative to a more pro-Western foreign policy course—a thinly veiled or outright threat if Washington did not pay greater attention to Moscow's interests.[8] Recall that in December 1999, during his last trip to China, Yeltsin pointedly warned the United States not to forget that Russia has a lot of nuclear weapons. Boris Yeltsin nicely captured China's position as a leverage point with the West when he said in 1995: "China is a very important state for us. It is a neighbor, with which we share the longest border in the world and with which we are destined to live and work side by side forever. Russia's future depends on the success of cooperation with China. Relations with China are extremely important to us from the global politics perspective as well. We can rest on the Chinese shoulder in our relations with the West. In that case the West will treat Russia more respectfully."[9]

The Russians are not the only ones with a proclivity of viewing China in a triangular format with the United States. This realist perspective has a long pedigree. Its most noted practitioner was Henry Kissinger during the Nixon administration, and the perspective can be seen in the emergence of the U.S.-Soviet-Chinese "strategic triangle" and triangular diplomacy in the early 1970s.[10] The balance-of-power approach to triangular relations continues to resonate in Washington, Beijing, and Moscow.[11] The Cold War's conclusion and the emergence of the United States as the clearly hegemonic power in the international system has presented Moscow and Beijing with a choice of bandwagoning with U.S. power or balancing against it. As nation-states, like people, prefer to "have their cake and eat it too," neither Russia nor China has made a clear choice, but rather both have preferred to hedge by balancing and bandwagoning simultaneously. Nevertheless, the desire to constrain, if not balance, U.S. unilateral power and to promote a multipolar world governed by international law rather than superpower *diktat* has been a consistent staple of Sino-Russian joint statements for the past fifteen years as the relationship has evolved from *partnership* to *constructive partnership* to *strategic partnership.*

Another staple line of Sino-Russian joint statements for the past ten years has been that their strategic partnership "is not an alliance directed against any third country" (with the obvious "third country" being the United States). This line has been repeated so many times that one is reminded of Queen Gertrude's oft-quoted response to her son, Hamlet: "the lady doth protest too much, methinks." Russian and Chinese leaders like to bill their partnership, as they do the Shanghai Cooperation Organization, as a new kind of phenomenon in international relations that transcends obsolete "bloc-style thinking" of mentalities that remain mired in Cold War logic. Deputy Foreign Minister Grigory Karasin, with responsibility for policy in Asia, summarized these points in commenting on the Sino-Russian joint declaration of 1996 that formally established the strategic partnership: "Especially pressing now, when the world society is still running across the inertia of the old mode of thought that was characteristic of the Cold War times with claims for sole leadership and attempts to steer the development of international relations in the direction of mono-popularity."[12]

"The Russian-Chinese Treaty of Good-Neighborliness and Friendly Cooperation," signed in July 2001, clearly outlined how far Moscow and Beijing were prepared to go in advancing their partnership. In contrast to the friendship treaty signed by Mao Zedong and Josef Stalin in 1950, there are no security guarantees in the 2001 treaty, and it does not lay the framework for an alliance. Russian deputy foreign minister Alexander Losyukov conveyed the official Russian view at the time of the signing: "A strategic partnership with China is not a union—neither a civilian nor a military one. . . . It is absolutely wrong to say that the partnership between Russia and China is aimed against anyone in the West. The West must understand that there is a certain line that neither we nor the Chinese are willing to cross."[13]

The U.S. deputy secretary of state at the time, Richard Armitage, reflected the nonchalant response of the Bush administration to the Sino-Russian treaty when he said, "This was clearly designed to boost both of their international standings without adding much real substance."[14]

For the most part, through the 1990s the United States and its allies remained fairly relaxed about the gradual rapprochement between China and Russia. Those skeptical of the likelihood of Moscow and Beijing engaging in a real alliance against the United States pointed to their long and complicated history involving intense competition and occasional conflict along their extensive border as well as their current competitive tendencies in Central

Asia and elsewhere. NATO secretary general George Robertson expressed this view in a lecture in Uzbekistan at the time of the Shanghai Five meeting being held in nearby Dushanbe in 2000 when he said, "The relationship between Russia and China is a matter for Russia and China but it [their alliance] has been tried before and has not always worked."[15] In U.S. policy circles, more concerned views about the Sino-Russian relationship tended to come from the right wing of the political spectrum.[16]

Predictably, the impulse of Moscow and Beijing to balance increased in response to exercises of U.S. power, such as the 1999 Kosovo war and the 2003 invasion of Iraq, or to policies or developments that appeared to increase U.S. power, such as NATO expansion, NMD, and support of "colored" revolutions in Eurasia (such as the Orange Revolution in Ukraine and the Rose Revolution in Georgia). The balancing impulse has been constrained both by the absence of perception of a sufficiently compelling threat as well as the reality, at least militarily, that a Sino-Russian alliance would not be capable of balancing U.S. unipolar power in the near- or midterm.[17] However, Russian arms sales to China have raised increasing concern among some in U.S. military circles about Russia's capacity to increase Chinese capabilities to hurt the U.S. Seventh Fleet in a showdown over Taiwan. In 2001 a U.S. military official was quoted as saying: "The sales are beginning to create concern . . . and could potentially hurt our aircraft carrier battle groups. . . . After a while, they start to build up. Of course, our real concern is in the things we can't see, the technical transfers, the help on China's cruise missile program, its rockets and strategic forces."[18]

Concern in U.S. policy circles would grow considerably in 2005 in response to the strong Chinese and Russian support for Islam Karimov's brutal suppression of the rioting in Andijan in May, the subsequent eviction of U.S. military forces from their Uzbek base in Khani-Karshabad, and the signing of the Russian-Uzbek security alliance in the fall. Many Russian analysts viewed these developments in Central Asia as a real turning point for Russia's influence in the region as well as for the role of the emerging Sino-Russian axis. One unnamed Kremlin-connected analyst said, "There is an impression that U.S. foreign policy expansion has reached its limits and now there begins an epoch of the gradual decline of American empire."[19]

Russians' confidence about their country's resurgence after its modern-day *Smutnoe Vremya* (Time of Troubles) during the traumatic decade of the 1990s grew tremendously throughout the first half of the 2000s. Indeed, the magnitude and the rapidity of Russia's revival have been as unexpected as they have been impressive. The numbers are staggering. According to Moscow-based investment bank Troika Dialog, from 1999 to 2009, Russia's nominal dollar GDP grew by a factor of 8, from less than $200 billion to more than $1.6 trillion.[20] Russia's foreign exchange reserves over this period grew thirty times, from about $20 billion when Putin became president to nearly $600 billion in autumn 2008. The Russian stock market was consistently one of the fastest growing in the world until the 2008–2009 financial crisis, growing about 1,000 percent, while average wages have grown fourfold.[21] With economic numbers like that, it is not a big surprise that Putin continues to enjoy high ratings above 70 percent. Whatever issue we look at—Iran, the Middle East peace process, gas and oil supplies to Europe and Asia, foreign investment in the energy sector—Russia is asserting its interests as it perceives them far more confidently than it did ten years ago, five years ago, or even one year ago. It is the combination of Russia's changing fortunes and U.S. foreign policy that has had the most significant influence on Russia's perception of and policy toward China.

Russian Domestic Politics, Regional Security, and Ideology

After the collapse of the Soviet Union, there was a strong correlation between Russia's more ardent reformers and an anti-China position.[22] The initial foreign policy orientation in 1992 under acting Prime Minister Yegor Gaidar and Foreign Minister Andrei Kozyrev leaned very heavily toward the West in the expectation of major aid and investment to support Russia's economic transformation. Russia's reformers viewed the liberal democracies of the West as both an economic and political model for reform and a source of financial support. Liberal reformers like Gaidar were also far more inclined to view China as a future security threat to Russia.[23] Alexei Arbatov, the deputy chair of the Duma's Committee on Security and a liberal member of the Yabloko Party, also expressed concern about the China threat: "In the mid-term perspective (five to ten years), China may present a more serious threat to Russian allies (Kazakhstan, Kyrgyzstan, and Tajikistan) and to neutral nations important for Russia (Mongolia), as well as a long-term threat (fifteen to twenty years) to the Russian territory (Transbaikal region, Primorsky Krai). This is the only scenario which presents a direct military threat to the Russian territory and demands preparations for a large trans-regional operation."[24]

More alarmist liberal as well as nationalist views of China stressed the massive demographic imbalance on the Sino-Russian border and the dangers of creeping Chinese influence through immigration and trade ties in the region.[25] Russia's flamboyant nationalist leader of the Liberal Democratic

Party of Russia (LDPR), Vladimir Zhirinovsky, often rants of the China threat and has imagined that "Russia has two main adversaries—the USA and China—who want to destroy us."[26] Alexander Dugin, a theorist of international relations who fancies himself a sort of geopolitical Dostoevsky, calls for a Russian-Muslim alliance to counter the threat emerging to Russia's "heartland" from China and the West.[27]

Those advocating a more gradual approach to reform and members of the Russian Communist Party looked more favorably on what Russia could learn from the Chinese reform experience. Centrist politicians like future foreign minister Yevgeny Primakov and Vladimir Lukin called for a more balanced Russian foreign policy that reached out to the East as well as the West, and centrist analysts like Yevgeny Bazhanov, vice director of the Diplomatic Academy in Moscow, have argued that China has no interest in threatening Russia as the Chinese will have their hands full for a long time with domestic socioeconomic development challenges.

While the Russian leadership in Moscow under Yeltsin and Putin has tended to positively view improved relations and increased contact with China as a strategic counterweight to the United States, perspectives of politicians and many analysts in the Russian Far East have viewed China more suspiciously. For example, President Putin views the Sino-Russian border agreement of 1991 and the final resolution of the border in 2004 as a remarkable and highly underrated achievement that resolved centuries of differences and decades of negotiations through wise mutual compromise.[28] For locals in the Russian Far East, however, the border agreements were extremely controversial as they called for handing over Russian land to the Chinese. As Elizabeth Wishnick wrote in her excellent study of Sino-Russian relations, "since 1994, the tensest negotiations on Russian-Chinese relations have been taking place between the Russian government and its regional representatives, not between leaders in Moscow and Beijing."[29] Russian feelings of economic and demographic vulnerability to China are naturally felt most acutely along their 2,600-mile border in the Russia Far East and in eastern Siberia, a thinly populated and economically depressed area of Russia. The Russian population and major centers of economic production are heavily weighted in the European area of Russia, west of the Urals. To those in the Russian Far East and eastern Siberia, Moscow feels far away because it is. A flight from Moscow to Khabarovsk is about seven hours, while the flight from Beijing to Irkutsk is only about two hours! Rather than viewing China as a strategic partner, residents of the Far East are more inclined to view China as a competitor and, in the longer term, as a threat.[30] Politicians in the Russian Far East have played upon the "China threat" scenarios to bolster local political support. Indeed, they are pushing on an open door given latent anti-Chinese sentiments and frequent press reports exaggerating the level of illegal immigration.[31]

Despite the differences cited above, Russia's view of itself as a declining power in the 1990s engendered a fairly broad consensus among Moscow's foreign policy elite that American alliances in Asia played a positive role since they view East Asia as a multipolar region in which the presence of U.S. forces help to preserve the status quo. This view starkly contrasted Russian views of NATO in Europe, which they believed was expanding both its membership and mission at the direct expense of Russian national interests. These stark differences in views of U.S.-led alliances principally had to do with Russian concerns about China as a rising power and, to a lesser extent, the possibility of Japanese remilitarization.[32] While Russian civilian and military analysts suggested that Russia would be a natural alliance partner of the West and Japan if conflict emerged with China, a wider consensus emerged that Russia's leverage is increased if it can present itself as a legitimate partner to all leading players in East Asia. Russian general A. F. Klimenko expressed this idea in 1997 in the influential military journal *Voennaia Mysl'* [Military Thought]: "It is logical to assume that should there be a confrontation between China and Russia the Western countries and Japan would side with the latter. One should believe that China is aware of this. It is therefore very doubtful that [China] is going to support an aggression on the part of the Western countries and Japan against Russia. It is for this reason that both Russia and China would prefer neutrality and mutually beneficial cooperation under any worsened situation."[33]

After 9/11 and Putin's decision to closely align with the U.S.-led coalition's war in Afghanistan—including agreement to allow U.S. military bases in Central Asia as well as a quiet acceptance of the U.S. withdrawal from the ABM Treaty and the second round of NATO expansion—a great deal of concern arose in Chinese foreign and security policy circles in 2001 and 2002 that President Putin had fundamentally altered Russia's balanced foreign policy to closely embrace Washington.[34] In May 2002, the second honeymoon of Russia and the United States reached its apex as President Bush traveled to Moscow, where he signed the Strategic Offensive Reduction Treaty (SORT), and the United States awarded Russia market-economy status.[35] In July 2002, Russian foreign minister Igor Ivanov clearly stated that Russia's threats are not from the West: "The threat for Russia hides in the Caucasus Mountains region and its Asian border. . . . One of the main threats we have seen has not been the United States or NATO, but Afghanistan."[36]

With the new China-Russia friendship treaty signed and the Shanghai Cooperation Organization formally established only six months before in the summer of 2001, it appeared that both agreements may have become somewhat obsolescent in the wake of the post-9/11 realignment.[37] The Chinese also aligned more closely with the United States after 9/11, as Chinese president Jiang Zemin made his visit to President Bush in Crawford, Texas, in October 2002 and China also approached NATO to seek a strategic dialogue for the first time in history.

Like the first U.S.-Russian honeymoon in 1992, the post-9/11 embrace would prove to be short-lived. Putin had made a bold decision to support the United States unequivocally in Afghanistan, going against the recommendations of the majority of the Russian foreign policy elite.[38] He and his colleagues in the Kremlin, however, quickly came to believe that the significance of this decision went underappreciated and virtually unrewarded by the Bush administration. The Bush administration's decisions to support another round of NATO expansion as well as to withdraw from the ABM Treaty in the fall of 2001 so soon after Putin had extended his support to his "friend George" left the Russians disappointed and feeling that they were receiving very little in return for their support.[39] As 2002 wore on, it became increasingly evident that the Bush administration would take military action against Iraq in defiance of Putin and much of the international community, including fellow UN Security Council member China. To rekindle the lost momentum in ties with China, Putin went to Beijing in December 2002, making himself the first prominent foreign visitor since the naming of Hu Jintao as leader of the Chinese Communist Party that fall. Speaking to a group of students at Peking University, Putin reaffirmed the importance of Russia's ties with China, saying that it is Russia's "biggest trade partner, our partner in the anti-terrorist coalition and our joint action in this direction is quite effective."[40]

The Cooling of U.S.-Russian Relations: Is a Beijing/Moscow Consensus Emerging?

Putin disagreed with the Bush administration's decision to invade Iraq, but both Washington and Moscow sought to insulate the U.S.-Russian relationship from a major fallout. A series of other events and trends, however, threw the U.S.-Russian relationship into a tailspin from which it has yet to escape. The past several years of deterioration in U.S.-Russian ties contrasts sharply with the continued improvement of Sino-Russian economic, security, and political relations. While Putin has said on several occasions in recent years that Sino-Russian ties have never been better, U.S.-Russian relations are chillier today than anytime since the collapse of the Soviet Union.[41] This is not to suggest that relations between Russia and China are entirely smooth; in fact, the Chinese probably have been as frustrated as the Americans over the unfulfilled promise of energy relations with Russia.

The arrest of Mikhail Khodorkovsky, CEO of the Yukos Oil Company—then Russia's most valuable company—on 25 October 2003 followed by parliamentary and presidential elections viewed as less fair and competitive than previous Russian elections drew increasing criticism from the Bush administration and other Western governments.[42] Alarm in the West about creeping authoritarianism in Russia and its growing influence on its periphery increased tremendously in response to the Orange Revolution at the end of 2004 in Ukraine. The Orange Revolution succeeded the Rose Revolution in Georgia, which brought pro-Western Mikhail Sakhashvili to power, and preceded the Tulip Revolution in Kyrgyzstan that toppled the Askar Akaev government in Bishkek. The Russian explanation for these events tended to emphasize the role of U.S.- and Western-supported NGOs and politicians, while the United States and its European allies argued that these events were catalyzed principally by falsified elections and the public's dissatisfaction with corrupt local governments and officials. The positions of Washington and Moscow on these events became increasingly polarized as officials and opinion leaders in Washington argued that Vladimir Putin's authoritarian inclinations led him to support dictatorship over democracy in countries on Russia's periphery. The quasi-official Russian view suggested that the United States was interfering in a hypocritical manner in countries that Moscow considered a part of its sphere of influence. The U.S. position was hypocritical in their view since the United States principally cared about regime change that brought about more pro-U.S. governments like that of Sakhashvili in Georgia and Viktor Yushchenko in Ukraine rather than real democracy. The fact that the Bush administration also came to justify the invasion of Iraq as part of its efforts at democracy promotion in the Middle East only added to the cynical skepticism that colored the Kremlin's view of U.S. foreign policy aims.

For the most part, the Chinese remained on the sidelines during this growing dispute between Washington and Moscow until the specter of color revolutions came to Central Asia in Kyrgyzstan in March 2005, and then with the civil unrest and brutal crackdown in Andijan, Uzbekistan, in May 2005. Chinese sensitivities about the potential for spillover from the civil unrest in

Central Asia to its own Muslim groups across the border in Xinjiang moved the leadership in Beijing to clearly support Karimov in Uzbekistan and the principles of order and sovereignty over the right of outside powers to interfere in domestic affairs. After the events in Andijan, the first places Karimov traveled to and where he received full support for his actions were Beijing and then Moscow. The dividing lines were sharpening between the West's support for democracy and human rights and the interests of an emerging "authoritarian internationale" led by Moscow and Beijing in Eurasia.

It is unclear at this point how far either Moscow or Beijing are prepared to go together to contest the interests of the United States in Eurasia, but what appeared as mainly rhetorical support for a "multipolar world" in the 1990s is now assuming greater substance, be it their cooperation in the UN Security Council on an increasing number of issues or the decision of the Shanghai Cooperation Organization in 2005 to request clarification from the United States about its plans for withdrawing from military bases in Central Asia established after 9/11.[43] The gathering of the SCO foreign ministers in Moscow in 2005 included those states that had recently acquired observer status—India, Iran, Mongolia, and Pakistan—in addition to full members. In his opening remarks, Putin crowed about how 3 billion people, virtually half the planet, were represented in the SCO gathering. While the number of people represented mostly carried symbolic value, Putin did note more seriously that the "SCO has gone far beyond the framework of the tasks initially set."[44]

Russian perspectives on the SCO reflect the broader ambivalence they hold in their views of China. This is natural since the China-Russia relationship is at the heart of the SCO. The mainstream Russian view is that the SCO is essentially a Chinese project, and that is even conveyed in the name of the organization. Russian preferences would certainly have an organization like the Collective Security Treaty Organization (CSTO), which has Russia as the clear hegemonic leader and which excludes Chinese participation, as the main multilateral organization with security responsibilities in Central Asia. But the Russian leadership is pragmatic and realistic and understands that Chinese influence in Central Asia, first of all economic and secondarily on security issues, is a natural outgrowth of expanding Chinese power and its geography. With this in mind, it is better to have Chinese regional engagement tied into an organizational format with the Russians, and the SCO serves this purpose. Only very significant developments that would push the Russians and Chinese closer to alliance would drive the SCO into becoming the "anti-NATO" as some analysts fear.[45] Azhdar Kurtov, a Moscow-based lawyer, in a

Mayak Radio discussion at the time of the Moscow SCO foreign ministerial meeting in October 2005, explained both the Russian sense that the balance of power is shifting and why the United States should pay attention:

> As for the U.S. position, there is indeed something for the United States of America, in my view, to be afraid of. It should be afraid of the fact that Russia is gradually getting on its feet, becoming stronger and claiming the role in international politics it deserves. In the 1990s the USA began to regard the Central Asian region as a zone of its interests, and some projects in the economic field were openly directed at pushing Russia out. ... Now on the other hand, as a result of the SCO getting stronger—and these aspects were among those discussed at the SCO summit—now the projects for laying railway routes or fiber-optic routes are in the interests of China, the Central Asian states, as well as Russia.[46]

There are striking similarities in the maturing ideological foundations of contemporary Russian and Chinese outlooks on the world and views of their respective roles. The emerging ideology promoted by the Putin administration is often described by the Russians as *Sovereign Democracy*.[47] The starting point in understanding the Kremlin's idea of Sovereign Democracy is the perception of the decade of the 1990s as a modern-day Russian "Time of Troubles" when domestically Russia was in chaos and very weak internationally, when foreign powers and organizations exerted too much autonomy/influence over Russian domestic and foreign policies. In this narrative, the leadership of Vladimir Putin restored stability to Russia and set it on the road to recovery, not by abandoning market democratic values and institutions, but by adapting them to Russian values and traditions. Former prime minister Yevgeny Primakov conveyed this in a major Russian television interview:

> You see, in the 1990s it was widely believed that Russia would be in tow of the United States. In the early 1990s the Russian Foreign Ministry, to quote the Foreign Minister [Andrei Kozyrev at the time], said that we had by all means to join the club of civilized nations while all the others are rabble. I am quoting. ... As you know, I was the government chairman and during my watch a representative of the International Monetary Fund came over and tried to impose certain models of development on us. They were trying to impose on us a system where the state was not to be involved in anything, everything was to be left at the mercy of the market and the market was supposed to take care of everything.[48]

The foreign policy analog to Sovereign Democracy was succinctly stated by current foreign minister Sergei Lavrov in a January 2007 speech to the

Moscow State Institute for Foreign Affairs (MGIMO): "The fundamental principles of Russia's foreign policy—pragmatism, multiple vector, and consistent but non-confrontational protection of national interests—have gained broad international recognition. . . . Many countries come to realize that a new safer, fair, and democratic world order, whose foundation we are laying together, can be only multipolar, based on international law, and regulated by the UN's unique legitimacy and central role."[49]

To be sure, this kind of rhetoric is hardly new, and, in fact, one can easily imagine a variant of it coming from the mouth of Yevgeny Primakov when he was foreign minister in the 1990s or that of Andrei Gromyko for the more than quarter century he served as Soviet foreign minister. But it does resonate with Chinese ideological formulations. It is telling that one of the most popular descriptions of the rhetorical and operational foundation for Chinese foreign policy has been described as the Beijing Consensus.[50] As engagingly described by Joshua Ramo Cooper, the Beijing Consensus is principally a socioeconomic development model that the Chinese have successfully implemented, one that differs considerably from the Washington Consensus as promoted by the U.S. government and multilateral organizations like the IMF and the World Bank. The Beijing Consensus has significant implications for foreign policy and international relations that resonate with the Kremlin's Sovereign Democracy. First, there is not just one correct path to development. A country must innovate and experiment to find the path best suited for its cultures and traditions, and no country or organization should seek to impose external models. The majority of Russians today view the advice of Western advisors and multilateral organizations as a failure that exacerbated Russia's socioeconomic problems. The typical Chinese interpretation of Russian development of the past two decades suggests that Moscow took the wrong path in the 1990s, but that the Putin administration learned many things from the Chinese reform experience and began to correct those past mistakes that devolved too much power away from the state.[51]

The other commonality between Moscow's and Beijing's views of the world concerns the ongoing shifting balance of power away from the unipolar moment of the 1990s to a genuine multipolar world. This rhetoric, as I noted earlier, is also not new, but the difference today is that there is a lot more evidence to support the conclusion that the global balance of power is shifting, and the Russians feel themselves to be one of the emerging powers. For several years now the financial and investment community has used the term BRICs to describe the large emerging economic world powers: Brazil, Russia, India, and China.[52] Putin himself recently alluded to the emergence of the BRICs as a powerful stimulus to a reordered multipolar world in his speech at the Munich security conference in February 2007: "The combined GDP measured in purchasing power parity of countries such as India and China is already greater than that of the United States. And a similar calculation with the GDP of the BRIC countries Brazil, Russia, India, and China surpasses the cumulative GDP of the EU. And according to experts this gap will only increase in the future. There is no reason to doubt that the economic potential of the new centers of global economic growth will inevitably be converted into political influence and will strengthen multipolarity."[53]

Political circles in Washington in particular have been slower to come around to this appreciation of Russian recovery, and the dominant view today is to see it as a malign phenomenon, as a more authoritarian Russia increasingly brandishing its energy "weapon" as Vice President Cheney stated in 2006 in Vilnius. On the basis of many discussions in recent years with Chinese and Russian scholars and analysts, my sense is there is a reasonably broad consensus in Russian and Chinese policy circles that the United States made a grave mistake and overextended itself in Iraq and has overplayed its hand in Central Asia and elsewhere in efforts to promote democracy.

Conclusion: The Enduring Ambivalence in Russia toward China

Despite perceptions of a shifting balance of power and the genuine cooling in U.S.-Russian ties described above, Russian elites remain at best ambivalent about the emerging Chinese superpower. The official line, however, from Putin and others in his administration tends to accentuate the positive, and it is debatable whether China-Russia relations today are better than ever. But the history of China-Russia relations does not set the highest of bars, so to speak. The kinds of lively debates we followed in Russia in the 1990s about China, whether dividing on ideological or regional perspectives, have largely disappeared. But that does not tell us much since public debate about most important domestic and foreign policy issues has muted during the Putin years. Much of the expert community built up during the Brezhnev years and still active in the 1990s has retired, died, or gone into business, and there is not a sizeable generation of younger scholars and experts to replace them.

Russian public opinion about China tends to be quite positive, but this is probably largely a reflection of the fact that most Russians get their information from national television, which is virtually controlled by the Kremlin and reflects the sunny outlook on China touted by the Russian leadership.[54] This may be a case where Russia's positive views of China are "a mile wide and an inch deep," as Richard Rose, on the basis of extensive survey research, has described the Russian public's support of Putin. Research conducted by the VTsIOM public opinion research center in July 2005 noted that while 56 percent of Russians view China as either a strategic partner or ally, 62 percent believe the increasing Chinese economic presence in Russia is negative, and 66 percent see the involvement of Chinese companies and workers in the development of the mineral resources in Siberia and the Russian Far East as dangerous for Russia.[55] Rather than viewing these results as cognitive dissonance, it probably reflects the strategic view of China's utility as a partner to contain the United States (Russian public opinion is quite negative on the U.S. role in the world under the Bush administration), combined with the sense of economic and demographic vulnerability of the Russian regions bordering China.[56]

The coverage of the Sino-Russian joint military exercises in August 2005 was extraordinary and also suggestive of ambivalence. For several nights in succession this was the number one news story on Russian television as footage of the beaming Russian defense minister, Sergei Ivanov, and his Chinese counterpart, Cao Gangchuan, observing the exercises was repeated over and over.[57] Coverage in the Russian print press and on the Internet, however, was much more nuanced and reflected the ambivalence in Russian foreign policy circles about the exercises and the relationship with China. The Russian daily *Kommersant* reported in the spring that the Russians and the Chinese had difficulties agreeing about the location of the exercises, as the Chinese wanted to hold them as close to Taiwan as possible in order to send a message to the islanders and their American allies.[58] Russian military analyst and journalist Alexander Golts insightfully concluded that the Russians and the Chinese had different goals for the exercises: "The Chinese want to use Russia in a complicated game with the U.S. and Taiwan. . . . China is expanding its military presence in the region. For Russia, this is mostly about selling weapons."[59] In another interview, Golts argued, "There is little doubt that in a real Taiwan crisis, Russia would step aside."[60] *Nezavisimaya Gazeta* questioned the relevance of antisubmarine and antiaircraft operations as well as cruise missile launches in what was billed as "Peace Mission 2005," supposedly an antiterrorist exercise.[61] Sergei Lusyanin of the Institute for International Relations, an institution closely affiliated with the Russian Ministry of Foreign Affairs, suggested a different explanation for the military exercises: "We're seeing a strategic shift which, if it continues, could change the whole picture of Eurasia. . . . Russia and China have many things in common. It's not just oil and arms; increasingly it's a shared concept of what the regional and global order should look like."[62]

The China-Russia energy relationship also reflects Russian ambivalence toward China, and a preference for the West. Look at which companies have major equity positions in upstream Russian oil resources. The American company Conoco-Philips owns 20 percent of Russia's largest oil company, Lukoil, while the country's third largest oil company, TNK-BP, is a 50/50 joint venture between Russian partners and British Petroleum. China has been trying to overpay for years for upstream Russian resources, and has consistently been turned away, most noticeably in the 2002 Slavneft auction.[63] It was only in 2006 that the Chinese finally broke through, when Sinopec cut a deal with Rosneft to get a 49 percent position in the smallish Udmurtneftgaz.[64] Also recall that in late 2005 President Putin himself offered former U.S. Secretary of Commerce (and close friend of President Bush) Donald Evans the position of chairman of the board of Rosneft, the designated state champion in the Russian oil industry.[65] While Evans ultimately did not accept the position, Putin was trying to send a message to Washington about Russian preferences. Much was made at the end of 2004 when the China National Petroleum Corporation (CNPC) lent Rosneft $6 billion to finance the purchase of the crown jewel of Yukos, the giant Yuganskneftgaz oil field, but the original plan was for Gazprom, Russia's state gas monopoly, to scoop up this juicy asset. A Houston bankruptcy court hearing calling for a temporary stay against companies participating in the Yugansk sale as part of a motion for Yukos bankruptcy protection prevented the participation of a coalition of Western banks that was prepared to loan the money to Gazprom for the purchase.[66] We can also point to the very lengthy deliberations about the direction of the Far Eastern oil pipeline (during which the Japanese and Chinese governments competed for Moscow's favor for several years) as evidence of deep ambivalence on the Russian part toward China. During the January 2003 visit of Japanese prime minister Junichiro Koizumi to Khabarovsk and Moscow, Japanese leaders and officials played quite openly on Russian sensitivities to overdependence on China.[67]

In conclusion, despite deep-seated ambivalence on the part of the Russian leadership and people, ties with China have significantly advanced under the leadership of both Boris Yeltsin and Vladimir Putin. The economic relationship, which already saw trade turnover increase since Putin became president by more than seven times to $55 billion in 2008, is likely to continue to grow rapidly as major oil and gas sales finally get more momentum.[68] What happens in the strategic relationship—from the Shanghai Cooperation

Organization to cooperation in the UN to arms sales—is harder to predict, as it will be contingent to a considerable extent on the actions of the United States. If, for example, the United States were to undertake military action against Iran not sanctioned by the United Nations, this would undoubtedly push Russia and China closer together strategically. A U.S.-China military conflict over Taiwan would place Russia in an awkward position, but I think Moscow would choose not to take sides. If the Europeans and/or the Americans removed the boycott on arms sales to China, over time this would undercut the dominant position Russian companies have as suppliers. A more aggressive posture by the United States toward confronting Russian interests in the post-Soviet space in the name of democracy promotion and human rights is also likely to push Russia and China closer together.

The second most important driver will be how the Russian oil and gas sector develops. Aside from money, which Moscow is not short of now, Chinese companies have little to offer the Russians in the development of greenfields that will include some of the largest capital expenditures and technically most challenging projects in history. Western companies do have management experience and technical expertise that can be useful, so it is more likely that, to the extent that foreign companies are allowed to participate in the development of the Russian hydrocarbon sector, Western firms have a significant comparative advantage. But if Russia's political relations with the West were to further deteriorate and/or the legal and business environment became more corrupt, the equation could change.

For historical, cultural, geographic, and economic reasons, Russia's preferred option is to lean west while improving ties with China both for intrinsic reasons as well as to enhance its leverage with the United States and Europe. Only events of quite a significant magnitude would alter the trajectory of Russia's path, which has been fairly consistent for nearly two decades after the brief lurch to the West with the collapse of the Soviet Union.

Notes

I thank Nathaniel Stice for his research assistance in preparing this chapter.

1. This generalization is principally based on my conversations with Russian and Chinese experts in Moscow, Beijing, and Shanghai in the fall of 2006.

2. For an excellent history of the evolution of Russian perceptions of China over the past three centuries, see Alexander Lukin, *The Bear Watches the Dragon* (Amronk N.Y.: Sharpe, 2003).

3. From Dostoevsky's article "Goek-Tepe: What Is Asia for Us," found in *Diary of a Writer,* translated and annotated by Boris Brasol (New York: Scribner, 1949).

This quote is also found in the interesting volume by Milan Hauner, *What Is Asia to Us? Russia's Heartland Yesterday and Today* (London: Routledge, 1992), 1.

4. For an analysis of this debate, see Tsuyoshi Hasegawa, Jonathan Haslamand, and Andrew Kuchins, eds., *Russia and Japan: An Unresolved Dilemma between Distant Neighbors* (Berkeley: Univ. of California Press, 2003).

5. A most striking juxtaposition of these views appeared in 1992 in published articles by Foreign Minister Andrei Kozyrev in *Foreign Affairs* and Vladimir Lukin in *Foreign Policy*. See: Andrei Kozyrev, "Russia: A Second Chance for Survival," *Foreign Affairs* 2 (1993), http://www.foreignaffairs.org/19920301faessay5864/andrei-kozyrev/russia-a-chance-for-survival.html; and Vladimir Lukin, "Remaking Russia: Our Security Predicament," *Foreign Policy* 88 (1992): 57–75.

6. Gareth Jones, "Putin's Asia Tour to Boost Russia's Role in the Region," Reuters, 16 July 2000.

7. On many occasions Putin and other Russian leaders have described Russia's main foreign policy goal as being recognized and respected as one of the world's great powers. This mentality echoes that of Soviet leaders like foreign ministers Molotov and Gromyko, who liked to boast that no major international relations challenge could be resolved without the involvement and/or approval of the Soviet Union. I was struck by this while working with a small working group of Russia's leading international relations thinkers and practitioners in the fall of 2004 who were tasked with outlining recommendations for improving U.S.-Russia relations. In response to my question "What does Russia want from the United States?" the unanimous response was help in getting Russia recognized as a great power. These deliberations resulted in the following report: Andrew Kuchins, Vyacheslav Nikonov, and Dmitri Trenin, *U.S.-Russia Relations: The Case for an Upgrade* (Moscow: Carnegie Moscow Center, 2005).

8. This kind of threat was clearly the overarching message of Mr. Putin's three-and-a-half-hour meeting with the Valdai Discussion Club in September 2006. See Andrew C. Kuchins, "Russian Spin Job?" *Carnegie Endowment for International Peace Web Commentary*, 18 September 2006, http://www.carnegieendowment.org/publications/index.cfm?fa=view&id=18715&prog=zru.

9. As quoted in Lukin, *The Bear Watches the Dragon*, 305.

10. The emergence of the "strategic triangle" in international relations theory is debatable, and even at the peak of triangular diplomacy in the late 1970s Kenneth Waltz argued that the triangle was not a helpful concept because China was too weak. Kenneth Waltz, *Theory of International Relations* (Reading, Mass.: Addison-Wesley, 1979): 180. Some scholars have suggested that the triangle emerged with the Sino-Soviet split in the 1960s. See Gerald Segal, "China and the Great Power Triangle," *China Quarterly* 83 (September 1980): 490–509. Others argued that the triangle emerged in the 1970s with the growth of China's nuclear arsenal and the improvement of Sino-U.S. relations. See, for example, Lowell Dittmer, "The Strategic Triangle: An Elementary Game Theoretical Analysis," *World Politics*, no. 33 (July 1981): 485–516.

11. Some Republican critiques of the Clinton administration's Russia policy were couched in these terms in the 2000 presidential campaign. See, for example, Paula Dobriansky, "Be Wary When the Bear Sides with a Dragon," *Los Angeles Times*, 18 September 2000.

12. G. Karasin, "A Glance of the Double-Headed Eagle Both at the West and at the East" [Vzglyad dvuglavogo oral I na Zapad, i na Vostok], *Rossiyski vesty*, 19 December 1996.

13. Agence France Presse, 15 July 2001.

14. Jane Perlez, "White House Unconcerned about China-Russia Pact," *New York Times*, 16 July 2001.

15. Mike Collett-White, "Few Easy Partnerships for Russia, China, and Central Asia," Associated Press, 6 July 2000.

16. See, for example, the reporting on arms sales and security cooperation by *Washington Times* reporter Bill Gertz. Analysts especially concerned about Chinese foreign policy and particularly China's military modernization viewed the Sino-Russian rapprochement as especially dangerous to U.S. interests. For a comprehensive presentation of this view, see Constantine C. Menges, *China: The Gathering Threat* (Nashville, Tenn.: Nelson Current, 2005). In the U.S. Congress, a right-wing Republican congressman from Southern California, Dana Rohrbacher, introduced legislation in 2000 to withhold aid to the Russians if they persisted with arms sales to China (U.S. Congress, House, *Report of the Select Committee on U.S. National Security and Military/Commercial Concerns with the People's Republic of China*, 80th Cong., 2nd sess., 1999, H. Doc. 105-851, http://www.house.gov/coxreport/cont/gncont.html).

17. For the strongest argument about the durability of U.S. hegemony, see William Wohlforth, "The Stability of a Unipolar World," *International Security* (summer 1999): 5–41.

18. John Pomfret, "Moscow and Beijing to Sign Pact: Stronger Ties Sought to Check U.S. Influence," *Washington Post*, 13 January 2001.

19. Igor Torbakov, "Analysts Debate Pros and Cons of 'Eastern Vector' in Kremlin's Foreign Policy," *Jamestown Report*, 15 July 2005. I published an article in September 2003 entitled "The Limits of Power" that received a great deal of attention in Russian policy circles, as the piece argued that the Iraq war likely represented the peak of U.S. hegemony in the post–Cold War period, as long-term economic prospects suggested that in the coming decades other great powers, including China and India as well as an increasingly unified Europe, would erode U.S. dominance. See Andrew C. Kuchins, *Nezavisimaya Gazeta* (fall 2003), www.ng.ru/courier/2003-10-27/14_peace.html. In many discussions with Chinese experts in 2006, I found that they generally believed that the United States had "overplayed its hand" in Eurasia promoting "color revolutions," and that the tide had turned against U.S. power in the region. For an excellent discussion of the global backlash against U.S. democracy promotion efforts, see Thomas Carothers, "The Backlash against Democracy Promotion," *Foreign Affairs* (March/April 2006), www.foreignaffairs.com/articles/61509/thomas-carothers/the-backlash-against-democracy-promotion.

20. In fact, in his introductory remarks before his annual press conference in 2006, President Putin ran through the very impressive numbers of the Russian recovery under his leadership. See Vladimir Putin, "Annual Press Conference," http://www.kremlin.ru/eng/speeches/2007/02/01/1309_type82915_117609.shtml.

21. Sebastion Alison, "Putin to Name Favored Successor When Campaign Begins," *Bloomberg*, 1 February 2007.

22. For two comprehensive analyses of the spectrum of views held by Russian politicians and analysts in the 1990s, see Alexander Lukin, "Russia's Image of China and Russian-Chinese Relations," *East Asia: An International Quarterly* 17 (1999): 5–39, and Evgenii Bazhanov, "Russian Perspectives on China's Foreign Policy and Military Development," in *In China's Shadow: Regional Perspectives on Chinese Foreign Policy and Military Development*, ed. Jonathan D. Pollack and Richard H. Yang, 70–90 (Santa Monica, Calif.: RAND, 1998).

23. Yegor Gaidar, *Gosudarstvo I evolyutsiya* [State and evolution] (Moscow: Evraziya, 1995).

24. A. Arbatov, "Military Reform: Doctrine, Troops, Finances" [Voennaia reforma: doktrina, voiska, finansy], *Mirovaia ekonomika I mezhdunarodnye otnosheniia*, no. 4 (1997): 11.

25. One of Russia's most celebrated Sinologists, Vilya Gel'bras, devoted a book to this threat. See: Vilya G. Gel'bras, *Asian-Pacific Region: Problems of Russia's Economic Security* [Aziatsko-Tikhookeanskiy Raion: problemy ekonomysheskoy bezopastnosti Rossii] (Moscow: Institut mikroekonomiki pri Minekonomiki RF, 1995).

26. As quoted in Lukin, *The Bear Watches the Dragon*, 30.

27. See the chapter on "The Fall of China" in Alexander Dugin, *The Fundamentals of Geopolitics: Russia's Geopolitical Future* [Osnovy geopolitiki: Geopoliticheskoe budushchee Rossii] (Moscow: Arktogeya, 1997). Frighteningly, Dugin's work has been used as a key text in Russian military education.

28. Heard by me at the Valdai Discussion Club's meeting with President Putin, 7 September 2006.

29. Elizabeth Wishnick, *Mending Fences: The Evolution of Moscow's China Policy from Brezhnev to Yeltsin* (Seattle: Univ. of Washington Press, 2001): 185.

30. Wishnick covers the center/regional differences over China well in chapter 9 of *Mending Fences*. See also Elizabeth Wishnick, "One Asia Policy or Two? Moscow and the Russian Far East Debate Russia's Engagement in Asia," *NBR Analysis* 13, no. 1 (2002): 39–101.

31. In a poll conducted in Primoriye in 2000, 74 percent of the respondents said they expect China to annex all or part of the region in the "long run." Another poll indicated the belief that Chinese immigrants already made up 10–20 percent of Primoriye's population when official data suggested a figure of no more than 3 percent—less than a third of the proportion at the beginning of the twentieth century. Robert Cotrell, "Islands of Contention: Russia's Eastern Border Has Become a Test of Her Relations with China," *Financial Times*, 27 August 2001.

32. For a full treatment of this argument, see Andrew C. Kuchins and Alexei

V. Zagorsky, *When Realism and Liberalism Coincide: Russian Views of U.S. Alliances in Asia* (Stanford, Calif.: Asia/Pacific Research Center, 1999).

33. A. F. Klimenko, "International Security and Character of Future Military Conflict," *Military Thought*, no. 1 (1997): 9.

34. This concern was expressed privately by a number of influential Chinese scholars in meetings in Beijing and Shanghai in April and June of 2002.

35. For a description of the U.S.-Russian relationship at that moment of promise, see Andrew C. Kuchins, "Summit with Substance," *Carnegie Endowment for International Peace Policy Brief*, no. 16 (May 2002): 1–7.

36. Angela Charlton, "Russia's Threats Come from Asia, not West, Foreign Minister Says," Associated Press, 10 July 2002.

37. This was certainly the mood reported in January 2002 at the time of the SCO Foreign Ministerial meeting. See "Low-Key Russian-Chinese Talks in Shanghai," *Jamestown Monitor*, 10 January 2002.

38. See Grigorii Yavlinskii, "Domestic and Foreign Policy Challenges of Russia Today," speech at Carnegie Endowment for International Peace, Washington D.C., 30 January 2002.

39. Alexander Voloshin, a former chief of staff in both the Yeltsin and Putin administrations, conveyed these views in a very candid and engaging fashion in a meeting at the Carnegie Endowment for International Peace in October 2006. I make reference to this in an article entitled "A Turning Point for U.S.-Russia Relations?" published in the Russian daily *Vedomosti* on 20 November 2006. For an English-language version of this article, see: http://www.carnegieendowment.org/publications/index.cfm?fa=view&id=18872&prog=zru.

40. Richard Balmforth, "Russia's Putin Explains Pro-West Policy in China," Reuters, 3 December 2002.

41. See Kuchins, "Look Who's Back." On 4 May 2006, Vice President Dick Cheney severely criticized Russia for using its energy resources as "tools of intimidation and blackmail," for its human rights violations, and for its antidemocratic tendencies. Cheney's words in Lithuania sharply contrasted with his warm treatment of Kazakhstan's authoritarian president the following day in Astana. See "Cheney, Visiting Kazakhstan, Wades into Energy Battle," *Washington Post*, 6 May 2006.

42. The U.S. secretary of state published an article in the Russian daily *Izvestiya* in January 2004 that included the first real critical remarks from a high-ranking figure in the Bush administration over the growing state control of politics and the economy under Putin. President Bush did not make his first critical remarks of Russia until his presidential debate with John Kerry in October 2004. See: Colin Powell, "Partnership under Construction," *Izvestia*, 26 January 2004, http://www.america.gov/st/washfile-english/2004/January/200401271056151ACnosnhoJ0.2891657.html, and the transcript of the 13 October 2004 presidential debate, http://www.debates.org/pages/trans2004d.html.

43. For a preliminary look at this question, see Andrew Kuchins, "Will the Authoritarians of the World Unite?" *Moscow Times*, 28 March 2006.

44. Natalya Alekseyeva, "Putin Assembles Half the Planet in the Kremlin," *Izvestiya,* 26 October 2005.

45. For a balanced Russian view on the SCO, see Dmitri Trenin, "The Post-Imperial Project," *Nezavisimaya Gazeta,* 15 February 2006. For a piece that outlines the potential dangers of the SCO to U.S. security interests, see Ariel Cohen, "What to Do About the SCO's Rising Influence," Eurasianet, 4 October 2006, http://www .eurasianet.org/departments/insight/articles/eav092106.shtml.

46. See "Russian Pundits Speculate on Shanghai Organization Military Ambitions," *Mayak Radio,* 29 October 2005.

47. As is typical of emerging ideologies, there has been considerable controversy over the term Sovereign Democracy and its meaning. The former deputy head of the presidential administration, Vladislav Surkov, has been the most vocal proponent of the notion, and his behind-the-scenes role has been compared to that of Mikhail Suslov during the Brezhnev years. Surkov laid out his understanding of Russian Sovereign Democracy in a fascinating, nearly stream-of-consciousness speech he gave at a party meeting for United Russia in February 2006 ("Vladislav Surkov's Secret Speech to United Russia," *Moscow News,* 7 July 2005, http://www.mosnews.com/ interview/2005/07/12/surkov.shtml).

48. See interview with Yevgeny Primakov, president of the Commerce and Industry Chamber, Voskresny Vecher NTV Program with Vladimir Solovyov, 28 January 2007, www.fednews.ru.

49. Sergei Lavrov, "Address at Moscow State Institute of Foreign Affairs," speech delivered to the faculty and students of the MGIMO, 30 January 2006, http://www .ln.mid.ru/brp_4.nsf/spsvy.

50. See Joshua Cooper Ramo, *The Beijing Consensus* (London: Foreign Policy Center, 2004).

51. I heard this view expressed many times in visits to China in May, October, and December 2006.

52. An important publication highlighting the growth potential of these economies was published by Goldman Sachs in the fall of 2003. This was one of the first optimistic economic outlooks for Russia, going so far as to predict that Russian per capita GNP would be higher than that of Germany, Britain, and France by 2050. Goldman Sachs, *Global Economics Paper # 99* (New York: Goldman Sachs, October 2003).

53. See "Speech at the Munich Conference on Security Policy," 10 February 2007, http://www.securityconference.de/konferenzen/rede.php?menu_2007=&menu_ konferenzen_archiv=&menu_konferenzen=&sprache=en&id=179&.

54. See summary of meeting "How Russians and Americans View Each Other, Themselves, China, and Iran," Carnegie Endowment for International Peace, Washington, D.C., 31 May 2006. This discussion included a presentation of survey research data on the topic conducted by the Program on International Policy Attitudes (PIPA) at the University of Maryland. See Carnegie's website, http://www .carnegieendowment.org/events/index.cfm?fa=eventDetail&id=890&&prog=zru.

55. "Russian Opinion Poll: China Seen as Partner, Fear of Chinese Expansion," Interfax, 15 August 2005.

56. See PIPA data cited above in note 2.54.

57. I was living in Moscow at the time, and the coverage of this event was among the most extraordinary I viewed during my two and a half years of regular Russian television viewing. The only time I saw Sergei Ivanov as happy was at the Paul Mc-Cartney concert in Red Square in May 2003.

58. See "Taiwan Issue Clouds Russia-China Joint Military Exercises," *Jamestown Monitor*, 22 March 2005. It was reported that the Russians preferred holding the exercises in Xinjiang Province, close to Central Asia, to demonstrate the value of its airbase in Kant, Kyrgyzstan. In an article entitled "Goodwill Mercenaries," *Kommersant* said that the exercises were fully funded by the Chinese, and as Sergei Blagov summarized, "Moscow risked becoming a full-fledged political and military ally of China in an arrangement reminiscent of the Warsaw Treaty Organization, warning that Russia would become the junior partner in such an alliance." See Sergei Blagov, "Russian-Chinese War Game Meant to Boost Bilateral Partnership," *Jamestown Monitor*, 18 August 2005.

59. Peter Finn, "Chinese, Russian Militaries to Hold First Joint Drills: Alliance May Extend to Arms Sales," *Washington Post*, 15 August 2005.

60. Fred Weir, "Russia and China Meld Muscle for War Games: Shared Concerns of Regional Unrest Push Aside Differences," *Christian Science Monitor*, 17 August 2005.

61. *Nezavisimaya Gazeta*, 15 August 2005.

62. Quoted in Weir, "Russia and China Meld Muscle for War Games."

63. For an interesting debate between Stephen Blank and Ed Chow about the China-Russia energy relationship, see "Can Anyone Save This Marriage? Russo-Chinese Energy Relations," Carnegie Endowment for International Peace, Washington, D.C., 25 May 2006, http://www.carnegieendowment.org/publications/index.cfm?fa=view&id=18872&prog=zru.

64. For analysis of this deal and its significance for Sino-Russian energy relations, see Niklas Norling, "Russia's Energy Leverage over China and the Sinopec-Rosneft Deal," *China and Eurasia Forum Quarterly* 4 (2006): 31–38. Norling concludes by saying: "even if the Sinopec-Rosneft deal should be seen as one step forward in Sino-Russian energy relations one should not, at least in the short term, look at it as a breakthrough in Sino-Russian energy relations."

65. "Putin Woos Evans for Rosneft Job," *Wall Street Journal*, 16 December 2005.

66. For a good report of this transaction, see Catherine Belton, "Rosneft Seeks $6 billion from China's CNPC," *Moscow Times*, 19 January 2005.

67. For a useful overview of this heated competition, see Lyle Goldstein and Vitaly Kozyrev, "China, Japan, and the Scramble for Siberia," *Survival* 48, no. 1 (spring 2006): 163–78.

68. "Russia and China Eye Booming Bilateral Trade and Investment Ties," RIA Novosti, 15 June 2006.

3
Why a "Strategic Partnership"?
The View from China
Elizabeth Wishnick

Chinese leaders claim that their country pursues a global foreign policy that does not favor any particular country. Indeed, China has established various types of partnerships with many countries, including the United States, Great Britain, France, Italy, South Korea, Indonesia, Algeria, and Argentina.[1] Nevertheless, what is unique about the strategic cooperative partnership [zhanlue xiezuo huoban guanxi] that has characterized Sino-Russian relations since 1996 is its cross-cutting influence. This chapter evaluates how the partnership fits into key tenets of Chinese foreign policy: peaceful development, win-win diplomacy aiming toward multipolarization, and the creation of a harmonious world based on the democratization of international relations. While Chinese leaders note that the Sino-Russian relationship has never been better, the study takes a critical look at the partnership, relying on the increasingly open discussion of its weaknesses among Chinese journalists and scholars, and on a comparison of Russian and Chinese positions on key political and economic issues. Finally, the chapter concludes that while the Sino-Russian partnership has certain distinctive features, it is losing its privileged position for China in particular.

Sino-Russian Partnership and Chinese Foreign Policy

To understand how the Chinese leadership views the Sino-Russian partnership, it is important to see how relations with Russia fit into China's overall foreign policy framework. In recent years, China's State Council has laid out the main principles of Chinese foreign policy in a series of white papers. "China's Peaceful Development Road," published in December 2005, explains how Chinese domestic and foreign policy goals are interrelated.

Although the 2005 white paper notes historical and cultural factors that reinforce the need for peaceful development, the report particularly stresses the need to create a peaceful environment for economic reform, with the aim of achieving a moderately well-off society at home and common development overseas.[2] The white paper goes on to explain that China contributes to world peace and international cooperation by basing its relations with other countries on the five principles of peaceful coexistence, being a friendly neighbor, using win-win diplomacy and multilateral cooperation to develop relations with major powers and developing states, and creating a harmonious world by democratizing international relations.[3]

The white paper on China's defense, issued in December 2006, highlights these same goals, but calls greater attention to the uncertainties and tensions that will pose challenges to their fulfillment. According to the 2006 white paper, "Guided by a security strategy of promoting both development and security, China strives to build a socialist harmonious society at home and a harmonious world to ensure both its overall national security and enduring peace in the world. It endeavors to enhance both development and security, both internal security and external security and both traditional security and non-traditional security; works to uphold its sovereignty, unity and territorial integrity and promote national development; and strives to sustain the important period of strategic opportunity for national development."[4]

The white paper notes that while China pursues a policy of peaceful development, "the world is not yet peaceful" due to the persistence of "hegemonism" and power politics as well as the growing complexity of non-traditional security threats and local wars.[5]

These white papers represent an effort to incorporate the cumulative foreign policy contributions of China's leadership. Each successive generation of Chinese leaders has put their stamp on foreign policy, with Deng Xiaoping developing the concept of "peace and development," Jiang Zemin devising a new security concept based on win-win diplomacy, mutual trust, equality, and cooperation, and Hu Jintao aiming to build a "harmonious world."[6] The following sections examine these concepts more closely in terms of their relationship to the evolution of the Sino-Russian partnership.

Peace and Development

Deng Xiaoping's commitment to peace and development was one of the factors that contributed to Sino-Soviet normalization in the 1980s and laid the foundation for the development of strategic partnership since the 1990s. In the Deng Xiaoping era, the nature of development—specifically the mutual desire to achieve socialist economic reform in both China and the Soviet Union—was just as important as the need for a peaceful environment in which to accomplish such reforms in prodding the two neighbors to end their costly antagonism and to cooperate instead in mutually beneficial ways. Thus evolving identities in China, the Soviet Union, and then post-Soviet Russia have served to deepen cooperation or accentuate differences between the two countries.

In recent years there has been considerable debate within China about the implications of China's spectacular economic growth. This debate reflected some soul-searching about Chinese identity as well as more pragmatic concerns about refuting "China threat" arguments. After briefly experimenting with the characterization "peaceful rise" in 2003–2004, Hu Jintao and Wen Jiabao settled on peaceful development as a less confrontational alternative.[7]

In late 2006, another debate emerged about the implications of a dragon as a symbol for China, which brought back earlier concerns about the need to express China's dynamism without alarming its partners and neighbors. The issue of the dragon came up in connection with the selection of the official mascots for the Beijing Summer Olympics. Wu Yaofu of Shanghai International Studies University argued that since, to Western minds, the dragon connotes a terrifying, aggressive beast, China should select symbols that are more in keeping with the harmonious image of a peacefully developing country. He later noted that one way out of this dilemma was to refer to the dragon only by its Chinese name, *long*, to distinguish it from the Western image.[8]

Scrapping the dragon led to a big debate in China's chat rooms and newspapers. Some experts, such as Pang Jin, director of the Research Centre on Dragon and Phoenix Culture, suggested that greater public education and promotion of Chinese dragons was needed.[9] Although 90 percent of 100,000 Sina.com readers voted to keep the dragon as a Chinese national symbol, the 2008 Beijing Olympics committee chose five less controversial mascots (or "five friendlies"): the fish, the panda, the Tibetan antelope, the swallow, and the flame.[10]

Nevertheless, a new mood of assertiveness appears to be taking root in China. While Deng Xiaoping contended that China needed to act modestly in its relations with other states to avoid provoking negative reactions to China's development, Chinese commentators today note that the current leadership increasingly projects an image of China as a global power with global reach.[11] As a review of Chinese foreign policy published in *Renmin Ribao* stated, "this administration under President Hu Jintao no longer tries to hide China's growing economic weight in global affairs and the role it will have to play in order to sustain growth."[12] In December 2006, for example, the Chinese president put on a military uniform and told a meeting of the Navy's 10th Communist Party Congress that China should develop a powerful navy.[13] China's limited naval force has long been viewed in the West as a constraint on its global ambitions. According to the U.S. Department of Defense's "2008 Annual Report to Congress," China's naval force improvements and operations indicate planning for contingencies well beyond Taiwan.[14]

How is China's evolving self-appraisal affecting Sino-Russian relations? Though China accepted the Soviet Union as the older brother in the 1950s, after Josef Stalin's death Mao Zedong chafed at the inequality in the Sino-Soviet relationship. In turn Soviet leaders criticized their Chinese counterparts for their "Sinocentrism." By the mid-1980s, Soviet and Chinese leaders appeared to be on the same page in terms of socialist reform, but in the 1990s China's economic reforms took off, while instability in Russia eroded its global role.[15] Although Russia has seen an economic boom in recent years, largely due to high oil prices, this has not necessarily smoothed Sino-Russian relations.

Chinese leaders continue to emphasize equality as a principle in Sino-Russian relations, but prominent journalists and scholars are reassessing their relative global weight.[16] Some analysts note that Russia remains a superpower due to its resources and military power.[17] Others, however, see Russia's over-reliance on energy as a potential source of weakness and argue that "there is still a long way to go for Russia to claim the status of a world-class big power."[18] Yan Xuetong of Qinghua University argues that in terms of comprehensive national power (military, economic, political), China is second only to the United States, though he admits that the two are in different classes: the United States is a superpower, while China is a major power.[19]

Russia's admission to the G-8, while China remains on the sidelines, rankled some. She Jiru of the Chinese Academy of Social Sciences' Institute of World Economics and Politics noted that while strengthening China's cooperation with the G8 would be mutually beneficial, Cold War thinking would make it difficult for China to become a member any time soon.[20] According to Ruan Zongze, the deputy director of the China Institute of International Studies, China takes exception to some of the group's entry requirements and it is unlikely that China will join in the short term. He noted that "Russia . . . does not mix well with the group. It joined the club in 1998 out of political needs, but was reduced into a second-class citizen, and has had little say on economic questions. So Russia is eager to establish itself as an equal member of the group by taking the opportunity as the host."[21] Another commentator, noting the significance of the Russia-India-China trilateral summit at the conclusion of the G-8 meeting, went so far as to group Russia with non-

Western developing countries. According to *Renmin Ribao* columnist Chu Shulong, *"Not belonging to the developed Western nations,* the views and positions of China, Russia, and India on regional and world issues can reflect better the interests and aspirations of the developing countries" (emphasis added).[22] Indeed, some Chinese Russia experts emphasized that because Russia and China are both developing countries, there were greater complementarities between them, facilitating mutually beneficial cooperation.[23]

Win-Win Diplomacy, Mutual Support, and Foreign Policy Consensus

While Deng Xiaoping succeeded in setting aside the past history of Sino-Soviet conflict and normalizing relations, it was Jiang Zemin who developed the Sino-Russian partnership in a series of meetings with President Boris Yeltsin. Jiang then codified it with President Vladimir Putin in the "Sino-Russian Treaty of Good-Neighborliness and Friendly Cooperation" on 16 June 2001. Beginning in the mid-1990s, President Jiang Zemin also elaborated a new security concept for China, based on "mutual trust, mutual benefits, equality and cooperation."[24] Sino-Russian dialogue and deepening partnership proved an important laboratory for fine-tuning Chinese concepts about the changing world order while providing a key source of support for Chinese positions. Indeed, many of the ideas that would emerge as central to the new security concept can be found in Sino-Russian partnership documents. As one Chinese diplomat and scholar noted, "China and Russia have discarded the Cold War mentality favoring zero-sum game rules and created a brand new concept in international relations."[25] Because the partnership does not target any third country and is characterized by nonalignment and nonconfrontation, China-Russia relations can be viewed as the prototype of a new Chinese model of post–Cold War state-to-state relations.[26] There are three aspects of the Chinese approach: win-win diplomacy, mutual support, and foreign policy consensus.

1. Win-Win Diplomacy

Chinese commentators hold up the Sino-Russian partnership as a "good example for the harmonious coexistence and the win-win cooperation among different countries."[27] To reassure China that Sino-Russian cooperation would continue beyond the Putin presidency, his successor, Dmitry Medvedev, made a state visit to Beijing an early priority. According to Chinese deputy foreign minister Li Hui, Medvedev's visit would help ensure the sustained development of the China-Russia partnership, define the next steps in its development, enhance mutual trust, provide mutual support on issues of territorial integrity and sovereignty, and deepen cooperation in a number of practical areas.[28]

In 2006, China and Russia celebrated a decade of partnership, based on "the principles of mutual respect for sovereignty and territorial integrity, mutual non-aggression, mutual non-interference in internal affairs, mutual benefit as equals, and peaceful coexistence."[29] As Hu Jintao told President Putin during his March 2006 visit to Beijing, one of the most important achievements of the Sino-Russian partnership in his view was that the two countries agreed "they will be friends for generations to come and will never be enemies."[30]

This partnership has involved resolving the border dispute between the two neighbors, opening the border regions to trade and cooperation, institutionalizing regular dialogue among national and regional officials, developing a multifaceted military relationship, and instilling a long-term commitment to Sino-Russian friendship among the two peoples. None of these goals has proved trouble-free for either side. On 14 October 2004, Russia and China at long last ended their border dispute by resolving the fate of the three islands that had remained outside the scope of earlier demarcation agreements for the 4,300-kilometer border. Chinese and Russian leaders agreed to split the largest island, Bolshoi Ussuriysky/Heixiazi Dao (320 square kilometers), though demarcation efforts continue. China has proposed creating a visa-free trade zone on the island.

China also regained control over the two smaller islands, the swampy and as yet uninhabited Bolshoi Island in the Argun River, as well as Tarabarov/Yinlong Island (46.4 square kilometers) in the Amur River.[31] Nonetheless, the specific territorial disposition was never published in Chinese media. Some Chinese scholars attributed such caution to concern over a potentially hostile reaction by the public to any territorial concessions to Russia, even though China received land in return.

If demarcating the border proved long and complex, opening it to economic cooperation has turned out to be even more challenging. Chinese enthusiasm for developing its economically backward border areas led to booming but at times poorly regulated border enclaves. Russian caution about opening up its sparsely populated border regions to cross-border cooperation with China created an imbalance in development that has further increased distrust of China on the Russian side. One glaring example of this is the rapid development of Heihe and Heihe Island into modern boomtowns, while

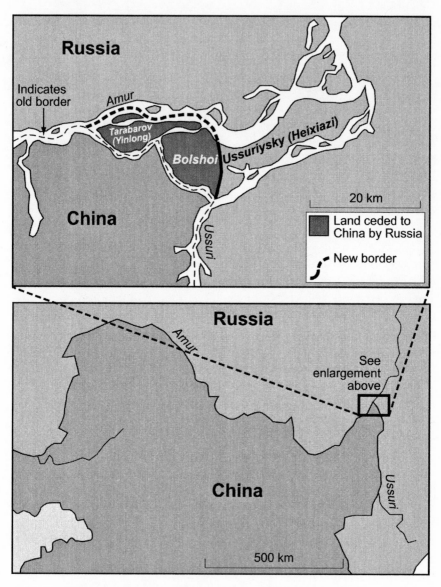

Map 3.1. China-Russia Border Dispute.

Blagoveshchensk across the Amur on the Russian side retains a nineteenth-century frontier town feel. A bridge connecting Heihe and Blagoveshchensk, discussed for more than a decade, is no closer to construction.

More significantly, due to continued concern over the problem of Chinese illegal immigration to Russia in the guise of "economic tourism," visa-free travel for Chinese tourists, allowed for thirty days since 1994, was curtailed to fifteen days in November 2006.[32] According to Konstantin Romodanovsky, head of Russia's Federal Migration Service, Chinese account for nearly one quarter of the 1 million illegal immigrants in the country.[33]

In 2007, the Russian government changed the country's migration laws, imposing stiff fines on employers for hiring foreign workers illegally and prohibiting foreigners from selling goods at Russian retail markets. Markets have had to scale down operations in some cities; in Vladivostok, for example, half of the stalls in a popular flea market were shut down.[34] Despite the higher prices that resulted, particularly on food, an April 2007 poll by VTsIOM showed strong support for the new laws: 75 percent supported them, while only 16 percent were opposed.[35]

On 1 June 2007, President Putin also reinstituted Soviet-era financial incentives for resettlement of Russians and Russian-speakers from the former Soviet Union to cities in the Russian Far East and other regions with worker shortages.[36] Migration officials claim that the new laws have reduced crime, increased tax revenue, and encouraged migrants to move out of the shadows and acquire work permits and citizenship legally. Nonetheless, it costs $1,000 to expel an illegal immigrant, and corruption remains an obstacle to enforcement of migrant laws.[37]

Chinese officials and scholars on both the national and regional level typically have questioned Russian motives in labeling Chinese migration to Russia a security threat, though a few urge Chinese leaders to take Russian concerns more seriously and implement measures to address the problem.[38] To explain why Russians view Chinese migration as threatening, many Chinese scholars attribute Russian concerns over Chinese migrants to the popularity of "China threat" views in the Russian Far East.

According to one Chinese expert, Russian allegations of Chinese expansionism in the region stems from trends within Russia, such as nationalism, Eurocentrism, and concern with Russia's weak position in the Northeast Asian balance of economic power.[39] Reflecting some Chinese concern over the consequences of the post-9/11 improvement in Russian-American relations, another scholar attributed the continued Russian securitization of the migration issue to the influence of discussion of the "China threat" in the United States. According to this analysis, American "China threat" views were then transplanted to Russia and refocused on the imbalance in population between China and Russia, China's territorial claims, the lack of democracy in China, and the historical tendency for the most populous countries to be expansionist.[40]

Although they disagree over the severity of the migration issue, Russia and China agree that it is in the mutual interest of the two countries to expand their economic relations. How to do so has long been a source of dispute, however. Chinese officials in Beijing and in the Chinese Northeast advocate taking advantage of the complementarities [hubuxing] between the two countries: China faces a labor surplus, but shortages of land and natural resources, while Russia has an abundance of such resources, but a labor shortage. While not contesting these facts, Russian officials tend to view abundant Chinese labor as a threat rather than an opportunity, and, as previously mentioned, have taken steps to restrict it, while opting instead for costlier labor resettlement policies for Russian speakers in the CIS.

After years of stagnation, leading to what Chinese observers called an imbalance between "hot" political relations and "cold" economic relations,[41] the volume of Sino-Russian trade has been growing steadily in recent years, increasing by 44.3 percent in 2007 to a record $48.17 billion, the highest annual increase since 1993.[42] According to Liu Huaqing, a Russia expert at the Chinese Ministry of Commerce's Research Institute on International Trade, one of the main reasons for the rapid growth in Sino-Russian trade since 2003 is the increase in prices for energy and other commodities, which artificially inflates the value of total bilateral trade. She notes that in the event these prices should fall significantly, this would have a major impact on Sino-Russian economic ties since current trade volume heavily depends on Russian resource exports to China.[43]

Despite the many twists and turns in major oil and gas projects of late, many scholars continue to view Sino-Russian energy cooperation as generally promising.[44] Some, however, continue to warn of the danger of growing Chinese dependence on Russian energy supplies.[45] Russian officials also are dissatisfied with the composition of Sino-Russian trade, and have unsuccessfully sought preferential treatment to boost Russian exports of machinery (civilian aircraft, nuclear reactors, hydroelectric turbines, etc.). According to former Russian economic development minister German Gref, "The increasing share of commodities in our exports to China is a potential threat to the stability in our trade relations."[46] Russia largely exports oil, oil products, and timber to China, which increasingly sells machinery and electrical appliances to Russia. This is a recent trend, however, and some Chinese observers view the relatively low-tech consumer products that constitute the lion's share of China's exports to Russia with concern, since the production of such goods relies on low-skilled, low-wage labor and aggravates income disparities in China.[47]

Due to its weak industrial exports and caution in resource deals with the Chinese, for the first time since the early 1990s Russia had a trade deficit with

China in 2007 ($8.8 billion). China is Russia's second-largest trade partner, accounting for 9.4 percent of its imports and 5.2 percent of its exports in 2007, while Russia is China's eighth-largest trade partner. By comparison, Chinese trade with Russia is one-sixth of its trade with the United States and one-quarter of its trade with South Korea.[48]

2. Mutual Support

From the Chinese perspective, the Sino-Russian partnership plays a key role in providing mutual support on important domestic concerns that are the target of international criticism—Chinese policies on Taiwan, Tibet, and efforts to counter terrorism in Xinjiang. In exchange for Russian support on these issues, China has pledged its support for Russian positions on Chechnya. In a series of joint declarations, China and Russia outlined their commitment to national sovereignty and unity, and noninterference in the domestic affairs of other states.[49] Such statements also evolved into a rejoinder to the Bush doctrine, in that they reject "double standards on terrorism," "unilateral action," and depicting the main trend of the world as a "clash of civilizations."

Statements of mutual support at times mask disagreements, however. From 2004 to 2006, Sino-Russian joint statements specified that Russia would not sell weapons to Taiwan, reflecting a 2004 report that President Putin had agreed to sell diesel submarines to the United States, which would then be resold to Taiwan.[50] Russia also refused to agree to hold the first Sino-Russian joint military exercise in Zhejiang Province across from Taiwan, as the Chinese side had proposed, fearing the location would be too provocative. The Russian military had hoped to hold the exercise in Xinjiang to address antiterrorism concerns in Central Asia and involve air units stationed at its Kant base in Kyrgyzstan, but Chinese leaders were opposed to the idea.[51] The Peace Mission 2005 exercise was eventually held on the Jiaodong Peninsula in Shandong Province, giving the impression that it was designed to focus on a potential crisis on the Korean Peninsula, when in fact this was a compromise location. Ultimately the exercise was most successful in showcasing Russian weapons systems for Chinese purchase and in providing training opportunities for Chinese forces using Russian military technology.[52]

3. Foreign Policy Consensus

In their joint declarations, China and Russia typically pledge their agreement on foreign policy issues of the day, most recently on ballistic missile defense, the militarization of outer space, and the Iranian and North Korean nuclear crises. The May 2008 Sino-Russian joint statement, for example, asserted that the two partners agreed that "International security is comprehensive and inalienable, and some countries' security cannot be guaranteed at the cost of some others."[53] As will be shown below, China and Russia have overlapping, but not necessarily identical foreign policy interests. Moreover, it is becoming increasingly less likely that either one will defer to the other as each state more strongly articulates its own national interests.

On North Korea, Chinese leaders assert that Russia and China hold identical views on Pyongyang's nuclear tests, the desirability of a nonnuclear Korean Peninsula, the peaceful resolution of the North Korean crisis through UN efforts and diplomacy, and the importance of maintaining the nonproliferation regime.[54] However, the two countries have squared off as competitors for access to North Korean ports, and China has been content to play the lead role in mediating between the United States and North Korea, first in trilateral and then in six-party talks. While Russia stands to gain from greater integration of the Korean Peninsula in its energy pipeline and transportation networks, China has a major stake in the status quo.

China's economic, political, and security interests have been more directly engaged by the crisis than have Russia's. China is well-known as North Korea's main trading partner, accounting for more than 30 percent of North Korea's total trade and as well as 40 percent of its food aid, and may provide as much as 90 percent of its energy supplies.[55] China was also South Korea's largest trading partner—bilateral trade in 2007 amounted to $145 billion—and Chinese leaders have a major economic stake in maintaining the status quo on the Korean Peninsula for economic reasons.[56] The Chinese leadership also fears that a collapse of the North Korean regime could lead to a massive influx of North Korean refugees into China: there are already at least one hundred thousand North Koreans seeking refuge in China's Yanbian Korean autonomous prefecture, which borders North Korea.[57]

Rejecting regime change out of concern for domestic stability in North Korea, the Chinese government has instead been showcasing its economic model and urging the North Korean leadership to adopt similar reforms as a way of improving its economic prospects. The North Korean leader's 2006 visit included a stop in Shenzhen, for example, one of the early Chinese special economic zones. Some of the limited economic opening in North Korea, particularly the use of development zones and private markets, appears to be patterned on the Chinese model.

After the Chinese leadership expended considerable political capital to convince North Korea to forego missile and nuclear tests, the failure of the Chinese diplomatic effort not only caused a loss of face for Chinese leaders, but also threatened to worsen China's security environment. China has opposed the nuclearization of the Korean Peninsula, in part to prevent Japan's remilitarization and a pretext for closer U.S.-Japan defense ties. As a consequence, China agreed to UN resolutions condemning North Korean missile and nuclear tests.

Despite Beijing's clear opposition to the 9 October 2006 nuclear test, Chinese permanent representative to the UN Wang Guangya, joined by his Russian colleague, negotiated hard to remove any mention of the use of force and to allow for adjustments in the sanctions imposed in the event of a change in North Korea's behavior.[58] Wang also stated that Chinese authorities would not participate in cargo inspections mandated by the 14 October resolution "because it could easily lead by one side or the other to a provocation of conflict."[59] Facing criticism for that position, the Chinese Foreign Ministry later amended the statement to indicate that China would implement the resolution responsibly and seriously, but would take its own commercial regulations into account.[60] Wang then backtracked and clarified that he meant that China would not participate in naval interdictions and interceptions, such as those involved in the U.S.-led Proliferation Security Initiative, but would carry out cargo inspections at border crossing points.[61] Unlike China, however, Russia has been a member of the U.S.-led Proliferation Security Initiative since 2004, although Moscow noted upon joining that the effort "Should not and will not create any obstacles to the lawful economic, scientific, and technological cooperation of states."[62]

Regarding Iran, China and Russia have taken the same restrictive position on United Nations sanctions, resulting in a weaker resolution than the United States wanted.[63] Although in this case both China and Russia have significant economic interests in Iran, China's considerable dependence on Middle East oil imports gives Chinese leaders a stronger stake than Russia in maintaining the regional balance of power in the Persian Gulf.

When Iranian president Mahmoud Ahmadinejad visited Beijing in early 2007, Wen Jiabao rejected his claim that the UN resolution imposing sanctions on Iran "Was a mere piece of paper," and then after his guest's departure, met with Israeli prime minister Ehud Olmert, who came away unexpectedly pleased with the Chinese leadership's position on the Iranian nuclear issue.[64] China has become increasingly active in the 5+1 meetings on the problem, involving the Security Council permanent members plus Germany. Although the Chinese government initially kept a low profile within the group, for the first time, Beijing played host in April 2008, a week after Iran announced it was expanding its nuclear program.[65]

Although both China and Russia have sought to improve relations with Saudi leaders in recent months, Saudi Arabia is becoming more important economically for China. Saudi Arabia is China's largest crude oil supplier, providing 16 percent of its total imports (Iran is third, with 12.5 percent).[66] China increased its oil imports from Saudi Arabia by 10 percent in 2007 to fill its planned oil reserves and contribute to a major joint venture refining project involving Saudi Arabia's Aramco, ExxonMobil, and Sinopec in Fujian Province.

Much like the European Union, China has been watching Russia discuss energy partnerships with its own key suppliers, Iran and Algeria, and seeking to ensure diversity of supply. Moreover, Saudi Arabia and China also are discovering common political interests, including a concern for political stability, resistance to American pressures for democratization, and an interest in counterbalancing U.S. influence in the Middle East and Central Asia.[67]

One surprising new area of foreign policy cooperation that has attracted relatively little attention is the emerging Sino-Russian-Indian trilateralism. When Prime Minister Yevgeny Primakov first raised the idea in 1998, it seemed wildly optimistic considering the history of Sino-Indian tensions. However, after five years of unofficial meetings among Chinese, Russian, and Indian leaders, and a foreign ministers' summit in Vladivostok in June 2005, their first high-level summit at the G-8 meeting marked a new chapter in their relations. Their most recent foreign ministerial meeting in May 2008 emphasized the unique contribution that the three multinational states can make to conflict resolution and multilateral efforts to resolve global problems.[68]

Chinese commentators were sober-minded in their initial assessments of the new trilateral cooperation, noting that while the three countries shared a common vision of a more inclusive international order, they had "dissimilar or even immense differences" on some issues, such as their differing perspectives on democracy, and continue to face many challenging bilateral issues—in particular, border demarcation and Tibet.[69] Some Chinese observers stress complementarities,[70] while others note areas of competition (for the most advanced Russian weapons, for example, where India typically prevails).[71]

Sino-Indian cooperation has accelerated in trade in recent years—China has overtaken the United States as India's largest trading partner, and bilateral trade reached $51.9 billion in 2008. In December 2007, China and India held their first joint antiterrorism exercise in Kunming.[72] Many differences remain, especially over border demarcation, India's desire to expand civilian nuclear cooperation outside the Nuclear Non-Proliferation Treaty framework, the Tibet issue, and India's growing security dialogue with the United States, Japan, and Australia.[73]

Considering that China and India are in a similar position as rapidly emerging economies, can they cooperate rather than compete for energy resources or markets for their computer industries? In 2006, also known as the "China-India Friendship Year," the two countries emphasized new perspectives for cooperation. In July 2006, they reopened border trade through Tibet's Nathu La pass, which had been closed for forty-four years.[74] During Hu Jintao's November 2006 visit to India, the first by a Chinese leader in ten years, the Chinese president and Indian prime minister, Manmohan Singh, agreed to a long list of cooperative endeavors, including strengthening cooperation in the computer and energy sectors. Interestingly, trilateral dialogue with Russia received only a brief mention in the joint declaration as a mechanism the two states "positively assess" and agree to continue further through exchanges and cooperation.[75]

For both China and India, trilateral dialogue with Russia is viewed as just one context for Sino-Indian cooperation, which now occurs in a varied set of bilateral and multilateral fora, including the Shanghai Cooperation Organization (where India is an observer), the ASEAN Regional forum, and the Conference on Interaction and Confidence-Building Measures in Asia (CICA). The Indian media talk of including Brazil in future dialogue, given the increasing economic clout of the "BRIC group." According to some financial analysts, Brazil, Russia, India, and China could overtake the G-8 in terms of GDP by 2040.[76] For China, improving relations with India coincides with efforts to firmly integrate Tibet into the Chinese economy and to develop China's western regions by expanding transnational trade, transportation, and energy networks.

Harmonious World

Building on Jiang Zemin's "new security concept," President Hu Jintao and Prime Minister Wen Jiabao have elaborated a conception of a "harmonious world," the foreign policy counterpart to their domestic agenda, aimed at creating a harmonious, moderately well-off socialist society. According to the Chinese leadership, a "harmonious world" involves encouraging multilateralism to ensure common security, aiming for common prosperity through mutually beneficial cooperation, and democratizing international relations by respecting the diversity of civilizations and each country's right to choose its own development path.[77] One component of this effort is to reassure foreign audiences that China's rise—what Chinese leaders now call "peaceful development"—will be beneficial for the international community.[78] During a speech at Yale University, Chinese president Hu Jintao explained that "harmony" is a longstanding Chinese value, underlying its priority on social stability at home, and a foreign policy based on mutual benefit.[79]

China's involvement with the Shanghai Cooperation Organization (SCO) best reflects this approach, and the group's conception of the "Shanghai Spirit" practically restates verbatim key aspects of the "harmonious world." As the 15 June 2006 SCO declaration affirms, "The SCO owes its smooth growth to its consistent adherence to the 'Shanghai Spirit' of 'mutual trust, mutual benefit, equality, consultation, respect for multi-civilizations and pursuit of common development.' This spirit is the underlying philosophy and the most important code of conduct of SCO."[80]

In practice, however, the "Shanghai Spirit" has not succeeded in overcoming conflicting interests in the region. Although Russian and Chinese leaders agree on the priority of combating the "three evil forces" of terrorism, separatism, and fundamentalism, Russia remains suspicious of China's interest in developing multilateral economic cooperation in Central Asia and has rejected Chinese proposals to set up a free trade zone in the region. Some Chinese analysts see instead a Russian effort to regain its influence in Central Asia, which they view as an obstacle to deepening economic cooperation.[81] Chinese critics have likened Russian views to a "siege mentality" and "old thinking,"[82] though others note that Central Asian leaders are equally suspicious of Chinese intentions.[83] During his May 2008 visit to Beijing, Medvedev told students at Beijing University that the SCO presented an opportunity for new forms of cooperation, particularly in energy, but this may really reflect Russia's effort to check China's progress in bilateral energy ties with Central Asian states.[84]

Despite the new attention to nontraditional security issues in the harmonious world concept, such problems present some of the greatest challenges for Sino-Russian partnership. When asked whether he was uneasy about China's economic rise, President Putin replied, "One is more concerned about the environmental situation in the border areas. . . . In addition to this . . . one has to attentively look at illegal migration."[85] Such concerns remained in evidence in the first communiqué signed by Medvedev and Hu Jintao, which pledged to expand their cooperation in environmental protection and immigration.[86]

Russian officials, especially in the Far East, have long expressed concern about China's environmental footprint. Such fears were confirmed in November 2005 and August 2006, when toxic chemicals from factories in China's Jilin Province spilled into the Songhua River, a tributary of the Amur, threatening water resources in Russia's Khabarovsky Krai. After the first spill on 13 November 2005, the more serious of the two, Chinese prime minister Wen Jiabao apologized to President Putin and the two countries set up a hotline to monitor the progress of the one hundred tons of benzene and other toxic chemicals heading toward Russian shores.[87] Russia and China then signed an agreement in June to cooperate in monitoring water quality in all of their shared waterways. Nonetheless, many Russian officials, especially on the regional level, accused their Chinese counterparts of being slow to release information.[88]

In fact, the Jilin Petrochemical Corporation, a subsidiary of the China National Petroleum Corporation (CNPC), regional environmental officials, and the State Environmental Protection Agency (SEPA), failed to inform the Chinese population about the water pollution for five days. Instead local authorities, citing routine maintenance needs, turned off the water in nearby areas, including major cities like Harbin, causing panicked water buying and angry web postings. More than ten thousand people reportedly fled their homes.[89] As a Shanghai scholar noted, the Chernobyl case demonstrated that efforts to avoid public panic may cause the accident to have an even greater impact.[90] Ultimately, the head of SEPA, several regional officials in Jilin and Heilongjiang provinces, and senior executives at CNPC lost their jobs over their mishandling of the accident. The vice mayor of the city of Jilin, where the accident occurred, committed suicide before he could be questioned about his responsibility for the cover-up.[91]

After the second spill on 20 August 2006 into a tributary of the Songhua River, the Chinese government set up a pollution control dam to prevent the ten tons of untreated toxic waste released by a Jilin chemical plant from reaching the Songhua. Although the Chinese government claimed they had contained the problem, Russian officials in neighboring Khabarovsk complained that they were not allowed to take samples from the Songhua River for more than a week after the accident.[92]

Conclusion: Prospects for Future Cooperation

Ironically, now that Sino-Russian ties are perhaps their best ever, the relationship is losing its privileged position. Military cooperation, which expanded dramatically after the collapse of the USSR, is now stalled. Russian arms exports to China fell by 63 percent in 2007, according to the SIPRI Arms Transfers Database, and no new orders for big-ticket items were placed that year.[93] Both sides have their own sources of dissatisfaction with military cooperation, formerly one of the drivers of strategic partnership.[94] Russia has seen China copy its aircraft designs and, consequently, hesitates to transfer its latest technology, particularly since Russian arms exporters are no longer dependent on the Chinese market for their survival, as they were in the 1990s.

Chinese defense companies are producing more of their own equipment and have complained about Russia's failure to deliver on a $1.5 billion contract for aircraft tankers.

Uncertainty about the routing of Siberian oil and gas pipelines and disagreements over pricing caused delays in cooperation, leading to greater Chinese diversification and setting limits to economic integration. Moreover, as Russia becomes more assertive with its energy diplomacy, China has all the more reason to be cautious about excessive dependence on any one supplier. In 2007, Russian oil accounted for 8.9 percent of China's total imports and China received no Russian gas, a 9 percent decline from 2006 levels.[95]

As negotiations over major oil and gas projects continue, Russian and Chinese officials can point to one promising success, the conclusion of a $1 billion nuclear cooperation agreement to provide enriched uranium and assistance with the completion of a uranium enrichment plant in China.[96] Nevertheless, economic relations have long lagged behind political cooperation, and Chinese experts note that optimistic targets for doubling or even tripling bilateral trade will require a major expansion in border infrastructure (especially transportation) as well as a commitment to improve trade administration.

The celebration of the "Year of Russia" in China in 2006, involving some two hundred cultural, trade-related, and athletic events as well as a series of high-level visits, and the "Year of China" in Russia in 2007, is as much a testimony to the progress in bilateral relations between the two neighbors as to its limits. The "friendship generation" in China, who studied Russian in the 1950s and often had work experience in the Soviet Union, is now retiring. They are nostalgic for Russian songs that are no longer sung and are familiar with Russian classics, but few Chinese know much about contemporary Russia.[97]

Currently English is mandatory in Chinese secondary education, while Russian language education has been in decline for many years. Until Sino-Russian economic cooperation began to show some dynamism in recent years, Chinese Russian language students faced difficulties in finding jobs, although Chinese education minister Zhou Ji claims that now Chinese Russian speakers face excellent job prospects.[98]

Nevertheless, Sino-Russian educational exchanges remain weak. There were 65,582 Chinese students in the United States in 2006, but that same year just 15,000 chose to study in Russia.[99] According to the Chinese Ministry of Education, there are only 1,224 Russian students in China, just 25 more than from Nepal (the United States has 3,693 in China, while the ROK leads with 35,353, and Japan, despite its difficult relations with China, has 12,765).[100]

To encourage Sino-Russian educational exchanges, the Chinese government is establishing Confucius Institutes in Russia to promote Chinese language and culture. At present, some 10,000 Russians study Chinese, compared to more than 60,000 Americans.[101] Russia has also set up a Russian Information Center in Beijing to promote knowledge of the country. China plans to make 2009 "Russian Language Year," while Russia will celebrate "Han Language Year" in 2010.

Greater mutual knowledge will help, but many of the future challenges awaiting Sino-Russian relations will involve coping with unpredictable external developments, such as political change in Central Asia, the impact of U.S. policies, developments in the Middle East, and future transnational problems such as epidemics, environmental disasters, and migratory flows. For Chinese leaders, this will require balancing three sets of goals: achieving economic development without leading to instability at home or inciting external pressures to contain China's rise, pursuing national interests while achieving mutually beneficial outcomes, and, perhaps most difficult of all, matching the rhetoric of a "harmonious world" with the policy measures and transparency needed to address nontraditional security concerns.

Notes

1. Avery Goldstein notes that China has established such partnerships to expand its own leverage as well as to develop mutually beneficial economic relations. See Goldstein, *Rising to the Challenge: China's Grand Strategy and International Security* (Stanford, Calif.: Stanford Univ. Press, 2005), 175; David M. Finkelstein, *China Reconsiders Its National Security: "The Great Peace and Development Debate of 1999"* (Alexandria, Va.: CNA Corporation, October 2000), CME D0014464.A1/Final, 10.

2. PRC State Council Information Office, "White Paper on Peaceful Development Road Published," 15 December 2005, www.china.org.cn/english/2005/Dec/152669.htm, page 3.

3. Ibid., 5, 11, 13. The five principles of coexistence are mutual respect for sovereignty and territorial integrity, mutual nonaggression, noninterference in the domestic affairs of states, equality and mutual benefit, and peaceful coexistence (Wen Jiabao, "Carrying Forward the Five Principles of Peaceful Coexistence in the Promotion of Peace and Development," www.fmprc.gov.cn/eng/topics/seminaronfiveprinciples/t140777.htm).

4. PRC State Council Information Office, "China's National Defense in 2006," Xinhua, 29 December 2006, 4, www.xinhuanet.com/english/.

5. Ibid., 3.

6. Xiong Guankai, "Deputy Army Chief Says China's Development, Peaceful, Open, Cooperative," Xinhua, 28 December 2005, www.xinhuanet.com/english/.

7. Zheng Bijian, a prominent Chinese Communist Party intellectual, first introduced the term "peaceful rise" [heping jueqi] on 3 November 2003 at the Boao Forum. Hu Jintao and Wen Jiabao incorporated the concept into their speeches in early 2004, but by April the leadership opted instead to use the term "peaceful development" [heping fazhan]. Robert L. Suettinger, "The Rise and Descent of 'Peaceful Rise,'" *China Leadership Monitor*, no. 12 (fall 2004): 1–6; Zheng Bijian, "China's 'Peaceful Rise' to Great-Power Status," *Foreign Affairs* 84, no. 5 (September/October 2005): 18–24; Wu Guogang, "The Peaceful Emergence of a Great Power?" *Social Research* 73, no. 1 (spring 2006): 318–20; Bonnie Glaser and Evan Madeiros, "The Changing Ecology of Foreign Policy-Making in China: The Ascension and Demise of the Theory of 'Peaceful Rise,'" *China Quarterly* 190 (June 2007): 292–96.

8. Benjamin Robertson, "Dragon Debate Reflects Beijing's Growing Sense of Image," *South China Morning Post*, 4 January 2007, http://www.scmp.com.

9. "Dragon Debate Stirs Public's Imagination," *China Daily*, 12 December 2006, http://english.peopledaily.com.cn; Joel Martison, "Dragons and Branding," 6 December 2006, www.danwei.org.

10. "Dragon Debate Stirs Public Imagination," *China Daily*, 12 December 2006, http://english.people.com.cn.

11. Deng Xiaoping, "With Stable Policies of Reform and Opening to the Outside World, China Can Have Great Hopes for the Future," 4 September 1989, *Selected Works of Deng Xiaoping*, vol. 3 (1982–1992), edited by *People's Daily Online*, http://english.peopledaily.com.cn/dengxp/.

12. "China Takes Its Place on the International Stage," *People's Daily Online*, 30 December 2006, http://english.people.com.cn.

13. "Hu Calls for Strengthened, Modernized Navy," *People's Daily Online*, 28 December 2006, http://english.people.com.cn/200612/28/eng20061228_336476.html; "Coming over the Horizon: Why China Wants a Bigger Navy," *The Economist*, 6 January 2007, 34.

14. Office of the Secretary of Defense, *Military Power of the People's Republic of China 2008*, page 39, www.defenselink.mil.

15. I discuss the changing patterns of Sino-Russian bilateral and regional relations in detail in *Mending Fences: The Evolution of Moscow's China Policy: 1969–1999* (Seattle: Univ. of Washington Press, 2001).

16. As Jiang Zemin explained after signing the 16 July 2001 Treaty of Good-Neighborliness and Friendly Cooperation, "treating each other on an equal footing and mutual respect are the prerequisite for building mutual trust," one of the cornerstones of good-neighborly relations. "Full Text of Jiang Zemin Speech at Moscow University," Xinhua, 17 July 2001, www.xinhuanet.com/english/. For a more recent discussion of the importance of equality, see Wang Baofu, "Bright Prospects for Sino-Russian Strategic Cooperation," *Jiefangjun Bao*, 27 April 2006, www.chinamil.com.cn.

17. Kou Hui, "China, Russia, India Begin Strategic Cooperation," *Ta Kung Pao*, 16 August 2006, www.takungpao.com.

18. Yu Sui, Senior Research Fellow, Research Center on Contemporary International Relations, "Resurgent Russia Takes Journey of Development," *Renmin Ribao*, 22 March 2006, http://www.english.peopledaily.com.cn/200603/22/ENG20060322_252582.html.

19. Yan Xuetong, "The Rise of China and Its Power Status," *Chinese Journal of International Politics* 1, no. 1 (2006): 21, 30.

20. "Experts Say China-G8 Ties Promote International Stability," *China Daily*, 17 July 2006, www.chinadaily.com.cn.

21. Ruan Zongze, "Comment: How China Should Get Along with G8?" *Renmin Ribao* (overseas edition), 17 July 2006, www.english.peopledaily.com.cn./200607/17/ENG20060717_283930.html.

22. Chu Shulong, "Right Time to Strengthen Cooperation," *Renmin Ribao*, 19 July 2006, www.peopledaily.com.cn.

23. Interviews, Beijing, 30 June 2006.

24. "Xiong Guangkai: The Road of Peaceful Development Determines That China's Development Is 'Peaceful, Open and Cooperative' Development," Xinhua, 28 December 2005, www.xinhuanet.com/english/.

25. Chen Yurong, "A Model of the New-Type State-to State Relationship," *Liaowang*, 28 March 2006 (World News Connection).

26. Ibid.

27. *Renmin Ribao*'s commentator's article, "Jointly Adding a New Chapter to China-Russia Friendly Relations—Extending Warm Congratulations to the Complete Success of China-Russia 'National Year' Activity," Xinhua, 7 November 2007.

28. Li Shijia and Chang Lu, "The Chinese Foreign Ministry Says the Russian President's Visit to China Will Achieve Four Goals," Xinhua, 20 May 2008.

29. Article 1, "Text of Sino-Russian Treaty," Xinhua, 16 July 2001, www.xinhuanet.com/english/.

30. Luo Hui, Li Zhongfa, and Rong Yan, "Hu Jintao Holds Talks with Russian President Vladimir Putin," Xinhua, 22 March 2006, www.xinhuanet.com/english/.

31. Pyotr Ivanchisin, "Are There Any Problems on the Russian-Chinese Border?" *Granitsa Rossii*, no. 41 (8 November 2006): 6–7; Vladimir Soskyrev, "Duma Communists Want to Know about the Russian-Chinese Solution to the Problem of Disputed Territories," *Nezavisimaya Gazeta*, 25 October 2004, 4. The islands had summer homes belonging to Russians in Khabarovsk, but no permanent residents.

32. Lyudmilla Yermakova, "Russia, China Shorten Bilateral Visa-Free Visits from 30 to 15 Days," ITAR-TASS, September 2006, www.itar-tass.com/eng/.

33. "Chinese Make Up Quarter of Illegal Migrants in Russia: Official," RIA Novosti, 15 September 2006 (ISI Emerging Markets).

34. Interview with Vyacheslav Potavnin, deputy director of the Federal Migration Service, *Rossiyskaya Gazeta*, 13 April 2007.

35. "Rynki bez inostrantsev," *VTsIOM Press-vypusk*, no. 672 [All Russia Center for the Study of Public Opinion Press Release 672], 12 April 2007, www.wciom.ru.

36. The Russian government will pay a flat sum of 60,000 rubles ($2,300) to

those willing to relocate to strategically important border areas (including three on the Sino-Russian border), plus 20,000 rubles ($750) for each family member and a monthly grant equivalent of 50 percent of the cost of living in their area of relocation. Sergei Dmitriyev, "Migration Aggravation," *Moscow News*, 19 January 2007, www.mosnews. com. The fines are 1,100 rubles ($40) for individuals violating migration laws, 44,000 rubles ($1,690) for employers, 550,000 roubles ($21,136) for officials, and 5,550,000 rubles ($211,365) for legal entities. See Tai Adelaja, "New Immigration Rules Aimed at CIS Migrants," *St. Petersburg Times*, 16 January 2007, www.sptimes.ru.

37. "Almost 8 Million Foreigners Were Registered in 2007—Russian Federal Migration Service" [Pochti 8 mln inostrantsev postavleno na uchyet v 2007 godu—FMC RF], RIA Novosti, 31 January 2008; "Russian Official Comments on Migration Figures in 2007," *Ekho Moskvy*, 23 August 2007.

38. Wang Yizhou, deputy director of the Institute of World Economics and Politics, "Three Demands of the New International Order: Some Views on the New Era in Sino-Russian Relations" [Guoji xin zhixu zhi sange yaodian—jianlun xin shiqi de ZhongE guanxi], in *Proceedings from the International Conference on Sino-Russian Relations: Past, Present, Future* [ZhongE guanxi: lishi, xianshi yu weilai. Guoji Huiyi], Chinese Academy of Social Sciences and Russian Academy of Sciences (Beijing: Chinese Academy of Social Sciences [cited hereafter as CASS], 19–20 June 2006), 79–80. I discuss the disconnect between Chinese and Russian views of the migration issue in "The Securitization of Chinese Migration to the Russian Far East: Rhetoric and Reality," in *Migration and Securitisation in East Asia*, ed. Melissa Curley and Wong Siu-lun (New York: Routledge Press, 2008).

39. Li Zhuanxun, director, Institute of Russian Studies, Heilongjiang University, "Current Issues in Sino-Russian Regional Economic Cooperation" [ZhongE quyu jingji hezuo mianlin de wenti], in *Sino-Russian Economic Relations* [ZhongE jingji guanxi], ed. Xue Jundu and Lu Nanquan, 237–45 (Beijing: CASS, 1999).

40. Xia Huanxin, Harbin City Academy of Social Sciences Research Institute for Northeast Asia, "Key Aspects of the Role of Siberia and in the Russian Far East in Sino-Russian Relations" [Xiboliya yu yuandong zai ZhongE guanxizhong de zhongyaoxing], in *Russian Siberia and Far East—The Development of International Political and Economic Relations* [Eluosi xiboliya yu yuandong—guoji zhengzhi jingji guanxi de fazhan], ed. Xue Jundu and Lu Nanquan, 229 (Beijing: World Knowledge Publishing House [Shijie zhishi chubanshe], 2002).

41. On this point, see Li Jingjie (a former director of the Institute of Russia, Eastern Europe and Central Asia, CASS), "A New Era of Sino-Russian Relations" [Xin shijie de ZhongE guanxi], in *Proceedings from the International Conference on Sino-Russian Relations* [ZhongE Guanxi], 96; and Guan Xiulin, professor, Beijing University, "Conditions for Boosting the Level of Sino-Russian Economic Cooperation" [Jin yi bu tuijin ZhongE jingji hezuo shuiping de tiaojian],) in ibid., 135.

42. "China to 'Continuously Promote Strategic Partnership' with Russia—Minister," Xinhua, 21 March 2008.

43. Liu Huaqin, "Prospects for the Complementarity and Development of Sino-

Russian Trade" [ZhongE maoyi hubuxing yu fazhan qianjing], in *Proceedings from the International Conference on Sino-Russian Relations*, 119.

44. Lu Nanquan, senior researcher, Institute of Russia, Eastern Europe and Central Asia, CASS, "The Future of Sino-Russian Energy Cooperation" [ZhongE nengyuan hezuo qianjing], *Xuexi Shibao*, 15 May 2006, 2; Lu Nanquan, "China, Russia Benefit from Energy Cooperation," *China Daily*, July 2006, 4.

45. Chen Wei, president, Liaoning University, "Sino-Russian Economic Cooperation Must Shift from Complementarity to Strategic [Cooperation]" [ZhongE jingji hezuo gai cong hubuxing wang zhanlue], in *Proceedings from the International Conference on Sino-Russian Relations*, 171.

46. "Russian-Chinese Relations: On Right Track," RIA Novosti, 11 September 2006, www.en.rian.ru.

47. Chen Wei, "Sino-Russian Economic Cooperation Must Shift from Complementarity to Strategic [Cooperation]," 172.

48. "Factbox—China-Russia Trade Relations," Reuters, 19 May 2008.

49. "Text of Sino-Russian Joint Communiqué Issued 3 July 2005," Xinhua, 4 July 2005, www.xinhuanet.com/english/; "Full Text of China-Russia Joint Statement on 21st Century World Order," 1 July 2005, Xinhua, 2 July 2005, www.xinhuanet. com/english/; "China and Russia Issue a Joint Statement, Declaring the Trend of the Boundary Line Has Been Completely Determined," Ministry of Foreign Affairs of the People's Republic of China website, 14 October 2004, www.fmprc.gov.cn/ en/wjdt/2649/tl65266.htm; "Chinese, Russian Leaders Sign Joint Declaration text," Xinhua, 27 May 2003; "Xinhua Carries Full Text of 2 December Sino-Russian Joint Declaration," Xinhua, 2 December 2002, www.xinhuanet.com/english/; "Text of Sino-Russian Treaty," Xinhua, 16 July 2001, www.xinhuanet.com/english/.

50. This language had not been seen in the joint statements since 2000. On the report about possible Russian diesel submarine sales to the United States, see Bill Gertz and Rowan Scarborough, "Inside the Ring," *Washington Times*, 25 June 2005, www.washingtontimes.com.

51. Ivan Safronov and Andrei Ivanov, "China Is Aiming to Use the Russian Military to Promote Its Own Objectives," *Kommersant*, 17 March 2005, 9; Anna Arutunyan, "Russia-China War Games a Rehearsal for Invasion?" *Moscow News*, 24 August 2005, www.mosnews.com.

52. Of the ten thousand troops participating, just eighteen hundred were Russian. For a detailed analysis of these exercises, see Elizabeth Wishnick, "Brothers in Arms? Assessing the Sino-Russian Military Exercises," *PACNet* 35, 18 August 2005, http://www.csis.org/pacfor/pacnet.cfm.

53. "International Security Inalienable: Sino-Russian Joint Statement," Xinhua, 23 May 2008.

54. "Russian President Putin Meets Chinese Envoy on N Korea Nuclear Test," Xinhua, 14 October 2006, www.xinhuanet.com/english/.

55. International Crisis Group, *China and North Korea: Comrades Forever?* Crisis Group Asia Report 112, 1 February 2006, 3.

56. "Korea, China Upgrade Partnership," *Korea Herald*, 28 May 2008.

57. International Crisis Group, *China and North Korea*, 28.

58. Liu Libin and Wang Bo, "Chinese Permanent Representative to the UN Says the Security Council Resolution on the DPRK Nuclear Test Expresses a Firm and Appropriate Response," Xinhua, 15 October 2006, www.xinhuanet.com/english/.

59. Cited in Maggie Farley, "Confronting North Korea: Security Council Vote Is Unanimous on Sanctions," *Los Angeles Times*, 15 October 2006, 10.

60. "China to Abide by UN Sanctions against N Korea Foreign Ministry," *AFX Asia*, 17 October 2006 (LexisNexis Academic).

61. "China Reportedly Begins Inspecting Cargo Bound for North," *Yonhap*, 17 October 2006.

62. Wade Boese, "Russia Joins Proliferation Security Initiative," *Arms Control Today*, July/August 2004, www.armscontrol.org.

63. United Nations Department of Public Information, "Security Council Imposes Sanctions on Iran for Failure to Halt Enrichment, Unanimously Adopting Resolution 1737," 23 December 2006, http://www.un.org/News/Press/docs/2006/sc8928.doc.htm.

64. M. K. Bhadrakumar, "China's Middle East Journey via Jerusalem," *Asia Times*, 13 January 2007, www.atimes.com.

65. Sim Chi Yin, "China No Longer 'Spoiler' on Iran N-Issue; It Has Taken Active and Constructive Role to Defuse the Nuclear Crisis," *Straits Times*, 19 April 2008.

66. "China's Top Crude Suppliers in 2007," *Platts Oilgram News*, 28 January 2008.

67. Harsh V. Pant, "Saudi Arabia Woos China and India," *Middle East Quarterly* 13, no. 4 (fall 2006), www.meforum.org/1019/saudi-arabia-woos-china-and-india.

68. "'Text' of Joint Communiqué of China, Russia, India Foreign Ministers' Meeting," Xinhua, 15 May 2008.

69. Kou Hui, "G8 Summit Fosters Strategic Cooperation between China, India, Russia," *Ta Kung Pao*, 16 August 2006 (World News Connection).

70. Chu Shulong, "Right Time to Strengthen Cooperation," *Renmin Ribao*, 19 July 2006 (World News Connection).

71. Chen Jiangyang, deputy director of the Center for Strategic Studies at the China Institute for Modern International Relations, "Draw Up New Periphery Strategy as Soon as Possible," *Liaowang*, 22 July 2006 (World News Connection). Russia provided 95 percent of China's weapons in 2000–2004 and 78 percent of India's during the same period, according to the Stockholm International Peace Research Institute data, www.sipri.org.

72. "Trust Is Key to India-China Relations," *China Post*, 30 January 2008; "Scholars Comment on China-India Ties Ahead of Indian PM's Visit," Xinhua, 12 January 2008.

73. Jim Yardley, "Two Giants Try to Learn to Share Asia," *New York Times*, 13 January 2008, 10; Rama Lakshmi, "For India, Tibet Poses Some Delicate Issues," *Washington Post*, 2 April 2008, A9.

74. "China, Russia, India Hold Trilateral Summit," *China Daily*, 18 July 2006, www.Chinadaily.com.cn.

75. "Full Text of China-India Joint Declaration during Hu Jintao's State Visit," Xinhua, 21 November 2006, www.xinhuanet.com/english/.

76. Dominic Wilson and Roopa Purushothaman, "Dreaming with BRICs: The Path to 2050," Global Economics Paper No. 99, Goldman Sachs, 1 October 2003, www.gs.com.

77. "Build towards a Harmonious World of Lasting Peace and Common Prosperity," speech by Hu Jintao to the United Nations Summit, 15 September 2005, www.fmprc.gov.cn. Also see "Turning Your Eyes to China," speech by Premier Wen Jiabao at Harvard University, 10 December 2003, http://losangeles.china-consulate .org/eng/news/topnews/t56336.htm; Shi Yonming, "Rational Order," no. 51, 21 December 2006, www.beijingreview.com.

78. Jia Qingguo, "Peaceful Development: China's Policy of Reassurance," *Australian Journal of International Affairs* 59, no. 4 (December 2005): 494–95.

79. Hu Jintao, "Speech by Chinese President Hu Jintao, Yale University," 21 April 2006, http://www.fmprc.gov.cn.

80. "Declaration on the Fifth Anniversary of the Shanghai Cooperation Organization," 15 June 2006, http://english.scosummit2006.org, 3.

81. Sun Zhuangzhi, researcher, Russia, Eastern Europe and Central Asia, CASS, "China and Russia Cooperation in the Framework of the SCO: Achievements and Problems" [Zhongguo yu Eluosi zai Shanghai hezuo zuzhi kuangjia nei de hezuo: chengjiu yu wenti], in *Proceedings from the International Conference on Sino-Russian Relations*, 99–100; "World Powers' Relations Feature Cooperation, Competition in 2006," *People's Daily*, http://english.peopledaily.com.cn./299701/03/ENG20070103_337857.html.

82. Interviews with Chinese scholars, Beijing, June 2006.

83. Liu Yantang, "The Misunderstood 'SCO': The Shanghai Cooperation Organization Has Never Sought Confrontation with Any Party," *Liaowang*, 16 June 2006 (World News Connection).

84. "Medvedev Pledges to Build Strategic Partnership with China," RIA Novosti, 24 May 2008.

85. "Putin Says Shanghai Cooperation Organization Not New Warsaw Pact," *Agentstvo Voyennykh Novostey*, 16 June 2006, www.armscontrol.ru.

86. "Text of Joint Communiqué on Meeting between Chinese, Russian Presidents," Xinhua, 24 May 2008.

87. For detailed analysis of the August 2005 spill see United Nations Environment Programme, "The Songhua River Spill, China, December 2005—Field Mission Report," http://www.reliefweb.int/library/documents/2005/unep-chn-31dec

.pdf; and Hans Bruynincks, Sofie Bouteligier, and Stefan Renckens, "Environmental Accidents in China: Virtual Reality's Challenge to the Chinese State," unpublished paper presented to the 48th annual convention of the International Studies Association, 28 February–4 March 2007.

88. Il'ya Sergeev, "Chemical Reaction" [Khimicheskaya reaktsiya], *Vremya Novostey*, 31 August 2006, 4, www.vremya.ru.

89. For blog entries covering the November accident, see EastWestNorthSouth, http://www.zonaeuropa.com/20051123_1.htm.

90. Fu Yong, "Songhuajiang Water Pollution: China Experiences a Test of Its Emergency Capacity" [Songhuajiang shui wuran: Zhongguo gai dui tufa shijian nengli jingshou kaoyan], in *International Status Report 2006* [2006 Zhongguo Guoji Diwei Baogao], ed. Zhang Youwen and Huang Renwei, 321 (Shanghai Academy of Social Sciences, 2006).

91. Shi Jiangtao, "Vice-Mayor of Spill City Kills Himself," *South China Morning Post*, 5 December 2005, A5.

92. "Russia Seeking Tests of China River Slick—Governor," RIA Novosti, 28 August 2006 (ISI Emerging Markets).

93. Paul Holtom, "The Beginning of the End for Deliveries of Russian Major Conventional Weapons to China," 31 March 2008, RIA Novosti, http://en/rian/ru/analysis/20080331/102440239.html.

94. Sergey Luzyanin, "Russian-Chinese Military-Technical Cooperation, Past, Present, Future," *Moskovskiye Novosti*, 17 August 2007; David Lague, "Russia-China Arms Trade Wanes; Fears of Rivalry and a Push for Self-Sufficiency Raise Doubt," *New York Times*, 3 March 2008, 3; Nikita Petrov, "Russian-Chinese Military Relations at a Low Point," RIA Novosti, 27 May 2008.

95. "China's Top Crude Suppliers in 2007," *Platts Oilgram News*, 28 January 2008.

96. Artur Blinov, "Medvedev Finds a Common Language with Hu Jintao," *Nezavisimaya Gazeta*, no. 104, 26 May 2008, 23.

97. Dmitri Kosyrev, UPI commentator, "Outside View: Putin's China Strategy," 20 March 2006, www.spacewar.com.

98. "Chinese Students in Russia Sought After in Job Market," Xinhua, 18 October 2006, www2.chinadaily.com.cn/china/2006-10/17/content_710450.htm.

99. Institute of International Education, "New Enrollments of Foreign Students in the U.S. Climbs in 2005/6," 13 November 2006, http://opendoors.iienetwork.org/?p=89251.

100. Ministry of Education of the People's Republic of China, "International Students in China," http://www.moe.edu.cn/english/international_3.htm (no date but appears to be from late 2006).

101. "China to Set Up Confucius Institutes in Russia," Xinhua, 17 October 2006, www.chinaview.cn.

Part Two

★

Economic Relations and the Energy Factor

4

Economic Integration of China and Russia in the Post-Soviet Era

Richard Lotspeich

Introduction

Although both the People's Republic of China and the Russian Federation have been extensively examined by economists since the advent of the transition from central planning, research on the economic relations between the two countries is relatively scarce. Much of the recent economic literature that treats both countries is concerned with comparing and explaining the different experiences under economic transition. Yet as Russia and China have followed their respective paths away from central planning, their economies have also become increasingly integrated. This is quite natural, as they have a long physical border and a history of economic relations that began in the seventeenth century. Understanding the extent and potential of their economic integration is important because each is a major force in the world economy and geopolitics.

The purpose of this chapter is to add to the existing literature on this subject, primarily from an empirical point of view, and to provide an economic setting for the other contributions to this volume. Features of geography, policy, and the historical relationship between the countries are briefly examined to reveal their influence on economic interactions. Quantitative measures of integration are reviewed and deficiencies in the data are identified. Throughout the chapter I provide perspective on the bilateral relationship by comparing China's and Russia's relations with other countries. Special focus is provided on trade in energy and armaments, as well as on interaction in the border region. Integration through bilateral investment is much less developed than integration through trade, and data are much sketchier here, but some quantitative indicators are reviewed. Finally, a third facet, labor flows and remittances, must be examined for a thorough assessment of integration. While the data here are dodgier still, large-scale labor movement is not evident. But the potential for labor to move from China into Russia is a significant challenge for both governments.

The conception of economic integration I use is simple: when economic transactions involve actors in separate countries, so that an international border is crossed as a consequence of the transaction, this is economic integration.[1] International trade is the quintessential example, but foreign investment, migration of labor, transmittal of remittances, and the extension of foreign aid are other examples of economic integration. Two countries are considered economically integrated when the extent of transactions across their national borders reaches a threshold that is arbitrarily determined. As with integration into the world economy, there is no distinct dividing line. Rather, there is a continuum of integration that is measured by such variables as the share of GDP comprised by imports and exports, the extent of total capital formation supported by cross-border flows of finance or the share of national income coming from remittances, and profit repatriation.

Economists have used other concepts of integration to analyze economic relations between countries or regions. These involve the coordination of economic policies, such as tariffs, labor laws, or a common currency, that support flows of products or factors of production across borders. Construction of infrastructure, like transport and communication facilities, that link economies is another feature of integration. Establishment of common policies or linking infrastructure indicates more extensive and durable economic integration and a long-term commitment to international or interregional ties. The main contemporary case is the European Union. The Council for Mutual Economic Assistance (CMEA), which operated during the Soviet era to promote economic coordination among communist countries, is another example. This kind of policy coordination is not currently a feature of the economic relations between China and Russia, and China was never a member of the CMEA. Moreover, transport ties between China and Russia are not extensive.[2] Yet substantial cross-border transactions have emerged in the post-Soviet era.

Ideally, one would be able to measure all transactions in a bilateral relationship to evaluate the extent of economic integration. This could also be compared to the extent of integration between the countries of interest and the rest of the world to assess the relative importance of the particular bilateral relationship. This would be difficult for any pairing of countries and is even more challenging for the case of China and Russia. Yet, while data is incomplete, there is still plenty of information on which to base an informed assessment. That is the basic objective of this chapter. The best available data

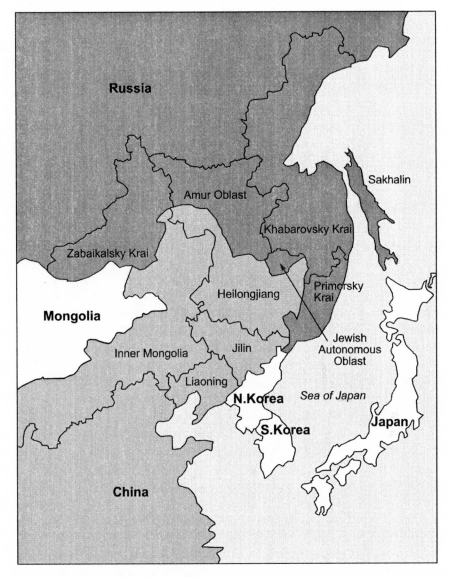

Map 4.1. China-Russia Border Region.

for measuring integration in the present case are bilateral trade flows, but I examine the incomplete data for other indicators as well.

I begin by considering fundamental forces affecting integration of the Chinese and Russian economies. Policies that promote or hinder integration are considered in section 2, although some points of policy are noted elsewhere. The remainder of the chapter is concerned with an assessment of quantitative measures of integration, considering in turn trade, investment, and labor movement. I examine some particular features of integration in detail, including trade in energy and armaments, and the role of the border regions in economic integration.

1. Geography and History

The geographic space that Russia and China occupy brings them together along a short border to the west of Mongolia and along a much longer border (4,300 kilometers) that begins on the eastern end of Mongolia and extends almost to the Pacific coast (see map 4.1). Only a narrow slice of land where Russia has a border with North Korea keeps the frontier between China and Russia from extending to the Pacific Ocean. The short western border is remote from significant populations in both countries and has little economic significance. The eastern border, however, is quite significant economically. This separates Northeast China from the Russian Far East and runs between three political units of China (Jilin and Heilongjiang provinces and the Inner Mongolian Autonomous Region) and five constituent subjects of the Russian Federation (Primorsky and Khabarovsky krais, the Jewish Autonomous Oblast', Amur Oblast', and Zabaikalsky Krai [formerly Chita Oblast']). On the Chinese side, regional economic links with Russia are dominated by Heilongjiang Province, although economic activities related to this border are also present in Jilin and Inner Mongolia and extend even into Liaoning Province. On the Russian side, regional economic links with China are spread across the five subjects, but connections with Zabaikalsky Krai, which borders on Inner Mongolia, are relatively underdeveloped. The more northern parts of the Russian Far East are little affected at present by the border with China.

A second important geographic feature that affects economic integration is the long distance between China and the main economic and population centers of the Russian Federation. The overland distances to western Russia from Northeast China run to thousands of kilometers, and the only significant transportation infrastructure currently spanning this distance is the trans-Siberian railroad. Trade between the dominant economic areas of the two countries occurs as much through maritime transport as across their contiguous border. This suggests that economic integration between China and

Russia is not likely to develop any more rapidly than integration between the European Union and China. Integration that does develop will be highly influenced by economic conditions in the southern part of the Russian Far East.

The historical relationship between the two countries also has played a role in limiting economic integration. Antagonism prevailed in state relations during much of both the tsarist and Soviet periods. From 1960 to 1985 the borders between China and Russia were highly militarized and essentially closed to economic activity.[3] Yet there was a degree of trade between the two communist countries, with the volume growing from around $2 billion in 1985 to around $4 billion by the end of the *perestroika* period.[4] A critical turning point came in 1989 with the historic visit of Mikhail Gorbachev to Beijing, during which essential agreements were reached that lessened security tensions between the countries. These led to further negotiations on economic relations and eventually to the relaxation of strict border controls. After the dissolution of the Soviet Union and the advent of economic transition in Russia, bilateral trade volume began a gradual rise, which was dominated initially by the growth of exports from Russia to China.

While communities in the border region began to take advantage of economic opportunities that liberalization presented, the legacy of tension and suspicion of the Chinese on the part of Russians in the region slowed the rate of economic integration, especially regarding the labor market. The sharp demographic distinctions suggest there would be a significant flow into the Russian Far East from the bordering regions of China, but resistance to this by local residents and regional leaders has prevented a large flow from materializing. This resistance has, at times, placed local government in the Russian Far East at odds with the central authorities in Moscow.

This reveals an essential facet of policy-making in both China and Russia that one must appreciate in order to understand the extent and shape of economic integration between them. Although they have been engaged in transition from centrally planned systems for decades, the legacy of a strong degree of control over economic affairs by both central governments persists. The move toward liberalized economies has freed individuals, private firms, and locally controlled public enterprises to seek economic opportunities across the Chinese-Russian border. But when this activity has raised concerns in Moscow or Beijing, authorities have been able to exert administrative control to impose limits.

While there are tariffs applied on each side, these are not necessarily the primary means of governing bilateral flows between the countries. Controlling access to export or import licenses, travel restrictions imposed on entrepreneurs and laborers, and the development of infrastructure to support integration are mechanisms influencing integration that are at least as important as tariff rates. Yet it is true today, just as during the era of central planning, that control by the center is far from perfect.[5] A striking example of this is the construction of illegal coal-fired power plants in Inner Mongolia.[6] Nonetheless it remains the case in both countries that control over economic activity, especially where it involves international integration, is more extensive than in developed capitalist countries, such as those in the Organization for Economic Cooperation and Development (OECD).

2. Policy Measures Affecting the Bilateral Economic Relationship

Although the Chinese project in economic liberalization started two decades before Russia's, the Chinese proceeded at a much slower pace. In 1992 Russia leapt into a decentralized, market-based economic system and undertook a rapid and widespread privatization that was largely completed by 1997. However, in contrast to policies under Boris Yeltsin, the Vladimir Putin administration took steps to reassert control from the center in several ways that had an important impact on economic relations with China. The more recent transition experience in Russia, in both economic and political dimensions, has much in common with the Chinese approach: tight political control coupled with reliance on market mechanisms and a significant state presence in industries of strategic importance.

Regional representatives of the Russian president were granted increased powers to override decisions by local administrations and even to replace personnel. In the wake of the Beslan hostage crisis in September 2004, the election of local governors was replaced by presidential appointments that are then approved by local legislatures. Potential dissent by local leadership was countered by increasing the influence of the Kremlin over political parties and the media. Finally, the central administration took steps to recapture control over the disposition of natural resources, which is especially relevant to Siberia and the Russian Far East since extractive activity is a key part of those regional economies. As analysis of the commodity composition shows, natural resources figure prominently in Russia's trade with China. Despite some expectation that President Dmitry Medvedev might be more supportive of Russia's private entrepreneurs, it is likely that the general directions set by Putin will continue under Medvedev.

Centralized Administration of Trade

What then are the goals and main policies of the central governments with respect to each other? First, both governments generally treat each other in an objectively commercial fashion, although they are wary of each other in strategic geopolitical terms. While they have made statements about forming an alliance as a counterweight to the United States and have pursued security cooperation through the Shanghai Cooperation Organization and bilateral treaties, in economic relations these concerns are not as important as the commercial advantages from integration. There is little likelihood of subsidized energy exports from Russia as a way of strengthening the political alliance. Both Putin and Yeltsin, and more recently Medvedev, made public statements supporting increased bilateral trade.[7] Putin made similar statements about the goal of increasing bilateral investment.

Although in 1994 Yeltsin declared an objective of $20 billion for trade volume by 2000, it did not reach this level until 2004. By 2007 volume was at around $48 billion, and trade flows at the rate of the first quarter of 2008 would have put the annual trade volume just above $50 billion.[8] There are good reasons to believe that bilateral trade will continue to expand and may increase the relative importance of Russia and China as trade partners. In November 2006, Prime Minister Mikhail Fradkov visited Beijing to conclude economic agreements with Chinese authorities in a variety of areas, including trade, mining, and infrastructure. During this visit, Vice Premier Wu Yi expressed the hope that trade volume would reach $80 billion by 2010.[9] If Russia's energy transport infrastructure were successfully developed, such a target would be reasonable. However, delays in these projects make this an unlikely outcome. (See the chapter by Erica Downs for more details.)

Trade between China and Russia has a peculiar bifurcated structure.[10] On one hand, there is a decentralized trading relationship driven by the interests of individual enterprises, both private and public. This kind of trade plays a dominant role in the border region. On the other hand, there are certain critical sectors where trade is closely governed by the two central governments, and these are more directly influenced by policy. The most important of these are armaments and energy. In recent years China has been Russia's largest customer for military hardware, and Russia has been China's largest external supplier of arms, from tanks and aircraft to submarines. (Section 3 of this chapter evaluates the scale of the armaments trade.)

The greatest unrealized potential in bilateral trade is export of petroleum and natural gas from Russia. This could change a great deal in the near future if Russian pipeline infrastructure is developed to support export to the

Asia-Pacific region and as deliveries from the Sakhalin fields expand. Even during the Soviet era, petroleum and natural gas were leading exports, and they continue to dominate Russian trade. Since 1993 China has been a net importer of oil, and over the past decade Chinese consumption and imports of oil have grown to make it a major importing country. The two countries are natural trading partners in this sector; however, while Russian crude and refined products have been sold to Chinese customers since 1995, export has been restricted by the expense of delivery by train from eastern Siberia and marine routes originating in western Russia. Improvement of the required infrastructure has been delayed by Russia's internal politics of control over natural gas and oil exports.

A number of policies in China may influence its energy imports from Russia. Recent emphasis on building up a domestic automotive industry and growth in household ownership of automobiles will increase demand for automotive fuels from all sources. China is also undertaking early steps to increase the share of natural gas in the national energy mix, partly in response to environmental concerns. As of 2004 there were thirty-nine gas-fired power plants under construction or planned in China.[11] As imports of energy have increased, Chinese officials have grown more concerned with energy security. Two policy responses are likely to increase imports from Russia. One is the establishment of strategic petroleum reserves, which are mostly to be located along the coastal area. This will provide some increase in Chinese demand for crude imports.[12] More significantly for imports specifically from Russia, Chinese authorities seek to diversify their sources of oil and especially want to reduce their reliance on sources in the Middle East and Africa, which transit sea-lanes in the Indian and Pacific oceans beyond the protective reach of the Chinese navy. A pipeline from Russia would help a great deal in this regard.

Tariff Policies

The central governments of both China and Russia exert a great deal of influence over their decentralized trade through both tariff and nontariff measures. According to the World Trade Organization (WTO), in 2005 Russia applied average duties of 8.8 percent on agricultural imports and 9.6 percent on imports of nonagricultural goods. By 2007 Russia had raised these rates to 14.5 percent and 10.5 percent, respectively.[13] China's analogous tariff rates for 2005 were 15.9 percent on agricultural goods and 9.1 percent on non-agricultural goods. In 2007 China's average tariff on agricultural goods was slightly lower, at 15.8 percent.[14] China thus appears more protective of its agricultural sector than Russia, while Russia applies higher tariffs on non-agricultural imports.

However, these are simple average rates rather than trade-weighted averages. A comparison of import duties collected as a proportion of total merchandise suggests Russia has been more restrictive overall. Import duties collected across 2002–2004 amounted to 7 percent of total merchandise imports, but the figure for China came to 2.7 percent for all imports across 1996–1998.[15] The WTO provides limited information on tariffs applied to Russian exports in the bilateral trade since China is a major destination. In 2007 the simple average Chinese tariff that Russian exporters of nonagricultural goods faced was 6.9 percent, but the trade-weighted average was much lower at 2.9 percent. Duty-free imports from Russia comprised 61.4 percent of the total.[16]

A more complete assessment of tariff rates in bilateral trade can be gleaned from the current tariff profiles provided by the WTO combined with commodity composition data from Chinese customs authorities.[17] Using data for 2007, a rough calculation based on the main product groups in bilateral trade results in a trade-weighted average tariff imposed by Russia on Chinese exports at 14.4 percent. The analogous calculation for tariffs that China applies to Russian exports is 7.9 percent. Thus Russia is substantially more protectionist in the bilateral trade than China.

Because both countries utilize a variety of administrative controls and tariffs specific to commodities and to countries in their conduct of trade policy, simple comparison of average tariff rates, weighted or not, is not an adequate assessment of which country may be more protectionist or how tariff policy affects bilateral trade. For example, in 2000 China introduced new duties on certain steel products from Russia as an antidumping action. Two years later the authorities fixed import quotas for Russian steel.[18] China also restricts the amount of refined oil products that nonstate firms can import, with the limit in 2006 set at 22 percent of the total.[19] In the early years of the post-Soviet period, China extended special privileges to the border provinces pertaining to trade with Russia. More recently these have been abolished, supporting a trend toward increased trade with Russia by the more distant provinces of China's southern and eastern regions.[20]

China's policies for international trade have moved toward lower tariffs, greater simplicity, and more transparency in accordance with the rules of the WTO. Economists Eswar Prasad and Thomas Rumbaugh write that Chinese tariffs declined from an average of 40 percent in the early 1990s to 12 percent in 2002.[21] Further reductions have been achieved since then. Yet China need not apply these policies to trade with Russia. Russia has had observer status at the WTO for a number of years but is not yet a member, so assessing the role of tariffs and other trade-related policies in the bilateral relationship requires detailed information on how Russia, in particular, is treated in Chinese trade policy.[22] Similarly, from the Russian perspective there is no uniform policy that applies to China as well as other trading partners. Moreover, in the Russian case regional governments have been especially active in establishing policies that impact foreign trade, primarily toward stimulating exports and protecting local industries from foreign competition.[23]

Administrative Influence on Bilateral Investment and Labor Movement

Policies also affect Chinese-Russian economic integration through foreign direct investment (FDI). As in trade, one can identify a dual structure in which some investment projects are directed closely by central governments and others are undertaken by independent firms. A primary interest of centrally controlled outward Russian FDI is gaining access to energy export infrastructures, particularly for natural gas. Since this is currently a small part of China's energy mix, there is not much interest in investment into China by Gazprom. The centrally directed investment from China is also much concerned with energy, and the Chinese have made repeated efforts to acquire production assets in the Russian energy sector. They have not been greatly successful in this endeavor, however, as the Russian federal authorities have made it increasingly clear that energy resources are considered a strategic asset that should remain under the firm control of the state or at least under the control of domestic producers, who can be closely monitored.

Regarding private, decentralized FDI activities, the central role of policy is to influence the overall business climate. China has been somewhat more successful in attracting FDI than Russia has. This is partly due to the difference in risks foreign investors perceive in the two countries. Russia has been rather unfriendly to foreign firms, while China has nurtured an environment that is conducive to foreign business interests.[24] These policies affect FDI generally, as well as FDI in the bilateral relationship.

The flow of labor between China and Russia consists primarily of Chinese citizens. Although some Russians have relocated in China to manage investment projects and to develop trade connections, there is not broad interest among Russian workers to seek opportunities in China. On the other hand, demographic conditions in the border region and the relative status of agriculture in the two countries provide natural pressures for Chinese to move into Russia. Although the central authorities seek to control this movement and influence it with visa policies and enforcement of worker rights, there is no kind of central policy guiding integration through labor movement, in contrast to many areas of trade.

In the early years of Russian transition Chinese citizens were allowed to enter Russia without visas, leading to a surge in trade, investment, and workers in search of opportunities across the border. Popular reaction against the influx of Chinese nationals into the Russian Far East was followed by tightening of border restrictions in 1994, including a reimposition of visa requirements. Consequently, bilateral economic activity fell off, although it has since recovered and now far exceeds the peak reached before 1994. Russian policy also restricts labor flows by limiting the number of migrant worker visas. Permits for Asians working in the Russian Far East in 2004 were limited to 41,000.[25] Some Chinese workers have reacted by entering Russia on tourist visas instead, making them illegal migrants.

3. Bilateral Trade Problems

In seeking data to describe quantitatively the growing integration of the Chinese and Russian economies one finds illuminated and dark areas. Data on bilateral trade are fairly complete, including both aggregate amounts and observations on commodity composition. For trade in armaments, essentially an export from Russia to China, good data are available from the Stockholm International Peace Research Institute (SIPRI).

Aggregate Trade Volumes

Aggregate data on bilateral trade is presented in table 4.1. Because there are discrepancies between the Russian and Chinese reporting, I present four time series: Chinese data on import from and export to Russia, and Russian data on export to and import from China. These figures are derived from the IMF's *Direction of Foreign Trade Statistics* and adjusted to real dollar terms using a GDP deflator for the United States.[26] Several comments are pertinent.

First, through 2006 Russia consistently ran a trade surplus with China, unlike most industrialized economies. But for 2007 and the first quarter of 2008, the Russian trade balance with China was in deficit. This remains so even when we add in Russia's exports of armaments to China, which are not recorded in standard trade statistics (see table 4.6). If the substantial potential for additional energy exports is actualized, it is likely that Russia will again run a surplus in trade with China. Second, all four data series reveal significant increases in trade. According to Chinese data, imports from Russia increased by a factor of around 4 and exports to Russia by a factor of around 9 from 1992 to 2007.[27] These correspond to annual average growth rates of 10 and 16 percent, respectively, above Chinese growth in real GDP as reported

Table 4.1. Chinese–Russian Bilateral Trade, 1992–2008

	1992	1993	1994	1995	1996	1997	1998	1999	2000	2001	2002	2003	2004	2005	2006	2007	est.[a] 2008	Period Growth[b] Factor	Rate[c]
Chinese Data																			
Export to Russia	2,705	3,046	1,748	1,817	1,804	2,133	1,900	1,530	2,233	2,651	3,380	5,672	8,315	11,688	13,567	23,773	21,743	8.8	15.6
Import from Russia	4,066	5,641	3,840	4,124	5,494	4,281	3,759	4,315	5,769	7,773	8,067	9,141	11,081	14,054	15,032	16,383	19,484	4.0	9.7
As Shares of Total Trade (%)																			
Export to Russia	2.7	2.9	1.3	1.1	1.1	1.1	1.0	0.8	0.9	1.0	1.1	1.4	1.5	1.7	1.6	2.3	2.2		
Import from Russia	4.3	4.8	3.0	2.9	3.7	2.9	2.6	2.5	2.6	3.3	2.8	2.4	2.2	2.4	2.2	2.1	2.2		
Russian Data																			
Export to China	3,169	3,471	3,144	3,666	4,991	4,173	3,259	3,552	5,233	3,926	6,517	7,670	9,154	11,544	13,485	14,519	17,713	4.6	10.7
Import from China	1,932	2,642	1,055	939	1,061	1,321	1,188	909	948	1,573	2,286	3,074	4,324	6,404	11,046	25,434	23,917	13.2	18.7
As Shares of Total Trade (%)																			
Export to China	6.9	7.0	4.5	4.4	5.6	4.7	4.4	4.8	5.1	4.9	6.3	6.2	6.0	5.5	5.4	5.1	5.3		
Import from China	4.8	8.7	2.5	1.9	2.2	2.4	2.7	2.9	2.8	4.4	5.2	5.8	6.9	7.4	9.7	12.7	10.5		
Data Discrepancy[d] (%)																			
Rus. Imp. vs Chin. Exp. (D1)	-40	-15	-66	-94	-70	-61	-60	-68	-136	-69	-48	-85	-92	-82	-23	7	9		
Chin. Imp. vs Rus. Exp. (D2)	22	38	18	11	9	3	13	18	9	49	19	16	17	18	10	11	9		

Sources: Trade data: IMF, *Direction of Trade Statistics Database*, accessed 7 August 2008.
Price index: U.S. GDP deflator, Bureau of Economic Analysis, U.S. Department of Commerce: http://www.bea.gov/bea/dn/nipaweb/NIPATableIndex.asp, accessed 28 September 2008.

Note: Trade levels are in millions of constant 2000 US$. Shares are in percent of total export and import.

[a] Estimate calculated as four times first quarter trade flows.
[b] Growth calculations exclude 2008 data to avoid seasonality bias.
[c] Average annual growth rate in % for 1992–2007.
[d] Calculated as percentage of recorded imports.

from official sources.[28] The Russian data begin with smaller trade flows in 1992 and show roughly comparable growth across the period. Russian exports to China increased by a factor of around 5, and imports from China by a factor of 13. Third, growth paths for all series are rather volatile. Standard deviations of the annual growth rates are over twice the period average, with some year-on-year changes in the trade flows being negative. This has not been a steady path of increasing integration.

Comparing these increases against the growth in total trade for China and Russia shows shifts in the relative importance of the bilateral relationship, reviewed below in comparison to these countries' trade with other key trading partners. The basic lesson from the shares presented in table 4.1 is that while the Chinese and Russian economies have become more integrated since 1992, there is no special story here. The pattern essentially follows their integration with the world economy, which has been substantial for both since the advent of economic transition. Across the same period China's exports to the world (in real terms) grew at an average annual rate just below 17 percent, slightly above growth in Chinese exports to Russia. Russia's exports to the world grew at an average annual rate of 13 percent, well above the growth of Russian exports to China. Chinese imports from the world grew at just above 15 percent, well above the growth of imports from Russia, and Russian imports from the world increased at just over 11 percent, while imports from China grew at about 19 percent. These different growth rates are evident in the changes in trade shares shown in table 4.1.[29]

Discrepancies in reporting from the two countries are intriguing. A rough measure is reported in the lower rows of table 4.1. The discrepancy in the flow of goods from China to Russia is calculated as the difference between Russia's reports of bilateral imports and Chinese reports of bilateral exports divided by Russia's import figures. Because imports are reported in c.i.f. terms and exports are f.o.b., one expects Russia's reports of imports from China to be slightly larger than China's reports of exports to Russia. The rule of thumb in international trade statistics is 10 percent, which accounts for freight and insurance charges. A similar measure is constructed for the flow of goods from Russia to China. Thus the figures in the two bottom rows ought to run close to 10. In trade statistics from the Soviet period this pattern prevailed, but from the advent of transition in Russia (1992) discrepancies emerged that were well outside this range and highly variable.[30] In recent years Chinese and Russian reporting of their trade relations seem to have reestablished consistency.

The data show that Russian reports of imports from China were much less than Chinese reports of exports to Russia. A similar discrepancy measure for the flow of goods from Russia to China (relative to Chinese import reporting) also indicates that Russian statistics were low compared to China's, but the discrepancy here was not nearly as large. Russian economist Liudmila Popova suggests that these discrepancies were due to "unorganized trade."[31] However, this does not really explain why they did not enter the trade statistics, as balance of payments accounting would require. Explanations are likely to be found in how local currency measures were converted into dollar terms, by attempts to avoid tariffs or other restrictions on trade, and possibly activity in the shadow economies. Smuggling appears to be part of the explanation.[32]

It is widely known, for example, that Russian fishing vessels sell product abroad without reporting it to the Russian authorities.[33] The level of fish imports from Russia reported in Chinese customs statistics was sufficiently high to remove the discrepancy in the last line of table 4.1, at least for the years in which I have data on fish imports. Resolving all the discrepancies, however, will require further research, especially regarding Russia's imports from China. Given the recent reversion to normal differences due to f.o.b. versus c.i.f. reporting, this anomaly may apply only to the early Russian transition period. As there is little gain to traders from over-invoicing foreign transactions, I suggest that the Chinese data is more reliable and I use this to construct figure 4.1 showing the trend in bilateral trade for the past seventeen years.

To illustrate the relative importance of trade between China and Russia, table 4.2 presents data comparing the shares and ranks of key trading partners against the bilateral Chinese-Russian trade shares. Since Japan is a major economy close to both Russia and China, I include it in this comparison. Examination of the distribution of trade does not reveal any surprises. Russia's trade is predominantly with Europe and the former Soviet republics, although the United States was also an important partner in the middle and late 1990s. In recent years China ranks ahead of the United States as a Russian trade partner, for both imports and exports. Chinese trade has a strong orientation to Asia, especially Japan and South Korea, but the United States also figures prominently in China's trade, particularly in regard to exports; the United States has absorbed roughly a fifth of Chinese exports since 2000. China's trade with the United States remains at several multiples of China's trade with Russia. Figures 4.2 and 4.3 show these relative trade positions graphically for 1992 and 2007.

Data across the past decade and a half indicate that in the bilateral relationship China is somewhat more important in Russia's trade than is Russia in China's trade. Although in 1992 Russia was ranked fourth as both destination and source in Chinese trade, in 2007 Russia was ranked as the

Figure 4.1. China's Trade with Russia, 1992-2008

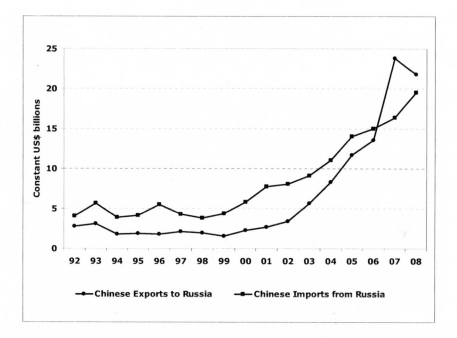

ninth largest trade partner, for both imports and exports. A stronger trade connection is seen in Russian exports to China. Since 1992 China has consistently been ranked in the top five destinations for Russian exports. In recent years China has also become a leading source of Russia's imports, displacing not only Japan and the United States, but also Ukraine and Kazakhstan. Completion of Russian infrastructure for delivery of oil and natural gas to the Pacific Ocean would enhance the position of Russia as an import source for China and of China as an export destination for Russia. But aside from this potential, which is uncertain, there is little reason to expect further enhancement of their relative positions in each other's trade relations.

Commodity Structure of Bilateral Trade

Further understanding of the trade relationship is revealed by examination of the commodity composition of the bilateral trade flows. Data on this are presented in table 4.3 (page 101) and illustrated in figures 4.4 and 4.5 (pages 102–3).[34] Industrial materials (base metals, chemicals, wood, and pulp and paper) and energy have dominated the flow of goods from Russia to China, although the share of metals and chemicals has fallen in recent years. The level of chemicals has almost doubled, but as a fraction of total trade it fell

Table 4.2. Shares for Key Trading Partners and Chinese-Russian Bilateral Trade

	1992		1995		2000		2005		2007	
	Share	Rank	Share	Rank	Share	Rank	Share	Rank	Share	Rank
Russian Export to:		b								
Germany	14.7	1	7.8	2	9.0	1	8.3	2	9.5	1
China	6.9	3	4.4	5	5.1	5	5.5	4	5.1	5
United States	1.7	16	6.6	3	7.7	2	3.1	12	4.8	7
Japan	3.9	9	4.1	8	2.7	13	1.6	19	2.6	14
Totalª	27		23		24		18		22	
Chinese Export to:		c								
United States	10.1	2	16.6	2	20.9	1	21.4	1	19.1	1
Japan	13.7	1	19.1	1	16.7	2	11.0	2	8.4	2
South Korea	2.8	4	4.5	3	4.5	3	4.6	3	4.6	3
Russia	2.7	5	1.1	10	0.9	16	1.7	8	2.3	9
Totalª	29		41		43		39		34	
Russian Import from:		b								
Germany	19.2	1	14.1	2	11.5	1	13.6	1	16.2	1
China	4.8	5	1.9	15	2.8	9	7.4	3	12.7	2
Japan	4.8	4	1.6	17	1.7	14	6.0	4	4.8	5
United States	8.2	3	5.7	4	8.0	4	4.7	6	3.4	9
Totalª	37		23		24		32		37	
Chinese Import from:		c								
Japan	16.7	1	22.0	1	18.4	1	15.2	1	14.0	1
South Korea	3.2	25	7.8	3	10.3	2	11.6	2	10.9	2
United States	10.9	2	12.2	2	9.9	3	7.4	3	7.3	3
Russia	4.3	4	2.9	5	2.6	5	2.4	7	2.1	9
Totalª	35		45		41		37		34	

Source: Calculations based on data from IMF, *Direction of Trade Statistics Database,* accessed 7 August 2008.

Note: Shares are percentage of total export or import. Ranks are based on shares relative to all trading partners.

ªTotal across countries represented.
ᵇRanking for 1992 excludes Russian trade with former Soviet republics.
ᶜRanking is for 1990.

by two-thirds. The share of base metals has fallen from over a third of imports to only 7 percent, with the absolute level remaining roughly constant. As noted elsewhere in this volume (chapters by Gilbert Rozman and Elizabeth Wishnick), China's imports of engineering products from Russia (vehicles and mechanical machinery) have fallen off considerably, to the disappointment of Russia's leaders. In the 1990s such products comprised as much as a fifth of China's imports from Russia, but recently they make up less than 1 percent.

Another interesting element is the significant presence of fish, which reflects the proximity of China to the fishing industry of the Russian Far East.

Figure 4.2. Comparison of Chinese and Russian Export Shares, 1992 and 2007

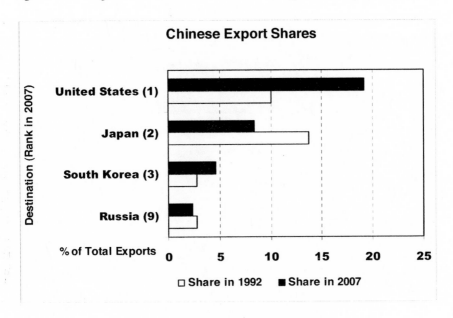

Chinese Export Shares

Russian Export Shares

Figure 4.3. Comparison of Chinese and Russian Import Shares, 1992 and 2007

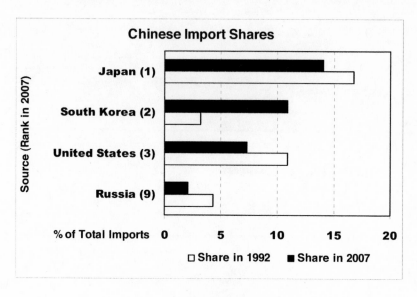

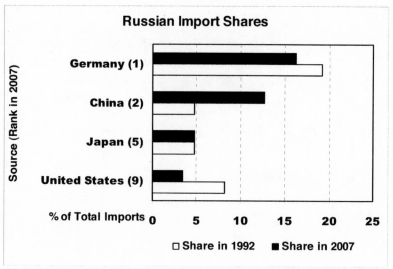

Table 4.3. Evolution of Commodity Composition in Chinese-Russian Bilateral Trade, 1995–2008

Chinese Imports from Russia	1995		1998		2002		2004		2006		2007[a]		2008[a,b]	
Product Group[a]	Value	Share	Value	Share	Value	Share	Value	Share	Value	Share	Value	Share	Value	Share
Base Metals (XV)	1,351	36	940	26	1,395	17	2,074	17	1,133	6	1,331	7	1,785	7
Mineral Fuels (V:27)	201	5.3	116	3.2	1,284	15	4,188	35	9,464	54	9,298	47	13,534	52
Chemicals (VI)	1,193	31	778	21	1,217	14	1,668	14	1,790	10	2,005	10	2,278	9
Wood (IX)	35	0.9	134	3.7	1,059	13	1,437	12	2,162	12	2,984	15	3,074	12
Vehicles (XVII)	94	2.5	414	11	994	12	347	2.9	19	0.1	25	0.1	14	0.1
Fish (1:03)[c]	116	3.0	277	8	623	7	779	6	1,211	7	1,337	7	1,197	4.6
Mech. Machinery (XVI: 84)	240	6	399	11	598	7	162	1.3	124	0.7	157	0.8	166	0.6
Pulp & Paper (X)	54	1.4	268	7	505	6	550	4.5	638	4	775	3.9	946	3.7
Other	515	14	317	9	733	9	922	8	1,012	6	1,718	9	2,889	11
Total	3,799	100	3,641	100	8,407	100	12,127	100	19,630	100	19,630	100	25,883	100

Chinese Exports to Russia	1995		1998		2002		2004		2006		2007		2008	
Product Group[a]	Value	Share	Value	Share	Value	Share	Value	Share	Value	Share	Value	Share	Value	Share
Apparel & Textiles (XI)	340	20	512	28	890	25	2,376	26	4,228	27	9,625	34	5,810	19
Leather Goods (VIII)	323	19	477	26	588	17	2,314	25	1,082	7	807	3	691	2
Footwear (XII)	145	9	174	9	495	14	834	9	1,422	9	1,891	7	1,818	6
Elec. Mach. & Electronics (XVI:85)	59	3.6	54	2.9	310	9	839	9	2,158	14	3,720	13	4,738	16
Meat & Prep. Food (1:02+IV:16-22,24)[d]	383	23	222	12	261	7	314	3.5	437	3	691	2	754	2
Mech. Machinery (XVI: 84)	34	2.1	26	1.4	196	6	534	6	1,540	10	2,655	9	4,369	14
Vegetable Products (II)	101	6	87	4.7	172	4.9	244	2.7	346	2	404	1	532	2
Base Metals (XV)	59	3.5	18	1.0	85	2.4	327	3.6	1,108	7	2,354	8	3,116	10
Vehicles (XVII)	8.3	0.5	3.9	0.2	25	0.7	104	1.1	668	4	2,003	7	2,686	9
Other	213	13	267	14	498	14	1,211	13	2,843	18	4,334	15	5,787	19
Total	1,665	100	1,840	100	3,521	100	9,098	100	15,832	100	28,484	100	30,302	100

Sources: China Customs *Statistics Yearbook*, 1995, 1998, 2002, 2004, and 2006. Calculations by the author.

[a] Data for 2007 and 2008 are from the China database of CEIC Data Co., Ltd., which is derived from the Chinese General Administration of Customs. Since the same level of detail was not available, strict comparability with earlier data is not possible for two categories. See [d].

Note: Values in millions of current US$; shares are percent of total trade activity with Russia.

[a] Commodity classification codes given in parentheses, based on Harmonized System of product nomenclature developed by the World Customs Organization.

[b] Figures for 2008 are estimates based on data for January–August.

[c] Figures for 2007 and 2008 are inferred from Section I total by applying the share of fish (I:03) from 2006. This was 99.7%.

[d] Figures for 2007 and 2008 are for Section IV total, which excludes meat and includes div. 23—waste from food industry.

Figure 4.4. Commodity Composition of Chinese Imports from Russia, 1995 and 2007

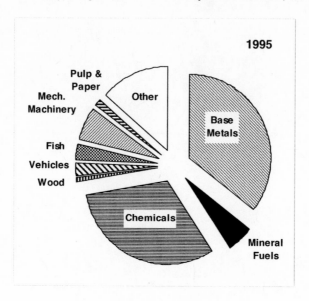

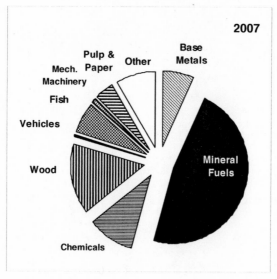

Figure 4.5. Commodity Composition of Chinese Exports to Russia, 1995 and 2007

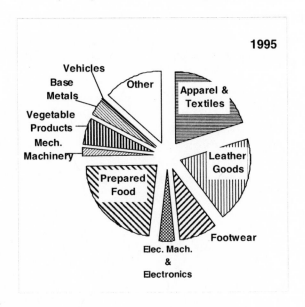

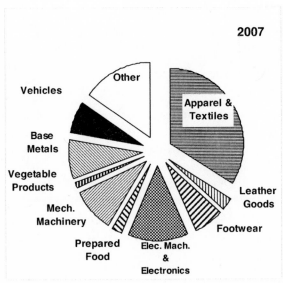

In nominal dollar terms this element of the import mix increased by a factor of 11 from 1995 to 2007, with the share roughly doubling. Although the rate of increase has slowed recently, fish will likely continue to be prominent in China's imports from Russia. The share of wood has also grown, from around 1 percent in 1995 to 15 percent in 2007.[35] As of 2003, China replaced Japan as the main destination of Siberian timber, receiving 80 percent of the total exports from the region.[36]

The most significant change in composition is the growing share of mineral fuels (primarily petroleum, although there is also some coal and a very small amount of gaseous hydrocarbons), which increased from 5 percent of China's imports from Russia in 1995 to around half of all imports in 2006–2008. This share could increase further if Russia's transport infrastructure to the east is developed and as product flows from Sakhalin oil and gas projects reach their potential. It is nearly certain that energy will continue to dominate Russia's exports to China.

Consumer goods make up most of the flow of commodities from China to Russia. Three categories—leather goods, textiles and apparel, and footwear—account for 40 to 60 percent between 1995 and 2007. In the mid-1990s, there was also a significant share of food in the mix, which was likely driven by trade activity in the Russian Far East. This was especially notable in 1995, when the share of prepared foods reached 23 percent of the total. The main force behind this was the collapse of the Russian commodity distribution system inherited from the Soviet Union. Due to its distance from western Russia as well as generally chaotic conditions in product distribution, the Russian Far East experienced particular hardship in obtaining consumer goods, including food. The solution was to turn to China. Although this flow abruptly diminished in the late 1990s, partly in response to ruble devaluation, from 1998 to 2007 food imports from China increased by a factor of 3 (in nominal dollar terms) even as food's share fell from 12 to 2 percent.

The increase in China's exports of vehicles and other transportation equipment to Russia has been extraordinary, albeit starting from a small base. From 1995 to 2007 the value in nominal dollars rose by a factor of 241 and reached 7 percent of all exports to Russia in 2007. Given that Chinese industrial leaders seek to raise their level of manufacturing technology, including in the automotive sector, a significant part of the growing Russian demand for cars may well be met by Chinese producers in the future. Finally, it is worth noting that other machinery (both mechanical and electrical) and electronics comprise a substantial part (20 to 30 percent in 2006–2008) of China's exports to Russia. However, China's exports to many other industrialized countries show much larger shares of such manufactures.

Table 4.4. Comparing the Composition of China's Trade: Russia vs. EU, United States, and World

					Percent Shares[a]			
Chinese Imports from:	Russia		European Union		United States		World	
Product Group[b]	2004	2007	2004	2007	2004	2007	2004	2007
Animals & Animal Products (I)	6.4	6.8	0.6	0.7	1.2	2.1	0.7	0.7
Mineral Fuels (V:27)	35	47	0.3	0.3	0.7	0.6	8.6	11.6
Chemicals (VI)	14	10	8.5	8.6	12	11	7.6	7.6
Plastics & Rubber (VII)	3.5	2.8	4.2	5.1	6.0	7.5	5.8	6.1
Wood (IX)	12	15	0.4	0.4	0.8	0.9	0.9	0.9
Base Metals (XV)	17	7	8.0	10.3	5.7	6.6	8.7	8.6
Mechanical Machinery (XVI: 84)	1.3	0.8	34	27.7	18	16	16	14
Elec. Machinery & Electronics (XVI: 85)	0.5	0.3	18	16.8	18	19	25	29
Vehicles, Aircraft, Trans. Equip. (XVII)	2.9	0.1	11	14.1	7.1	10.9	3.5	3.9
Instruments (XVIII)	0.1	0.1	5.8	5.3	7.8	7.1	7.4	7.9
Other	8	10	9	11	24	19	15	10
Total value in US$ millions	12,127	19,630	70,093	111,041	44,657	68,589	561,229	899,301

Chinese Exports to:	Russia		European Union		United States		World	
Product Group[b]	2004	2007	2004	2007	2004	2007	2004	2007
Leather Goods (VIII)	25	3	2.4	1.7	2.6	1.8	2.3	1.3
Apparel & Textiles (XI)	26	34	10	11	7.3	9.9	15	14
Footwear (XII)	9.2	6.6	2.7	2.4	5.7	4.3	3.1	2.5
Base Metals (XV)	3.6	8.3	6.8	10	7.0	7.7	7.4	9.5
Mechanical Machinery (XVI: 84)	5.9	9.3	27	24	24	22	20	19
Elec. Machinery & Electronics (XVI: 85)	9.2	13	22	23	21	24	22	25
Vehicles, Aircraft, Trans. Equip. (XVII)	1.1	7.0	4.3	5.0	4.3	3.8	3.5	4.5
Misc. Manufactures (XX)	3.6	3.7	6.9	6.8	12	11	6.0	5.7
Other	16	15	18	16	16	15	21	19
Total value in US$ millions	9,098	28,484	107,152	245,231	124,942	232,272	593,326	1,214,530

Sources: Data for 2004 are from the *China Customs Statistics Yearbook*. Calculations by the author. Data for 2007 are from the China database of CEIC Data Co., Ltd., derived from the Chinese General Administration of Customs. Calculations by the author.

[a]Shares are percent of total trade activity with designated country/region.
[b]Commodity classification codes given in parentheses, based on Harmonized System of product nomenclature developed by the World Customs Organization.

Table 4.4 compares the commodity composition of Chinese-Russian bilateral trade with the composition of China's trade with the European Union, the United States, and the world. There are both similarities and distinctions. Distinctions are more prominent in China's import mix. The main categories imported from Russia (mineral fuels and wood) are barely represented in China's imports from the European Union and the United States. In earlier years, basic industrial goods like chemicals and metals were a larger part of China's import mix from Russia vis-à-vis imports from other industrialized economies. However, data for 2007 show the EU and the U.S. proportions are roughly the same. Another contrast is the high share of engineering products (machinery and vehicles) coming from Europe (about 60 percent of China's imports from the EU) and the United States (about 45 percent). These categories made up less than 5 percent of imports from Russia in 2004, and the share fell to 1.2 percent in 2007.[37] China's imports of instruments are likewise more strongly represented in trade with the EU and the United States than with Russia.

The significant share of consumer goods in China's export mix is found in all three destinations represented here, but the share is magnified in the case of Russia, where leather goods, textiles, and footwear comprised over 60 percent of Chinese exports in 2004 and 43 percent in 2007. Machinery and electronics are strongly represented in China's exports to all three destinations, but their share of export to Russia was much smaller.

These limited comparative data suggest four general conclusions. First, as is well known from anecdotal evidence, China's imports from Russia are more strongly oriented to primary products. Second, China relies much more on the European Union and the United States than on Russia for imports that are technologically sophisticated. Third, the composition of Chinese exports to Russia is trending toward the pattern in exports to other developed economies. Fourth, the composition of China's trade with Russia, for both exports and imports, is much more dynamic, showing larger changes than the relatively stable compositions seen in China's trade with both the EU and the United States.

Chinese Imports of Energy from Russia

The basic energy relationship between China and Russia is straightforward. China needs foreign energy supplies and Russia has the natural resources to offer. Moreover, several oil and gas fields are located relatively close to China. However, political considerations complicate this straightforward economic situation. The chapter by Erica Downs addresses both energy trade and the politics surrounding it in more detail, while the chapter by Gilbert Rozman also touches on energy in the context of strategic geopolitical relations. Attention here is narrowly focused on the economics and available statistical information.

Table 4.5 contains data on bilateral energy trade. Although coal is a part of the mix, China has abundant coal resources of its own. The level of coal imports has fluctuated with no discernible trend, reaching a high in 2005 of $58 million. But across the entire period the share of coal in the total energy imports from Russia averaged only 2.5 percent by value. The share of electricity is even smaller, averaging less than 0.5 percent, and summing to only $51 million for all fourteen years. Chinese customs data show negligible amounts of gaseous hydrocarbons imported from Russia, totaling only $1.8 million.

As this commodity group includes natural gas, in the long term it could grow substantially, but up to the present it has essentially not been a part of the import mix.

The main story of energy trade is the huge growth of China's petroleum imports from Russia, both crude oil and refined products. The physical quantity data from table 4.5 are also shown in figure 4.6. From 1995 to 2008 the physical quantity of refined products nearly quadrupled, and crude oil increased by a factor of 343. During the Soviet period and the early post-Soviet years, China may have imported some refined products and possibly some crude oil from Russia, but consistent data begins in 1995 when crude and refined products combined were less than 5 percent of China's imports from Russia. This grew rapidly across the past thirteen years, reaching a share of 54 percent by 2008. Russian companies provided only 0.1 percent of China's crude oil imports in 1995; by 2005 this share was over 10 percent, although more recently it has fallen to around 8 percent. A few years ago Chinese oil industry analysts believed it beneficial and possible for this share to rise to 30 percent as early as 2010.[38] This now seems extremely unlikely given both technical transport problems and heightened concern over the reliability of Russia as an energy partner.

The technical problem of expanding this trade lies in infrastructure development that will facilitate Russian energy exports to Asia. Pipelines for both oil and natural gas are either under construction or in planning stages to begin product delivery by 2010–2011. There are also issues of a political nature. First, China faces competition from Korea and Japan for access to energy resources, including Russian exports of oil and gas. This was especially evident in the competing eastern oil pipeline proposals reported in the press throughout 2004. With Gazprom and Rosneft taking ascendant roles in the development of Sakhalin hydrocarbons, Japan's intent to import from that source becomes more vulnerable to Chinese offers to buy product. Second, the political climate between China and Russia could influence this commercial relationship. The diplomacy around the dismantling of the Yukos oil company in 2003–2004 suggests that governments in both countries will seek to preserve commercial ties, but cautious Chinese leaders seeking energy security may choose to limit their exposure to uncertain Russian suppliers.[39] The decline of Russian oil deliveries to China since 2006 may indicate that a plateau has been reached at which China will rely on Russia for only about 10 percent of imports.

Some other features of table 4.5 bear mentioning. Refined oil products continue to be a significant part of Russian oil exports to China. From the Soviet period through 2002 they constituted the major part, but with the

Table 4.5. China's Energy Imports from Russia, 1995–2008

	1995	1996	1997	1998	1999	2000	2001	2002	2003	2004	2005	2006	2007	2008[h]	Period Growth Factor	Rate[i]
Dollar Value[a,b,sa]																
Coal	9.0	17.6	8.0	7.8	n.a.	n.a.	5.9	37.2	25.2	34.1	58	n.a.	20.6	0.001	--	--
Crude Oil	4.8	49	66	16	82	320	327	664	1,102	2,938	4,958	7,491	7,220	9,290	1953	79
Refined Oil Products	82	165	341	85	240	444	462	717	946	1,189	1,513	1,881	2,044	3,539	19	26
Electrical Power	3.1	2.6	2.3	0.40	3.0	2.3	3.0	3.0	3.0	5.9	9.6	10.0	2.7	0.12	--	--
Total	199	234	418	109	324	767	798	1,421	2,076	4,167	6,539	9,383	9,287	12,829	64	38
Energy Share (%)[y,sb]	5.2	4.5	10.2	3.0	7.7	13	10	17	21	34	41	53	47	54	10	20
Physical Quantity[b,sa]																
Crude Oil[d]	37	319	475	145	572	1,477	1,766	3,478	5,255	10,777	12,776	15,966	14,526	12,537	343	57
Share of Total (%)[e,sc]	0.10	0.71	0.70	0.25	0.88	1.5	1.9	3.4	4.0	8.8	10.1	8.21	n.a.	n.a.	--	--
Refined Products[d]	1,309	1,235	3,450	888	2,069	2,511	2,911	4,414	4,996	5,548	5,128	5,163	4,920	4,935	3.8	11
Total Crude & Products	1,346	1,554	3,925	1,033	2,641	3,987	4,677	7,892	10,251	16,325	17,904	21,128	19,446	17,472	13	22
Crude Oil (1,000 bpd)[f]	0.8	6.6	9.8	3.0	12	30	36	71	108	221	263	328	298	258	--	--
Refined Products (1,000 bpd)[f]	27	25	71	18	43	52	60	91	103	114	105	106	101	101	--	--
Electrical Power[g]	139	124	89	17	132	122	167	158	152	315	491	479	121	4.6	--	--
Implicit Prices																
Crude Oil ($/met. ton)	130	154	140	110	143	217	185	191	210	273	388	469	497	741	5.7	14
Refined Oil Products ($/met. ton)	139	134	99	96	116	177	159	162	189	214	295	364	415	717	5.2	13
Crude Oil ($/bbl)[f]	17.4	20.6	18.6	14.6	19.0	28.9	24.7	25.5	28.0	36.3	51.7	62.6	66.3	98.8	--	--
Electrical Power ($/mwh)[f]	22.6	21.4	25.6	23.1	23.1	19.3	18.0	18.8	19.5	18.8	19.6	21.0	22.4	26.0	--	--
OPEC crude price[sd] $/bbl	16.9	20.3	18.7	12.3	17.5	27.6	23.1	24.4	28.1	36.1	50.6	61.1	69.1	106.3	6.3	15

Sources:

[a][b]Customs General Administration of P.R. China, data provided by EIA CCS Information Service Center, Hong Kong. Data for 1994–2006 received 31 January 2007. Data for 2007 and 2008 received August 2008. Coal data for 1995–2006 received 15 February 2007, via personal communication with Liu Junting, visiting scholar from Liaoning University.

[a][b]Total imports derived from IMF, *Direction of Trade Statistics Database*, accessed 7 August 2008.

[b][c]Total Chinese imports of crude oil from Asian Development Bank, Key Indicators, http://www.adb.org/Documents/Books/Key_Indicators/2008/Country.asp, accessed 18 October 2008.

[c][d]OPEC website: http://www.opec.org/home/basket.aspx, accessed 30 January 2007 and 18 October 2008.

[a]Millions of current US$, in c.i.f. terms.

[b]Coal represented by HS code 2701; crude by HS code 2709; refined products by HS code 2710; electricity by HS code 2716. HS code 2710 may include small amounts of refined products for nonenergy uses, such as pentanes, as well as waste oils.

[c]Share of total imports from Russia. Excludes coal in 1999, 2000, and 2006 from energy imports.

[d]Thousands of metric tons per year.

[e]Share of China's total crude oil imports.

[f]Converted using 7.5 bbl/ton and 365 days/year.

[g]Gigawatt hours per year.

[h]Annual estimate based on imports for January to June. Calculated as two times January–June totals.

[i]Average annual growth rate in %.

Figure 4.6. China's Imports of Petroleum from Russia, 1995-2008

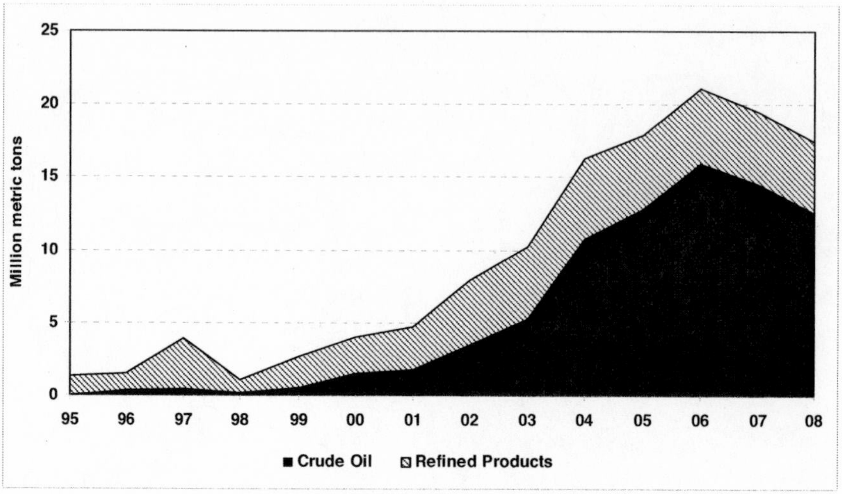

tripling of crude deliveries from 2003–2006, refined products more recently comprise only around a third of the total. But this is still substantial at $2.0 and $3.5 billion in 2007 and 2008. Although the value of oil deliveries, both crude and products, have increased hugely, a part of this is due to price increases. The implicit prices calculated from the data on values and quantities show increases by factors of 5.7 for crude and 5.2 for products, which still leaves quantity as the dominant force in the increase of import value for crude oil.

It is also interesting to note how closely the implicit price paid by China for Russian crude follows world prices. The correlation coefficient between the implicit price from the trade data and the OPEC basket price (bottom row of table 4.5) is equal to 0.998. Moreover, the Russian price is within $2/barrel of the OPEC price for almost all years. What these observations make clear is that China is not getting any special price deals on Russian crude. An anomaly here is that refined products are priced below crude for all years except 1995, sometimes substantially so.[40]

A pipeline from eastern Siberia to Daqing (as had been proposed) would link Russia and China in a close energy trading relationship subject to holdup threats. Without firmly established cooperative political relations, this could inject a great deal of uncertainty into the energy trade. China can reduce this risk by pursuing imports through marine routes and other pipelines, such as the new one from Kazakhstan, which transports Russian as well as Kazakh oil.[41] Russia's best risk reduction is to construct a pipeline to the Pacific coast, from which oil can be exported all around the Pacific rim, including to China.

There is considerable unrealized potential for Russian exports of natural gas to China. In addition to being another energy source, natural gas offers environmental benefits that are desperately needed. Its share in China's energy mix will likely increase substantially in the future. Consumption rose from 15 billion cubic meters per year in 1990 to 56 billion in 2006.[42] China's internal production met these needs, but as the use of natural gas increases, imports will become necessary. Journalists have cited preliminary agreements between China and Gazprom to begin deliveries in 2011, with volumes increasing gradually to as much as 80 billion cubic meters per year.[43] At a price of $240 per 1,000 cubic meters (roughly the price to Europe in 2006), this would have a market value of $19.2 billion, about double the value of Russia's energy exports to China in 2007.

Like the case of oil, actualizing this potential requires development of transportation infrastructure. Because the potential is so large, it is likely that the necessary investment will occur, and some of it is already under way. But as with an oil pipeline, trade supported by a natural gas pipeline locks parties into a relationship that may increase risk if political relations are uncertain. Planning has begun for the construction of a pipeline to bring Russian gas to both China and Korea with capacity at 40 billion cubic meters per year. Initial proposals describe the feedstock coming from the Kovytka field in eastern Siberia, but with connections to the existing gas pipeline system in Russia there are several other sources that could be tapped to provide this export. Another pipeline to China proposed by Gazprom would deliver gas from western Siberia and have the same capacity.[44] Gas deliveries could also include up to 8 billion cubic meters annually supplied from the Sakhalin-1 project, which would be delivered to the Russian mainland via pipeline and subsequently to consumers in the Russian Far East and Korea as well as China.[45] China has also been constructing terminals for importing liquefied natural gas (LNG), the first of which began operation in 2006.[46] These would allow China to purchase Russian LNG from the Sakhalin-2 project when that facility comes onstream.

China has notable deficiencies in its electrical power supply, and Russia is able to offer exports of this form of energy as well. Although the market value and energetic content of electricity imports from Russia are small compared to oil, and minuscule in relation to China's total use of electricity, the quantity increased by 3.4 times from 1995 to 2006. In the 1990s Russia provided as much as 35 percent of China's imports of electricity, but from 2000 to 2006 this share averaged around 9 percent. Data for 2007 and 2008 show imports have plunged to a fraction of the 2006 level. This is odd in that additional electrical power grid connections with Russia were under construction, suggesting that growth would continue. Moreover, an agreement announced in 2005 would allow Chinese companies to construct power plants in Russia.[47] There is potential for Russia to become a larger supplier of electricity to China, especially in the border region, but the recent changes suggest uncertainty in whether this will emerge as an important component of integration. Like pipelines, linking power grids binds parties into long-term bilateral dependence.

Armaments

Russia's provision of military hardware to China evolved into one of the most important economic and strategic connections between the countries. Yet it is not clear that this aspect of economic integration will endure, as political and strategic concerns exert primary influence. The chapters by Kevin Ryan and Jing-dong Yuan provide both technical detail and a military context for this part of the Chinese-Russian economic relationship, which must be understood from a strategic perspective. My comments address this trade from a narrow economic viewpoint.

Over the past sixteen years, and especially the last nine, China has been a key customer of the Russian military-industrial complex, and Russia has been by far China's main external supplier of military goods. Across the period 1992 to 2007, China was the destination of one-third of Russia's aggregate export of armaments, and Russia provided over four-fifths of China's arms imports.[48] Technology transfer through production licensing is a part of this trade, although this was small compared to the expenditures on hardware. The mix of specific equipment is extensive and more details can be found in the chapters by Ryan and Yuan. Technical specifics are also described in the yearbooks from the Stockholm International Peace Research Institute.[49]

Exporting arms to China has generated a degree of controversy in Russia because some Russians perceive China as a strategic threat. But the extreme stress on the Russian military industrial sector during economic transition and the aggressive quest for export markets by Rosoboronexport (the state enterprise responsible for all Russian armaments exports) have largely overridden these security concerns. On the Chinese side, authorities are pursuing the goal of improving the technological level of the military and expanding their naval capability beyond the coastal zone. Armaments from Russia can assist a great deal in achieving these objectives. Essentially, Russia exports these products to China in response to offers that are generated by the in-

Figure 4.7. China's Imports of Armaments from Russia, 1992-2007

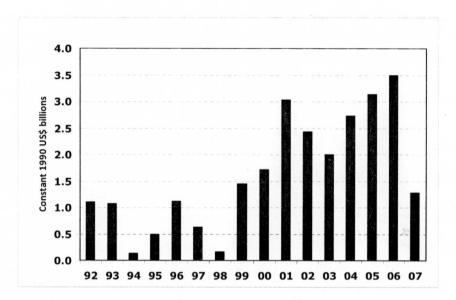

creasing wealth that can support Chinese national political and security objectives. Notable among these goals are energy security, resolving the Taiwan
issue, countering competing claims to offshore energy resources, and expanding outward in a contemporary neocolonial search for raw materials.

Data on armaments trade are presented in table 4.6 and displayed visual-
ly in figure 4.7. Although measured in real dollar terms, these figures are not,
strictly speaking, comparable to data on nonmilitary exports from Russia.
The unit of measurement is intended to allow for an aggregation across armament types and is based on a particular methodology developed by SIPRI.[50]
Moreover, trade in armaments is not included in the standard accounting of
foreign trade that China and Russia report to the International Monetary
Fund, which is the basis of data on nonmilitary exports in table 4.6. Despite
the difference in accounting unit, comparing the series directly is accurate
enough to provide perspective on the importance of armaments in the overall
trade relationship. The third row of table 4.6 calculates the armaments import value as a share of China's total imports from Russia, combining arms
and nonmilitary goods. Across the years shown, arms averaged 20 percent
of China's imports from Russia, and in some years this share rose to nearly
a third. Although including the arms trade substantially widened Russia's
current account surplus with China from 1992 to 2006, arms sales were not
enough to prevent the emergence of a trade deficit in 2007.

Table 4.6. China's Armaments Imports from Russia, 1992–2007

	1992	1993	1994	1995	1996	1997	1998	1999	2000	2001	2002	2003	2004	2005	2006	2007	Avg. 1992–2007
Armaments[a,aa]	1,098	1,077	130	498	1,115	628	166	1,446	1,718	3,037	2,429	1,996	2,735	3,132	3,498	1,290	1,625
Nonmilitary Imports[b,ab]	3,317	4,603	3,133	3,365	4,482	3,493	3,067	3,520	4,707	6,342	6,582	7,458	9,041	11,467	12,265	13,367	6,263
Arms Share of Imports (%)[c]	25	19	4	13	20	15	5	29	27	32	27	21	23	21	22	9	20
As Share of Total Arms Trade																	
Share from Russia[d]	91	87	45	78	88	85	57	86	92	94	92	97	94	94	94	91	85
Share to China[e]	41	31	9	15	31	21	8	37	41	54	45	37	43	56	54	28	34

Sources:

[aa]SIPRI Arms Transfers Database, August 2008, http://www.sipri.org/contents/armstrad/access.html, accessed 7 August 2008.
[ab]Trade flows: IMF, *Direction of Trade Statistics Database*, accessed 7 August 2008. Based on Chinese reporting. Deflator: Bureau of Economic Analysis, U.S. Department of Commerce, http://www.bea.gov/bea/dn/nipaweb/NIPATableIndex.asp, accessed 28 September 2008.

[a]Trend indicator values expressed as millions of constant 1990 US$. Methodology available at http://web.sipri.org/contents/armstrad/at_data.html.
[b]In millions of constant 1990 US$.
[c]Share of combined arms and nonmilitary imports.
[d]Imports from Russia as share of total Chinese armaments imports.
[e]Exports to China as share of total of Russian armaments exports.

In my view, the prospects for Russian exports of arms to China are less certain than those for energy. The substantial decline from 2006 to 2007 (63 percent) was followed by a smaller reduction from 2007 to 2008 (15 percent). However, two observations are a weak basis to infer a trend, and this data series is rather erratic annually due to the idiosyncratic nature of trade in major armaments systems and timing of the associated accounting. Yet given China's strategic and developmental objectives, the most cogent understanding of the arms trade between China and Russia sees it as a temporary reliance by China in the face of: (1) the European and U.S. arms embargos in place since 1989; and (2) the time required to develop indigenous capacity for the sophisticated engineering and manufacturing that modern armaments require. As either or both of these constraints are relaxed, China will most likely reduce purchases of armaments from Russia. The license to manufacture Sukhoi aircraft that China acquired from Russia suggests this direction, as does China's growth as an arms exporter in its own right.

Summary of the Bilateral Trade Relationship

To summarize the trade picture, the temporal pattern shows increasing integration of the Chinese and Russian economies by means of trade, but the increase is not significantly different from the increasing integration of these two countries with the rest of the world. With regard to shares of aggregate trade, Russia is not a particularly important destination for Chinese exports. Since the main part of Chinese exports to Russia is consumer goods, the relatively small population and low income in the Russian Far East and the long distance to markets in western Russia are key factors. In contrast, China is an important destination for Russian exports, largely because much of the Russian export mix consists of raw materials (such as energy and wood) and semifinished industrial goods (such as chemicals and metals). China, as a major manufacturing platform for the world economy, has a large appetite for such goods. Yet China has other sources of these materials, so the relative importance of Russia in total Chinese imports (excluding the special case of armaments) is not as large. Finally, China as a source of imports for Russia has become quite significant in the twenty-first century, rising to the rank of number two in the latest data. The Russian Far East relies more heavily on China as a source of imported goods than the rest of the country. Basic geography drives this pattern.

China's imports of crude oil and refined petroleum products from Russia increased by large multiples in the past thirteen years, and the potential for Russian exports of natural gas to China is huge. Considering the basic energy positions of the two economies and proposed pipelines for oil and natural gas, Russia's energy exports to China could increase again by multiples within the next decade, and investment in the necessary infrastructure is under way. Yet as Erica Downs notes in her chapter, the outlook for energy trade is uncertain, and shipments in 2007 and 2008 were below the peak reached in 2006.

Armaments in bilateral trade are a special case. Although economic circumstances certainly play a role, the main driver of this trade is the Chinese goal of increasing the technological capacity of its armed forces. Geopolitical and strategic considerations are more influential here than in other areas of trade. As China increases its indigenous capacity to manufacture sophisticated weapons, arms imports from Russia will likely decline.

4. Bilateral Investment and Labor Flows

While bilateral trade data is readily available and fairly complete, the investment and labor flow linkages between China and Russia are not as well documented in published sources. The *World Investment Reports* from the United Nations include the total aggregate flows and stocks of foreign direct investment for the two countries, but they do not provide detail on bilateral flows. The OECD tracks bilateral FDI, but only for member countries, excluding Russia and China. There is even less information available on bilateral portfolio investment. This may be because the amounts are quite small or perhaps because there is a stronger interest in FDI. Data from Chinese authorities show Russian portfolio investment into China at zero. Nevertheless, with limited quantitative data on bilateral investment and several anecdotal observations, we can construct a useful perspective on integration via cross-border asset holdings. Full analysis of the Chinese-Russian investment relationship will require more complete data. What we can conclude with reasonable confidence is that bilateral trade flows are at least two orders of magnitude larger than bilateral investment flows.

Similarly, available data on labor movement and remittances between the countries are less than required for analysis of integration on this score. Border authorities record figures on the number of Chinese citizens entering Russia, but we have only fragmentary evidence on how long they stay, what they do there, and the scale of remittances sent back to China. As with FDI, accumulating comprehensive and accurate data is an important and challenging project, but nonetheless required to fully understand the economic relationship between these countries.

Bilateral Investment

Anecdotal evidence from journalists and limited work of scholars clearly shows that bilateral capital commitments in both directions have taken root in the post-Soviet period, but the composition and dynamics of bilateral investment are elusive. The picture that emerges from consideration of available information suggests investment relations between China and Russia are at an early stage and not yet extensive. But they are growing.

Most of the capital flight from Russia in the early transition era was destined for portfolio investment, primarily in Europe and the United States. China, until recently, placed most of its earnings of foreign currency on current account transactions into financial investments abroad. Neither China nor Russia is a particularly attractive destination for these purposes. It is only recently that significant capital flows from these countries have emanated in pursuit of FDI projects. Outflows from both countries reached billions of dollars by the late 1990s, and across 2000 to 2007 averaged $8.9 billion per year from China and $14.3 billion per year from Russia.

Integration by means of capital flows, particularly FDI, is more significant than by trade because it creates a more durable linkage. Such commitment also entails greater risk, which is a key factor limiting the extent of integration by means of investment. University of North Carolina economist Steven Rosefielde contends that China and Russia are distinguished in the transition experience by their different abilities to attract FDI, and risk plays a key role in this.[51] Much of China's relative economic success is attributed to its ability to provide a political and legal environment sufficiently secure to attract large amounts of FDI, while Russia's chaotic political conditions and lack of rule of law have dissuaded many potential foreign investors. Yet the size of the countries also plays a role; China's population is roughly ten times larger than Russia's, and the Chinese GDP is around five times the Russian. Adjusting for these scales, China is not so much more successful than Russia in attracting FDI. Moreover, Russian outward FDI is much larger than Chinese, especially when adjusted for population and gross output.

Table 4.7 (reverse) provides comparison of aggregate FDI flows and stocks. The striking feature is the much larger inflow to China, which is nearly four times that for Russia across 2000–2007. Naturally the inward stock position is much higher for China as well. With regard to outward FDI, on the other hand, the average flow from Russia was about twice that of China, as was the Russian outward stock position. On a per capita basis, FDI inflow has been substantially higher in Russia, while the outflow was larger by an order of magnitude. To compare FDI flow relative to GDP it is

Table 4.7. Comparison of Aggregate FDI for China and Russia, 1995, 2000–2007

Part A. Flows[sa] (US$ billion)	1995	2000	2001	2002	2003	2004	2005	2006	2007	Mean 2000–2007	Mean Ratios: China/Russia[a] Levels	Per Capita[ab]	Per GDP[sc]
Inward FDI to:													
China	35.85	40.72	46.88	52.74	53.51	60.63	72.41	72.72	83.52	60.39	3.7	0.41	1.54
Russia	2.02	2.71	2.71	3.46	7.96	15.44	12.89	32.39	52.48	16.25			
Outward FDI from:													
China	2.00	0.92	6.88	2.52	-0.15	5.50	12.26	21.16	22.47	8.94	0.6	0.07	0.20
Russia	0.36	3.18	2.53	3.53	9.73	13.78	12.77	23.15	45.65	14.29			

Part B. Stock Position[sa] (US$ billion)	1995	2000	2001	2002	2003	2004	2005	2006	2007	Mean 2000–2007	Mean Ratios: China/Russia Levels	Per Capita	Per GDP
Inward FDI to:													
China	137.4	193.3	395.2	448.0	501.5	245.5	317.9	292.6	327.1	340	3.0	0.4	1.4
Russia	5.5	32.2	20.1	51.4	52.5	98.4	132.5	197.7	324.1	114			
Outward FDI from:													
China	15.8	27.8	32.7	35.2	37.0	38.8	46.3	73.3	95.8	48	0.5	0.06	0.2
Russia	3.0	20.1	14.7	4.7	51.8	81.9	120.4	156.8	255.2	88			

Sources:

[sa]FDI data from United Nations, *World Investment Report*, 2001, 2003, 2004, 2005, 2006, 2007, and 2008. Some figures are estimates; some are based on accumulating and subtracting flows. See source for details.

[ab]China population from: China database of CEIC Data Co., Ltd. Derived from the Chinese National Bureau of Statistics, accessed 30 September 2008. Russia population from: Russia database of CEIC Data Co., Ltd. Derived from the Russian Federal State Statistics Service (Rosstat), accessed 30 September 2008.

[sc]GDP and exchange rates from IMF, *International Financial Statistics*, web service, accessed 15 August 2008.

[a]Mean ratios are China mean for 2000–2007 divided by Russia mean for same years.

[b]Conversion of GDP to dollars used the IMF annual average exchange rate. IMF data accessed 26 March 2007.

Table 4.8. Comparisons of Foreign Investment into China

	1998	1999	2000	2001	2002	2003	2004	2005	2006
Direct Investment[a] (US$ million)									
World	45,463	40,319	40,715	46,878	52,743	53,505	60,630	60,325	63,021
Japan	3,400	2,973	2,916	4,348	4,190	5,054	5,452	6,530	4,598
Europe	4,309	4,797	4,765	4,484	4,049	4,272	4,798	5,643	5,712
Russia	19	20	16	30	39	54	126	82	67
United States	3,898	4,216	4,384	4,433	5,424	4,199	3,941	3,061	2,865
Portfolio Investment[a] (US$ million)									
World	2,095	2,128	8,641	2,795	2,268	2,635	3,443	3,480	4,055
Japan	44	91	145	161	166	88	67	117	119
Europe	100	170	2	19	42	41	4	14	n.a.
Russia	0	0	0	0	0	0	0	0	0
United States	275	7	1	109	132	173	3	13	11
Russian Shares of Direct Investment (%)									
of World	0.043	0.048	0.040	0.063	0.073	0.10	0.21	0.14	0.11
of Europe	0.45	0.41	0.34	0.66	0.95	1.3	2.6	1.5	1.2

Source: *China Statistical Yearbook:* 2000, 2002, 2005, 2006, and 2007.

[a]"Actually used foreign direct and other investment"; "other" is interpreted as portfolio investment.

necessary to convert the countries' GDP levels into dollars. Using the IMF's annual average official exchange rates, I find by this measure that China's inward FDI flow is 1.5 times Russia's, while Russia's outward FDI flow exceeds China's by a factor of 5.

But what can we say about the *bilateral* FDI relation? Unfortunately, a long data series for Chinese investment into Russia is not readily available, but table 4.8 provides data on Russian investment into China and comparisons with some other key sources. The presumption noted above, that portfolio investment between the countries is not an important route of integration, is borne out here. For the world as a whole, portfolio flows into China were around only 5 percent of the FDI flow, but for Russia there were none at all. Neither is Russia an important source of direct investment into China. Russia's share of European FDI into China averaged only 1 percent, and Russia's share of the world flow was less than 0.1 percent. Japan alone supported nearly 10 percent of world FDI into China. Although Russia's relative importance to China in this regard is very low, the data show increases in the absolute amount of FDI and a tripling of the relative share. Figure 4.8 provides a visual representation of this trend.

By comparing the figures in table 4.8 with the Russian outward totals in table 4.7 we can assess the importance of China as a destination for Russian FDI. Here, too, China plays a minor role. From 2000 to 2006 China was a

Figure 4.8. Russian Foreign Direct Investment into China, 1998-2006

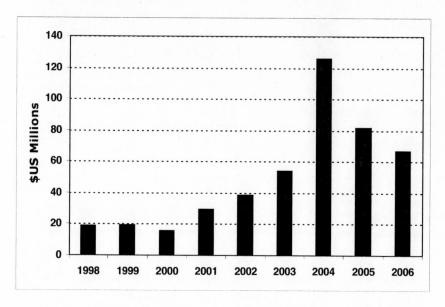

destination for less than 1 percent of Russian outward FDI, ranging from a low of 0.2 percent in 2006 to a high of 1.2 percent in 2001.

The reverse relationship (Chinese FDI into Russia) is more significant. According to the *China Statistical Yearbook,* Chinese FDI into Russia was $77.3 million, $203 million, and $452 million in 2004, 2005, and 2006, respectively.[52] Although for 2004 this was below the Russian FDI into China, in 2005 and 2006 Chinese FDI into Russia greatly exceeded Russian FDI into China. Chinese FDI into other European countries is small by comparison. Indeed, the recent flows to Russia constitute 45, 40, and 76 percent of the total FDI into Europe by Chinese firms (for 2004, 2005, and 2006, respectively). If we subtract China's FDI into Hong Kong, the Cayman Islands, and the Virgin Islands from the total outward FDI, the shares of this adjusted total going to Russia are 7, 8, and 19 percent. In 2006 Russia was the primary destination for FDI originating from China.[53] In 2004 and 2005, Russia was ranked at number four and number three, respectively, as a destination for China's outward FDI. The conclusion from this short time series is that Russia is significant for Chinese outward FDI and growing in importance.

Estimates of bilateral FDI are also cited in research by economists Li Jianmin and Liudmila Popova.[54] Li reported that by midyear 2003, Chinese firms' accumulated FDI stock in Russian-based affiliates was $350 million, and that Russian enterprises' accumulated FDI stock in Chinese affiliates stood at $329 million. Popova reports a much smaller stock of Chinese assets in Russia, $91.9 million as of the end of 2004.[55] Her figure for Russian investment in China is roughly consistent with Li's, showing an accumulated stock at $460 million as of 2004. Although precise comparisons are not possible, these researchers' estimates are broadly consistent with published statistical evidence, with the exception of Popova's figure for assets in Russia held by Chinese firms, which seems too low. Stock holdings accumulated from 2004 to 2006 would come to around $733 million.

Systematic sectoral distribution of bilateral investment is not provided in any source, although some anecdotal evidence is noted below. It may be the case that bilateral foreign investment has a significant presence in particular sectors or regions, but in the aggregate, bilateral FDI between China and Russia is small by world standards. It comprises only a fraction of a percent of the total inward and outward stocks of the countries. The figures overall indicate another route through which the two economies are becoming integrated, but judging by this data, the bilateral investment connection is not currently robust. The strongest potential seems to be Chinese investment into Russia.

Investments are often related to specific features of the overall economic relationship between China and Russia. First, the border region is important because proximity reduces risk by facilitating the gathering of relevant information and monitoring of projects. Most FDI projects ought to be found near the border, and this is precisely what Popova reports.[56] Second, there is a tendency for investment projects to be linked with trade between the countries. Third, a general feature of Chinese outward FDI is emphasis on natural resource projects and agriculture in an attempt to secure supplies of materials to support domestic needs. For example, a private Chinese firm spent $125 million in a joint venture into an oil refinery in the Amur Oblast' with the intention of marketing the product inside China.[57] Another Chinese oil firm, Sinopec (China Petroleum and Chemical Company), is engaged in a joint venture on Sakhalin with Rosneft for oil and natural gas production with the objective of supplying China's energy markets.[58]

More extensive participation of Chinese firms in Russian energy projects would likely have developed, but the Putin administration and the Duma obstructed attempts by Chinese oil firms to acquire assets in Russia. It was not until June 2006 that any Chinese oil firm was able to acquire a production asset in the country. In this case Sinopec, which purchased a property from the joint venture TNK-BP, immediately sold a 51 percent stake to Rosneft.[59] Another acquisition, a portfolio investment, occurred in July 2006 when the

China National Petroleum Corporation bought $500 million of stock in the initial public offering of Rosneft.[60] China is a welcome customer for Russia's oil and natural gas, but, given the political economy of Russian energy, FDI in this sector by Chinese firms will be constrained.

Of course, Chinese investment into the Russian economy is not limited to energy and the border region. Popova notes a new interest of Chinese investors in real estate in Moscow and St. Petersburg, and both Li and Popova cite projects in wood processing, telecommunications equipment, microelectronics, consumer appliances, and agriculture.[61] The main sectors where Russian enterprises invest in China are chemicals, agricultural machinery, automobiles, construction, and nuclear power.[62] Popova indicates Russian investment positions also in construction materials and river transportation as well as primary sectors (agriculture, forestry, and fishing). In terms of the number of enterprises, Chinese affiliates supported by Russian investment grew from 1,000 in the year 2000 to 1,687 by 2004. Russian affiliates supported by Chinese investment grew from 430 to 575 across the same period.[63]

Since 2003 the Chinese government has supported a policy aimed at promoting investment into the Russian economy and as a part of this effort sponsored investment forums in 2004 and 2005.[64] Contracts signed in these forums reached $1 billion and $1.5 billion, respectively. A notable (and controversial) project concerns property development in St. Petersburg. The "Baltic Pearl" complex was described as the largest prospective project in Russia undertaken by Chinese firms, with an estimated cost of $1.25 billion.[65] There have even been proposals for Chinese investment of $100 million into production enterprises in Chechnya.[66] These projects are likely still in planning stages, and it remains to be seen whether the full amounts cited will actually be invested. If carried out, they would constitute a large increase in bilateral FDI.

Labor Flows

One of the greatest contrasts between the Chinese Northeast and the Russian Far East is population density. Table 4.9 presents population and density data for the administrative units that lie along the border. Density in China is almost twenty times higher; if Inner Mongolia (which is largely remote from the border region) is excluded, Chinese density is nearly forty times higher. Moreover, population in the Russian region has declined since the advent of transition, while in China it has increased slightly. These stark distinctions suggest substantial pressure for labor migration. However, there are more obstacles to economic integration through the movement of labor than through trade and investment. A key obstruction is the threat that many Russians associate with immigrants from China, even though many Chinese immigrants stay for only short periods in Russia and provide badly needed trade services and other forms of labor. There are undoubtedly some Russians migrating to China for work, but this flow is minor compared to the reverse direction. It has not been mentioned in any of the sources consulted for this chapter and will not be treated here.

Given the size of the potential, the actual flow of labor from China into Russia has been modest. Data are sketchy, but estimates of the total number of Chinese citizens living in Russia are in the low hundreds of thousands, including 50,000 to 70,000 in Moscow.[67] Wishnick cites a government estimate in 2004 of 150,000 to 200,000 Chinese "living in Russia on a permanent basis," but also notes that the recent census recorded only 35,000. But many more could presumably be present on a temporary basis.[68] Mikhail Alexeev, an associate professor at San Diego State University, provides more detailed and carefully considered estimates for Primorsky Krai in the late 1990s, concluding that the number of Chinese citizens present in the krai at any given time was around 15,000 in 1997 and 35,000 in 1998.[69] He also cites a federal migration official's estimate for 1999 as 5,000 Chinese in this krai. Pavel Minakir, director of the Institute of Economics Research in Khabarovsk, provided upper limit estimates of 50,000 to 80,000 Chinese citizens in the Russian Far East in 1992–1993.[70] While the border region is most favored by those migrating to Russia, Chinese can be found throughout the country. Major cities are an expected destination, but Chinese nationals have also pursued rural income opportunities thousands of kilometers from the border region, where land has fallen into disuse after the collapse of state or collective farms.[71]

Table 4.10 contains relevant data from the *China Statistical Yearbook* on the turnover of foreign economic cooperation, including labor compensation. A clear interpretation of these figures is not possible because they aggregate flows in both directions and the total includes a number of elements of "foreign economic cooperation" that are not clearly defined. Still, the data are another indicator of economic integration, and labor transactions account for a large part of this turnover. Roughly half of the total turnover was compensation for labor in the case of Russia, putting Russia's share relative to the world at around 3.4 percent. Relative to Europe, Russia's share of labor compensation was around half.

It is unfortunate that this data is not disaggregated by direction of flow. They are the only quantitative indicators published for the exchange of labor between China and Russia, a matter that has gained increased political attention. Given the anecdotal evidence we have, it is likely that a large fraction

Table 4.9. Populations in the Chinese-Russian Border Region

Variable Unit Year	Area[a] (1,000 km²) 1999	Population[ab] (1,000s)					Density (people/km²)				
		1990	1995	2000	2005	2007	1990	1995	2000	2005	2007
China											
Heilongjiang Province	469	35,430	37,010	38,070	38,200	38,240	76	79	81	81	82
Jilin Province	187	24,402	25,509	26,273	26,694	27,298	130	136	140	142	146
Liaoning Province	146	39,173	40,340	41,353	41,892	42,980	268	276	283	287	294
Inner Mongolia	1,200	21,626	22,844	23,724	23,864	24,051	18	19	20	20	20
All Regional Units	2,002	120,631	125,703	129,420	130,650	132,569	60	63	65	65	66
Russia											
Amur Oblast'	364	1,059	1,033	998	888	830	2.9	2.8	2.7	2.4	2.3
Jewish Aut. Oblast'	36	216	210	197	189	186	6.0	5.8	5.5	5.2	5.2
Khabarovsky Krai	789	1,611	1,577	1,506	1,420	1,378	2.0	2.0	1.9	1.8	1.7
Primorsky Krai	166	2,279	2,271	2,172	2,036	1,978	13.7	13.7	13.1	12.3	11.9
Zabaikalsky Krai (Chita)	432	1,320	1,296	1,256	1,128	1,119	3.1	3.0	2.9	2.7	2.7
All Regional Units	1,786	6,485	6,387	6,129	5,661	5,491	3.6	3.6	3.4	3.2	3.1

Sources:

[a]Chinese figures from Benewick and Donald, *State of China Atlas*. Russian figures from Goskomstat, *Demograficheskii Ezhegodnik Rossii*, 2002.

[ab]Chinese population data for 1990–2005 from All China Data Center on-line service, Yearly Provincial Macroeconomic Statistics, accessed 14 March 2007. Chinese data for 2007 from China database of CEIC Data Co., Ltd., which is derived from the Chinese National Bureau of Statistics, accessed 30 September 2008. Russian population data for 1990–2000 from Goskomstat, *Rossiiskii Statisticheskii Ezhegodnik*, 2001; data for 2005 from Goskomstat, *Regiony Rossii: Osnovnye Sotsial'no-Ekonomicheskie Pokazateli Gorodov, 2005*. Data for Zabaikal Oblast' for 2005 and 2007 and Jewish Aut. Oblast' for 2007 from Russia database of CEIC Data Co., Ltd., which is derived from the Russian Federal Statistics Service (Rosstat), accessed 30 September 2008. Population figures for Amur, Khabarovskii and Primorskii for 2007 are estimates based on growth rates from 2002 to 2005.

Table 4.10. Comparisons of Turnover of China's Foreign Economic Cooperation

	1998	1999	2000	2001	2002	2003	2004	2005	2006
Total Turnover of Foreign Economic Cooperation (US$ million)[a, b]									
World	11,773	11,235	11,325	12,139	14,352	17,234	21,369	26,776	35,695
Japan	332	288	397	488	594	705	860	1,190	1,531
Europe	489	306	542	767	1,107	1,415	1,645	2,451	3,811
Russia	214	91	111	151	186	205	340	454	662
United States	306	323	351	399	707	301	359	497	1,216
of which — Labor Compensation (US$ million)[b]									
World	2,390	2,623	2,813	3,177	3,071	3,309	3,753	4,786	5,373
Japan	327	283	381	469	543	677	804	1,089	1,393
Europe	246	171	184	202	178	250	250	298	373
Russia	128	58	67	61	86	119	148	180	243
United States	191	220	223	158	143	145	122	87	74
Russian Shares of Total Turnover (%)									
of World	1.8	0.8	1.0	1.2	1.3	1.2	1.6	1.7	1.9
of Europe	44	30	21	20	17	15	21	19	17
Russian Shares of Labor Compensation (%)									
of World	5.3	2.2	2.4	1.9	2.8	3.6	3.9	3.8	4.5
of Europe	52	34	36	30	48	47	59	60	65

Source: *China Statistical Yearbook*, 2000, 2002, 2005, 2006, and 2007.

[a]Turnover of economic cooperation includes several activities, such as construction and engineering contracts, contracted labor, and other items.
[b]Both Total Turnover and Labor Compensation include payments in both directions.

of the labor compensation turnover shown in table 4.10, which averaged $121 million annually, is a flow from Russia to China. But clear interpretation will require additional research. What we can say here is that bilateral payments for labor are more than twice the volume of FDI flow from Russia into China, although they are a small fraction (0.1 percent) of the foreign trade turnover.

Although population density is an easily measured indicator of migration pressure, differentials in economic opportunity are the fundamental driver, and density is a very imperfect measure of this. In early economic models of labor migration, which were primarily interested in rural-urban movements in developing countries, the incentive was expressed as a differential in expected lifetime earnings.[72] Later literature expanded on this by considering the role of familial relations and how migration could serve as a risk reduction mechanism.[73] The choice to migrate across international borders rather than between rural and urban locations within a country involves additional variables but is influenced by similar fundamentals. The present chapter cannot address either theoretical models or the full range of considerations that face potential labor migrants from China into Russia. But it is in the spirit of this earlier research that I compare indicators of labor market conditions on both sides of the Chinese-Russian border.

Table 4.11 presents these comparisons. Although differences in official unemployment rates are large, they should be interpreted with skepticism because the methodologies used by Chinese and Russian labor statisticians are different. Moreover, it is widely recognized that labor markets in China generally, and the northeast region in particular, experience considerable underemployment not captured by official statistics. Comparative changes in the unemployment rates are more reliable as indicators of the direction of labor markets. Unfortunately, provincial-level unemployment rates in China could only be obtained for 2001. With the exception of Jilin, the northeast region had higher unemployment than China as a whole, with the weighted regional average at 4.3 percent compared to the national rate of 3.6 percent. Nationally, unemployment in China increased through 2005, although it fell by 0.2 percentage points by 2007. It is reasonable to assume that the northeast experienced a similar trend, but these changes are modest. Although unemployment rates in the Russian border region increased in the late 1990s, more recently they decreased to levels well below those reached in 2000. Moreover, unemployment rates in the border area have been consistently higher than the Russian national rate, which is one factor leading to the outmigration of Russian citizens from this region to other parts of Russia, reducing labor supply. Therefore, judging by unemployment rates, relative conditions along the border have shifted in favor of labor migration from China to Russia.

The dynamic of average real wages, on the other hand, suggests conditions have shifted against such migration. Since 1995, the Russian border regions have seen significant increases in real wages, with most of the gains occurring since 2000. Across the twelve years ending in 2007, the regional average real wage increased by 192 percent. Yet the Chinese border region experienced stronger growth, with the regional average real wage increasing by 292 percent. In China the growth pattern was more even, with real wages roughly doubling in each five-year period. Chinese wage data primarily reflect the experience of workers employed outside of agriculture. The real wage dynamics suggest nonagricultural labor in particular will be only weakly attracted to the Russian labor market. Agricultural labor markets are treated in more detail below.

Table 4.11 also compares income per capita, converted from local currencies to U.S. dollars using purchasing power parity exchange rates.[74] Incomes on the Russian side of the border were about three times larger on average than in the Chinese border provinces.[75] These figures suggest a strong incentive for Chinese workers and farmers to seek economic opportunities across the border. Moreover, unlike the case of real wages, income per capita has grown faster in Russia, indicating a strengthening of this incentive.

The Chinese figures are averages of urban and rural per capita incomes, a breakdown not available in the Russian data. Nonetheless it is informative to compare these categories separately against the Russian incomes. Urban incomes in the Chinese border region averaged 2.1 to 2.6 times rural incomes. Thus the attraction of earning opportunities in Russia is much stronger for the Chinese rural population. Indeed, for China, the average urban income in the region for 2000 was $1,290 compared against $1,441 in the Russian border region, barely any differential at all. In 2005 income per capita in Russia ($6,340) was more than double that for urban residents in China ($2,562), but it was over six times higher for rural Chinese residents ($967).[76] Given the restrictions on rural to urban migration within China, this suggests that Chinese rural residents are more likely to migrate to Russia than are Chinese living in cities.

What opportunities are available in Russia to Chinese workers? There are three main sectors in which they have found work: agriculture, construction, and services, especially trade. A small proportion works in forestry. A 2004 survey of 250 Chinese workers in the Russian Far East found that 14 percent were construction workers, the largest fraction after entrepreneurs.[77] Chinese participation in Russian construction projects is usually organized through labor recruiters. This mode of labor migration is subject to restrictions placed by Russian authorities on the number of foreign workers who may be granted work visas. The largest share of Chinese citizens in Russia is engaged in trading activity. This includes both individuals trading on their own account as well as those who work as representatives of enterprises in China that import from or export to Russia. In the same 2004 survey, 48 percent were individual traders and 16 percent identified themselves as a "business person." Whether the latter were engaged in trade activities is not clear, but there must be representatives of Chinese enterprises in Russia to facilitate trade.

In agriculture, Chinese citizens in Russia are sometimes contracted workers, but often they are independent farmers. One feature driving migration is the decline in Russian agriculture, particularly in the Russian Far East.[78] The agricultural sector performed poorly in many of Russia's regions during transition, especially in the early years. As a result, many private farms formed out of the collective and state farms have failed, and many enduring state and collective farms have reduced the areas of land that they cultivate. For Chinese farmers this unused land is a great opportunity. Table 4.12 con-

Table 4.11. Labor Conditions in the Chinese–Russian Border Region

Variable Unit / Year	Unemployment Rate %[sa]						Average Real Wage[a, ab, ac] constant 2000 rubles or yuan/month						Annual Income per Capita US$[d, ae, b, c]					
	1995	2000	2001	2005	2006	2007	1995	2000	2005	2006	2007	% change 1995–2007	1995	2000	2005	2006	2007	% change 1995–2007
China																		
Heilongjiang Province	2.9	3.1	3.6	4.2	4.1	4.0	369	653	1,136	1,260	1,383	275	604	859	1,721	n.a.	2,404	397
Jilin Province	n.a.	n.a.	4.7	n.a.	n.a.	n.a.	393	660	1,114	1,253	1,475	275	558	826	1,783	n.a.	2,570	460
Liaoning Province	n.a.	n.a.	3.2	n.a.	n.a.	n.a.	442	734	1,368	1,527	1,687	282	650	975	2,003	n.a.	3,138	481
Inner Mongolia	n.a.	n.a.	4.9	n.a.	n.a.	n.a.	332	581	1,227	1,393	1,545	365	446	829	1,717	n.a.	2,590	580
All Regional Units[d, af]	n.a.	n.a.	3.7	n.a.	n.a.	n.a.	391	667	1,223	1,369	1,530	292	581	884	1,823	n.a.	2,710	466
Russia																		
Amur Oblast'	8.9	10.7	9.1	7.6	7.2	n.a.	2,100	2,232	4,986	5,569	6,313	201	1,762	1,395	5,145	5,600	7,037	398
Jewish Aut. Oblast'	13.4	13.4	12.2	10.5	8.2	6.4	1,806	1,982	4,092	4,602	5,457	202	1,430	1,138	5,492	5,726	6,718	469
Khabarovsky Krai	17.0	15.2	9.5	8.0	6.0	5.9	2,460	2,800	5,544	5,979	6,900	181	1,842	1,911	8,278	9,299	11,586	628
Primorsky Krai	11.4	11.6	10.3	6.8	8.0	7.0	2,343	2,383	5,043	5,881	6,700	186	1,857	1,376	6,242	6,999	8,472	455
Zabaikalsky Krai (Chita)	10.0	11.9	8.6	9.0	8.8	10.1	1,856	2,106	4,448	5,118	5,834	214	1,500	1,074	5,156	5,419	6,625	441
All Regional Units[d, af]	11.0	12.6	11.4	9.2	7.7	7.4	2,216	2,391	5,010	5,661	6,473	192	1,751	1,441	6,340	7,000	8,601	490

Sources:

[aa] Chinese national unemployment data from Asian Development Bank, on-line service, http://www.adb.org/Documents/Books/Key_Indicators/2008/Country.asp, accessed 18 October 2008. Regional un-employment data from provincial statistical services (for 2001): *Statistical Communique of National Economy and Social Development in Heilongjiang Province, 2001*; *Statistical Communique of National Economy and Social Development in Jilin Province, 2001*; *Statistical Communique of National Economy and Social Development in Liaoning Province, 2001*; *Statistical Communique of National Economy and Social Development in Inner Mongolia Aut. Region, 2001*. Russian national unemployment data from IMF, *International Financial Statistics*, on-line service, accessed 8 August 2008. Regional unemployment data for 1995, 2000, 2001, and 2005 from Goskomstat, *Ekonomicheskaia Aktivnost' Naseleniia Rossii, 2002*, and *Regiony Rossii: Sotsial'no-Ekonomicheskie Pokazateli, 2005*. Regional unemployment data for 2006 and 2007 from Russia database of CEIC Data Co., Ltd., which is derived from the Russian Federal Statistics Service (Rosstat), accessed 30 September 2008.

[ab]Chinese nominal wage for 1995, 2000, and 2005 from All China Data Center: Yearly Provincial Macroeconomic Statistics, accessed 17 March 2007. Chinese nominal wage for 2006 and 2007 from China database of CEIC Data Co., Ltd., which is derived from the Chinese Ministry of Labour and Social Security, accessed 30 September 2008. Russian nominal wage data for all years from Russia database of CEIC Data Co., Ltd., which is derived from the Russian Federal Statistics Service (Rosstat), accessed 30 September 2008.

[ac]Chinese price level (CPI) for 1995–2005 from All China Data Center: Yearly Provincial Macroeconomic Statistics, accessed 17 March 2007. Chinese CPI for 2006 and 2007 from China database of CEIC Data Co., Ltd., which is derived from the Chinese Ministry of Labour and Social Security, accessed 30 September 2008. Russian price level (CPI) for 1995 and 2000 from Goskomstat, *Regiony Rossii: Satsial'no–Ekonomichaskie Pokazateli, 2005*. Data for 2005 from Goskomstat, *Statisticheskoe Obozrenie*, 2005. No. 4 (55). CPI for 30 September Russian price level (CPI) for 2006 and 2007 from Russia database of CEIC Data Co., Ltd., which is derived from the Russian Federal Statistics Service (Rosstat), accessed 30 September 2008.

[ad]Chinese income data for 2000 and 2005 from All China Data Center: Yearly Provincial Macroeconomic Statistics, accessed 17 March 2007. For 1995 from from: *China Statistical Yearbook, 2001, 2006*. For 2007 from China database of CEIC Data Co., Ltd., which is derived from the Chinese National Bureau of Statistics, accessed 30 September 2008. Russian income data for all years from Russia database of CEIC Data Co., Ltd., which is derived from the Russian Federal Statistics Service (Rosstat), accessed 30 September 2008.

[ae]Exchange rate is the Big Mac Index from *The Economist*: for 15 April 1995, vol. 335, no. 7910: 74; for 27 April 2000, on-line service, accessed 6 February 2007; for 6 November 2005, vol. 375, no. 8430, on-line service; for 25 May 2006, on-line service, accessed 6 February 2007; for 7 July 2007, on-line service, accessed 20 October 2008.

[af]Chinese population data for 1995–2005 from All China Data Center on-line service: Yearly Provincial Macroeconomic Statistics, accessed 14 March 2007. Chinese data for 2006–2007 from China database of CEIC Data Co., Ltd., which is derived from the Chinese National Bureau of Statistics, accessed 30 September 2008. Russian population data from Goskomstat. For 1995–2001: Goskomstat, *Rossiiskii Statisticheskii Ezhegodnik*, 2001. For 2002: Goskomstat, *Demograficheskii Ezhegodnik Rossii*, 2002. For 2005: Goskomstat, *Regiony Rossii: Osnovnye Satsial'no–Ekonomicheskie Pokazateli Gorodov, 2005*. Data for Zabaikalskii krai for 2003–2007 and Jewish Aut. Oblast' for 2003–2004 and 2006–2007 from Russia database of CEIC Data Co., Ltd., which is derived from the Russian Federal Statistics Service (Rosstat), accessed 30 September 2008. Population figures for Amur, Khabarovskii, and Primorskii for 2006 and 2007 are estimates based on growth rates from 2002 to 2005.

[a]Nominal monthly wages adjusted by local CPI to real 2000 rubles and yuan.

[b]Annual income expressed in dollars, converted from local currencies using a PPP exchange rate, the Big Mac Index. See [ae].

[c]For China: converted from yuan values that are urban and rural averages weighted by urban and rural population shares.

[d]Regional averages weighted by population (see [a] for sources).

Table 4.12. Agriculture in the Chinese-Russian Border Region: Sown Areas

	1,000s of hectares					% change	
	1995	2000	2005	2006	2007	1995–2006	2000–2006
China[sa]							
Heilongjiang Province	8,647	9,329	10,084	10,468	n.a.	21	12
Jilin Province	4,060	4,542	4,954	4,985	n.a.	23	10
Liaoning Province	3,624	3,622	3,797	3,767	n.a.	4	4
Inner Mongolia	5,079	5,914	6,216	6,297	n.a.	24	6
All Regional Units	21,410	23,408	25,050	25,517	n.a.	19	9
Russia[sb]							
						1995–2007	2000–2007
Amur Oblast'	1,082	660	586	636	672	-38	2
Jewish Aut. Oblast'	122	80	92	96	100	-18	25
Khabarovsky Krai	110	103	88	91	88	-20	-15
Primorsky Krai	565	448	361	350	335	-41	-25
Zabaikalsky Krai (Chita)	747	340	285	278	257	-66	-24
All Regional Units	2,625	1,630	1,411	1,451	1,451	-45	-11

Sources:

[sa]Chinese figures from *China Statistical Yearbook, 2001, 2006, 2007,* except 1995. Figures for 1995 from from All China Data Center: Yearly Provincial Macroeconomic Statistics, accessed 17 March 2007.

[sb]Russian figures from Russia database of CEIC Data Co., Ltd., which is derived from the Russian Federal Statistics Service (Rosstat), accessed 30 September 2008.

tains data showing the trend in sown areas in the border region to provide quantitative evidence. From 1995 to 2007 the planted area in the border region declined by 45 percent on the Russian side, with each krai and oblast experiencing such a decline. On the Chinese side, however, sown areas all increased, with the regional total rising by 19 percent. The relative shift in the intensities of cropland use suggests an incentive for agricultural labor in China to seek opportunities in Russia, and anecdotal evidence on migrants supports this conclusion.[79]

Chinese who work in Russian agriculture are typically paid in a sharecropping arrangement. In areas close to the border they may export their crops back into China, but in some cases their crops are marketed in Russia. Foreign citizens are not legally entitled to own agricultural land in Russia, but leases are available. Usually these are short term, often for a single season. A law adopted in 2003 allows foreigners to lease land for up to forty-nine years, so this pattern may shift. But all these observations are based on spotty anecdotal evidence. Understanding the extent and economic significance of Chinese participation in Russian agriculture will require substantially more effort in gathering data.

For both prospective and current migration, the Russian Far East is the principle destination because its proximity to China reduces the cost and risk to migrants seeking opportunities. Workers, farmers, and entrepreneurs are more familiar with this part of Russia and can easily return to China if prospects turn out worse than expected. But this is by no means the only destination for Chinese labor migrants moving into Russia. If labor flows increase substantially, there will likely be a greater regional diversity of Chinese living and working in Russia. However, there is significant political resistance to accepting an increased number of Chinese workers. Many Russians perceive immigrants as a threat, and politicians have been willing to reflect this popular view in restrictive policies. A recent example is the April 2007 regulation that forbids foreign citizens from participating in Russia's retail markets as independent entrepreneurs.[80] Although this new regime is not directed at Chinese specifically, they are subject to its provisions.

In summary, there is a large potential for labor to flow from China into Russia, but migration has not been extensive thus far. Although indicators of labor market conditions suggest opportunities may be better on the Russian side of the border region, the decision to migrate in search of work involves a complex set of factors, including access to the opportunities, restrictions on movement imposed by authorities, and coping with a different cultural and linguistic environment. Comprehensive and reliable estimates on the number of migrants are not readily available, and there is little information about what the economic impact of the migrants has been, on either their own lives or the local economy. A deeper analysis of economic integration via labor markets will require substantially improved data on the economic outcomes for Chinese migrants to Russia and consideration of the range of factors that influence decisions to migrate.

5. The Role of the Border Regions in Economic Integration

The regions of Russia and China that lie along their mutual border have historically played an important role in the economic integration of the two countries and will continue to have a major influence. Three aspects of proximity to the border drive this. First, economic opportunities of cross-border activity are more apparent to actors close to the border. Entrepreneurs in Heilongjiang, for example, are generally more aware of economic conditions and profitable opportunities in the Russian Far East than are entrepreneurs in southern China. This applies to potential labor migrants as well. Second, the transport costs of international trade are lower for the border regions. Third, proximity to the border can reduce uncertainty and the attendant risk, which is relevant to foreign investment as well as labor migration. Closeness facilitates monitoring and reduces transaction cost. It is no surprise, then, that much of the bilateral economic activity is closely attached to the border regions.

Although well-organized and complete quantitative data on integration in the border region are not available, a brief survey of trade connections, trade intensity of regional production, and anecdotal evidence of cross-border activity are informative. Research by David Kerr in the mid-1990s provides perspective on the relative importance of the border regions in the overall trading relationship between China and Russia. In 1995, the three provinces of China's northeast accounted for 71 percent of China's exports to Russia. While the Russian Far East accounted for only 5 percent of Russia's exports to China in 1995, by 1996 this share had increased to 16 percent. The share of Russia's imports from China received by the Russian Far East was larger at around 20 percent in both years.[81]

If proximity to a border with a significant trading partner drives a strong international trade dynamic, economic activity there should be relatively intensive in exports and imports. Data in tables 4.13 and 4.14 are mixed on this score. These tables show the regional volumes of exports and imports as well as their shares of regional GDP. For comparison, the shares of national export and import shares in national GDP are also provided. In the early 1990s the Chinese Northeast was slightly less oriented toward trade than China as a whole, but in recent years this difference has widened. Exports and imports in regional GDP are only around half the national average. Only Liaoning province approaches the national shares, which is partly due to its location on the coast rather than proximity to Russia. Inner Mongolia is the least trade intensive, which is not surprising given its geographic location.

More than any other unit on the Russian side, Khabarovsky Krai has an economy oriented toward exporting, with an export share of GDP consistently above the national average. Primorsky Krai also has a strong export presence in its economic structure, but less than Russia as a whole.[82] If unreported sales of seafood products were included in the official GDP and trade statistics, the export share would be even higher than shown in table 4.14. Regarding imports, Russia's border region with China has been less intensive than the national average, with the exception of Primorsky Krai, where the share has risen to well over twice the national.[83] But taken as a whole, the Russian side of the border region is less trade intensive than the national

Table 4.13. Foreign Trade Intensity in the Border Region: Chinese Areas

	1998	2000	2001	2002	2003	2004	2005	2006	2007	est.[b] 2008	Period Growth Factor	Rate[c]
Levels[a, aa, ab]												
Exports												
Heilongjiang	2,071	2,383	2,129	2,313	3,503	3,377	5,123	6,018	8,385	7,449	3.6	14
Jilin	1,148	1,486	1,493	1,793	2,264	1,741	2,446	2,672	3,365	3,876	3.4	13
Liaoning	7,902	10,568	10,740	11,624	14,151	17,909	21,837	24,348	29,780	34,723	4.4	16
Inner Mongolia	541	1,113	900	984	1,436	1,726	2,023	2,310	3,175	3,651	6.7	21
Total Border Region	11,662	15,549	15,263	16,714	21,353	24,752	31,428	35,349	44,706	49,699	4.3	16
Imports												
Heilongjiang	1,238	1,569	1,879	2,183	2,340	3,159	4,140	6,051	6,987	9,451	7.6	23
Jilin	1,139	1,498	1,926	2,126	4,127	4,780	3,989	4,786	6,068	7,644	6.7	21
Liaoning	6,359	9,471	10,056	10,917	13,929	18,572	19,790	20,583	24,585	33,192	5.2	18
Inner Mongolia	439	1,272	1,259	1,574	1,598	2,270	2,671	2,992	4,465	4,981	11.3	27
Total Border Region	9,175	13,810	15,120	16,799	21,995	28,781	30,590	34,412	42,104	55,269	6.0	20
As Share of GDP (%)[ac, ad, ae, af]												
Exports												
Heilongjiang	6	6	5	5	8	6	9	9	11			
Jilin	6	6	6	7	7	5	6	6	6			
Liaoning	16	19	18	18	21	24	25	24	25			
Inner Mongolia	4	6	4	4	5	13	5	4	5			
Total Border Region	10	11	11	11	12	13	14	13	14			
Total for China	18	21	20	22	27	31	33	35	38			
Imports												
Heilongjiang	4	4	5	5	5	6	7	9	9			
Jilin	6	6	8	8	14	14	10	10	11			
Liaoning	13	17	17	17	20	25	23	21	20			
Inner Mongolia	3	7	6	7	6	7	6	6	7			
Total Border Region	8	10	10	11	13	15	13	13	13			
Total for China	13	19	19	20	25	29	29	29	29			

Sources:

[aa] Regional trade flows from China database of CEIC Data Co., Ltd., which is derived from the Chinese General Administration of Customs, accessed 30 September 2008.

[ab] U.S. GDP deflator from Bureau of Economic Analysis, U.S. Department of Commerce, http://www.bea.gov/bea/dn/nipaweb/NIPATableIndex.asp, accessed 28 September 2008.

[ac] Regional GDP from China database of CEIC Data Co., Ltd., which is derived from the Chinese National Bureau of Statistics, accessed 30 September 2008.

[ad] Exchange rate is annual average, rf series: IMF, *International Financial Statistics*, on-line service, accessed 8 August 2008.

[ae] China total GDP from IMF, *International Financial Statistics*, on-line service, accessed 8 August 2008.

[af] China total exports and imports from IMF, *Direction of Trade Statistics Database*, accessed 7 August 2008.

[a] In millions of constant 2000 US$. Conversion from current to constant 2000 dollars using the U.S. GDP deflator. Deflator for 2008 is based on first quarter.

[b] Estimate based on trade from January–August 2008. Calculated as 12/8 times January–August sum.

[c] Average annual growth rate in % from 1998 through 2008.

Table 4.14. Foreign Trade Intensity in the Border Region: Russian Areas

	1998	2000	2001	2002	2003	2004	2005	2006	2007	Period Growth Factor	Rate[b]
Levels[a, sa, sb]											
Exports											
Amur Oblast'	47	58	94	68	72	91	146	134	175	3.7	16
Jewish Aut. Oblast'	3	12	16	8	8	5	7	10	15	4.8	19
Khabarovsky Krai	895	1,308	2,297	1,128	1,506	1,681	2,485	2,946	1,463	1.6	6
Primorsky Krai	566	612	1,119	758	714	739	926	919	922	1.6	6
Zabaikalsky Krai (Chita)	99	104	83	84	84	77	140	215	295	3.0	13
Total Border Region	1,610	2,095	3,610	2,046	2,384	2,593	3,704	4,224	2,871	1.8	7
Imports											
Amur Oblast'	53	17	21	23	35	46	101	124	232	4.4	18
Jewish Aut. Oblast'	4	5	4	4	4	4	8	15	14	3.2	14
Khabarovsky Krai	191	122	142	207	258	261	498	757	878	4.6	18
Primorsky Krai	511	329	455	728	880	1,234	1,956	2,526	3,517	6.9	24
Zabaikalsky Krai (Chita)	110	60	257	198	100	93	145	213	335	3.1	13
Total Border Region	869	533	880	1,161	1,276	1,639	2,708	3,635	4,977	5.7	21
As Share of GDP (%)[sc, sd, se, sf]											
Exports											
Amur Oblast'	3	6	7	5	4	4	6	5	n.a.		
Jewish Aut. Oblast'	2	9	11	4	3	1	2	2	n.a.		
Khabarovsky Krai	28	54	84	36	41	39	49	48	n.a.		
Primorsky Krai	17	27	45	25	19	15	16	14	n.a.		
Zabaikalsky Krai (Chita)	7	10	7	6	5	4	6	8	n.a.		
Total Border Region	17	31	46	22	22	19	23	22	n.a.		
Total for Russia	26	40	27	31	30	28	31	30	27		

Imports									
Amur Oblast'	3	2	2	2	2	2	4	4	n.a.
Jewish Aut. Oblast'	3	4	3	2	2	1	2	3	n.a.
Khabarovsky Krai	6	5	5	7	7	6	10	12	n.a.
Primorsky Krai	15	14	18	24	24	25	33	38	n.a.
Zabaikalsky Krai (Chita)	8	6	21	14	6	5	7	8	n.a.
Total Border Region	9	8	11	13	12	12	17	19	n.a.
Total for Russia	16	13	12	13	13	13	13	13	19

Sources:

[aa]Regional export and import for 1998 from Goskomstat, *Regiony Rossii: Sotsial'no–Ekonomicheskie Pokazateli*, 2002. Regional export and import for 2000–2007 from Russia database of CEIC Data Co., Ltd., which is derived from the Russian Federal Statistics Service (Rosstat), accessed 30 September 2008.

[ab]U.S. GDP deflator from Bureau of Economic Analysis, U.S. Department of Commerce, http://www.bea.gov/bea/dn/nipaweb/NIPATableIndex.asp, accessed 28 September 2008.

[ac]Regional GDP for 1998–2002 from Goskomstat, *Regiony Rossii: Sotsial'no–Ekonomicheskie Pokazateli*, 2005. Regional GDP for 2003–2006 calculated as GDP per capita times population. GDP/cap from CEIC Russia database of CEIC Data Co., Ltd., which is derived from the Russian Federal Statistics Service (Rosstat). Populations from the same source. Accessed 30 September 2008.

[ad]Exchange rate used is annual average: IMF, *International Financial Statistics*, on-line service, accessed 8 August 2008.

[ae]Russia total GDP from IMF, *International Financial Statistics*, on-line service, accessed 8 August 2008.

[af]Russian total export and import from IMF, *Direction of Trade Statistics Database*, accessed 7 August 2008.

[a]In millions of constant 2000 US$.
[b]Average annual growth rate in % from 1998 through 2007.

economy, although the difference is less than what table 4.13 shows for the Chinese side.

It is also interesting to compare the growth rates of trading activities. Exports from the Chinese side of the border have tended to grow faster than exports from the Russian side, 16 percent compared to 7 percent annually. An exception to this is the Jewish Autonomous Oblast', which had an average export growth rate of 19 percent. But this is a very small regional unit, and at their largest, exports from this oblast' were only 0.5 percent of the regional total. With regard to imports, growth rates on the Chinese and Russian sides of the border region have been roughly the same: 20 and 21 percent, respectively.

While the indicators in tables 4.13 and 4.14 provide perspective on the regional economies, they do not directly address the question of bilateral trade in the region. We can, however, offer some qualitative observations on limited quantitative data from 1995.

On the Chinese side the province most integrated with Russia is Heilongjiang. It has the longest border with Russia and a significant history of occupation by Russians, during both the tsarist and Soviet periods. Jilin has only a short border with Russia, and is more integrated with South Korea. Yet the Tumen River project, involving China, Russia, and North Korea in collaborative industrialization where the three countries come together, has the potential to increase this province's economic connections with Russia. Liaoning Province, the most industrialized province in the Chinese Northeast, does not border Russia. But as an important member of the regional economy, it possesses a degree of integration with Russia that is greater than in most of China outside the northeast. Moreover, Liaoning is the only province in the region with a seacoast, so trade involving marine transport has potential to play a role in this province's integration with the Russian economy. Inner Mongolia, an autonomous region within the PRC, also has an international border with Russia, all of it with the Zabaikalsky Krai. However, most of Inner Mongolia lies far away from Russia, and it is not as industrialized as the rest of the northeast.

David Kerr at the University of Durham provides provincial-level data of China's trade with Russia for 1995.[84] The share of exports and imports having Russia as a destination or origin were highest for Heilongjiang, at 41 and 51 percent, respectively. For Jilin both shares were 6 percent, while for Liaoning they were only 1.5 and 2.4 percent. Inner Mongolia had trade shares with Russia of 8.8 percent for exports and 47 percent for imports. The north central provinces had Russian trade shares at around 4 percent, but only for exports (Beijing) or imports (Hebei and Shanxi). Some provinces outside of the northeast and north central regions had Russian shares a bit larger than Liaoning's, but only for Henan, in the central southern region, was the dollar value of trade volume with Russia ($159 million) comparable to that of Liaoning's ($194 million). Understanding how this regional pattern has changed over the past decade will require further research along the lines of what Kerr accomplished in the mid-1990s.

On the Russian side interaction with China is more evenly spread among the five units that border China. The longest stretch of border lies in the Amur Oblast', which also has the greatest potential to attract Chinese farmers. Over 70 percent of the exports of soy from the Russian Far East go to China, and much of it is produced in Amur.[85] Just to the west lies Zabaikalsky Krai, where wood exports to China are an important influence on the local economy.[86] Forestry products are also an important export from Khabarovsky Krai, but here there is also a substantial industrial sector, including production of military goods. As noted above, China is a major customer of Russian armaments producers and wood products, and Khabarovsk City benefits from this trade. Primorsky Krai is the major source of China's imports of fish from Russia, which has been one of the largest sectors of the local economy for decades.[87] Primorsky also attracts Chinese agricultural labor and is a source of agricultural exports to China. The remaining unit, the Jewish Autonomous Oblast', is a small part of the region, comprising 2 percent of land area and 3.3 percent of population. As a landlocked and relatively isolated area, international trade activity is not prominent, but there are commercial connections with China and probably some labor migration from China. Agriculture and forestry are the most important sectors with relevance for economic integration.

6. Conclusion and Prospects

It is clear from this review of the evidence that the Chinese and Russian economies have become more integrated during the post-Soviet era. The main means of integration is trade, with investment and labor flows playing a relatively minor part thus far. Yet FDI has grown substantially since the 1990s, with investment from China into Russia emerging as more significant than the reverse flow. Both countries have also become more integrated with the world economy during this time. Despite their proximity and complementary resource bases, bilateral integration has not proceeded more rapidly or deeply than their separate integrations with the rest of the world. The reasons for this are related to geography, social features, and policy.

Although the countries share a long border, it is distant from the economic and population centers of Russia. This is particularly relevant for Chinese exports to Russia, primarily consumer goods. Distance is less of a factor for Russian exports to China because much of the related production activity occurs in the eastern regions of Russia, where extractive industries are dominant. Official pronouncements supporting increased trade have been part of the bilateral dialogue throughout this era, but at the same time policies have been put in place that restrict it. My perception is that protectionist policies have not severely limited development of trade and it is likely to continue expanding in the next decade. The greatest potential is in energy exports from Russia, primarily of oil and natural gas, but also including electricity. Export of armaments is a special case, which is driven more by strategic military concerns than economic development. The significant arms trade that developed over the past sixteen years may continue in the near term, but in the long term China will probably reduce this dependence by developing indigenous capacity to produce the armaments needed by the Chinese military.

Integration by investment is more sensitive to government actions because of the exposure to risk that committing capital across borders entails. Neither China nor Russia are attractive destinations for portfolio investment given the options of more developed and better-governed capital markets. Direct investment is another matter, as it could take advantage of particular features of the broader economic relationship, such as Chinese firms acquiring natural resource properties in Russia or enterprises to facilitate trade. In the case of FDI, however, Russia has not provided a hospitable environment, particularly in its energy sector, a key objective of China's outward FDI. Moreover, both countries are at an early stage of outward direct investment and their opportunities in other countries have often proven more attractive. There is potential for more bilateral FDI, but this connection will probably develop more slowly than integration through trade.

Labor flow from China to Russia has great potential but also faces great obstacles. Like investment, integration through labor markets is highly sensitive to policy. It is also sensitive to the social environment in the destination country. Russians and Chinese are culturally distant and Russian society is noted for its xenophobic tendencies. Even with a relatively authoritarian government, Russian leaders must respond to attitudes of the citizenry, and their attitudes toward Chinese immigration are not favorable. Policy steps such as limiting the amount of contract labor and implementing difficult visa procedures have served to constrain the flow of Chinese workers seeking opportunities in Russia.

Yet as the demographic and labor market conditions in the border region show, there are fundamental forces that press Chinese citizens to look to Russia for economic opportunity, especially among the rural Chinese population. The population decline in the Russian Far East and the reduction of farming activity across the eastern regions present the Russian government with a very challenging situation. If a way is found to manage this challenge and accommodate the international demographic pressure, there could be substantial economic benefits to both countries. But the prospect of an effective policy in this complex social environment is not particularly auspicious. Benefits through trade are much easier for the Russian leadership to manage.

Notes

1. I use the idea of an international border in a broad sense, which is not limited to the physical perimeter of a country's territory. The essential feature for economics is the crossing from one regime of law, regulation, and culture into another. Electronic transfers of funds and FDI activity make such crossings without any contact with the physical boundary. Trade in products, of course, involves the physical border as well as movement between national regimes.

2. As Elizabeth Wishnick notes in chapter 3, a much discussed bridge across the Amur River that could connect the Russian and Chinese border towns of Blagoveshchensk and Heihe is not yet under construction.

3. For more on relations between China and Russia in the Soviet period, see: M. I. Sladkovskii, *History of Economic Relations between Russia and China*, trans. M. Roublev (Jerusalem: Israel Program for Scientific Translations, 1966); O. A. Westad, ed., *Brothers in Arms: The Rise and Fall of the Sino-Soviet Alliance, 1945–1963* (Washington, D.C.: Woodrow Wilson Center Press, 1998); Richard Lotspeich, "Perspectives on the Economic Relations between China and Russia," *Journal of Contemporary Asia* 36, no. 1 (2006): 48–74.

4. IMF, *Direction of Trade Statistics Yearbook* (Washington, D.C.: International Monetary Fund, 1992).

5. See: Shai Oster, "Illegal Power Plants, Coal Mines in China Pose Challenge for Beijing," *Wall Street Journal*, 27 December 2006, A1, A2.

6. Oster, "Illegal Power Plants, Coal Mines in China Pose Challenge for Beijing."

7. Aside from a brief stop in the former Soviet republic of Kazakhstan, Mevedev's first official visit abroad as Russian president was to China.

8. These figures are in nominal terms, to maintain consistency with the official pronouncements. Data are from International Monetary Fund, Direction of Trade Statistics Database, accessed 7 August 2008. Given the global downturn in economic activity that emerged in 2008, it is likely trade volume fell short of this projected amount.

9. *Newsline* (Radio Free Europe/Radio Liberty electronic news service) 10, no. 208, Part I (9 November 2006).

10. Judith Thornton, "Reform in the Russian Far East: Implications for Economic Cooperation," in *Rapprochement or Rivalry: Russia-China Relations in a Changing Asia*, ed. S. W. Garnett, 257–311 (Washington, D.C.: Carnegie Endowment for International Peace, 1998).

11. James Brooke, "China and Japan Jockey for Share of Russian Gas," *New York Times*, 4 November 2004, W1, W7.

12. A recent report noted a delivery of crude by a Russian tanker to the reserve facility located at Zhenhai. See: Shai Oster and David Winning, "China's Oil Imports Surge amid Relentless Demand," *Wall Street Journal*, 13 October 2006, A3.

13. *Country Profile for Russia*, website of the World Trade Organization, http://stat.wto.org/CountryProfiles/CN_e.htm, accessed on 15 January 2006.

14. *Country Profile for China*, website of the World Trade Organization, http://stat.wto.org/CountryProfiles/CN_e.htm, accessed on 14 January 2007.

15. *Country Profile for China*, website of the World Trade Organization, http://stat.wto.org/CountryProfiles/CN_e.htm, accessed on 14 January 2007; *Country Profile for Russia*, website of the World Trade Organization, http://stat.wto.org/CountryProfiles/CN_e.htm, accessed on 15 January 2006.

16. These are Most Favored Nation averages. Analogous figures are not reported for Chinese imports of agricultural goods from Russia or either category of Russian imports from China.

17. *Country Profile for China*, website of the World Trade Organization, http://stat.wto.org/CountryProfiles/CN_e.htm, accessed on 14 January 2007; *Country Profile for Russia*, website of the World Trade Organization, http://stat.wto.org/CountryProfiles/CN_e.htm, accessed on 15 January 2006.

18. Liudmila Popova, "Recent Trends in Russian-Chinese Economic Cooperation," *World Economic Papers* (special issue), no. 7 (2006): 37–46.

19. "China's Xinghe Inks Refinery Deal with Moscow's Lanta," *Platts Oilgram Price Report* 84, no. 121 (26 June 2006): 1.

20. Popova, "Recent Trends in Russian-Chinese Economic Cooperation."

21. Eswar Prasad and Thomas Rumbaugh, "Beyond the Great Wall," *Finance and Development* (December 2003): 46–49.

22. Russia's armed conflict with Georgia has made WTO membership more remote.

23. *Trade Policies in Russia: The Role of Local and Regional Governments* (Paris: Organization for Economic Cooperation and Development, 2003).

24. Steven Rosefielde, "The Illusion of Westernization in Putin's Russia and Wen's China," conference paper presented at the annual meetings of the Association for Comparative Economic Studies, Chicago, 7 January 2007.

25. James Brooke, "New Face of Farming in Russia's Far East," *New York Times*, 8 July 2004, W1, W7.

26. My analysis does not attempt to account for price level behavior in China and Russia. Trade statistics are typically reported in nominal dollar terms. Use of the U.S. GDP deflator is simply a device to measure the flows in a fixed unit of account.

Greater precision of this measurement is possible, but would not affect the conclusions reached regarding what the trade data imply about economic integration.

27. The numbers in table 4.1 for trade volumes in 2008 are estimates calculated as four times the first quarter amounts. Given the decline in global economic activity, both the Chinese and Russian economies have slowed to below previous trends, so this rough estimate may overstate the volume of trade between them. Given this, and since there may be some seasonality in trade activity, I exclude the 2008 data from calculations of growth factors and growth rates.

28. Official Chinese growth rates are disputed by some economists. The prevailing view is that they are overstated. For a review of the issues, see: Harry X. Wu, "China's GDP Level and Growth Performance: Alternative Estimates and the Implications," *Review of Income and Wealth* 46, no. 4 (2000): 475–99.

29. These growth rates are based on nominal dollar figures (IMF 2008) adjusted to real terms using the U.S. GDP deflator. As in the table, growth statistics exclude the 2008 estimates.

30. Richard Lotspeich, "Perspectives on the Economic Relations between China and Russia," *Journal of Contemporary Asia* 36, no. 1 (2006): 48–74.

31. Popova, "Recent Trends in Russian-Chinese Economic Cooperation."

32. As a clandestine activity, smuggling is difficult to prove. One case revealed in the press involved officers from the Russian Federal Customs Service and Chinese nationals working in Russia. See: *Newsline* (Radio Free Europe/Radio Liberty electronic news service) 10, no. 76, Part I (26 April 2006).

33. Anthony Allison, "Sources of Crisis in the Russian Far East Fishing Industry," *Comparative Economic Studies* 43, no. 4 (2001): 67–93.

34. Commodity composition is based on statistics from the Chinese Customs Administration. Chinese data are more comprehensive and probably more reliable than available Russian statistics.

35. As an indicator of the natural resource intensity of Russian exports, 91 percent of the wood exports to China were in the form of roundwood. See: Popova, "Recent Trends in Russian-Chinese Economic Cooperation."

36. Peter Wonacott, "China Saps Commodity Supplies," *Wall Street Journal*, 24 October 2003, C1, C9.

37. As can be seen from table 4.3, this decline in the share of engineering products is due both to a substantial increase in petroleum and an absolute decline in China's imports of machinery and vehicles from Russia.

38. Popova, "Recent Trends in Russian-Chinese Economic Cooperation."

39. Up to 2003, Yukos was the main Russian supplier of oil to China, shipping its product by rail, which is expensive. The original pipeline proposal (from Angarsk, Russia, to Daqing, China) was a Yukos project and a challenge to the export monopoly of Transneft, the state oil pipeline company. When these shipments were put at risk by the seizure of Yukos assets by the federal Russian government, authorities were careful to ensure that product would continue to be delivered to China and even invited China to participate as a part owner in the main producing subsidiary

of Yukos, Yugankneftgaz. There is evidence also that Chinese authorities facilitated this state seizure by helping to finance the purchase of Yugankneftgaz by the state oil firm, Rossneft, through a $6 billion loan from Chinese banks. But the press contains conflicting reports. For more details see: "Russian Oil: King Solomon's Pipes," *The Economist*, 7 May 2005, 59–60; Gregory White and Bhushan Bahree, "Kremlin Moves to Nationalize Yukos's Chief Unit," *Wall Street Journal*, 31 December 2004, A1, A2; Gregory White and Guy Chazan, "China Lends Russia $6 Billion to Help Finance Yukos Deal," *Wall Street Journal*, 2 February 2005, A2, A6.

40. One possible explanation is that the imports in this classification include a substantial amount of waste oils. HS code 2710 includes waste oils as well as refined products. Finding a definitive resolution to this question will require further research into the fine details of the commodity composition and pricing practices.

41. "Russia's Monopoly Mentality Makes It an Unreliable Partner," *Platts Energy Economist*, no. 299 (1 September 2006): 35.

42. *People's Republic of China—Key Indicators*, Asian Development Bank, 2008, www.adb.org/statistics/, accessed on 15 October 2008.

43. Gregory White, "Exxon, China Reach Tentative Deal on Russian Gas," *Wall Street Journal*, 24 October 2006, A2.

44. "Russia Plans Two Lines to China," *Platts International Gas Report*, no. 545 (24 March 2006): 1.

45. White, "Exxon, China Reach Tentative Deal on Russian Gas."

46. "Russia and China Are So Near but So Far Apart," *Platts International Gas Report*, no. 549 (19 May 2006): 3.

47. *Newsline* (Radio Free Europe/Radio Liberty electronic news service) 9, no. 64, Part I (6 April 2005).

48. Calculations by the author based on data from SIPRI 2007. Details available on request. See: Arms Transfers Database, SIPRI (Stockholm: Stockholm International Peace Research Institute, 2008), http://www.sipri.org/contents/armstrad/access.html, accessed 7 August 2008.

49. SIPRI, *SIPRI Yearbook: Armaments, Disarmament and International Security* (New York: Oxford Univ. Press, [various years]); earlier years of the armaments relation between China and Russia are examined in Bill Gill and Kim Taeho, *China's Arms Acquisitions from Abroad: A Quest for Superb and Secret Weapons* (New York: Oxford Univ. Press, 1995), and Alexander A. Sergounin and Sergey V. Subbotin, "Sino-Russian Military-Technical Cooperation: A Russian View," in *Russia and the Arms Trade*, ed. Ian Anthony, 194–216 (New York: Oxford Univ. Press, 1998).

50. Explanation of the SIPRI methodology can be found at the SIPRI Arms Transfers Project Internet site: http://web.sipri.org/contents/armstrad/at_data.html.

51. Rosefielde, "The Illusion of Westernization in Putin's Russia and Wen's China."

52. *China Statistical Yearbook* (Beijing: China Statistics Press, [2006 and 2007]).

53. This excludes Hong Kong, the Cayman Islands, and the Virgin Islands. I assume that these destinations do not actually absorb Chinese FDI in the usual sense.

54. Li Jianmin, "Russian Efforts to Attract FDI: The Current Situation," *Russian, Central Asian and East European Markets*, no. 2 (2004): 8–14 (in Chinese); Popova, "Recent Trends in Russian-Chinese Economic Cooperation."

55. Ibid.

56. Popova, "Recent Trends in Russian-Chinese Economic Cooperation."

57. "China's Xinghe Inks Refinery Deal with Moscow's Lanta," *Platts Oilgram Price Report* 84, no. 121 (26 June 2006): 1.

58. "Russia and China Are So Near but So Far Apart."

59. *Newsline* (Radio Free Europe/Radio Liberty electronic news service) 10, no. 113, Part I (21 June 2006).

60. "Rosneft's Share Offering," *The Economist*, 20 July 2006, 71.

61. Li Jianmin, "Russian Efforts to Attract FDI"; Popova, "Recent Trends in Russian-Chinese Economic Cooperation."

62. Li Jianmin, "Russian Efforts to Attract FDI."

63. Popova, "Recent Trends in Russian-Chinese Economic Cooperation."

64. Ibid.

65. *Newsline* (Radio Free Europe/Radio Liberty electronic news service) 9, no. 110, Part I (10 June 2005).

66. *Newsline* (Radio Free Europe/Radio Liberty electronic news service) 10, no. 53, Part I (22 March 2006).

67. By "presently" Larin presumably means the year 2004 for these figures. See: Victor Larin, "Chinese in the Russian Far East: Regional Views," in *Crossing National Borders: Human Migration Issues in Northeast Asia*, ed. T. Akaha and A. Vassilieva, 47–67 (New York: United Nationals Univ. Press, 2005).

68. Elizabeth Wishnick, "Migration and Economic Security: Chinese Labour Migrants in the Russian Far East," in *Crossing National Borders: Human Migration Issues in Northeast Asia*, ed. T. Akaha and A. Vassilieva, 79 (New York: United Nations Univ. Press, 2005).

69. Mikhail Alexseev, "Chinese Migration in the Russian Far East: Security Threats and Incentives for Cooperation in Primorskii Krai," in *Russia's Far East: A Region at Risk*, ed. Judith Thornton and Charles Ziegler, 319–47 (Seattle: Univ. of Washington Press and National Bureau of Asian Research, 2002).

70. Pavel A. Minakir, "Chinese Immigration in the Russian Far East: Regional, National and International Dimensions," in *Cooperation and Conflict in the Former Soviet Union: Implications for Migration*, ed. J. R. Asrael and E. A. Payin, 94 (Santa Monica, Calif.: RAND, 1996).

71. Guy Chazan, "Border Crossings: Giant Neighbors Russia, China See Fault Lines Start to Appear," *Wall Street Journal*, 14 November 2006, 1.

72. Michael Todaro, "A Model of Labor Migration and Urban Unemployment in Less Developed Countries," *American Economic Review* 59, no. 1 (1969): 139–47;

John R. Harris and Michael P. Todaro, "Migration Unemployment and Development: A Two-Sector Analysis," *American Economic Review* 60, no. 1 (1970): 126–42.

73. Oded Stark, *The Migration of Labor* (Cambridge, Mass., and Oxford: Blackwell, 1991); Oded Stark and David E. Bloom, "The New Economics of Labor Migration," *American Economic Review* 75, no. 2 (1985): 173–78.

74. The Big Mac Index published by *The Economist* was used for these conversions (Big Mac Index, various years). While perhaps not as precise as some other PPP exchange rates, it is close enough for the comparisons made here. As the publisher of the Big Mac Index notes, "more sophisticated analysis comes to broadly similar conclusions" about whether official exchange rates are over- or undervalued. Thus a more refined PPP exchange rate would not change the fundamental conclusion that average incomes are higher on the Russian side of the border. See: "The Big Mac Index" (various years), *The Economist*, 15 April 1995, 27 April 2000, 6 November 2005, 25 May 2006, 7 July 2007, and 24 July 2008.

75. In 2000, Russian income per capita was only 1.6 times higher. This seems to be an artifact of currency conversion, but it may have partial basis in actual incomes as well. Using the PPP exchange rates from the Penn World tables raises the relative per capita income in Russia to 2.4 times the Chinese. The same comparison for 2001 and 2003 shows the Russian level at 2.5 and 3.0 times the Chinese. This suggests a temporary disequilibrium in the Moscow hamburger market, the main Russian location for McDonald's. In contrast to Russia, McDonald's is ubiquitous in all areas of China.

76. Conversions to dollar measures of the average urban and average rural incomes in China used the same methodology as applied in table 4.11.

77. Wishnick, "Migration and Economic Security: Chinese Labour Migrants in the Russian Far East," 68–92.

78. Jennifer Duncan and Michelle Ruetschle, "Implementing Agrarian Reform in the Russian Far East," *Comparative Economic Studies* 43, no. 4 (2001): 95–121.

79. Brooke, "New Face of Farming in Russia's Far East"; Chazan, "Border Crossings," 1.

80. "Immigrants in Russia: Market Forces," *The Economist*, 20 January 2007, 61.

81. David Kerr, "Problems in Sino-Russian Economic Relations," *Europe-Asia Studies* 50, no. 7 (1998): 1133–56.

82. An exception occurred in 2001 when the Primorsky share was higher than the national average. This was an unusual year for exports from the Russian Far East; export shares were at their highest in all four governmental units.

83. This may partly reflect the krai's role in Russia's international transport, with some imports recorded here actually moving on to other destinations in Russia. Yet it is also well known that foreign countries supply significant consumer goods to residents in Primorsky Krai. Japan in particular plays an important role in this regard.

84. Kerr does not indicate the source of his data. Judging by his remarks, they

come from provincial level economic reports that he collected during a research tour through the region. See: Kerr, "Problems in Sino-Russian Economic Relations."

85. Duncan and Ruetschle, "Implementing Agrarian Reform in the Russian Far East."

86. The Zabaikalsky Krai is formally part of the Eastern Siberian Federal Region rather than the Russian Far East.

87. Allison, "Sources of Crisis in the Russian Far East Fishing Industry."

Sino-Russian Energy Relations

An Uncertain Courtship

Erica S. Downs

Introduction

The China-Russia energy relationship has not reached the level of development their geographical proximity and economic complementariness implies. In terms of forging an energy partnership, China and Russia appear to be a perfect match. China, the world's second largest oil consumer and third largest oil importer and a small but growing consumer and importer of natural gas, is seeking "security of supply" and the diversification of its imports away from the Persian Gulf and the sea lines of communication. Russia, the world's second largest oil producer and exporter and the world's top producer and exporter of natural gas, is pursuing "security of demand" and the diversification of its exports away from Europe. However, the development of the infrastructure necessary for the cost-effective delivery of large volumes of energy from Russia to China has not yet materialized despite more than a decade of bilateral negotiations and repeated statements by both Beijing and Moscow of their intention to tighten their energy embrace.

China-Russia energy relations are stuck in a protracted and uncertain courtship because the forces driving China and Russia apart outweigh, but do not fully mitigate, the forces propelling them together. Despite the attraction each holds for the other as an energy partner, the enormous potential for bilateral energy cooperation remains largely unfulfilled. Not only have historically developed mutual mistrust and lack of understanding contributed to commitment fears in both countries, but China and Russia also have not been equally interested in deepening bilateral energy ties at the same time. During the 1990s, when oil prices were low, Russia pushed for expanded energy cooperation, but China—which was reluctant to invest in expensive infrastructure projects and was intent on taking advantage of the buyer's market to extract maximum price concessions from the Russians—was in no hurry to make binding commitments to cross-border pipelines. The rise in world oil prices after the turn of the century turned the tables. China, motivated by its surging energy demand and concerns that energy might become a constraint on the country's rapid economic growth, became more eager to "settle down" with its neighbor to the north. In contrast, Russia became increasingly reluctant to commit to deeper energy integration with its neighbor to the south in large part because of the intersection of fears about China's rise with the role that energy exports play in Russian foreign policy and domestic politics. The global financial crisis and the fall in world oil prices, however, facilitated a breakthrough in bilateral energy relations, with China lending cash-strapped Russian energy companies US$ 25 billion in exchange for the completion of an oil pipeline to China and a 20-year oil supply contract. This chapter examines the current state of China-Russia energy trade, the forces of convergence and divergence shaping their energy relations, the role that energy plays in the broader bilateral relationship, and some of the factors that might strengthen or weaken energy cooperation between China and Russia.

The State of the Energy Relationship

China-Russia energy trade has grown rapidly over the past decade. Russian crude oil exports to China increased from less than 1,000 barrels per day (b/d) in 1995 to 321,000 b/d in 2006, only to fall to 292,000 b/d in 2007, largely because Russian firms found it more profitable to sell to European customers (see figure 5.1).[1]

In 2005, Russia accounted for 11 percent of China's crude oil imports and China accounted for about 4–5 percent of Russian crude exports. Almost 80 percent of China's crude oil imports are supplied by the Persian Gulf and Africa (see figure 5.2), and a little more than 80 percent of Russian crude exports are delivered to Europe (see figure 5.3). Russia currently does not send any natural gas to China.

Forces of Convergence

There is great potential for the expansion of China-Russia energy trade. China's rapidly growing demand for oil and natural gas complements Russia's substantial reserves of both. Beijing seeks to diversify China's energy imports away from the Persian Gulf, while Moscow aims to diversify its energy

Figure 5.1. China's Crude Oil Imports from Russia, 1995-2007

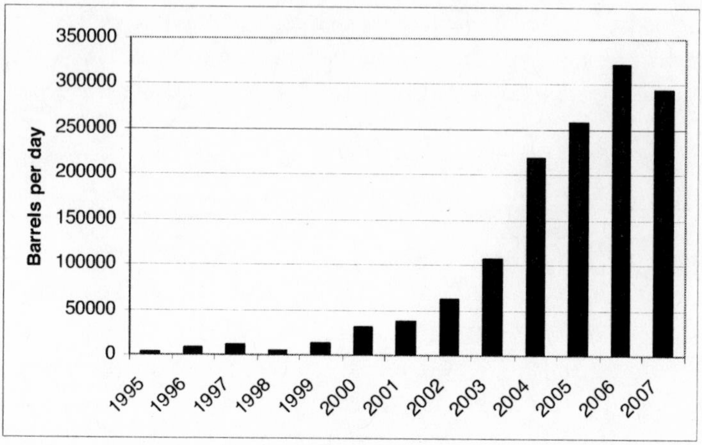

Sources: Data from the General Administration of Customs, People's Republic of China, cited in *International Petroleum Economics* (*guoji shiyou jingji*), various issues, and provided by EIA CSS Information Service Center, Hong Kong.

exports away from Europe. Additionally, geographical proximity allows for direct, cross-border deliveries of energy without third-country transit.

China's Energy Demand

China, self-sufficient in oil as recently as 1993, is the world's second largest oil consumer behind the United States and the world's third largest oil importer after the United States and Japan. Between 1997 and 2007, China accounted for about one-third of world oil demand growth.[2] In 2007, China consumed 7.9 million b/d, with imports of 4.1 million b/d supplying more than 50 percent.[3]

China's oil demand and imports are expected to increase markedly. The International Energy Agency (IEA) projects that by 2030 China's oil demand will climb to 16.5 million b/d and its production will decline to 3.4 million b/d. Consequently, net oil imports will rise to 13.1 million b/d, and China's dependence on imported oil will increase to 80 percent.[4]

China's demand for natural gas, which accounted for just 3 percent of China's total primary energy demand in 2007, has also grown dramatically in recent years.[5] Both consumption and production of natural gas more than tripled between 1997 and 2007, with consumption increasing from 19.5 bcm

Figure 5.2. China's Crude Oil Imports, 2005

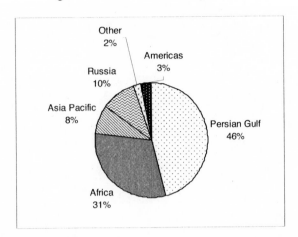

Source: Tian Chunrong, "Analysis of China's Oil Imports and Exports in 2005" (2005 *nian zhongguo shiyou jinchukou zhuangkuang fenxi*), *International Petroleum Economics* (*guoji shiyou jingji*), no. 3 (2006):4.

Figure 5.3. Russia's Crude Oil Exports, 2005

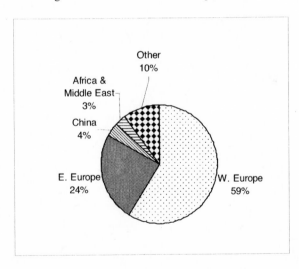

Source: *Almanac of Russian and Caspian Petroleum 2006* (New York: Energy Intelligence Group, 2007).

to 67.3 bcm and production growing from 22.7 bcm to 69.3 bcm.[6] China began to import liquefied natural gas (LNG) from Australia in 2006.

China's demand for and imports of natural gas are also expected to grow substantially. The IEA projects that in 2030 China's natural gas demand of 238 bcm will be more than double its production of 111 bcm. As a result, China's dependence on natural gas imports will exceed 50 percent.[7]

Russia's Energy Supply

Russia has the potential oil and natural gas resources to help satisfy China's burgeoning demand. The country, which holds the world's sixth largest crude oil reserves, is the world's second largest oil producer and exporter after Saudi Arabia.[8] Russian oil output has experienced a dramatic change in fortune since the late 1990s. Production plummeted from 11.5 million b/d in 1987 to 6.1 million b/d in 1996, largely because of reduced investment after the collapse of the Soviet Union.[9] Recovery began in 1999, with the application of advanced production technologies at existing fields.[10] The rise in world oil prices also encouraged expanded output. Between 1999 and 2007, Russian oil production grew by more than 50 percent from 6.2 million b/d to 10 million b/d.[11] Over this period, the increase in Russian oil production alone supplied about 40 percent of the total world oil demand growth and exceeded Chinese demand growth.[12] Russian oil exports have also increased from 3.5 million b/d in 1999 to 7.0 million b/d in 2007.[13]

The IEA expects Russia's oil production and exports to modestly increase, reaching 11.2 million b/d and 7.9 million b/d, respectively, in 2030.[14] However, there is great uncertainty about how much Russia will be able to expand output. There have been no major oil field discoveries over the past decade, and most of the low-cost opportunities to increase production have already been exploited. The development of East Siberia, which the Russian government and oil companies regard as a potential major new production province, involves many challenges, including the remoteness of prospective areas, lack of infrastructure, and the harsh climate.[15]

Russia has the world's largest natural gas reserves—more than 25 percent—and is the world's largest natural gas producer and exporter.[16] In 2007, Russia produced 607 bcm and exported 148 bcm by pipeline to Europe.[17] The IEA projects that in 2030 Russia's natural gas production will reach 823 bcm, with exports of 237 bcm.[18] Although Russia is expected to remain the world's top gas exporter in 2030, domestic and international energy experts are concerned that Gazprom, the Russian state gas monopoly, may have trouble meeting its future export commitments if it does not make the necessary investments in new production and transportation infrastructure.[19] In recent years, the company has focused on downstream investments in foreign countries.

Complementary Trade Diversification Strategies

China and Russia feature prominently in each other's energy trade diversification strategies. China is eager to diversify its oil imports away from the Persian Gulf—which supplies almost half of its crude imports—and away from the sea lines of communication through which more than 85 percent of its crude oil imports flow because of their vulnerability to disruption on the high seas by various modern navies.[20] Consequently, the construction of an oil pipeline from Russia is a high priority for China not only because Russia is located outside of the Persian Gulf region, but also because Russian oil is primarily shipped to China overland. Although Beijing is undoubtedly pleased with the growth in Russian oil exports over the past decade, it probably does not consider rail and tanker deliveries to be a perfect substitute for pipeline deliveries. Not only does a pipeline imply a larger, more stable, longer-term supply of crude, but pipeline deliveries are more cost-effective.[21]

Russia wants to diversify its energy exports away from Europe—the destination for the vast majority of Russia's oil exports and all of its natural gas exports—to have greater flexibility in energy trade. China is an attractive customer to Russia because of the expectation that China's demand for oil and natural gas will grow much more quickly than that of Europe. Viktor Khristenko, Russia's former minister of industry and energy, has projected that by 2020 the Asia-Pacific region's share of Russian crude oil exports will increase from 3 percent to 30 percent and its share of Russian natural gas exports will rise from 5 percent to 25 percent.[22] Most of this oil and gas will probably go to China.

Geographical Proximity

The fact that China and Russia are neighbors is a compelling reason for expanded energy exports from Russia to China. The two countries share a 4,200 kilometer (km) border. This geographical proximity allows for direct trade free from third-party countries, which require transit fees and have the power to withhold supplies.

The Lack of Critical Infrastructure

China and Russia need to construct additional infrastructure to expand energy trade and to make it more cost-effective in the long term. Currently, the majority of Russia's oil exports to China are delivered by rail, which is about two and a half to three times as expensive for Russian oil producers as shipments by pipeline and may not be economical in the absence of high oil prices.[23] A pipeline or LNG facilities are also required for the delivery of natural gas from Russia to China.

Chinese and Russian officials and oil companies have been discussing the construction of a cross-border oil pipeline since the mid-1990s. The initial plan was for a pipeline from Angarsk in East Siberia to Daqing in northeastern China, which Chinese and international observers expected to be finalized during the meeting between Jiang Zemin and Vladimir Putin in December 2002.[24] However, Moscow's interest in the Angarsk-Daqing pipeline had begun to wane by the time of the Jiang-Putin summit. Not only was Moscow increasingly concerned about building a pipeline to a single customer and about the involvement of a private oil company—Yukos—in the project, but also the Russian state pipeline monopoly Transneft had developed a proposal for a rival pipeline from Angarsk to Russia's Pacific coast, which became the objective of an active lobbying campaign by Japan. Moscow subsequently abandoned the Angarsk-Daqing pipeline in favor of a pipeline from East Siberia to the Pacific coast, with a spur to China. This project, known as the East Siberia–Pacific Ocean (ESPO) pipeline, is being built in stages. In 2006, Transneft began work on the first leg from Taishet to Skovorodino. A 70-kilometer spur from Skovorodino to the Chinese border, currently being built by Transneft and which will be extended to Daqing by China National Petroleum Corporation (CNPC), is scheduled for completion in 2010. Moscow has not yet made a final decision about the construction of the second leg from Skovorodino to the Pacific coast. There is great uncertainty among industry experts about whether there is sufficient oil in East Siberia to make the construction of the ESPO commercially viable.[25] Moreover, the timetable for construction is vague.[26]

The most advanced proposal for the export of natural gas from Russia to China is for a 4,000-kilometer pipeline that would supply 30 bcm per year of natural gas to China (20 bcm) and South Korea (10 bcm) from the Kovykta gas field in East Siberia near the Chinese border. Kovykta, which holds about 1.9 trillion cubic meters of gas, is the third largest undeveloped gas field in Russia. TNK-BP, the Russian-British joint venture which has a controlling share (62.9 percent) of Russia Petroleum, the consortium that holds the license to develop Kovykta, has championed the construction of a pipeline to China and South Korea for almost a decade; these countries are the most

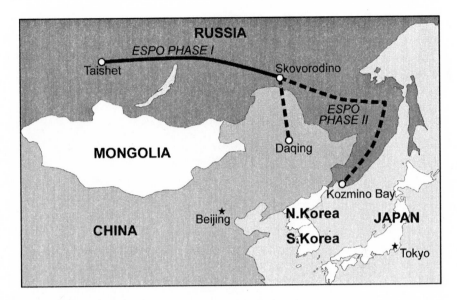

Map 5.1. Proposed East Siberia–Pacific Ocean Pipeline.

Table 5.1. Segments of the East Siberia–Pacific Ocean Oil Pipeline

Segment	Length (kilometers)	Design Capacity (barrels per day)
Taishet-Skovorodino	2,300	600,000 (initial)
		1,600,000 (if other segments built)
Skovorodino-Pacific Coast	2,000	1,000,000
Skovorodino-Daqing	900	600,000

logical markets for Kovykta gas.[27] However, TNK-BP does not have the right to export gas, which is monopolized by Gazprom.

Forces of Divergence

Transnational pipelines are large, complex, and expensive projects that require the active support of both the buyers and sellers. In the case of the proposed China-Russia pipelines, Beijing and Moscow have not been equally supportive of these projects at the same time. Over the past decade, the waxing of China's interest and the waning of Russia's interest in finalizing agreements for these pipelines is due to several factors, including the fall and rise of world oil prices and the inability of both countries to agree on oil and natural gas pricing formulas, Russia's use of energy exports and pipelines as a foreign policy tool, mutual mistrust between the two countries, struggles between Russian energy and transportation companies for control over energy deliveries to China, and a lack of understanding by energy officials and companies in both countries about how their counterparts operate.

The Fall and Rise of Oil Prices

The dynamics of the China-Russia energy relationship have been shaped by fluctuations in world oil prices. In the 1990s, when world oil prices were low and the Russian oil industry was starved for capital, Russia was more interested in selling oil and natural gas to China than China was in buying. As Chinese analysts are fond of pointing out, it was the Russians who first proposed constructing an oil pipeline from Russia to China in 1994.[28] The Russians, according to Chinese analysts, were also willing to sell CNPC a stake in Russia Petroleum at a "reasonable price."[29] The Chinese hesitated, and BP purchased a 10 percent stake in 1997.

The Chinese, however, were in no hurry to finalize the negotiations for oil and gas pipelines that became a regular feature of meetings between Chinese and Russian leaders or to acquire upstream assets in Russia. Not only did the Chinese consider Russia to be a particularly risky country in which to invest,[30] but they were not preoccupied with securing oil supplies because of the low world oil prices, especially in the late 1990s when oil prices fell below $11 per barrel in December 1998.[31] In the last two years of the twentieth century there was a reluctance among the Chinese leadership, notably then-Premier Zhu Rongji, who was in charge of China's economy, to invest in transnational pipelines—the project economics of which are less attractive the lower the price of oil—and the acquisition of oil exploration and production assets abroad when oil could be purchased so cheaply on the international market.[32] Chinese officials and CNPC were also content to discuss the proposed Kovykta pipeline at a leisurely pace because China was not ready to absorb the 20–30 bcm of natural gas it would deliver annually and they felt they had a captive supplier in TNK-BP.[33] The Chinese also stalled the oil and gas pipeline negotiations in hopes of gaining price concessions from the Russians.[34] They would later come to regret this tactic when the oil pipeline, which they had thought was firmly in their grasp, seemed to suddenly slip through their fingers.[35]

The rise in world oil prices over the past decade shifted the power in the China-Russia energy relationship from China to Russia. The increase in the average annual price of oil from $14 per barrel in 1998 to $72 per barrel in 2007 and China's own oil consumption and import growth over this period—a source of upward pressure on world oil prices—created anxiety in Beijing about the security of China's oil supply.[36] This energy insecurity made Beijing increasingly eager to finalize the oil and gas pipeline negotiations.[37]

Unfortunately for China, the feeling in Russia was not mutual. The rise in oil prices fueled the growth of resource nationalism in Russia, motivating Moscow to expand its control over oil and natural gas resources. While this phenomenon has emerged, to varying degrees, in hydrocarbon-rich states around the world, it took a decidedly more political bent in Russia.[38] For Moscow, greater state control of energy assets is not only a way to revitalize its economy but also a means to achieve international political and economic gains. (In his 1997 doctoral dissertation, former president and current prime minister Vladimir Putin argued that Russia's energy resources were an important vehicle for revitalizing Russia's economy and restoring Russia's great power status.)[39]

The emergence of higher oil prices and Russian resource nationalism were an unwelcome surprise to China. It was a surprise because the Chinese government and NOCs were caught off guard by how quickly the world oil and natural gas markets changed from buyer's to seller's markets.[40] Moreover, the news was unwelcome because it contributed to delays in the pipeline negotiations that the Chinese had limited ability to influence.

Indeed, both the oil and gas pipeline projects have been hindered by the involvement of private companies, whose control of export pipelines would undermine Moscow's ability to use energy exports for foreign policy leverage. In the case of the oil pipeline, an important factor behind the abandonment of the Angarsk-Daqing route—and its replacement with the ESPO pipeline and spur to China—was the fact that the principal Russian supporter of the Angarsk-Daqing oil pipeline was Yukos, a private oil company increasingly resented by the Kremlin and Russian state oil companies. Not only had Yukos become the country's largest oil producer through questionable privatizations in the 1990s (which left the state-owned companies indignant that they had been cheated out of assets they maintained rightfully belonged to them), but it also threatened to break the state's export pipeline monopoly.[41] Moreover, Yukos had been exploring the possibility of establishing a joint venture with ExxonMobil, and Moscow was opposed to an American oil company having even indirect ownership of an export pipeline.[42] Additionally, with the reassertion of state control over the energy sector, the Kremlin and the Russian state energy firms became increasingly irritated with CNPC for continuing to negotiate with Yukos rather than the Russian state.[43] (Indeed, one of the lessons China learned from the "Yukos Affair" was to only negotiate with Russian state energy companies.)[44] In the case of the natural gas pipeline, opposition from Gazprom has substantially delayed the plans of the private and half-foreign firm TNK-BP to export gas from the Kovykta field.[45]

The sharp rise in natural gas prices also contributed to the lack of progress on the Kovykta pipeline by rendering the low prices insisted on by the Chinese even more unattractive to the Russians. Sino-Russian negotiations over the export of Russian natural gas to China have collapsed repeatedly over China's refusal to pay internationally competitive prices for natural gas.[46] In 2007, for example, the price CNPC offered Gazprom ($5.28 per million Btu) was about 60 percent of the price at which Gazprom sold gas to Europe in mid-2008 ($13–14 per million Btu).[47] Historically, CNPC has insisted that Gazprom sell natural gas to China at a price that is competitive with China's low domestic coal prices, while Gazprom wants CNPC to pay natural gas prices that are tied to oil prices, like its customers in Europe do.[48]

Russian Energy Diplomacy and the "China Card"

Moscow's use of oil and natural gas exports as a means to gain economic and political benefits from energy importers is another reason for the delay in the construction of an oil pipeline from Russia to China. The emergence of Japanese support for the pipeline from East Siberia to the Pacific coast provided Russia with the opportunity to exploit the competition between China and Japan. Moscow has delayed making a final decision about the ESPO pipeline and its China spur to maximize concessions from both countries.

Japan initially appeared to offer the larger prize. Tokyo launched its campaign for the ESPO pipeline by indicating its willingness to consider financing the pipeline with preferential loans and to help fund oil exploration in East Siberia.[49] However, a formal financing offer has yet to be made. Japanese willingness to foot the bill for the project seems to have waned with growing uncertainty about the availability of sufficient oil in East Siberia and Moscow's refusal to guarantee that the pipeline to the Pacific coast will be built before the spur to China.[50] Individuals from the Japan Bank for International Cooperation have indicated that they are not in favor of supporting the project if it involves heavy subsidies.[51] Additionally, the substantial increase in Russian revenue from oil and natural gas since the Japanese first made their offer to fund the project in early 2003 has made Japanese financing less attractive.[52]

The Chinese, however, have delivered more. First, in December 2004, CNPC loaned Rosneft $6 billion as an advance payment for oil supplies through 2010. Rosneft used the money to help fund its $9.4 billion purchase of Yuganskneftegaz, the main production unit of Yukos, which the Kremlin had seized as payment for back taxes. The Chinese loan was especially valuable as Rosneft was unable to borrow from Western banks because Yukos had filed for chapter 11 bankruptcy protection in the United States. (This first "loans for oil" deal later became a source of tension between Rosneft and CNPC. Rosneft, which claimed that changes in world oil prices were causing it to lose money on crude deliveries to China, pressured CNPC to renegotiate the oil pricing formula.)[53] Second, in July 2006, CNPC subscribed to $500 million worth of Rosneft shares during the company's initial public offering. CNPC's participation helped make the auction a "success" despite the absence of institutional investors because of the controversy over Rosneft's acquisition of Yuganskneftegaz.[54] Third, CNPC financed the $37 million feasibility study of the ESPO branch from Skovorodino to the Chinese border and agreed to foot the bill for the pipeline spur, estimated to cost $436 million.[55] Fourth, and most importantly, in 2009 the China Development Bank loaned $15 billion to Rosneft and $10 billion to Transneft, providing them with money to refinance debts and make large-scale investments at a time when both companies were having trouble raising capital. In return, Transneft approved the construction of the long-awaited spur from the ESPO to China and Rosneft agreed to supply CNPC with 300,000 b/d of oil for twenty years to fill the spur.

China has also been valuable to Russia as a tool to pressure Europe to think twice about attempting to reduce its dependence on Russian energy. The energy pricing disputes between Russia and the Ukraine (2005–2006) and Belarus (2006–2007) resulted in brief supply disruptions to Europe when Russia temporarily suspended pipeline deliveries, raising doubts in Europe about the reliability of Russia as an energy supplier and inciting discussions about the need to diversify energy imports away from Russia. In response, the Russians signed a nonbinding agreement with the Chinese in March 2006 for the construction of two pipelines to deliver up to 80 bcm of natural gas per year (more than half the amount it ships to Europe) from West and East Siberia to China by 2011. The proposed pipelines were intended, at least in part, to remind Europe that Russia might develop an alternate market for its natural gas.[56]

Meanwhile, China has turned to Central Asia for its first pipeline imports of oil and natural gas. In 2003, when Chinese hopes for the Angarsk-Daqing oil pipeline dimmed with growing Russian interest in and intense Japanese lobbying for an alternative pipeline to Russia's Pacific coast, they dusted off their plans to build an oil pipeline from Kazakhstan to China.[57] The eastern leg of this multistage project—which runs from Atasu, Kazakhstan, to Alashankou, China—began sending oil to China in 2006. The pipeline has helped increase China's oil imports from Kazakhstan from 26,000 b/d in 2005 to 120,000 b/d in 2007, but it is still operating below its design capacity of 200,000 b/d.[58] The western leg of the pipeline, which runs from Atyrau to Kenkiyak, was finished in 2003 and currently flows from east to west. The construction of the middle leg of the pipeline from Kenkiyak to Kumkol, completed in 2009, will double the capacity of the pipeline and provide oil companies operating in the Caspian Sea region with an eastern export route.

In 2007, construction began on a pipeline from Turkmenistan to China, which is slated for completion in late 2009. This project appeared to be extremely ambitious when the two countries signed the initial agreement in April 2006 because of questions about whether there would be sufficient gas available to fill the pipeline, designed to carry 30 bcm per year, by its planned start-up date and whether the countries through which the pipeline must cross would agree to the project.[59] However, both sides have worked hard to make the pipeline a reality. CNPC, which has provided US$2 billion in funding for the US$7 billion project, will supply 13 bcm of gas from its operations at the Bagtiyarlyk field on the right bank of the Amu Darya River. Turkmenistan has pledged to provide the remaining 17 bcm from the Samandepe and Altyn Asyr deposits (CNPC reportedly secured tough penalty clauses should Turkmenistan fail to meet its obligations).[60] CNPC also negotiated transit agreements with Uzbekistan and Kazakhstan.

Some industry analysts maintain that Russia has featured prominently in China's decisions to build oil and natural gas pipelines from Central Asia, with several arguing that these projects are a hedge against the failure of the proposed pipeline deliveries of oil and natural gas from Russia to China and others asserting that China pursued the Central Asian pipelines, especially the Turkmenistan-China gas pipeline, to strengthen its hand in its negotiations with Russia by reminding its northern neighbor that China has alternate sources of overland energy supplies.[61] Both of these arguments probably overstate the role that Russia played in China's decisions to build the Kazakhstan-China oil pipeline and the Turkmenistan-China natural gas pipeline. Although China's frustration with the slow progress in pipeline negotiations with Russia has increased Chinese enthusiasm for the Central Asian pipelines, China has had a longstanding interest in oil and natural gas imports from both the north and west. Progress on the pipelines from Central Asia has not dampened Chinese enthusiasm for the Russian pipelines.[62] Moreover, it is also highly unlikely that CNPC would invest the time and money to negotiate, let alone build, a pipeline as expensive and challenging as the one from Turkmenistan in a bid to increase its leverage in negotiations with Russia.[63] Indeed, CNPC's main motivation for building the Turkmenistan-China natural gas pipeline is to secure supplies for its second West-East Natural Gas

Map 5.2. Pipeline Connecting Kazakhstan and China.

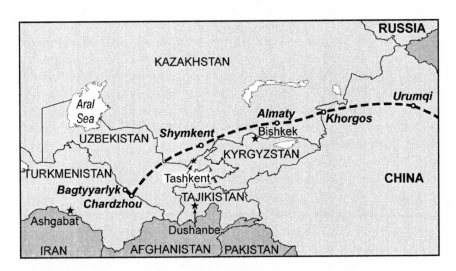

Map 5.3. Proposed Pipeline Connecting Turkmenistan and China.

Pipeline.[64] It certainly would be icing on the cake for CNPC if the supply of natural gas from Turkmenistan to China happens to aid CNPC in its negotiations with Gazprom, although both companies undoubtedly realize that there will always be room for Russian gas in China.[65]

Mutual Mistrust

Mistrust between China and Russia has hindered energy cooperation between the countries.[66] Russia's suspicions of China have been a much greater impediment than China's suspicions of Russia. Moscow fears that increasing dependence on China as an energy export destination will eventually constitute a threat to national security. In contrast, Beijing is primarily concerned with whether Russia will fulfill its promises.

Moscow has been reluctant to make binding commitments to construct oil and natural gas pipelines to China largely because of concerns that by doing so Russia will be directly helping to fuel the rise of a country that poses a serious long-term threat to Russian national security.[67] Russia fears becoming an "energy appendage" to China (a concept traditionally associated with Europe), which is at odds with its self-proclaimed status as a global superpower. Russia's energy resources are intended to enhance rather than diminish Russia's international status.[68] Moscow is irritated that China purchases little machinery and manufactured goods from Russia. Putin, during his March 2006 visit to China, called the fact that the bulk of Russian exports to China are natural resources and raw materials a "serious problem" in bilateral relations and urged China to diversify its imports from Russia.[69]

Russia's anxieties about supplying ever larger quantities of energy to China were reflected in the Kremlin's indecision about the routing of the ESPO pipeline. One of the reasons the Pacific coast route appeals to Moscow is the hope that it would facilitate the development of the sparsely populated Russian Far East.[70] Many Russians are convinced that this part of the country will increasingly become a Chinese sphere of influence if larger numbers of the hundreds of millions of inhabitants of China's northeast move north in search of additional "living space."[71] Moscow also vacillated on the construction of a pipeline to China because it would make Russia a "captive supplier," subject to pressure from China on volume and price. (Russia's experience with the Blue Stream natural gas pipeline to Turkey taught the country about the perils of selling to just one customer: after the project was completed, a recession triggered a downgrading in Turkish natural gas demand projections and Turkey took advantage of its single-buyer status to renegotiate prices.)[72]

Chinese officials and oil companies, while eager to expand energy trade with Russia, are deeply skeptical of Russia's intentions because of the slow progress on the development of the transnational oil and natural gas pipelines.[73] Russia's credibility with the Chinese arguably has been most damaged by its failure to deliver the Angarsk-Daqing oil pipeline.[74] The Chinese have been reluctant to criticize the Russians—lest they further jeopardize their chances for an oil pipeline—and instead initially directed much of their anger toward the Japanese for their support of a pipeline to the Pacific coast. In a rare public expression of official dissatisfaction with the Sino-Russian energy relationship, Zhang Guobao, the vice minister of the National Development and Reform Commission (NDRC) in charge of energy until June 2006, voiced frustration[75] with Russia's wavering over deeper energy cooperation with China on the eve of Putin's visit to Beijing in March 2006:

- "One moment Russia is saying they have made a decision, the next saying that no decision has been made. To date, there has been no correct information. This is regrettable."
- "Currently, the Sino-Russia pipeline is one step forward, two steps back. Today is cloudy with a chance of sun while tomorrow is cloudy with a chance for clouds, just like a weather forecast."
- "Even though there have been a lot of promises expressing Russia's interest in exporting natural gas to China, in truth no real progress has been made."[76]

Russia's use of energy exports as a foreign policy lever has also raised China's doubts about Russia's trustworthiness.[77] Its cutoff of natural gas exports to pressure Ukraine to pay higher prices raised concerns about the extent to which China should rely on Russian energy supplies. Although the incident did not dampen China's enthusiasm for pipelines from Russia, it did serve as a reminder that China should avoid becoming overly dependent on Russian energy through continued supply diversification.

Russian Corporate Infighting

Struggles between Russian companies for control over energy flows to China have also impeded the construction of cross-border oil and natural gas pipelines. The Angarsk-Daqing oil pipeline was a victim of the competition between Yukos and Transneft. The Yukos-backed project threatened to break Transneft's monopoly on pipeline oil exports. In response, Transneft developed its own proposal for a rival pipeline to the Pacific coast. This proposal would preserve Transneft's monopoly and, unlike the Angarsk-Daqing proposal, would avoid the risks associated with building a pipeline to a single customer.[78]

After the demise of Yukos, Russian Railways—whose president, Vladimir Yakunin, is a close associate of Putin—emerged as a rival to Transneft. Russian Railways has been a prime beneficiary of the oil pipeline project delays, and the company is loath to lose its lucrative oil freight business to Transneft.[79] The rail company claims that additional investments will allow it to ship 600,000 b/d,[80] double the initial capacity of the proposed pipeline spur to China from Skovorodino. Yakunin even published a book that assesses all possible energy transportation routes to Asia and concludes that rail deliveries are the best option.[81] Moscow's decision to construct the ESPO pipeline in phases, with the first leg terminating at Skovorodino rather than at the Chinese border or on the Pacific coast, may reflect a deliberate effort to balance the interests of Transneft and Russian Railways.[82]

Gazprom has actively undermined TNK-BP's plans to export natural gas from the Kovykta field to China via pipeline. Gazprom, which seeks to gain a majority stake in the project—in which it is not currently invested—and to maintain its export monopoly, has refused to grant export rights to the TNK-BP-led consortium.[83] TNK-BP repeatedly sought to negotiate with Gazprom over the company's role in the project, recognizing that Kovykta gas will not be exported unless Gazprom is brought in.[84] The two companies reached an agreement in principle in June 2007 for Gazprom to buy TNK-BP's controlling stake in Kovykta, but the deal has not been finalized. Gazprom has not been in a hurry to do so, probably because it does not want to enter the project on a commercial basis.[85]

Mutual Lack of Understanding

Many Chinese analysts argue that one of the principal factors behind China's difficulties in expanding energy cooperation with Russia is that China's NOCs have insufficient knowledge about Russian energy companies and energy decision-making.[86] Both China's NOCs and Chinese foreign policy experts have noted that China's NOCs do not always fully grasp the political environments in which they seek to invest.[87] They maintain that this lack of understanding has played an especially prominent role in China's setbacks in Russia.

For Chinese analysts, the event that epitomizes the failure of China's NOCs to understand Russia was CNPC's aborted attempt to acquire a controlling share in the Russian oil company Slavneft in December 2002, which played out in the same way as the unsuccessful bid by China National Offshore Oil Corporation (CNOOC) for the U.S. oil company Unocal did in 2005.[88] CNPC, like CNOOC, was willing to pay a much higher price than its chief competitor. Although CNPC reportedly was ready to offer US$3 billion for a 74.59 percent stake in Slavneft, the company was sold to Russian oil companies for just US$1.86 billion.[89] CNPC, like CNOOC, also withdrew from the competition in the face of strong opposition from the host country. Russian parliamentarians, unnerved by the prospect of a state-owned company from a strategic rival gaining control of Russian oil reserves, recommended that CNPC be barred from the Slavneft auction.[90] The Russian oil companies vying for Slavneft shared their opposition.[91]

China's NOCs are not the only ones that have had difficulties navigating the Russian energy sector. Gazprom and Rosneft are also opaque to Western investors.[92] Several international oil companies have suffered from the lack of clear and transparent rules on investment, which Russian bureaucrats have exploited to support Russia's state energy firms in their efforts to acquire stakes in the remaining foreign-controlled projects in Russia, including ExxonMobil's Sakhalin I, Shell's Sakhalin II, and Total's Kharyaga.[93]

Chinese officials have also voiced frustration with the opaqueness of Russian energy policy making. Zhang Guobao has observed that despite the fact that the NDRC has been in contact with Russia for a long time on energy matters, the NDRC did not understand Russia and had difficulty locating decision makers.[94] According to Zhang, "We have contacted government officials. We've even talked to Putin and department heads. We've talked to everyone in the government. They say they can't make a decision, and we should talk to the private sector. We've met with every company. They say they can't sign an agreement and we should talk to the government. We don't know who can make decisions."[95]

Just as the Chinese are flummoxed by Russian energy decision making, the Russians are somewhat mystified by how the Chinese do business. According to Bobo Lo at the Centre for European Reform, the Russians have little understanding of how the Chinese operate. In contrast, the Russians have been selling natural gas to European countries for more than forty years.[96] One example of how the Russians have found dealing with the Chinese different from the Europeans is in the sequencing of the components of transnational pipeline projects. The Russians prefer to sign supply agreements first and then construct pipelines. The Chinese, however, have a history of building pipelines first and then securing supplies to fill them. CNPC, for example, built both the West-East Natural Gas Pipeline, which transports natural gas from Xinjiang to Shanghai, and the Kazakhstan-China oil pipeline without firm supplies for either project. CNPC is comfortable constructing the spur from the ESPO pipeline to the Chinese border without a supply contract with Rosneft, while Rosneft insists that a supply contract for deliveries must be signed before the spur can be built. Negotiations between the two companies are deadlocked over the issue of the price formula.[97]

The Role of Energy in the Bilateral Relationship

Energy has not been a major force of convergence in China-Russia relations to date. The political and military dimensions of the bilateral relationship are much more important than the economic one. Consequently, concerns that China-Russia energy ties are bolstering cooperation on other issues are misplaced; energy is a weak link in the chain that binds the two countries together.[98]

The strongest element of the bilateral relationship is shared political interests. China and Russia see eye-to-eye on a variety of international issues, including resistance to U.S. hegemony, cooperation in the United Nations Security Council, respect for each other's territorial integrity (Beijing supports Moscow's position on Chechnya, and Moscow supports Beijing's position on Taiwan), and the promotion of stability in Central Asia, including efforts to reduce the American military presence in the region. Both countries view their relations with each other in the context of their relations with the United States. Since 2001, Beijing and Moscow have prioritized their relationships with Washington over their relationships with each other.[99]

Military cooperation has also been a strong component of the bilateral relationship, especially in the areas of border demarcation and arms sales. In terms of border demarcation, China and Russia have worked to resolve the disagreement over their shared boundary since 1991, with a final agreement reached in 2005. In terms of arms sales, China has been a major market for Russian weapons over the past decade. These sales provide Russia with an important source of foreign currency and China with relatively inexpensive equipment that is compatible with its existing inventory.[100] However, Moscow is reluctant to sell China the more advanced military hardware and technology it supplies to India and to coproduce a new generation of fighters because of concerns about increasing the capabilities of a potential adversary, which frustrates the Chinese.[101]

The economic relationship between China and Russia is a source of bilateral friction. Although trade between the two countries has grown substantially over the past decade, it is dissatisfying to both Russia and China. Moscow fears Russia will become China's "energy appendage," and Putin has urged Beijing to import more machinery and technology, in which the Chinese are not particularly interested. China, meanwhile, is quite content to have Russia as a raw materials and natural resources base but is very disappointed that bilateral energy relations have developed more slowly than was anticipated. Indeed, it is the stalled energy cooperation between Russia and

China where Russia's ambivalence about China's rise and China's concerns about Russia's fickle international behavior clearly manifest themselves.

Conclusion: Whither China-Russia Energy Relations?

Over the past decade China-Russia energy relations have been stuck in an uncertain courtship. Both countries continue to pursue the relationship because each views the other as an attractive energy partner for the long term. However, this engagement has not yet led to marriage because neither country has been ready to settle down at the same time. Whether and when China and Russia develop closer energy relations may depend on several factors, including changes in world oil prices, China's willingness to pay more for natural gas, China's willingness to play by Russia's "rules of the game" for energy cooperation, and Russian concerns about the "China threat."

A. Changes in the Price of Oil and Natural Gas

Higher oil and natural gas prices are likely to frustrate closer energy cooperation. A high energy price environment might encourage Moscow to delay progress on cross-border pipelines in an attempt to maximize concessions from China and other stakeholders. Higher prices are also likely to facilitate the continued consolidation of Russian state control over the oil and natural gas industry, which will limit upstream investment opportunities for foreign investors. Additionally, a Russia flush with windfall energy profits may be emboldened to seek to renegotiate the terms of the loans-for-oil agreements, which Russia signed during a period of weakness.

A prolonged period of lower oil and natural gas prices, however, might foster closer China-Russia energy cooperation. Lower prices might make Russia, whose economic health is highly dependent upon energy prices, more willing to build pipelines to China—to ensure "security of demand"—and more receptive to financing offers from abroad. A lower energy price environment may also motivate Moscow to open the door wider to foreign investment in the Russian oil and natural gas industry. Whether international oil companies will be more welcome than China's NOCs will depend on a number of factors, including the nature of the project (the more complex the project and the more advanced the technology and the management skills required, the more likely the edge will go to an international oil company) and Russian attitudes toward China (the greater the anxiety about China, the less the enthusiasm about Chinese investment).

B. China's Willingness to Pay Internationally Competitive Prices for Natural Gas

An agreement by China to pay internationally competitive prices for Russian natural gas would remove one of the major obstacles to the realization of the Kovykta pipeline. Although the Chinese have long insisted that Russia sell gas to them at a price substantially lower than that paid by Russia's European customers, there is a growing realization in Beijing that the window of opportunity to secure subsidized gas exports from Russia has closed.[102] After 2006, Gazprom stopped subsidizing natural gas export to all Commonwealth of Independent States with the exception of Armenia and Belarus, which are on schedule to fully transition to market prices by 2012.[103]

Moreover, China's oil companies have already grudgingly come to terms with the fact that they must pay internationally competitive prices for LNG. CNOOC signed China's first two twenty-five-year LNG contracts—with Australia's Northwest Shelf project in 2002 and with Indonesia's Tangguh project in 2003—at a time of historic overcapacity in the global LNG market. Consequently, it secured the impressively low prices of US$3.00 per million British thermal units (MMBtu) and US$2.80 per MMBtu (later raised to about US$3.5 MMBtu in 2006), respectively, which the company expected would set a precedent for future contracts.[104] However, the sharp rise in global LNG prices forced CNOOC and its domestic peers to agree to pay more. According to industry analysts, the LNG supply contracts that China's NOCs signed with Qatargas in 2008 reflected international prices for long-term contracts.[105]

The LNG supply agreements signed with Qatar make it more likely that CNPC will have to pay internationally competitive prices for Russian natural gas. The prices the companies were paying for Qatari LNG were on par with the prices at which Russia was selling natural gas to European customers in mid-2008, and the Russians took notice. In June 2008, Gazprom deputy CEO Alexander Medvedev stated, "We know that China buys LNG at market world prices. We don't see any reason why pipeline gas must be sold cheaper."[106]

Russia's hand in price negotiations with China may also be strengthened by Turkmenistan. In the summer of 2008, Gazprom reportedly agreed to pay Turkmenistan European-level prices for natural gas, which appear to be substantially higher than the price at which CNPC agreed to buy gas from Turkmenistan.[107] Gazprom is hoping that the plan of Turkmenistan and other Central Asian natural gas producers to increase their gas price to European levels will prompt Ashbagat to renegotiate its supply contract with CNPC.[108]

According to Medvedev, "Given that Russia and Turkmenistan sell their gas at international market price, I think that China will have to buy gas at the similar price."[109] Gazprom is probably content to hold off on full development of Kovykta until CNPC is ready to pay European-level prices for gas.

C. China's Willingness to Play by Russia's "Rules of the Game" for Energy Cooperation

China's continued willingness to play by Russia's "rules of the game" for energy cooperation might help China's NOCs secure additional upstream investment opportunities. Although Chinese officials and NOCs have repeatedly stated that they do not understand the Russian energy sector, they appear to have realized that, especially in a higher oil price environment, Russia will only welcome those foreign investors who are willing to play by its rules. These include taking minority stakes in projects on terms highly favorable to Russian state firms, such as Sinopec's acquisition of Udmurtneft from TNK-BP in 2006,[110] and exchanging downstream access for upstream access, such as the nonbinding agreements CNPC and Rosneft signed in 2006 for cooperation in China's downstream sector and the establishment of a joint venture for exploration and production in Russia.[111] Indeed, one Chinese analyst has described CNPC's plan to build a refinery in Tianjin with Rosneft as an example of "exchanging market for energy."[112]

D. The "China Threat"

Increased anxiety in Russia about Chinese exploitation of Russia's demographic vulnerabilities in East Siberia and the Russian Far East may thwart the expansion of China-Russia energy cooperation. Russian nationalists at the central and local levels might be able to delay or deter deeper energy cooperation between China and Russia on the grounds that supplying China with more energy would help fuel China's continued rise and the threat China poses to Russia's sparsely populated eastern regions. Although China can provide Russia with "security of demand" and help diversify Russia's oil and natural gas exports away from Europe, fears of a rising China may continue to influence Russian energy decision-making.

Notes

The author would like to thank Edward Chow, Igor' Danchenko, Scott Harold, Elena Herold, and Robert Sutter for helpful discussions and comments.

1. Song Yen Ling, "China's Oil Imports Soar," *International Oil Daily*, 25 Janu-

ary 2008; and data from the General Administration of Customs of the People's Republic of China, cited in Tian Chunrong, "Analysis of China's Oil Imports and Exports in 2007" [2007 nian Zhongguo shiyou jinchukou zhuangkuang fenxi], *International Petroleum Economics* [Guoji shiyou jingji] 17, no. 3 (2008): 40, and provided by EIA CSS Information Service Center, Hong Kong, 17 January 2007 and 8 August 2008.

2. *BP Statistical Review of World Energy*, June 2008, 11. Available at www. bp.com.

3. Ibid., 11, 20.

4. International Energy Agency, *World Energy Outlook 2007* (Paris: OECD/ IEA, 2007), 80, 82, 325–26.

5. *BP Statistical Review of World Energy*, June 2008, 28, 40.

6. Ibid., 24, 27.

7. IEA, *World Energy Outlook 2007*, 85, 87, 332.

8. *BP Statistical Review of World Energy*, June 2006, 6.

9. *BP Statistical Review of World Energy*, June 1997, 7; *BP Statistical Review of World Energy*, June 2006, 8.

10. Clifford Gaddy, Fiona Hill, Igor' Danchenko, and Dmitry Ivanov, *Brookings Foreign Policy Studies Energy Security Series: The Russian Federation*, October 2006, 12; http://www.brookings.edu/fp/research/energy/2006russia.htm; and International Energy Agency, *World Energy Outlook 2004* (Paris: OECD/IEA, 2004), 303.

11. *BP Statistical Review of World Energy*, June 2008, 8.

12. Ibid., 8, 11.

13. Ibid.

14. IEA, *World Energy Outlook 2007*, 80, 82.

15. I thank Igor' Danchenko for these points.

16. *BP Statistical Review of World Energy*, June 2008, 22.

17. Ibid., 24, 30.

18. IEA, *World Energy Outlook 2007*, 85, 87.

19. "Former Minister Draws Bleak Future for Russian Energy Sector," *International Oil Daily*, 4 December 2006; and Anna Shiryaevskaya, "IEA Calls on Gazprom to Look Closer Home; Agency Urges More Investment in Domestic Upstream Operations," *Platts Oilgram News*, 2 November 2006.

20. Tian Chunrong, "Analysis of China's Oil Imports and Exports in 2007," 40.

21. "China, Russia Face Energy Challenge: Russia May Not Have Natural Gas for China" [ZhongE mianlin nengyuan kaoyan: E dui Hua tianranqi keneng wu qi ke gong], *Nanfeng Chuang*, 24 April 2007, http://finance.ifeng.com/news/domestic/200704/0423_193_107468.shtml.

22. Nelli Sharushkina, "Russia Targets More Downstream Capacity in Consumer Markets," *International Oil Daily*, 4 April 2006. Viktor Khristenko, "Energeticheskaya strategiya Rossii: Proryv na Vostok" [Russia's Energy Strategy: Breakthrough to the East], *Vedomosti*, no. 19 (6 February 2006). I thank Igor' Danchenko for locating and translating this document.

23. John Webb, "The New Baltic Crude Export Game: What Role Will Vent-spils Play?" *CERA Insight,* 17 April 2003, 2, 6.

24. Zhao Renfeng, "Sino-Russian Oil Link Proposed," *China Daily,* 30 December 2002; and Peter Wonacott, "Thirsting for Oil, China Is Eyeing Russian Supplies—This Week's Beijing Summit Is Expected to Yield Accord on a 1,500-Mile Pipeline," *Wall Street Journal,* 2 December 2002.

25. See, for example, United Financial Group, "Russian Oils 2005: Red Star Rising," United Financial Group (Moscow: UFG, 7 April 2005); and Matthew J. Sagers, John Webb, and Philip Vorobyov, "Oil Pipeline Duel in Eastern Russia Entering Decisive Phase," *CERA Decision Brief,* May 2003.

26. Transneft plans to complete the second phase of the line to the Pacific coast in 2015 and to be operating at the full capacity of 1.6 million b/d by 2025. "ESPO Gets More Oil," *International Oil Daily,* 18 September 2008.

27. Shawn McCormick, "East Siberia-Regional Resource Potential," in *Russia in Asia—Asia in Russia: Energy, Economics, and Regional Relations,* Kenan Institute Occasional Paper #292, ed. F. Joseph Dresen, 24 (Washington, D.C.: Woodrow Wilson International Center for Scholars, 2005).

28. See, for example, Yu Bin, "The Russia-China Oil Politik," *Comparative Connections* 5, no. 3 (October 2003): 138; "*China Business Post*: High-Level NDRC Official Says Plans for the China-Russia Oil Pipeline Have Not Changed" [Caijing shibao: Fagaiwei gaoceng cheng ZhongE shiyou guandao jihua bubian], 20 September 2003,   http://news.xinhuanet.com/newscenter/2003-09/20/content_1091056.htm; and "'Background on the Angarsk-Daqing Pipeline" [AnDa xian' de laili], *Nanfang Zhoumo,* 10 September 2003, http://finance.sina.com.cn/b/20030910/0906439774 .shtml.

29. Xu Haiyan, "Russia's 'Eastern-Oriented' Energy Export Strategy and Sino-Russian Oil and Gas Cooperation—An Analysis Based on Geopolitics and Economics" [Eluosi 'dongxiang' nengyuan chukou zhanlue yu ZhongE youqi hezuo—jiyu diyuan zhengzhijingjixue de fenxi], *Fudan Xuebao (Shehui kexue ban),* no. 5 (2004): 104.

30. Interview with Chinese foreign policy expert, Washington, D.C., 25 January 2007.

31. "Sheng Shiliang: China and Russia Welcome the Best Period in Bilateral Relations" [Shen Shiliang: ZhongE huanlai liangguo guanxi zuihao shiqi], Xinhua, 23 March 2006, http://news.xinhuanet.com/misc/2006-03/23/content_4336459.htm.

32. Interview with Chinese energy and foreign policy experts, Beijing, China, 4 April 2006 and 11 April 2006; Xu Haiyan, "Russia's 'Eastern-Oriented' Energy Export Strategy," 104.

33. Telephone interview with industry insider, 12 January 2007.

34. See, for example, Andrei Glazov and Doug Rohlfs, "China Doll—China Pipeline Talks Stall Despite State Initiative," *Nefte Compass,* 16 November 2006.

35. Xia Yishan, a Chinese diplomat specializing in Russia who currently heads the Centre for the Study of Energy Strategy at the China Institute for International

Studies, the research arm of the Ministry of Foreign Affairs, has argued that if China had had great foresight in the 1990s, then perhaps an oil pipeline from Russia to China would already exist. Zheng Min and Chu Fujun, "Is the Ministry of Energy Almost Here?" [Nengyuanbu huzhiyuchu], *Zhongguo Shiyoushihua*, no. 1 (2005): 24.

36. *BP Statistical Review of World Energy*, June 2008, 16.

37. "Expert: The Change in Gas Pipelines Does Not Affect the Overall Sino-Russian Energy Situation" [Zhuanjia: shuqi guandao shengbian wushang ZhongE nengyuan daju], *Nanfang Zhoumo*, 12 October 2006, http://finance.people.com.cn/GB/1038/59942/4911706.html.

38. "Resource Nationalism: Then and Now," *Petroleum Intelligence Weekly*, 8 January 2007.

39. For more on Putin's views on energy, see Stephen Boykewich, "The Man with the Plan for Russia, Inc.," *Moscow Times*, 6 June 2006; and "Vladimir Putin's Academic Writings and Natural Resource Policy," *Problems of Post-Communism* 53, no. 1 (January–February 2006): 48–54.

40. Telephone interview with industry insider, 12 January 2007; and Liu Li, "Sino-Russian Energy Cooperation" [Lun ZhongE nengyuan hezuo], unpublished master's thesis, School of Public Policy and Management, Tsinghua University, Beijing, China, May 2006, 50.

41. "Russian Politics: Khodorkovsky, Yukos and the Kremlin," *EIU ViewsWire*, 19 May 2005; and Philip Vorobyov, "Russian-Japanese Relations and Oil Pipeline Politics: Much Hope, Much Uncertainty," *CERA Insight*, 8 March 2005, 4.

42. I thank Elena Herold for this point.

43. Interview with Elena Herold, PFC Energy, Washington, D.C., 7 February 2007.

44. "International Herald Leader: The Sino-Russian Natural Gas Pipeline Plan Is Complex" [Guoji Xianqu Daobao: ZhongE tianranqi guandaoxian fangan cuozong fuza], *Guoji Xianqu Daobao*, 28 October 2004, http://news.sina.com.cn/2004-10-28/11574734703.shtml.

45. In April 2005, BP announced that it did not expect to begin exports from the Kovykta field until 2014, six years after the original start-up date of 2008. Andrew Neff, "BP Sees Delay in Gas Exports from Russia's Kovykta Field until 2014," *World Markets Analysis*, 27 April 2005.

46. See, for example, "Russia's Putin Tells China Gas Price Offer Too Low," Reuters, 23 August 2002.

47. Mark Smedley, "Slump in Sino-Russian Gas Relations Has Wide Reverberations," *World Gas Intelligence*, 2 July 2008.

48. "Gazprom makes BP Offer It Can't Refuse," *International Petroleum Finance*, 6 July 2007; Mark Smedley, "Gazprom Stresses China Prospects, Sees Gas Deal This Year," *International Oil Daily*, 7 July 2006; and "Hardball: Deal Looms for Russia-China Gas Connection," *Nefte Compass*, 16 March 2006.

49. "Japan Courts Russia for Siberian Oil Pipeline Project," *BBC Monitoring*

Asia Pacific, 8 January 2003; and Sagers, Webb, and Vorobyov, "Oil Pipeline Duel in Eastern Russia Entering Decisive Phase," 8.

50. Nelli Sharushkina, "Russia Denies Japan Secure Pipeline Access," *International Oil Daily,* 19 July 2006; "Japan, Russia Plan to Cooperate on Oil Export Pipeline," *Platts Oilgram Price Report,* 22 November 2005; and James Brooke, "The Asian Battle for Russia's Oil and Gas," *New York Times,* 3 January 2004.

51. Email correspondence with Peter Evans, 8 February 2007.

52. Peter C. Evans, "The Brookings Foreign Policy Studies Energy Security Series: Japan" (Washington, D.C.: Brookings Institution, December 2006), 16, http://www.brookings.edu/fp/research/energy/2006japan.htm.

53. "Rosneft and CNPC to Discuss 2004 contract price revision – source (part 2)," *Russia & CIS Energy Newswire,* 15 November 2007.

54. Andrew Neff, "Fresh from 'Success' of IPO, Russia's Rosneft Promises Expansion," *Global Insight Daily Analysis,* 17 July 2006; and Jason Bush, "Rosneft IPO: Less Than Meets the Eye," *BusinessWeek Online,* 17 July 2006.

55. "Govt Review of Feasibility Study on ESPO Branch to China to Be Completed Soon—Transneft (Part 2)," *Russia and CIS Business and Financial Newswire,* 2 October 2008; and Nelli Sharushkina, "Price Dispute Stops Russia and China Agreeing Oil Pipeline Spur," *International Oil Daily,* 7 November 2007.

56. "Russia-China Gas Deal to Curtail EU Leverage over Moscow—Analyst," RIA Novosti, 23 March 2006; "China, Russia Using Gas Deal for Vastly Different Reasons—Analysts," *AFX International Focus,* 22 March 2006; and "Gazprom, China Deal Has Western Angle," *World Gas Intelligence,* 22 March 2006.

57. Li Xin, "'Saboteur' Japan Clears the Way for the Kazakhstan-China Pipeline" ['Pohuaizhe' Riben chengjiu ZhongHaxian], *21 Shiji Jingji Daobao (21st Century Business Herald*), 9 August 2004.

58. Tian Chunrong, "Analysis of China's Oil Imports and Exports in 2007," 40.

59. "Turkmenistan/China Economy: Gas Accord?" *EIU ViewsWire,* 5 April 2006; and Andrew Neff, "Planned Gas Pipeline Advances with Turkmenistan-China Gas Deals," *Global Insight,* 18 July 2007.

60. John Roberts, "Turkmenistan Set to Unveil Large Gas Reserves Focusing on Yoloten," *Platts Oilgram News,* 16 September 2008; "Turkmenistan Moves Ahead with China Pipeline," *Nefte Compass,* 21 February 2008; and Michael Ritchie, "China Pumps Cash into Turkmen Gas Pipe," *International Oil Daily,* 31 December 2007.

61. See, for example, Chen Aizhu and Tom Miles, "China Courts Turkmens, Myanmar as Russian Gas Stalls," Reuters, 22 August 2007; and "Turkmenistan/China Economy: Gas Accord?"

62. Tom Grieder, "CNPC Expresses Hope of Siberia Gas Project Speed-Up," *Global Insight Daily Analysis,* 11 September 2008; and "CNPC Wants Russian Govt to Help Break Deadlock on ESPO Branch to China," *Russia and CIS General Newswire,* 24 April 2008.

63. Conversation with longtime observer of China's energy sector, Washington, D.C., 7 October 2008.

64. "China Speeds Plans for West-East Gas Pipe; Costing Nearly $20 Billion, Pipeline to Distribute Gas from Turkmenistan," *Platts Oilgram News*, 21 January 2008.

65. See, for example, "China Will Not See Gas Oversupply Despite Upsurge in Projects—CNPC Researcher," *China Energy Newswire*, 8 September 2008.

66. For a discussion of the mistrust between China and Russia, see Bobo Lo, "China and Russia: Common Interests, Contrasting Perceptions," *CLSA Asia-Pacific Markets Special Report*, May 2006. Available at: http://www.chathamhouse.org.uk/files/6609_pacificrussia.pdf.

67. Yu Bin, "China and Russia: Normalizing Their Strategic Partnership," in *Power Shift: China and Asia's New Dynamics*, ed. David Shambaugh, 238–39 (Berkeley: Univ. of California Press, 2005).

68. For Russia's "energy appendage" concerns, see "Pundit criticizes Russia-China oil deal," *BBC Monitoring Former Soviet Union —Political*, 18 June 2009; and Bobo Lo, "China and Russia: Common Interests, Contrasting Perceptions," 5.

69. "Russia's Putin Calls for Broader Trade with China, Warns against Instabilities," *Xinhua Financial Network News*, 23 March 2006.

70. "Russia Energy: Turning Japanese," *Economist Intelligence Unit—Executive Briefing*, 17 January 2005.

71. For more on the perceived Chinese threat to the Russian Far East, see Clifford G. Gaddy, "As Russia Looks East: Can It Manage Resources, Space, and People?" *Gaiko Forum*, January 2007, http://www.brookings.edu/views/articles/gaddy/200701.pdf; Arkady Ostrovsky, "Fears Grow of Chinese Moving into Russian East," *Financial Times*, 1 December 2006; Yu Bin, "China and Russia," 239; and Fiona Hill and Clifford Gaddy, *The Siberian Curse: How Communist Planners Left Russia Out in the Cold* (Washington, D.C.: Brookings Institution Press, 2003), 171, 180–81.

72. "Russia Energy: Turning Japanese."

73. Telephone interview with industry insider, 19 January 2007.

74. "Chinese Wall: China Falls Out with Russia over Pipeline," *Nefte Compass*, 16 September 2003.

75. On the rarity of Chinese officials publicly expressing dissatisfaction with the Sino-Russian energy relationship, see "China Is Dissatisfied with the Delay in Energy Projects, Putin Fulfills His Commitments" [Nengyuan xiangmu tuota Zhongguo buman, Putin fang Hua duixian chengnuo], *Sing Tao Net*, 21 March 2006.

76. All three quotes are found in Tom Miles and Emma Graham-Harrison, "Frustrated China Seen Getting No Promises from Putin," Reuters, 20 March 2006.

77. This paragraph is based on my interview with a Chinese foreign policy expert, Washington, D.C., 25 January 2007; interview with industry insider, Beijing, China, 11 April 2006; and "The Russia-Ukraine Natural Gas Dispute Provides

Some Enlightening Guidance for China" [EWu tianranqi zhi zheng gei Zhong-guo de yidian qishi], *Beijing Zhenbao,* 9 January 2006, http://finance.sina.com.cn/roll/20060109/0220485014.shtml.

78. "Tough Cookie: Moscow Faces Tough Choice over Eastern Pipe," *Nefte Compass,* 11 December 2002; and "Transneft Chief Foresees Pacific Pipeline," *Pipeline and Gas Journal,* 1 December 2001.

79. "Russia: Opponents Queue Up to Block Pipeline," *Energy Compass,* 14 April 2006; and Sergei Blagov, "Russian Railways Fears Losing Oil Shipments to China," *Eurasia Daily Monitor* 3, no. 42 (2 March 2006). Available at www.jamestown.org.

80. "RZD, Transneft Scramble for Oil Transmission to China," *SinoCast China Business Daily News,* 2 March 2006.

81. V. I. Yakunin, B. N. Porfiriev, A. A. Arbatov, M. A. Belova, S. S. Sulak-shin, and V. I. Feigin, *Energy Vector of Russia's Eastern Geopolitics: Choosing Routes for Transportation of Oil to the Far East, China, and States of the Asian-Pacific Region* [Energeticheskii vektor vostochnoi politiki Rossii: Vybor putei transportirovki nefti na Dal'nii Vostok, v Kitai, i strany Aziatsko-Tiho'okeanskogo regiona] (Moscow: Economika, 2006). I thank Igor' Danchenko for identifying and summarizing this book and for translating the citation into English.

82. Igor' Danchenko, "Russian-Chinese Energy Relations (Russia's Position)," unpublished document, 18 January 2007.

83. Andrew Neff, "TNK-BP Faces Revocation of License to Key Russian Gas Field," *Global Insight,* 26 September 2006; Neil Buckley and Richard McGregor, "TNK-BP optimistic on Kovykta," *Financial Times,* 26 March 2006; and "Gazprom Lays on Pressure in Talks to Join Kovykta Project," *International Oil Daily,* 29 January 2004.

84. See, for example, Andrew Neff, "TNK-BP Offers Gazprom Controlling Stake in Kovykta Holding Company," *World Market Analysis,* 15 March 2006; and "Members Only: Gazprom Invited to Join Kovykta," *Nefte Compass,* 9 December 2003.

85. Andrew Neff, "Renewed Threat to Kovykta License; Gazprom May Pull out of Deal with TNK-BP," *Global Insight,* 17 October 2008; and email correspondence with Elena Herold, PFC Energy, 27 February 2007.

86. See, for example, Wang Xiaoyu, "Sino-Russian Energy Cooperation Viewed from CNPC's Purchase of Rosneft Shares" [Cong Zhongshiyou cangu Eshiyou kan ZhongE nengyuan hezuo], *Zhongguo Qingnian Bao,* 26 July 2006, http://news.xinhuanet.com/comments/2006-07/26/content_4878617.htm.

87. Interview with representative of a Chinese national oil company, Beijing, China, 2 April 2006; and interview with a Chinese foreign policy expert, Beijing, China, 11 April 2006.

88. Zheng Min and Chu Fujun, "Is the Ministry of Energy Almost Here?" 23–24; "Correctly Understand and Diligently Strengthen the Sino-Russian Strategic Partnership Relationship" [Zhengque renshi he nuli jiaqiang ZhongE zhanlue huo-ban guanxi], (an excerpt from a symposium cohosted by the China Institute for In-

ternational Relations and the Russian Embassy in Beijing in commemoration of the 55th anniversary of the establishment of diplomatic relations), 10 September 2004, http://www.china.com.cn/zhuanti2005/txt/2004-10/13/content_5678818.htm; and Wang Yichao, "Background to CNPC's Retreat from Russia" [Zhongshiyou bingbai Eluosi muhou] *Caijing*, no. 3–4 (2003): 134.

89. "China Wounded by Icy Blast of Rejection," *Nefte Compass*, 14 May 2003; and Wang Yichao, "Background to CNPC's Retreat from Russia," 134.

90. "Contest Heats Up for Russia's Slavneft; Deputies Call for CNPC Ban," *International Oil Daily*, 16 December 2002.

91. Email correspondence with Igor' Danchenko, 12 February 2007.

92. According to one industry insider, CNPC has repeatedly complained that it does not understand Gazprom (telephone interview, 19 January 2007). For Western commentary on the opaqueness of Russian state energy firms, see "Russia's Energetic Enigma Gazprom," *The Economist*, 8 October 2005; and Andrew E. Kramer, "Putin Plays Headhunter for Oil Company," *New York Times*, 17 December 2005.

93. Arkady Ostrovsky, "Oil and Gas: Long on Resources but Short on Clear Rules," *Financial Times*, 10 October 2006.

94. "China's NDRC Despairs on Energy Cooperation Plans with Russia," *Platts Commodity News*, 9 March 2006.

95. Ibid.

96. Bobo Lo, "Russia-China: Axis of Convenience," 20 May 2008, www.opendemocracy.net.

97. "Price Dispute Stops Russia and China Agreeing Oil Pipeline," *International Oil Daily*, 7 November 2007; and "Price Is Sticking Point in New Rosneft, CNPC Oil Contract," *Interfax Russian and CIS Energy Newswire*, 14 March 2008.

98. See, for example, U.S. Congress, Senate, Committee on Energy and Natural Resources, "The Geopolitics of Oil and America's International Standing," testimony by Flynt Leverett, 110th Cong., 1st sess., 10 January 2007; and Irwin M. Stelzer, "The Axis of Oil," *Weekly Standard* 10, no. 20 (7 February 2005), http://www.weeklystandard.com.

99. During the 1990s, China and Russia partnered with each other against the United States on a variety of issues. In 2001, Putin signaled that Russia's relationship with the United States was more important than Russia's relationship with China when he did not oppose the Bush administration's withdrawal from the Anti-Ballistic Missile Treaty, a move staunchly opposed by Beijing. However, China followed suit in prioritizing relations with the United States after realizing that no other major powers wanted to actively resist American hegemony. Conversation with Robert Sutter, 24 January 2007.

100. Robert G. Sutter, *Chinese Policy Priorities and Their Implications for the United States* (Lanham, Md.: Rowman and Littlefield, 2000), 66–67.

101. Yu Bin, "China-Russia Relations: Back to Geostrategics," *Comparative Connections* (April 2005): 136.

102. See, for example, "Russia Factor Could Make Gas Dearer," *Industry Up-*

dates, 8 January 2007; and Chen Wenxian, "Impossible for China to Receive Russia's Gas at Low Price," *Xinhua China Oil, Gas and Petrochemicals,* 25 January 2007.

103. Email correspondence from Igor' Danchenko, 9 July 2009.

104. Wood Mackenzie, "China's LNG Market Development at Risk," *Gas Insight North America,* January 2006, 4.

105. Vanda Hari and John McIlwraith, "LNG Prices Converge as Oil Prices Rise," *International Gas Report,* 5 May 2008; and "Qatar in China," *World Gas Intelligence,* 16 April 2008.

106. Nadia Rodova and Anna Shiryaevskaya, "Gazprom, E.ON to Review Asset Swap Deal; High Oil Prices Prompt Rethink on Assets Involved," *Platts Oilgram News,* 19 June 2008.

107. "Miller Confirms Gazprom Plans to Buy Turkmen Gas at Market Price," Interfax, 4 July 2008; and Mark Smedley, "Caspian: China Sets the Pace," *Energy Compass,* 11 July 2008.

108. For more on the planned increases in Central Asian natural gas prices, see Nadia Rodova and Stuart Elliott, "Central Asian States to Hike Gas Price in 2009; Turkmenistan, Uzbekistan, Kazakhstan Plan European Prices," *Platts Oilgram News,* 12 March 2008; and "Central Asian Gas Pricing," *World Gas Intelligence,* 19 March 2008.

109. Rodova and Shiryaevskaya, "Gazprom, E.ON to Review Asset Swap Deal."

110. Sinopec reportedly paid US$3–4 billion for the asset and then immediately transferred a 51 percent stake to Rosneft, which will repay Sinopec in either production or in company shares. Chinese industry analysts, who are uncertain whether this will prove to be a profitable venture for Sinopec, viewed this investment as a long-term strategic investment aimed at getting the company's foot in the door. See: Xiao Yu, "Why Does the Search for Oil Overseas Suffer Setbacks in Russia?" [Haiwai xun you weihe shouzu Eluosi] *Quanqiu Caijing,* 17 August 2006, http://finance.sina.com .cn/review/20060817/09592828282.shtml; and Wang Xiaoyu, "Sino-Russian Energy Cooperation Viewed from CNPC's Purchase of Rosneft Shares."

111. "China Play: Rosneft Cements Energy Ties with China," *Nefte Compass,* 16 November 2006.

112. Ming Qian, "The Largest Sino-Russian Joint Venture Refinery Project Goes to Tianjin: CNPC Initiates 'Market in Exchange for Energy'" [ZhongE zuida hezi lianyou xiangmu jiang luohu Tianjin; Zhongshiyou lakai 'shichang huan nengyuan' damu], *21 Shiji Jingji Daobao (21st Century Business Herald),* 24 September 2008, http://www.21cbh.com/HTML/2008/9/24/HTML_P5LCIRX51O1M.html.

Part Three

★

The Bilateral Defense Relationship

6

Russo-Chinese Defense Relations

The View from Moscow

Kevin Ryan

If you look carefully at a picture of a Russian troika you will see that the horses are harnessed in a way that causes each of them to pull in a slightly different manner. The horse in the middle pulls straight ahead at a trot while the other two horses are canted to the outside pulling at a gallop: horses running at different speeds in different directions. Some would say this is less than efficient cooperation, but a troika is a good model for how Russia conducts military cooperation with China. Despite built-in tension (or maybe because of it) the team moves forward.
—Fred Burnaby, *A Ride to Khiva*, 1877

Introduction

When the dissolution of the Soviet Union in 1991 put Russia and China on different vectors to post–Cold War development—one democratic, one communist—the two countries might have drifted farther apart as they found their place in a globalized world. However, common concerns such as economic growth, national security, and demographic change have pulled these two giants together, closer than when they were professed comrades in communism. For those trained to see social progress through the Marxist dialectic, Russia and China have become the "thesis and antithesis," which the most imaginative believers could not have foreseen.

Russian-Chinese military cooperation has been typical of the broader, sometimes-hesitant, rapprochement between the two countries. Officials planning and building military cooperation have struggled against historical obstacles while exploring new opportunities for a profitable partnership. The view from Moscow of military relations with China varies depending on the organizational viewpoint of the individual. Like horses in a troika, different observers each want relations to develop in a slightly different direction and at a slightly different speed. A General Staff officer may advise caution in selling the newest military technologies to an historic adversary, while the chairman of a state-owned aircraft enterprise urges coproduction of Russia's newest fighter jets. Both, however, want military sales to continue. As much as possible, this chapter attempts to capture the predominating view within Russia's defense establishment toward cooperation with China.

Konstantin Makienko, a Russian defense specialist who follows military-technical cooperation with China closely, has warned, "a non-governmental expert, researching Russian arms trade with China on the basis of open sources inevitably runs up against a lack of verifiable information."[1] According to Makienko, deputy director of the Moscow-based Center for Analysis of Strategies and Technologies, secrecy clouds military cooperation with China much more than similar relations with countries like India or Malaysia. For that reason, this chapter draws as much as possible on published data, but does not shy from introducing some conjecture or opinion where it can fill gaps.

The Catalysts for Russian-Chinese Military Cooperation

In 1989 two events occurred that laid the basis for a rapid development of Russian-Chinese military-technical cooperation in the 1990s. In May, Soviet leader Mikhail Gorbachev made an historic visit to Beijing, normalizing relations between the two long-time adversaries. Gorbachev's initiative opened the door to exchanges and dialogues for many Russian institutions, including the defense establishment. In June of that same year, after months of escalating pro-democracy protests, Chinese leaders ruthlessly suppressed a popular demonstration on Tiananmen Square, leading to an embargo on arms sales by the United States and the European Union.[2] China, which had embarked on a military modernization program in 1985, now had no access to modern military technologies from the West.[3] The timing was perfect for Soviet, and later Russian, arms dealers eager for contracts.

Russian arms sales to China blossomed in the early 1990s and grew from there. Makienko estimates that the first Chinese contracts for military equipment (Su-27 fighter interceptors) were signed in 1991 before the fall of the

Soviet Union, with the first deliveries (26 aircraft) arriving in China in 1992.[4] When the Soviet Union collapsed, the new Russian government was unable to generate the domestic orders for equipment necessary to sustain the bloated military-industrial complex, and Russian companies turned increasingly to foreign sales to stay afloat. Russia already had a positive experience with military sales to India and saw China as its next big customer. Over the next four years Russia expanded its military-technical relationship with China, selling an average of just under $1 billion worth of arms per year.[5]

Even before the resumption of arms sales in 1991, reasons to cooperate with China on military and security matters were mounting. During the 1980s a steady flow of extremist groups to Chinese and Soviet borders was generated by the Soviet war in Afghanistan. Under Mikhail Gorbachev's "perestroika" reforms, Soviet foreign policy focused on neutralizing external threats to marshal scarce resources for internal domestic problems. Soviet leaders hoped that agreements demilitarizing borders with China would free up thousands of Soviet troops and facilitate the government's effort to downsize the military and its budget. Border issues, however, became even more complicated for Russia and China in 1991 with the emergence of new Central Asian states. When the Cold War ended, the United States was left as an unchallenged superpower, causing Russia and China to seek each other's support in creating a multipolar response. For example, as early as the inauguration of the Shanghai Five in 1996, President Boris Yeltsin and Chinese Premier Li Peng jointly denounced a world dominated by one (American) power.[6] These kinds of issues also served to bring the Russian and Chinese military establishments closer together and eventually generated joint activities across the full spectrum of military cooperation.

The Russian Understanding of Military Cooperation

Military cooperation is a broad term encompassing various activities by different agencies and bureaucracies. Defense Minister Sergei Ivanov provided insight into the Russian understanding of military cooperation when he explained Russian-Chinese cooperation to reporters following their first joint Peace Mission exercise in August 2005. "Our military cooperation with Beijing has three aspects: military-political consultations, practical actions of the troops during military exercises, as well as military-technical cooperation."[7]

In terminology more familiar to U.S. defense observers, Russian military cooperation has three components. (1) Military-political cooperation deals with the overarching strategic and political goals of the two militaries and states. An example is an activity that promotes a multipolar world order—a strategic goal of the Russian state. (2) Military-practical cooperation refers to those activities such as exercises, joint training, or even joint operations, in which two or more states participate. And (3) military-technical cooperation consists of foreign arms sales and technology transfers from one state to another.

Russia has experience with foreign military cooperation dating well back into its military history. In the post–World War II period, the Soviet Union sold arms to its satellite countries, conducted joint exercises and war games, and even licensed production of selected defense items with other states. China was initially one of those favored nations, but a political falling out between Nikita Khrushchev and Mao Zedong after the death of Josef Stalin resulted in a three-decade freeze in military relations. Gorbachev's visit in 1989 and Russia's break with its communist past in 1991, however, caused a reordering of old alliances and a reexamination of many aspects of Russian policy, including military cooperation with China. To understand post–Cold War Russian perspectives on military cooperation with China, a good starting point is the Russian Federation's military doctrine, published by the Ministry of Defense (MoD). The military doctrine identifies the threats to the nation and the tasks before the military, including the goals in foreign military cooperation.

The military doctrine of the Russian Federation has been undergoing revision since 2000 and a new version is expected soon. However, examining the still-active 2000 edition of the doctrine and its 1993 predecessor reveals that post–Cold War Russian officials have consistently emphasized the military-technical (economic) goals of military cooperation. Both the 1993 and 2000 military doctrines clearly saw the key role of military cooperation in facilitating the recovery and survival of Russia's defense industry. Both doctrines referred to cooperation with foreign militaries as "military-technical cooperation," underscoring the predominant role of the transfer and sale of military technology. Notably, both doctrines dealt with military cooperation in the third section of the document, which addressed economic and technical issues facing the Russian military.

The 1993 military doctrine provides the best illustration of the relationship between foreign military cooperation and economic issues. It lists five specific aims for military cooperation, four of which address concerns about the defense industry:

Strengthening the Russian Federation's military-political positions in various regions in the world; earning foreign currency for state requirements, the development of conversion, military production, the dismantling and salvaging of weapons, and the structural restructuring of enterprises in the defense sectors of industry; maintaining the country's export potential in the sphere of conventional weapons and military hardware at the necessary level; developing the scientific, technical, and experimental base of the defense sectors of industry and their scientific-research and experimental design work institutions and organizations; providing social protection for the personnel of enterprises, institutions, and organizations developing and producing weapons, military and special hardware, and other equipment.[8]

The term "military-technical cooperation" was used to describe the entirety of foreign military cooperation in 1993, but by 2000 terminology had changed and, rather than one, two aspects of military cooperation—military-political and military-technical—were highlighted in the doctrine: "The Russian Federation executes international military [military-political] and military-technical cooperation in accordance with its national interests and the requirement for balanced resolution of the tasks of military security. Military-political and military-technical cooperation are the prerogatives of the state."[9]

The 2000 military doctrine is less specific than the 1993 version about the economic aims of military cooperation but still lists the subject under the chapter on economic issues. The 2000 doctrine, however, elevates "military-political" as a distinct aspect of cooperation.

The existence of a military-political aspect to foreign military cooperation was not a new discovery for the Russian military leadership in 2000. The Directorate of International Military Cooperation, led by Colonel-General Leonid Ivashov in 2000, had the twofold responsibility of ensuring that guidance from the government's national security concept was followed in the conduct of military cooperation as well as providing MoD input in the development of that security strategy. In fact, Russia's international security and political goals (military-political) have long been recognized as parameters determining the kinds of military-technical cooperation that were permissible with foreign militaries. What was different about the wording of the 2000 doctrine was that the military-political realm was not only the context within which military cooperation would occur, but it was mentioned as an active part of the military's cooperation program.

Bringing Coherence to Military Cooperation with China

We are not privy to the notes of the drafters of the 2000 doctrine, but there are a couple of possible reasons why the military-political aspect of cooperation was elevated in the doctrine that year. One possibility is that the 2000 document was a refinement of the earlier 1993 doctrine, and the authors may have been simply correcting a deficiency in the earlier document. More likely though is that the introduction of this aspect of cooperation in the document's text reflected an effort to rein in the many actors involved in military-technical cooperation—state arms producers, politicians, government officials, private businessmen, etc.—particularly in dealings with China. According to Russian General Staff chief Yuri Baluyevsky, one of the tasks of the military doctrine is to provide that kind of guidance and unity of effort.[10] While not wishing to curtail foreign technical sales in general, the military's leaders were trying to introduce coherence to the decisions about what was sold, by whom, and to whom.

Coherence in Russian policy, particularly military-technical cooperation with China, was hard to come by in the mid-1990s. The Russian government and political elites were divided, sometimes even within bureaucracies, over the direction the Russian-Chinese relationship should take. In June 1996, immediately after joining China in the "Shanghai Five" group, former minister of foreign affairs Andrei Kozyrev spoke against tilting too far in the direction of China, noting, "there are those in the bureaucracy who want, outright, to shift Russia's foreign policy toward the East and give a cold shoulder to the West and thus gain more weight in international relations."[11] According to Sergey Makienko, while Russian military industrialists pushed for upgrading exports to China in order to retain business, "the power ministries, which were concerned about an inappropriately strengthened demographic giant" across the border, blocked the transfer of more modern equipment.[12] A former chairman of the Duma Subcommittee on International Security and Arms Control, Vyacheslav Nikonov, echoed concern among the Russian military, saying Russia must preserve its arms markets, but also avoid new security threats to itself.[13]

Eurasia specialist Stephen Blank may have captured the situation best in his 1997 paper "The Dynamics of Russian Weapon Sales to China," where he observed that the early Russian-Chinese military relationship was driven as much "by the private interests of Russian arms dealers . . . as by any reasoned calculation of Russian strategic or national interests."[14] Blank presented several illustrations of the lack of coordination exercised by the government over military sales to China at that time. The Sukhoi Aircraft Design Bureau, for example, admitted in 1996 to transferring Su-27 production licenses to China without government authorization. In another incident in 1995, according to reports in the journal *Military Space,* the Ministry of Defense sold upper-stage rocket engines to China without notifying the company that produces them and in violation of the Missile Technology Control Regime.[15]

While it is clear that Russian military sales during the 1990s were sometimes uncontrolled and unsynchronized between firms and government authorities, that did not mean that Russian strategic goals were not being developed or ironed out within the government. On the contrary, those goals were evolving rapidly and in the direction of a strategic partnership with China. Blank cites Russian defense correspondent Pavel Felgenhauer, who said that the General Staff, MoD, and defense industrialists believed China's need for military technology would "become not only a way for our hapless military-industrial complex to preserve jobs and earn money, but also the start of a long-range strategic partnership and a new balance of forces in Asia that would favor Russia."[16] The reality is that both China and Russia were actively trying to leverage the growing relationship between the two states into something which would benefit their strategic interests—many of which were increasingly common.

By 2000, Blank accurately projected that security assessments of the Russian military would more and more converge in the direction established by military-technical cooperation with China, leading to a closer strategic partnership.

> We can expect that the Russian army . . . will show a much warmer attitude towards China. Threat perceptions of a resurgent China have diminished even as Chinese-Russian positions on major issues of international security have come together. Military exchanges have picked up considerably since late 1998 and there are visible signs of enhanced military as well as political cooperation against the United States on issues like national missile defense (NMD) and theater missile defense (TMD). Therefore we can anticipate, if all things remain equal, greater Sino-Russian military cooperation and Russian weapons and technology transfers to China that are openly targeted deliveries against U.S. policies and interests.[17]

At the same time that Ministry of Defense officials were redefining China from the category of strategic threat to strategic partner, they were also beginning to emplace the mechanisms to regain control over military-technical cooperation. By 2001, the MoD had reoriented its Directorate of Military Cooperation, now headed by General Anatoly Mazurkevich, to provide more supervision over military sales. In the fall of that year, Mazurkevich told the U.S. defense attaché in Moscow that his expanded duties made him responsible for overseeing sales of MoD surplus equipment and upholding MoD responsibilities in providing repair parts and equipment training for foreign customers.[18]

The Ministry of Defense also dedicated a deputy minister, KGB-trained General Mikhail Dmitriev, to run the central government's newly formed office of Military Technical Cooperation with Foreign Governments (December 2002).[19] Dmitriev's office oversaw sales of the three main practitioners of military-technical cooperation in Russia: state defense industries, private industries, and the Ministry of Defense. The office's mission, which was broader than Mazurkevich's in MoD, was to ensure that no strategic materials (as defined by the government) were sold without the government's knowledge and permission. This was not an easy task for a new office working among thousands of ex-Soviet defense enterprises. In one case, it was the U.S. Defense Department itself which alerted Dmitriev's organization to the illegal sale of jamming devices by a private Russian firm to the Iraqi government in 2003.[20] Since 2004, Dmitriev's office has graduated to a separate agency, the Federal Service for Military-Technical Cooperation, meeting regularly with foreign governments, not the least of which is China, to coordinate military sales and technical assistance programs. The Russian state also exercises control over sales and licenses through state-owned Rosoboronexport, the largest Russian exporter of military equipment.[21] These developments, together with a coalescing of Russian elite thinking on the strategic relationship with China, have strengthened the role of military-political considerations in bringing the overall cooperation program into alignment with external and internal national interests.

Using Military Cooperation with China to Build the Russian Economy

In 2005, according to the Congressional Research Service, Russia surpassed America for the first time and moved into first place among world arms exporters to developing countries, signing agreements for $7 billion worth of exports. China comprised 40 percent of those agreements in 2005—about $2.8 billion—and is expected to remain a strong market in the future.[22]

The military-industrial complex is one of the few Russian economic sectors capable of successfully building and exporting finished products. The government sees military exports as essential not only to the survival of the defense sector but to the long-term development of the overall economy. In a 2005 interview with the state newspaper *Russian Gazette,* Chief of the Russian General Staff Yuri Baluyevsky asserted that the system of foreign military sales provided much needed money to keep Russian defense firms "off their knees." He explained that profits from sales are distributed partly to the development of the industrial-technological base, partly to the development of new weapons systems, and partly to the Ministry of Defense as revenue. According to Baluyevsky, growing sales to China will not threaten Russia's own security because export versions of new Russian equipment are less capable than the versions made for Russian consumption.[23] Baluyevsky claimed that continuing sales between Russian producers and the Chinese military prevented other foreign arms sellers from "taking away our customer."[24]

Under President Putin, Russia continued to invest time and energy in streamlining the military-industrial sector in a two-pronged effort to control strategic assets and to "ride this horse" to a stronger and more diversified economy. In 2001, Putin eliminated state contracts with half of the roughly eighteen hundred enterprises in the military-industrial complex, concentrating the surviving companies into fifty firms and holding companies.[25] In November 2006, Putin challenged leaders of the aircraft industry, the most successful exporters of the military-industrial complex, to spread their insights throughout Russian industry. Putin called for the military-industrial enterprises to lead the development of innovation in the country: "It is necessary to take the experience, which has already been gathered in the aviation industry, and spread it among the other spheres of the economy. We have to think about the role of the defense industries in the development of the most important technological areas of the economy as a whole; how to utilize defense enterprises to solve the problems of innovative development of the country."[26]

Sergei Ivanov embodies this view of the interdependence of defense and civilian industries. By December 2006, Ivanov, who was already minister of defense, deputy prime minister, and head of the Russian Federation's Military Industrial Commission, added an additional title when he was chosen to head the consortium of state-owned aviation companies.[27]

Ivanov told Russian media in January 2007 that in order for Russia to return as "a great power" it must create a competitive economy which can win in world markets. He went on to say the military-industrial complex is not only the guarantor of Russian defense capabilities, but "the most important

instrument of effective resolution of [Russia's] social-economic problems. . . .
The military industrial complex has the potential to propel the entire economy."[28] Under Ivanov, the aviation sector, which today is 90 percent owned
by the government and 70 percent focused on military production, has the
task of increasing private investments to reduce government ownership to 75
percent and increase the share of civilian production to 50 percent.[29] China,
with its sizeable arms market and even larger energy requirements, has the
potential of being Russia's long-term partner in its endeavor to grow economic capacity.

Some Russian strategists, like Konstantin Makienko, urge goals beyond
economic ones in expanding the strategic relationship with China. In 2005,
Makienko suggested that modern Russian equipment in the hands of the
Chinese would enhance Russian national interests by providing a more capable opponent of U.S. military power in the Pacific and Asia. He chided
conservatives in the MoD for not seeing the benefit of a militarily stronger
China, and suggested that in the near future China and Russia could "syn-
chronize their foreign policy operations for reestablishment of sovereignty
over lost territory," having in mind Russia's ethnic enclaves in former Soviet
territories and China's Taiwan.[30]

Central Asia—The Stage for Military-Political and Military-Practical Cooperation with China

Those of us who initially looked for Chinese-Russian military cooperation to
develop most prominently along their mutual Siberian and Far East borders
were surprised when instead it emerged in Central Asia. Central Asia, being a nexus of threats common to both Russia and China, quickly showed
itself to be the more important stage for cooperation. All of the twelve basic
external threats to security identified in Russia's military doctrine are present
in Central Asia.[31] Separatist groups consisting of nationalists and religious
extremists fight open conflicts with authorities in Kyrgyzstan, Uzbekistan,
and Tajikistan, and feed terrorist activities in both China and Russia. Drugs
and criminal activity flow across the borders in the same manner, taking
advantage of the difficult terrain and weak policing capabilities of the new
Central Asian states. In 2001, nascent American interest in the region esca-
lated to continuous U.S. troop presence in support of the war in Afghanistan
and is seen today as a threat to Russian and Chinese influence in the region.
Add to these concerns Russian and Chinese interest in protecting energy and

natural resource flows into and out of the region, and one has an appreciation for the attention that both countries give to the area, and the reasons behind the rapid rise of the Shanghai Five and its successor, the Shanghai Cooperation Organization (SCO).

Many scholars credit China with being the driving force behind the creation of the Shanghai Five and the SCO, but Russia has certainly been an active participant in shaping the organizations' direction. China sees the SCO development in three stages: resolving border issues; focusing on security problems; and finally, establishing a single economic space.[32] From the Russian perspective, the Shanghai Five and the SCO were first and foremost efforts at addressing regional security problems. China and Russia had been battling separatist movements throughout the 1990s: the Uyghurs in China's northwest and the Chechens in Russia's south. By 2000, Russia, China, and the three Central Asian members of the Shanghai Five had already begun the process of creating a counterterrorism center.[33] The deputy chief of the Kremlin administration in 2001, Sergey Prikhodko, emphasized that the SCO had a "very serious role in the formation of general approaches of member states in the building of a security model in Asia and in the world as a whole."[34] During the first SCO summit in June 2001, President Putin noted the important contribution of military-political cooperation among member states in enhancing trust within the group.[35] In the summit's declaration, the presidents of all the member states reaffirmed their commitment to another key military-political objective, a multipolar world, and attached "special importance and . . . greatest effort to safeguarding regional security, [by] . . . cracking down on terrorism, separatism and extremism."[36] These threats closely match threats identified in Russia's own military doctrine and make the SCO an excellent forum within which to channel military cooperation with member nations—especially China.

President Putin also laid down markers for increasing military-practical cooperation: exercises and operations. Putin declared that the Shanghai Cooperation Organization should focus its work on security, economics, and antiterror cooperation. He said the states must "actively and efficiently fight international terrorism, ethnic separatism and religious extremism, and illegal arms and drug trafficking." Putin challenged the organization to expand cooperation into "active joint work."[37] Putin's comments on joint practical cooperation reflected the more activist role Russia was assuming in response to the terrorist threat in the region in 2001, and presaged the series of Russian-Chinese led military exercises that started four years later under the auspices of the SCO: "Peace Mission 2005" and "Peace Mission 2007" (examined later in the chapter).

At the June 2001 SCO summit, Putin also declared that member states "realize that threats to international stability and security are not limited to the Central Asian region."[38] A year before, Russia had called for a rapid reaction force among the Tashkent Collective Security Treaty (CST) states (Armenia, Belarus, Kazakhstan, Kyrgyzstan, Russia, and Tajikistan) to combat terrorism, with Putin hinting that such forces might launch preemptive strikes on Afghan terrorist bases. (Recall that for several years before 9/11, Russia and China were much more concerned than the United States about spillover threats from the Taliban in Afghanistan.)[39] The CST began joint training and conducted an initial combined exercise in 2004 called "Rubezh 2004."[40] In 2005, Russia and China conducted their first major SCO exercise, "Peace Mission 2005." Initial proposals for the follow-on "Peace Mission 2007" would have combined the efforts of the SCO and CSTO (Collective Security Treaty Organization renamed from the earlier Tashkent group) toward counterterrorism, but eventually the two exercises remained separate.[41] From Russia's perspective, this vector of activities has the potential to combine antiterror cooperation in Central Asia with cooperation in the rest of Russia's southern tier, leading to a more integrated approach to a widespread threat.

At a 2006 conference on the achievements and future of the SCO, Alexander Lukin, director of the Russian Foreign Ministry's training institute (MGIMO), noted the shift of the SCO focus from border issues to broader regional concerns: terrorism, separatism, and religious extremism.[42] According to Lukin, joint SCO exercises like "Peace Mission" are the beginning of the organization's "practical work" toward countering the region's threats. Lukin predicted that the military forces of member states would continue to "coordinate their positions" and conduct joint antiterrorist exercises.[43]

Russian-Chinese Joint Exercises— A New Level of Cooperation

"Peace Mission 2005," the first joint ground, sea, and air exercise in history involving Russian and Chinese forces, was held in August 2005 under the auspices of the Shanghai Cooperation Organization. The exercise was designed around a joint operation to assist a third state battling separatist activities by terrorists.[44] Conducted in three stages over eight days, the exercise involved over 9,000 Russian and Chinese forces (1,800 Russian and 7,200 Chinese).[45] The first stage of the exercise consisted of military and political consultations held in the Russian Pacific port of Vladivostok between the two General Staffs. The next two stages consisted of amphibious and airborne landings conducted on China's Shandong Peninsula on the Yellow Sea.[46] "Peace Mission 2005" accomplished goals across the span of military cooperation: practical, technical, and political.

The announced reason for conducting the "Peace Mission" exercise was to improve counterterrorism cooperation between China and members of the SCO, and the exercise was a tangible step in that direction. According to General Staff chief Yuri Baluyevsky, the first "Peace Mission" exercise worked out procedures for cooperation at the company level.[47] The follow-on "Peace Mission" exercise in 2007 involved battalion-sized elements from both countries as well as company-sized units from other SCO members. After the 2005 exercise, some skeptics claimed that the exercise's location on China's Shandong Peninsula near the Yellow Sea revealed the activities were not connected to Central Asia but intended to threaten Taiwan. However, the location of the 2007 follow-on exercise near Cheburkal, along Russia's border with Kazakhstan, put that suspicion to rest. According to General Baluyevsky, the "Peace Mission" exercises are a serious effort to build a multinational capability that can unite the Central Asian security forces. Baluyevsky said, "I do not rule out that by decision of the Shanghai Cooperation Organization, of which both Russia and the People's Republic of China are members, the armed forces of our countries may be committed to solving certain tasks," referring to countering terrorist activity in SCO member countries.[48] Baluyevsky was quick to add, though, that he did not foresee the need for Russia or China to deploy their forces into each other's territories to quell terrorist threats there.

Another Russian aim in conducting the exercises was the much-publicized goal of sustaining Chinese military-technical cooperation. In January 2005, seven months before the first exercise, Russian Air Force chief General Vladimir Mikhailov told journalists that one of the main reasons for the participation of Tu-22M and Tu-95 strategic bombers in the exercise was to encourage the Chinese to buy them.[49]

According to Deputy Prime Minister Sergei Ivanov, the joint military capability demonstrated by Russia and China through the Peace Mission exercises provides a new dimension to the work of creating the multipolar world.[50] Conducting the exercises under the auspices of the Shanghai Cooperation Organization boosts the importance of that organization as one of those "alternate poles." At this early stage, the joint exercises are more significant politically than operationally, but over time they could achieve their goal of creating an authentic counterterrorism capability; one that could also be an alternate power pole in a multipolar world.

The Russian Domestic Context for Military Cooperation with China

In the Siberian district of Krasnoyarsk, where Russian workers are scarce, regional authorities have invited Chinese immigrants into the district and given them plots of land so that they can raise produce, principally vegetables. But local Russians have held meetings and accused the Chinese farmers of poisoning the ground and selling unsafe produce: "The Chinese themselves do not eat the vegetables they grow. They sell their tomatoes across the region but eat the tomatoes grown by Russian locals. Its enough to note that on the ground where Chinese hot houses have been used, grass will no longer grow . . . because of the poisonous fertilizer they use."[51]

Historic Russian ethnic and cultural biases against the Chinese have the potential to short-circuit more pragmatic thinking in managing the future direction of cooperation, including military cooperation. For Russians in general, and for the Russian military establishment in particular, China is a double-edged sword. One edge represents China's capacity to help Russia cut through obstacles to regain its status as a global power, but the other edge represents the potential harm a rising China could do to Russian interests in the Far East, Siberia, and Central Asia. An historical and racial distrust of the Chinese permeates the Russian culture. Add to this a national xenophobia against foreigners in general, and one can begin to appreciate how conflicted today's Russian strategists must feel.

Across Siberia and the Far East, the demands of commerce are opening up connections between Russia and China. At the Siberian crossing site of Zabaikalsk-Manzhouli, where a decade ago thousands of troops stood guard, 770 passenger buses and an average of 5,800 people cross the border every day.[52] By 2010, trade along both sides of the border is estimated to increase about eightfold, from the current $2.5 billion to $15–$20 billion dollars, according to the Chinese Ministry of Commerce.[53] In the Siberian district of Zabaikalsky Krai, where the Russian Siberian Military District is headquartered, China accounts for about 96 percent of external trade ($400 million).[54] Russian officials in the Siberian city of Irkutsk near Lake Baikal hired a Chinese construction company to build mass housing as part of Russia's national "Affordable Housing" program. Part of the deal requires the Chinese company to pass along construction expertise which Russian companies do not have.[55] These and other examples underscore the growing economic integration of Chinese and Russian communities in the Far East and Siberia.

Nonetheless, these steps toward economic integration come against a backdrop of strategic concern over Russian territory, resources, and jobs. At a December 2006 Security Council meeting, President Putin declared that Russia's Far East was increasingly isolated from the rest of the country, and that failure to properly exploit the region's vast natural resources threatened national security. Putin noted that Chinese immigrants were filling the vacancies left by a disappearing Russian population. "All of these things pose a serious threat to our political and economic positions in the Asia-Pacific region, and to Russia's national security, without exaggeration."[56]

Russian MFA official Andrey Kondakov observed that Russian-Chinese trade relations are in danger of becoming "colonial in nature." Russian exports to China consist primarily of natural resources (35 percent), and machine-building equipment has fallen from 20 percent to about 2 percent. Meanwhile Chinese machine-building exports to Russia have risen to about 20 percent of the total.[57]

According to Russian interior minister Rashid Nurgaliyev, there are between 8 and 12 million immigrants, only 705,000 of whom are legal.[58] President Putin said in October 2006 that the government must protect the jobs of Russian citizens and control the flow of immigrants into the country. "Our economy was and will remain absolutely open and transparent . . . but we must regulate the flow of immigrants. [Russian citizens] should not feel infringed upon in the labor market and other areas."[59]

Russian military leaders also operate in this same dynamic environment. Driven to cooperate in arms sales to save the defense industry and forced into a closer political relationship to balance U.S. power, they nevertheless remain concerned about growing Chinese influence in the Russian economy and the physical presence of Chinese workers in Russia's eastern regions. Thus far, military officers have supported the sale of modern weapons but hedged against the risk of a future conflict with their neighbor by withholding the latest military technologies. According to Russian military observer Dmitry Litovkin, "the General Staff of Russia (which is approving the list of arms allowed for exportation) has been accounting for discrimination of China with a fear for rapid economic development of our neighboring state." Asked by journalists in advance of the "Peace Mission 2005" exercise whether he thought China would ever use Russian-sold weapons against Russia, General Staff chief Baluyevsky dodged the question and only noted that weapons sold abroad were export versions with simplified technologies.[60] Asked in November that same year whether Russia would ever consider selling China its latest military technologies, Baluyevsky intimated that he drew the line at fielding weapons to China that had not first been put in service in the Russian military.[61]

The Future of Russian-Chinese Military Cooperation

In 2006, on the anniversary of the end of WWII, General Staff chief Yuri Baluyevsky said that Russia should not follow the example of either Asia or Europe in the international arena: "Russia should follow its own path. It has always been, is and will be Russia, because not a single country that is considered a political trendsetter has the same history as our country does."[62]

Baluyevsky's prescription for Russian advancement reflects the resurgent pride of the military and the country's aspiration to be a global power once again. Nevertheless, Russia cannot yet achieve that goal by itself and must align with trusted partners. Former Deputy Minister of Foreign Affairs Kozyrev cautioned in 1996 against leaning too far in the direction of China, but a decade later the fear of a military conflict with China has largely receded among security strategists. The Russian defense establishment today wants military cooperation with China to continue and expand. The only question is how fast and in what areas. Over the next decade we might expect the following developments:

Given the mission of the defense industry to propel the rest of the economy forward, government leaders will likely seek to sustain and increase sales of military equipment. Notwithstanding General Baluyevsky's cautions above, as China becomes sated with fourth-generation aircraft and submarines, Russian military leaders will be under pressure from Chinese buyers and Russian producers to share the latest fifth-generation technologies, even if they have not been fielded to Russian units. As president, Putin put a huge burden in the rucksack of the military-industrial complex, in particular the aircraft companies, to expand their success of the 1990s and lead the development of an "innovation-based" economy for Russia. Russia has already offered the opportunity to jointly develop its most advanced aircraft, not yet in service, to India. China will likely be next.

As Chinese aviation and naval needs are met, Russia will likely expand military-technical cooperation in space and nuclear industries. Russia's MoD is already selling access to GLONASS, a satellite navigation system, to China and India. According to Nikolai Testoyedov, general director of the Federal Space Agency's Scientific-Production Facility, Russian specialists have been part of the development of every phase of China's space program and further cooperation is only understandable.[63] Russian nuclear-powered submarines could eventually be put on the list of approved exports to China, a major improvement to Chinese sea power.

The growing importance of energy and natural resources in the Russian conception of vital national interests will generate additional military cooperation tasks—security of natural resources and their delivery systems. As Russian and Chinese militaries become more capable in joint antiterrorist operations through the SCO, we might expect that they will apply that capability to protecting energy flows that transect their borders and regions. Such cooperation could augur for sharing more power projection capabilities in aviation and shipping. On 7 February 2007, Defense Minister Ivanov announced an eight-year, $189 billion modernization plan, which includes new power projection capabilities: additional ships, aircraft, and aircraft carriers.[64]

Russian military observers who have seen drafts of the new military doctrine, not published at the time of writing, have hinted that it will be more specific about which countries are considered partners and which are threats.[65] China has proven to be a willing partner in balancing American power in world bodies and regional forums. This closer cooperation with China in the military-political realm may be captured in the new military doctrine. The outcome could be a newly defined strategic relationship between Russia and China, which could, in turn, accelerate military cooperation across the entire spectrum, including technical (sales), practical activities (exercises and operations), and political.

There are, however, negative developments, which could derail or reverse some aspects of military cooperation between the two countries. First among these would be a decision by China to reduce or eliminate major arms purchases from Russia. Russian observers like Sergey Makienko have been warning about such a possibility since Russian aircraft sales to China appeared to top out in 2004.[66] A loss of income from arms sales could change the calculus of Russian strategists trying to weigh the pluses and minuses of military cooperation with China. Likewise, an end to the EU arms embargo against China could also encourage China to diversify its military purchases among European countries, putting a dent in Russian exports.[67]

Another potential problem might be the inability to resolve the business and immigration issues for Chinese laborers working in Russia's Far East and Siberia. Failure there would not only risk alienating China but would harm Russian long-term economic growth by denying the region the labor force it desperately needs.

Conclusion

As much as anything else, Russian military cooperation with China is a product of the diminished capabilities of the post–Cold War Russian state: diminished capability to defend itself from external threats, diminished ability to counter NATO expansion, diminished capacity to build and export finished material goods, and a diminished ability to counter relentless Chinese demographic pressure in Russia's Far East. In a January 2007 speech to Russian MoD officers working on the new military doctrine, General Baluyevsky said that Russia must account for this diminished capacity in its strategic calculations. According to Baluyevsky, threats to Russia come not only from the United States, but from developing countries with modern military capabilities.[68]

China has proven a trusted partner to Russia in balancing U.S. power by helping to construct other "power poles" in a multipolar world. A strategic partnership with China also offers Russia significant opportunities for the growth of its economy and security against threats from the south—particularly from the instabilities of Central Asia.

Yet partnership with China also carries risks. Russia could be arming today an opponent of the future. This would not be the first time Russia miscalculated in its choice of allies. After World War I, the Soviet and German militaries cooperated across a wide range of activities. German units and officers trained on Soviet territory. That relationship backfired and contributed to Russia's enormous losses in WWII. After World War II, the Soviet Union pursued a strategic partnership with China, even sending troops and equipment to help fight the war in Korea against American forces. That alliance also ended in disappointment and is only now being reconsidered. With such glaring failures in recent history, Russian security elites might prefer today to be more cautious about the extent of Chinese military cooperation, but seeing few alternatives, they appear to have shelved their concerns for now.

Notes

Epigraph source: Fred Burnaby, *A Ride to Khiva: Travels and Adventures in Central Asia* (New York: Harper and Brothers, 1877), 50.

1. Konstantin Makienko, "Is It Dangerous to Trade in Weapons with China?" [Opasno li torgovat' oruzhiem s Kitaem?] (Moscow: Center for Analysis of Strategy and Technology [Tsentr Analiza Strategiy i Tekhnologiy], 1 December 1999), 1.

2. Ian Hayes, "ISN Security Watch. Lifting the China Embargo: The EU's Trade Gambit," 16 March 2005, http://www.isn.ethz.ch/news/sw/details.cfm?ID=10950. The embargo did not fully stop arms sales between the EU and China, but did allow Russia to occupy first place among suppliers to China.

3. Statement of Harold J. Johnson, associate director, International Relations and Trade Issues, National Security and International Affairs Division, "China, U.S. and European Union Arms Sales since the 1989 Embargoes," GAO Testimony be-

fore the Joint Economic Committee, GAO/T-NSIAD-98-171, 1: "In 1985, China adopted a military doctrine that emphasizes the use of modern naval and air power in joint operations against regional opponents. It later began buying foreign military hardware to support its new doctrine."

4. Ibid.; Makienko, "Is It Dangerous to Trade in Weapons with China?"

5. Between 1992 and 1996 China purchased a total of 2 ships, 48 aircraft, and 144 missiles from Russia. See: ibid.; GAO Testimony, 10. For information on equipment types, see also: United Nations Register of Conventional Arms, http://disarmament.un.org/cab/register.html.

6. "China Hails Russia Ties, Warns against U.S. Domination," Agence France-Presse, 29 December 1996.

7. "Russia Considering SCO Joint Military Exercise," Organization of Asia-Pacific News Agencies, 31 August 2005.

8. "Basic Provisions of the Military Doctrine of the Russian Federation," adopted by edict No. 1833, 2 November 1993, hosted on the website of the Federation of American Scientists, http://www.fas.org/nuke/guide/russia/doctrine/russia-mil-doc.html.

9. Directive of President of Russian Federation, 21 April 2000, No. 706, http://www.mil.ru/849/11873/1062/1347/1818/index.shtml.

10. In a January 2007 speech to conferees working on the new military doctrine, General Baluyevsky said that the purpose of military doctrine is to "consolidate the efforts of state power in solving the tasks of providing military security." See: Yuri Baluyevsky, "Structure and Basic Content of the New Military Doctrine of Russia" [Struktura i osnovnoe soderzhanie novoy Voennoy Doktriny Rossii], website of the Russian Federation Ministry of Defence, http://www.mil.ru/847/852/1153/1342/20922/index.shtml.

11. "Playing Russia's China Card," New Perspectives Quarterly 13, no. 3 (1 June 1996): 41.

12. Konstantin Makienko, "Commentary from Centre for Analysis of Strategies and Technologies," Kommersant 151 (16 August 2005).

13. John Helmer, "Shift in Russia's Strategy on Asia," Straits Times, 18 April 1996.

14. Stephen Blank, "The Dynamics of Russian Weapon Sales to China," U.S. Army War College Strategic Studies Institute, 4 March 1997, vi.

15. Ibid., 4–5. Blank's own footnotes for the same information are: Kommersant-Daily, 18 July 1996, FBIS-SOV-96-140, 19 July 1996, 20–22, and Military Space, 21 August 1995, 1.

16. Ibid., 3.

17. Stephen Blank, "Threats to Russian Security: The View from Moscow," U.S. Army War College Strategic Studies Institute, July 2000, 38–39.

18. Conversation between Mazurkevich and the author during the conduct of business at the Ministry of Defense in September 2001.

19. In 2001, a few days after 9/11, waiting outside the Russian Minister of De-

fense's office in Moscow I met the recently assigned new head of Russian Military Cooperation, General Anatoly Mazurkevich. When I congratulated him on his assignment heading military cooperation, he stopped and corrected me, pointing out that he was in reality in charge of "military-technical" cooperation and not just "military cooperation" as his predecessor had been. Mazurkevich explained that his new responsibilities in monitoring contracts and sales with foreign countries was now the major part of his duties and prevented him from spending much time on more traditional political cooperation issues. I expressed surprise at his additional responsibilities in technical cooperation, and to prove his point Mazurkevich took out one of his business cards to show me the official title of his position. Unfortunately for Mazurkevich, the renaming of his position was so recent that the cards in his pocket still bore the old directorate's name, Upravleniye Voennogo Sotrudnichestra. But, the incident underscored the changes MoD was making to gain influence over Russian foreign military sales.

20. Diana Lynne, "GPS Jammer Contractor Plays Both Sides of War," WorldNetDaily.com, 29 March 2003, http://www.worldnetdaily.com/news/article .asp?ARTICLE_ID=31773. During my tour as defense attaché in Moscow from 2001 to 2003, I had several occasions to meet with Dmitriev's Office to discuss both cooperation and complaints concerning arms sales by Russian enterprises. In the case of jammers, it appeared the Russian government was unaware of the sales by Aviaconversiya until informed by the United States.

21. The primacy of policy over sales is demonstrated by Rosoboronexport's reviewing China's request to resell Klimov RD-93 jet engines made under license to Pakistan. Russian policy had been not to sell engines to Pakistan. See: "Beijing Is Confident that Russia Will Agree to a Resale of Russian Engines to Pakistan" [Pekin uveren shto Moskva dast dobro na pereprodazhu rossiyskikh dvigateley Pakistanu], *Financial Times*, 9 November 2006, article reprinted on Rosoboronexport website.

22. Together China and India account for about 80 percent of Russian arms sales. India was the leading purchaser over 2002–2005 of foreign arms, with $12.9 billion. China ranked second during the same period in arms transfer agreements with $10.2 billion. Most of China's and India's arms purchases come from Russia. The $7 billion represents Russia's arms agreements to the developing world, not deliveries. The United States still leads in deliveries to the developing world and leads overall in arms sales due to sales to developed countries. See: "Conventional Arms Transfers to Developing Nations 1998–2005," Congressional Research Service, 23 October 2006, 35, 54.

23. The extent to which Russian military technology is shared is difficult to determine. Although Russia has not sold China the latest versions of its hardware, such as the S-400 Air Defense system or its most advanced fighters, Russia has agreed to let India be a codeveloper of its newest aircraft, a fifth-generation Sukhoi fighter. In addition, Baluyevsky's claim that equipment sold to China is less modern than that provided to Russian units is undercut by the fact that almost no new equipment is

provided to Russian units. According to the 2002 edition of *Military Balance* by the International Institute for Strategic Studies, London, UK, 314 percent more equipment was sold abroad than provided to Russian units in 2001. See also: "Russian and Indian Aircraft Builders Will Jointly Develop a Fifth-Generation Fighter and Medium Transport Aircraft" [Rossiyskie i indiyskie aviastroiteli budut sovmestno rasrabatyvat' istribitel' pyatogo pokoleniya i sredniy transportnyi samolyot], Interfax, 25 January 2007, and "S-400 Air Defense Systems to Be Put on Duty in 2006," RIA Novosti, 30 March 2006.

24. "We Don't Intend to Fight with NATO" [s NATO voevat' ne sobiraemsya], *Rossiyskaya Gazeta*, 1 November 2005.

25. *Military Balance 2002*, International Institute for Strategic Studies, London, UK, 274.

26. Sergey Belov, "Aircraft to Sergey Ivanov" [Samolyoty Sergeyu Ivanovu], *Rossiyskaya Gazeta*, 11 October 2006.

27. Ivanov was elected by the United Aircraft Corporation (OAK) board, but only after Putin made public his support for Ivanov. The OAK incorporates the Sukhoi Aircraft Company, Aviaexport Association, Ilyushin Finance Licensing Company, Irkut Corporation, Gagarin aircraft amalgamation in Komsomolsk-on-Amur, Ilyushin Interstate Aircraft Company, Sokol Aircraft Factory in Nyzhny Novgorod, Chkalov aircraft amalgamation in Novosibirsk, Tupolev Company, and the Financial Leasing Company.

28. "Russian Defense Complex Is an Instrument for Solving Social-Economic Tasks—Sergey Ivanov and Vice Premier RF Ivanov Consider the Military-Industrial Complex a Locomotive for the Russian Economy" [Rossiyskaya "oboronka" yavlyaetsya instrumentom resheniya sotzial'no-ekonomicheskikh zadach—Sergey Ivanov, and Vitse-prem'er RF Ivanov shchitaet oboronno-promyshlennyi kompleks lokomotivom rossiyskoy eknomiki], Interfax, 25 December 2006. See also http://www.arms-expo.ru/site.xp/049051124050050056.html.

29. Ibid.; Sergey Belov, "Aircraft to Sergey Ivanov."

30. Konstantin Makienko, "Restoration of Historical Russia, the Role of China and the Instruments of Military Technical Cooperation" [Restavratsiya istoricheskoy Rossii, rol' Kitaya i instrumentariy VTS], *Glavaya Tema*, no. 7, 21 October 2005.

31. "Military Doctrine of the Russian Federation" [Voennaya doktrina Rossiyskoy federatsii], *Nezavisimaya Gazeta*, 21 April 2000.

32. Dosym Satpayev, "The Organization of 20 Hieroglyphs," *Novoye Pokoleniye*, 3 September 2004, reprinted by BBC Monitoring Asia Service, 9 September 2004.

33. "Patterns of Global Terrorism—2000," U.S. Department of State, 30 April 2001, http://www.state.gov/s/ct/rls/crt/2000/2433.htm.

34. "Shanghai Cooperation Organization to Be Set," ITAR-TASS, 14 June 2001.

35. "Shanghai Six Form New Pole of International Politics," ITAR-TASS, 14 June 2001.

36. "Declaration of Shanghai Cooperation Organization," website of the Peo-

ple's Republic of China Consular General Office in Houston, 15 June 2001, http://www.chinahouston.org/news/2001615072235.html.

37. "Putin Says Shanghai Six to Focus on Security, Economy," ITAR-TASS, 14 June 2001.

38. Ibid.

39. Heather Clark, "Russia, China, Three Central Asian States Pledge," Agence France-Presse, 25 August 1999.

40. Jim Nichol, "Central Asia: Regional Developments and Implications for U.S. Interests," Congressional Research Service, 4. Updated 12 May 2006.

41. "At the Exercises in the 'SCO-ODKB' Format, the Largest Contingents Are Russian and Chinese" [Na Ucheniyakh v Formate "SHOS-ODKB" samye krupnye voinskie kontingenty predstavyat Rossiya i Kitay], Interfax, 11 July 2006.

42. "Countering NATO Is Not a Task of the SCO—Expert" [V zadachu SHOS ne vkhodit protivostoyat' NATO—eksperty], Interfax, 30 November 2006.

43. Ibid.

44. "Interview on Russia-China Military Cooperation with Yuri Baluyevsky, Chief of the Armed Forces General Staff," ITAR-TASS, 10 August 2005.

45. "Russia-China Military Relations Aimed at Strategic Partnership," Organization of Asia-Pacific News Agencies, 18 August 2005.

46. Viktor Litovkin, "Rossiysko-kitayskie Ucheniya: Ataka Na Lyaodunsky Poluostrov," Ria Novosti, 22 March 2005.

47. Ibid.; Marina Shatilova, "Language Barrier Major Difficulty in Russia-China Military Drill," ITAR-TASS, 18 August 2005.

48. "Interview on Russia-China Military Cooperation with Yuri Baluyevsky, Chief of the Armed Forces General Staff," ITAR-TASS, 10 August 2005.

49. Less than a month after the exercise, at the scheduled meeting of the Russian-Chinese Intergovernmental Commission for Military-Technical Cooperation, the two defense ministers, Ivanov and Gangchuan, met with President Putin and announced their commitment to strengthening military-technical cooperation and continuing joint exercises within the framework of the Shanghai Cooperation Organization. China reportedly did not buy the strategic bombers on display during the exercise but did sign contracts worth $1.5 billion for thirty-nine Il-76 and 78 transport aircraft. China also discussed the possible purchase of Su-30 MK3 aircraft with the highly advanced Zhuk-MSE radar system: a potentially significant upgrade in technology transfer. See: "Russia-China Military Exercise in Aug–Sep—Reports," Dow Jones International News, 28 January 2005; Vasiliy Kashin and Anna Nikholaeva, "Putin Earned $1.5 billion; Agrees to Sell 38 Aircraft to China" [Putin zarabotal $1.5 mlrd. Dorovorilis's kitaytsami o prodazhe 38 samolyotov], Vedomosti, 8 September 2005.

50. "Russia, China to Expand Military Cooperation," Vietnam News Agency Bulletin, 7 September 2005.

51. Local deputy Petr Medvedev, quoted in "Krasnoyarsk Deputies Are Dissatisfied with the Quality of Chinese Vegetables" ["Krasnoyarskie deputaty nedovol'ny

kachestvom 'kitayskikh ovoshchey'"], Regnum.ru, 8 November 2006, www.regnum
.ru/news/735487.html.

52. "More Than 7,000 People a Day Cross the Border at Zabaykalsk-Manchzhuria" [Bolee 7000 chelovek v sutki peresekayut granitsu na punkte Zabaykalsk-Manchzhuria], Taiga.Info, 14 December 2006, http://tayga.info/news/16809/.

53. "The Volume of Border Trade between the Russian Federation and China by 2010 could reach $15 Billion—PRC Ministry of Commerce" [Ob'em prigranichnoy torgovli RF i KNR k 2010 mozhet dostich' $15 mlrd—Minkommertsii KNR], Interfax, 8 September 2006.

54. "A New Bridge over the Argun Connects China and Siberia" [Kitay i Sibir' svyazal noviy most cherez Argun'], Taiga.Info, 29 November 2006, http://tayga .info/news/16169/.

55. "Irkutsk Attracts Chinese Builders for Realization of the National Project 'Affordable Housing'" [Irkutsk privlichet kitayskikh stroiteley dlya realizatsii natsproekta 'Dostupnoe zhil'e'], Taiga.Info, 12 November 2006, http://tayga.info/ news/15378/.

56. "Putin Sees East Fading Away," Associated Press, 21 December 2006.

57. "Trade with China Reminds one of a Colonial Exchange—Russian Diplomat" [Torgovlya s Kitaem napominaet kolonial'nyi obmen rossiyskiy diplomat], Taiga.Info, 6 November 2006, http://tayga.info/news/15128/.

58. "Putin Prods Ministers on Immigration," Reuters, 17 October 2005.

59. "Putin Seeks Curbs on Immigration," Moscow Times, 5 October 2006.

60. "Interview with Gen Yuri Baluyevskiy," S NATO Voevat Ne Sobiraemsya, Rossiyskaya Gazeta, 2005.

61. "Interview on Russia-China Military Cooperation with Yuri Baluyevsky, Chief of the Armed Forces General Staff," ITAR-TASS, 10 August 2005.

62. "Top General Sees Role of Russian Army to Prevent New World War," MosNews, 5 September 2006.

63. Little data was uncovered describing Russian-Chinese space or nuclear cooperation, but based on Testoyedov's comments it seems reasonable to believe it has been occurring. See: "The Head of the NPO PM Is Certain That Participation by the Russian Side in the Creation of the Chinese Analog to the GLONASS System Is Possible and Necessary" [Uchastie Rossiyskoy Storony V Sozdanii Kitayskogo Analoga Sistemy GLONASS Vozmozhno i Neobkhodmo, Uveren Glava NPO PM], AKOR, 9 November 2006.

64. Simon Saradzhyan, "Military to Get $189Bln Overhaul," Moscow Times, 8 February 2007.

65. Yuriy Kirshin, "Generals Discuss New Military Doctrine" [Generaly verstayut novuyu voennuyu doktrinu], Nezavisimaya Voennoe Obozrenie, 25 August 2006.

66. Makienko, Kommersant, 16 August 2005.

67. Dmitry Litovkin, "Russia Could Be Ousted from the Chinese Arms Market," Izvestia, 29 January 2004.

68. Ibid.; Yuri Baluyevsky, "Structure and Basic Content of the New Military Doctrine of Russia" [Struktura I Osnovnoe Soderzhanie Novoy Voennoy Doktriny Rossii], originally published on the website of the Russian Ministry of Defence, www.mil.ru/847/852/1153/1342/20922/index.html. The article has since been removed.

Sino-Russian Defense Ties

The View from Beijing

Jing-dong Yuan

Introduction

The end of the Cold War has witnessed perhaps one of the most significant transformations in interstate relations. In the course of almost two decades, and especially since Russian president Boris Yeltsin's visit to China in December 1992, Beijing and Moscow have formed a strategic and cooperative partnership, resolved their boundary disputes, and cooperated on many important international issues where both countries support the role of the United Nations and multipolarity, promote a new international order, and oppose unilateralism, the "Cold War mentality," and power politics. In 2001, the two countries signed the "Treaty of Good Neighborliness and Friendly Cooperation." The two countries have also played a central role in the establishment and development of the Shanghai Cooperation Organization (SCO).

Perhaps the most salient and tangible aspect of the Sino-Russian strategic partnership is the defense relationship that was initiated in the final days of the Soviet Union, was nurtured and blossomed during the Yeltsin years, and was expanded and further strengthened under the Vladimir Putin administration. China has become an important customer of Russian weaponry since the early 1990s, with major imports of fighter aircraft, destroyers, submarines, missiles, and aerial early warning systems. In addition, Beijing has also been able to secure military technology transfers from Russia as part of the arms trade arrangements. China has benefited from this relationship, as Russian weapons systems fill important gaps in the People's Liberation Army's (PLA) existing inventories of equipment and hence help develop pockets of excellence in both aerial and naval capabilities for offshore military operations, especially in the context of a possible military conflict over the Taiwan Strait. This relationship becomes all the more critical in the context of continuing U.S. and European Union arms embargoes on China, imposed since 1989. Second, given that China's defense industry was set up with Soviet assistance in the 1950s, bilateral defense ties reestablished since the early 1990s have helped support Chinese efforts in renovating existing defense industrial infrastructure and participating in coproduction projects. Third, closer Sino-Russian defense ties, including joint military exercises and other close defense consultations, also support the broader objectives of reinforcing and strengthening the strategic and cooperative partnership in response to U.S. dominance in the post–Cold War international system.

However, Beijing also recognizes both the limitation of its defense ties with Russia, where Moscow remains cautious regarding the types of weapons systems it is willing to sell out of concerns over U.S. and regional reactions, and the risk of overdependence on Russian supplies of arms. In addition, there are also issues of after-sale services, repairs, and spare parts supplies that could become bottlenecks to fully utilizing Russian weapons systems to advance China's strategic interests in the short to medium term. Likewise, the PLA's inability to fully integrate Russian equipment into its existing orders of battle has also cautioned Beijing against purchases of Russian armaments on a large scale. The recent downward trends confirm this assessment.

This chapter will discuss and analyze various aspects of Sino-Russian defense ties in terms of their evolution, current programs, future projections and limitations, and the implications for regional security and U.S. policy. I argue that Sino-Russian defense ties will continue in the coming years, barring (and even despite) dramatic developments such as the lifting of the EU arms embargo, with China continuing to make sizeable albeit selective purchases of Russian weapons systems. However, Beijing will seek to leverage its position as a key customer to demand more advanced systems and greater technology transfers in an effort to further improve its own domestic defense industrial base.

Chinese Arms Acquisitions from Russia since the 1990s

Chinese perspectives on security underwent drastic transformation with the end of the Cold War. The normalization of Sino-Soviet relations in 1989 and the subsequent disintegration of the Soviet empire in 1991 effectively removed an external threat that had been a major Chinese security concern in the previous decades. Consequently, Chinese defense strategists and policy-makers shifted their focus from preparing for a large-scale land war to building a modern defense force capable of deterring major aggression and winning local wars under modern conditions. What emerged was the doctrine of peripheral defense, which called for limited but effective military operations in regions bordering China. A most noticeable result of this doctrinal change has been the increasing importance assigned to the People's Liberation Army Navy (PLAN), which has been asked to broaden its traditional mission of coastal defense to include offshore operations across the Taiwan Strait and force projection into the South China Sea and beyond. Likewise, the requirement of an air force able to provide effective cover and maintain air control over regions of particular Chinese interest also reflects Beijing's changing defense priorities.[1]

Given the new military missions as a result of the changed defense posture, the deficiency of the PLA's equipment at the end of the Cold War became obvious and indeed was made all the more glaring during the Gulf War of 1990–1991, which showcased how the United States executed modern warfare with a synchronization of modern weapons, superior command, control, communications, and intelligence (C^3I), and the air-land battle (ALB) doctrine. The lessons of Desert Storm were not lost on the PLA leadership.[2] Indeed, one major lesson China has learned from the Gulf War is the decisive power of high technology. A commentary in the PLA's official newspaper, *Jiefangjun Bao*, claimed:

> New and developing science and technology are energetically giving impetus to a revolution in weapons. This revolution has widened the gap between weapons and has extended the qualitative difference in military power. The technological gap of weapons and equipment between the opposite sides finds its expression in the battlefield in information gap, space gap, time gap and precision gap. . . . The development of the war in the direction of high technology has become an irreversible trend. . . . The future war will be characterized by the intensive use of high and new technology and will give increasing prominence to and find its expression in the contest in science and technology. The role of quality confrontation will be greatly raised in the process of war as well as its conclusion and the stress on quality buildup will be the only option for any army.[3]

This concern over the apparent mission capability gap has been a key driver behind the double-digit increases in Chinese defense expenditure over the past two decades and large purchases of Russian weaponry during the same period. Clearly, a poorly equipped infantry groomed for protracted land wars and attrition could hardly carry out the new missions of protecting

China's newly found maritime interests and fighting and winning local wars under the informationalized environment. Accordingly, Chinese defense modernization has been heavily concentrated in its naval and air force development and on several main systems. These consist of sea platforms including submarines, new-generation destroyers, frigates, and corvettes; aircraft (fixed and rotary wing, fighter jets with powerful radar, airborne early warning [AEW], command and control, and in-flight refueling equipment and technology); weapon suites (guns, ammunition, torpedoes, cruise missiles, modern surface-to-air missiles, and target vehicles); and sensor arrays (radar, sonar, communications gear, and navigation equipment).[4]

For Chinese military leaders in the early 1990s, to redress this mission capability problem meant choosing either or both of the following two tactics. For the short term, the needs of the armed forces could be met by imports of advanced weapons systems from abroad. However, there were several inhibiting factors that would dismiss such a quick-fix strategy as unpractical. To begin with, there was the question of resource limitation. To raise the equipment level of the PLA to that of major powers—not to mention the superpowers—would be a monumental task. However, the more important question was whether, and to what extent, China was willing and ready to forgo the principle of self-reliance and accept dependence on foreign suppliers. Another external constraint would be the willingness of major foreign suppliers to sell advanced equipment and transfer sensitive military technology to China out of concerns over nonproliferation and other national security and foreign policy considerations. Indeed, China's ability to acquire advanced military technology was constrained by the Western arms embargoes imposed in the aftermath of the 1989 Tiananmen incident.[5]

Predictably, a long-term tactic would be to enhance the overall technological level of the domestic defense industrial base. However, it was an acknowledged fact that the ability of the PRC defense industry to meet the PLA's equipment requirements in qualitative terms was limited due to their weak indigenous technological and industrial base, which lagged ten to twenty years behind those in the West and Japan.[6] In addition, catching up would take time, and given the priorities accorded to economic development at the time, China's defense industry was unlikely to receive more funding.[7] What would be appropriate, then, would be to combine imports of weapons and military technology with the medium- and long-term development strategies of the defense industry.[8]

In the end, a combination of factors guided Beijing's arms procurement decisions. These factors included the need to quickly modernize the PLA in selected areas; China's steadily growing economy moving into the 1990s, making it possible to devote more resources for off-the-shelf purchases; the buyer's market in international arms trade, which allowed Beijing to cut better deals in arms imports and be less concerned with overdependence on any particular supplier; and finally, the inadequacy of the domestic defense industrial base as a reliable source to fill PLA equipment orders. The purchases would be limited and selective in those high-priority and bottleneck areas. However, this import-assimilation would be combined with the longer-term goals of reverse-engineering that put more emphasis on the importation of technology, licensed production, coproduction, and codevelopment of weapons to gradually supplement if not replace completely off-the-shelf purchases.[9]

Given the U.S. and EU arms embargoes, China naturally turned to the former Soviet Union and, later, Russia for help. While Moscow's early post–Cold War foreign policy had a strong tilt toward the West, the Yeltsin administration nonetheless continued the detente with China that had been initiated by Mikhail Gorbachev and Deng Xiaoping in the late 1980s. The relationship would continue to evolve and improve, culminating in the 1996 establishment of the strategic partnership and the Shanghai Agreement on military confidence-building measures.[10] The two countries targeted expansion of trade as an important element of strengthening the bilateral relationship, but in the end it was the Russian arms sales to China that became the hallmark of this budding relationship.[11]

In March 1990, Xie Guang, deputy director of the Commission of Science, Technology, and Industry for National Defense (COSTIND), led a delegation to visit the Soviet Union in exploration of military technology cooperation and arms purchases. This was followed by Premier Li Peng's visit in late April, during which the Sino-Soviet Mixed Commission on Military Technology Cooperation was established. Admiral Liu Huaqing, a former PLAN commander and vice chairman of the Central Military Commission (CMC), was appointed the head from China's side. Admiral Liu studied for four years in the Soviet Union in the 1950s and was an active promoter of science and technology in Chinese defense modernization. He proposed to the Chinese leadership that Beijing and Moscow sign an agreement on defense science and technology cooperation and that China approach the Soviets to purchase Su-27 fighter aircraft. Liu led a delegation to the Soviet Union in May–June 1990. This was the first time in thirty years that China sent such a high-level military delegation to the Soviet Union. The two governments signed the Agreement on Military Technology Cooperation. Moscow in principle agreed to sell Su-27s to China.[12]

There were ample reasons as to why China chose Russia as its main weapons supplier. Russian weapons were relatively inexpensive, especially in a largely buyers' market with the end of the Cold War; Moscow was willing to accept flexible payment arrangements, including barter trade; the PLA was largely armed with former Soviet weapons systems and hence compatibility issues could be easily handled; and Russia did not attach any political strings for its arms exports, while the U.S. decision to suspend all military exchanges with China after Tiananmen imposed significant constraints on China's defense modernization. These considerations prompted Beijing to seek Soviet/Russian arms imports.[13]

During his December 1992 visit to China, Russia's President Yeltsin and China's Premier Li Peng signed the "Memorandum on the Principles of Military and Technical Cooperation between China and Russia." The two countries also established an intergovernmental mixed commission on military technology cooperation. Since then, top military leaders from both countries have engaged in regular visits; between 1992 and 2009, the vice chairman of the Chinese Central Military Commission (CMC) and defense minister visited Russia ten times. Admiral Liu himself would make another two trips to Russia (see table 7.1 on pages 210–13 for selected high-level military exchange visits between the two countries). Eleven rounds of consultations between the two countries' General Staff departments have been held over the years. At the functional levels, such exchanges are even more frequent. Since 1996, for instance, more than two thousand PLA officers have studied at various levels of Russian command and staff schools as well as military academies; Russia has also sent its military officers to study in China. In 2000, during Chinese defense minister Chi Haotian's visit to Russia, the two countries reportedly drafted a fifteen-year military cooperation plan to jointly research and manufacture military equipment.[14] These activities have paved the way for extensive Sino-Russian military cooperation over the past seventeen years. According to the Stockholm International Peace Research Institute arms transfers database, China spent over $26 billion between 1992 and 2006 on the purchase of Russian weapons, about 89 percent of its total foreign arms imports during the same period.[15] China has ordered a sizeable number of advanced Russian weapons and weapons technologies, many of which have been delivered to date. These include:

- 44 Ilyushin Il-76M/Candid-B medium/long-range transport aircraft (10 delivered in 1993) and 4 Il-78 tanker-transport aircraft;[16]
- 3 A-50U/Mainstay AEW&C aircraft ordered;
- 173 Su-27SK/Flanker long-range strike fighters (including 95 assembled in Shenyang as part of the prelicensed production out of the originally agreed 200; China has cancelled the rest);[17]

- 100 Su-30MK/Flanker FGA aircraft;
- 154 AL-31FN turbofan engines ordered for Chinese J-10 combat aircraft;
- 200 D-30 turboprop engines imported from Uzbekistan for 40 IL-76 transport and IL-78 tanker/transport aircraft;[18]
- 100 RD-33/RD-93 turbofan engines ordered for Chinese-made FC-1 and JF-17 combat aircraft (on the condition that the engines not be reexported by China);
- 8 batteries of S-300PMU-1/SA-10D SAM systems;
- 8 batteries of S-300PMU-2/SA-10E SAM systems ordered;
- 35 Tor-M1/SA-15 Mobile SAM systems;
- 50 T-72 tanks, 200 T-80U main battle tanks, and 70 BMP-1 armored infantry fighting vehicles;[19]
- 4 Sovremenny class destroyers;[20]
- 10 Type-636E/Kilo class submarines; and
- 2 Type-877E/Kilo class submarines.

In addition to these arms purchases, for which the Russian defense-industrial complex has received both hard currency and consumer goods through barter trade, Beijing and Moscow have also engaged in negotiations on other advanced weapons systems, either for off-the-shelf purchases, licensed production, or technology transfers. These negotiations and discussions reportedly include potential future purchases and licensed production of MiG-31 long-range interceptors (negotiated but not yet materialized), MiG-29 (Fulcrum) interceptors, and Su-24 ground attack aircraft (under negotiation).[21] China has purchased Ka-27PL/Helix-A antisubmarine warfare (ASW) helicopters for its navy, some A-50 airborne warning and control aircraft and long-range early warning radar systems, and signed contracts for the purchase of close to 300 SA-10 Grumble (S-300) air-defense missile systems.[22] In addition, the Russians reportedly offered to sell China supersonic Tu-22M Backfire long-range bombers. There are reports that China agreed to buy 440 T-72M main battle tanks (MBTs) and 70 BMP vehicles.[23] Russia reportedly has even offered Sukhoi Su-33 and Su-35 combat aircraft to China for use on aircraft carriers. The offer is significant because the aircraft are still in development, which suggests that Russia is willing to share its latest technology with China.[24]

The acquisitions of Russian weapons systems have enhanced the PLA's power projection capabilities. For instance, the Su-27 is an air superiority fighter designed for air-to-air combat and equipped with Russia's most advanced avionics. It has a range of 4,000 kilometers in internal fuel tanks and a

Table 7.1. China-Soviet/Russia Military Exchange Visits, 1990–2007

Date	Visit	Comment
06/1990	CMC Vice Chairman Liu Huaqing visited the Soviet Union.	Discussed possible purchase of 24 SU-27s.
05/1991	Soviet Defense Minister Dmitri Yazov visited China.	Continued discussion of the Su-27 and other military hardware sales.
08/1991	PLA Chief of the General Staff Chi Haotian visited the Soviet Union.	
02/1992	CIS Joint Armed Forces Chief of Staff Viktor Samsonov visited China.	Discussed the reduction of military forces along the Sino-Russian border.
04/1993	Chinese PLAN Commander Zhang Lianzhong visited Russia.	Discussed PRC interest in purchasing Russian naval armaments.
06/23/1993	CMC Vice Chairman Liu Huaqing visited Russia.	
11/07/1993	Russia's Defense Minister Pavel Grachev conducted a four-day visit to China.	Signed a five-year agreement on military cooperation.
04/19/1994	Russia's Chief of Staff, Col.-Gen. Mikhail Kolesnikov, visited Beijing.	
06/11/1994	PRC Defense Minister Chi Haotian visited Russia.	Signed agreement on the prevention of dangerous military activity.
11/02/1994	Commander-in-Chief of the Russian Navy Feliks Gromov visited Beijing.	
05/15/1995	Russian Defense Minister Pavel Grachev visited China.	
12/02/1995	CMC Vice Chairman Liu Huaqing visited Moscow.	
10/12/1996	Lieutenant General Guo Boxiong, Deputy Commander of the Beijing Military Region, visited Russia.	
04/14/1997	Russian Defense Minister Igor Rodionov visited Beijing.	
08/24/1997	CMC Vice Chairman Liu Huaqing arrived in Moscow for an official visit.	Signed deal for aircraft spare parts and follow-on maintenance for recently purchased advanced Russian Su-27 fighter jets.
01/21/1998	Russia's State Military Inspector and Secretary of the Russian Defense Council Andrei Kokoshin visited China.	

Table 7.1. China-Soviet/Russia Military Exchange Visits, 1990–2007 (cont'd)

Date	Visit	Comment
10/20/1998	Russian Defense Minister Igor Sergeyev visited China.	Agreed that Russia will provide technological assistance as needed in China's domestic production of high-tech weapons; reached preliminary agreement on the delivery of Su-30MKK fighters to China.
05/22–29/1999	Admiral Vladimir Kuroyedov, Commander-in-Chief of the Russian Navy, visited Beijing and Shanghai.	
05/31/1999	Deputy Chief of the General Staff of the Russian Armed Forces Valentin Korabelnikov visited China.	
06/07–17/1999	CMC Vice Chairman Zhang Wannian visited a division of Russian Strategic Missile Troops near Novosibirsk.	Signed a cooperation agreement on the training of military personnel. General Zhang also visited Russia's Strategic Missile Troops and the Russian Pacific Fleet.
08/24–28/1999	Russian Vice Prime Minister Ilya Klebanov, responsible for supervising the military-industrial complex, visited Beijing.	Finalized details for China's purchase of 50 Su-30 fighter jets.
10/11/1999	Two Russian warships commanded by Pacific Fleet Commander Mikhail Georgevich Zakharenko visited China.	
10/18–25/1999	PLA Navy Commander Shi Yunsheng conducted a week-long visit to Russia.	
01/16–18/2000	PRC Defense Minister Chi Haotian visited Russia, met Russian Defense Minister Igor Sergeyev and Vice Premier for the military-industrial complex Ilya Klebanov.	Formulated fifteen-year military cooperation plan; signed MOU on further strengthening military cooperation.
11/14/2000	First Deputy Chief of the General Staff of the Russian Armed Forces Valeri Manilov visited Beijing.	
12/04–08/2000	Commander of Russia's Airborne Forces Georgi Shpak conducted five-day visit to China.	Visited an elite paratroop brigade in Wuhan.
02/19–22/2001	CMC Vice Chairman Zhang Wannian traveled to Moscow on a four-day visit.	
09/04/2001	Deputy Commander Zhu Shuguang led a People's Armed Police delegation to Russia.	

Table 7.1. China-Soviet/Russia Military Exchange Visits, 1990–2007 (cont'd)

Date	Visit	Comment
10/19–21/2001	Anatoly Kvashnin, Deputy Defense Minister and Chief of the General Staff of the Russian Armed Forces, met Chief of the PLA General Staff Fu Quanyou in Shanghai.	
11/25/2001	Deputy Chief of the General Staff Xiong Guangkai visited Russia.	
05/31/2002	Russian Defense Minister Sergei Ivanov visited China.	
07/03/2002	Victor Chechevatov, President of the Military Institute of the General Staff of the Russian Armed Forces, visited Beijing and met Chief of the General Staff Fu Quanyou.	
12/16/2002	Deputy Chief of the General Staff Xiong Guangkai and First Deputy Chief of the General Staff Yuri Baluyevsky jointly presided over the 6th round of Sino-Russian military consultations.	
05/30/2003	Russian Defense Minister Sergei Ivanov held talks with PRC Defense Minister Cao Gangchuan in Moscow.	
12/15/2003	Defense Minister Cao Gangchuan visited Moscow.	
03/15/2004	Russia First Deputy Chief of the General Staff of the Russian Armed Forces Yuri Baluyevsky visited China.	
04/20/2004	Russian Minister of Defense Sergei Ivanov met PRC Defense Minister Cao Gangchuan in Beijing.	
05/17–23/2004	PRC Chief of the General Staff Liang Guanglie visited Moscow and toured Russia's Baltic Fleet.	
06/23/2004	PRC military delegation from the PLA's Jilin Provincial Military District visited Sakhalin Island in Russia's Far East.	
07/05/2004	CMC Vice Chairman Guo Boxiong visited Moscow and met Russian Defense Minister Sergei Ivanov and Chief of General Staff of the Russian Armed forces Anatoly Kvashnin.	
12/13/2004	Russian Defense Minister Sergei Ivanov visited Beijing.	Announced plans to hold a joint exercise.

Table 7.1. China-Soviet/Russia Military Exchange Visits, 1990–2007 (cont'd)

Date	Visit	Comment
03/17–20/2005	Russian Chief of General Staff Yuri Baluyevsky visited Beijing; met with PRC Premier Zhu Rongji and PLA Chief of Staff Liang Guanglie.	Discussed details of the planned joint military exercise.
08/18/2005	PLA Chief of Staff Liang Guanglie and Chief of Staff Colonel Yuri Baluyevsky held a press conference at the headquarters of the Russian Pacific Fleet in Vladivostok and met with journalists covering the "Peace Mission 2005" Sino-Russian joint military exercise.	
02/16/2006	Lieutenant General Yevgeny Buzhinsky, Vice Director of the International Military Cooperation Bureau and Director of the International Treaty and Law Bureau under the Ministry of National Defense, visited China.	
03/25–29/2006	Commander-in-Chief of Russia's Ground Troops Alexei Maslov visited China.	Discussed military cooperation.
04/23/2006	Russian Vice Premier and Defense Minister Sergei Ivanov visited China.	
05/22–24/2006	PLA Chief of Staff Liang Guanglie visited Moscow; met Russian Chief of Staff Yuri Baluyevsky.	
05/30/2006	Deputy Chief of Staff Alexander Rukshin and Deputy Chief of the General Staff Zhang Qinsheng held 10th round of consultations between the two general staffs in Beijing.	
03/03–04/2007	Russian Armed Forces Chief of Staff Yuri Baluyevsky visited China.	Discussed bilateral military technical cooperation and planning of "Peace Mission 2007."
11/07–10/2007	PLA Deputy Chief of the General Staff Ma Xiaotian visited Russia.	Participated in 11th round of Sino-Russian strategic consultations.
06/16–19/2008	Head of the Russian Armed Forces' Air Defense Force Nikolai Frolov visited China.	Inspected Russian-made surface-to-air missile systems.
12/09–11/2008	Russian Defense Minister Anatoly Serdyukov visited China.	Discussed bilateral military cooperation.
04/25–29/2009	Chinese Defense Minister Liang Guanglie visited Russia.	Attended the meeting of SCO defense ministers.

Sources: Pacific Forum-CSIS, *Comparative Connections,* chapters by Yu Bin on Sino-Russian relations, various years, at http://www.csis.org/pacfor/ccejournal.html; Jeanne L. Wilson, *Strategic Partners: Russian-Chinese Relations in the Post-Soviet Era* (Armonk, N.Y.: Sharpe, 2004), 93–113; and author's own compilation.

combat radius of approximately 1,500 kilometers. With aerial refueling technology, the PLAAF could extend air control over the Spratly island group. The Kilo class submarine has a range of 9,650 kilometers and an ability to remain at sea for up to forty-five days. China already purchased twelve Kilos and may plan to buy up to a total of twenty-two of the diesel-powered submarines (SSKs) from Russia. The Sovremenny class destroyers are equipped with SS-N-22/Sunburn antiship cruise missiles, which are designed to defeat the U.S. Navy's Aegis air-defense system, thereby enhancing China's antiaircraft carrier capabilities.[25]

While China has spent significant amounts on the purchases of major Russian weapons systems, Beijing is also interested in acquiring the necessary military technologies from Russia, as well as from elsewhere, to enhance its indigenous defense industrial capabilities.[26] Russia is an ideal provider, given the past ties between the two countries in the defense industrial sector. China's defense industry was built in the 1950s with Soviet assistance through massive imports of plants, prototypes, blueprints, the training of personnel, and organization and management structure. By the late 1970s, when economic reforms were implemented, China had established a behemoth defense industrial base that contained about 25 percent of the country's capacity of heavy industries and produced 10 percent of its gross national product (GNP).[27] However, the quantitative growth had not been accompanied by qualitative progress. Most of the weapons the Chinese defense industry manufactured were of Soviet prototypes of the 1950s and 1960s vintage. In overall terms, China's defense industrial base and military technology base remained weak and has been further weakened by the process of economic reforms that began in the late 1970s.[28]

China has adopted a number of approaches toward acquiring military technologies from Russia. One is to seek licensed production. The Su-27 licensed production is one example. A 1995 agreement allowed China to produce 200 Su-27s at its Shenyang aircraft factory. In addition, technology transfers and technical know-how from Russian defense manufacturers have proved instrumental in Chinese development of major weapons systems. This is particularly the case with the new generation of Chinese fighter aircraft, where Russian companies have provided designs in avionics and airframes. A second approach is to have Russian defense technicians work in Chinese defense research institutes and factories. It has been widely reported that as many as two thousand Russian technicians have been employed by China to work on laser technology, nuclear weapons miniaturization, cruise missiles, space-based weaponry, and nuclear submarines. Meanwhile, many Chinese defense technicians have gone over to Russia for training or other forms of work in Russia's major aerospace research and development centers.[29] China has been able to incorporate Russian technologies in the development of several of its own weapons systems, such as infantry fighting vehicles (IFV), conventional diesel-powered submarines, and the J-10 combat aircraft.[30]

China's manned space program has benefited from close cooperation with, and assistance from, Russia. In March 1994, Beijing and Moscow signed an agreement on space cooperation between the Russian Space Agency and the China National Space Administration. Russia agreed to provide certain equipment, technologies, expertise, and training to the burgeoning Chinese manned space program.[31] Chinese sources identified a number of areas of specific cooperation, including "docking system installations, model spaceships, flight control, and means of life support." Chinese astronauts received training at the Gagarin Cosmonaut Training Center in Star City outside Moscow.[32] In addition, the Chinese reportedly copied Russian pressure suits. Western analysts point to the remarkable similarity between the Russian *Soyuz TM* and the Chinese spacecraft *Shenzhou*, although many also agree that the Chinese have made modifications in addition to selected purchases and copying.

There has been some speculation about the military significance of China's successful manned space program and on Sino-Russian cooperation on military space programs.[33] For instance, western analysts point to the fact that the Chinese manned space program has always been under the command of the head of the PLA's General Armament Department—General Cao Gangchuan for Shenzhou V and General Chen Bingde for Shenzhou VI. Many of the programs carried out through the Shenzhou series are suspected of having dual-use significance, such as the high-resolution imaging system and reconnaissance capabilities.[34] The July 2005 U.S. Defense Department's *Annual Report to Congress: Military Power of the People's Republic of China* voiced concerns over China's space program, pointing out that military capability and strategy "is likely one of the primary drivers behind Beijing's space endeavors and a critical component" of the country's financial investment in space.[35] U.S. analysts are also concerned that growing Chinese space capabilities would enable the country to develop and deploy antisatellite weapons.[36]

Related to space cooperation are ballistic and cruise missile programs, where China could also benefit (and reportedly already has benefited) from technical assistance from Russia and elsewhere. There have been unconfirmed reports of Ukrainian missile experts working in China, and Russia may have shared technical data on its own fourth-generation ICBMs (SS-18 and SS-25).[37] While such information is difficult to verify, recent developments in Sino-Russian and Sino-Ukrainian military cooperation are openly reported. From the Russian/Ukrainian perspective, there is much to gain through such assistance. It could further strengthen the so-called strategic partnership. Economic factors are also important as Russia and Ukraine seek to maintain the viability of their defense-industrial complexes. Research and development on future weapons could also be funded through greater cooperation with and assistance to China.

Obviously, for a country like China, defense modernization cannot be realized by buying weapons and equipment. Consequently, China will always adhere to the fundamental guideline that the development of defense science and technology should mainly depend on its own strength.[38] This has been an unwavering principle strongly held among the Chinese military leadership. While the past seventeen years have seen a modification of the self-reliance principle, this slight change results from the lessons of the Gulf War and the fact that indigenous efforts have been adequate in quickly turning around the defense industry, enabling it to produce high-quality, high-tech weaponry and other military equipment. As mentioned above, the Gulf War left an indelible impact on the PLA high command. What is most obvious is the urgency to upgrade weaponry. China's defense-industrial complex has been called upon to invest heavily in research and development. Meanwhile, a new line of upholding the principle of integrating self-reliance with the vigorous import of advanced technology from abroad has been put forth to quicken the pace of modernization of weapons and equipment.[39] There have been reports that COSTIND won an intensive internal debate over the question of military procurement. While the navy and air force had advocated substantial off-the-shelf purchases of Russian weapons systems, COSTIND opted for upgrading China's defense industrial base through technology transfers, licensed production, and coproduction, with the help of Russian scientists and technicians.[40]

China has clearly benefited from Russian military technology transfers. These have enabled the Chinese defense industry to reverse-engineer the purchased Russian systems as well as modify and improve upon indigenous prototypes and come up with new and better systems.[41] According to Richard Fisher, a close watcher of the PLA, the Chinese military has been able to leverage foreign military technologies it has acquired to significantly transform itself into a formidable military force.[42] Indeed, Chinese media, citing Russian experts, suggest that Russian technologies have been critical in some of China's recent breakthroughs in new indigenous weapons systems. For instance, the J-10 multirole fighter aircraft are equipped with Russian

AL-31FN turbofan engines, and Chinese analysts advocate for joint production of military aircraft to form economies of scale that would benefit the air forces of both countries.[43]

Sino-Russian Defense Cooperation: Issues and Prospects

While Sino-Russian defense ties since the end of the Cold War have remained robust and China has received its weapons systems predominantly from Russia, this relationship is not without its problems. There have always been debates and indeed misgivings about arms transfers to China within Russia's military and security community.[44] While Russian defense-industrial complexes are eager to make money just to stay alive, Russian policymakers have remained cautious regarding the types of weapons systems to allow for export to China, have continued to keep a lid on the level of technology transfers, and have tried to influence or even impose conditions on where the Chinese-acquired weapons could be deployed so as to minimize any threats to Russia's security interests. Several issues stand out. One is whether Russia should help an already strong economic power become a military one and what potential threats that would pose to Russian security. This security consideration has informed Moscow's decision to turn down Chinese requests to purchase Tu-22M Backfire supersonic tactical strike bombers (despite unconfirmed reports that Moscow had offered to sell them to China in the 1990s) while being willing to sell them to India. Similarly, Russia has declined to export Su-35 fighters to China, and the Chinese proposal to coproduce 150 sets of Tor-M1/SA-15 mobile SAM systems was also turned down by Moscow.[45] Chinese media reports and analyses have noted, with regret, that Russia tends to be very cautious in its arms sales to China, whereas it has been more liberal in its arms exports to countries such as India and Vietnam. Russian concerns about future Chinese threats are a key variable influencing Moscow's decisions.[46]

A second issue is the impact of Russian arms transfers to China on East Asian regional military balance and stability.[47] China's growing military activities on the high seas may place it directly on a collision course with other powers. China is enhancing its capabilities not only to develop a green water navy capable of asserting itself in future maritime disputes and protecting what it considers to be its maritime territories stretching between islets and atolls in the South China Sea, but also to establish effective control over critical sea lines of communication in the region. China's growing assertiveness in the South China Sea in the early 1990s also increased the chance for accidents. One missile-firing exercise in the mid-1990s, for instance, almost hit a drilling platform off the Hainan coast. The increasing frequency of such exercises could likely disrupt and endanger both oil exploration and sea lines of communication.[48]

And the third issue is the U.S. factor, in that Moscow must be sensitive to Washington's concerns, but also sensitive to how Sino-Russian defense ties could be leveraged as a counterforce against U.S. dominance. Chinese acquisitions of Russian arms have important implications for U.S. security interests in the region. For Beijing, these arms acquisitions are principally aimed at enhancing its military projection capabilities in Asia, and its ability to influence events throughout the region, including both the Taiwan Strait and the South China Sea, where territorial disputes exist between China and a number of Southeast Asian states. U.S. policy in the region remains one of maintaining close security relationships with key allies, continuing a sizeable military presence against any security contingencies, combating the proliferation of weapons of mass destruction, and assuring allies and friends of its commitments to their defense, hence influencing and shaping the region's security. Within this context, Washington continues to provide appropriate military equipment to allies and friendly states in Asia to help offset any prospective threat China may pose to such nations, while keeping the U.S. military aware of any threat it may face in any confrontation with China. Any significant shifts in the military balance will either raise doubts in the confidence in U.S. security guarantees and commitments or raise the costs of U.S. intervention. In this context, China's growing military capabilities during a period of continued stalemate over the allocation of Taiwan's special defense budget is a cause of concern for Washington.[49]

Perhaps the most serious U.S. concern relates to reported Russian contemplation of transferring ballistic missile technologies to China. For instance, U.S. Defense Secretary William Perry warned in 1996 that it would be "a significant mistake" if Russia were to transfer SS-18 technology to China, as western analysts suspect that China had obtained the components, engine, and guidance technology of the SS-18.[50] The 2006 Department of Defense report on China's military power explicitly spells out the implications of Sino-Russian military cooperation: "China also relies on critical Russian components for several of its weapon production programs and, in some cases, has purchased the production rights to Russian weapon systems. Russia continues to cooperate with China on technical, design, and material support for numerous weapons and space systems." And, "Russia has historically refrained from transferring its most sophisticated weapons systems to China. However, China's persistent pressure on Russia to make available more advanced military equipment—particularly using Russia's dependence on Chinese arms purchases as leverage—could cause a shift in Sino-Russian military cooperation."[51]

These considerations will clearly affect Russian decisions on arms sales to China. At the same time, it remains to be seen if, in the foreseeable future, the Chinese naval buildup could pose any serious threat to U.S. interests in the region and significantly change the regional balance of power. Chinese purchase of Russian submarines and destroyers cannot fundamentally change the fact that the PLAN remains years away from becoming a truly blue water navy. Nor is the PLAN able to pose a serious challenge to even its neighbors, whose purchase of European-designed submarines are an effective counterforce to the PLAN's newest fleet of destroyers and frigates. There remains weakness in terms of early warning, naval defense, command and control, and ASW capabilities that require years, if not decades, to overhaul and improve upon.[52]

The Sino-Russian defense relationship has sometimes experienced unrealized high expectations and subsequent disappointments. The much-anticipated financial benefits through arms sales have not been fully accrued due to payment arrangements that China insists on, including barter trade. For instance, only 35 percent of the $1 billion for the first batch of twenty-six Su-27s was actually paid in hard currency, with the balance in the form of barter trade in Chinese consumer goods, such as running shoes and canned meat, among others. Some of the Russian weapons systems have been delivered to China to write off existing debts. Finally, while Russian weapons systems initially proved to be cost-effective due to their competitive pricing, rising costs and disputes over prices and delivery delays have not made either side happy. The negotiation on the Sovremenny class destroyers took more than three years to conclude, mainly due to disagreements over pricing. The Chinese side has also reportedly complained about the differences in the unit price of the Su-27SKs ($35 million) it received in the early 1990s and the Su-30MKKs ($30 million) that Russia has sold to Vietnam. There have also been delays in the delivery of the Il-76MDs, and the quality of Russian fighter aircraft has been questioned as fires in the engine system have led to serious incidents costing the lives of Chinese pilots and the loss of planes.[53]

Chinese acquisitions of complete Russian weapons systems seem to have reached a saturation point over the last few years, with deliveries rather than new contracts being reported. Indeed, no significant orders have taken place since 2005, while Beijing pushes for more advanced arms or a greater share of the technological components of any new deals. Recent reports indicate that Russian sales to China dropped by 62 percent in 2007.[54] This presents serious dilemmas for Russia. On the one hand, Moscow cannot afford to sell its most advanced weapons systems to China out of concerns over the potential future Chinese threat to Russian security interests, regional repercussions, and likely strong U.S. response. On the other hand, Beijing increasingly insists that production licenses and technology transfers should be part of the bilateral arms sale arrangements. For instance, China reportedly suspended or deferred deliveries of some of the big-ticket deals, such as the Il-78 transport aircraft and Il-78 airborne tankers.[55] To retain China's arms market, Russia has to make its offers more attractive. For instance, recent reports suggest that the two countries are finalizing Chinese purchases of the Su-33, an advanced carrier-based version of the Su-27.[56] From Beijing's perspective, it is not an ideal situation for Russia to be virtually the sole source of Chinese foreign military acquisitions. Political considerations aside, the continued EU arms embargo on China means that for the foreseeable future, China will have to look to Russia as its key arms supplier, making the buyer's market elusive as far as selection, price, and after-sale services are concerned. But this is the reality that Beijing has to live with.[57]

Russia seeks to retain China as its major customer of arms. During the August 2005 "Peace Mission 2005" Sino-Russian joint military exercises, Russia showcased a number of weapons systems in the hopes of securing future Chinese purchases. These included Tu-95 strategic bombers and Tu-22M long-range bombers.[58] It was reported that Chinese defense minister Cao Gangchuan led high-ranking PLA officers to review the advanced weapons systems that the Russian military used during the exercises and soon concluded an arms deal for Ilyushin Il-76 transport aircraft and Ilyushin Il-78 aerial refueling tankers worth $1.8 billion.[59] There have been reports that China and Russia may sign a contract allowing China licensed production of the Tu-22M.[60] Indeed, Russia may be forced to either offer more advanced weapons systems or upgrade the technological components and allow more technology transfers. For instance, Russia reportedly is selling weapons systems that only a few years ago it would decline even to discuss, let alone sell, including the Klub-S (SS-N-27) antiship and land-attack cruise missile, an improved version of the Moskit (SS-N-22) antiship missile, and the Su-30MMK2 and the Su-30MKK3 combat aircraft that even the Russian military is not equipped with. Indeed, there have been reports that Russia has proposed that China participate in the program to design a fifth-generation multirole fighter. The two countries have also entered into discussion on the joint use of the Russian GLONASS global navigation satellite system.[61]

However, despite the slowdown or even setbacks in Russian weapons sales to China, the past two decades have seen growing Sino-Russian defense cooperation not confined to arms transfers alone. These areas include regular high-level defense consultation (see table 7.1), joint military exercises conducted either bilaterally or held under the auspices of the SCO, and converging interests on important international security issues such as missile defenses and space weaponization.

As noted above, "Peace Mission 2005" represented the first ever large-scale joint military exercises between the two countries, with over 9,000 Russian and Chinese forces participating and the deployment of major weapons systems, such as Tu-22 and Tu-95 bombers, missile destroyers, and AWACS, among others. In August 2007, over 6,500 troops from Russia, China, and the other SCO member states held a two-phase joint antiterrorism military exercise that began in the Xinjiang Uyghur Autonomous Region and concluded in the Russian Chelyabinsk region.[62] China, in particular, benefited from the exercises. Not only did the PLA for the first time dispatch a 1,600-member unit to a foreign location over long distance, which tested its air-lift power projection capabilities, but the participating Chinese troops as well as headquarters staff officers observed firsthand, coordinated with, and executed assigned tasks from the multinational joint exercise headquarters. Chinese military analysts and media readily admitted that the PLA strengthened its capacities in dealing with nontraditional security threats and contingencies through the exercises and interactions with its Russian and other SCO counterparts. The exercises also strengthened the SCO's four capabilities: strategic consultation, power projection, joint command, and joint operations.[63]

Another area of close Russian-Chinese cooperation focuses on their shared opposition to U.S. missile defense developments and deployments, whether these are in East Asia, Europe, or on U.S. territories. Beijing and Moscow view such developments as highly destabilizing and essentially as undermining the strategic balances among major powers. Indeed, prior to the U.S. withdrawal from the ABM Treaty in 2002, China and Russia had closely cooperated in various international fora, including at the United Nations and the Conference on Disarmament, in submitting resolutions opposing missile defenses.[64] In recent years, Beijing and Moscow have expressed deep concerns over U.S. plans to deploy missile defenses in Europe. Indeed, the joint statement issued during Russian president Dmitry Medvedev's visit to China in May 2008 strongly condemned the U.S. missile shield in Europe, arguing that such systems "do not support strategic balance and stability, and harm international efforts to control arms and the nonproliferation process."[65] Likewise, the two countries have also joined hands in proposing international negotiations leading to a treaty on preventing the weaponization of outer space.[66]

Conclusion

Sino-Russian defense ties have been and remain the most salient aspect of their strategic partnership. Both countries have benefited from this close military cooperation since the late 1980s, when bilateral relations were normalized. Chinese purchasing orders of Russian weapons systems have helped sustain Russia's massive defense-industrial complexes, while acquisitions and integration of advanced Russian weaponry have filled in the gaps in the PLA's orders of battle in selected areas at reasonable prices and with favorable payment arrangements, enhanced its power projection capabilities, and contributed to the renovation of China's defense industrial base with technology transfers. As long as the EU and the United States maintain post-1989 arms embargoes on China, Beijing will have to remain dependent on critical military technologies and advanced weapons systems from Russia, even though Chinese preferences will increasingly be leaning toward technology transfers rather than off-the-shelf purchases.

However, there are limitations to this relationship due to politico-strategic, security, and commercial considerations.[67] Russia remains wary of China's future trajectory as a rising power and is therefore cautious in making arms sales decisions. Regional balance of power and U.S. reactions are additional factors that inform and influence Russian arms sales to China. Tension arises where buyer-seller expectations and preferences diverge, and future arms trade between the two countries will largely be shaped by their ability to strike mutually satisfactory deals, taking into consideration all relevant factors. For the United States, the critical issue is less what Beijing purchases off the shelf, and more its ability to acquire, absorb, and integrate military technologies that can transform its defense industrial base, making it capable of designing, testing, and manufacturing large quantities of new-generation weaponry indigenously.

The future direction of Sino-Russian defense ties will continue to be determined by the overall politico-strategic relationship of the two countries. Beijing and Moscow maintain close consultation and cooperate on a range of international and regional issues, driven by their shared interests of countering U.S. dominance. The two countries are therefore expected to continue defense cooperation that encompasses not only military sales but also joint military exercises, high-level consultations, and other exchange programs. Within the broader contexts of growing political, strategic, and economic contacts, defense ties will retain their commercial as well as strategic salience.

Notes

1. Paul H. B. Godwin, "From Continent to Periphery: PLA Doctrine, Strategy and Capabilities towards 2000," *China Quarterly* 146 (June 1996): 464–87.

2. Harlen Jencks, "Chinese Evaluations of 'Desert Storm,'" *Journal of East Asian Affairs* 6, no. 2 (summer/fall 1992): 447–77.

3. This commentary is cited in Chen Xiaogong and Liu Xige, "Several Questions concerning China's National Defense Policy," *International Strategic Studies* (Beijing), no. 2 (1993).

4. David Shambaugh, *Modernizing China's Military: Progress, Problems, and Prospects* (Berkeley: Univ. of California Press, 2002).

5. Shirley Kan, *U.S.-China Military Contacts: Issues for Congress*, Congressional Research Service (CRS) Report for Congress, RL32496, updated 15 April 2009; Kristin Archick, Richard F. Grimmett, and Shirley Kan, *European Union's Arms Embargo on China: Implications and Options for U.S. Policy*, CRS Report for Congress, updated 26 January 2006.

6. Eric Arnett, "Military Technology: The Case of China," in *SIPRI Yearbook 1995: Armament, Disarmament and International Security* (Oxford: Oxford Univ. Press, 1995), 359–86; John Frankenstein, "The Peoples Republic of China: Arms Production, Industrial Strategy and Problems of History," in *Arms Industry Limited*, ed. Herbert Wulf, 271–319 (Oxford: Oxford Univ. Press, 1993); John Frankenstein and Bates Gill, "Current and Future Challenges Facing Chinese Defence Industries," *China Quarterly* 146 (June 1996): 394–427.

7. Bates Gill, "The Impact of Economic Reform upon Chinese Defense Production," in *Chinese Military Modernization*, ed. C. Dennison Lane, Mark Weisenbloom, and Dimon Liu, 144–67 (New York: Kegan Paul International, 1996).

8. This second aspect of the tactic may prove the more difficult to undertake. There are two related issues confronting China's defense industry. One is the ability of the industries to translate foreign weapons and technology acquisitions into a more advanced indigenous production capability. Second is how economic reforms have affected the defense industry. Defense conversion—or the rush toward commercialization and consumerism—probably has weakened the overall ability of the domestic defense industry to develop advanced weapons systems. It has been observed that the focus on civilian production to make profits may erode the industry's ability to produce and integrate foreign weapons technologies. For an excellent discussion, see

Evan S. Medeiros et al., *A New Direction for China's Defense Industry* (Santa Monica, Calif.: RAND, 2005).

9. Bill Gill and Kim Taeho, *China's Arms Acquisitions from Abroad: A Quest for Superb and Secret Weapons,* SIPRI Research Report No. 11 (Oxford: Oxford Univ. Press, 1995); Richard D. Fisher Jr., "Foreign Arms Acquisition and PLA Modernization," in *China's Military Faces the Future,* ed. James R. Lilley and David Shambaugh, 85–191 (Armonk, N.Y.: Sharpe, 1999).

10. Elizabeth Wishnick, *Mending Fences: The Evolution of Moscow's China Policy from Brezhnev to Yeltsin* (Seattle: Univ. of Washington Press, 2001); Sherman W. Garnett, ed., *Rapprochement or Rivalry? Russia-China Relations in a Changing Asia* (Washington, D.C.: Carnegie Endowment for International Peace, 2000); Jeanne L. Wilson, "Strategic Partners: Russian-Chinese Relations and the July 2001 Friendship Treaty," *Problems of Post-Communism* 49, no. 3 (May/June 2002), 3–13; Jing-dong Yuan, "Sino-Russian Confidence-Building Measures: A Preliminary Analysis," *Asian Perspective* 22, no. 1 (spring 1998): 71–108.

11. Alexander A. Sergounin and Sergey V. Subbotin, *Russian Arms Transfers to East Asia in the 1990s* (Oxford: Oxford Univ. Press, 1999), 70–92; Sergounin and Subbotin, "Sino-Russian Military-Technical Cooperation: A Russian View," in *Russia and the Arms Trade,* ed. Ian Anthony, 194–216 (SIPRI: Oxford Univ. Press, 1998); Pavel Felgengauer, "An Uneasy Partnership: Sino-Russian Defense Cooperation and Arms Sales," in *Russia in the World Arms Trade,* ed. Andrew J. Pierre and Dmitri V. Trenin, 87–103 (Washington, D.C.: Carnegie Endowment for International Peace, 1997).

12. Liu Huaqing, *The Memoir of Liu Huaqing* (Beijing: Liberation Army Publishing House [Jiefangjun chubanshe], 2004), 590–94.

13. Ibid. For an overview of Sino-Russian military cooperation, see Ming-yen Tsai, *From Adversaries to Partners? Chinese and Russian Military Cooperation after the Cold War* (Westport, Conn.: Praeger, 2003).

14. Wang Zhong, "Sino-Russian Military Security Cooperation Just Beginning to Develop, with No Sign of Letting Up," *Jiefangjun Bao,* 28 March 2006, 6; Ching-wei Lin, "China-Russia Military Cooperation: A Probe into China-Russia Joint Military Exercises" [Zhonge junshi hezuo de zhuanbian ong zhonge lianhe junyan tantao], *Zhongguo Dalu Yanjiu* 49, no. 4 (December 2006): 55; Kenneth W. Allen and Eric A. McVadon, *China's Foreign Military Relations* (Washington, D.C.: Stimson Center, October 1999), 59–63; Taeho Kim, *The Dynamics of Sino-Russian Military Relations: An Asian Perspective,* CAPS Papers, no. 6 (Taipei: Chinese Council of Advanced Policy Studies, November 1994).

15. Unless otherwise cited, information on Russian arms sales to China is drawn from the SIPRI database on arms sales; relevant chapters in the annual *SIPRI Yearbook,* various years; and the CRS Report for Congress on conventional arms transfers, various years.

16. Siemon T. Wezeman et al., "International Arms Transfers," *SIPRI Yearbook*

2007: Armaments, Disarmament and International Security (Oxford: Oxford Univ. Press for SIPRI, 2007), 393.

17. Robert Kamiol, "China Is Poised to Buy Third Batch of Su-27s," *Jane's Defence Weekly*, 24 April 1996, 10; "Made in China Deal Is Forged for Su-27s," *JDW*, 6 May 1995, 3.

18. "Military Official Says Russia Will Supply 40 Ilyushin Aircraft to China," *Novosti*, 9 August 2005.

19. Sergounin and Subbotin, "Sino-Russian Military-Technical Cooperation: A Russian View," 205, 208–9; Tsai, *From Adversaries to Partners*, 127.

20. Simon Saradzhyan, "China to Double Its Order of Russian-Made Destroyers," *Defense News*, 27 March 2000, 17.

21. See: Yu Bin, "Sino-Russian Military Relations: Implications for Asian-Pacific Security," *Asian Survey* 33, no. 3 (March 1993): 307–8; David A. Fulghum and Paul Proctor, "China Seeks to Build Mig-31," *Aviation Week and Space Technology*, 5 October 1992, 27.

22. SIPRI arms transfer database; David Boey, "China Seeks Purchase of Russian S-300Ps," *Defense News*, 18–24 April 1994, 29.

23. International Institute for Strategic Studies, *The Military Balance 1997/1998* (Oxford: Oxford Univ. Press, 1997), 170–72.

24. P. Butowski, "China Interested in Ship-Borne Su-33" [La Chine s'intéresse au Su-33 embarqué], *Air and Cosmos*, 16 September 2005, 19.

25. Starr, "China's SSK Aspirations Detailed by U.S.N. Chief," 3; Shirley A. Kan, Christopher Bolkcom, and Ronald O'Rourke, *China's Foreign Conventional Arms Acquisitions: Background and Analysis*, CRS Report for Congress, October 2000.

26. Michael J. Barron, "China's Strategic Modernization: The Russian Connection," *Parameters* 31, no. 4 (winter 2001/2002), 72–86; Vladimir Ivanov and Vladimir Shvarev, "China Needs Our Technologies. Beijing Sets Strategic Course of Acquiring Licenses and Own Production," *Nezavisimaya Gazeta* (Moscow), 17 December 2003, in FBIS-CEP20031217000164.

27. Harlan W. Jencks, "The Chinese Military-Industrial Complex and Defense Modernization," *Asian Survey* 20, no. 10 (October 1980): 966. For general surveys of China's defense industry, see David L. Shambaugh, "China's Defense Industry: Indigenous and Foreign Procurement," in *The Chinese Defense Establishment: Continuity and Change in the 1980s*, ed. Paul H. B. Godwin, 43–86 (Boulder, Colo.: Westview Press, 1983); Gill and Kim, *China's Arms Acquisitions from Abroad*, chapter 2; Ronald D. Humbe, "Science, Technology and China's Defense Industrial Base," *Jane's Intelligence Review*, January 1992, 3–11; Wendy Frieman, "China's Defense Industry," *Pacific Review* 6, no. 1 (1993): 51–62; John Frankenstein, "The People's Republic of China: Arms Production, Industrial Strategy and Problems of History," in *Arms Industry Limited*, ed. Herbert Wulf, 271–319 (Oxford: Oxford Univ. Press for SIPRI, 1993).

28. Eric Arnett, "Military Technology: The Case of China," in *SIPRI Year-*

book 1995: Armament, Disarmament and International Security (Oxford: Oxford Univ. Press, 1995), 359–86; Medeiros et al., *A New Direction for China's Defense Industry,* chapter 1.

29. Jim Mann, "Russia Boosting China's Arsenal," *Los Angeles Times* (Washington ed.), 30 November 1992, 1; Tai Ming Cheung, "China's Buying Spree," *Far Eastern Economic Review,* 8 July 1993, 24; John J. Fialka, "U.S. Fears China's Success in Skimming Cream of Weapons Experts from Russia," *Wall Street Journal,* 14 October 1993, 12; John Pomfret, "China, Russia Solidifying Military Ties," *Washington Post,* 10 February 2000, 17; Tsai, *From Adversaries to Partners?*

30. Siemon T. Wezeman and Mark Bromley, "International Arms Transfer," *SIPRI Yearbook 2005: Armament, Disarmament and International Security* (Oxford: Oxford Univ. Press for SIPRI, 2005), 424.

31. Brian Harvey, *China's Space Program: From Conception to Manned Spaceflight* (Chichester: Springer, 2004), 248–89; International Institute for Strategic Studies, "China's Space Ambitions: Pride and Practicalities," *Strategic Comments* 8, no. 6 (August 2002).

32. James Oberg, "Great Leap Upward," *Scientific American* 289, no. 4 (October 2003): 81.

33. Li Ku-cheng, "The Militarization of Space Technology and the Transformation of Missile Technology," *Kai Fang,* no. 162 (June 2000): 17–18, in FBIS-CPP20000613000037.

34. Craig Covault, "The Historic Chinese Shenzhou Manned Flight also Has Military Objectives," *Aviation Week and Space Technology,* 19 October 2003.

35. Office of the Secretary of Defense, *Annual Report to Congress: The Military Power of the People's Republic of China 2005,* 19 July 2005, http://www.dod.mil/news/Jul2005/d20050719china.pdf. See also: Arun Sahgal, "China in Space: Military Implications," *Asia Times,* 5 November 2005.

36. "China's Space Ambitions Potential Threat to U.S.: Analysts," Agence France Presse, 12 October 2005.

37. Author's private correspondence with former Soviet/Russian officials.

38. COSTIND, *China Today: Defense Science and Technology* (Beijing: National Defense Industry Press, 1993), 890, 892, cited in Arnett, "Military Technology," 361.

39. Liu Huaqing, "Unswervingly Advance along the Road of Building a Modern Army with Chinese Characteristics," *Qiushi,* no. 15 (1993), in FBIS-CHI, 18 August 1993.

40. David Shambaugh, "The Insecurity of Security: The PLA's Evolving Doctrine and Threat Perceptions towards 2000," *Journal of Northeast Asian Studies* 13, no. 1 (spring 1994): 3–25.

41. John Pomfret, "Russians Help China Modernize Its Arsenal; New Military Ties Raise U.S. Concerns," *Washington Post,* 10 February 2000, A17.

42. Richard Fisher Jr., "People's Liberation Army Leverage of Foreign Military Technology," International Assessment and Strategy Center, 22 March 2006, http://www.strategycenter.net/research/pubID.97/pub_detail.asp.

43. Cited from *Dongfang Junshi,* 13 February 2008, http://mil.eastday.com/m/20080213/ula3400773.html?index=1.

44. Robert H. Donaldson and John A. Donaldson, "The Arms Trade in Russian-Chinese Relations: Identity, Domestic Politics, and Geopolitical Positioning," *International Studies Quarterly* 47, no. 4 (December 2003): 709–32; Jeanne L. Wilson, *Strategic Partners: Russian-Chinese Relations in the Post-Soviet Era* (Armonk, N.Y.: Sharpe, 2004), 93–113.

45. Paradorn Rangsimaporn, "Russia's Debate on Military-Technological Cooperation with China: From Yeltsin to Putin," *Asian Survey* 46, no. 3 (May/June 2006): 477–95; Joseph Y. S. Cheng, "Challenges to China's Russia Policy in Early 21st Century," *Journal of Contemporary Asia* 34, no. 4 (2004): 493–94; Tsai, *From Adversaries to Partners?* 123–26.

46. Vladimir Shlapentokh, "China in the Russian Mind Today: Ambivalence and Defeatism," *Europe-Asia Studies* 59, no. 1 (January 2007): 1–21; Qian Chengcan, "Russia's Global Arms Sales Break the $6 Billion Mark; Numerous Restrictions on China" [Equanqiu junshou tupo 60 yimeiyuan, duizhongguo xianzhi poduo], mil.eastday.com, 19 December 2006; Wu Dahui, "Cooperation amidst Precaution—The Psychology of Russia's View of China's Peaceful Rise" [Fangfan zhongde hezuo—eluosi guanyu zhongguo heping jueqi de xinli tujie], *Eluosi Zhongya Dong'ou Yanjiu,* no. 5 (2005): 52–60.

47. See: Jyotsna Bakshi, "Russia-China Military-Technical Cooperation: Implications for India," *Strategic Analysis* 24, no. 4 (July 2000): 633–67.

48. Nayan Chanda, "Too Close for Comfort," *Far Eastern Economic Review,* 5 October 1995, 16.

49. Tyler Marshall, "Chinese Raise the Arms Stakes with $500-Million Destroyer," *Los Angeles Times,* 12 February 2000; Liz Sly, "China's New Warship Makes Waves off Taiwan," *Chicago Tribune,* 12 February 2000.

50. "Alleged ICBM Transfer from Russia to China," *Disarmament Diplomacy,* no. 6 (June 1996): 45.

51. Office of the Secretary of Defense, *Annual Report to Congress: Military Power of the People's Republic of China 2006,* June 2006, 21–22.

52. Jason Glashow, "U.S. Says Chinese Naval Threat Is Years Away," *Defense News,* 23–29 October 1995, 12.

53. Nikolai Novichkov, "Tor-M1s Help Pay Debt to Beijing," *JDW,* 15 March 2000, 13; "Military Trade: Prospect of Russia-China Military Cooperation in 2007," *Kanwa Defense Review* (Toronto), 1 January 2007, in CPP20070129715035, accessed on 30 January 2007, through Open Source Center; see also, Tsai, *From Adversaries to Partners?*

54. Stephen Fidler, "Russian Weapons Sales to China Fall," *Financial Times,* 31 March 2008, http://us.ft.com/ftgateway/superpage.ft?news_id=fto033020081712146238, accessed on 30 May 2008.

55. Yu Ping, "Sino-Russian Military Cooperation Replaces Weapons Sales with Technology Cooperation" [Zhonge junshi hezuo you jishu hezuo qudai wuqi

maimai], *Junshi Wenzhai*, 6 November 2007, http://mil.eastday.com/m/20071106/ula3210238.html, accessed on 13 February 2008; David Lague, "Russia and China Rethink Arms Deals," *New York Times*, 2 March 2008, http://www.nytimes.com/2008/03/02/world/asia/02iht-arms.1.10614237.html.

56. Richard Weitz, "The Sino-Russian Arms Dilemma," *China Brief* 6, no. 22 (8 November 2006): 9–12; Nabi Abdullaev, "China No Longer Reliant on Russia for Weapons," DefenseNews.com, 23 October 2006; "Chinese Purchases of Russian Weapons at Saturation Point: Report," Agence France-Presse, DefenseNews.com, 13 October 2006.

57. Wu Dahui, "EU's Lifting of Arms Ban on China and Sino-Russian Cooperation on Military Technology" [Oumeng jiechu duihua wuqi jinyun yu zhonge junji hezuo], *Russian, Central Asian and East European Studies*, no. 1 (2005): 33–38.

58. "Sino-Russian Military Exercises Said Commercial Opportunity for Moscow," Agence France-Presse, 24 August 2005, FBIS-CPP20050824000027; "Sino-Russian Joint Military Exercises Aim at Taiwan Independence," *Yazhou Zhoukan*, 27 October 2005.

59. Bai Hua, "Sino-Russian Arms Deals and Other Military Exchanges" [Zhonge junhuo hetong he qita junshi jiaoliu], *Voice of America* (Chinese Online), 8 September 2005, http://www.voanews.com/chinese/archive/2005-09/w2005-09-08-voa47.cfm.

60. "Russian Commentator Says PRC Negotiating for Tu-22M Bomber Licensed Production," *Tokyo Sankei Shimbun*, 26 August 2005, in FBIS-JPP20050826000026.

61. Siemon T. Wezeman and Mark Bromley, "International Arms Transfer," *SIPRI Yearbook 2005: Armament, Disarmament and International Security* (Oxford: Oxford Univ. Press for SIPRI, 2005), 422–25; Alexander Shlyndov, "Military and Technical Collaboration between Russia and China: Its Current Status, Problems, and Outlook," *Far Eastern Affairs* 33, no. 1 (January–March 2005): 1–20; Alexei Nikolsky, "The Last Billion from China: Russia Will Now Be Compelled to Share New Technologies," *Defense and Security* (Russia), 16 October 2006.

62. Roger N. McDermott, *The Rising Dragon: SCO Peace Mission 2007*, Occasional Paper (Washington, D.C.: Jamestown Foundation, October 2007); M. K. Bhadrakumar, "SCO Is Primed and Ready to Fire," *Asia Times Online*, 4 August 2007, http://www.atimes.com/atimes/Central_Asia/IH04Ag01.html, accessed on 6 August 2007.

63. Li Xuanliang and Shan Zhixu, "Chinese Expert: Peace Mission 2007 Enhances Four Capabilities of the SCO" [Zhongguo zhuanjia: 'heping shiming-2007' tisheng shanghe zuzhi sizhong nengli], Xinhua, 7 August 2008, http://mil.eastday.com/m/20070807/ula3024608.html, accessed on 13 August 2007; Cao Zhi and Li Xuanliang, "Military Exercises Enhance the Chinese Military's Capacities to Fulfill Its Historical Mission" [Junyan tisheng zhongguo jundui lvxing lishi shiming nengli], *Jiefangjun Bao*, 17 August 2007, http://www.chinamil.com.cn/site1/xwpdxw/2007-08/17/content_922938.htm, accessed on 3 June 2008.

64. Jing-dong Yuan, "Chinese Responses to U.S. Missile Defenses: Implications for Arms Control and Regional Security," *Nonproliferation Review* 10, no. 1 (spring 2003): 75–96.

65. Edward Wong and Alan Cowell, "Russia and China Attack U.S. Missile Shield Plan," *New York Times*, 24 May 2008, http://www.nytimes.com/2008/05/24/world/24china.html?partner=rssnyt&emc=rss.

66. "Russia, China Challenge U.S. with Proposal to Ban Space Weapons at Disarmament Conference," *International Herald Tribune*, 12 February 2008, available at http://www.highbeam.com/doc/1A1-D8UOVRJG1.html.

67. Richard Weitz, "China and Russia Hand in Hand," *Global Asia* 2, no. 3 (winter 2007): 52–63; Andrew Kuchins, "Russia and China: The Ambivalent Embrace," *Current History* 106, no. 702 (October 2007): 321–27; Peter Ferdinand, "Sunset, Sunrise: China and Russia Construct a New Relationship," *International Affairs* 83, no. 5 (September 2007): 841–67.

Part Four

★

China, Russia, and Regional Issues

Central Asia, Japan, and the Two Koreas

Map 8.1. Central Asia.

8

Russia and China in Central Asia

Charles E. Ziegler

Conceptualizing Russian and Chinese relations with Central Asia is a difficult task. The leaderships of these two major powers approach foreign policy in largely realist terms, seeking to maximize their power, jealously guarding their national sovereignty, and engaging in balancing against a superior adversary. Yet neither country fully fits the standard realist model in its foreign policy behavior. Russia had been a power in decline, until Vladimir Putin and other Russian officials found that energy resources gave their country far more leverage in world politics than military power, the old Soviet staple. China is a rising power, but its foreign policy has been oriented toward preserving the status quo, fostering the conditions for strong economic growth and social stability domestically. Both Russia and China have become strong advocates of multilateral organizations, from regional groupings like the Shanghai Cooperation Organization and Collective Security Treaty Organization to the United Nations on a global scale.

Surprisingly, these two powers have found their interests coincide remarkably well in Central Asia, at least in the short term. Russia and China are now aligned together against a hegemonic United States that seeks both to preserve stability and to transform the political landscape of Central Asia. Moscow and Beijing perceive these two goals as contradictory, and have opted to support repressive Central Asian regimes as the best hedge against the new security threats of terrorism and extremism.

This chapter will explicate Chinese and Russian interests in and policy toward Central Asia. I address the various elements in Russian and Chinese relations with the countries of post-Soviet Central Asia (Kazakhstan, Uzbekistan, Kyrgyzstan, Tajikistan, and Turkmenistan), examine the roles of China and Russia in the Shanghai Cooperation Organization and other regional groupings, and assess the implications of Chinese and Russian policies and activities in Central Asia for U.S. national interests. The chapter first considers political and security issues, then turns to the various forms of economic cooperation and rivalry in the region, particularly in energy. Finally, I assess the important role of diaspora politics and population issues for Russia, China, and Central Asia.

Political and Security Issues

Relations with Central Asia in the 1990s were not central to Russian foreign policy. The reformers affiliated with Boris Yeltsin who dominated politics regarded the former republics as an unnecessary burden on Russia, politically and economically. Central Asian elites tended to mirror this perspective.[1] Integration through the Commonwealth of Independent States and its affiliated organizations stalled early on. Moscow frequently adopted a neo-imperial posture toward its former republics, but the state clearly lacked the military or economic capability to implement policies abroad, as the first Chechen venture (1994–1995) demonstrated. Russia's influence reached a new low in 1998–1999 with the collapse of the ruble and Moscow's inability to counter NATO's campaign against the Serbs.

Vladimir Putin was clearly a stronger leader than Boris Yeltsin, but his "restoration" of Russian power was aided by developments largely beyond the new president's control. Oil prices surged from a low of about $12 per barrel in 1998 to over $140 per barrel in 2008, resulting in a windfall for the Russian treasury. Russia's economy posted record growth rates, even if the growth was somewhat uneven. Russian nationalism and confidence grew as the United States became bogged down in Iraq, without first stabilizing Afghanistan. Putin enhanced Russia's position by effectively wielding the energy and infrastructure levers to enhance Russian influence in Central Asia (and in the western and Caucasian republics), while strengthening the "power vertical" and concentrating authority in the hands of the executive. Since Putin's successor, Dmitry Medvedev, served as chairman of the board of Gazprom, Russia's largest energy company, he too is likely to appreciate the critical role of energy in ties with Central Asia, and in Russian foreign policy more broadly.

China's regional policy toward Central Asia, and indeed its foreign policy more broadly, experienced a transformation nearly as sweeping. In the early 1990s Beijing's focus was largely regional, with most of its attention devoted to Taiwan and the western Pacific. China was only beginning to appreciate the implications of globalization and its growing role in the world's economy. Deng Xiaoping had rejected Mao Zedong's revolutionary activism, and instead crafted a pragmatic policy of concentrating on internal development while maintaining a low profile internationally. Deng advised the Chinese to conceal their capabilities, guard their weaknesses, and never claim leadership, all the while waiting patiently for the opportune moment to make a comeback.[2]

Jiang Zemin and Hu Jintao, Deng's successors, have undertaken a more active, confident foreign policy to enhance China's influence regionally. China's rapidly growing economy and its extensive trade relations throughout the world ($2.17 trillion in 2007) have encouraged Beijing's leaders to develop a global perspective on foreign affairs. China's rapidly growing energy dependence has also made its foreign policy more globally oriented. A sustained military modernization program has improved the PLA's capabilities, which, while far from global, have at least become significant along China's entire periphery. Finally, American assertiveness and the global war on terror have combined to heighten Chinese concern with regional developments, such as those in Central Asia, which would not have commanded Beijing's attention a decade earlier.

Russia and China find that their interests overlap on many security issues in the Central Asian region, as they do in global politics. As autocratic powers experiencing dynamic economic growth, Moscow and Beijing are frequently aligned together in opposition to democratic influences from the United States and Europe.[3] Authoritarian rulers in the five Central Asian states share their larger neighbors' antipathy toward democracy, while seeking to play Russia and China off against the United States. One shared concern is stability. Beijing constantly reiterates its opposition to the three forces (often called the "three evils") of terrorism, separatism, and extremism. Although China is developing more global interests, regional concerns still take precedence. China seeks stability along its periphery to maximize conditions for internal economic growth.

China's regional foreign policy is strongly conditioned by domestic factors—namely, the possibility of border territories (Taiwan, Xinjiang, and Tibet) agitating for separation. Chinese leaders are determined not to repeat the Soviet experience, where ethno-nationalist territories were hived off from the Russian core. Another fear is the "extremism" of national or religious groups, such as Muslims, Buddhists, Falun Gong, or Uyghurs, who advance demands inconsistent with state priorities, or who have demonstrated a capability to organize and resist state control. It bears emphasizing that China's terrorism threat is not the diffuse, global threat faced by the United States and Europe, but rather is domestic, centered on violent Uyghur opposition to Han domination of Xinjiang, a cause supported in the past by some Central Asian elements and by the Taliban.

For Beijing, instability in Central Asia is dangerous primarily because of the potential impact on the Muslim Uyghur population in the Xinjiang Uyghur Autonomous Region of western China. Uyghur ethnic identity, which came under extreme duress during the Cultural Revolution, experienced resurgence in the more relaxed reform era under Deng Xiaoping. Economic development brought a large influx of Han Chinese, who threatened Uyghur identity, while the disintegration of the Soviet state facilitated links with coethnics in Central Asia.[4] During the 1990s trade between the newly independent states of Central Asia and Xinjiang expanded significantly. This brought the restive Uyghurs into contact with the large Uyghur diaspora in Central Asia.[5] Renewed contacts raised expectations among China's Uyghurs and contributed to growing demands for autonomy or even independence. In the early to mid-1990s Uyghur resistance leaders found sanctuary among their Muslim compatriots in Central Asia.[6]

Beijing rejects all forms of separatism, whether in Taiwan, Tibet, or Xinjiang, and has dealt harshly with Uyghur separatists. After the 11 September attacks the Chinese government was quick to portray Uyghur activists as terrorists, lumping together Muslim fundamentalism, extremism, and separatism as the three major threats to stability. In summer 2002, Washington and the United Nations backed China's claim that the Xinjiang-based separatist East Turkestan Islamic Movement (ETIM) was a terrorist organization, and the U.S. State Department added the ETIM to its list of terrorist organizations, claiming it had a close financial relationship with al-Qaeda. But China's leaders share an expansive definition of terrorism. Kyrgyzstan's Tulip Revolution (March 2005) and the Andijan uprising in Uzbekistan (May 2005) were viewed with sympathy in the West as popular reactions to corrupt and repressive regimes. From Beijing's perspective, these movements were inspired by terrorist and criminal elements, and were indicators of the potential for instability, which could spill over into China.[7] Consistent with its domestic policies, China unreservedly supports the use of repressive measures to maintain order.

Russia's perspective is similar to China's, deriving from its experience in Chechnya. Putin sought to link the Chechen conflict to the international terrorist movement. The Chechens have received support from Middle Eastern extremists, but Chechen terrorism, like that in Xinjiang, has not spread beyond Russian borders. Muslim extremism in Central Asia has to date been relatively weak, with the notable exception of Uzbekistan, where Hizb-ut-Tahrir and the Islamic Movement of Uzbekistan (IMU) have been active. The U.S. campaign in Afghanistan disrupted the Taliban's support for the IMU, and repressive measures throughout Central Asia have largely contained the threat of political Islam.[8] Nonetheless, Russian concern with Chechen terrorism has been generalized into a broader resentment of Caucasians and Central Asians, as reflected in public statements about immigrants and racist attacks on peoples of the south in Russian cities.

The real sources of instability in Central Asia relate more to poor governance, corruption, and dismal economic performance than to terrorism. All the Central Asian states, with the possible exception of Kazakhstan, have serious political, social, and economic problems. In 2003, nearly half the population of Turkmenistan and Uzbekistan lived below the poverty line; the figures for Kyrgyzstan and Tajikistan were 70 percent and 74 percent, respectively.[9] Per capita incomes have risen across Central Asia since 1998, but the global financial crisis of 2008 and 2009 inflated prices for food and energy, and tighter credit slowed growth. The poorest Central Asian states also have weak, ineffective governments. In 2008 Uzbekistan ranked twenty-sixth on the Fund for Peace's Failed States Index (in the "alert" category), while Tajikistan, Kyrgyzstan, and Turkmenistan were slightly better, with scores in the "warning" category. Only Kyrgyzstan received a Freedom House rating of "partly free" in 2008; the other four Central Asian states were judged to be "not free." While Central Asia's pattern of corrupt, authoritarian government has complicated relations with the democratic West, other factors have conditioned ties with Russia and China.

Uzbekistan

Uzbekistan's authoritarian government would seem to position it closely with the alliance of autocracies, but in practice its relationships with the great powers have fluctuated over the years since independence. In the 1990s, President Islam Karimov distanced his country from Russia in an attempt to preserve Uzbek independence and strengthen his pretensions to a position of leadership in Central Asia. During that time, Uzbekistan developed cordial, albeit quiet, military ties with the United States and NATO. As the IMU threat increased late in the decade, Karimov broadened his search for allies against the Muslim extremists, all the while jealously guarding Uzbekistan's sovereignty. In 1999 and early 2000, Putin visited Tashkent twice and signed a pact on deepening military cooperation, but Uzbekistan remained wary of Moscow's intentions. Uzbekistan joined the anti-CIS GUAM (Georgia, Ukraine, Armenia, Moldova) pact, thus creating GUUAM in 1999, and welcomed military cooperation with the United States, China, and Turkey, Russia's competitors in Central Asia. Uzbek-Russian ties remained anemic until spring 2004; U.S.-Uzbek collaboration against the Taliban in Afghanistan was deemed more important for the country's foreign policy.[10]

Yet security cooperation with the United States was complicated by inconsistent tendencies in Washington's Central Asia policy. The State Department's annual reports on human rights were highly critical of Uzbekistan's record, while the Defense Department under Donald Rumsfeld praised Tashkent's cooperation in the war on terror. The bloody repression of the 2005 uprising in Andijan (an uprising that Tashkent blamed on CIA interference) led to a sharp downturn in U.S.-Uzbek relations. When the heads of the Shanghai Cooperation Organization declared at their June 2005 meeting that temporary coalition forces stationed in Central Asia should set a timeline for withdrawal, Karimov used the opportunity to request that American forces leave the Kharshi-Khanabad base by the end of the year.[11]

Russia's relations with Uzbekistan improved dramatically as Tashkent's ties with the United States were deteriorating. In June 2004, Russia and Uzbekistan signed a treaty on developing a strategic partnership. Tashkent announced its decision to withdraw from GUUAM in May 2005, and in 2006 Uzbekistan concluded a treaty of alliance relations with Russia. Military interoperability was part of this agreement, as was the struggle against terrorism and narcotics smuggling. In June 2006, Uzbekistan rejoined the Collective Security Treaty Organization, Russia's proclaimed counterpart to NATO, and in December of the same year Uzbekistan agreed to allow the Russian Air Force use of its new airfield near Navoi to set up an air defense system, for CIS operations.[12] Public declarations of friendship continued under President Medvedev, who described Uzbekistan as a key strategic partner in Central Asia. Karimov, in St. Petersburg for a meeting with the new president, voiced his enthusiastic support for Russia's foreign policy, asserting that the two nations had similar positions on all major issues.[13] At the same time, Uzbekistan and the West were moving to rebuild ties that had frayed in the aftermath of Andijan.

Moscow and Tashkent agree on the importance of strengthening the state to ensure stability, and the Putin administration manifested scant concern for human rights abuses in Uzbekistan, so their political positions are more closely aligned than those of Tashkent and Washington. However, Karimov, like his fellow autocrats in Central Asia, has been careful not to sever the links to Western democratic states, resisting complete bandwagoning in favor of balancing.[14] As a weak and vulnerable state, Uzbekistan takes advantage of the competition among its larger, more powerful partners. Although Karimov expelled U.S. forces at Karshi-Khanabad, he allowed the Germans to maintain a refueling station at Termez in exchange for development aid worth millions of euros. By early 2008, Admiral William Fallon, head of U.S. Central Command, had visited Tashkent, and American military personnel were quietly returning to Uzbekistan, sharing the Termez base with their German counterparts.[15] The Western democracies were rethinking sanctions, based on modest improvements in Tashkent's human rights practices. Memories of Andijan were fading, and Washington realized cooperating with Tashkent would strengthen its hand in the competition for control over Central Asia's energy resources.[16]

Relations between China and Uzbekistan are uncomplicated by political issues. Chinese and Uzbek leaders agree on the need to exercise strict control over domestic extremists. The coincidence of Chinese and Uzbek interests was apparent when Beijing welcomed President Islam Karimov for a state visit just two weeks after the Uzbek government brutally repressed the Andijan uprising. Chinese president Hu Jintao signed a treaty of friendship and cooperation with his Uzbek counterpart, and told Karimov that China "honored" Uzbekistan's efforts to preserve its independence, sovereignty, and territorial integrity. At the Shanghai Cooperation Organization meeting in June 2005, Foreign Minister Li Zhaoxing expressed "delight" that the situation in Andijan had returned to normal.[17] During Prime Minister Wen Jiabao's November 2007 visit (which also included stops in Turkmenistan, Belarus, and Russia), he reiterated China's opposition to human rights pressures as interference in Central Asian internal affairs. Uzbek and Turkmen officials pledged to support Beijing on Tibet and Taiwan, and firmly rejected the cause of East Turkestan (i.e., Uyghur) separatism.[18]

Turkmenistan

As a small, isolated country, Turkmenistan has a weak position in the Central Asian region. Turkmenistan had been stable and neutral under the totalitarian control of Saparmurat Niyazov (the "great Turkmenbashi"), but following his death in December 2006 his successor, Gurbanguly Berdymukhammedov, eased controls over the population, allowing greater access to the Internet, restoring the normal school year, and releasing political prisoners. However, there has been virtually no movement toward political liberalization under Berdymukhammedov. All opposition parties are outlawed, NGOs are severely restricted, and the president dominates the courts and legislature.[19]

In foreign affairs, Turkmenistan had maintained a state of permanent neutrality, recognized by the United Nations in 1995. From the start of independence in 1991 Niyazov rejected ideas of Islamism and Panturkism, creating his own unique ideology of a paternalistic state led by an infallible figure (Niyazov himself), legitimized through his spiritual guidebook, the Rukhnama. Ideology under Niyazov was nationalistic and anti-Russian, blaming Turkmenistan's weakened position on repressive Russian and Soviet colonial history.[20] With Niyazov's death, Berdymukhammedov has followed his own "multi-vectored" policy of opening the country to foreign investment in natural gas. Turkmenistan needs foreign investment and technology to develop its huge gas reserves, and the government has signaled its willingness to do business with companies and states around the globe. Berdymukhammedov has frustrated Moscow's efforts to monopolize natural gas exports by alternately agreeing to and then backing off from Russian plans such as the South Stream pipeline. In a clear rebuff to Moscow's Central Asia policy, the new Turkmen president attended NATO's Bucharest summit in May 2008, raising the possibility that Turkmen facilities might be used for the Afghanistan campaign.[21]

Tajikistan

Tajikistan settled into a corrupt and moderately repressive pattern following its five-year civil war, but political and ethnic divisions continue to threaten stability. Although the country has posted impressive growth rates in recent years, about two-thirds of the population lives in poverty, and the country remains the poorest of the former Soviet republics. Tajiks were disturbed by the prospect of spillover from the events in Kyrgyzstan and Uzbekistan, and few complaints, either domestic or international, were voiced over the stage-managed reelection of Emomalii Rahmon as president in November 2006.[22]

Tajikistan is most closely allied with Russia, which has kept the 201st Motorized Rifle Division in the country since independence and has provided additional peacekeeping and border security forces, for a total of about twenty thousand troops. However, Tajikistan's relations with Russia cooled after Dushanbe cancelled a $2 billion deal with RusAl to finish construction of the Rogun Dam.[23] China is making inroads and its investments are more than twice those of Russia's. Tajikistan's key location next to Afghanistan makes it vitally important as a buffer against Islamic radicalism in Central Asia. Russia, China, and the United States are all interested in preserving stability in this war-torn country. Even India is establishing a modest military presence in Tajikistan.[24] The United States plans to tie Tajikistan into Greater Central Asia (Central Asia, Afghanistan, Pakistan, and India) through economic, security, and energy and transportation networks, with the ultimate goal of strengthening Afghanistan's prospects for building a stable democracy.[25]

Kyrgyzstan

Kyrgyzstan remains fragile. The country is far smaller than Uzbekistan or Kazakhstan, and its formerly nomadic peoples do not have the strong religious traditions that might translate into radicalism. Kyrgyzstan started its

Table 8.1. Proportion of Central Asian States' Trade with the Russian Federation and the People's Republic of China, 2004, by Exports and Imports (% of total trade)

	Imports from Russia	Exports to Russia	Imports from China	Exports to China
Kazakhstan	37.7	14.1	5.9	9.8
Kyrgyzstan	31.2	19.2	8.5	5.5
Tajikistan	24.2	6.6	4.1	0.7
Uzbekistan	25.4	12.6	7.4	2.1

Source: *Central Asia: Increasing Gains from Trade through Regional Cooperation in Trade Policy, Transport, and Customs Transit,* Asian Development Bank, 2006, Appendix 1, http://www.adb.org /Documents/Reports/CA-Trade-Policy/ca-trade-policy.pdf. Data for Turkmenistan was not available.

era of independence with great promise, and the West enthusiastically supported President Askar Akaev's efforts to transform his country into "the Switzerland of Central Asia." By the late 1990s, however, this poor nation of 5 million had become increasingly corrupt and authoritarian. The popular uprising in March 2005 known as the Tulip Revolution that toppled the Akayev government ushered in a period of chaos and uncertainty. A number of political and cultural figures were assassinated, criminal and drug-related groups engaged in violence, and the new president, Kurmanbek Bakiyev, engaged in a prolonged struggle with opposition forces in parliament.[26] Kyrgyzstan's Central Asian neighbors viewed these events with apprehension, as did Russia and China.

Although Russia and China criticized the protests and supported Akayev, the new government under Kurmanbek Bakiyev moved quickly to strengthen relations with Moscow. President Bakiyev made his first official state visit to Russia, meeting with then-President Putin, Prime Minister Mikhail Fradkov, and Duma Speaker Boris Gryzlov. While this 2006 visit was meant to strengthen relations with Moscow at a critical political juncture, the new Kyrgyz leader also used the opportunity to put some pressure on Washington by calling for a massive increase in rent for the Manas airbase, used by U.S. and NATO military forces for the Afghanistan campaign. After some bargaining, Washington eventually agreed to raise the amount of U.S. aid to Kyrgyzstan. In February 2009, the Kyrgyz government again announced plans to shut Manas but changed its mind after Washington agreed to triple annual rent payments for the facility to $60 million.[27]

Kyrgyzstan is also host to the first Russian military base established in the post-Soviet period, at Kant, just thirty-five kilometers from the U.S. base at Manas, and only three hundred kilometers from the Chinese border. The ostensible purpose of the base was to provide logistical support for a rapid reaction force operating under the Collective Security Treaty, but Russia's interest in renovating the base was clearly a reaction to the American presence in Kyrgyzstan. Russia upgraded the base in 2006, adding a ground force element to the air forces. Moscow pays $4.5 million annually for Kant, and in early 2009 promised Bishkek an aid package worth over $2 billion, an offer that may have been linked to closing Manas. Russia plans to continue to improve the facilities at Kant, and the two countries have conducted joint antiterrorism exercises.[28]

Beyond the military link, Russian-Kyrgyz relations revolve around the energy-economic relationship, and the situation of an estimated 650,000 Russian ethnics living in Kyrgyzstan. During his 2006 meeting with Bakiyev, then-president Putin raised the question of the status of Russian language in Kyrgyzstan.[29] Laws mandating the use of Kyrgyz in government positions, widespread emigration of ethnic Russians, and poor funding for Russian language instruction have led to Kyrgyz and Uzbek supplanting Russian as the primary languages, with the exception of in higher education.[30] On the energy front, Russian companies receive preferential treatment; in exchange, Moscow provides financial and humanitarian assistance. But as in Tajikistan, China is fast making inroads. Trade between Kyrgyzstan and the PRC is increasing rapidly—in 2006 it was nearly three times the volume of trade with Russia. China's President Hu Jintao made his first official state visit to Bishkek in July 2007, in connection with the Shanghai Cooperation Organization summit, and was warmly received.[31]

Kazakhstan

Kazakhstan is the bright spot in Central Asia, with its prosperous economy and stable society, mildly authoritarian regime, and people who are tolerant of ethnic and religious diversity. Kazakhstan's President Nursultan Nazarbayev has followed a careful policy of balancing among the great powers that are so keenly interested in his country's vast energy wealth. Oil and gas give Kazakhstan a great deal of international leverage. Kazakhstan cooperates with Russia, China, and the United States on security issues, and engages each economically. The United States is the largest investor in the oil and gas sector (about $15 billion as of the end of 2006), the two countries have worked closely together on nuclear nonproliferation, and Astana has been responsive, at least rhetorically, to Washington's position on democracy and human rights. In 2003 the United States and Kazakhstan signed a five-year program to provide military equipment and assistance to modernize Kazakhstan's forces. In return, the Kazakh government deployed a small contingent of troops supporting the U.S. effort in Iraq. Kazakhstan also cooperates on security matters with Russia and China through the SCO, and has conducted separate anti-terrorism exercises with China.

Kazakhs retain strong cultural and linguistic ties to Russia, even though Kazakhstan arguably suffered more during the Soviet era than any other former republic—some 40 percent of the population perished during the 1932–1933 famine, Kazakh culture and language were suppressed, and severe ecological damage (Semipalatinsk, Baikonur, and the Aral Sea) resulted from Soviet central planning. Yet educated Kazakhs speak Russian rather than Kazakh, and 30 percent of the population is ethnic Russian. Russia is Kazakhstan's largest trade partner—about one-quarter of Kazakhstan's total trade turnover is with Russia—and in the Putin era the two countries pursued a wide range of cooperative ventures, in uranium production, ship building, and energy. Nazarbayev has described the Kazakh-Russian relationship as advancing to a new level of strategic partnership under Vladimir Putin.[32] Official Astana was delighted that Dmitry Medvedev chose Kazakhstan for his first (admittedly brief) foreign visit after becoming president. From Astana Medvedev went directly to China.

However, Nazarbayev does not clearly favor Russia over the United States, China, or Kazakhstan's Central Asian partners.[33] Kazakhstan was the first Central Asian nation to sign an Individual Partnership Action Plan with NATO, for example, and the country's foreign policy is frequently described by officials as "multi-vectored," having good ties with all nations. Kazakhstan has cooperated closely with the International Security in Afghanistan Forces (ISAF) operation, allowing coalition forces to transit its territory. During Nazarbayev's visit to NATO headquarters in December 2006 he met with Secretary-General Jaap de Hoop Scheffer and pledged Kazakhstan's support in the war on terror. Finally, Kazakhstan's determination to play an international role beyond its size is reflected in the country's successful campaign to chair the Organization for Security and Cooperation in Europe in 2010. In August 2008 the Kazakh government announced a "Road to Europe" plan linked to the OECD chairmanship.[34] This move may also have been part of Astana's balancing strategy in the wake of the Russia-Georgia conflict.

Kazakhstan's continuing support for the U.S. and NATO campaign in Afghanistan, and its deployment of a small contingent of troops to Iraq, contrasts with Moscow's retrenchment. Russia initially supported the American-led invasion of Afghanistan to topple the Taliban, including the deployment of limited troop contingents in Central Asia. Putin reportedly did not oppose the establishment of U.S. bases in Uzbekistan and Kyrgyzstan, although elements in the military and some Russian nationalists voiced concerns. Since the war in Iraq, however, Russian opposition to American presence in the region has grown. Putin has consistently criticized American involvement in Iraq. During his speech to the Munich security conference in February 2007 the Russian president condemned the United States for "overstepping its national borders in every way" and pursuing a unipolar model of world politics.[35] Putin also asserted that the Bush administration was concocting a Russia threat in order to secure funding for military operations in Afghanistan and Iraq, and to justify installing a missile defense system in Eastern Europe.[36]

The Shanghai Cooperation Organization

As president, Medvedev has promised to follow Putin's foreign policy line, assigning priority to strengthening ties with the CIS countries.[37] Russia's neo-imperial foreign policy is competitive in nature, designed to achieve hegemony in the CIS countries, to constrain American and NATO presence and influence, while (at least in the short term) partnering with China. Given the constraints on its military capabilities, Moscow has developed an appreciation for the utility of multilateral organizations that preserve a place for Russia in Central Asia, and constrain U.S. actions in the region. The main security organizations relevant to Central Asia are the Shanghai Cooperation Organization (comprised of Russia, China, Kazakhstan, Uzbekistan, Kyrgyzstan, and Tajikistan) and the Collective Security Treaty Organization (Russia, Kazakhstan, Uzbekistan, Kyrgyzstan, Tajikistan, Armenia, and Belarus).

The Shanghai Cooperation Organization has quickly evolved into the most prominent multilateral organization in Central Asia. Originating in 1996 talks to resolve border disputes between the Central Asian states and China, the SCO formalized operations in 2001, with the accession of Uzbekistan to membership. The SCO now deals with a full range of issues, including politics, economics, transportation, education, culture, and environmental protection. Security concerns are addressed in the SCO's two permanent structures, the Regional Anti-Terrorist Structure (RATS), headquartered in Tashkent, and the Secretariat, headquartered in Beijing. In August 2007 the SCO held large-scale military exercises in Russia's Ural Mountains, with some 6,500 Chinese troops participating.

Both Russia and China see their regional interests threatened by NATO expansion eastward. The more conservative forces in Russia's military, and many moderates, are disturbed by NATO's addition of new members in Eastern Europe and the former Soviet Union, and by its stated interest in Central Asia. While Moscow perceives NATO actions as limiting Russia's

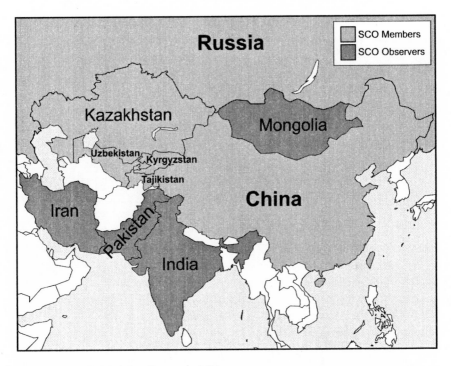

Map 8.2. SCO Member States and Observers.

options in the west and south, Beijing perceives U.S. and NATO involvement in Central Asia and in Afghanistan as part of an encirclement plan, when combined with the strong U.S.-Japan alliance in the east. For China the SCO is a means of securing and stabilizing the periphery, while providing a counterbalance to U.S., NATO, and Japanese power.[38] Russia and China also fear that American and European support for "color revolutions" such as those in Ukraine, Georgia, and Kyrgyzstan will destabilize Central Asia and weaken their influence in the region. SCO documents stress the principles of sovereignty and noninterference in domestic affairs, effectively denying the legitimacy of criticism over human rights abuses and external democracy-building efforts in member nations.

The possibility that the SCO might limit U.S. options in Central Asia only became apparent to the U.S. government after 2005; prior to that the organization had received minimal attention in Washington. The Bush administration was mildly supportive of SCO efforts to combat extremism and terrorism in Central Asia, but for the most part had adopted a wait and see approach.[39] After U.S. forces were expelled from Uzbekistan, however, members of the U.S. foreign policy community began to discuss the organization as a possible threat, particularly with the inclusion of Iran as an observer. Congress organized hearings to determine whether the Shanghai Cooperation Organization was undermining American interests in Central Asia, and to assess the impact of the organization on democratic development in the region.[40] Trepidation mounted when Russia, China, and the other members held "Peace Mission 2007" in Urumqi and Chelyabinsk during August 2007. Russian and Chinese leaders denied these large-scale military exercises were directed against the United States or NATO; they claimed the joint operation was designed to counter terrorism, separatism, and religious extremism, and was not targeted against any third country.[41]

The four Central Asian participants in the SCO have goals similar to those of Russia and China, although they have less scope for maneuver than do their giant neighbors. Membership in the SCO allows them to balance Russia and China against each other, while the big two counterbalance American hegemony. The smallest states (Tajikistan and Kyrgyzstan) are weak and fear the region's potential for extremism, so they appreciate the organization's security provisions. The larger Central Asian members realize benefits in terms of security and prestige—serving in leadership positions or hosting facilities.[42] In addition, the SCO may constrain a more aggressive Russia. At the SCO Dushanbe summit in August 2008 the member states refused to endorse Moscow's military action in Georgia, asserting, "None of the modern international problems can be solved by force," and calling for the two sides to resolve their problems peacefully, through dialogue. The SCO members snubbed Moscow by refusing to grant diplomatic recognition to the breakaway regions of Abkhazia and South Ossetia, reiterating instead their support for the concept of territorial integrity.[43]

The Collective Security Treaty Organization

The Collective Security Treaty (signed in 1992) was reinvigorated in 2002 when the CST members agreed to upgrade the grouping into a regional security organization, renaming it the Collective Security Treaty Organization (CSTO). The organization evolved into an increasingly important element of Russia's foreign policy strategy under Putin, providing a counterweight to NATO and a security forum that Moscow could dominate, in contrast to the SCO. The CSTO's utility became apparent after the Russia-Georgia conflict of August 2008, when Moscow needed international support for its military attack and recognition of Georgia's breakaway republics. At the September CSTO summit in Moscow, the member states placed most of the blame for the conflict on Tbilisi, and voiced support for Russia's actions in the region, including ensuring lasting security for Abkhazia and South Ossetia. CSTO members also strongly warned NATO against any further eastward expansion, and criticized the planned missile defense deployments in the Czech Republic and Poland. Still, aside from Russia, not one of the CSTO member states was willing to grant diplomatic recognition to Abkhazia or South Ossetia.[44]

The CSTO charter is modeled on NATO's, and top Russian foreign and defense officials have proposed that NATO and the CSTO delineate spheres of responsibility for security. NATO's anti-Taliban operations in Afghanistan are in Russia's interest, but Russian leaders are opposed to a more diffused NATO influence in the Central Asian region.[45] Moscow has become increasingly strident in its demands that NATO confine its operations to Europe, asserting that the CSTO can cover the Russian periphery, particularly the less stable southern arc that includes Central Asia and the Caucasus. With Moscow's attack on Georgia, NATO membership is far more problematic for Ukraine and Georgia, while CSTO members such as Armenia and Kazakhstan may rethink their relationship with the Atlantic alliance.

One area of potential cooperation for the CSTO and NATO is in combating narcotics trafficking. Russian analysts have long proposed that the two organizations could cooperate on stemming the Afghanistan drug trade, and the September 2008 CSTO summit described such potential cooperation as "an important step."[46] The drug trade in Central Asia has become an important security issue for Russia, China, the United States, and the vulnerable Central Asian states. Opium production in Afghanistan increased dramatically after the 2001 invasion, peaking at an estimated 8,200 tons in 2007, twice the figure for 2005 and well above preinvasion levels.[47] Narcotics trafficking has contributed to the corruption and criminalization of weak Central Asian states—the most vulnerable being Kyrgyzstan and Tajikistan—by insurgent and terrorist organizations who fund their operations by selling heroin.[48] Russia's 201st Motorized Rifle Battalion in Tajikistan is tasked with protecting borders and interdicting narcotics, but corrupt troops often facilitate the drug trade. Over 2 million Russian citizens suffer from drug addiction, and approximately 80 percent of the heroin entering Russia originates in Afghanistan and is funneled through Central Asia.[49]

Russian and Chinese membership in multilateral institutions should not be viewed as diluting or limiting their national sovereignty. These states are strictly realist in the sense of supporting the original Westphalian concept of strong central control to preserve social cohesion within a territorial unit. For Moscow and Beijing, membership becomes a means of ensuring their presence and representation in regional affairs, while generating a counterweight to forces (such as the United States or NATO) that might seek to contain

their exercise of power. Collective benefits also include promulgating organizational norms that counter a trend toward absolute sovereignty in favor
of humanitarian intervention and "responsible sovereignty" in international
affairs.[50]

Russia, China, and the Central Asian governments also advocate strong
state structures not simply because they favor repression and the status quo
(which they do), but because strong states are needed to deal with the serious threats posed by narcotics traffickers, extremists, and criminal gangs.
The weaker states in the region have government bureaucracies that are thoroughly penetrated by criminal elements, and so pose a genuine threat to their
neighbors. Color revolutions in Central Asia would undermine state authority, leading to chaos and violence comparable to what Kyrgyzstan experienced in the wake of the Tulip Revolution. It is debatable whether this sort
of "democratization" is in America's best interest, much less that of the states
directly involved. Russian and Chinese leaders clearly believe it is not in their
interest.

Energy and Economics

In relative terms, the Central Asian states are, with the exception of Kazakhstan, economically weak. According to World Bank figures, the total
GDP for all five countries in 2007 was approximately $146 billion, about the
same as Ukraine, less than half that of Denmark, and about one-tenth that of
Spain. Great power interest centers on energy—estimates are that Kazakhstan, which accounts for fully 70 percent of the region's GDP, may have 39
billion barrels of oil (about 10 billion barrels more than the United States, but
with a population of only 15 million), while Turkmenistan has natural gas
reserves of about 3 trillion cubic meters. China and the United States, as oil
importing nations, seek access to the region's energy wealth to diversify their
supplies. Russia approaches the region from the perspective of an oil and gas
exporter seeking to control the transit routes of natural resources lost when
the Soviet Union fragmented.

Former president Vladimir Putin proved adroit at leveraging Russia's energy reserves, its energy companies, and its energy infrastructure into foreign
policy influence. Massive increases in the price of oil and natural gas since
1998 have given Russia new clout internationally. In Central Asia, Russia's
energy diplomacy is multifaceted. Moscow's policy is to control export and
import routes, relying on state-owned Gazprom for natural gas and Transneft
for oil. Russian companies—Gazprom, Lukoil, Rusal, Unified Energy Sys-

tems—have invested in various energy projects throughout Central Asia. This web of energy ties, together with trade in other goods and labor migration (to be discussed in the following section), constitutes what one knowledgeable observer has described as Moscow's "soft power approach."[51]

Much has been written recently on China's growing demands for energy, particularly oil and natural gas. Since 1997, Chinese energy companies have pursued an aggressive strategy of securing upstream energy holdings in various parts of the world—Southeast Asia, Africa, Latin America, and Central Asia. Central Asia has considerable potential for the export of oil and natural gas, and has the advantage of geographical proximity. China has already reduced its dependence on Middle East oil—about 50 percent of China's imports came from this volatile region in 2003, compared with 40 percent in 2007.[52] Pipelines from Central Asia, while expensive to construct, would be more reliable than seaborne supplies, assuming the restive Uyghur movements in western China can be contained (80 percent of China's oil transits the Strait of Malacca, where pirates and terrorists threaten shipments). Central Asia cannot replace the Middle East in China's energy calculations, since the Gulf region holds two-thirds of the world's total reserves, but it can help diversify supplies while tying Central Asia into a network of commercial and political relations that enhance stability on China's western border.[53]

Chinese interest in Central Asian oil stems from a desire to promote overall economic regional integration, and to build a land bridge between Central Asia and Russia that would be more reliable than maritime shipments of Persian Gulf crude. China has a number of energy projects in various stages of planning or completion in Central Asia. Chinese companies are interested in both oil (in the short term) and natural gas (in the longer term). At present, gas accounts for only a small fraction of China's energy needs, but as the energy balance changes and pipelines come on stream this will change. China is planning to import gas from Turkmenistan, Kazakhstan, and Uzbekistan.

The most prominent project is an oil pipeline from Atasu in central Kazakhstan to Alashankou in Xinjiang, which will eventually be linked to the rich Kashagan field near Atyrau. This joint venture between the Kazakh state oil company Kazmunaigaz and the China National Petroleum Corporation (CNPC) began delivering crude oil in July 2006. Construction started on the second phase of the pipeline in late 2007; about 220,000 tons per month was being delivered in early 2008, and at full capacity it is expected to carry 20 million tons per year. Part of the oil supplied to China is Russian, produced by TNK-BP and Gazprom Neft, and routed through Samara to the Atyrau pipeline. Russia's Ministry of Industry and Energy predicted deliveries of up to 100,000 barrels per day of crude oil to China via the Samara-Atyrau pipeline in 2008, but price regulations in China and differences between Transneft and the Kazakh government make this export option relatively unattractive for Russian companies.[54]

Purchasing foreign upstream assets is an important component of China's energy policy. The largest foreign acquisition by any Chinese company was the $4.18 billion CNPC takeover of Canada's PetroKazakhstan in 2005, a move contested by Russia's Lukoil. The third largest acquisition also involved Kazakh oil, as China's CITIC Group acquired the Kazakh oil assets of Canada's Nations Energy Company for $1.91 billion in late 2006 (and shortly thereafter was forced to sell a controlling interest in the company to Kazmunaigaz). Other Chinese energy projects in the region include a $152 million gas exploration deal between CNPC and Turkmenistan concluded in November 2006, and a similar agreement for $200 million signed between the China National Offshore Oil Corporation (CNOOC) and Uzbekistan in December 2006.[55] Construction on a 7,000-kilometer natural gas pipeline that would deliver Uzbek and Turkmen gas through Kazakhstan got under way in July 2008. When operating at full capacity (in 2013), the pipeline is to deliver 40 billion cubic meters of gas per year to China and South Asia.

Kazakhstan's energy cooperation with China is a balancing strategy on President Nazarbayev's part. He is seeking to maximize Kazakhstan's freedom of action and security given the pressures emanating from Moscow, Washington, and Beijing. Russia's key advantage has been its monopoly over the existing pipeline routes for Kazakh oil, which disappeared with the completion of the Atasu-Alashakou and Baku-Tblisi-Ceyhan (BTC) pipelines. Moscow bitterly opposed BTC, and the opening of the pipeline presumably has contributed to tensions in Russian-Georgian relations. Russia's military action against Georgia demonstrated the vulnerability of pipelines through the Caucasus, and may force Central Asian exporters to rely more on Russian and Chinese routes.

While the BTC was a coup for the United States, Chinese pipelines undercut American influence in Central Asia since the flow of oil and gas eastward will divert supplies away from BTC and the planned Nabucco pipeline, which Washington and the Europeans favor. Russia is determined to maintain its monopoly over export routes. Moscow exerted strong diplomatic pressure to convince Kazakhstan, Uzbekistan, and Turkmenistan to develop the South Stream gas pipeline, which would run parallel to the Caspian and would ensure Gazprom's dominant position. The Central Asian states formally signed on to South Stream in December 2007, but alternative export routes are preferable to exclusive reliance on Russia. Prior to 2008, Russia was unwilling to pay world market prices for Central Asian gas, but that changed with Gazprom's decision in March 2008 that it would double remuneration to Central Asian producers.[56] Still, Central Asia's leaders continue their efforts to balance the great powers while preserving maximum freedom to maneuver.

Turkmenistan's huge gas reserves are of great interest to both China and Russia. Gazprom, with Russian diplomatic support, pursued a strategy of acquiring Turkmen gas at concessionary prices, while charging close to market rate for Russian gas exported to Europe and the near abroad. A twenty-five-year deal to purchase gas at $44 per thousand cubic meters was negotiated in 2003 and renegotiated two years later at Ashgabad's insistence. Gazprom acceded to additional price increases as world prices spiked in 2007 (Turkmenistan exported about 50 billion cubic meters of gas to Russia in that year). Not satisfied with Russian prices, Niyazov and his successor Berdymukhammedov also sought export routes through China and Iran. The 2006 Turkmen-Chinese deal to construct a 30 bcm natural gas pipeline to Guangdong and Berdymukhammedov's diplomatic initiatives toward Europe and the United States were instrumental in convincing Gazprom to shift its pricing policies.

Kyrgyzstan has neither the oil nor the gas resources of its neighbors, but this impoverished country, along with Tajikistan, does control the water supply for much of Central Asia, and both countries have considerable hydroelectric potential. In Kyrgyzstan, Moscow wants preferential treatment for its energy companies, which have negotiated on plans to finish construction on the Kambar-ata 1 and 2 hydroelectric stations. Gazprom, which holds exploration licenses in southern Kyrgyzstan and hopes to participate in the privatization of Kyrgyzneftegaz, also has significant stakes in the country.[57] But Russia has not followed through on pledges of economic support, and Bishkek may feel it can get better deals from the Chinese or South Asians. Kyrgyzstan and Tajikistan are developing plans to export electricity to Afghanistan and Pakistan, in line with Washington's Great Central Asia plan. Moreover, China is working on several electric power projects with Kyrgyzstan with the goal of importing electricity to the Kashgar region of Xinjiang.

Tajikistan has good political and security ties with Russia, but economic links are relatively anemic. As the data in table 8.2 show, total Tajik-Russian trade turnover in 2007 was just $772 million compared with nearly $17 billion in Russian-Kazakh trade. As with Kyrgyzstan, there is potential for cooperation in hydroelectric power production and export to China and Afghanistan. The Tajik government worked with Russia's Unified Energy Systems to finish construction on the Sangtuda-1 hydroelectric station, and Tajik-Russian firms are cooperating in aluminum production and developing

Table 8.2. Russia's Trade with Central Asia (US$ millions)

Total Turnover	1995	2000	2001	2002	2003	2004	2005	2006	2007
Kazakhstan	5,230	4,447	4,796	4,349	5,754	8,093	9,735	12,807	16,576
Kyrgyzstan	206	192	145	178	265	418	542	755	1,169
Tajikistan	357	293	199	134	198	259	335	504	772
Turkmenistan	272	603	179	175	250	285	301	309	453
Uzbekistan	1,713	937	993	797	996	1,380	1,765	2,379	3,180
Total	7,778	6,472	6,312	5,633	7,463	10,435	12,678	16,754	22,150

Source: Russian Federation State Statistical Service, http://www.gks.ru/bgd/regl/b08_11/IssWWW.exe/Stg /d03/26-06.htm.

the Bol'shoi Koni Mansur silver deposit. Tajikistan had been deeply indebted to Russia, but Moscow agreed to expunge the debt in exchange for ownership of the Nurek space control center and a 75 percent share in the Sangtuda-1 plant.[58]

Dushanbe is looking to its neighbors—particularly China, Pakistan, and India—and to the United States for additional investment and technical assistance in developing its hydroelectric power industry. Tajikistan has proposed the formation of an electric energy consortium that would bring together the United States, Pakistan, and India to construct the Dashtidzhumskii hydroelectric station. Iran has also invested in the energy, transport, finance, construction, and raw materials branches of the Tajik economy, primarily the Sangtuda-2 hydroelectric station and the Shakhristan automobile tunnel. Support for Tajikistan's infrastructure has come from the Asian Development Bank, which in late 2006 provided a concessionary loan to Tajikistan and Afghanistan totaling $56.5 million for a power line stretching from the Vakhsh River to Kabul. Additional infrastructure development plans include building a railroad from Tajikistan to China, via Vakhdat, Irkeshtam, Kashgar, and Urumchi.[59] Highways linking Central Asia with China and South Asia are also currently under construction.

Russia's energy-based foreign policy seeks to limit the influence of competing powers in Central Asia. As president, Putin had suggested that the Shanghai Cooperation Organization could form an "energy club" of suppliers and consumers that would coordinate prices and stabilize supplies. Were India, Pakistan, and especially Iran with its huge natural gas reserves granted membership in the SCO, a Eurasian energy club could prove to be a potent organization. While Washington has focused on Russia's assistance to the Iranian nuclear program and its weapons sales to the radical Islamic state, less attention has been paid to the possibility of collusion in oil and natural gas.[60] Russia and Iran have the largest and second largest natural gas reserves, respectively, and together with the Central Asian states would control over half of the world's supply. Iran has invited Russia to participate in the con-

Table 8.3. China's Trade with Central Asia (US$ millions)

Total Turnover	1995	2000	2001	2002	2003	2004	2005	2006	2007
Kazakhstan	391	1,557	1,288	1,955	3,292	4,498	6,806	8,358	13,800
Kyrgyzstan	231	178	119	202	314	602	972	2,226	3,780
Tajikistan	24	17	11	12	39	69	158	324	524
Turkmenistan	18	16	33	88	83	98	110	179	350
Uzbekistan	119	51	58	132	347	576	681	972	1,130
Total	783	1,819	1,509	2,389	4,075	5,843	8,727	12,359	19,584

Source: *Chinese Statistical Yearbook* (Beijing: National Bureau of Statistics of China), 1997, 2002, 2003, 2005, 2006, 2007; ITAR-TASS, 20 May 2008; "China-Kazakhstan Cooperation Continues," 7 July 2008, http://www.china.org.cn/business/news/2008-07/11/content_15995033.htm; "Uzbekistan: Tashkent Strives to Diversify Its Trade Partners," 19 March 2008, http://www.eurasianet.org/departments/insight/articles/eav031908.shtml; 2007 data from the Website of the PRC Ministry of Commerce, http://oz.mofcom.gov.cn/accessory/200801/1201137340455.xls.

struction of a gas pipeline from Iran through Pakistan to India, and Gazprom has entertained the possibility of participating in the project with India's Oil and Natural Gas Company.[61]

The Shanghai structure could improve relations between traditionally hostile India and Pakistan, were they to be admitted as members. However, China may be reluctant to accept full membership for India and there seems to be some reluctance to confront the United States by welcoming Teheran into the SCO fold. More importantly, Beijing would strongly resist formation of a gas cartel within the SCO. As a natural gas importer, China prefers to deal with Russia, Iran, and the Central Asian states on a bilateral basis, rather than being faced with taking cartel prices.

Trade and economic cooperation between Central Asia and Russia and China is fairly limited outside the energy and raw materials sector, as is evident from tables 8.2 and 8.3. Trade with the Central Asian states constituted only 4.6 percent of Russia's total trade turnover in 2004, and only 0.5 percent of China's. Chinese trade with Central Asia has grown dramatically in recent years and in the case of Kyrgyzstan has surpassed trade with Russia. Russia remains the more important trading partner for the other Central Asian states, but it is fast losing ground. Many parts of Central Asia have become highly dependent on cheap goods from China, Beijing provides larger loans on more favorable terms than does Moscow, and Chinese traders have become an integral part of Central Asian markets. Low-priced Chinese goods raise Central Asian living standards, but the simultaneous influx of ethnic Chinese and China's economic dominance raises fears among Central Asians that they will be submerged by their giant eastern neighbor.[62]

Central Asian trade has a significant local impact on western China, too. The Xinjiang Autonomous Region, which is geographically distant from the powerhouse economies of China's coastal regions, accounts for more than 40 percent of China's overall trade with Central Asia. Beijing is promoting Xinjiang as an economic bridgehead between Central Asia and China, based on the assumption that economic cooperation will promote stability in the less developed western border provinces, while strengthening international ties. One final observation—the official statistics may be somewhat misleading. Russian figures for trade with Turkmenistan, for example, would not include natural gas imports, which probably totaled $5 billion in 2007. There is also a great deal of unrecorded border trade, and Central Asians often travel to China to purchase consumer goods directly. These exchanges are not likely to be registered in government accounts.

To summarize, Russia is using its control of the pipeline infrastructure and the economic power of companies like Gazprom and Transneft to extract revenue from the Central Asian states and to reassert political influence over the former republics. China is looking to Central Asia as a long-term, stable source of oil, gas, and electricity to supply its rapidly growing economy, and it is willing to invest heavily in Central Asia's energy sector. There is an inherent tension in Russian-Chinese relations with reference to the energy situation that is less apparent in politics and security, although Russia and China do cooperate on some regional energy projects.

In terms of U.S. interests, the development and export of Central Asian energy resources westward diversifies world supplies, lowers prices, and reduces the unhealthy reliance on Middle Eastern oil. The United States has been critical of Russia's heavy-handed energy diplomacy in Europe and Central Asia, and is increasingly attentive to the implications of China's aggressive search for new supplies of oil and gas. For Washington, the creation of an energy bloc within the Shanghai Cooperation Organization would be highly problematic, particularly if this arrangement included Iran. Washington is already critical of Moscow and Beijing's willingness to deal bilaterally with Teheran, which undercuts U.S. strategy in the Middle East and Central Asia.

Population Dynamics, Diasporas, and Political Influence

Population dynamics is a critical yet often neglected dimension of domestic and international politics in Central Asia. The five Central Asian states cover huge territories but have relatively small populations. To the east lies the most populous country in the world, with a highly mobile workforce. Their neighbor to the north has some 7 million compatriots still living in the region, and is undergoing an unprecedented decline in population. To complicate matters, wide variations in economic performance have stimulated massive labor migration.

The Russian diaspora in Central Asia is a minor yet increasingly important component of Moscow's relations with the region, in line with Russia's growing use of soft power.[63] Russian nationalism and ethnic chauvinism became prominent in Russian politics under Putin, and this trend is continuing under Medvedev. The rise of nationalism in the 1990s seemed to be linked to frustration arising from Russia's lack of influence on world politics, including in the unstable southern arc. Russian nationalism is fueled by terrorist actions in the Islamic areas of Central Asia and the Caucasus, such as the Beslan massacre of September 2004, and it surged in the wake of Russia's brief war with Georgia in August 2008. President Putin's cautious embrace of nationalism, his hard-line approach to terrorism and instability on Russia's borders, and his pledge to defend the interests of Russians abroad resonated with a large segment of the population, and President Medvedev has shown little inclination to change course.

Russian diaspora communities in Central Asia are weak and fragmented, but their large numbers and concentration in the north of Kazakhstan make that border a potential source of friction between Astana and Moscow. Nearly 5 million ethnic Russians live in Kazakhstan, and there are about 1.2 million in Uzbekistan. In recent years nationalists in Russia have been pushing the cause of their compatriots abroad, whether in Latvia, Ukraine, or Turkmenistan.[64] While the Russian military incursion in Georgia was justified as a defense of Russian citizens (many Abkhazians and Ossetians hold Russian Federation passports), the Russian government is not likely to advance irredentist claims elsewhere in the former Soviet space. Asserting a vocal role as protector of compatriots abroad and providing them with funding for Russian language and cultural studies is relatively low-cost compared to military action, and it gives Moscow an opportunity to claim the role of protector in Central Asia. Promoting Russian language, education, and culture may well prove to be a potent instrument of Russian statecraft over the long term, and these instruments are becoming more important in Moscow's foreign policy.[65] Moreover, Russia's willingness to use force in the Caucasus may encourage the Central Asians to be more accommodating to Moscow's interests.

Immigration from Central Asia and the Caucasus is becoming an increasingly important part of Russia's internal politics, resulting in a backlash against illegal and legal migrants and the criminal gangs who dominate much of Russia's consumer markets in the larger cities. An estimated 6 million Uzbeks, mostly working-age men, have left their country to take construction, service, agricultural, and other menial jobs (legally and illegally), largely in Russia and Kazakhstan. Attacks on Tajiks, Georgians, and other foreigners by skinheads and ultranationalists have become a regular occurrence. Resentment is also growing against Chinese immigrants who have opened small retail establishments in cities throughout the Russian Federation. In 2007 the Russian government established quotas for foreign workers in Russian markets and authorities started a campaign to deport many foreign workers. New migration rules limited the number of work permits issued for foreign laborers. This legislation could have severe consequences for the poorer Central Asian countries since remittances from emigrant workers are a major source of revenue.[66] More restrictive labor and immigration laws could exacerbate Russian labor shortages and erode an element of Moscow's soft power in Central Asia.[67]

The population dynamic is also important for China's relations with Central Asia, but it takes a much different form. Contrary to Russia's declining population, China's continues to grow, and its diasporas have become an important component of Beijing's new soft power approach to influence abroad.[68] The population of Han Chinese in Central Asia is relatively small, but rapidly expanding economic ties have led to the creation of modest Chinatowns or Chinese markets in various Central Asian cities. Up to 500,000 Chinese may be living in Kazakhstan, a significant number in a country with only 15 million people.[69] Given the small populations of these countries, even a modest influx of Chinese nationals could change the ethnic balance dramatically. Chinese diasporas have a record of dominating economies in Southeast Asia, and Central Asians fear that Chinese laborers employed in joint projects might stay on after their contracts are completed.[70]

While the Han Chinese presence in Central Asia is a means of extending influence, the Uyghur minority is a challenge to Beijing's governance. Kazakhstan and Kyrgyzstan are relatively tolerant of their ethnic Uyghur diasporas—in the 1990s the Kazakh government permitted Uyghur émigré groups opposing Chinese dominance of Xinjiang to operate freely, but it has since made it more difficult for these groups to advocate independence. Beijing has succeeded in getting the Shanghai Cooperation Organization's members, including Kazakhstan, to support its goal of quashing separatist movements. However, Uyghurs are fairly well integrated into Kazakh society and there is considerable popular sentiment in favor of the Uyghur cause.[71] By contrast, China and Uzbekistan are in close agreement on population issues and Beijing appreciates Tashkent's strict controls over the large Uyghur diaspora in Uzbekistan. In keeping with the country's repressive policies, Uyghurs have no right to form political organizations and positive media treatment of the Uyghur cause is forbidden.[72]

Conclusion

Russian and Chinese interests in Central Asia are closely aligned on political-security issues, at least in the short term, and both countries are thoroughly pragmatic in their foreign policies toward the region. Russia and China fear domestic terrorism (in Chechnya and Xinjiang, respectively), are concerned with instability in Central Asia, are opposed to "color revolutions" in Central Asia, and seek to limit U.S. and NATO influence in the region. The region is accorded high priority in Russian foreign policy, and Russia continues to have an edge over China and the United States in terms of influence. However, Russia's position appears to be slipping. In recent years China has secured a foothold in Central Asia through its participation in the Shanghai Cooperative Organization, through effective bilateral diplomacy with each of the Central Asian states, and most importantly by using trade, investment, and population migration as levers of influence. American influence waxes and wanes in line with regional dynamics and Washington's frequently shifting priorities.

From a neorealist perspective, the Shanghai Cooperative Organization encapsulates the dynamics of power politics in Central Asia. For Russia, a declining hegemon, this regional organization is a means "to pursue its interests, to share burdens, to solve common problems, and to generate international support and legitimacy for its policies."[73] For China, a rising power, the SCO constrains Russian and American power in the region, while legitimizing China's new role on its western periphery. The weaker member states value the organization as a mechanism for balancing off the great powers, including those who are members (China and Russia) and those who are not (the United States). Official Washington tolerates the SCO as long as it does not constrain America's regional security moves or exclude western firms from Central Asia's vast energy wealth.

In Central Asia, the Russian-Chinese maneuvering for energy is creating tensions. Russia is determined to monopolize the region's oil and gas export routes, to insert its powerful energy monopolies into the regional economies, and to restore lost political influence through energy diplomacy. China's rapidly growing need for energy and new investments in Central Asia make the region a vital part of its energy strategy over the longer term, even though at present Central Asia provides only a small fraction of China's energy imports. Both compete with the United States for Central Asia's energy resources, a fact that may contribute to future tensions.

Population dynamics constitute a small yet growing component of Russian and Chinese ties to Central Asia. An influx of Central Asian and Chinese workers prompted Russian nationalists to lobby (successfully) for legislation regulating immigrants. These nationalists are also pushing Moscow to defend the large Russian expatriate communities in Central Asia. China's major concern is with the expatriate Uyghur community in Central Asia and its possible links to separatist movements in Xinjiang. Central Asians are increasingly nervous about the demographic imbalance as China's regional presence and influence grow.

The war on terror and high global energy prices have made Central Asia an area of vital importance to American foreign policy. Political, economic, and security ties among the Central Asian states, Russia, China, and the United States are extremely complex and multifaceted. Crafting an effective policy is equally complicated. Washington seeks cooperation with the Central Asian states on security and energy issues, while pressing the leaders of these countries to respect human rights and enact democratic reforms. The geographical proximity of Central Asia's states to Afghanistan and their potential for Muslim radicalism constitutes a potential threat over the long term; conversely, the preponderance of moderate Islamic movements in these societies provides a model that other Muslim states might emulate. Central Asia's political systems are authoritarian, but their populations are highly educated and under the right circumstances could move, however gradually, toward more democratic forms of governance.

Notes

I would like to thank David Frost for his research assistance on this project.

1. A. A. Kurtov, "Rossiia i Tsentral'naia Azia," in *Rossiia v Azii: problemy vzaimodeistviia*, ed. K. A. Kokarev, 229 (Moscow: Russian Institute of Strategic Studies, 2006). I am indebted to Mikhail Troitsky for bringing this publication to my attention.

2. John W. Garver, "China's U.S. Policies," in *China Rising: Power and Motivation in Chinese Foreign Policy* (Lanham, Md.: Rowman and Littlefield, 2005), 201–5.

3. Robert Kagan argues that the twenty-first-century world is re-forming along nineteenth-century-balance-of-power lines, with the major division being between the "axis of democracies" (the United States and Europe) and the "association of au-

tocrats" (Russia and China). See: Robert Kagan, *The Return of History and the End of Dreams* (New York: Knopf, 2008).

4. See Elizabeth Van Wie Davis, "Uyghur Muslim Ethnic Separatism, in China," *Asian Affairs* 35 (spring 2008): 15–30.

5. Calla Weimer, "The Economy of Xinjiang," in *Xinjiang: China's Muslim Borderland*, ed. S. Frederick Starr, 171–72 (Armonk, N.Y.: Sharpe, 2004). The Uyghur diaspora in Central Asia is estimated at 500,000 to 1 million, with the bulk concentrated in Kazakhstan.

6. Author interview with a Uyghur resistance leader in Almaty, Kazakhstan, in 1995.

7. China warmly welcomed Uzbek president Islam Karimov on a state visit just a few weeks after the Andijan violence. President Hu Jintao told Karimov that China "honored" Uzbekistan's efforts to protect its national independence, sovereignty, and territorial integrity, and the two sides signed a treaty of friendship and cooperation. Chris Buckley, "China 'Honors' Uzbekistan Crackdown," *International Herald Tribune*, 27 May 2005.

8. For an excellent discussion, see: Adeeb Khalid, *Islam after Communism: Religion and Politics in Central Asia* (Berkeley: Univ. of California Press, 2007).

9. Jacek Cukrowski, "Central Asia: Spatial Disparities in Poverty," United Nations Development Programme, for 2003, http://www.developmentandtransition. net/index.cfm?module=ActiveWeb&page=WebPage&DocumentID=617.

10. Evgenii Abdullaev, "Ustoichivoe neravnovesie: otnosheniia s Rossiei v politike Uzbekistana," *Mezhdunarodnye protsessy* 3 (May–August 2005): 119–26.

11. For a discussion of the U.S.-Uzbek relationship, see: Seth G. Jones et al., *Securing Tyrants or Fostering Reforms: U.S. Internal Security Assistance to Repressive and Transitioning Regimes* (Santa Monica, Calif.: RAND, 2007), 49–88. It is not clear exactly what role the Russian and Chinese leaders played in formulating the language in the declaration. For the text of the declaration, see the SCO website, http://english.scosummit2006.org/EN_BJZL/2006-04/21/content_145.htm.

12. "Uzbekistan predostavliaet Rossii svoi aerodrome dlia vozhmozhnykh 'forsmazhornykh obstoiatel'stv'," Ferghana.ru, 21 December 2006.

13. At the same meeting, Karimov proposed merging the CSTO with the Eurasian Economic Community to create a single stronger organization. See: ITAR-TASS, 6 June 2008.

14. One Uzbek scholar, for example, argued that the development of a new alliance between Russia and Uzbekistan is more of a "defensive" measure on Tashkent's part than the outcome of an effective diplomatic offensive by Russia. See: Farkhod Tolipov, "The Strategic Dilemma of Central Asia," *Russia in Global Affairs* 4 (October–December 2006): 170–78.

15. "Steering by Karimov's Compass," *Transitions Online*, 24 March 2008, http://web.ebscohost.com.echo.louisville.edu/ehost/detail?vid=7&hid=21&sid=1e3d 9a44-7bf2-43ce-8beb-b4718ef026d1%40SRCSM2.

16. A prominent Russian analyst, Azhdar Kurtov, dismissed the argument that the U.S. government was primarily interested in Uzbekistan as a partner in the Afghan conflict, suggesting instead that Washington was trying to reassert its presence in Central Asia. In general, Kurtov downplayed the significance of a possible rapprochement between Washington and Tashkent, asserting that Karimov was simply pursuing a multivectored foreign policy and seeking to avoid isolation. See: Interview with Azhdar Kurtov, "Osnovanii dlia vyvodov o peremenakh vo vneshnei politike Tashkenta ia ne vizhu," Ferghana.ru, 6 March 2008, http://www.ferghana.ru/article. php?id=5620.

17. Xinhau News Agency, translated in BBC Monitoring Asia Pacific—Political, 4 June 2005.

18. Xinhau News Agency, translated in BBC Monitoring Asia Pacific—Political, 8 November 2007.

19. See Freedom House's 2008 Turkmenistan Country Report, http://www. freedomhouse.org/template.cfm?page=22&year=2008&country=7509.

20. For a discussion of Turkmen ideology under Niyazov, see: Slavomir Horak, "The Ideology of the Turkmenbashy Regime," *Perspectives on European Politics and Society* 6 (2005): 305–19.

21. Bruce Pannier, "Turkmenistan: NATO Finds New Partner in Central Asia," *Eurasia Insight,* http://www.eurasianet.org/departments/insight/articles/pp053008. shtml.

22. French president Jacques Chirac congratulated the Tajik leader on his contributions to democracy, while Assistant Secretary of State Richard Boucher met with the president just prior to the elections. The OSCE did, at least, describe the presidential elections as not up to international democratic standards. See: "Rakhmonov's Marathon Run," *Transitions Online,* 30 October 2006, www.tol.cz.

23. "Does Dushanbe Want to Distance Itself from Russia?" Eurasianet.org, 7 September 2007, http://www.eurasianet.org/departments/insight/articles/eav 090707aa.shtml.

24. In April 2002, India's defense ministry agreed to renovate the Ayni air base outside Dushanbe, building three hangars and possibly deploying MiG-29s and helicopters there, as part of trilateral agreement with Tajikistan and Russia. Although it is not clear how large the Indian military presence would be, this is the first Indian base outside its borders. Defenceindia.com (20 April 2006). India's primary concern is of course Pakistan, rather than Russia or China, and possible terrorist threats from the Afghan-Pakistan region.

25. Evan Feigenbaum, deputy assistant secretary of state for South and Central Asia, outlined the U.S. Great Central Asian approach in a speech to the Central Asia-Caucasus Institute in February 2007 (www.silkroadstudies.org/new/docs/ publications/2007/0702feigenbaum-CACI.pdf). S. Frederic Starr, director of the Institution, had first proposed the concept of a Greater Central Asia Partnership for Cooperation and Development in "A Partnership for Central Asia," *Foreign Affairs* 84, no. 4 (July/August 2005): 164–67. China views the plan as a scheme to break

up the SCO and deny influence to Beijing and Moscow: "U.S. Scheming for 'Great Central Asia' Strategy," *Renmin Ribao*, 3 August 2006, http://english.people.com. cn/200608/03/print20060803_289512.html.

26. For a useful chronicle of these events see the "Kyrgyzstan: Revolution Revisited" series of articles in Eurasianet.org. For a cogent analysis of the Tulip Revolution, see: Matthew Fuhrmann, "A Tale of Two Social Capitals: Revolutionary Collective Action in Kyrgyzstan," *Problems of Post-Communism* 53 (November–December 2006): 16–29.

27. The Russian-language website Lentu.ru claimed the U.S. embassy protested that the United States had already pumped over $850 million into the country since independence to support democracy, economic development, and humanitarian projects and to guarantee security. See: "SSHA gotovy platit' za bazu v 55 raz bol'she," http://www.lenta.ru/news/2006/07/14/pay/. Also see: Michael Schwirtz and Clifford J. Levy, "In Reversal, Kyrgyzstan Won't Close a U.S. Base," *New York Times*, 23 June 2009, http://www.nytimes.com/2009/06/24/world/asia/24base.htm?_r=1.

28. RIA Novosti, 21 February 2008; Vladimir Socor, "Russia Augmenting Air Base in Kyrgyzstan," Interfax, 21 February 2006, in *Eurasia Daily Monitor*, http://www.jamestown.org/single/?no_cache=1&tx_ttnews[tt_news]=31407; Ferghana.ru, http://ferghana.ru/article.php?id=4623.

29. Kuban Kalymbaev, "Udobnaia pozitsiia," 26 April 2006, http://www.lenta. ru/articles/2006/04/26/bakiev/.

30. Hamid Toursunof, "Tongue-Tied Schools," *Transitions Online*, 26 May 2008, www.tol.cz.

31. Su Qiang, "President Hu Begins Landmark Visit to Kyrgyzstan," *China Daily*, 15 August 2007, http://www.chinadaily.com.cn/china/2007-08/15/content_ 6026852.htm.

32. Nursultan Nazarbayev, "'Kazakh' and 'Kazan' Have the Same Root," *International Affairs* (Moscow) 51 (2005): 45–46.

33. The Kazakh presidential website lists congratulatory remarks from George W. Bush and Hu Jintao ahead of those from Vladimir Putin. Following the August 2008 Russo-Georgian War, Kazakhstan appeared supportive of Moscow, but Astana declined to grant diplomatic recognition to the breakaway republics of Abkhazia and South Ossetia, as Moscow wanted.

34. Andrew Iacobucci, "Kazakhstan: Astana Promotes Plan for Expanded Ties with Europe," Eurasianet.org, 23 October 2008, http://www.eurasianet.org/depart ments/insightb/articles/eav102308.shtml.

35. Vladimir Putin, "Speech at the 43rd Munich Conference on Security Policy," 10 February 2007, http://www.securityconference.de/konferenzen/rede. php?sprache=en&id=179.

36. Agence France Presse, 13 February 2007. One knowledgeable Russian observer, however, has suggested that Moscow and Washington are really not that far apart on Central Asia, and could improve cooperation in the region with some adjustments on each side. See: Mikhail Troitsky, "Institutionalizing U.S.-Russian

Cooperation in Central Eurasia," Kennan Institute Occasional Paper #293 (Washington, D.C.: Woodrow Wilson International Center for Scholars, 2006).

37. See his "Speech at the Meeting with Russian Ambassadors and Permanent Representatives to International Organizations," 15 July 2008, http://www.kremlin. ru/eng/speeches/2008/07/15/1121_type82912type84779_204155.shtml; and Nikolaus von Twickel, "Medvedev Plugging CIS on First Trip," *Moscow Times*, 23 May 2008.

38. See: Robert G. Sutter, *China's Rise in Asia: Promises and Perils* (Lanham, Md.: Rowman and Littlefield, 2005), esp. 249–63.

39. See: Charles Ziegler, "Strategiia SShA v Tsentral'noi Azii i Shanghaiskaia Organizatsiia Sotrudnichestva," *Mirovaia ekonomika i mezhdunarodnye otnosheniia* 4 (April 2005): 13–22; and "The Shanghai Cooperation Organization and the Future of Central Asia," remarks by Evan A. Feigenbaum, deputy assistant secretary of state for South and Central Asia, to the Nixon Center, 6 September 2007, http://dushanbe .usembassy.gov/sp_09062007.html.

40. Senator Sam Brownback (R-Kansas) chaired the Commission on Security and Cooperation in Europe hearings on the SCO in September 2006, commenting in his opening remarks on the July 2005 SCO summit's call for the withdrawal of foreign forces from Central Asia, and the negative implications of SCO activity for democratization and human rights in the region. However, Assistant Secretary of State for Central and South Asia Richard Boucher and the Central Asia specialists who testified at the hearing played down the possible threat to U.S. interests. See: U.S. Helsinki Commission website, http://www.csce.gov/index.cfm?Fuseaction= ContentRecords.ViewDetail&ContentRecord_id=381&Region_id=0&Issue_id=0 &ContentType=H,B&ContentRecordType=H&CFID=26037517&CFTOKEN= 20186348.

41. Yan Wei, "Partnership in Security," *Beijing Review*, 2 August 2007, http:// www.bjreview.com/world/txt/2007-08/02/content_71251.htm.

42. Kazakhstan's former ambassador to the United States, Bolat Nurgaliyev, was appointed to a three-year term as secretary general of the SCO, while Tashkent hosts the RATS center.

43. "Dushanbe Declaration of Heads of SCO Member States," 28 August 2008, accessed at the Russian version of the Shanghai Cooperation Organization website, http://en.sco2009.ru/docs/documents/dus_declaration.html.

44. "Declaration of the Moscow Session of the Collective Security Council of the Collective Security Treaty Organization," Moscow, 5 September 2008, http:// www.ln.mid.ru/brp_4.nsf/e78a48070f128a7b43256999005bcbb3/39ae7686f5ea11 26c32574c20032f125?OpenDocument.

45. At the 2006 meeting of heads of parliaments of SCO members in Moscow, Duma speaker Boris Gryzlov told his colleagues that Russia would not tolerate the creation of an American-led competitor to the SCO in Central Asia. See: Alexei Chebotarve, "Gryzlov Indentifies the Shanghai Cooperation Organization's Chief Rivals," *Nezavisimaya Gazeta*, 31 May 2006.

46. Vladimir Sergeyev, "The Leverage Is There: Can NATO Take Action at the Global Level?" *Rossiiskie vesti*, 15 December 2006; RIA Novosti, 1 December 2006.

47. United Nations Office on Drugs and Crime, Statistical Annex to the Note "Afghanistan Opium Survey 2007," http://www.unodc.org/pdf/research/AFG07_ExSum_web.pdf.

48. For an excellent discussion of the intersection of drugs, crime, and terrorism in Central Asia, see: Svante E. Cornell and Niklas L. P. Swanström, "The Eurasian Drug Trade: A Challenge to Regional Security," *Problems of Post-Communism* 53 (July–August 2006): 10–28. Beijing's concern with the drug trade in Central Asia is slightly different than Russia's. China receives heroin from Afghanistan primarily through Pakistan, with additional supplies originating in northern Burma, rather than through the Central Asian routes. Heroin transiting the Silk Road in Central Asia is destined primarily for Russia and Europe.

49. Aleksei Rogov, deputy director of the Ministry of Foreign Affairs' department for new challenges and threats, has called for a coordination center to fight drug trafficking. See: ITAR-TASS, 7 February 2006.

50. The concept of responsible sovereignty is developed in Francis M. Deng et al., *Sovereignty as Responsibility: Conflict Management in Africa* (Washington, D.C.: Brookings, 1996).

51. Fiona Hill, "Moscow Discovers Soft Power," *Current History* 105 (October 2006): 341–47.

52. "Chinese Oil Imports from Middle East Down," *China Daily*, 17 January 2008, http://www.china.org.cn/english/business/239753.htm.

53. Charles E. Ziegler, "China, Russia and Energy in the CCA Region and East Asia," in *Energy, Wealth and Governance in the Caucasus and Central Asia: Lessons Not Learned*, ed. Richard M. Auty and Indra de Soysa (London: Routledge, 2006).

54. "Russia to Boost Oil Exports to China," *NEFTE Compass*, 19 December 2007.

55. See: Charles E. Ziegler, "Competing for Markets and Influence: Asian National Oil Companies in Eurasia," *Asian Perspective* 32, no. 1 (2008): 129–63.

56. Gazprom had been paying $130–$180 per thousand cubic meters at the beginning of 2008, and in turn was selling its gas to Europe for about $350. The new deal promises to raise prices to at least $300 in 2009.

57. Anna Shiryaevskaya, "Gazprom Wins E&P Licenses in Kyrgyzstan," *Platt's Oilgram News*, 21 February 2008; Kalymbaev, "Udobnaia pozitsiia."

58. "Medvedev Signs Law on Settlement of Tajikistan's Debt," ITAR-TASS, 15 July 2008, http://www.asiaplus.tj/en/news/29/34651.html.

59. Farrukh Salimov, "Tadzhikistan v regional'noi politike," *Mezhdunarodnye protsessy* 4 (March–August 2006): 129–37; *Financial Times*, 24 December 2006.

60. See: Robert O. Freedman, *Russia, Iran and the Nuclear Question: The Putin Record* (Carlisle, Pa.: Strategic Studies Institute, U.S. Army War College, November 2006).

61. Guzel' Maitdinova, "Faktor ShOS v sisteme bezopastnost Tsentral'noi Azii (v kontekste Afganskikh problem)," paper presented to the International Conference on Afghanistan, Dushanbe, Tajikistan, December 2006, accessed at Ferghana.ru, 18 December 2006; RIA Novosti, 14 February 2007.

62. One Dushanbe observer noted that the influx of cheap items from China, together with a $600 million Chinese credit through the SCO, significantly reduced poverty rates in Tajikistan. See: Viktor Dubovitskii, "Tadzhikistan-Kitai: Ot nasto-rozhennogo otnosheniia k strategicheskomu partnerstvu," Ferghana.ru, http://www.ferghana.ru/article.php?id=4862&PHPSESSID=1f608c1967431640d4c97e62d2d1 dd35. A Kyrgyz political scientist, on the other hand, warned that China was seeking to conquer Central Asia by economic means. See: "Kyrgyz Pundit Warns against Chinese Expansion," *Delo No* (Bishkek), trans. in BBC Monitoring Central Asia Unit, 14 April 2008.

63. See Charles E. Ziegler, "The Russian Diaspora in Central Asia: Russian Compatriots and Moscow's Foreign Policy," *Demokratizatsiya* 14 (winter 2006): 103–26.

64. A conference of Russian compatriots living in Central Asia was held in Almaty in September 2006 (www.fergana.ru, 21 September 2006), and a worldwide conference of Russian compatriots was held in St. Petersburg in October 2006 (www.mid.ru).

65. Francesca Mereu, "Trading Hard Power for Soft Power," *Moscow Times*, 24 March 2005. In Ukraine, for example, the West's investment in building civil society proved to be more successful than Moscow's heavy-handed support for authoritarian forces. See: Adrian Karatnycky, "Ukraine's Orange Revolution," *Foreign Affairs* 84 (March/April 2005): 35–52.

66. For example, an estimated 1.5 million Tajiks work in Russia and remit somewhere between $400 million and $3.3 billion annually to their home country. See: Viktor Dubovitskii, "Tadzhikistan kak strategicheskii partner Rossii: 'Ispravlenie imen' ili o konkretizatsii poniatii," Ferghana.ru, http://www.ferghana.ru/article.php?id=4850.

67. Hill, "Moscow Discovers Soft Power."

68. For example, China has been establishing Confucius Centers in different regions of the world to promote the study of Chinese language and culture.

69. Author's interviews in Astana and Almaty, May–June 2008.

70. This fear was expressed to the author in discussions with Kazakh officials and experts about the Kazakh-China oil pipeline, in 2002 and 2004.

71. Kazakhstan has been relatively free of ethnic strife, and the government has made much of the harmony that exists among national and religious groups in this multiethnic country. In November 2006, however, more than three hundred Kazakh and Uyghur youth clashed in the village of Shelek, about one hundred kilometers from Almaty. The incident was reported in just one Kazakh periodical, the opposition paper *Svoboda Slova*. See: Bakhtiyar Gayanov, "Uchastivshiesya

mezhnatsional'nye konflikty po-prezhnemy ostaiutsya 'zapretnoi temoi' dlya SMI kazakhstana," http://www.ferghana.ru/article.php?id=4793&PHPSESSID=88242 d8a009c727633568d7cf0f0f415.

72. N. T. Tarimi, "China-Uzbek Pact Bad News for Uyghurs," *Asia Times*, 30 July 2004, www.atimes.com.

73. Andrew Hurrell, "Regionalism in Theoretical Perspective," in *Regionalism in World Politics*, ed. Louise Fawcett and Andrew Hurrell, 52 (Oxford: Oxford Univ. Press, 1995).

9

Overshadowed by China

The Russia-China Strategic Partnership in the Asia-Pacific Region

Leszek Buszynski

The Notion of a Strategic Partnership

Russian president Boris Yeltsin's second visit to Beijing, in April 1996, was indicative of a shift of foreign policy away from complete identification with the West toward a more balanced position. Yeltsin had supported a pro-Western policy since the collapse of the Soviet Union but had become disenchanted by the West because of its plans to expand NATO eastward, and also its intervention in the Bosnian conflict over 1993–1995 to the detriment of the Serbs. The significance of Yeltsin's turn toward China was little understood at the time, as it was regarded as a maneuver to bring about Chinese compliance with the Comprehensive Nuclear Test Ban Treaty then being discussed. The declaration of a "strategic partnership for the 21st Century" which arose from the visit was an afterthought; the Chinese side was hesitant to sign until the last moment in the negotiations. Yeltsin was effusive and declared that relations with China had been "elevated to a new level of mutual cooperation" and that "there were no disputes" between Russia and China.[1]

Despite initial hesitance, the Chinese later realized the value of a strategic partnership with Russia after the Clinton administration intervened in the Taiwan crisis of 1996. By the time of Jiang Zemin's return visit to Moscow in April 1997, each sought the support of the other in common opposition to U.S. hegemony. During that visit Yeltsin and Jiang Zemin signed a "Joint Declaration on a Multipolar World and the Formation of a New International Order," which, as they stressed, indicated mutual agreement over the key issues of international affairs.[2] The strategic partnership was affirmed on subsequent occasions when Yeltsin visited Beijing later in November 1997 and during Jiang Zemin's visit to Moscow in November 1998. By the time Vladimir Putin had established himself as Russia's president, a mechanism of consultation and coordination between Russia and China had been put in place; it involved regular meetings by the heads of state and prime ministers,

Map 9.1. China, Russia, and the Korean Peninsula.

annual meetings of foreign ministers, the formation of bilateral committees to oversee and monitor economics and trade relations, and other areas of co-operation.[3]

Putin's determination to revive Russia's international role required that greater value be attached to the strategic partnership with China. In this context Putin declared that the partnership's purpose was to defend the balance of power, and to check U.S. hegemony, which had threatened Russia's interests.[4] New areas of convergence arose with China over America's plans to deploy ballistic missile defense (BMD) at both the national and regional levels. On 17 July 2000 Putin and Jiang Zemin signed a declaration opposing any amendment to the ABM Treaty and condemning the possible deployment of BMD in Taiwan. At this level the partnership was a diplomatic alignment vivified by the sense of shared threat that Russia and China felt from America's unilateralism. Their intention was to impose constraints upon U.S. behavior by signaling the prospect of greater cooperation between them, particularly over issues brought to the UN Security Council, where they could employ their veto.[5] The parameters of the strategic partnership were defined on 16 July 2001 when a twenty-year treaty was signed during Jiang Zemin's visit to Moscow. In this treaty Russia and China agreed not to take action detrimental to each other's security, which was the core feature of their partnership.[6] For Russia the treaty was particularly important in obtaining China's agreement to its Far Eastern borders since under Article 6 the parties were to abjure territorial claims against each other.[7] Jiang Zemin revealed China's interest in an interview with the Russian press when he admitted that the treaty was his initiative intended to ensure China and Russia would never threaten each other again. The Chinese leader was concerned that the transition to a new leadership in Beijing which had little experience with Russia might result in the neglect of the relationship.[8] For both Russia and China geographical proximity was indeed inescapable, which meant that a concern for the security of their common border was their main priority in this relationship. Russia and China were determined to prevent a revival of their Cold War conflict, which was stimulated by lingering Chinese claims to the Russian Far East. Under Mikhail Gorbachev a Soviet-Chinese border treaty was concluded on 15 May 1991 which left the status of the 1,845 islands of the Amur, Ussuri, and Argun rivers undefined. (Their ownership would eventually be resolved over two stages, in 1999 and November 2005.) This strategic partnership also embraces the Shanghai Cooperation Organization (SCO), which, as Putin explained, is a means of ensuring border security between Russia, China, and Central Asia.[9] Putin outlined the value of the strategic partnership in terms of the removal of territorial claims and the harmonization of policy with China over the burning issues of international affairs.[10]

The United States was not the main factor in this partnership, and even without the challenge of U.S. unipolarity Russia and China would still be compelled to live together as neighbors, and would be concerned about the impact of their actions upon each other. They would still be obliged to devise a means of cooperation to deal with their common security. In any case, there were inherent limits to their willingness to cooperate against the United States, as both had important interests at stake. When Putin and Hu Jintao met in Moscow in May 2003 after the American invasion of Iraq, both were disturbed by this unilateral resort to military power and the sidelining of the UN Security Council, but they were careful not to condemn the United States.[11] Neither side was willing to alienate America or to threaten it with the prospect of a de facto alliance which would go against their interests. For China not only was the United States its major export market and the main driver of its economic growth, but America was also the arbiter of Asia-Pacific security and the principal external actor over issues of direct concern to Beijing, the Korean Peninsula, Taiwan, and Japan.[12] For Russia, cooperation with the Bush administration over terrorism was critical for its own efforts to deal with Chechen and Central Asian terrorism. Immediately after 9/11 Putin declared his support for the United States.[13] Deputy Foreign Minister Alexander Losyukov noted that Russia does not see the United States as an enemy, but a partner in the antiterrorist campaign.[14] Putin declared that the era of confrontation with the West had passed and that the main task of the future was the "internationalization" of Russia's economy, and in this context partnership with the United States was a priority together with the need to develop relations with the Asia-Pacific region, including India and China.[15]

According to the terms of the strategic partnership, both sides are obliged to avoid action which would impact negatively upon border security or which would detrimentally affect the security of the other. Nonetheless, Russia has revealed a greater need for the partnership than China, which reflects an inherent imbalance in the relationship. Russia has constantly sought Chinese support over the expansion of NATO, and though Beijing at times was worried about the unlikely prospect of Russia bandwagoning with NATO, it was otherwise less concerned. Putin consulted Jiang Zemin about the formation of the NATO-Russia Council on 28 May 2002, which was intended to reduce the tensions created by NATO's expansion eastward.[16] During Putin's visit to Beijing in March 2006 Moscow and Beijing agreed to harmonize their approaches toward regional conflicts, international terrorism, and also the expansion of NATO.[17] China, however, had little need for Russian support in the Asia-Pacific region and the coordination of policy was largely absent, except over the Korean Peninsula, and then only for a specific period. Beyond the Korean Peninsula, however, China revealed a marked disinterest in Russian regional concerns and the strategic partnership was largely irrelevant.

The Korean Peninsula

Russia was excluded from the Agreed Framework of 21 October 1994, which brought the first Korean nuclear crisis to an end. This agreement was conclud-

ed between the North and the United States, and though the Russians complained about their exclusion they had little influence on the situation. Russia
was also barred from the Korean Peninsula Energy Development Organization (KEDO), which was created to provide Light Water Reactors (LTRs)
to the North under the agreement. It was also sidelined from the four-party
talks which were conducted from April 1996 to August 1999 and included
the United States, China, and North and South Korea.[18] Putin, however, was
determined to involve Russia directly in the Korean Peninsula and for this
reason cultivated relations with Kim Jong-il during his visit to Pyongyang in
July 2000. The Russian president presented the North with a means of off-
setting pressure from the United States while minimizing dependence upon
China. Kim Jong-il reciprocated and visited Russia over July–August 2001
and August 2002, which revealed the extent to which the North's relationship with Russia had developed. Russia had intended to use the relationship
to gain entry into the negotiations relating to the nuclear program and also to
position itself as a mediator between the North and the United States.[19]

The second Korean nuclear crisis brought Russia and China together,
prompted by the fear that the Bush administration would resort to force.
This crisis was provoked on 4 October 2002 when U.S. assistant secretary of
state James Kelly presented the North with evidence of its purchase of gas
centrifuge technology relating to the development of a highly enriched uranium (HEU) nuclear program.[20] On 10 January 2003 the North announced
its withdrawal from the Non-Proliferation Treaty (NPT). Putin and Jiang
Zemin met in Beijing over the issue in December 2002 when Putin was introduced to Jiang's successor, Hu Jintao. Both leaders expressed their concern
over the Bush administration's intention to deploy ABM systems in East Asia
and agreed that the negotiations over the Korean issue should be broadened
to include "all interested governments."[21] The widening of the negotiations
over this issue had been a Russian objective since the first nuclear crisis. On
24 March 1994 the Russian Foreign Ministry proposed a multilateral conference on the Korean Peninsula that would include eight parties: Russia,
the United States, China, Japan, and both Koreas, as well as the IAEA and
the UN Secretary General.[22] At that stage, however, neither China nor the
United States expressed any interest, and though the North declared its "appreciation" of the proposal, it was more interested in the United States and
called upon Russia to press the United States into direct negotiations.[23] Much
later Deputy Foreign Minister Alexander Losyukov, during his visit to Seoul
on 1 October 2002, called for six-party talks for "creating an atmosphere"
that would help activate inter-Korean dialogue.[24]

Despite Putin's agreement with Jiang Zemin, the Chinese leader did not go out of his way to comply with the Russian request. The Russians discovered that the strategic partnership had its limits over the Korean Peninsula, and the mutual concern about an American resort to force did not immediately translate into Chinese support for Russia's involvement in the negotiations. Both Russia and China were distressed by the prospect of the nuclearization of the Korean Peninsula, which could provoke the Bush administration into using force and destabilize the peninsula, and with it their border territories.[25] China and Russia could work together to prevent an American resort to force, but beyond this common concern, however, there were significant differences. China had a special interest in supporting the Northern regime as a buffer state which was not shared by Russia. China's security establishment, and the military in particular, has regarded the North as an ally and buffer state for preventing American domination of the Korean Peninsula, and also as a means of keeping Japan at bay.[26] According to Chinese buffer state theory, the collapse of the North would make the United States the dominant power on the Korean Peninsula, in which case U.S. troops would be deployed along the Chinese border. To ensure the regime's survival China has provided the North with up to half of the 1 to 1.5 million tons of grain Pyongyang imports annually, and up to a third of the North's energy needs, estimated at 1 million tons of oil annually.[27] China has also pressed the North to take the path of economic reform as a means of averting the regime's collapse. The North's economic reforms of July 2002, when prices and wages were allowed to rise and markets were created, have been regarded as emulation of the Chinese model.[28] Nonetheless, attitudinal differences over North Korea have been noted in Beijing that are partly generational, as younger officials see less reason to support the North than do their older counterparts, and partly institutional, as the foreign and economic ministries do not share the PLA's sense of obligation to the North.[29]

Because of its close ties with both North and South Korea, China was better positioned to act as a mediator over the Korean nuclear issue, which would ensure it of influence over the peninsula. Under Yeltsin, Russia claimed this coveted position but failed because of its weak ties with the South.[30] Putin revived the effort to maneuver Russia as a mediator between the North and the international community, which was the objective of his personal diplomacy in cultivating Kim Jong-il over 2000–2002.[31] Putin's personal diplomacy showed signs of success, particularly after Kim Jong-il's visit to Vladivostok in August 2002. The Russian press certainly thought that Putin could act as a sponsor of the North and could mediate between the United States and

Japan to facilitate the North's integration into the international community.[32] When he met the North Korean leader, Putin attempted to lay the basis for a Russian economic role in the North to support these ambitions.

In August 2002 the Russian president opened negotiations with Kim Jong-il over the plan to link the inter-Korean railway system with the Trans-Siberian Railway, which would reduce freight time for South Korean exports to Europe. Putin had previously raised the issue with South Korean president Kim Dae-jung in New York in September 2000 and moved rapidly to pre-empt China over this project. The cost of linking the two systems was an estimated $3 billion, which would result in an estimated $500 million annually in freight and transit fees for Russia.[33] Nonetheless, particular difficulties had to be resolved as the proposal required North-South agreement; also, Russian and Korean railway gauges were different.[34] Despite the hope that this would be a bilateral Russian-South Korean project, the Russians were disturbed by China's interest in the Seoul-Sinuiju line, which had been agreed to by the two Korean leaders at their summit in June 2000.[35] Sinuiju is on the Chinese border, and the proposed railway would connect with Shenyang within China, and then a separate line would join the Trans-Siberian Railway at Zabaikalsk, effectively bypassing the Russian Far East.[36] Despite this anxiety, in May 2007 Russia and the North reached agreement over the reconstruction of the fifty-two-kilometer line from the North Korean port of Rajin to Hasan on the Russian border, which could then link the inter-Korean railway system with the Trans-Siberian Railway.[37] The Russians also planned to supply energy to the North, which would ensure them of additional leverage over Pyongyang, and for this purpose the proposal for a gas pipeline from the Kovytinsk field 350 kilometers northeast of Irkutsk was raised.[38] Proposals for energy projects, however, were hamstrung by the North's inability to pay and to offer funding for infrastructure development.

The long-term strategies of both Russia and China over the Korean Peninsula differed somewhat, which complicated the task of maintaining agreement beyond the urgent and immediate aim of preventing conflict. Indeed, alarm over the Bush administration's confrontational posturing over the North's nuclear program bound both Russia and China over short-term objectives and concealed possible disagreements that could emerge over the future of the Korean Peninsula. The Russians did not share China's attachment to the survival of the North or Kim Jong-il, and often looked ahead to the endgame on the peninsula when the two Koreas would face the prospect of reunification. The Russians maneuvered themselves to take advantage of this eventuality, as they were more confident that reunification would redound to their advantage. In their view, a reunited Korea would turn to Russia for support to avoid dependence upon powerful neighbors such as China, and it might also emerge as a strong ally against Japan. China, however, was a barrier to the fulfillment of these aims and, as Russian commentary lamented, Beijing looked on the Korean Peninsula as its own sphere of influence, and on Korea as a younger brother, which limited Russia's room for maneuvering.[39]

After the eruption of the second nuclear crisis in 2002, Russia was prompted to stake out a position of influence before any of the other powers could respond. Deputy Foreign Minister Alexander Losyukov visited the North in January 2003 in an attempt to fulfill Russian aspirations to become a mediator between Pyongyang and the outside world. He brought with him a "package" proposal that included the following steps: dialogue between the North and the United States, the removal of the North from the "axis of evil" to which President Bush had consigned it in his State of the Union address of 29 January 2002, an assurance that the United States would not attack the North, a trilateral guarantee of the North's security by the United States, China, and Russia, the opening up of the North to the external world, and the creation of a nuclear-free zone on the Korean Peninsula.[40] In effect, the Russian proposal demanded a return to the agreed framework of October 1994 that had terminated the first nuclear crisis.[41] Losyukov later claimed that as a result of his visit he was sure that there was no nuclear program in the North and therefore no reason to go to war.[42] Russia, however, was in no position to mediate over this issue because of its inability to offer incentives to the North, or to threaten penalties such as sanctions, which its leaders had vehemently opposed anyway. Losyukov lamented that the North was only interested in dialogue with the United States and an American security guarantee. Pyongyang was opposed to the internationalization of the issue in the way Russia had advocated because of its fear that a united front against it would be the result.

Heavily embroiled in Iraq, the Bush administration understood that it could not force the issue with Pyongyang and approached China to bring about a resolution of this issue.[43] This in itself was recognition of China's position of influence with the North and its potential as mediator over the issue. In January 2003 Assistant Secretary of State James Kelly visited Seoul and then flew to Beijing, which offered to host bilateral talks between the United States and the North, while Deputy Secretary Richard Armitage visited Tokyo to consult with the Japanese. Russia was not on the list, as the Americans considered it peripheral to the issue. On 8 February 2003 President Bush telephoned Chinese leader Jiang Zemin and urged him to help resolve the nuclear crisis by pressing the North into an agreement.[44] The Chinese leadership was sufficiently concerned about the nuclear issue to accept the role of mediator in a major conflict for the first time. China arranged the three-party talks, which brought it together with the North and the United States in Beijing over 23–25 April 2003.[45] Citing technical problems with the pipeline from Liaoning Province, China had cut off oil supplies for three days to the North in March 2003, which was interpreted as pressure on the North to agree to negotiate.[46] In this way China persuaded the North to drop its demand for bilateral talks with the United States and to accept a multilateral format, which was an American demand.

Russia's exclusion from the three-party talks revealed the limits to the coordination of policy that Moscow and Beijing had previously agreed upon. China did not feel obliged to involve the Russians and was very much bound by the North Koreans, who wanted to keep the talks limited to a few parties. A South Korean report claimed that neither Russia nor Japan were invited because the North at that stage only wanted bilateral talks with the United States and was opposed to any expansion of the talks to include Russia, let alone Japan, which it had publicly criticized. South Korea was interested in the "two plus two" format, which brought together the two Koreas at the core, and the United States and China on the outside of the talks. Russia and Japan were not regarded as relevant to the security situation on the peninsula and could be excluded.[47] The United States regarded trilateral talks as preliminary and pressed for five-party talks involving Japan and South Korea, but was not interested in including Russia. A Russian commentary opined that Russia's exclusion from the talks was a result of Putin's excessive encouragement of the North, which was impeding a resolution of the nuclear crisis.[48] Nonetheless, Putin had calculated (correctly as it turned out) that developing a relationship with the North would give Russia a foothold to join the talks, and without this Russia would have had no role in the issue. Japan came out in favor of involving Russia in the talks, which indicated an alignment between the two outsiders and mutual support over the talks. The Japanese Foreign Ministry revealed that Japan and Russia were in "close contact" over the issue.[49]

During the three-party talks the United States demanded that the North accept Comprehensive Verifiable and Irreversible Disarmament (CVID) before it would consider a security guarantee and economic assistance as Pyongyang had demanded. The North, however, declared that it was close to completing its nuclear weapons program and that it might conduct a "physical demonstration" of its capability. It claimed that the nuclear program would be dismantled only if the United States ended its hostile policy to the North and it demanded American diplomatic recognition, oil shipments, food supplies, and American security guarantees, after which the nuclear program would be terminated.[50] North Korea's behavior during the talks alarmed the Chinese leadership, which feared that the nuclearization of the Korean Peninsula could become irreversible. Chinese president Hu Jintao reacted in anger to the North's admission of a nuclear arsenal and stressed that China's support for the North was conditional on its not developing nuclear weapons. While America's invasion of Iraq was in progress, North Korea's Vice Marshal Cho Myong Nok visited Beijing and called for Chinese guarantees of the North's security against U.S. attack. The Chinese resisted the North's entreaties and countered that such guarantees would be offered only if the North dismantled its nuclear program and agreed to engage the United States in dialogue.[51] The result was a reassessment of priorities in Chinese policy, as more attention was given to the need to remove the nuclear program from the Korean Peninsula and less emphasis was placed upon the idea of using the North as a buffer state. China became more active over the issue and appointed Dai Bingguo, former head of the Communist Party's international liaison department, as mediator.

In these conditions of heightened concern China moved to coordinate policy with Russia once again, which showed that the strategic partnership was activated only when China needed additional support in an escalating situation. Had China been able to manage the situation alone as mediator it is doubtful that Russia would have been involved. The new Chinese leader, Hu Jintao, visited Moscow in May 2003 and with Putin stressed that the use of force to resolve the nuclear issue was unacceptable. Both called for guarantees of the North's security and for the creation of favorable conditions for its economic and social development. China and Russia both leaned toward the economic and diplomatic engagement of the North to create a conducive environment for its nuclear disarmament.[52] The urgency of their meeting was prompted by signals from U.S. vice president Dick Cheney and defense secretary Donald Rumsfeld, who felt betrayed by the Bush administration's acceptance of negotiations and hinted at a strike upon the North's nuclear facilities.[53]

Russia only became involved in the negotiations when the United States, seeking to avoid bilateral talks with the North, pressed for an expansion of the three-party talks to include South Korea and Japan. These three countries formed the Trilateral Coordination and Oversight Group (TCOG), which met in Hawaii on 12–13 June 2003 and called for five-party talks.[54] Russia then was included at the insistence of the North as a balancer between the others to create the six-party format.[55] The North wanted to prevent an imbalance between the parties to the talks that would allow the United States and its two allies to gang up against it. Putin's policy of cultivating relations with Kim Jong-il was indeed vindicated. Russia's value to the North was in deflecting pressure coming from the United States and Japan, and its use of the veto in the UN Security Council to prevent the imposition of sanctions. Significantly, Russia's inclusion in the Six-Party Talks was not at China's urging, though the Chinese did not object to Russia's presence. The Americans accepted the six-party format as a necessary price to bring the North to the negotiating table, though they evinced little enthusiasm over Russia's involvement.[56] Russian-Chinese consultations in preparation for the Six-Party Talks were activated when both agreed that the removal of the nuclear weapons program would be the main purpose, but with the provision of the necessary assurances and guarantees for the North.[57] The first round of the Six-Party Talks was conducted in Beijing over 27–29 August and was inconclusive.

Russia was included in the Six-Party Talks as a product of the North's attempt to bargain with the United States, and not because of the strategic partnership with China. Initially the North wanted to limit the negotiations to the United States only and was uninterested in widening the talks. Its threat to activate its nuclear program, intended to shock the United States into concessions, had the effect, however, of alarming China and prompted the United States into increasing the number of participants. The North then accepted Russia's presence as a balancer. Nonetheless, once involved in the Six-Party Talks, Russia was peripheral and its leaders were obliged to accept the mediating role of China and to forgo their own ambitions for this honor. The first four rounds of the Six-Party Talks over 2003–2005 followed a similar pattern, with the North threatening to declare itself a nuclear power and to conduct a nuclear test while the United States resisted these blandishments. China's role as mediator became critical for the fourth round, when the 19 September 2005 agreement was reached. Under this agreement the North agreed to abandon its nuclear weapons program in return for the provision of light water reactors, which the United States had refused to supply since the outbreak of the second crisis.[58] In this situation Russia was obliged to be passive but could, at least, obtain satisfaction in seeing the Bush administration bend to a Chinese-sponsored agreement.[59]

This passivity irked the Russians, who expected a more active role over the issue.[60] Not until the North conducted its ballistic missile tests on 5 July 2006, and then its first nuclear test on 9 October 2006, was Russia propelled into a more active role, but then in a support capacity. What is striking about this event is that the North disregarded Chinese warnings not to go ahead with the test. According to the Russians, China was given just a twenty-minute advance notice of the test, which they suspect may have been a failure. When senior Japanese Liberal Democratic member Taku Yamasaki visited Beijing before the test in September 2006 he was told that China was "absolutely against" any test and if the North went ahead regardless the Six-Party Talks would be destroyed as a consequence.[61] Nonetheless, China was opposed to any attempt to condemn the North and with Russian support diluted the wording of Resolution 1718 adopted by the UN Security Council on 14 October 2006.[62] A change in the relative negotiating strengths of the two major adversaries followed these events, as the North announced its return to the Six-Party Talks on 31 October. If the North's position had been strengthened, the Bush administration's position was undermined by the deteriorating situation in Iraq and the election of a Democratic Congress in November 2006. While the United States was under strong domestic pressure to terminate the standoff with North Korea it reached again to China for an agreement that was eventually negotiated on 13 February 2007. According to this agreement the North would close down its nuclear reactor at Yongbyon and declare all its nuclear facilities in exchange for shipments of heavy oil and the promise of eventual U.S. diplomatic recognition.[63] Russia contributed to the unblocking of the impasse created when the North refused to implement the agreement unless the United States released $25 million that had been frozen in its account with Banco Delta Asia in Macau. In June 2007 the United States agreed to allow the funds to be remitted via the Russian Central Bank to the North's account with Dal'kombank in Khabarovsk. This was, however, a result of an agreement with the United States and not with China. The North prevaricated and failed to meet the deadline of 31 December 2007 for a declaration of its nuclear programs and only complied on 26 June 2008. With the change of administration in the United States, the threat of American military action has now passed as the United States focuses attention on the negotiations.

What becomes of the Six-Party Talks is an important issue. Moscow had anticipated that they could serve as a basis for a new Northeast Asian regionalism that would preserve Russia's presence on the Korean Peninsula. The idea of a separate forum and a permanent peaceful regime on the Korean Peninsula was mentioned in the communiqué of the Six-Party Talks of 19 September 2005.[64] The Russian Foreign Ministry stated that the talks would lead to the formation of "a dialogue mechanism over the issue of security and cooperation in Northeast Asia."[65] However, if such a mechanism were created in the wake of a resolution of the Korean nuclear issue, it is doubtful that the Russian-Chinese partnership would be a main feature of it. Indeed, without the urgency of the nuclear crisis issue to bring them together, Russia and China are likely to diverge over the Korean Peninsula. China has the dominant position in the Korean Peninsula and by its very presence could marginalize Russia, or at least limit it to a supplementary and unsatisfactory role. Russia would then be prompted to activate ties with the North in terms of the railway project and energy support, but China holds all the economic cards in North Korea.[66] At this point rivalry may emerge and Russia would be tempted to revert to a hedging strategy in a search for alternative ways of strengthening its position on the Korean Peninsula.

Dealing with a Rising China

A rising China presents new challenges for Russia and the strategic partnership they have formed. Not only has China overshadowed Russia on the Korean Peninsula but it has emerged as key player in regional bodies in the Asia-Pacific, where Russia has been struggling to make its voice heard. China indeed threatens to crowd out Russia from the Asia-Pacific region, and the much vaunted strategic partnership provides Moscow with few benefits there. The logical step for a Russia that is steadily being overtaken by China is to develop a hedging strategy against the risk of exclusion from the region which would entail developing relations with regional actors such as Japan. Some Russian commentators have stressed the importance of Japan for Moscow in terms of "restraining" Chinese ambitions, and such comments are increasingly being made.[67] When Putin's successor, Dmitry Medvedev, visited Beijing in May 2008 the Russian press averred that Moscow should manage China by strengthening relations with other Asia-Pacific countries, including Japan and South Korea.[68] There are several difficulties with Russia's ability to develop an appropriate hedging strategy, however. In relation to Japan, the two countries' territorial dispute over the southern Kuril Islands demands resolution before Russia's relations with Tokyo can develop, and the Japanese have rejected all ways of circumventing this hurdle. The options beyond Japan are similarly restricted for different reasons, as South Korea is locked into a close relationship with China as the major actor on the Korean Peninsula and its main trading partner. Within ASEAN Malaysia and Indonesia have encouraged Russia to assume a role in the region, but they are distant and their ties with Russia are weak. Moreover, hedging against regional exclusion and balancing against China are different courses of action. An overt balancing strategy against China would undermine the strategic partnership and destroy the good relations that Russian and Chinese leaders have established over the past decade. Balancing against China by approaching Japan is risky for Russia in view of the suspicions that plague China's relationship with Japan (Russia might lose China's support). Nonetheless, Russia does want to broaden its own regional presence in a hedging strategy to avoid being over-shadowed by China, yet without appearing to challenge it.

The Siberian pipeline proposal gave Russia an opportunity to position itself between China and Japan and revealed Putin's inclination to resort to balancing tactics. The Angarsk-Daqing 2,400-kilometer pipeline was initially negotiated by Russian oil company Yukos and was agreed to by Putin and Jiang Zemin on 17 July 2001. Russia's state oil company Transneft promoted a Pacific Ocean route from Taishet to Perevoznaya Bay, which appealed to Putin because it would allow Russian oil to be shipped to other markets in the Asia-Pacific, including Japan. Japan's Prime Minister Koizumi visited Moscow in January 2003 and proposed funding if the pipeline were constructed to the Pacific. In March 2003 Transneft proposed that the Perevoznaya route be constructed with a spur line to Daqing. Putin vacillated over the pipeline's direction and postponed a decision several times. The Chinese were angered and accused the Russians of refusing to take into account China's economic needs in the strategic partnership.[69] There was economic logic in the Russian desire to ship to other markets in the Asia-Pacific region and also to avoid becoming locked into the Chinese market, which would permit Beijing to dictate prices. The Russians complained that energy negotiations with the Chinese were habitually difficult as they insisted on price reductions as part of the strategic partnership.[70] For Russia's Foreign Ministry the attraction of the Perevoznaya route was that it could tempt the Japanese into sidestepping the territorial dispute to develop energy relations with Russia.[71] On 15 November 2004 Russia offered a resolution of the territorial issue based on the Soviet declaration of November 1956, according to which two island groups, Shikotan and Habomais, would be returned to Japan while Russia would keep the two larger islands, Kunashiri and Etorofu.[72] The Russians surmised that the Japanese would be receptive to a compromise over the issue.[73] However, the Japanese rejected the demarche, demanding a return of all the islands, and there was little chance of squeezing diplomatic benefits from them over the pipeline route.[74] Irrespective of the Japanese response, Putin made his preference clear when he visited Beijing in March 2006 and told the Chinese that Russia would go ahead with the Pacific route, with a spur line to Daqing. The Chinese were disappointed but insisted that the communiqué with Hu Jintao mention the importance of energy cooperation, which was "one of the main components of the strategic partnership between the two governments."[75] Construction of the pipeline began in April 2006, and the Pacific route is scheduled for completion in 2014. Russia retains the hope that the pipeline will allow it to become a major oil supplier to other consumers in the

Asia-Pacific region, such as Japan, South Korea, and the ASEAN countries.[76] The problem is that Russia's oil production peaked in 2007 and unless taxes on oil are reduced and new fields in East Siberia are opened there may not be sufficient supply to support these ambitions.[77]

Russia has also developed ties with India, not only to promote arms sales but as part of a broader strategy of balance within multipolarity. During Putin's first visit to New Delhi in October 2000 he declared a strategic partnership with India. Moscow has repeatedly affirmed the Asian Triangle idea, which was proposed by then-Prime Minister Yevgeny Primakov in December 1998 to bring India and China together. Initially, it was a means of orchestrating China and India against U.S. hegemony, but it has also been regarded as a surreptitious way of balancing against China.[78] Indeed, Russia's defense collaboration with India has gone further than that with China and includes joint production of sea-based cruise missiles and a fifth-generation stealth fighter designated as the PAK-FA.[79] Russia has sold the Su-30 MKI to India, which is more advanced than the Su-30 MKK it sold to China, provoking a protest from the Chinese.[80] In 2000 Russia also agreed to Indian production of the Su-30 MKI under license, which the Russians would not consider with China in view of their concern about Chinese pilfering of their technology.[81] Russia has also contributed to the development of the Indian navy by agreeing to manufacture a total of six Krivak frigates under two contracts, which were signed in 1997 and 2006. Moreover, Russia transferred the *Admiral Gorshkov* carrier to India in 2004. It will be refitted with MiG-29K aircraft and relaunched in 2010 as the INS *Vikramaditya*. Nonetheless, Indian cooperation with the United States over atomic energy and terrorism has also developed, demonstrating that the days of exclusive alliances are now past. Russians lament that India is more interested in economic ties with the United States and China and that Russia's position there beyond the area of defense cooperation is weak.[82] India's role as a balance against China is uncertain, as New Delhi has made an effort to defuse past tensions, particularly since China has downplayed the Kashmir issue.

Overshadowed by China

Conditions have changed since the strategic partnership was first proclaimed in 1996. Then, a weakened Russia and an insecure China faced a confident and triumphant America whose hegemonic ambitions prompted them to seek each other's support. That moment has passed and America has lost this self-assurance as a result of the Iraqi quagmire, terrorism, and the economic crisis. The Bush administration sought Chinese mediation to untangle the Korean nuclear crisis, which was an admission that it could not resolve proliferation problems unilaterally. China is the emerging economic giant and Russia is a new energy superpower, which changes their relationship with the United States as the dominant power. China has less need for Russia in this situation and is increasingly regarding itself as a global player, one capable of dealing directly with a chastened America. China's role in the Korean Peninsula has been elevated by its active mediation there, and its influence in the Asia-Pacific region has been enhanced by its expanding economic presence and its role as a major trading partner of both Japan and Korea. China is a leading actor in the process of creating East Asian regionalism, from which Russia feels excluded. Russia, indeed, risks being overshadowed and sidelined by China in the Asia-Pacific region. Russia's efforts to hedge against regional marginalization require the development of relations with actors that may become rivals of Beijing over various issues; the strategic partnership may come under some strain as a result. In relation to Japan, options are circumscribed by the territorial dispute, while elsewhere Russia's generally feeble economic ties with the region do not stimulate much enthusiasm on its behalf. Russia's defense cooperation with India has advanced considerably, but India's ties with the United States and China have similarly developed.

Despite the anticipated vicissitudes, the strategic partnership between Russia and China is likely to survive, for it is too important for both nations to be cast aside. In sustaining this relationship both sides have been motivated by a concern for border security and the stability of outlying areas such as Central Asia. In addition, China's needs for Russian energy will increase and Russia's share of China's oil imports is expected to rise well beyond the current 10 percent. Moscow, in turn, may increasingly look to China to develop the Far East and Siberia. Though their foreign policies may diverge, they will continue to be bound by the proximity of each other's presence, which will act as an ultimate constraint upon their actions.

Notes

1. Vladimir Mikheev, "Boris Yeltsin vypolnil v Kitae osoboe zadanie 'semerki'," *Izvestiya,* 26 April 1996.

2. Dmitri Gornostaev and Alexander Reutov, "Moskva i pekin v sovmestnoi deklaratsii vyskazalis' protiv postroeniya odnopoloyarnogo mira," *Nezavisimaya Gazeta,* 24 April 1997.

3. "China and Russia: Partnership of Strategic Coordination," Ministry of Foreign Affairs of the People's Republic of China, 17 November 2000, www.FMPRC. gov.cn/eng/ziliao/3602/3604/tl8028.htm.

4. Svetlana Babaeva, "Kogda sosed luchshe rodsvennika," *Izvestiya*, 19 July 2000.

5. Peter Ferdinand, "Sunset, Sunrise: China and Russia Construct a New Relationship," *International Affairs* 83, no. 5 (2007): 841–67.

6. According to Article 8 the parties agreed not to enter into any activities, agreements, or alliances with third states detrimental to the interests of the other. They would also not allow their territory to be used against the other. In the event of a situation or threat to one of the parties they were obliged to contact each other and consult. Of major concern to the Chinese side was Article 5, according to which Russia upheld Beijing's position over Taiwan, while China was committed to Russia's territorial integrity in Article 4. For the text of the treaty see: "Dogovor o dobrososedstve, druzhbe i sotrudnichestve mezhdu Rossiiskoi Federatsiei i Kitaiskoi Narodnoi Respublikoi," *Rossiiskaya Gazeta*, 16 July 2001. On the treaty see also: Elizabeth Wishnick, "Russia and China: Brothers Again?" *Asian Survey* 41, no. 5 (September/October 2001): 797–821.

7. "Interv'yu zamestitelya Ministra inostrannykh del Rossiiskoi Federatsii A. P. Losyukova," Ministry of Foreign Affairs of the Russian Federation: Press and Information Department (henceforth cited as MFARF) [Ministerstvo inostrannykh del rossiiskoi federatsii departament Informatsii i pechati], no. 1700, 24 July 2003.

8. Sergei Luzyanin, "Kitai i Rossiya nodpishut novyi dogovor," *Nezavisimaya Gazeta*, 14 July 2001.

9. "Interv'yu Prezidenta Rossii V. V. Putina Kitaiskim gazetam 'Zhen'min' Zhibao'," *MFARF*, 13 October 2004.

10. Vladimir Putin, "Rossiya: Novye Vostochnyye Perspectivy," *Nezavisimaya Gazeta*, 14 November 2000.

11. Michail Petrov, "Sotrudnichestvo-priortetny kyrs RF i KNR," ITAR-TASS, 27 May 2003; Yevgenii Verlin, "Nefteprovod 'Rossiya-Kitai' zavis v vozdukhe," *Nezavisimaya Gazeta*, 26 May 2003; Yevgenii Verlin, "Putin I Khu ne budet ssorit'sya s bushem," *Nezavisimaya Gazeta*, 29 May 2003.

12. Chinese exports to the United States over 2002–2006 were 33.6 percent of total exports. Though the percentage dropped to 26 percent in 2007, China was strongly dependent upon the American market. See: *U.S.-China Trade Statistics and China's World Trade Statistics*, published by the U.S.-China Business Council, www.uschina.org/statistics/tradetable.html. In terms of security, China cooperated with the United States over terrorism and has evinced increased dependence on the security of the international sea lines of communication as guaranteed by the U.S. Navy. See: Robert Sutter, *China's Rise in Asia* (Lanham, Md.: Rowman and Littlefield, 2005), 77–80.

13. Marina Volkova, "Vtoroi front prezidenta," *Nezavisimaya Gazeta*, 26 September 2001.

14. "Interv'yu zamestitelya Ministra inostrannykh del Rossiiskoi Federatsii A. P. Losyukova," *MFARF*, no. 1700, 24 July 2003.

15. "Vystuplenie Presidenta Rossii V. V. Putina na plenarnom zasedanii soveshchaniya poslov I postoyannykh predstavitelei Rossii," *MFARF*, Moscow, 12 June 2004.

16. "Putin I Tsyan Tszemin pogovorili pro NATO," *Nezavisimaya Gazeta*, 17 April 2002, http://news.ng.ru/2002/04/17/1019039117.html.

17. "Vosmaya Vstrecha," *Rossiiskaya Gazeta*, 17 July 2001. The consultation extended to the political parties when United Russia leader and Russian Duma chairman Boris Gryzlov visited Beijing and discussed terrorism, the war in Iraq, and bilateral economic issues with Chinese Politburo members. See: "Novosti Kitaya," Interfax, 27 April 2004, www.interfax.ru/r/B/0/205.html?menu=8&id_issue=9694882.

18. Seung Ham Yang, Woosang Kim, and Yonggho Kim, "Russo-North Korean Relations in the 2000s: Moscow's Continuing Search for Regional Influence," *Asian Survey* 44, no. 6 (November/December 2004): 794–814.

19. Sergei Luzyanin, "Vostochnoaziatskii 'pas'yans," *Nezavisimaya Gazeta*, 21 October 2002.

20. James Kelly visited Pyongyang over 3–5 October 2002 and presented evidence of bills of sale for the importation of the equipment from Pakistan through what later was known as the A. Q. Khan network. See: George Gedda, "North Korean Weapons Program Prompt," *Washington Post*, 18 October 2002. Why did the North admit to the HEU program? U.S. national security advisor Condoleezza Rice thought that it may have signaled a desire to demonstrate transparency and to break out of economic isolation. Kim Jong Il admitted to the abduction of Japanese citizens during Japanese Prime Minister Junichiro Koizumi's visit to Pyongyang on 17 September 2002, so there may have been a connection. Another explanation is that it was a problem of translation from the Korean, as the particular phrase "entitled to have" was translated as actual possession. See: Brian Knowlton, "North Korea Arms Pact Is Now Dead," *International Herald Tribune*, 21 October 2002. The existence of the HEU program remained speculative and the United States could never identify the location of the facilities. Nonetheless, it came to have a life of its own and State Department spokesman Richard Boucher later said that there is "very conclusive information" that a covert HEU program exists. See: "China View on Arms in North Korea Puzzles U.S.," *International Herald Tribune*, 10 June 2004.

21. Natal'ya Melikova and Yevgenii Verlin, "Putin nakonets uvidel Podnebesnuyu," *Nezavisimaya Gazeta*, 3 December 2002.

22. "Russia Presses for Multilateral Talks on Korea," *Japan Times*, 31 March 1994.

23. "NK Calls on Russia to Push U.S. into Direct Talks," *Japan Times*, 2 April 1994.

24. "Russia Keen to Initiate Regional Talks in Northeast Asia," ITAR-TASS, 1 October 2002.

25. Eric A. McVadon, "Beijing's Frustrations on the Korean Peninsula," *China Brief* 7, no. 4 (25 March 2007): http://www.asianresearch.org/articles/3003.html.

26. For an explanation of buffer state theory see: Ming Liu, "China and the North Korean Crisis: Facing Test and Transition," *Pacific Affairs* 76, no. 3 (fall 2003): 347–73; Zhang Zuqian, "When Beijing Speaks, Kim Listens," *Japan Times,* 5 March 2005. For current challenges to buffer state theory see: Bonnie Glaser, Scott Snyder, and John Park, "Chinese Views on North Korea," *Japan Times,* 15 February 2008.

27. Charles Hutzler and Gordon Fairclough, "China Breaks with Its War-Time Past," *Far Eastern Economic Review,* 7 August 2003. Ming Liu claims that Western estimates of Chinese food and fuel shipments to the North have been exaggerated. See: Ming Liu, "China and the North Korean Crisis." A variant of buffer state theory has it that China is using the North against Japan and South Korea. See: Willy Wo-lap Lam, "China Diplomacy Hinging on 'Korea Option'" *CNN,* 3 June 2003, http://Taiwansecurity.org/CNN/2003/CNN-060303.htm; Jaewoo Choo, "Mirroring North Korea's Growing Economic Dependence on China: Political Ramifications," *Asian Survey* 48, no. 2 (March/April 2008): 344–72.

28. North Korean officials announced the market-based reforms to foreign diplomats which were introduced on 1 July 2002 as a means to overcome "severe economic difficulties." See: "North Koreans Confirm Shifts in Economy," *International Herald Tribune,* 31 July 2002; Christopher Torchia, "N. Korea Outlines Change to Economy," *Washington Post,* 30 July 2002; John Larkin, "Mysterious Reform," *Far Eastern Economic Review,* 8 August 2002.

29. John Pomfret and Glenn Kessler, "China's Reluctance Irks U.S.; Beijing Shows No Intention to Intervene in N. Korea Crisis," *Washington Post,* 4 February 2003.

30. For Russian efforts to act as mediator between North and South Korea under Yeltsin see: Seung-ho Joo, "Russian Policy on Korean Unification in the Post Cold War Era," *Pacific Affairs* 69, no. 1 (spring 1996): 32–48.

31. See Georgii Toloraya, "Svernaya Koreya: novy etap otnoshenii ili 'povtorenie proidennogo," Centre for the Study of Contemporary Korea, Far Eastern Institute, 9 December 2004, http://world.lib.ru/k/kim_o_i/a9620.shtml; Sergei Luzyanin, "Vostochnoaziatskii 'pas'yans," *Nezavisimaya Gazeta,* 21 October 2002.

32. For Russian expectations of Kim Jong-il's visit to Vladivostok in August 2002 see: Andrei Fedorov, "KNDR-na starte protsessa peremen," *Nezavisimaya Gazeta,* 22 August 2002; Georgi Bulychev and Aleksandr Vorontsev, "Severokoreiskii pas'yans," *Nezavisimaya Gazeta,* 26 August 2002.

33. Andrei Fedorov, "KNDR-na starte protsessa peremen," *Nezavisimaya Gazeta,* 22 August 2002.

34. Russian railways use a broad gauge at 1,520 mm while both Koreas use the standard gauge of 1,435 mm, though the North's line to Russia is a broad gauge.

35. Ahn Byung-Min, "Restoration of the Seoul-Shinuiji Line: Review and Outlook," *East Asian Review* 14, no. 1 (spring 2002): 107–19.

36. Luzyanin, "Vostochnoaziatskii 'pas'yans."

37. Kseniya Solyanskaya, "Spala-izgoi," *Gazeta.ru,* 24 April 2008, www.gazeta.

ru/politics/2008/04/24_a_2705768.shtml; "North Korea, Russia Sign Railway Reconstruction Deal," *Yonhap*, 31 May 2007, www.accessmylibrary.com.

38. Fedorov, "KNDR-na starte protsessa peremen." On the Kovytinsk gas fields, see: Bok-Jae Lee, Won-Woo Lee, and Chang-Won Park, "Energy Cooperation in Northeast Asia," summary of research paper, Korea Energy Economics Institute, May 2002.

39. Sergei Luzyanin, "Vostochnoaziatskii 'pas'yans."

40. "Stenogramma vystypleniya Zamestitelya Ministra inostrannykh del Rossii A. P. Losyukova na press-konferentsii no itogam vizita v Pkhen'yan," Moskva, 24 January 2003, in *MFARF*, no. 181, 25 January 2003; "Stenogramma vystypleniya Zamestitelya Ministra inostrannykh del Rossii A. P. Losyukova v programme V. Poznera 'Vremya' telekopanii 'pervyi kanal'," Moskva, 25 January 2003, in *MFARF*, no. 203, 28 January 2003; "Sverokoreiskaya problema: na kompromiss pridetsya idti vsem, schitaet ekspert," *Radio Mayak*, 25 April 2003, http://old.radiomayak.rfn.ru.archive/text?stream=interview&item=20386.

41. Also see: Andrei Napkin, "Possiya pomirit Ssha I KNDR," *Utro.ru*, 12 January 2003, www.utro.ru/articles/print/20030112170036121359.shtml (accessed 5 November 2004).

42. Interview with Alexander Losyukov in "Mydrosti ne khvataet ni Pkhen'yanu ni Vashingtonu," *Izvestiya*, 14 February 2003.

43. See Philip P. Pan, "China Treads Carefully around North Korea," *Washington Post*, 10 January 2002; Pomfret and Kessler, "China's Reluctance Irks U.S.; Beijing Shows No Intention to Intervene in N. Korea Crisis." Differences within the administration arose, but the neoconservatives were sidelined by the State Department, which called for negotiations. See: Glenn Kessler, "Bush Team Split on N. Korea Move," *Washington Post*, 11 January 2003. The administration's adjusted position was explained to its allies when James Kelly visited Seoul on 14 January 2003 and told his South Korean hosts that a guarantee of the North's security might pave the way for its return to the NPT. See: Seo Hyun-jin, "U.S. Envoy Sees Possible N.K. Security Guarantee," *Korea Herald*, 15 January 2003.

44. James Dao, "Bush Urges Chinese President to Press North Korea on Arms," *New York Times*, 8 February 2003.

45. Wang Jisi, *China's Changing Role in Asia* (Washington, D.C.: Atlantic Council of the United States, January 2004).

46. "China Leans on North Korea," *Japan Times*, 2 April 2003; "China Cuts Oil Supply to Warn Off North Korea," *Straits Times*, 29 March 2003.

47. "N Korea, China Want Japan, Russia Out of Talks," *Kyodo*, 15 April 2003.

48. Sergei Luzyanin "Vsesil'nyi Pekin i bespomoshchnaya Moskva," *Nezavisimaya Gazeta*, 23 June 2003.

49. Press Secretary Hatsuhisa Takashima said that Japan was in favor of having Russia in the talks and claimed that Russia and Japan were in close contact over the issue. See: Press Conference, The Ministry of Foreign Affairs of Japan, 15 April 2003, www.mofa.go.jp/announce/press/2003/4/0415.html.

50. Murray Hiebert, "Powell Says 'No,'" *Far Eastern Economic Review,* 8 May 2003; Joel Brinkley, "U.S. Rejects North Korean Proposal," *International Herald Tribune,* 30 April 2003.

51. The Chinese were "shocked" by the North's behavior and felt insulted when the North declared that it might export nuclear weapons or conduct a "physical demonstration"; the North also said that it had nearly completed reprocessing eight thousand fuel rods into weapons-grade plutonium. (In December 2002 the North had apparently withdrawn these fuel rods from the special storage into which they had been placed under the Agreed Framework of 1994.) See: Glenn Kessler and John Pomfret, "North Korea's Threats Prod China toward U.S.," *Washington Post,* 26 April 2003; see also Willy Wo-Lap Lam, "China Diplomacy Hinging on 'Korea Option,'" *CNN,* 3 June 2003; Ching Cheong, "China Offers North Korea Security from Any U.S. Attack," *Straits Times,* 3 May 2003; Murray Hiebert, "China Talks on Korea," *Far Eastern Economic Review,* 1 May 2003.

52. For the Putin–Hu Jintao agreement see: "Sovmestnaya Deklaratsiya Rossiiskoi Federatsii i Kitaiskoi Narodnoi Respubliki, Moskva, Kreml', 27 Maya 2003 Goda," *MFARF,* 27 May 2003; "Rossiay i Kitai podpisali sovmestnuyu deklaratsiyu," *Nezavisimaya Gazeta,* 27 May 2003; Mikhail Petrov, "Sotrudnichestvo-priortetny kyrs RF i KNR," ITAR-TASS, 27 May 2003.

53. Nicholas D. Kristof, "Secret, Scary Plans," *New York Times,* 28 February 2003; Ronald Reagan's former assistant secretary of defense, Richard Perle, stated that a surgical strike on the North's nuclear facilities similar to the Israeli attack on the Iraqi Osirak nuclear reactor of 7 June 1981 could not be excluded. Perle was a member of Defense Secretary Donald Rumsfeld's advisory panel ("U.S. Should Be Ready to Strike N. Korea: Rumsfeld Adviser," *Japan Times,* 14 June 2003).

54. "ROK, U.S., Japan push for 5 way talks with NK," *Korea Times,* 10 June 2003.

55. Alexander Vorontsov, *Current Russia-North Korea Relations: Challenges and Achievements,* Brookings Institution, Centre for Northeast Asian Policy Studies, Working Paper Series, February 2007.

56. James Kelly later noted that the six-party format would prevent the North from playing members against each other, but if anything it gave greater latitude to the North to do just that. See: James A. Kelly, assistant secretary of state for East Asian and Pacific Affairs, "Ensuring a Korean Peninsula Free of Nuclear Weapons," remarks to the "North Korea: Towards a New International Framework" research conference, Washington, D.C., 13 February 2004.

57. "V Pekine nachalis' Rossiisko-kitaiskie konsul'tatsii po KNDP," ITAR-TASS, 25 August 2003, www.itar-tass.com/different/hotnews/Russian/406797.html (accessed 25 August 2003).

58. The North was "committed to abandoning all nuclear weapons and existing nuclear programs and returning, at an early date, to the Treaty on the Non-Proliferation of Nuclear Weapons and to IAEA safeguards." The other parties "agreed to discuss, at an appropriate time," the supply of LTRs to the North, to

provide energy assistance to the North, and to promote economic cooperation with it. See: "Joint Statement of the Fourth Round of the Six-Party Talks, Beijing," 19 September 2005, U.S. Department of State, 19 September 2005, www.state.gov/p/eap/regional/c15455.htm.

59. Oleg Kir'yanov, "Pkhen'yanu Nastupili Na Koshelek," *Rossiiskaya Gazeta*, 19 September 2005.

60. Alexander Zherbin, "Amerikanstam neobkhodima severokoreiskaya problema," *Nezavisimaya Gazeta*, 22 May 2006.

61. Yamasaki met Xiong Guankai, former deputy chief of the General Staff of the PLA and head of the China Institute for International Strategic Studies. See: "China 'Absolutely Against' N. Korean Nuke Test: Japan Lawmaker," *Nikkei*, 2 September 2006.

62. After the test, U.S. representative to the UN John Bolton sought stiff UN sanctions on the North under Chapter 7 of the UN Charter. He pressed for international inspections of all cargo entering the North, which would require Chinese cooperation. The resolution banned the sale or transfer to the North of arms and nuclear-related technology and called upon member states to take "cooperative action, including thorough inspection of cargo" in accordance with their national laws. See: "UN Security Council Resolution 1718," 14 October 2006, Security Council, SC/8853, www.un.org/News/press/docs/2006/sc8853.doc.html.

63. On the 13 February 2007 agreement, see: "North Korea-Denuclearization Action Plan," U.S. Department of State, Office of the Spokesman, Washington, D.C., 13 February 2007; David E. Sanger, "Outside Pressures Broke Korean Deadlock," *New York Times*, 14 February 2007; Glenn Kessler and Edward Cody, "U.S. Flexibility Credited in Nuclear Deal with N. Korea," *Washington Post*, 14 February 2007; and Park Song-wu, "6 Way Talks Make Breakthrough," *Korea Times*, 13 February 2007.

64. According to the joint statement the Six Party Talks are committed to a "lasting peace in Northeast Asia," the parties will negotiate a "permanent peace regime on the Korean Peninsula at an appropriate separate forum," and the parties agreed "to explore ways and means for promoting security cooperation in Northeast Asia." See: "Joint Statement of the Fourth Round of the Six-Party Talks, Beijing," 19 September 2005, U.S. Department of State.

65. "Obzor Vneshnei Politiki Rossiiskoi Federatsii," *MFARF*, no. 431, 27 March 2007.

66. China's economic ties with North Korea have grown significantly over 2005–2006; Chinese investment, which was $1.1 million in 2003, increased to $90 million in 2005, China took 40 percent of the North's trade in 2005, trade with China reached $1.5 billion in that year, and as much as 80 percent of the consumer products in the North were Chinese. See: Robert G. Sutter, *Chinese Foreign Relations: Power and Policy since the Cold War* (Lanham, Md.: Rowman and Littlefield, 2008), 252.

67. Japan is an alternative for Russia in the Asia-Pacific region and a means

of restraining Chinese ambitions. See: Dmitrii Polikanov, "Yaponiya kak vazhnaya al'ternativnaya derzhava," *Nezavisimaya Gazeta*, 21 November 2005.

68. According to *Nezavisimaya Gazeta*, Moscow should deal with a rising China by strengthening relations with other governments of the Asia-Pacific region and should adopt a neutral position in relation to American problems with Japan, South Korea, and China; Moscow should promote the normalization of relations with Japan; and both Russia and Japan could formulate a more constructive approach to the resolution of their territorial dispute over the southern Kuril Islands on the basis of mutual concessions, following the example of the Russian-Chinese border agreement of 2005. This would not only improve the bilateral relationship but would positively impact upon the stability of the region. See: "Vostochnaya diplomatiya trebuet balansa," *Nezavisimaya Gazeta*, 26 May 2008.

69. Yevgenii Verlin, "Kitaitsy podarili Ivanovu poshliny," *Nezavisimaya Gazeta*, 16 January 2004.

70. China haggled over gas prices with Gazprom, which refused to lower prices below those charged to Europe. See: Sergei Pravosudov, "Kitaiskii gazovyi put," *Nezavisimaya Gazeta*, 11 March 2008.

71. Alexander Losyukov saw negotiations with China over the pipeline issue as a means of pushing Japan into a closer relationship over energy. He called on the Japanese to establish the same level of good relations with Russia as Russia has with China. See: "Interv'yu zamestitelya Ministra inostrannykh del Rossiiskoi Federatsii A. P. Losyukova," *MFARF*, no. 1700, 24 July 2003.

72. "Moskva gotova otdat' Yaponstam chast' Kuril," *Izvestiya*, 15 November 2004; "Otvety ofitsial'nogo predsavitelya MID Rossii A. V. Yakovenko na voprosy SMI otnositel'no pozitsii Rossii po probleme mirnogo dogovora s Yaponiei," *MFARF*, no. 2402, 15 November 2003.

73. For commentaries linking Russia's supply of energy with the territorial dispute with Japan, see: Natal'ya Melikova, "Tokiiskii razmen," 22 November 2005; Artur Blinov, "Iz khrama Yasukuni Yuzhnye Kurily ne vidny," *Nezavisimaya Gazeta*, 14 November 2005; and Alexander Sadchikov, "Kurily-ne glavnoe," *Izvestiya*, 21 November 2005.

74. Vaslii Golovnin, "Yapontsy reshili pomolchat," *Izvestiya*, 15 November 2004.

75. "Sovmestnaya Deklaratsiya Rossiiskoi Federatsii i Kitaiskoi Narodnoi Respubliki," *MFARF*, 22 March 2006.

76. Yelana Zamirskaya, "Rossiya namerena rasshiyat' masshtaby eksporta nefti v strany Azii," *RBK*, 30 April 2008, www.quote.ru/print_news.shtml?news_id=31918745.

77. The vice president of Lukoil, Leonid Fedun, claimed that Russian extraction of oil will fall in the coming years and that unless taxes on oil are reduced and new fields in eastern Siberia, the Caspian, and the Arctic are developed oil production may drop by 10–15 percent. See: "Rossiya nikogda ne smozhet dobyt stol'ko nefti,

skol'ko bylo dobyto v 2007 godu: obzor delovoi pressy. (16 Aprelya)," *Regnum,* 16 April 2008, http://regnum.ru/news/987212.html?forprint.

78. Yelena Tikhomirova, "Kitai nam drug, no istana dorozhe," *Nezavisimaya Gazeta,* 24 January 2006.

79. Russia and India have established a joint venture to produce the BrahMos antiship cruise missile ("New Russian Frigate May Be Fitted with BrahMos Cruise Missiles," RIA Novosti, 20 June 2008). In January 2007 Russian Defense Minister Sergei Ivanov and his Indian equivalent, A. K. Antony, signed an agreement for the joint production of the PAK-FA. See: Shiv Aroor, "Advanced Stealth Fighter Aircraft India-Russia's New Joint Venture," *India Express,* 25 January 2007.

80. Alexander Khramchikhin, "Rossiya schitaet Indiyu ideal'nom soyuznikom," *Nezavisimaya Gazeta,* 15 August 2007.

81. "Su-30 FLANKER (Sukhoi)," *GlobalSecurity.org,* www.globalsecurity.org/military/world/india/su-30.htm.

82. Igor' Naumov, "Deli menyaet Rossiyu na SsHA I Evropu," *Nezavisimaya Gazeta,* 14 February 2008.

Part Five

★

China, Russia, and Regional Issues

Taiwan

10

China, Russia, and the Taiwan Issue

The View from Moscow

Jeanne L. Wilson

Introduction

The development and steady upgrading of Russian-Chinese ties during the presidencies of Boris Yeltsin and Vladimir Putin meant that Russia had to devise a framework for its interactions with Taiwan that was acceptable to China. At the same time, the nature of Russia's relationship with the People's Republic of China (PRC)—most specifically the transfer of weaponry—had an impact on China's interactions with Taiwan, as well as the structural dynamics of the cross-Straits crisis. This chapter examines Russian foreign policy toward the China-Taiwan issue. The first section sets forward a chronological account of Russia's interactions with Taiwan and with China on the Taiwan issue. Then I briefly assess the extent of Russia's bilateral communications with Taiwan and their significance. The last section analyzes Moscow's perspective on the China-Taiwan issue. It is my contention that Russian foreign policy on this topic exhibits fundamental tensions that are inherent to Russia's overall relationship with China. The cross-Straits conflict between China and Taiwan is, in certain respects, highly advantageous to Russia. However, the intensification of ties between Russia and China in the 2000s has taken place against the backdrop of the rise of China as a global presence. The Russian leadership is faced with the challenge of negotiating a course of action in its relationship with China which ensures that it does not inadvertently become ensnared as a participant in a conflict in a region in which it has no substantive interests.

Sino-Soviet Relations and the Taiwan Issue

The Taiwan issue emerged as one of the many factors that contributed to the rift between the Soviet Union and the PRC in the 1950s. The opening of the Soviet archives has provided evidence to indicate, contrary to many previous Western assessments, that the Soviet Union was not opposed to the initial Chinese bombardment of the offshore islands held by the Republic of China (ROC) in 1958.[1] However, the Soviet leadership, as with its Chinese counterpart, did not anticipate the vigor of the U.S. response, and was decidedly uninterested in becoming drawn into a military confrontation with the United States. By one account, Nikita Khrushchev even went so far as to suggest to Mao Zedong that China simply accept Taiwan's independence.[2] In a 1959 meeting with Mao, Khrushchev was blunt about the limits of Soviet support, noting that although the Soviet Union would promise to defend China for outside consumption, "between us, in a confidential way, we say that we will not fight over Taiwan."[3]

As the Sino-Soviet conflict intensified, the level of hostility between the Soviet Union and Taiwan declined, with the two sides making several overtures toward each other.[4] Such activities indicated more of an effort to engage the attentions of the United States or China than a genuine desire to establish any sort of relationship. Sustained interactions between the Soviet Union and Taiwan did not commence until the late 1980s, when Mikhail Gorbachev's assumption of leadership in the Soviet Union coincided with the movement toward democratization on Taiwan. Under these circumstances, both states showed an interest in expanding bilateral contacts. By 1990, a steady stream of Soviet visitors began turning up in Taiwan, including some high-ranking politicians (although in an unofficial capacity).[5]

Nonetheless, the Gorbachev administration officially took a cautious approach to Taiwan, largely due to its concerns over alienating the PRC. Gorbachev's May 1989 visit to Beijing resulted in the normalization of relations between the two states, laying to rest a quarrel of three decades. Article 11 of the "Sino-Soviet Joint Communiqué" emphasized that the Soviet Union supported China's position that Taiwan was "part and parcel of the territory of the PRC."[6] Subsequently, China made it clear that Soviet interactions with Taiwan should remain of a strictly nonofficial nature, subject to Beijing's approval. The Chinese Foreign Ministry regularly registered complaints regarding the trips of Soviet political figures to Taiwan (a reflection of the erosion of mechanisms of state control) and pressured the Soviet authorities to prohibit corresponding visits of Taiwanese politicians. Thus, Moscow did not reciprocate after Taiwan lifted restrictions on direct trade in March 1990 and was resistant to Taiwanese efforts to set up bilateral representative offices connected with economic and cultural affairs.[7]

Russia, China, and Taiwan in the Yeltsin Era

In the wake of the Soviet collapse, the Russian Federation assumed the obligations pledged by the Soviet Union in its relationship with the PRC, set out in the joint communiqués signed by Gorbachev and PRC president Jiang Zemin in 1989 and 1991.[8] Nonetheless, the newly installed administration of Boris Yeltsin possessed no great enthusiasm for China, which was seen as a repressive, Communist state. Taiwan, meanwhile, looked upon the Soviet collapse as an unprecedented opportunity to make diplomatic inroads in the newly founded states of the former Soviet Union, a process aided by the political inexperience of nascent political leaderships operating in conditions of administrative upheaval. In January 1992, Vice Foreign Minister John Chiang appeared in Moscow, where he held private talks with a series of Russian officials. Chiang's main aim was to upgrade relations with the Russian Federation, but he also apparently investigated the possibility of arms purchases.[9]

By April 1992, the Taiwanese press was issuing reports that the ROC was close to its goal of setting up representative offices in the capitals of Russia, Ukraine, and Belarus.[10] However, the announcement in September 1992 that Russia had signed an agreement with the ROC to set up coordinating commissions in each other's capitals set off a minor diplomatic crisis in Moscow. Beijing objected strongly to the arrangements, which were undertaken without consultation with the Russian Foreign Ministry, and rather were the handiwork of Oleg Lobov, a close associate of Boris Yeltsin. The Russian Foreign Minister, Andrei Kozyrev, was compelled to contact the Chinese ambassador to emphasize that, contrary to the rumors sweeping Moscow, the organizations would be nongovernmental in nature, established for the purpose of promoting economic and cultural ties. On 19 September 1992 Yeltsin himself issued a decree that clarified the relationship between the Russian Federation and Taiwan, noting that all interactions proceeded "from the premise that there is only one China," that all interactions of the two entities would be nonofficial in nature, and that plans to open a Moscow-Taipei Coordinating Commission in Moscow would be delayed "until further notice."[11] This commitment was reconfirmed during Boris Yeltsin's first presidential visit to China in December 1992. The joint communiqué released by the two states included a clause that specified that Russia would not establish "governmental relations and ties with Taiwan," dictating that the PRC existed as the sole legitimate government representing the Chinese state.[12] In essence, Moscow indicated its acquiescence to Beijing's one-China policy as a precondition of the development of the Russian-Chinese relationship.

While Beijing maintained a constant watch over Russia's interactions with Taiwan, it did not in principle object to bilateral ties between the two entities, as long as they were devoid of political content and limited to informal nongovernmental communications. In June 1993, Taiwan succeeded in setting up a representative structure in Moscow to promote forms of economic and cultural cooperation. The Taiwanese, however, faced a formidable array of challenges in their struggle to establish the commission as a visible or indeed viable presence on the Russian scene. The Yeltsin presidency was preoccupied by a bitter struggle with the Congress of People's Deputies and wary of offending China. The Taiwanese soon discovered that they were virtually completely isolated, unable even to make contact with members of the Russian branch of the coordinating commission, who, in the words of one staff member, appeared "to have disappeared off the face of the earth."[13] Such obstacles, in addition to Russia's chronic economic difficulties, delayed the parallel opening of the Taipei branch of the commission until December 1996. After their initial diplomatic embarrassment, Russian officials in the Ministry of Foreign Affairs were cautious in their interactions with Taiwan, consulting with Beijing before undertaking any bilateral initiatives.[14]

The Yeltsin regime took a circumspect approach to the escalation of tensions across the Taiwan Strait in 1995–1996, indicating its preference for a peaceful resolution to the crisis. In a formal statement, Grigory Karasin, the Russian Foreign Ministry spokesman, emphasized that Russia saw the conflict as a Chinese "internal affair," but hoped for "serious and constructive dialogue" and a peaceful settlement of the dispute.[15]

By the late 1990s, however, the annual joint communiqués signed between Russia and China during presidential visits became more explicit in their references to Taiwan, reflecting rising tensions in cross-Straits relations brought on by the Taiwanese independence movement. In November 1998, Boris Yeltsin indicated his support for the "four no's," a formulation incorporated into the 1998 Russian-Chinese joint communiqué, which specified that Russia would not sell weapons to Taiwan, that it opposed Taiwan's admission into the United Nations and other international organizations, that it supported the stand of the PRC against "two Chinas" or "one China, one Taiwan," and that it would provide no backing to the concept of the "independence of Taiwan" in any form.[16]

The Putin Leadership and the Taiwan Issue

The Putin presidency followed upon the path set by the Yeltsin administration in its ties with China. In 2001, the two states signed a twenty-year Friendship Treaty (formally the Treaty of Good-Neighborly Friendship and Cooperation between the People's Republic of China and the Russian Federation) that included an obligatory reference by each party to upholding the national unity and territorial integrity of the other. In Article 5, Russia confirmed its adherence to the stance on Taiwan established during the Yeltsin era, as outlined in the series of communiqués signed between 1992 and 2000. The Taiwan issue, always a top priority to China, became even more of an obsession with the 2000 victory of the proindependence Democratic Progressive Party (DPP). In March 2005, Moscow was quick to express its support, both in a formal statement from the Foreign Ministry and in comments by Putin himself, for an "Anti-Secession Law" passed by the Chinese National People's Congress that granted Beijing the authority to attack Taiwan should it move further toward independence.[17] Russia also followed China's lead in March 2006 in condemning Taiwanese president Chen Shui-bian for his decision to discontinue the National Unification Council and the application of the National Unification Guidelines, which specified that Taiwan was a part of China. Although largely a symbolic move, this action nonetheless set Taiwan further along the path toward a formal declaration of independence.

The DPP's quest for international recognition of Taiwan as a sovereign state intensified in 2007, as the government applied for membership in the World Health Organization (WHO) in the name of Taiwan instead of seeking observer status as a "health entity" as it had done for the past ten years. The Chen administration also elected for the first time to make its annual appeal for membership in the United Nations as Taiwan rather than as the Republic of China, the constitutionally correct designation. Moreover, in the spring of 2007 the DPP began making plans to put forward a referendum to gather public support for its application to join the UN under the designation "Taiwan." All these measures challenged the Chinese leadership's interpretation of the Anti-Secession Law, which considered any effort of Taipei to change its constitutional status as a de jure statement of independence. Russia's response was to line up squarely in China's camp.

The Russian delegation put forward the motion to strike discussion of Taiwan's membership off the agenda of the World Health Assembly, the decision-making body of the WHO. The Russian Foreign Ministry subsequently issued numerous statements condemning Taipei's bid for UN status and its intention to put forth a referendum on the topic. Moscow reiterated its opposition to Taiwan's membership in any international organizations that consisted of sovereign states, noting its steadfast opposition to any sort of independence activities on the part of Taiwan, which it viewed as "a dangerous game" with potentially disastrous consequences.[18] Moscow, along with most other members of the international community, expressed relief at the victory of the Kuomingtang in the March 2008 elections, and the election of the more moderate Ma Ying-jeou as president, as well as the resounding defeat of the Taiwan UN referendum.[19]

Bilateral Ties between Russia and Taiwan

Taiwan was not able to capitalize on the original gains that it made in Russia because the Russian leadership soon came to realize that developing cordial ties with China was an imperative necessity that took precedence over any interactions with the Taipei authorities. In the early 2000s, Oleg Lobov, the former close colleague of Boris Yeltsin and the signatory to the Russian side of the agreement to set up bilateral structures, still played a key role as an intermediary, serving as the chairman of the Moscow side of the Moscow-Taipei Economic and Cultural Coordinating Commission. But his influence was long diminished. Taiwan made its greatest inroads on the Russian domestic political scene with the Liberal Democratic Party of Russia (LDPR), courting its members, and hosting them on numerous trips to Taiwan. In June 1998, the LDPR put forward an initiative (dubbed the Taiwan Relations Act), prepared by the Duma's Geopolitics Committee under the chairmanship of LDPR member Alexei Mitrofanov, which in effect sought to acknowledge the existence of Taiwan as an independent state. The proposal, although defeated, elicited a protest from the PRC, as did a subsequent trip by LDPR leader Vladimir Zhirinovsky to Taiwan, where he met with ROC president Lee Teng-hui. The Putin leadership, however, was successful at co-opting the LDPR into a tamed and nonthreatening opposition. Duma lawmakers rushed to praise the Putin administration's support of China's Anti-Secession Law in March 2005. Zhirinovsky, in his capacity as the vice-chairman of the State Duma, noted that the "Taiwanese authorities should agree to a solution for the issue in accordance with the principle of 'one country, two systems,'" a statement that conformed to a standard mantra of Beijing.[20]

Lacking any realistic potential to forge a direct political relationship, Taiwan devoted a renewed attention in the 2000s to developing economic and cultural links with Russia. In 2002, Taiwan established the Taiwan-Russia Association drawn from Taiwanese business and academic circles to step up bilateral exchanges with the Russian Federation. The designation of

Chang Chun-hsiung as the association's chairman, however, indicated that Taiwan still hoped to gain some political mileage from this appointment. The high-profile Chang was not only a former premier and the secretary-general of the DPP, but also concurrently served as the chair of the Taiwan side of the Straits Exchange Foundation in its dealings with the PRC. In the 2000s, the Chen Shui-bian presidency also identified Russia as a rapidly growing economy—one of the so-called BRIC countries, along with Brazil, India, and China—and a key target for the development of economic relations. As table 10.1 indicates, the total value of Taiwanese-Russian trade notably increased in the 2000s, despite the fact that it was largely transported via third countries. Total trade between the two reached a high of $2.909 billion in 2004. Taiwanese imports from Russia, however, invariably exceeded exports, leaving a sizeable deficit in the balance of trade in Russia's favor. As table 10.2 indicates, Russia, conforming to its global trade profile, predominantly exported raw materials to Taiwan. Although the Taiwanese press has stressed the growing demand for Taiwanese consumer products in Russia, and Russia has emerged as a growing market for home appliance manufactures, table 10.3 reveals that machine parts comprised the largest single export item to Russia in 2007. Despite the efforts of the Taiwanese authorities, the scale of foreign investment in Russia by Taiwanese entrepreneurs has remained negligible. In 2002, there were an estimated twenty-five Taiwanese firms operating in Russia, with a combined capital investment of $3.5 million, while seven Russian firms were registered in Taiwan, none of them connected with manufacturing.[21] Although Taiwan was often singled out as Russia's fourth largest trading partner in the Asia-Pacific region, Russian-Taiwanese trade figures were dwarfed by Russia's trade profile with China. After years of relative stagnation in the 1990s, Russian-Chinese trade volume grew rapidly in the 2000s, reaching an estimated total of $48.2 billion in 2007.[22]

Taiwanese efforts to develop trade relations with Russia are more a reflection of political considerations than economic ones. With a total trade volume of $508 billion in 2007 (over $90 billion of which was with the PRC), Taiwan's trading relations with Russia are of little importance.[23] But Russia does loom large as a foreign policy preoccupation of Taiwan, given its close ties with China and the large quantity of arms that it provides to the PRC. Similarly, Russia's bilateral interaction with Taiwan is of marginal importance in itself. Unlike Japan and the United States, Russia has no financial interests in Taiwan that would be threatened in the event of an escalation of hostilities between Taiwan and China. Taiwan, however, is relevant to Russia insofar as it exercises a significant indirect impact on its relations with China.

Table 10.1. Taiwanese-Russian Trade, 1992–2007 (US$ millions)
(Reimports and reexports included)

Year	Exports	Imports	Total
1992	23,013	344,977	367,991
1993	72,889	641,092	713,982
1994	163,562	1,097,721	1,801,989
1996	141,241	1,063,842	1,205,084
1997	172,496	1,236,800	1,409,296
1998	137,536	843,982	981,518
1999	107,837	1,183,240	1,291,077
2000	265,006	1,379,611	1,565,685
2001	265,006	603,706	868,712
2002	265,006	927,365	1,182,500
2003	305,009	1,299,896	1,604,905
2004	436,575	2,473,122	2,909,697
2005	516,438	2,196,398	2,712,837
2006	604,051	1,902,961	2,507,012
2007	807,291	1,904,320	2,711,612

Source: Bureau of Foreign Trade, Republic of China, http://cus93
.trade.gov.tw.

Cross-Straits Tensions as a Positive Benefit

In certain respects, the conflict between China and Taiwan is advantageous
to Russia. In the early 1990s, China turned to Russia as a source of weaponry.[24] This was in large part a matter of necessity due to the arms embargo imposed on China by the West after the June 1989 Tiananmen events. Russian
arms manufacturers, facing a dearth of domestic orders, were eager suppliers,
and China rapidly became Moscow's best customer. The bulk of Russian arms
sales to China have consisted of technologically advanced naval, aviation, and
missile systems. This list includes scores of Su-27 and Su-30 fighter aircraft,
four destroyers, and twelve Kilo class submarines. After 2002, with the demand for fighter aircraft sharply attenuated, China increasingly focused on
the purchase of weaponry for the Chinese navy. In contrast, China has indicated little interest in purchasing land-based equipment. Between 1992 and
2002, the only purchases that China made from Russia in land-based arms
consisted of thirty-five transport helicopters and an assortment of artillery
shells and artillery platforms.[25]

Although China's growing global presence creates a sense of unease in
many sectors of Russian society, the Russian government, including the Russian General Staff, appears to have reached the conclusion that China does
not pose a discernable threat to Russia for the present. The distrust that many
sectors of the Russian military felt toward China at the onset of the Russian

Table 10.2. Taiwanese Imports from Russia by Product, 2007 (US$ millions) (Reimports included)

Items by Type	Ranking	Value
Iron and Steel	1	717,903
Organic Chemicals	2	306,357
Nickel	3	239,427
Naphtha	4	190,985
Scrap Iron and Steel	5	171,760
Bituminous Coal	6	145,790
Pig Iron	7	112,501
Nickel Alloys	8	99,215
Semifinished Iron and Steel Products	9	53,516
Stainless Steel Scrap Products	10	42,787

Source: Bureau of Foreign Trade, Republic of China, http://cus93.trade.gov.tw.

Table 10.3. Taiwanese Exports to Russia by Product, 2007 (US$ millions) (Reexports included)

Items by Type	Ranking	Value
Machine Parts	1	57,077
Sound Recording Equipment	2	55,836
Data Recording Equipment	3	42,096
Screws and Bolts	4	35,895
Electric Burglar Alarms	5	34,436
Self-Adhesive Products	6	34,173
Data Processing Equipment	7	29,796
Bicycles	8	25,660
Polyester Fibers	9	22,345
Assorted Machine Parts	10	19,154

Source: Bureau of Foreign Trade, Republic of China, http://cus93.trade.gov.tw.

Federation underwent a shift in the late 1990s. At this time, members of the Russian military high command subscribed to the position that it would take decades for China to emerge as a "first-class military power."[26] Russia's nuclear forces are seen to provide a deterrent to the risks of a Chinese attack. Equally important, the pattern of Chinese arms purchases clearly indicates that the focus of China's military orientation is directed at Taiwan and the South China Sea rather than a land-based conflict along the Sino-Russian border. As the Sino-Soviet split intensified, Soviet leaders found that Chinese-Taiwanese animosity was in their interest insofar as it compelled the PRC to divert troops to Fujian Province who might otherwise have been placed along the Sino-Soviet border. Almost four decades later, under very different circumstances, a similar structural dynamic still applies. Moscow gains a sense of security from China's focus on Taiwan as its most likely military target. Simultaneously, it also reduces the potential negative consequences of the large-scale transfer of arms to China.

In the last several years, the proportion of Russian arms sales to China has declined. Recent contracts have been comprised largely of spare parts and component equipment rather than big ticket items such as fighter aircraft, which have reached a point of market saturation. According to SIPRI statistics, Russian arms sales to China fell from $3.498 billion in 2006 to $1.29 billion in 2007. Nonetheless, China was still Russia's largest customer for the year, constituting about 28 percent of total sales.[27]

Military-technical cooperation with China remains a priority, insofar as arms sales provide a means of survival for certain enterprises in the remnants of the Soviet military-industrial complex. In 2006, for example, the Russian military reportedly purchased six intercontinental ballistic missiles, thirty-one tanks, 120 armored vehicles, one airplane, and eight helicopters, a situation which starkly highlights the dependence of armaments factories on foreign customers for survival.[28] In this context, the maintenance of cross-Straits tensions gives Russia reason to anticipate that China will continue to look to Russia as a source of arms. By the same token, Russia could welcome moves by Taiwan to upgrade its weaponry, based on the assumption that it would spur Beijing toward reciprocal measures, serving to rejuvenate Russian weapons sales.

Cross-Straits Tensions: Potential Dangers to Russia

Although the maintenance of tensions between China and Taiwan serves to alleviate Russian security concerns, as well as to provide a venue for arms sales to China, the escalation of the conflict into outright military confrontation is not in Russia's interest (nor presumably in the interest of any of the other relevant actors, including China itself). In its days as a superpower, the Soviet Union resisted becoming entangled in a Chinese confrontation with Taiwan, viewing the conflict as peripheral to its overall geostrategic concerns. Since the collapse of the Soviet Union, the Russian Federation has pursued a considerably less ambitious foreign policy that is essentially defined by a preoccupation with regional rather than global issues. Russia's influence in the East Asian region is minimal, and it seems improbable that it would be willing to expend its resources there—especially at the cost of confrontation with the United States.[29]

A key problem for Moscow is that China not only expects Russia's formal acquiescence to the one-China policy, but also desires more tangible signs of support from its strategic partner in its mission to reunite Taiwan with the mainland. As a matter of geopolitical strategy, the Chinese leadership seeks to portray Russia as a potential source of support in any military venture it might undertake in the Taiwan straits, regardless of the empirical reality. This tendency was evident in the joint military exercises between the two states in August 2005. The exercises, code-named "Peace Mission 2005," were the first war games conducted between Russia and China (although technically they took place under the auspices of the Shanghai Cooperation Organization).[30] The eight-day games, located in China's Shandong Peninsula, involved nearly ten thousand Chinese and Russian troops (eighteen hundred were Russian) in a three-stage war game that involved an impressive variety of Russian military equipment. Although the games were ostensibly directed against a terrorist foe, speculation inevitably ensued that Taiwan was the real target of the exercise.

In fact, the scale of the Russian-Chinese war games and their coastal location did not lend credence to the notion that they were directed against terrorists, but rather gave the impression that China had secured an increased level of support from Russia in its quest to liberate Taiwan.[31] Russia, for its part, made a concerted effort to dispel this sort of message. The negotiations over the conduct of the exercises were reportedly extended, with China pushing its agenda onto the Russians.[32] China's original hopes were to hold the exercises opposite Taiwan, a move that the Russians steadfastly resisted.[33] The Russian side, moreover, took care to specify that the maneuvers were in no way directed against Taiwan. Sergei Ivanov (the minister of defense), Colonel General Vladimir Moltenskoy (the Russian commander of the exercises), and Sergei Lavrov (the minister of foreign affairs) all released statements emphasizing that the war games were unrelated to the Taiwan issue. Ivanov, moreover, pointedly specified during the maneuvers that "Peace Mission 2005" should in no way be construed as evidence that Russia was prepared to be involved in joint combat operations with China. According to Ivanov, "This is a purely training affair."[34]

If the Chinese sought to promote "Peace Mission 2005" as a signal to Taiwan—and by extension the United States—a motivating factor on the Russian side was apparently financial. The Chinese offer to pay the expenses for the war games was apparently an irresistible carrot for the Russian Ministry of Defense, which could not afford to undertake such large-scale maneuvers independently. Second, the exercises provided yet another opportunity for Russia to showcase Russian military hardware for Chinese purchase and to get a sense of the ability of the Chinese military to integrate Russian equipment into their operational systems. In particular, the Russians were interested in demonstrating aviation and naval systems for sale.[35] According to an unnamed source in the Russian defense industry, one of the main goals of the exercises was to "improve the competitiveness of Russian weapons in international markets."[36]

Despite a barrage of positive publicity surrounding the exercises, a number of Russian analysts indicated concern that Russia risked becoming a pawn of China in its efforts to exert pressure on Taiwan. Writing in *Kommersant,* journalists Ivan Safranov and Andrei Ivanov argued (in an article subtitled "Russia Will Participate in Anti-American Maneuvers on Chinese Money") that "China is trying to play its own game, using Russia."[37] That these sentiments possibly extended into the Kremlin itself was suggested by an article appearing in the government daily newspaper *Rossiiskaia Gazeta.* Advancing a similar argument, Sergei Oznobishchev maintained that joint maneuvers with China were harmful to Russia's long-term defense objectives, which lay in stabilizing military relations with the West.[38]

In comparison to 2005, the next round of military exercises between Russia and China—"Peace Mission 2007"—was notably devoid of any particular Taiwan referent. Held in Urumqi in the Xinjiang Autonomous Region and Chelyabinsk in Siberia from 8–17 August 2007, these were the first exercises under SCO auspices to include participants from all the SCO states, although the presence by other parties besides Russia (two thousand troops) and China (sixteen hundred troops) was minimal.[39] Billed as a means to combat terrorism, the exercises were based on the uprising in Andijan in Uzbekistan in May 2005. The exercises also served as an implicit rebuke to the U.S. presence in Central Asia. In contrast to the 2005 exercises, "Peace Mission 2007" bore the earmarks of Russian planning. The Russian side reportedly selected the Andijan scenario and bore the predominate costs—$78 million—of the exercises.[40] "Peace Mission 2007" marked the first time that China had sent such a large number of troops to a foreign territory, including an air force combat group to collaborate with foreign troops. It also indicated, on the Russian side, an unprecedented willingness to accommodate troops from the PRC on Russian soil, suggesting an increased level of military cooperation between Russia and China.[41]

Conclusion

In the 1990s, Russian-Chinese relations developed on the basis of newly found convergent interests. These included a joint desire to constrain U.S. hegemony, as indicated by their promotion of a multipolar world, a mutual desire to maintain stability (while minimizing the U.S. presence) in Central Asia, the resolution of longstanding border conflicts, and the development of bilateral ties, most notably in the economic sphere. Russia's support for a one-China policy did not in itself entail any significant sacrifice insofar as Moscow had no significant stake in Taiwan. In return for Russia's pledge to uphold the territorial integrity of China, Moscow also benefited from China's vigorous backing of Russia in its ongoing struggle against separatist factions in Chechnya. Russia, moreover, has not hesitated to pursue certain actions that contravene Chinese interests regarding Taiwan. While China has been a vehement opponent of theater missile defense, fearing that it could be deployed to protect Taiwan, Russia began its own development of theater missile defense systems, based on S-300 missiles, in the 1990s.

This does not indicate, however, that Russia faces no dilemmas in its effort to forge a coherent policy on the cross-Straits issue. In a fundamental sense, Russia does not possess a comprehensive articulated foreign policy approach to the question. As the Russian academic Yuri Tsyganov has noted, "Russia lacks a clear conception of a political course with respect to the unification of China; in fact it is trying to ignore the Taiwan problem."[42] To be sure, the cross-Straits dilemma is shrouded in ambiguity, some of it deliberate. The U.S. reaction to a Chinese attack on Taiwan has been subject to endless speculation, but is not the topic of any definitive policy statement. Russia's interaction with China on the China-Taiwan issue highlights the tensions Russia faces between short-term and long-term objectives. Certain policies, most notably arms sales to China, which are advantageous for the present, carry some risk over time of compromising Russian independence as an actor.

Russian arms manufacturers and their representatives exert considerable pressures to expand the scale and technological level of arms sales to China. This position is shared by the Russian government, which is also concerned to keep the most advanced segments of its military-industrial complex operational. This stance is devoid of any ideological orientation or even a particular liking for China. Rather it, like many other Russian policies, is driven by economic considerations. Adherents to this position argue that Russia should eliminate the prohibitions on the transfer of technology to China, offering China its most advanced types of equipment. As Konstantin Makienko, vice director of the Centre for Analysis of Strategies and Technologies (CAST) has noted, "any obstacles which the military places in the way of further exports of weapons and military equipment to China will lead to the collapse of the only living part of the nation's defense capacity, that is its military-industrial complex, which has preserved its relative effectiveness precisely because of Chinese contracts for arms."[43] Simultaneously, joint development projects would provide capital and serve to bind Chinese operational systems to Russian prototypes, thus helping to maintain China as a customer in the event that the European Union or the United States lifts its arms embargo.

The potential for China to serve as a major source of capital for the military-industrial complex is accompanied by the prospect that Beijing could exercise decisive control over the evolution of weapons systems for the Russian military. Such proposals, if realized, would have the inevitable effect of more closely integrating the operations of the Russian and Chinese militaries, with the consequent prospect that Russia could inadvertently be drawn into a military confrontation in the Taiwan Strait. These, however, are hypothetical scenarios, not the current situation. Present assessments indicate that the Russian military-industrial complex would be hard pressed even to resupply China with armaments in a timely manner in the case of a military confrontation in the Taiwan Strait.[44] Nonetheless, the fact remains that any independent military action by China directed against Taiwan would be fought with Russian-made weapons.

As Beijing's strategic partner, Russia is compelled to tread a fine line on the cross-Straits issue. The military-technical relationship between the two states injects its own dynamic into calculations of Moscow's motivations, serving at times to convey the impression that Russia's stance could extend to military support in the case of confrontation. This is a perception that Beijing, engaged in a complex game of geostrategic positioning, has occasionally encouraged, hoping that it would provide Taipei with an additional incentive to dampen its proindependence activities. Russia also faces a challenge in defining its relationship with China as a rising power, with the consequent danger —especially if it increases in its dependence on China as a source of capital for the military-industrial complex—that it could be reduced to the permanent status of a junior subordinate partner. In the 1990s and early 2000s, the initiatives for developing the relationship largely rested with China. This pattern was somewhat redressed in the second half of the Putin administration as rapid economic growth contributed to Russia's administrative capacity and led to an increasingly assertive foreign policy stance. Russia's ability to hold its own in future interactions with China is dependent on a combination of effective governance domestically, the continued rejuvenation and modernization of the Russian economy (beyond a reliance on energy as a source of growth), and skillful diplomacy that reflects Russia's core interests.

However, the widespread congruence of Russian and Chinese interests in the foreign policy sphere does not extend to Taiwan in any fundamental sense. Since the late 1990s, Russia has scrupulously adhered to the "four no's," denying the legitimacy of Taiwanese independence and endorsing the peaceful unification of Taiwan with the PRC. Moscow's position is to advocate the peaceful resolution of the cross-Straits issue. This support is rendered through the channels of political diplomacy. It does not signify a willingness to participate in a military operation in the region.[45] The Soviet Union, formally committed to an alliance with China, perceived that it had no interest in aiding China in its bid to recover Taiwan in the 1950s. It is even less credible that its successor state, Russia, can find any tangible gains to be derived from involvement in a potential military conflict.

Notes

1. For earlier assessments, see Thomas J. Christenson, *Useful Adversaries: Grand Strategy, Domestic Mobilization, and Sino-American Conflict, 1947–1958* (Princeton, N.J.: Princeton Univ. Press, 1996), 231–46; and Donald S. Zagoria, *The Sino-Soviet Conflict, 1956–1961* (New York: Athenaeum, 1966), 200–221. The Cold War International History Project (CWIHP) provides analyses and documentation of the impact of Taiwan on Sino-Soviet relations based on Soviet archival evidence. See in particular: Vladislav M. Zubok, "The Khrushchev-Mao Conversations, 31 July–3 August 1958 and 2 October 1959," *Cold War International History Project Bulletin (CWIHPB)* 12/13 (fall/winter 2001): 243–72; and "New Evidence on Sino-Soviet Relations," *CWIHPB* 6/7 (winter 1995): 148–207. Also see Czeslaw Tubilewicz, "Taiwan and the Soviet Union during the Cold War," *Communist and Post-Communist Studies* 38 (2005): 457–73.

2. John W. Garver, *The Sino-American Alliance: Nationalist China and American Cold War Strategy in Asia* (Armonk, N.Y.: Sharpe, 1997), 141–42.

3. "Document No. 3. Memorandum of Conversation of N. S. Khrushchev with Mao Zedong, Beijing, 2 October 1959," *CWIHPB* 12/13 (fall/winter 2001): 264.

4. Viktor Louis, a Soviet journalist with close ties to the Kremlin, visited Taiwan in 1968, becoming the first Soviet citizen to step on Taiwanese soil since 1949. The following year, a former deputy minister of education for the ROC visited Moscow.

5. For example, Gavril Popov, the mayor of Moscow, visited Taiwan in October 1990.

6. "USSR-PRC Joint Communiqué on Summit Issued," ITAR-TASS, 18 May 1989, in FBIS-SOV-89-095, 18 May 1989.

7. In April 1992, for example, Vice Foreign Minister John Chiang optimistically (and erroneously) predicted that the Republic of China would set up a consulate in Moscow. See "Taipei to Open Offices in Moscow, Kiev, Minsk," Central News Agency, 18 April 1992, in FBIS-CHI-92-077.

8. The 1991 joint communiqué included a reference, similar to that of the 1989 version, upholding the Soviet commitment to a one-China policy.

9. See: Alexander A. Sergounin and Sergey V. Subbotin, *Russian Arms Transfers*

to East Asia in the 1990s, SIPRI Research Report No. 15 (Oxford: Oxford Univ. Press, 1999), 18. In July 1992, Vice Foreign Minister Chiang, implicitly acknowledging the veracity of such reports, noted that Taiwan had encountered numerous difficulties in finding reliable sources to discuss arms purchases in a volatile and unstable Russia. Chiang added it was more realistic for Taiwan to study the feasibility of developing academic and technological exchanges. See "Military Cooperation with Russia Not Likely," Central News Agency, 14 July 1992, in FBIS-CHI-92-135.

10. The ROC's most impressive foreign policy coup among the states of the former Soviet Union was the temporary—until 1994—establishment of consular ties with Latvia in January 1992 (an action that caused the PRC to break off diplomatic contacts).

11. "Decree of the President of the Russian Federation on Relations between the Russian Federation and Taiwan," *Rossiiskaia Gazeta*, 19 September 1992, in FBIS-SOV-92-183.

12. "Information on the Results of the Official Visit Paid by Boris Yeltsin, President of the Russian Federation, to the People's Republic of China," ITAR-TASS, 19 December 1992, in FBIS-SOV-92-245, 21 December 1992.

13. Interview with staff member, Taipei-Moscow Coordinating Commission for Economic and Cultural Cooperation, Moscow, Russia, 14 October 1993.

14. The Chinese ambassador to Moscow, Li Fenglin, announced in 1996 that China and Russia had "preliminarily agreed on the exchange of unofficial representations between Moscow and Taipei." Similar consultations were held by the two states before Russia signed a protocol with Taiwan in 1997 that permitted direct air links. See: Andrey Varlamov and Andrey Kirilov, "Contacts with Taiwan Will Not Harm Relations with China," ITAR-TASS, 23 October 1996, in FBIS-SOV-96-206, 23 October 1996; "To Taipei without Symbols," *Rossiiskaia Gazeta*, 16 September 1997, 1, in FBIS-SOV-97-259; and Yuri Savenkov, "Taibei Fog" [Taipei tuman], *Izvestiia*, 13 August 1996, 3.

15. "Russia Says Taiwan 'Inalienable' Part of China," Xinhua, 21 March 1996, in FBIS-CHI-96-057, 21 March 1996. Also see: Alexander Lukin, *The Bear Watches the Dragon* (Armonk, N.Y.: Sharpe, 2003), 295.

16. "Text of China-Russia Joint Statement," Xinhua, 24 November 1998, in FBIS-CHI-98-327, 24 November 1998; Czeslaw Tubilewicz, "The Little Dragon and the Bear: Russian-Taiwanese Relations in the Post–Cold War Period," *Russian Review*, no. 61 (April 2002): 292.

17. For Putin's comments, see "Putin Reiterates Support of China's Stance on Taiwan Issue," Xinhua, 19 March 2005, via World News Connection (hereafter cited as WNC) 20050318.

18. See, for example, the statements of Deputy Foreign Minister Aleksander Losyukov in "Russia Condemns Taiwan's 'Referendum on UN Membership," Xinhua, 5 February 2008, via WNC 20080204, and First Deputy Foreign Minister Andrey Denisov in "Russia Criticizes Taiwan's UN Referendum Plans," Interfax, 19 March 2008, via WNC 20080319.

19. Technically, there were two UN referendums on the ballet, one put forward by the DPP, and one by the KMT which proposed membership in the UN as the Republic of China. Both failed to receive a high enough percentage of votes to validate the referendum.

20. "Russian Lawmakers Say China Has Right to Safeguard Territorial Integrity," Xinhua, 14 March 2005.

21. Kvo Bupin, "Trade-Economic Relations between Taiwan and Russia" [Torgovo-ekonomicheskie otnosheniya mezhdu taivanem i rossiei], *Mirovaia ekonomika i mezhdunarodnye otnosheniia*, 2004-07-31IMEO-No. 007, 3 July 2004, 68–69. Also see *Financial Times*, 12 December 2005, www.lexisnexis.com. In 2005, the Taiwan-Russia Association reported that business contracts worth $375 million had been signed during a delegation visit, but the extent to which these have been realized is not clear. See: *Asia Pulse*, 6 October 2005, www.lexisnexis.com. Also see: Sergey Vradiy, "Russia's Unofficial Relations with Taiwan," *Slavic Research Center News* 14, no. 3 (December 2006): 229.

22. "China-Russia Bilateral Trade Hits $48 bln in 2007," RIA Novosti, 22 May 2008, at http://en.rian.ru/business/20080522/108086671.html.

23. Bureau of Foreign Trade, Republic of China, http://cus93.trade.gov.tw.

24. In fact, China sought to purchase Su-27 fighter aircraft from the Soviet Union after the normalization of relations in 1989, with negotiations in progress at the time of the Soviet collapse.

25. Konstantin Makienko, "Military-Technical Cooperation between Russia and the PRC, 1992–2002: Results, Tendencies, and Prospects" [Voenno-tekhnicheskoe sotrudnichestvo Rossii i KNR v 1992–2002 godakh: dostizheniia, tendentsii, perspektivy], Document No. 2 (Moscow: Russian Office of the Center for Defence Analysis, October 2002), 46–47.

26. See, for example: Dmitri Trinin, "Russia and Global Security Norms," *Washington Quarterly* 27, no. 2 (spring 2004): 73; and Alexei Arbatov, "Russian Military Policy Adrift," *Carnegie Moscow Center Briefing* 8, no. 6 (November 2006): 3; Paradorn Rangsimapom, "Russia's Debate on Military-Technological Cooperation with China," *Asian Survey* 46, no. 3 (May–June 2006): 486–89.

27. Furthermore, Russia was the source of over 90 percent of all arms deliveries to China for the year. See: http://armstrade.sipri.org/arms_trade/values.php.

28. Arbatov, "Russian Military Policy Adrift," 5.

29. Trenin, "Russia and Global Security Norms," 65.

30. A joint operation between the Russian and Chinese navies, however, took place in 1999.

31. Some analysts chose to focus on the Korean Peninsula as the object of Russian-Chinese attentions.

32. Yu Bin, "China-Russia Relations: Back to Geostrategies," *Comparative Connections* 7, no. 1 (2005), http://csis.org/component/option,com_csis_pubs/task,view/id,4660/type,1/; Igor Plagatarev, "He That Pays Also Orders Exercises," *Nezavisimoye Voyennoye Obozhreniye*, 24 August 2005, WNC 20050824.

33. Hung Mao-hsiung, "How Will War Games Affect Security?" *Taipei Times*, 22 August 2005, 8, http://www.taipeitimes.com; Wu Min-chieh, "Choice of Venue for Military Exercises 'Kills Two Birds with One Stone,'" *Wen Wei Po*, 19 August 2005, WNC 20050829; Elizabeth Wishnick, "Brothers in Arms Again? Assessing the Sino-Russian Military Exercises," *PacNet*, no. 35 (18 August 2005).

34. "Joint Exercise Does Not Mean Russia Can Join China on Battlefield," ITAR-TASS, 23 August 2005, via WNC 20050823.

35. Plagatarev, "He That Pays Also Orders Exercises"; "Analysis Center Head Comments on Sino-Russian Exercise," *Agentstvo Voyennykh Novostey*, 22 August 2005, WNC 20050822. A number of reports indicated that Russian expenses for the exercises were $5.5 million dollars. See, for example: Artur Blinov and Viktor Myasnikov, "Bear Dancing with Dragon" [Tantsy medvedya s drakonom], *Nezavisimaya Gazeta*, 1 September 2005.

36. Weapons on display for sale included Tu-95 and Tu-22M3 strategic bombers, A-50 radar aircraft, Il-78 tankers, Su-24MK frontline bombers, and Su-27CKM multipurpose single-seat fighters. See: "Russian-Chinese Maneuvers Seen to Enhance Russian Arms Export Potential," *Agentstvo Voyennykh Novestey*, 26 August 2005, via WNC 20050826. Also see Richard Weitz, "The Sino-Russian Arms Dilemma," *China Brief* 6, no. 22 (8 November 2006): 9.

37. Ivan Safronov and Andrei Ivanov, "International Debt: Mercenaries of Good Will" [Internatsional'yi dolg: naemniki doproi voli], *Kommersant*, 18 August 2005, 9; also Alexander Golts, "Russia's Economic Maneuvers," *Moscow Times*, 15 August 2005, 8.

38. Report by Vladimir Bogdanov and Vladimir Belousov citing Sergei Oznobishchev, "The World and Russia: Russia Risks Playing in an Alien Game" [Mir I Rossiia: Rossia rickuet cygrat' v chuzhuyu igru], *Rossiiskaia Gazeta*, 19 August 2005, 8.

39. Some discrepancy exists in reports of the actual number of troops taking part in the mission. According to Andrei Chang, "Peace Mission 2007" involved sixteen hundred troops from China, two thousand from Russia, one hundred from Kazakhstan, two hundred from Tajikistan, and a dozen from Uzbekistan. Uzbekistan, however, sent staff officers rather than troops. "Analysis: Is SCO New Warsaw Treaty Group," UPI, 10 August 2007.

40. Roger N. McDermott, *The Rising Dragon: SCO Peace Mission 2007*, Occasional Paper (Washington, D.C.: Jamestown Foundation, October 2007), 3, 16.

41. After Kazakhstan refused transit rights, Chinese troops were compelled to undertake a 10,300-kilometer journey to reach Chelyabinsk.

42. Y. Tsyganov, "Russian-Chinese relations and Taiwan" [Rossiisko-Kitaiskie otnosheniia i Taivan'], *Mirovaia ekonomika i mezhdunarodnye otnosheniia*, no. 3 (1998): 122–28.

43. Konstantin Makienko, "The Russian-Chinese Arms Trade: An Attempt at Qualitative Analysis," *Moscow Defense Brief*, no. 2 (2004): 3.

44. See: Yuri Baskov, "Russia's Capability to Supply Ammunitions to China," *Kanwa Asian Defense Review*, 24 January 2008, WNC 20080124; and Andrei Chang and Jeff Chen, "China's Capacity to Produce Advanced Equipment vs. PLA's Capability to Sustain Warfare," *Kanwa Asian Defense Review*, 24 January 2008, WNC 20080124.

45. Interview with Gennadiy Chufrin, 28 April 2008, Moscow, Russia.

11

The Taiwan Issue and the Sino-Russian Strategic Partnership

The View from Beijing

Shelley Rigger

The purpose of this chapter is to determine what the government of the People's Republic of China expects from Russia, vis-à-vis Taiwan, and to what extent Moscow's current policy and behavior meet those expectations. Regrettably, the Chinese leadership has not yet published a white paper on the topic, so answers must be divined from other sources. As a starting point for collecting and analyzing evidence on the topic, this chapter assumes that China's policy toward Taiwan rests on the following logic:

1. For the PRC leadership, preserving and protecting China's national sovereignty and territorial integrity are matters of national and regime survival. Therefore, maintaining the viability of unification between Taiwan and the Chinese mainland is a top priority of China's foreign and domestic policy at all times.[1]

2. Unification will become unviable if Taiwan changes its international status in such a way as to sever permanently its connection to the Chinese nation; this is the meaning of "Taiwan independence." Therefore, "Taiwan independence" must be prevented at all cost.

3. Taiwan's international isolation makes Taiwan independence infeasible. Therefore, Beijing should maximize Taiwan's isolation, both by preventing it from gaining membership in international organizations and by requiring China's diplomatic partners to accept Beijing's view of Taiwan's status (there is but one China, Taiwan is part of China, and the sole legal government of China is the PRC).

4. A primary obstacle to the achievement of unification (and the eradication of the Taiwan independence threat) lies in the United States' policy of enabling effective deterrent and defense capabilities for Taiwan. Therefore, to eliminate the danger of Taiwan independence and secure unification, China must increase its power relative to both Taiwan and the United States.

Given this logic, Beijing's expectations regarding Russia's Taiwan policy can be divided into five components. First, like all countries that wish to establish normal diplomatic ties with China, Russia must adopt a correct political and rhetorical approach to the Taiwan issue. It must acknowledge the one China principle, and it must oppose Taiwan independence. In addition, although this is not a requirement for normalized relations, China prefers that Russia assign blame for instability in the Taiwan Strait to Taiwan and its protector, the United States. Second, China expects Russia to adopt a correct relationship with Taiwan. Russia cannot have diplomatic relations with Taipei, nor should it sell weapons to Taiwan. Also, as we shall see, China has encouraged Russia to exercise restraint in its economic and substantive ties with Taiwan.

Third, Beijing has revealed an expectation that Russia will support China's global strategic orientation. China has encouraged Russia to join an alliance, or at least to conclude a formal agreement that ensures friendly relations between Moscow and Beijing. Internationally, China prefers multilateralism and the UN system to unilateralism and hegemonism, and it strongly opposes separatist movements. It has sought Russia's endorsement of these principles. The two nations have agreed to strengthen regional cooperation, including through the Shanghai Cooperation Organization.

A fourth element of China's policy involves military cooperation. China's actions reveal a preference for a Russian policy toward arms sales and military-technological cooperation that will assist China's military modernization. Beijing shows particular interest in persuading Russia to sell weapons and transfer technology and know-how that will help China develop weapons systems and tactical capabilities to deter or defeat both Taiwan and the United States in the event of armed conflict in the Taiwan Strait. In addition to acquiring weapons and military technology from Russia, China has shown a keen interest in carrying out joint military exercises with Russia, especially exercises designed to demonstrate China's resolve and capability to counter Taiwan independence.

We can discern these four elements by looking at Beijing's rhetoric and behavior toward Russia. In addition, I will argue that China has an interest in encouraging Russia to commit itself to intervene on China's behalf in the event of a Taiwan Strait conflict. This desire does not rise to the level of an expectation, and there is little evidence to suggest that Russia has made such a commitment. Not least because the goal is unlikely to be achieved, Beijing does not express it openly, either in public statements or in its behavior. Nonetheless, I will argue that China would like Russia to make such a commitment—or at least to create sufficient uncertainty on the issue that the

United States and Taiwan are forced to consider it in their own military planning. Mechanisms for bringing this situation into being would include entering into a mutual defense pact with China, integrating Russian and Chinese forces, and transferring weapons that require Russian cooperation to use.

Adopt a Correct Political and Rhetorical Approach

In the waning years of the Soviet Union and the early post-Soviet era it seemed that Russia might not fully accommodate China's preferences on the Taiwan issue. Under Mikhail Gorbachev, Russia flirted with Taiwan, apparently attracted by the possibility of trade, but the Kremlin was ultimately unwilling to sacrifice its rapprochement with China, and interactions with Taiwan stalled. In the early 1990s, Taiwanese officials hoped they would be able to formalize relations with the Soviet Union's successor states; for a while, it seemed such a policy might succeed. One reason for Taipei's optimism was the evident disarray in Russian foreign policy–making circles: "Sensing emerging disagreements in Moscow over the 'one China' principle, in early 1991 [Taiwan's] Executive Yuan formed a Working Group on Relations with the Soviet Union . . . to facilitate 'unofficial' interaction with Moscow."[2]

These trends were noted in the PRC. "Beijing also had suspicions that Yeltsin's government would switch its allegiance to Taiwan. Taipei authorities doubled efforts, hoping to woo Russia and its neighbors with economic incentives. Russian democrats and technocrats also turned toward Taiwan. Some were so inexperienced and naïve that they did not even suspect Beijing's possible reaction to the moves toward Taipei. Chinese politicians and diplomats noted with contempt that Yeltsin, together with his close associates, had been on record denouncing the People's Republic and praising Taiwan."[3]

President Boris Yeltsin's tendency toward independent action, combined with his pro-Western leanings and suspicion of China, encouraged Taiwan's diplomatic effort. Also, Yeltsin's associate Oleg Lobov had a long-standing relationship with Taiwan, which Taipei used to its advantage. While the PRC channeled its diplomacy through Russia's Foreign Ministry, Taiwan used Lobov and other connections in the Russian government to work around the ministry. Vladimir Zhirinovsky's Liberal Democratic Party of Russia (LDPR) also championed Taiwan's cause. The LDPR tried to press Taiwan's interests in the Duma—even sponsoring a "Russian Taiwan Relations Act" in 1998—but it was not powerful (or persuasive) enough to win. According to Alexander Lukin, Taiwanese diplomats wanted to believe that the LDPR's support could bring about a breakthrough, but as it turned out, its close association with the unpopular Zhirinovsky ended up hurting Taiwan's cause.[4]

During the upheaval of the early 1990s, Taiwan scored some important successes. In April 1992, Lobov negotiated an agreement to allow for the exchange of quasi-official representative offices (the Moscow-Taipei Economic and Cultural Coordination Commission [MTC] and the Taipei-Moscow Economic and Cultural Coordination Commission [TMC]). Yeltsin approved the exchange in September. This event was a high point in relations between Moscow and Taipei. Taiwan opened its representative office in Moscow (the TMC) in July 1993. Yeltsin appointed Lobov to head the MTC in 1993, but Russia did not open its own office in Taipei until December 1996, a delay which "signified Moscow's waning interest in relations with Taipei."[5]

By the time President Vladimir Putin took office it was clear that Russia was determined to secure good relations with Beijing. Since then, Moscow has adjusted its rhetoric over time to reflect Beijing's positions.[6] In 1998, Yeltsin announced his "four no's": no "two Chinas" or "one China, one Taiwan"; no Taiwan independence; no support for Taiwan's entry into international organizations that had statehood as a membership requirement; and no arms sales to Taiwan. Repudiating arms sales was significant, because for years rumors had circulated that Taiwan was interested in buying weapons from Russia, and that Russia might be interested in selling. Russia's unequivocal statement did not put these rumors entirely to rest, but it was an important affirmation to Beijing that Moscow was prepared to "recite the catechism."

Russia added more detail to its pronouncements in a summit statement signed by Jiang Zemin and Vladimir Putin in July 2000. The statement stressed that "China and Russia believe that the Taiwan issue is China's internal affair [and] . . . no outside force should be allowed to interfere in resolving the Taiwan issue." The statement also criticized U.S. theater missile defense plans, stating, "the incorporation of Taiwan into any foreign missile defense system is unacceptable and will seriously undermine regional stability."[7]

In 2001, China and Russia signed the "Treaty of Good-Neighborliness, Friendship and Cooperation between the People's Republic of China and the Russian Federation." In addition to calling for strategic cooperation between the two sides and affirming the Anti-Ballistic Missile Treaty, the treaty reiterated Russia's commitments to China vis-à-vis Taiwan. In Article 4 the two sides promised to support one another's policies regarding national unity and territorial integrity. In Article 5 Russia affirmed its previous statements upholding Beijing's "one China principle" and promised to oppose Taiwan independence.

A joint statement signed by the two presidents in December 2002 fleshed out these commitments. According to the statement, "national independence, sovereignty, and territorial integrity are the basic elements of the international law, the essential principles of international relations, and the necessary conditions for each nation's existence. It is the legal right of every nation to firmly condemn and strike against any attempt or activity that sabotages the above-mentioned principles. China and Russia firmly support each other's policy and actions on maintaining national unification and territorial integrity. The Russian side reiterates that the government of the People's Republic of China is the only legitimate government representing the whole China, and Taiwan is an integral part of the Chinese territory. Russia will not form any official relations or have official exchanges with Taiwan. Russia always recognizes that Tibet is an integral part of China. China supports Russia's efforts in striking against Chechnya terrorists and separatists. China and Russia will not allow the establishment of any organization or group in their own territories that will sabotage each other's sovereignty, security and territorial integrity. They will prohibit such activities."

Subsequent summit documents, including the "2005–2008 Outline for the Implementation of the Good Neighbor Treaty," have reaffirmed these commitments. In 2005 Moscow made an even more fulsome statement of support for China's position, explicitly stating its opposition to Taiwan's United Nations bid as well as its support for China's Anti-Secession Law. The statement included a clause placing the Taiwan issue into the context of the Sino-Russian strategic partnership: "The two sides believe that the extensive support which the two countries give each other on the major issues of national sovereignty, national security, and territorial integrity is a major feature of the strategic cooperative partner relationship between China and Russia." To realize that support, the two sides agreed to deepen military and technical cooperation and conduct joint military exercises. President Putin repeated the mantra yet again in a statement signed in March 2006.

As part of its policy of taking a correct rhetorical line toward Taiwan, Moscow has followed Bejing's lead in attributing heightened tensions in the Taiwan Strait to Taiwan and the United States. During the Taiwan Strait crisis in 1995 and 1996, Russia declined to criticize or condemn China's actions and specifically said that the crisis would not affect Yeltsin's planned visit to China in April—although it did reiterate its support for peaceful reunification. Russia's deputy chief of the General Staff "criticized the United States for stationing a naval battle group in the immediate vicinity of China's 'military exercises,' which he characterized as 'local,' claiming that the American presence was destabilizing and could lead to 'undesirable incidents' in the

Asia-Pacific region."[8] In March 2005, when the PRC passed an Anti-Secession Law authorizing the use of force to prevent Taiwan independence, the Russian foreign minister said that Russia understood the reasoning behind the law, and affirmed that Moscow viewed the Taiwan issue as China's internal matter.[9] Likewise, a year later, the Foreign Ministry criticized Taiwanese president Chen Shui-bian's decision to freeze the National Unification Council.[10]

While Moscow's statements conform very closely to China's preferred language, small areas of difference do exist. Russia consistently emphasizes the importance of resolving the Taiwan issue peacefully. Its response to the 1996 crisis is a good example: "At that time, the Russian Foreign Ministry issued an official statement: (1) announcing that Moscow was 'attentively following' the events in the Taiwan strait; (2) recognizing that the Taiwan question was a Chinese internal issue; (3) expressing hope that a serious and constructive dialogue would be initiated; and (4) pointing out that the official Russian position called for a peaceful resolution of hostilities."[11] Moscow's representative in Taipei affirmed this position in 1998. According to Lukin, "Most major political forces in Russia share this point of view."[12] Nor are all Russian officials equally sympathetic to China's position. After Zhirinovsky visited Taiwan in 1998, the Foreign Ministry supported a measure in the Duma to censure him, but despite Zhirinovsky's unpopularity with many of his Duma colleagues, the measure failed. Similarly, while the Foreign Ministry expressed its "understanding" of the Anti-Secession Law, the chairman of the Duma's international affairs committee suggested that the law could "seriously aggravate" regional tensions.[13]

Adopt a Correct Relationship with Taiwan

The Kremlin's words are clear: There is only one China—the PRC—and Taiwan is part of it. But what about its actions? For the PRC, it is important that diplomatic partners' behavior toward Taiwan match their rhetoric. Still, given its global economic weight, it is unrealistic to think that other states will cut off ties with Taiwan completely. Instead, Beijing presses its partners to make sure their behavior conforms to certain expectations, most of which boil down to keeping relations with Taiwan unofficial and accommodating Beijing when it makes specific demands regarding Taiwan. In this regard, Russia could serve as a model, for, as Lukin put it, "today, an understanding between Moscow and Beijing dictates that Russia will not take any significant steps to develop its relations with Taiwan without Beijing's consent."[14]

No Diplomatic Relations with Taiwan

Although Gorbachev preferred not to let the Taiwan issue disrupt the Sino-Russian rapprochement in the late 1980s, others in the Russian government were eager to open channels with Taiwan. One of the most enthusiastic was the Moscow city government. In 1990, the Moscow City Soviet Chairman visited Taiwan; the Soviet government tried to hide the visit, but it was reported in the Taiwan press.[15] In 1992 Taiwan reached out to Russia again, through Yeltsin's friend Oleg Lobov. On 9 September, the two sides announced that they would establish economic and cultural coordinating committees, with Lobov at the head of the Russian group. In an interview, Lobov implied that Moscow and Taipei would develop ties similar to diplomatic ones, including diplomatic immunity for Taiwan's representatives in Russia, and direct air links. The Chinese reacted sharply. Beijing's ambassador delivered a strong demarche to Russian Foreign Ministry officials and Yeltsin backed down. On 15 September, he issued a statement "confirming adherence to Moscow's traditional 'one China policy.'"[16] Subsequent efforts to upgrade Russia-Taiwan relations—including the LDPR's proposal for a "Russian TRA"—have failed.

President Chen Shui-bian took a number of actions in his first term of office that suggest he hoped for a breakthrough in Taiwan's relations with Russia. Under Chen, Taiwan reinvigorated negotiations on a number of economic issues, invited numerous trade delegations to Taiwan, and reached out to the Russian public. Among other actions, Taipei aggressively promoted Russia's bid for WTO membership. In July 2002, the Central News Agency (Taiwan) published an article headlined "President Hoping for Breakthrough in Taipei-Moscow Relations."[17] The vehicle for that breakthrough was the "Taiwan-Russia Association," founded in July 2002 to great acclaim (in Taipei) under the leadership of DPP Secretary-General (and soon-to-be premier) Chang Chun-hsiung. Also present at the founding was Taiwan's longtime friend and ally Oleg Lobov. Despite Chang and Lobov's best efforts, however, the Chen administration did not manage to upgrade the relationship between Taipei and Moscow.

No Weapons Sales to Taiwan

Despite persistent rumors to the contrary, there is no evidence to suggest that Russia has seriously considered breaking its pledge not to sell weapons to Taiwan.[18] In June 2001, a Foreign Ministry spokesman rebuffed reports from Britain and Hong Kong that Russia was helping Taiwan build submarines. He said, "with regard to Taiwan, Russia clearly adheres to a stance that rules out the authorization of any military-technical cooperation with the island, including the dual-purpose products sector. . . . During the past few years, the foreign media have been regularly publishing untruths whenever important Russian-Chinese meetings are forthcoming."[19]

Exercise Restraint in Economic Ties with Taiwan

Beijing has made it clear that Moscow may pursue unofficial, substantive relations with Taiwan. A joint statement released by the prime ministers of Russia and China in 2000 said, "China does not object to Russia's unofficial links with Taiwan in economic, trade, scientific, technologic, cultural, and sports areas."[20] Nonetheless, Beijing reportedly has interfered to keep those unofficial links limited in scope. Two good examples are the unresolved issues of direct flights between Russia and Taiwan and the establishment of a Taiwan representative office in Vladivostok. In both cases, Taipei is eager to move forward, but Russia has dragged its feet, apparently under Chinese pressure.

Russia and Taiwan signed a draft aviation accord in 1993, but the promise of regular direct flights is still unrealized. The official explanation for the delay cites problems with tax arrangements and landing rights fees, as well as a disagreement over whether flights could continue through to other European destinations (a condition Taiwanese airlines believe is necessary to make the routes profitable). In 2002, Russia confirmed that its deliberations on the issue included consultations with Beijing. According to the Foreign Ministry, "the launch of the aforementioned flights is exclusively related to unofficial commercial air service in order to expand unofficial trade, economic, culture and tourism ties with Taiwan."[21] When a charter flight made its way to Moscow in August of that year, Taiwan's transportation minister complained, "The goal originally could have been realized in 1997 but was later foiled due to political factors." Negotiations over direct flights have now dragged on for more than a decade; discussions about opening a Taipei representative office have been in progress almost as long. According to an official in Taiwan's presidential office interviewed in early 2007, the Vladivostok office will open "any day now," but in June 2009, Taiwan's foreign minister told reporters that Taipei had given up the effort to open an office in Vladivostock.[22]

Support China's Efforts to Isolate Taiwan Internationally

Russia has not been as active as Beijing might like on this front, although it has done nothing to raise Taiwan's international status. The strongest allegation in this regard comes from University of Adelaide professor Czeslaw Tubilewicz, who asserts that "Russia removed the question of Taiwan from the agenda of the Group of Eight Nations [at its 2000 meeting in Okinawa, Japan], which no longer could discuss the implications of regional security posed by Beijing's 'belligerent' Taiwan policy." I have not been able to verify this report.[23] Other sources blame other countries—mainly the meeting host, Japan—for removing Taiwan from the agenda, under pressure from Beijing. A Reuters report quoted University of Tokyo professor Takashi Inoguchi as saying that "the Japanese government is not interested in making too much noise about the Taiwan issue." He said the Japanese government sees the issue as "noisy, difficult, and troublesome, so better not to discuss it."[24] In the same article, however, Reuters differentiated Russia from the G7 countries, pointing out that Russia "fully backs Beijing's hard line."

Support China's Global Strategic Orientation

Another of China's objectives for its relationship with Russia is to encourage Moscow to support its overall approach to international relations. In particular, it hopes to enlist Russian support in opposing unilateralism and hegemonism, supporting multilateralism and the United Nations system, strengthening regional cooperation, and opposing separatist movements. For the most part, Russia has met these expectations.[25]

That said, former U.S. deputy assistant secretary of defense for Russia, Ukraine, and Eurasia Sherman Garnett makes an important point: China does not really need much from Russia in this regard, because "China's main advantage in having Russia as a friendly partner is its elimination as a military threat. China does not need more from Russia than basic stability and the continued absence of military pressure."[26] Still, as Georgia Tech professor John Garver points out, securing good relations with Russia is very valuable to Beijing: "Strategic partnership with Russia . . . strengthened China's position in the event of a confrontation with the United States over Taiwan. . . . In the event of such a confrontation, strategic partnership with Russia would guarantee China secure rear areas and open lines of international transportation, considerably diminishing prospects that a U.S. naval blockade might force China into submission."[27]

Undertake Military Cooperation with China

Sell Arms to China, Especially Weapons That Would Be Useful in Deterring/Defeating the United States in a Taiwan Scenario

To achieve the goals of its Taiwan policy, China must deter Taiwan from seeking independence. Failing that, it must be able to defeat Taiwan militarily. To do so, Chinese military planners assume that they will have to counter a U.S. intervention, too. Their options are to deter the United States from entering the conflict, deny the United States access to the battle space, or defeat the United States in battle. China's arms purchases from Russia in recent years reflect these objectives. Whether or not Russia has met China's needs is a matter of debate, but the evidence suggests that Russia has not sold China all of the weapons Beijing would like to have in order to maximize its chances of succeeding in a Taiwan Strait conflict.

Defeating Taiwan militarily—whether to block an independence bid or to coerce Taiwan into accepting unification on Beijing's terms—would require China to improve its air power and its amphibious lift capability. Keeping the United States out of the fight would require sea denial capabilities. As Garver's summary makes clear, these are precisely the capabilities China is purchasing from Russia:

> During the 1997–2001 period, China was the second-largest importer of weapons, purchasing over $7.1 billion in weapons during that five-year period. . . . Most of that amount came from Russia. From Russia the PLA purchased a dazzling array of weaponry, including seventy-eight Sukoi-27 and seventy-six [Sukoi]-30 air-supremacy fighters; air-to-air, anti-ship, surface-to-air, and antiradar missiles; combat radars; and two extremely capable Sovremenny-class destroyers, specifically designed by the Soviet Union to destroy U.S. aircraft carriers. Many of these Russian-supplied weapons were appropriate to air-naval battles around Taiwan. PLA modernization was driven by scenarios of a conflict over Taiwan, including deterring or, if deterrence failed, actually defeating U.S. military forces.[28]

The fact that these weapons could be used against the United States in a Taiwan conflict is not lost on their Russian manufacturers. There is evidence of a debate within Russia about the wisdom of some of these sales. For example, "government spokesmen denied in September 1996 that Moscow was selling Sovremenny destroyers equipped with Moskit anti-ship missiles, weapons designed to take out the U.S. Seventh Fleet and Aegis systems. In December sales of both to China were announced. . . . While there were reports that advanced weapons systems such as the Granit—Russia's newest anti-ship missile system that could seriously undermine American regional naval supremacy—was being considered, government spokesmen denied this. Russian military experts ruled out this sale possibility for the time being as it 'would require a substantial change in policy' on Moscow's part."[29]

Most sources that look at Russia's arms sales to China imply that Russia is arming China generously. Wittenberg University politcal scientist Yu Bin, in contrast, says, "in the case of Russian arms sales and technology transfers to China, however, Moscow has so far refrained from treating Beijing as a 'normal customer.' Its arms supplies to China have been inferior to those for other nations, such as India, despite the fact that both Asian nations are Moscow's 'strategic partners.'"[30] Paradorn Rangsimaporn agrees, arguing that the Russian debate on military-technological cooperation (MTC) with China reveals that Russia is ambivalent about the strategic relationship with China, and that economics—not a strategic calculus—is the main driver of MTC policy. He argues: "The impetus to MTC cannot thus be seen as a conscious result of the Kremlin's strategic calculus but rather as a case of economic interest dictating policy. . . . Although the official perception is that there is no Chinese military threat, this view reflects not consensus but rather an acceptance of short-term economic gains amid hopes that Russia can still control the process and thereby preserve its national interests."[31]

So while Russia has become the major foreign supplier of weapons and technologies for China's military modernization, it has not thrown open its arsenals to Chinese arms buyers. It has not sold China Tu-22M Backfire supersonic tactical strike bombers or Su-35 fighters, and it has withheld certain items from Chinese military expos.[32] Not all Russian security experts agree with this approach; some have even advocated arming China to take on the United States in the Taiwan Strait. In March 2006, Russian security expert Konstantin Makienko of the Center for Analysis of Strategies and Technologies in Moscow listed weapons China might acquire: Su-27SK and J-11 aircraft, phased array radars Shtil, Shtil-1 and Rif-M air-defense systems, Zubr and Murena-E air-cushion ships for amphibious operations; even an aircraft carrier and support craft, including Russian Tu-22M3 bombers and Project 949A Oscar II nuclear submarines. In Makienko's view, it is in Russia's interest to help China gain the ability "to neutralize possible engagement of a third party into its conflict with Taiwan."[33]

Since 2006, the likelihood that China will obtain Russia's most advanced weapons systems has waned; Chinese reliance on Russian weapons sales seems to have peaked that year. Evidence from 2007 and 2008 suggests that China has decided to build an independent arms manufacturing capability to wean itself off Russian weapons. According to the Stockholm International Peace Research Institute (SIPRI), Russian arms sales to China fell 62 percent in 2007. According to SIPRI researcher Paul Holtom, "with no new contracts for big-ticket aircraft or ships in 2007, this may be the beginning of the end for the high-volume of arms transfers from Russia to China."[34] One reason, says Princeton University's Jason Lyall, is that Russian arms sales experts suspect China is reverse-engineering and copying Russian systems for domestic manufacture.[35] The Chinese international relations specialist Shen Dingli encouraged this suspicion when he told the *International Herald Tribune*, "we want to buy better-quality weapons, but they refuse. If I was Russian, I would do the same thing. We are a country that is very capable of using their technology to build our own versions and competing with them."[36] The decline in arms sales may indicate an overall deterioration in trust and cooperation between the two countries, or it may be that Russia is guarding its technology more closely while China is building its domestic capacity. In any case, it shows that both sides are willing to compromise the pace of China's military modernization (and by extension its goals in the Taiwan Strait) to protect other interests.

Conduct Joint Military Exercises (Ideally Aimed at Taiwan)

Sino-Russian military cooperation extends beyond arms sales. In 2001, Hong Kong's *Wen Wei Po* ran a long piece by Zheng Yu, the director of the Russian Research Center of the Chinese Academy of Social Sciences, outlining Sino-Soviet relations since the early 1990s. According to Zheng, "[China-Russia] ties and contacts in the military field have already expanded to logistic support, communications, topographic mapping, and military education as well as those fields like military science, medicine, army building and deployment, aviation, and so on. The contacts between various military services and the adjacent military regions of China and Russia are also many and varied and the cooperation of military technology in many fields is also increasing."[37]

China and Russia carried out their first joint military exercises in August 2005. The exercises, which were conducted on the Shandong Peninsula, had many objectives, but for China, demonstrating its resolve and capability to suppress Taiwan independence clearly was one of them. The exercise was billed as an antiterror drill, but the activities that were practiced—including amphibious landing and naval assault—were far more relevant to a conflict in the Taiwan Strait than to an antiterrorist strike. Even more telling was China's preferred location for the exercises: the coast of Zhejiang Province, just north of the Taiwan Strait. According to the Russian newspaper *Kommersant*, Beijing's proposal showed "its clear intent to use the Russian army to pressurize Taiwan," a goal the newspaper called "scandalous." *Kommersant* characterized the drill as "rehearsing the capture of Taiwan."[38]

Moscow rejected the Zhejiang plan, and throughout the exercise Russian officials stressed that it was not aimed at any third party. Nonetheless, press reports continued to interpret it as a warning to both Taiwan and the United States. As Hong Kong's *Zhongguo Tongxun She* put it, "the outside has associated the exercise of the forced beach landing of Chinese troops to be covered

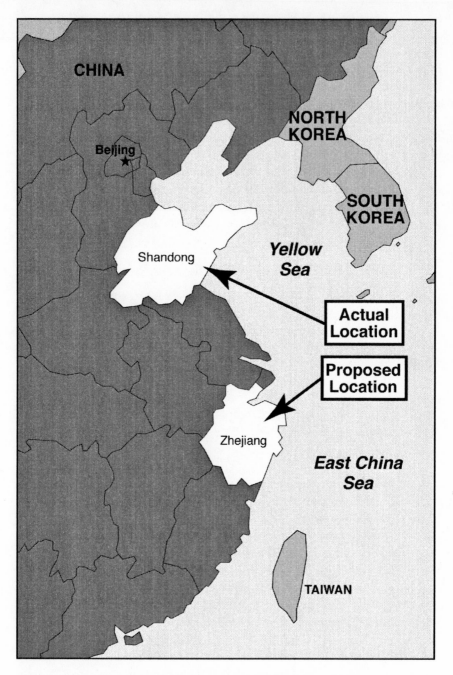

Map 11.1. Proposed and Actual Locations of "Peace Mission 2005."

by Russian troops with many other issues, and has even speculated that in the future, Russian troops may help defend the mainland if a war breaks out in the Taiwan Strait."[39] The article quoted Chinese military officials who said that such speculation was overblown, but such comments had little effect.[40] This is hardly surprising since, as the *Washington Post* pointed out, the Chinese government itself was sending mixed messages. For example, the Xinhua News Agency said the exercise was aimed at "international terrorism, extremism, *or separatism*."[41] The American military expert Peter Brookes noted a similar quotation from General Cao Gangchuan: "The exercise will exert both immediate and far-reaching impacts." According to Brookes, a former U.S. deputy assistant secretary of defense, "Beijing clearly wanted to send a warning to Washington (and, perhaps, Tokyo) about its support for Taipei, and hint at the possibility that if there were a Taiwan Strait dust-up, Russia might stand with China."[42]

What Else Might China Want?

As Brookes says, Russia's actions to date *hint* at the *possibility* that Russia might assist China militarily in the event of a Taiwan Strait conflict. But Russia has never explicitly stated that it would do so—at least not in public. Thus, for China to be confident of Russia's full support, Moscow needs to go beyond the actions it has taken to date. While China has not explicitly stated further actions as goals or expectations, there are a number of things Russia could do that clearly would advance China's interests.

Enter into a Mutual Defense Agreement That Would Obligate Russia to Take China's Side in a Taiwan Strait Conflict

Although the media sometimes use the term "military alliance" to describe the relationship between Moscow and Beijing, the two sides do not, in fact, have a mutual defense agreement. The 2001 "Treaty of Good-Neighborliness" obligates the two sides only to "make contact and hold consultations" if a threat to security should arise; it does not require military assistance. As Elizabeth Wishnick has written, the 2001 treaty, "sets very low benchmarks for international cooperation. . . . The treaty falls short of codifying a new alliance, and Russian and Chinese leaders have rejected any such intention."[43] Nonetheless, Peter Brookes argues that the joint military exercises in 2005, while falling short of a mutual defense pact, "represent a new, more intimate phase in the Sino-Russian relationship. And China's growing political/economic clout mated with Russia's military would make for a potentially potent anti-American bloc."[44]

An explicit, public pledge by Russia to take China's side in a military conflict—including one in the Taiwan Strait—would significantly enhance China's deterrence of both Taiwan and the United States. Tubilewicz quotes a report in Hong Kong's *Ming Pao* in which a Chinese military official observed that "once Beijing used force against Taiwan, Russia's support for China would induce the United States to think twice before taking 'reckless actions.'"[45] This military official is right: a deterrent effect already exists, because both Taipei and Washington are watching the Sino-Russian relationship carefully. Still, formalizing the alliance seems unlikely, because for both Moscow and Beijing a formal commitment carries significant risks.

As much as China might appear to stand to gain from a military alliance, there is danger even for China in such an arrangement. Although China seeks to weaken the U.S. commitment to Taiwan, Beijing is not prepared (at least not now) to sacrifice good relations with Washington to accomplish this aim, not least because trade with the United States is vital to China's economic survival. As Garver puts it, "China's Russian card has to be played carefully. Too close an anti-United States partnership with Russia—a military alliance perhaps—might stimulate rather than deter U. S. hostility. Thus virtually every Sino-Russian joint declaration and virtually every Chinese analysis of the Sino-Russian strategic partnership contain a politically de rigueur disclaimer to the effect that the partnership 'is not directed against any third country.'"[46]

The risks for Russia are even more obvious. A military alliance would antagonize the United States (and other neighbors), and it could encourage China to act provocatively. Ultimately, China's actions could drag Russia into a war with the United States. Even if the situation did not deteriorate to that extent, rising tensions would hurt Russia's economic relations with Taiwan and the United States, both of which are significant players in the Russian economy. Russia's attitudes toward theater missile defense, the U.S.-Japan alliance, and other issues make it clear that Moscow will take positions that displease China when it is in Russia's interest to do so.[47]

Offering rhetorical and moral support for China's unification agenda is one thing; sacrificing Russia's own national interests in pursuit of that agenda is another. According to Alexander Lukin at the Moscow State Institute for Foreign Affairs, Russians have little stomach for a more active posture on the Taiwan issue. He argues that most Russian media commentators either think unification is happening naturally, so China should just be patient, or it is a very long way off, and what China ought to do is to make more efforts to attract or seduce Taiwan:

> While Russian journalists usually do not question Beijing's position that Taiwan is a part of China, when Beijing's threats create tension, sympathies go to the weaker and democratic Taiwan. . . . Beijing is often characterized as the initiator in crisis situations, increasing the possibility of a military conflict in the Taiwan strait, although more conservative commentators traditionally continue to blame the U.S. for fueling tensions. During the times of tension, Russian journalists are more likely to discuss political differences between Taiwan and mainland China, and these comparisons are usually not favorable to Beijing . . . the interference of outside forces, pressure and threats of the use of military force are not welcome in Russia; and in the case of a serious conflict initiated by the PRC, Russian sympathies would probably be on the side of Taiwan.[48]

A more Machiavellian outlook (one that is well represented among Russian analysts) holds that Russia benefits most from the status quo: a simmering, unresolved conflict that whets China's appetite for weapons even as it directs Beijing's attention away from Russia. If the issue were resolved, China's military strength would increase, and its strategic focus might well shift toward its northern border. Anxiety about a stronger China is driven by ongoing Russian concerns about China's intentions in the Russian Far East. Also, as Tubilewicz points out, "China's unification would augment the PRC's economic power, remove the major obstacle to closer Sino-American ties and, thus, render Russia's strategic friendship less significant in the new geopolitical context."[49] State Duma president Konstantin Kosachyov expressed this view after China passed its Anti-Secession Law: "Taiwan is a territory with de-facto independence from China, but its independence has not been legally confirmed, while most countries, including Russia, regard Taiwan as a part of China from a juridical point of view. . . . [T]he 'neither war, nor peace' situation, which has existed until now, is more preferable than any attempts to unfreeze the conflict which has lasted for several decades."[50]

Although the status quo appears to serve Russia's national interests, some analysts believe that Moscow already has secretly promised its support for China's unification plans. However, the evidence for this assessment is weak. According to Tubilewicz, "Putin . . . went beyond Yeltsin's 'four "No"s' policy on Taiwan by pledging Russian military support for China in the event of U.S. intervention in Sino-Taiwanese conflict. According to reports by the ROC-based Central News Agency, such a pledge followed the Putin-Jiang meeting in Dushanbe in July 2000. The Russian president allegedly issued special instructions for the Russian military to be prepared for a deployment in the Taiwan Straits to block the intervention of the American navy in the 'internal Chinese affair.'"[51] Unfortunately, none of these allegations can be confirmed, and the sources Tubilewicz cites are questionable. Tubilewicz also mentions a report published in the *Washington Times* in February 2001 that "the Russian military conducted exercises which included large-scale simulated nuclear and conventional attacks against U.S. military units 'opposing' a Chinese invasion of Taiwan."[52] Again, the source's reliability is open to doubt.

Integrate Russia's Forces with China's

Another way that China could secure Russia's cooperation in the event of a Taiwan Strait war would be to integrate its forces with Russia's. Again, there is little evidence to suggest that this is happening. According to press reports, Russia and China have undertaken intelligence cooperation, but there is no evidence that it is aimed at Taiwan.[53] Also, some of the armaments (and licensing rights for local manufacture) that China has bought from Russia require Russian parts, and "all of the Su-27s and Su-30s also receive overhauls in Russia, after approximately 800 hours of flight time."[54] This suggests that China would need Russian assistance to maintain equipment in the event of a protracted conflict. Noting the need, however, is not enough to prove conclusively that Russia would actually provide the assistance in the event of war.

Conclusion

Russia's policy toward Taiwan incorporates much of what China has demanded. Moscow is a vigorous and vocal supporter of Beijing's "one China policy." Its relationship with Taiwan is subject to China's veto, and it has supported China's efforts to keep Taiwan out of the community of nations. Russia has sold China weapons it would need to defeat Taiwan and to deny U.S. aircraft carrier battle groups access to a Taiwan Strait battlefield. Military cooperation between China and Russia has progressed to the point where some Western analysts suggest that Taiwan—and the United States—should be concerned. Still, there is no firm evidence to show that Russia has pledged to support China militarily in a Taiwan Strait conflict.

Ultimately, Moscow is unlikely to take that final step, for the simple reason that it is not in Russia's interest to do so. As Alexander Lukin put it, "one can predict that if peaceful reunification occurs, there will be little reaction from Russia apart from congratulations. At the same time, a military conflict between Taiwan and China will put Russia in a difficult situation, especially if mainland forces attack Taiwan and the U.S. throws its support behind Taipei. In this case, Russia is unlikely to interfere, since any interference will endanger its relations with either Beijing or Washington. But, without denying Beijing's legal right to Taiwan, Russia would frown upon any use of force and may try to caution it or persuade Beijing to moderate its position."[55] Yu Bin takes a similar view: "At the strategic level, it is unlikely that President Putin would decisively tilt toward either Japan or China. What Moscow seems to be maneuvering for is milking maximum profit from both rich Asian neighbors while maintaining a balanced posture between them, particularly while Russia is weak."[56]

American academics Robert Donaldson and John Donaldson, assessing the situation from the perspective of international relations theory, agree with Lukin and Yu that the tie between China and Russia is weak, and a closer alliance is not in Russia's interests. They point out that while some Russians, including former defense minister Pavel Grachev, say that China poses no threat to Russia, or even that an arms race in the region is good because it increases demand for weapons, most in Russia's current leadership disagree. The views of Grachev's successor, Defense Minister Igor Rodionov, reflect the thinking of many Russians: "From the perspective of these observers . . . by closely associating with China and by selling it arms, Russia risks upsetting the delicate military balance in Asia and even being drawn into China's territorial disputes with Taiwan, Vietnam, Japan, and ultimately the United States."[57] Pulling Russia into those conflicts may be China's ultimate objective, but it is unlikely to happen.

Notes

1. For a description of China's posture toward Taiwan, see: Wang Jisi, "China's Changing Role in Asia," Occasional Paper published by the Atlantic Council of the United States Asia Program's project on China, the United States, and the Changing Strategic Environment, 2004, 12–13.

2. Czeslaw Tubilewicz, "The Little Dragon and the Bear: Russian-Taiwanese Relations in the Post–Cold War Period," *Russian Review*, no. 61 (April 2002): 282.

3. Eugene Bazhanov, "Russian Policy toward China," in *Russian Foreign Policy since 1990*, ed. Peter Shearman, 164 (Boulder: Westview, 1995).

4. Alexander Lukin, *The Bear Watches the Dragon: Russia's Perceptions of China and the Evolution of Russian-Chinese Relations since the Eighteenth Century* (Armonk, N.Y.: Sharpe, 2003), 287–89.

5. Tubilewicz, "The Little Dragon and the Bear," 284.

6. Agreeing with China on the sovereignty issue suits Russia's own interests,

since it, too, faces separatist movements. Nor have Taiwanese always shown sensitivity to Moscow's situation. For example, in 1998, Taiwan's opposition Democratic Progressive Party invited Chechen representatives to attend a meeting of the Unrepresented National People's Organization in Taiwan. Russia strongly protested Taipei's decision to grant visas to the Chechen activists. See: "MOFA Denies Interfering in Russian Internal Affairs," Central News Agency, in National Technical Information Service (cited hereafter as NTIS) Number: DRCHI09221998000750, 22 September 1998.

7. Paul Eckert, "China-Russia Pact Condemns U.S. Missile Shield," Reuters, 18 July 2000, http://cndyorks.gn.apc.org/yspace/articles/china11.htm.

8. Tubilewicz, "The Little Dragon and the Bear," 291–92.

9. "Russia Understands China's Position on Taiwan Issue," Xinhua, 14 March 2005, FBIS Document Number: 200503141477.1_6f4500205514a5.

10. "Russia Assails Taiwan's Decision to Halt Reunification Efforts," Interfax, 1 March 2006, FBIS Document Number: 200603011477.1_3fe50a003c434618.

11. Lukin, *The Bear Watches the Dragon*, 295.

12. Ibid.

13. "Russian Official Says China's Law on Territorial Integrity May Lead to Tension," *Agentstvo Voyennykh Novostey*, 14 March 2005, FBIS Document Number: 200503141477.1_120b001e9ee57750.

14. Lukin, *The Bear Watches the Dragon*, 294.

15. Ibid., 267.

16. Bazhanov, "Russian Policy toward China," 177.

17. "President Hoping for Breakthrough in Taipei-Moscow Relations," Central News Agency (Taiwan), 27 July 2002, AFS Document Number: CPP20020727000052.

18. For example, in October 2002, the DPP secretary-general said Taiwan might be able to benefit from "contradictions" between Moscow and Beijing to secure better relations with Moscow. That same month, a Taiwanese newsmagazine reported that sub-rosa military contacts between Taiwan and Russia were common. And in 2004, the *Washington Times* reported that Russia might be a source of submarines for Taiwan.

19. "Russia Denies Reports on Helping Taiwan Build Submarines," Interfax, 27 June 2001, AFS Document Number: CEP20010627000297.

20. "Joint Communiqué of the 5th Sino-Russian Regular Meeting," Xinhua, 13 November 2000, AFS Document Number: CPP20001103000123.

21. "Russian Foreign Ministry Announces Charter Flights between Moscow, Taipei," Interfax, 19 August 2002.

22. "China Airlines Launches Maiden Direct Flight to Moscow," Central News Agency, 24 August 2002, AFS Document Number: CPP20020824000054; "Taiwan to Shut Representative Offices in Five Countries," *Earthtimes*, 6 June 2009, http://www.earthtimes.org/articles/show/272016,taiwan-to-shut-representative-offices-in-five-countries.html (accessed 15 June 2009).

23. Tubilewicz, "The Little Dragon and the Bear," 291.

24. "G8 Bow to China, Keep Taiwan off Agenda," Reuters, 11 July 2000.

25. A detailed discussion of these topics can be found in John W. Garver, "China's U.S. Policies," in *China Rising: Power and Motivation in Chinese Foreign Policy,* ed. Yong Deng and Fei-ling Wang, especially 226–27 (Lanham, Md.: Rowman and Littlefield, 2005).

26. Sherman Garnett, "Challenges of the Sino-Russian Strategic Partnership," *Washington Quarterly* 24, no. 4 (2001): 51.

27. Garver, "China's U.S. Policies," 227.

28. Ibid., 229; Other experts also emphasize the relationship between China's weapons purchases and the Taiwan issue. See, for example, Paradorn Rangsimaporn, "Russia's Debate on Military-Technological Cooperation with China: From Yeltsin to Putin," *Asian Survey* 46, no. 3 (2006): 491–92, and Robert H. Donaldson and John A. Donaldson, "The Arms Trade in Russian-Chinese Relations: Identity, Domestic Politics, and Geopolitical Position," *International Studies Quarterly,* no. 47 (2003): 723.

29. Rangsimaporn, "Russia's Debate on Military-Technological Cooperation with China: From Yeltsin to Putin," 491–92.

30. Yu Bin, "China and Russia," in *Power Shift: China and Asia New Dynamics,* ed. David Shambaugh, 240 (Berkeley: Univ. of California Press, 2005).

31. Rangsimaporn, "Russia's Debate on Military-Technological Cooperation with China: From Yeltsin to Putin," 495.

32. Ibid., 489.

33. "Russian Expert: China to Remain Largest Buyer of Russian Weapons in Future," Interfax, 20 March 2006, NewsEdge Document Number: 200603201477.1_00340062b2a17479.

34. "Arms Transfers Data for 2007," *SIPRI,* press release dated 30 March 2008, http://www.sipri.org/contents/armstrad/PR_AT_data_2007.html.

35. Andre de Nesnera, "Russia-China Ties Grow," *VOA,* 4 June 2008, http://www.voanews.com/english/NewsAnalysis/2008-06-09-voa8.cfm.

36. David Lague, "Russia and China Rethink Arms Deals," *International Herald Tribune,* 2 March 2008, http://www.iht.com/articles/2008/03/02/asia/arms.php.

37. Zheng Yu, "CASS Professor Reviews Sino-Russian Relations, Strategic Cooperation," *Wen Wei Po,* 16 July 2001, NTIS Document Number: CPP20010716000039.

38. Ivan Safronov and Andrey Ivanov, "Things Taiwanese Become Clear—China Wants to Use Russian Army for Its Own Ends," *Kommersant,* 17 March 2005, BBC Monitoring International Reports, ACC Number: A200503171B6-ADBD-GNW.

39. Yu Song, "China-Russia Military Exercises Serve as a Warning to the United States and Japan," *Zhongguo Tongxun She,* 22 August 2005, NewsEdge Document Number: 200508221477.1_db7f00c90cf24a20.

40. Articles calling the exercises a warning to Taiwan and the United States

were published in outlets as diverse as the *Washington Post* and Taiwan's *Shangye Zhoukan.*

41. "Joint Drill with Russia Named 'Peace Mission 2005,'" Xinhua, 15 August 2005, emphasis added.

42. Peter Brookes, "An Alarming Alliance: Sino-Russian Ties Tightening," *Military.com,* 15 August 2005, http://www.military.com/Opinions/0,,Brookes_081505,00.html.

43. Elizabeth Wishnick, "Sino-Russian Relations in a Changed International Landscape," *China Perspectives* 43 (September–October 2002).

44. Brookes, "An Alarming Alliance."

45. Tubilewicz, "The Little Dragon and the Bear," 292.

46. Garver, "China's U.S. Policies," 228.

47. Elizabeth Wishnick, "Russia and China: Brothers Again?" *Asian Survey* 41, no. 4 (2001): 816.

48. Lukin, *The Bear Watches the Dragon,* 292–93.

49. Tubilewicz, "The Little Dragon and the Bear," 297.

50. "Russian Official Says China's Law on Territorial Integrity May Lead to Tension," *Interfax-AVN,* 14 March 2005, NewsEdge Document Number: 200503141477.1_120b001e9ee57750.

51. Czeslaw Tubilewicz, "The Little Dragon and the Bear," 295.

52. Ibid.

53. Stanislav Lunev, "Is China Russia's New Ally?" *Prism,* 3 May 1996, 4.

54. Elizabeth Wishnick, "Sino-Russian Relations in a Changed International Landscape."

55. Lukin, *The Bear Watches the Dragon,* 298.

56. Yu Bin, "China and Russia," 241.

57. Donaldson and Donaldson, "The Arms Trade in Russian-Chinese Relations," 723.

Contributors

James Bellacqua is an Asia Security Analyst at the CNA Corporation. He holds a B.A. in East Asian Studies from Lewis and Clark College in Portland, Oregon, and has an MBA from American University. Prior to joining CNA, Bellacqua served as a senior Chinese media analyst and linguist for the Foreign Broadcast Information Service examining PRC media treatment of Chinese domestic politics and legal affairs. Having lived, worked, studied, and traveled extensively throughout the People's Republic of China for several years, he speaks, reads, and writes Mandarin Chinese fluently. Bellacqua is also a graduate of the Johns Hopkins-Nanjing University Center for Chinese and American Studies and has studied Mandarin Chinese in Guangxi and Heilongjiang provinces. His numerous research interests include Chinese foreign policy, internal security, and media reform.

Leszek Buszynski is Professor of International Relations at the Graduate School of International Relations at the International University of Japan. He was also Senior Research Fellow and Coordinator of the Graduate Program in Strategic Studies at the Strategic and Defence Studies Centre (SDSC) at the Australian National University (ANU), Canberra, Australia. Before then he was a lecturer and later senior lecturer at the Department of Political Science at the National University of Singapore (NUS). He has published widely on Asia-Pacific security issues and has focused particularly on Russia's relations with the Asia-Pacific region. He is the author of *Asia-Pacific Security: Values and Identity* (Routledge, 2004) and more recently has published various articles in refereed journals on Russia's policy toward China and Japan, and also toward Southeast Asia.

Erica S. Downs is the China Energy fellow in the John L. Thornton China Center at the Brookings Institution. She previously worked as an energy analyst at the Central Intelligence Agency, a political analyst at the RAND Corporation, and a lecturer at the Foreign Affairs College in Beijing, China. She earned a Ph.D. and an M.A. from Princeton University and a B.S. from Georgetown University. Her current research and writing focuses on the Sino-Russian energy relationship, institutional change in China's energy bureaucracy, and the relationship between the Chinese party-state and China's national oil companies.

Andrew C. Kuchins is Director of the Russia and Eurasia Program and a senior fellow at the Center for Strategic and International Studies (CSIS). Previously, Kuchins was a senior associate at the Carnegie Endowment for International Peace (CEIP) in Washington, D.C., directing its Russian and Eurasian Program. Kuchins also directed the Carnegie Moscow Center in Russia during his time at CEIP. He conducts research and writes widely on Russian foreign and security policy and is working on a book entitled *China and Russia: Strategic Partners, Allies, or Competitors?* Kuchins is also an adjunct professor at Georgetown University. Prior to his time at the Endowment, Kuchins served from 1997 to 2000 as Associate Director of the Center for International Security and Cooperation at Stanford University. From 1993 to 1997, he was a senior program officer at the John D. and Catherine T. MacArthur Foundation, where he developed and managed a grant-making program to support scientists and researchers in the former Soviet Union. From 1989 to 1993, he was Executive Director of the Berkeley-Stanford Program on Soviet and Post-Soviet Studies.

Richard Lotspeich is associate professor of economics at Indiana State University. He holds an undergraduate degree in economics with a minor in Russian from Georgetown University (Washington, D.C.) and a Ph.D. in natural resource economics from the University of New Mexico (Albuquerque). He began his working career in the Systems Analysis Group at the Los Alamos National Laboratory and later engaged in postdoctoral studies on the Soviet economy at Indiana University. He has twice been awarded Fulbright lecturing fellowships for Russian universities in St. Petersburg, and was a visiting scholar at the Kennan Institute for Russian Studies (part of the Woodrow Wilson International Center for Scholars, Washington, D.C.) in 1995 and again in 2005. His research interests focus on environmental policy, transitional economies, the economics of conflict, and the interface between criminality and economics.

Shelley Rigger is the Brown Professor of East Asian Politics at Davidson College in Davidson, North Carolina. She has a Ph.D. in government from Harvard University and a B.A. in public and international affairs from Princeton University. She has been a visiting researcher at National Chengchi University in Taiwan (2005) and a visiting professor at Fudan University in Shanghai (2006). Rigger is the author of two books on Taiwan's domestic politics—*Politics in Taiwan: Voting for Democracy* (Routledge, 1999) and *From Opposition to Power: Taiwan's Democratic Progressive Party* (Lynne Rienner Publishers, 2001). She has published articles on Taiwan's domestic politics, the national identity issue in Taiwan-China relations, and related topics. Her current research studies the effects of cross-Straits economic interactions on the Taiwan people's perceptions of mainland China. Her monograph *Taiwan's Rising Rationalism: Generations, Politics and "Taiwan Nationalism"* was published by the East West Center in Washington, D.C., in November 2006.

Gilbert Rozman is Musgrave Professor of Sociology at Princeton University, where he studied in the junior-year Critical Languages Program, received his Ph.D., and has taught since 1970. After a series of comparative historical projects, he turned in the 1980s to studies of Soviet debates on China, Chinese debates on the Soviet Union, and Japanese debates on the Soviet Union. In the following decade, he examined prospects for regionalism in Northeast Asia, covering cross-border ties, mutual perceptions, great-power relations, and strategies toward regional cooperation. In addition to using Chinese, Japanese, and Russian sources, he began to read Korean sources in order to incorporate South Korean views into his analysis. Recently he has worked on a series of books on strategic thought on Asia, including Russian, Japanese, and Korean strategic thought toward Asia and strategic thinking toward the Korean nuclear crisis. A book on China will follow.

Kevin Ryan is a senior fellow at Harvard's Belfer Center for Science and International Affairs. A career military officer, he has extensive experience in political-military policy, air and missile defense, and intelligence. He is a trained foreign-area specialist for Eurasia and speaks fluent Russian. He has served as Senior Regional Director for Slavic States in the Office of the Secretary of Defense, as Chief of the U.S. POW/MIA Office in Moscow, and as Defense Attaché to Russia. He has also served as Chief of Staff for the Army's Space and Missile Defense Command and as Assistant Professor of Russian Language at the U.S. Military Academy. In his last active-duty assignment, General Ryan was Deputy Director of the Army's Directorate of Strategy, Plans, and Policy, managing War Plans, Policy, and International Affairs. General Ryan holds a B.S. from the U.S. Military Academy and master's degrees from Syracuse University and the National War College.

Jeanne Wilson is Professor and Chair of the Department of Political Science at Wheaton College in Norton, Massachusetts, and a research associate at the Davis Center for Russian and Eurasian Research at Harvard University, Cambridge, Massachusetts. Her research interests include the politics of transition in Russia and China, and Russian-Chinese relations. Recent publications include "Emerging Capitalism in Russia and China: Implications for Europe" (with Sheila M. Puffer and Daniel J. McCarthy), *European Journal of International Management* 1 (May 2007); "China's Economic Transformation: Toward the Liberal Market Economy," in *Varieties of Capitalism in Post-Socialist Countries*, ed. David Lane and Martin Myant (Palgrave, 2006); and *Strategic Partners: Russian-Chinese Relations in the Post-Soviet Era* (Sharpe, 2004). Currently she is working on a research project examining the impact of internationalization on domestic policy in Russia and China. She has a B.A. from the University of Michigan and an M.A. and Ph.D. from Indiana University.

Elizabeth Wishnick is assistant professor of political science at Montclair State University and a research associate at the Weatherhead East Asian Institute, Columbia University. She was a Fulbright fellow at Lingnan University, Hong Kong, and a research fellow at Taiwan's Academia Sinica, the Hoover Institution, and the Davis Center at Harvard University. Her current book project, *China as a Risk Society*, examines how transnational problems originating in China (environment, resource scarcity, public health, migration) shape Chinese foreign relations with neighboring states and involve Chinese civil society in foreign policy. In the summer of 2007 she spent a month in residence at Beijing University and Keio University (Tokyo) to pursue related research on environmental and energy issues in Sino-Japanese relations, thanks to a fellowship from the East Asian Institute in Seoul, South Korea. Dr. Wishnick is the author of *Mending Fences: The Evolution of Moscow's China Policy from Brezhnev to Yeltsin* (Univ. of Washington Press, 2001) and has contributed numerous articles on great-power relations and regional development in Asia. She received a Ph.D. in political science from Columbia University, an M.A. in Russian and East European studies from Yale University, and a B.A. from Barnard College. She speaks Chinese, Russian, and French fluently.

Jing-dong Yuan is the Director of the East Asia Nonproliferation Program at the James Martin Center for Nonproliferation Studies, and Associate Professor of International Policy Studies at the Monterey Institute of International Studies, where he also coordinates the Certificate in Nonproliferation Studies program. A graduate of the Xi'an Foreign Language University, People's Republic of China (1982), he received his Ph.D. in political science from Queen's University in 1995 and has had research and teaching appointments at Queen's University, York University, the University of Toronto, and the University of British Columbia, where he was a recipient of the prestigious Izaak Killam Postdoctoral Research Fellowship. Professor Yuan's research and teaching focuses on Asia-Pacific security, global and regional arms control and nonproliferation issues, U.S. policy toward Asia, and China's defense and foreign policy, in particular its defense and nuclear modernization efforts. He has published over sixty monographs, journal articles, and book chapters, and his op-eds have appeared in the *International Herald Tribune, Japan Times, Los Angeles Times, South China Morning Post,* and *Far Eastern Economic Review,* among others. He is the coauthor of *China and India: Cooperation or Conflict?* (Boulder, Colo., and London: Lynne Rienner Publishers, 2003) and is currently working on a book manuscript on post–Cold War Chinese security policy.

Charles E. Ziegler is Professor and Chair of the Political Science Department at the University of Louisville, founder and Director of the Institute for Democracy and Development, and founder of the Center for Asian Democracy. A specialist on Russia and Eurasia, Ziegler is coeditor (with Judith Thornton) of *The Russian Far East: A Region at Risk* (Univ. of Washington Press, 2002) and author of *The History of Russia* (Greenwood Press, 1999), *Foreign Policy and East Asia* (Cambridge Univ. Press, 1993), and *Environmental Policy in the USSR* (Univ. of Massachusetts Press, 1987). In addition, he has written more than fifty book chapters and articles for such professional journals as *Comparative Politics, Political Science Quarterly, British Journal of Political Science, Problems of Post-Communism, Asian Survey, International Politics, Policy Studies Journal,* and *Pacific Review.* Ziegler has held an International Research and Exchanges Board Advanced Individual Research Opportunity grant, a Senior Fulbright Fellowship to Korea, a Council on Foreign Relations International Affairs Fellowship, and the Hoover Institution National Fellowship. He currently serves as Executive Director of the Louisville Committee on Foreign Relations.

Index